# Astro Equations
# for
# Specific Profession

# Science of Light

# Astro Equations for Specific Professions

Mridula Trivedi
T.P. Trivedi
R. Asthana

MOTILAL BANARSIDASS PUBLISHERS
PRIVATE LIMITED • DELHI

*Second Revised Edition: Delhi,* ***2016***



ISBN: 978-81-208-4077-5

MOTILAL BANARSIDASS
41 U.A. Bungalow Road, Jawahar Nagar, Delhi 110 007
8 Mahalaxmi Chamber, 22 Bhulabhai Desai Road, Mumbai 400 026
203 Royapettah High Road, Mylapore, Chennai 600 004
236, 9th Main III Block, Jayanagar, Bengaluru 560 011
8 Camac Street, Kolkata 700 017
Ashok Rajpath, Patna 800 004
Chowk, Varanasi 221 001

*MLBD Cataloging-in-Publication Data*
SCIENCE OF LIGHT – 2
ASTRO EQUATIONS FOR
SPECIFIC PROFESSIONS
MRIDULA TRIVEDI
T.P. TRIVEDI, R. ASTHANA
in *Science of Light Series*
ISBN : 978-81-208-4077-5

*Printed in India*
by Replika Press, India,
and published by Motilal Banarsidass Publishers (P) Ltd,
www.mlbd.com • mlbd@mlbd.com

Dedicated
to our beloved daughter

**Deeksha**

Who, like a gentle breeze,
has caressed our lives
with unfathomable love and unabated joy.

# Foreword

The present work by the authors may be deemed to be a sequel to their earlier title POINTERS TO PROFESSION and deals in greater detail with the subject of career choices. Based on combinations given in classical works and suitably adapted to present time options, the authors deal in some detail with the clues needed to identify specific professional lines such as of doctors, lawyers, engineers, teachers, bureacrats, as also businessmen, sports persons, film stars , politicians and other vocations. The content of the volume carries the weight of their wide experience, research and study of a large number of charts from across the globe and needs to be studied with diligence.

One's calling –whether it is one of service and employment, or in the nature of business or of a professional – is a very important part of one's life. It calls for a careful decision to be able to choose one's career properly. Such a decision may be necessary even as a student when one has to choose the line of study that would bring one not only satisfaction as an achiever but also is financially comfortable. Many parents believe what is good for them is good for their children too but this may not be true always. They often, in a move that is well-meant but ill-conceived, foist their vocational preferences on the youngsters. As a result, these young people with great hopes of a successful career, are forced into a line of study dictated by parental suggestions, peer pressure and other extraneous considerations and which leave them finally frustrated. The best help one can get in such circumstances so as to be able to choose the profession that is best for one is from the horoscope. It is in this context that the present volume fulfills a long felt need.

Different houses, signs and planets as also the role of Jaimini Atmakaraka have been extensively dealt with reference to specific vocations. Yogas such as Sakata, Kemadruma and others have been critically examined and their power to create setbacks and impediments in one's vocational life have been lucidly explained.

In short, the volume proves to be a benchmark work and an important addition to extant literature on the subject of vocational guidance.

Bangalore
July 22, 2016

Gayatri Devi Vasudev
Editor: MODERN ASTROLOGY

सरसिजनिलये सरोजहस्ते धवलतमांशुकगन्धमाल्यशोभे।
भगवति हरिवल्लभे मनोज्ञे त्रिभुवनभूतिकरि प्रसीद मह्यम्।।

*Beloved of Lord Vishnu, O Goddess Laxmi ! You sit on a lotus and also hold lotus flowers in your hands. You are dressed in new soft silken clothes and are adorned with a garland and fragrance. Your appearance is extremely pleasing. Giver of prosperity of all the universe, O Bhagvati ! Be pleased (shower your blessings) on us.*

# Preface

**"Astro Equations For Specific Professions"** is, in a true sense, continuation of our previous book on the vocational aspect of life 'Pointers to Profession : An Astrological Exposition'. 'Pointers to Profession : An Astrological Exposition' deals with the combinations, constellations and houses for the judgment of professional aspects and prospects of the native. This work includes dictums and sutras of yore, supplemented by observations from our experience and supported by more than hundred case studies. How to time the different events in the professional life like commencement of career, time of promotion etc have all been dealt in quite detail, with practical illustrations. But the study of astrological combinations, in relation to various aspects of profession, would not be complete without the understanding of planetary set up for different professions. Being aware of it we have, after analysis of thousands of birth charts of persons from different occupations, delineated specific planetary configurations responsible for specific professions. What are the combinations which make one a doctor, or an engineer, or a teacher, or a lawyer have all been worked out. We have been able to work out the combinations making one successful in IAS, IPS, IFS and the like, and all this vital information has been incorporated in the present book titled **'Astro Equations For Specific Professions'.**

**'Astro Equations For Specific Professions'** is again a monumental work on one of the most important aspect of life - the means of livelihood or the profession of the native, who can be benefited by selecting appropriate and suitable occupation on the basis of planetary set up of their birth chart. In the earlier times, only a few vocations existed such as agriculture, engineering, medicine or law, in addition to various kinds of business etc. However, the selection of appropriate profession is largely in demand, generally from the very beginning of schooling, by one and all.

The most commonly asked question, even to a child, is 'बड़े होकर क्या बनोगे?' i.e. what would you like to become when grown up?, which simply means, what profession you would join? Small kids reply with any profession, which has caught up their fancy lately but for students in higher classes, the question is a nightmare with everyone suggesting something or the other. So great is the focus today on a 'right' choice of career and such wide spectrum of professions are available to choose from that students get baffled. More often than not the real potential takes a back seat and the professions in vogue are unwillingly chosen. Now-a-days numerous techniques, psychoanalytical assessment and aptitude tests are being used by career counselors to identify the right career for an individual. **"Astro Equations For Specific Professions"** is an effort to refine the choice of career using principles of Astrology.

Like every other aspect of life, a right and appropriate profession can also be chosen using the amazing and authentic *Sutras* of the sublime science of astrology. **"Astro Equations For Specific Professions"** discusses in detail about various astrological combinations and corresponding careers viz. business, agriculture, service, medicine, engineering, administrative services and so on. It also talks on the suitability of a profession to an individual by considering native's birth chart.

However, to find out one's profession on the basis of his birth chart is truly a tough exercise. It requires vast experience, wide study and practical applications on thousands of nativities that will make one adept in making correct observation, with regard to most suitable and appropriate profession of the subject. It is a general belief that the tenth house deals with profession. It is absolutely true. However, in the present scenario when the numbers of vocations are so varied, many other concerning houses are to be taken into consideration for correct and precise interpretation. A few planets, which signify a particular occupation, should also be examined carefully to find out the most suitable occupation as indicated by the planets of the native. The tenth house, its lord and the *navamsa* of the lord of the tenth house are most important in finding out a suitable occupation. Anyway, in addition to the tenth house, the lords of the second and eleventh house should also be taken into account. These two houses indicate the means of livelihood. Thus, indirectly second and eleventh houses too play a vital role in the judgement of the native's occupation. The effect of these two houses has been demonstrated in the discussions for various professions in "**Astro Equations For Specific Professions**", which will help to pin-point the most probable and suitable job for the native.

Equally important are the roles of sixth and eighth houses in predicting career progression of individuals. The sixth and eighth houses are most misunderstood houses with regard to profession, though both have a lot of influence on the native's career progression. The sixth house governs the professional fortune that is promotion, demotion, termination and the like. The eighth house is tenth from the eleventh house and eleventh from the tenth house. Eleventh house rules over accomplishment of ambitions. Therefore, the professional ambitions should be judged by the eighth house, especially if one has to enter into Civil Services on top or Ministers, Presidents, top industrialists, film actors, multi-millionaires etc. have a vital concern with the eighth house in their horoscope. Generally, it is believed that if the lord of tenth house occupies the sixth or the eighth house it spoils the career of the native. But our research oriented observations, which are based on the practical study of more than twenty five thousand horoscopes, are eye openers for one and all. Instead of adversities, the relationship of the lord of the tenth house with sixth or the eighth house promotes the career of the native to an appreciable height. In fact, the sixth house indicates future of the professional career, whereas the eighth house shows professional prosperity. Eighth house is always found involved with the combinations of profession, where the native has may people under his control

"**Astro Equations For Specific Professions**" largely covers the planetary combinations for various types of career. What makes one a Doctor, Engineer, Lawyer, Banker, Teacher, I.A.S., I.P.S., Businessman, Sports Person, Film actor and actresses, Musicians, Singers, Dancers, Journalist, Politician, Minister, President, M.P. or M.L.A., M.B.A's, C.A's etc. Which will be the most successful profession for the native and why? What kind of business will suit the subject?

In fact, "**Astro Equations For Specific Professions**" is our dream work, which has been carried out on the basis of our thirty five years wide study, vast experience and unaccountable practical applications in the field of sublime Science of Astrology. This is a vast research oriented work with regard to most important aspect of one's life i.e. the means of livelihood. The subject was highly in demand by the readers and students of astrology. We had received innumerable mails for an authentic work on the professional aspect of individuals during last so many years. It has taken a time of almost eight years to bring out "**Astro Equations**

**For Specific Professions**" in the present shape and size, which will largely fulfill the demand of the serious readers of astrology.

We believe that our sincere endeavor will help the readers and students of astrology to find out the most suitable and appropriate occupation at the right time.

**'Astro Equations For Specific Professions'** is a perfect treatise of paramount importance on professional prospects of people, containing profound research observations based on the practical examination of thousands of birth charts of individuals of all over the World. These observations are perfectly accurate, appropriate, authoritative and authentic as these findings have been carried out after a wide and thorough study of all classical works of various sages. We have tried to explain the planetary configurations of as many as specific professions as it was possible, keeping limited space and scope of this book in view. Much literature is not available on the professional aspects in Astrology. There were only a few engagements and professional employments during earlier period, therefore our sages, who were blessed with *Siddhies* have stated only about the prevalent professions of that period in their classical texts. However, we have classified all kinds of vocations in different groups and we have covered as many as practically possible.

**'Astro Equations For Specific Professions'** contains eighteen chapters on varied professions like I.A.S., Doctors, Engineers, Lawyers, Journalists, Teachers, Police Personnel, Industrialists, Scientists, Mathematicians, Consultants, Politicians, Players, Actors, Actresses and Artists, Bank Personnel, M.B.As., C.As. and persons involved in various kinds of business etc. We have found and explained in this work that specific profession can be precisely pointed out. Most suitable and appropriate profession, in which the native will prosper and progress properly, can certainly be worked out after a through examination of the birth chart. 'Astro

Equations For Specific Professions' will enable the scholars to foretell about the profession pertaining to planetary placements in the horoscope of the individuals, which will help them to select concerning subjects for their advanced studies.

Though, certain books on the aspect of profession are available in the market but all these books are quite ambiguous and lacking in necessary information. A few of these explain number of professions indicated by the nine planets, whereas others explain the group of planets for each profession but these works have not tried to emphasize the concerning house and signs, along with planetary conjunctions and combinations, as required for specific professions. We have made sincere and honest, thought provoking and research oriented endeavor on each and every point and planetary combinations, in respect of the particular houses and signs, for the examination of specific professions. We have also concentrated on the constellations and *navamsa* occupied by the concerning planets, in addition to the signs and their dispositors etc., so that there may not be any kind of error in the judgement of most appropriate and suitable profession of the native.

*Atmakaraka* planets do play a prominent role in the judgement of professional pointers for appropriate profession. The study of any birth chart will remain incomplete and erroneous, especially in the matters of profession, if *Atmakaraka* planets are not analyzed properly and precisely. This assists a lot in the confirmation of the findings, after the judgement of the professional aspect of Astrology. The principles for proper judgement for professional aspects of the native have been fully explained in our other book **'Pointers to Profession: An Astrological Exposition'.**

'Astro Equations for Specific Professions' deals with minute details and precise observations of each and every profession separately, with illustrative discussions of the natal charts of the concerning professionals. Various rules for different occupations have been propounded quite categorically and significantly, which will help the scholars of astrology, in finding out most appropriate and suitable profession of one and all, by applying least efforts and doing very less exercise, comparatively, in this regard.

Some *Yogas* or planetary combinations like *Kaalsarpa Yoga*, *Sakat*, *Kemadrum* and *Baadhak Yogas* create problems and obstacles in the career of the native. However, suitable and timely remedial measures can help the subject to prevent the negative effects of such *Yogas*. Hence, it is important for one to know the career progression and the probable ups & downs in one's professional life. It is the personal experience of the authors that suspension and other adversities can be avoided by undertaking suitable remedial measures, well in time. Various spiritual measures, to avoid obstacles in the career and to become more prosperous and rich, are also detailed in "**Astro Equations For Specific Professions**".

Any research work of this enormity requires inspiration from inside and affection from outside. Had such inspiration not come from someone, whose divine beauty is beyond any description, the work of mortal being would have never seen the light of the day. She was none but Goddess of learning, who fired our imagination when after the day's hard work, body was fatigued and refused to obey the orders of mind, it was her blessings and motivation that infused new life.

Any organized work of this mammoth dimension would require the assistance of sincere co-workers. We thank all associates who have assisted in one or the other way during the process of research carried out in this work.

We offer our thanks to Mr. Sada Shiv Tiwari for making flawless CRC of the book and also to Mr. Rajesh Tyagi for their assistance in typing and carrying out the enormous spade work, so essential to complete this comprehensive book.

M/s. Motilal Banarasi Dass Publishers, Delhi are renowned to be the largest and the best publishers of not only India but that of whole Asia. Mr. Rajeev Prakash Jain, who is a very worthy son of his worthy father, has expressed his valuable acceptance with regard to publication of **'Pointers to Profession: An Astrological Exposition'** and **'Astro Equations For Specific Professions'.** For this gracious gesture of his, we are extremely indebted to him and M/s. Motilal Banarasi Dass Publishers.

With this, we present this work in the hands of our astute and able readers and are sure that they will find it very informative. If some professions have been left out, we will work on them and present our views, as and when the opportunity arises. It is an aspect of life where interminable research is called for. We are, more than anybody else, conscious of many defects and blemishes – which would have inadvertently crept in this book. For this we shall be extremely grateful to accept any suggestion from the valuable readers. Satisfaction of our intelligent readers will be the fruit of our labor.

**Rakesh Asthana**
C-43A, Sector-A
Mahanagar
Lucknow - 226 006
Tel: 0522-2323686

**Mridula Trivedi & T.P. Trivedi**
*'Mridul Vatika'*, 24 Mahanagar Extn.
Opp. E-40, Corporation Quarters,
Pili Colony, Lucknow - 226 006
Tel: 0522-2326625

Dated: March 30th, 2016

# Contents

# About the Book

**'Astro Equations For Specific Professions'** is a perfect treatise of paramount importance on professional prospects of people, containing profound research observations based on the practical examination of thousands of birth charts of individuals, and after a wide and thorough study of all classical works of various sages. There were only a few professional employments during earlier period, therefore our sages, who were blessed with Siddhies have stated only about the prevalent professions of that period in their classical texts. Authors, in this book, have tried to explain the planetary configurations of as many as specific professions as it was possible.

The most commonly asked question, even to a child, is 'बड़े होकर क्या बनोगे?' i.e. what would you like to become when grown up, which simply means, what profession you would join? Small kids reply with any profession, which has caught up their fancy lately but for students in higher classes, the question is a nightmare with everyone suggesting something or the other. So great is the focus today on a 'right' choice of career and such wide spectrum of professions are available to choose from that students get baffled. More often than not the real potential takes a back seat and the professions in vogue are unwillingly chosen. Now-a-days numerous techniques, psychoanalytical assessment and aptitude tests are being used by career counsellors to identify the right career for an individual. **'Astro Equations For Specific Professions'** is an effort to refine the choice of career using principles of Astrology.

**'Astro Equations For Specific Professions'** contains eighteen chapters on varied professions like I.A.S., Doctors, Engineers, Lawyers, Journalists, Teachers, Police Personnel, Industrialists, Scientists, Mathematicians, Consultants, Politicians, Players, Actors, Artists, Bank Personnel, M.B.As., C.As. and persons involved in various kinds of business etc., explaining that how can specific profession be precisely pointed out. Which will be the most successful profession for the native and why? What kind of business will suit the subject? All these questions are vividly answered in this book.

**'Astro Equations For Specific Professions'** deals with minute details and precise observations of each and every profession separately, with illustrative discussions. Various rules for different occupations have been propounded quite categorically and significantly, which will help scholars of astrology, in finding out most appropriate and suitable profession by applying least efforts and doing very less exercise, comparatively, in this regard.

Various spiritual measures, to avoid obstacles in the career and to become more prosperous and rich, are also detailed in **'Astro Equations For Specific Professions'.**

## Chapter-1

# Planetary Configuration and Classification of Occupation

Undoubtedly, one's career is of foremost importance. Everyone wants to get a bright career, so that he may earn name, fame, honour, position, prosperity, popularity, power and pelf in the society. A good career is a dream of one and all. A few get their desires and ambitions accomplished, while others fail to do so.

Reverting to the major topic of this book, we examine and discuss the various parts of a horoscope, which collectively determine the occupation.

We may begin with the examination of the *lagna* or the first house of the horoscope, which is quite important in this connection. It gives us a general impression of the potentiality of the horoscope. It is the house of one's own efforts. It shows the amount of energy, will and determination one has, to carry out his aims and to execute his plans. It shows the quantity and quality of one's ambitions. The nature and mental temperament are amply reflected and projected by this house. Independence of nature, the will to lead, the ambition to live with honour and dignity – these and other similar traits, the first house detects and the other parts and constituents of the horoscope confirm.

Again, it is for the first house to determine the measure of success, which will attend one's efforts. A strong first house makes the entire horoscope strong, and it is one of very good arguments in the favour of a successful, purposeful and eventful life, and consequently success in one's occupation.

The next spot in the horoscope, which should attract our attention, is the $10^{th}$ house. It is generally called the house of occupation. We feel once again to emphasize the peculiar aspect of the science of Astrology, even at the cost of repetition, that it is the science of exceptions, and one factor alone does not decide anything conclusively. Thus, even if the 10$^{th}$ house is generally called the house of occupation, the occupation of a person cannot be, and should not be, determined, fixed and predicted after the study of the 10$^{th}$ house alone. It is only one of the considerations, which help us to frame our opinion regarding the occupation of the person in question.

A good and strong 10$^{th}$ house improves a good deal one's chances of enjoying the correct occupation; it reduces considerably the chances of going astray and of wasting precious time elsewhere. The ruler of the 10$^{th}$ house gives a lead in the right direction to the astrologer, to direct his search for the occupation among the categories and sub-divisions, the occupational activities have been divided. The position of the lord of the 10$^{th}$ house throws light over the matter and further directs and guides our search. The nature and the strength of the planets, which occupy the 10$^{th}$ house, are also important and should be thoroughly studied.

The 10$^{th}$ house indicates the father or the guardian, the mental caliber of the father or the guardian, his social standing and status and consequently his financial position. The social standing and the status of the father and his financial position determine the environments of the person in question, during his childhood and early youth, which is the formation period for the person concerned. To understand the factors, which contribute to the formation of one's character, is to understand and visualize one's character itself. Thus, it further adds to the importance of the study of the 10$^{th}$ house.

The 11$^{th}$ house indicates the benefits, which one is likely to derive from one's occupational activities. The strength of the 11$^{th}$ house should be measured and gauged, in order to ascertain the monetary aspect of the occupation. The 11$^{th}$ house also informs us about the financial position of the father or the guardian.

The $4^{th}$ house is the house of mother. It reveals the temperament. The person in question has sucked the milk of his mother. The ways of thinking, the methods of work, and the approach to problems, the whims and fancies are fully displayed by the $4^{th}$ house. The $4^{th}$ house also indicates the inheritance, the landed property and the means of conveyances and transport at one's disposal.

The $4^{th}$ house indicates educational qualification, achievements, and certificates. In fact, the $4^{th}$ house reveals the education received in school, college or university, whereas the $5^{th}$ house signifies intelligence, brilliance, sharpness of brain, retentive memory or afflicted thought, positive or destructive trend of mind, foresight, intuition, flexibility of brain, imagination and the education received through experience.

The $9^{th}$ house is the house of general prosperity and the $2^{nd}$ house is the house of ready cash and the accumulation of money. A strong $9^{th}$ house indicates that the prosperity lies away from the place of birth and the lord of the $9^{th}$ house and the planet, if any, which occupies the $9^{th}$ house, shows the direction where prosperity can be expected. The negative traits of the father or the guardian and the hostile influences, likely to obstruct the occupational progress, are linked with the $9^{th}$ house. A hostile and weak $9^{th}$ house also points to the hostile and unco-operative blood relations or the partners, if any, and slow progress or retardation may be safely attributed to their intrigues.

The $9^{th}$ house is a very important spot in the horoscope and in importance, it is only second to the $1^{st}$ house. It is a very important trine and its connection with any of the *Kendra* is considered very auspicious. If a malefic happens to own it, the malefic loses much of its evil effect and a benefic adds considerably to its good effects by virtue of its ownership of the $9^{th}$ house.

The $9^{th}$ house is the house of higher thinking. This house represents people, who live in the upper world, the world of the soul; the people who do not think only of the material gain. This house is diagonally opposite to the 3rd house, which is the house of the material gain and which represents people whose only aim of life is to earn money. The 9th house indicates the higher education.

The 5th house speaks about one's social standing and status. It shows ready credit, which one may enjoy in one's dealing in the world of commerce and trade. It reflects the reputation one has earned in one's lifestyles. It indicates the aptitude for studies and the education at the school level.

Among the **planets**, the first to attract our attention is the Moon. The position of Moon, in the house and the sign, is considered the 2nd *lagna*, which is equally important as the *lagna*. It represents the temperament of the person concerned, both mentally and otherwise.

The second in importance, among the planets, is the Sun. The position of the Sun, by virtue of the house and the sign, helps us to measure energy, vitality and stamina one has, at one's disposal, to work out one's way through this world of hard facts and better realities. The position of the Sun enables us to measure the quality and quantity of efforts one can put in. It reveals the legality and the moral standards of one's thinking and one's ways and means of livelihood. Self-respect, self-sufficiency, self-centeredness, pride, vanity, arrogance, etc., all these traits of human character and thinking are fully reflected by the Sun, and the house and the sign the Sun occupies in the horoscope.

Next, we shall examine the mental equipment of the person concerned, to measure and gauge his capacity to think, to imagine, to perceive mentally; to plan, to chalk out the course of action, and the most important of all, to execute and translate his plans into action and practice. To this end, we shall have to consult our very good friend – the Mercury. Mercury, by its position in the horoscope, tells us quite eloquently, about all the points raised above.

The success that our efforts are likely to achieve depends upon our capacity to try and try again. We are to ascertain the quantity and quality of patience and perseverance, one has to work and strive steadfastly by, in one particular direction to achieve one's goal. We are to be sure if one can fight a losing battle. And it is precisely the role of the Saturn. All these characteristics of human nature are represented by Saturn, and the position of Saturn by house and sign indicates the presence or absence of these vital characteristics in the person whose horoscope is under consideration. Saturn also helps us to work out the ratio in which one's efforts achieve the results.

The study of the $5^{th}$ house, along with Jupiter and Mercury, unfolds the chances that may fall in one's way to acquire things by the sheer stroke of luck; it reveals the chances to lead a carefree and effortless life; it informs us about the chances to achieve one's aims and to fulfill one's ambitions by mere asking. Jupiter represents people born with the golden spoon in their mouth. Jupiter signifies honesty, fairness, frankness, outspoken nature, which seldom stoops low to achieve any material gain; it represents a nature, which is absolutely devoid of craze for money at any cost.

A planet, which happens to own a *Kendra* and a Trine, and happens to occupy a good house and sign, may be earmarked as one of the strong arguments in favour of the field of occupational activity, the planet in question points to.

Again, the relation of the lords of a *Kendra* and a Trine, which occupy a good house and a sign, may be listed as one of the strong arguments pointing to the specific field and sphere of occupational activities, where the success awaits the person concerned.

Various classical works like "*Vrihadhora Parashar* of Maharishi Parashar; *Sarawali* of Kalyan Verma; *Phaldipika* of Mantreshwar; *Jatak Parijaat* of Vaidyanath; *Vrihadjatak* of Varahmihir; *Jatak Tattwam* of Mukund Daivagya; and *Phalit Martand*" etc. contain very important rules and results of innumerable planetary combinations with regard to one's professional aspects. These classical works have classified innumerable occupations under the signification of nine planets and twelve signs. First, we feel it essential to study these planetary combinations of concerning classical works, in absence of which one can never be expert in the examination of the professional aspect of the native. We are confident that with the help of the rules, as prescribed in various classics, the suitable and most appropriate occupation can be pin pointed. Thus, the astrology will be of immense benefit to the native, who want to select the profitable and appropriate profession for themselves or for others. The concerning aphorism and rules are given hereunder:-

## 1.1 Consideration of the Tenth House

कर्मभावाधिपो नीचे षडादित्रयगोऽपि चेत् ।
करोति कर्मवैकल्यं स्वोच्चस्वर्क्षपदं विना ।।

(*Bhavakotuhalam,* Ch-15, Vers-43)

If, the lord of the tenth house is debilitated or occupies any other sign, other than his own or sign of exaltation, in the 6$^{th}$, 8$^{th}$ or the 12$^{th}$ house, the native is a failure in the sphere of his occupation.

कर्माधिपे केन्द्रनवात्मजर्क्षे बुधेज्यदृष्टे सबले नराणाम् ।
तुरङ्गमातङ्गनवाम्बराणि भवन्ति नानाधनसंयुतानि ।।

(*Bhavakotuhalam,* Ch-15, Vers-44)

If the lord of the 10$^{th}$ house occupies a *Kendra* or *Trikona* (1$^{st}$, 4$^{th}$, 7$^{th}$, 10$^{th}$, 5$^{th}$ or 9$^{th}$) and is aspected by Mercury, Jupiter or Venus, the native is bestowed with new clothes, horses, elephants, different kinds of wealth and affluence.

कर्मपः केन्द्रकोणस्थो ज्योतिष्टोमादियज्ञकृत् ।
कूपायतनकर्त्ता च देवतातिथिपूजकः ।।

(*Bhavakotuhalam,* Ch-15, Vers-45)

If the lord of the 10$^{th}$ house occupies a *Kendra* or

*Trikona,* the native performs *Yagya* and *mantras* for planets, builds wells and Dharmshalas, respects Devtas and guests, and is very religious.

लग्नादिन्दोर्दशमभवने जन्मकाले नराणा-
मादित्याद्यैः क्रमत उदिता जीविका खेचरेन्द्रैः।
तातान्मातुर्निजरिपुकुलान्मित्र पक्षात्सहोत्थात्
पत्न्याः पुत्रादपि बुधवरैर्जातकज्ञैर्विशेषात्।।

(*Bhavakotuhalam,* Ch-15, Vers-46)

The placement of planets like Sun etc in the 10th, as reckoned from the *lagna* or the position of Moon, decides the means of livelihood of the native, so say the Acharyas.

If the Sun resides in the 10th house, from the *lagna* or Moon, the native earns his livelihood with the help of his father, if Moon mother, if Mars enemies, if Mercury friends, if Jupiter brother, if Venus wife and if Saturn is in the 10th, native earns his livelihood with the help of his servants.

रविशीतकराङ्गकर्मपानां नरवृत्तिः कथिता लवेशवृत्या।
कनकोर्णतृणौषधैर्दिनेशे कृषिदाराम्बुसमाश्रयाच्च चन्द्रे।।

अथ साहसवह्निधातुशस्त्रैः क्षितिजे काव्यकलापतो ज्ञे।
लवणद्विजकाञ्चनेभदेवैर्मणिरौप्यचयैः क्रमाच्च गुर्वोः।।

रविजे श्रमभारनीचतः स्यादिह कर्मेशभवांशनाथवृत्तिः।
हितवैरिनिजर्क्षतुङ्गसंस्थैर्हितवैरिस्ववशाद्धनाप्तिरुच्चैः ।।

(*Bhavakotuhalam,* Ch-15, Vers-47 to 49)

The native's occupation depends on the nature of the lord of *navamsa* in whose *navamsa* the 10th lord, as reckoned from *lagna,* Moon or the Sun, falls. If the 10th lord, from *lagna,* Moon or Sun, obtains the *navamsa* of Sun, the native's livelihood is earned through trading in gold, wool or woolen clothes or herbal medicines; if *navamsa* lord is Moon, through agriculture or trading in agro products, cereal, fish etc, dealing in or related with water, navy, or with the help of wife; if Mars is the *navamsa* lord, fire (trading in electrical products), through courageous deeds, or trading in articles made of metals, firearms etc; if Mercury is the *navamsa* lord, through poetry, painting, or writing etc.; if Jupiter is the *navamsa* lord, through salt or products made of salt, gold, elephants or performing *yagya, anushthan* or *mantra* japa etc.; if Venus is the lord of *navamsa*, through trading in jewels, gems, or silver; and if Saturn is the *navamsa* lord, the native earns through laborious works (servant, manual labour, slavery), coolie like works of low dignity etc. The said lord of the *navamsa,* if occpies the friendly sign, then with the help of friends, in inimical sign through enmies, if in own house through his own endeavours, or if exalted, then sudden gains are there with the help of high class persons.

## Rajyoga :

आज्ञास्थानाधिपे सौम्ये शुभदृष्टयुतेऽपि वा।
शोभनांशगते वापि जातस्त्वाज्ञाधिपो भवेत्।।

(*Sarvarth Chintamani,* Ch-8, Vers-15)

The 10th house is also called the house of authority. Therefore, if the 10th lord, being a natural benefic, is aspected by or conjoined with auspicious planets, or obtains *navamsa* of benefic planets, the native born with this combination is and administrative officer or a magistrate.

आज्ञास्थानगते सूर्ये भूमिपुत्रेन वा युते।
केन्द्रान्विते तदीशेऽपि क्रूरामाज्ञाकरोति सः।।

(*Sarvarth Chintamani,* Ch-8, Vers-16)

If Sun and Mars, both, occupy the 10th house, and the tenth lord is in *Kendra,* the native's commands are nasty and intend punishment.

**Note:** Cruel orders would mean that the native, being a senior officer asks for ardous work from his subordinates, and in case they do not perform, he suspends or even terminates them.

आज्ञाधिपे मन्दयुते रन्ध्रनाथेन संयुते।
क्रूरांशे केन्द्रराशौ वा क्रूरमाज्ञाङ्करोति सः।।

(*Sarvarth Chintamani,* Ch-8, Vers-17)

If the 10th lord conjoins with Saturn or the 8th lord, occupies a cruel *navamsa* or a *Kendra,* the native is used to pass rude orders.

मानाधिपे केन्द्रयुते शुभयुक्तेक्षितेऽपि वा।
शरषष्टयंशसंयुक्ते सौम्यामाज्ञाकरोति सः।।

(*Sarvarth Chintamani,* Ch-8, Vers-18)

If the 10th lord occupies a *Kendra,* is aspected by or conjoined with a benefic and falls in the fifth *Shashthiamsa,* the native passes refined orders.

राहुमान्दियुते माने रन्ध्रे राहौ ध्वजेऽपि वा।
नीचस्थे धर्मभावेशे क्रूरामाज्ञाङ्करोति सः।।

(*Sarvarth Chintamani,* Ch-8, Vers-19)

If Rahu or Gulika occupy the 10th house or Rahu-Ketu fall in the 8th house and the 9th lord obtains a cruel *navamsa,* the native is in habit of passing rude orders.

मानाधिपे चरांशस्थे सदाचारसहितो भवेत्।
स्थिरांशे स्थैर्यमुद्दिष्टं मृगयात्रा द्विदेहगे।।

(*Sarvarth Chintamani,* Ch-8, Vers-29)

This *shloka* has three combinations: 1. If the 10th lord obtains movable *navamsa,* the native always shifts in his profession. 2. If the 10th lord falls in a fixed *navamsa,* the native remains at a permanent place and is not interested in movements or traveling. 3. If the 10th lord acquires common *navamsa,* the native travels like deers (*'Mrag yatra').*

**Note :** As all animals move from their places for grazing etc and come back to their original place, similarly the naitve, whose 10th lord falls in a common sign in *navamsa,* goes out for earning his livelihood and in the evening comes back home after selling his products or after work (Like hawkers or vendors). This is called *'Mrag yatra'*.

## Earning or livelihood :

लग्नाब्जयोर्बलवशात्पदसद्म कर्म्म यत्तत्स्वभावजनितं तदधीशवृद्ध्या।
वृद्धिर्भवेदितरथाऽपचितिर्निरुक्ता कर्म्म स्वनाथशुभखेचरयुक्तदृष्टम्।।

तत्सौख्यजीवनदमुग्रयुतेक्षितं चेत्प्रोक्तं प्रयासभववृत्तिकरं बुधेन्द्रैः।
होरेन्दुतो दशमगेऽम्बरपेऽथ वाऽभ्राङ्कांशाधिपे स्वभलवे निजतुङ्गभागे।।

स्यात्सौख्यवृत्तिररिनीचगृहांशकेऽल्पं सौख्यं च पुण्यमुपचारकदासभृत्यः।
मानेऽमलेष्वखिलकर्म्मण एव सिद्धिर्भूनाथलब्धविभवो जनितो मनुष्यः।।

(*Jyotish Tattwam,* Ch-23, Vers 116-118)

The 10th house, as reckoned from the stronger among the *lagna* or Moon, is the *'Karma sthana'* i.e. the house of profession. The native is engaged in an occupation accordingly. The strength of the 10th lord brightens the prospects and weakness of the 10th lord dims the prospects of profession. If the *'Karma sthana'* or the 10th house is aspected by its own lord or is occupied or aspected by benefic planets, the native's profession is comfortable. And, if the same is occupied or aspected by evil planets, the professional sphere is full of struggles. If the 10th lord, from the *lagna* or Moon, falls in the 10th itself, or if the lord of *navamsa* occupied by the 10th lord acquires the sign or *navamsa* of his own, or his exalted sign or *navamsa,* the profession is blissful. If the *navamsa* lord of the 10th house occupies the inimical sign or *navamsa,* or the sign or *navamsa* of debilitation, the native serves others as a servant or labourer and gets least contentment from his work. If benefics occupy the 10th place, all his endeavours are fruitful and he gets wealth from the King.

सादभ्रपङ्के दुरितेक्षिते दृशि तत्पे गतोर्ज्जे सखलेऽङ्गपे त्रिके।
तज्जीवनं केन भवेन्न तुङ्गभे स्वपेऽशुभेऽसाधुयुतेक्षितेऽङ्गपे ।।

विप्राणिनि क्रूरयुतेऽस्य जीवनोपायेऽपरो नास्ति सहायकस्तदा।
व्ययेऽरिपे राहुयुतेऽथ वा रवियुक्ते कुवृत्तिर्वसतिः परालये।।

(*Jyotish Tattwam,* Ch-23, Vers 119-120)

If malefics occupy the *'Dhan sthana'* i. e. the 2nd house, and they are aspected by evil planets, lord of the 2nd house is weak, and the ascendant lord falls in *Trik* houses with evil planets, the native born under this combination is not happy with his profession. The 2nd lord is a malefic, occupies its own or exalted sign and is aspected or conjoined with malefics, the native born in this combination does not get the help of others in earning his livelihood. If lord of the sixth house falls in the 12th, with Rahu or Sun, the native born in this *yoga* performs condemnable acts and lives in other's house.

## Livelihood through famous or condemned vocations

छायासूनौ कारकांशे प्रसिद्धकर्माजीवी धिष्ण्यपाद् धीनिधाने।
गीर्वाणेड्ये कालधर्म्मेऽमले वाऽसत्याजीवि नीचकर्मादितो ना।।

(*Jyotish Tattwam,* Ch-23, Vers 121)

If Saturn occupies the *karkansha lagna,* the native is engaged in a high-class occupation. If Jupiter occupies the 2nd or 5th from Moon, and benefic or malefics occupy the 8th house, the native born in this combination earns his livelihood through despicable means.

चेदेकस्मिन्खेचरे मित्रराशौ जातो जन्मी चान्यजीवी प्रसूतौ।
कोणः कोणेऽर्थेऽङ्गपे खे क्षयेऽघैः स्यादाजीवी पूरुषो नीचवृत्त्या।।

(*Jyotish Tattwam,* Ch-23, Vers 122)

In whose birth chart, only one planet occupies the friendly sign, the native earns his livelihood through others. If Saturn is in 2nd or *Trikona, lagnesh* is in the 10th and malefics occupy the 8th, the native born under this combination earns his livelihood through lowly and mean acts.

## 1.2 Results of Sun in the Tenth House

कर्माश्रितस्तीक्ष्णकरः स्वतुङ्गे करोति कर्म व्रतकृत्यमेव।
तदंशकस्थो वधबन्धजं च षड्वर्गशुद्धः सकलं कलाजम्।।

(*Vridh Yavan Jatak,* Ch-34, Vers-1)

If Sun occupies his exalted sign in the 10th house, the native works as a *Purohit,* performs religious *anushthans, vrat etc.*

If Sun acquires his exalted *navamsa,* the native executes killings, murders, detentions and abduction etc.

If Sun occupies the 10th house and is powerful and auspicious in *Shadvargas,* the native is deft in various skills and earns his livelihood through exhibition of his talent.

**Yoga for business:**

नीचाश्रितस्तीक्ष्णकरोऽम्बरस्थो नृणां विधत्ते बहुदासकर्म।
तस्यैव भागे वणिजोद्भवं च वर्गोत्तमस्थो वणिजप्रसूतम्।।

(*Vridh Yavan Jatak,* Ch-34, Vers-2)

If Sun occupies the 10th house in debilitation, the native serves others as servant.

If Sun in the 10th house obtains the *navamsa* of debilitation, the native enters into business.

If Sun in the 10th is *vargottam,* the native earns through his family business.

**Yoga for agriculture or government job:**

मित्राश्रयस्थो दिनकृत् खसंस्थः करोति पुंसां कृषिजं च कर्म।
मित्रस्य भागे कुनृपस्य सेवजं पापस्य वर्गे वधबन्धजं सदा।।

(*Vridh Yavan Jatak,* Ch-34, Vers-3)

If Sun falls in the 10th house, in a friendly sign, the native eanrs his livelihood through agriculture.

If Sun occupies the 10th house in an evil *navamsa,* the native servs a cruel king.

If Sun occupies malefic *vargas*, the native earns through murder, abduction etc.

**Yoga for Condemned professions:**

शत्र्वाश्रयस्थो दिनपो नराणां ददाति कर्माशुभमेव नित्यम् ।
तस्यैव भागे जनगर्हितं च मूलत्रिकोणे खरसेवजं च ।।

(*Vridh Yavan Jatak,* Ch-34, Vers-4)

If Sun falls in an inimical sign in the 10th house, the native performs lowly deeds. If Sun obtains his inimical *navamsa*, the native always performs acts condemned by others.

If Sun occupies the 10th house in his *Mooltikona* sign, the native serves cruel people.

## Nature of Sun

भैषज्यवादोर्णतृणाम्बुधान्यहिरण्यमुक्ताक्रयविक्रयेण ।
मंत्रोपदेशेन रसैर्विनोदमार्गैरसौ जीवति भास्करांशे ।।

(*Jyotish Tattwam,* Ch-23, Vers-128)

If the lord of *navamsa* of the said 10th lord is Sun, the native earns his livelihood through medicines, conflicts, trading in wool, grass, water, cereal, gold, pearl or through preaching of *Mantras,* art or means of entertainment.

## 1.3 Results of Moon in the Tenth House

**Highly acclaimed and benevolent occupations:**

कर्माश्रितः शीतकरः स्वतुङ्गे करोति कर्म प्रथितं नृलोके ।
तस्यैव भागे द्विजदेवजं च षड्वर्गशुद्धो वरदानभाजम् ।।

(*Vridh Yavan Jatak,* Ch-34, Vers-5)

If the Moon occupies the 10th house, in the sign of its exaltation, the native engages himself in an occupation, generally highly praised or considered dignified by the people.

If the Moon occupies the 10th house, in his own or exalted *navamsa,* the native is employed in a vocation that delights Devtas or Brahmins.

If the Moon is in beneficial *vargas,* the native takes on charity and donation.

**Combinations for Commission agent:**

नीचाश्रितः शीतकरोऽम्बरस्थो ददाति कर्मातिसलज्जमेव।
तस्यैव भागे क्रयविक्रयोत्थं पापस्य वर्गे व्यसनोद्भवं च।।

(*Vridh Yavan Jatak,* Ch-34, Vers-6)

If Moon falls in the 10th house, in the sign of debilitation, the native takes up a vocation, which he himself is ashamed of.

If Moon obtains the *navamsa* of debilitation, the native earns through brokerage, deals in cereals or sale and purchase of cars.

If Moon falls in the 10th house in evil *vargas,* the native takes up the job of corrupt practices.

**Knowledge of Shastras :**

मित्राश्रयस्थो यदि शीतरश्मिः कर्माश्रितः कर्म ददाति सौम्यम्।
तस्यैव भागे बहुशास्त्रभाजं वर्गोत्तमस्थो मखजं सदैव।।

(*Vridh Yavan Jatak,* Ch-34, Vers-7)

If Moon in the 10th house joins a friendly sign, the native is engaged in gentle and worthy profession.

If Moon acquires a friendly *navamsa,* the native earns his livelihood through his knowledge of various Shastras.

If Moon obtains the *vargottam navamsa,* the native performs *Yagya* etc.

शत्र्वाश्रयस्थोऽम्बरगो निशेशः कर्म प्रसूते सुतरां नृशंसम्।
तस्यैव भागे वनितोद्भवं च मूलत्रिकोणे नृपदैत्यजातम्।।

(*Vridh Yavan Jatak,* Ch-34, Vers-8)

If Moon occupies the $10^{th}$ house in inimical sign, the native takes up cruel and callous works.

If Moon joins the inimical *navamsas,* the native earns through the help of females or deals in objects meant for women.

If Moon joins the sign of her *Mooltrikona,* the native serves the king or a wicked person.

## Nature of Moon

वस्त्रक्रयाद्वारिसमुद्भवानां व्यापारतो राजवधूश्रयेण।
विनोदमृद्वादकृषिक्रियादे र्वार्मण्डलांशे कथयन्ति वृत्तिम्।।

(*Jyotish Tattwam,* Ch-23, Vers-129)

If Moon is the significator, the native earns through the trade of things grown in water, through the shelter of king or ladies, entertainment, work of clay and soil, and through agriculture.

## 1.4 Results of Mars in the Tenth House

**Livelihood through speculation, lottery or war:**

भौमोऽम्बरस्थो यदि तुङ्गसंस्थो युद्धोद्भवं कर्म ददाति पुंसाम्।
तस्यांशके द्यूतसमुद्भवं च षड्वर्गशुद्धः स्मरजं नितान्तम्।।

(*Vridh Yavan Jatak,* Ch-34, Vers-9)

If Mars occupies the $10^{th}$ house in the sign of exaltation, the native earns his livelihood through war i.e. trading in material used in battles and war, or by serving in army.

If Mars in the $10^{th}$ obtains exalted *navamsa,* the native trades in lottery, gambling and speculation.

If Mars occupies the $10^{th}$ in beneficial *vargas,* the native deals in trades satisfying the sex needs.

**Livelihood through prostitution :**

नीचाश्रितो भूतनयोऽम्बरस्थः कर्म प्रसूते परदारजातम्।
तदंशकस्थो गणिकोद्भवं च पापस्य वर्गे ह्युभयं सदैव।।

(*Vridh Yavan Jatak,* Ch-34, Vers-10)

If Mars occupies the 10th house in inimical sign, the native earns livelihood through the contact with other's wives.

If Mars occupies the 10th in debilitated *navamsa*, the person earns through prostitution.

If Mars occupies the 10th house in evil *vargas*, the native does both the above.

मित्राश्रयस्थः क्षितिजोऽम्बरस्थः कर्म प्रसूते ऽक्षममुद्भवं च।
तस्यांशकस्थो बहुभारजातं वर्गोत्तमस्थः प्रणयेन हीनम्।।

(*Vridh Yavan Jatak,* Ch-34, Vers-11)

If Mars in the 10th joins his friendly sign, the native earns through gambling.

If Mars obtains friendly *navamsa*, the native has to execute the work of great responsibility.

If Mars falls in *vargottam navamsa*, the native dispassionately enters into an apt enterprise.

**Yoga for beggars and uncertain income:**

शत्र्वाश्रयस्थः क्षितिजो नभोगः कर्म प्रसूते बहुदैन्यजातम्।
तस्यैव भागे त्वथ भिक्षजं च मूलत्रिकोणे ऽम्बरकाष्ठजातम्।।

(*Vridh Yavan Jatak,* Ch-34, Vers-12)

If Mars occupies the inimical sign in the 10th house, the native's profession is pathetic.

If Mars acquires his debilitated *navamsa*, the native earns through begging.

If Mars in the 10th house joins his *Mooltrikona* sign, the native takes up the works related with wood and with irregular or uncertain income.

## Nature of Mars

व्योमोल्मुकांशे समरप्रहाराद्धविर्भुजा साहसधातुमूलात्।
विवादतः स्तब्धकलिप्रवृत्त्या जीवेदसौ मोषकवृत्तितो वा।।

(*Jyotish Tattwam,* Ch-23, Vers-130)

In the navamsa of Mars, the earning is through war, assault, fire, courage, metals, conflicts, or fraud or theft.

## 1.5 Results of Mercury in Tenth House

**Agriculture or rearing of animals:**

सौम्यः स्वतुङ्गे यदि कर्मसंस्थः कर्म प्रसूते धनधान्यजातम्।
तस्यैव भागे च चतुष्पदोत्थं षड्वर्गशुद्धो गजवाजिजातम्।।

(*Vridh Yavan Jatak,* Ch-34, Vers-13)

If Mercury occupies the 10th house in the sign of exaltation, the native earns his livelihood through money or cereals i.e. earns interest on money and grows cereals in his agriculture and earns through its trading.

If Mercury in the 10th obtains exalted *navamsa,* the native earns through animal keeping.

If Mercury occupies the 10th in beneficial *vargas,* the native earns livelihood through elephants or horses.

**Combination for self-employed persons:**

नीचाश्रितः सोमसुतोऽम्बरस्थः कर्म प्रसूते निजमेव पुंसाम्।
तस्यैव भागे परदेशजातं पापस्य वर्गे खलजं सदैव।।

(*Vridh Yavan Jatak,* Ch-34, Vers-14)

If Mercury occupies the 10th house in inimical sign, the native is a self-employed person.

If Mercury occupies the 10th in debilitated *navamsa,* the person earns in a foreign land.

If Mercury occupies the 10th house in evil *vargas,* the native earns through contact with dishonest and wicked people.

**Business of Horses or silver:**

मित्राश्रयस्थः शशिजो ऽम्बरस्थः कर्म प्रसूते हयविक्रयोत्थम् ।
तस्यैव भागे रजतं नराणां वर्गोत्तमस्थो ऽद्भुतमंत्रजातम् ।।

(*Vridh Yavan Jatak,* Ch-34, Vers-15)

If Mercury in the 10th joins his friendly sign, the native earns through the sale and purchase of Vehicle or horses etc.

If Mercury obtains friendly *navamsa*, the native trades in silver.

If Mercury falls in *vargottam navamsa*, the native earns his livelihood through amazing *Mantras* and strong inner power.

शत्र्वाश्रयस्थः शशिजोऽम्बरस्थः कर्म प्रसूते बहुकष्टजातम् ।
तस्यैव भागे गुणवर्जितं च मूलत्रिकोणे सुयशोद्भवं च ।।

(*Vridh Yavan Jatak,* Ch-34, Vers-16)

If Mercury occupies the inimical sign in the 10th house, the native earns through hard toil and laborious work.

If Mercury acquires his debilitated *navamsa*, the native spends quality time.

If Mercury in the 10th house joins his *Mooltrikona* sign, the native takes up the works bestowing him much distinction.

## Nature of Mercury

नवांश के चान्द्रमसस्य काव्य-ज्ञानेन शास्त्रागममार्गरूपात् ।
पुरोहितत्वेन जपात्प्रवृत्तिः पाठाच्छ्रुतेः शिल्पकलादिभिः स्यात् ।।

(*Jyotish Tattwam,* Ch-23, Vers-131)

In the *navamsa* of Mercury, the earning is through the knowledge of poetry, Shastras & Vedantas, priesthood, recitation of *Mantras,* Vedas and arts and crafts.

## 1.6 Results of Jupiter in the Tenth House

जीवो ऽम्बरस्थो यदि तुङ्गसंस्थो ददाति कर्म प्रचुरं प्रधानम्।
तदंशकस्थो द्विजपूजनोत्थं षड्वर्गशुद्धः सुजनार्चनोत्थम्।।

(*Vridh Yavan Jatak,* Ch-34, Vers-17)

If Jupiter occupies the 10th house in the sign of exaltation, the native significantly grows in his profession.

If Jupiter obtains exalted *navamsa,* the native respects and serves Brahmins and learned.

If Jupiter occupies the 10th in beneficial *vargas*, the native serves gentle men.

नीचाश्रितो देवगुरुः खसंस्थः करोति कर्माधमलोकसेव्यम्।
तदंशकस्थोऽद्भुतचौर्यजातं पापस्य वर्गेऽर्थविवर्जितं च।।

(*Vridh Yavan Jatak,* Ch-34, Vers-18)

If Jupiter occupies the 10th house in the sign of debilitation, the native serves and helps wicked and downtrodden.

If Jupiter occupies the 10th in debilitated *navamsa*, the person is engaged in theft etc.

If Jupiter occupies the 10th house in evil *vargas*, the native performs gratuitous work i.e. his vocation does not earn him money.

मित्राश्रयस्थो दशमे सुरेज्यः करोति कर्माणि शुभानि नित्यम्।
तदंशसंस्थो नृपतेः समुत्थं वर्गोत्तमस्थो महिषीगवोत्थम्।।

(*Vridh Yavan Jatak,* Ch-34, Vers-19)

If Jupiter in the 10th joins his friendly sign, the native always earns through beneficial and auspicious works.

If Jupiter obtains friendly *navamsa*, the native servs in government.

If Jupiter occupies the 10th in *vargottam navamsa*, the native keeps cows and buffaloes and earns through them.

**Combinations for fraud and jobs dear to king:**

शत्र्वाश्रयस्थो दशमे सुरेज्यः कर्म प्रसूते सततं कृतघ्नम्।
तस्यैव भागे परवंचनेन मूलत्रिकोणे नृपतेरभीष्टम्।।

(*Vridh Yavan Jatak,* Ch-34, Vers-20)

If Jupiter occupies the inimical sign in the 10th house, the native performs thankless jobs.

If Jupiter occupies the 10th house in inimical *navamsa,* the native deceives and swindles others.

If Jupiter in the 10th house joins his *Mooltrikona* sign, the native takes up the works dear to the King i.e. works in conformity with the government.

## Nature of Jupiter

महामतेर्नन्दलवे पुराणशास्त्रागमानां पठनात्स जीवेत्।
देवद्विजोपासकनीतिधर्म्मोपदेशतोऽध्यापकमार्गरूपात्।।

(*Jyotish Tattwam,* Ch-23, Vers-132)

In the *navamsa* of Jupiter, livelihood is through narration of Vedas, Puranas & Shastras; the service of Brahnins & Devtas; preaching of Dharma & ideals, and teaching.

## 1.7 Results of Venus in the Tenth House

**Trading in gems and diamond:**

तुङ्गाश्रयस्थो ऽम्बरगो भृगुश्च कर्म प्रसूते जनवल्लभं च।
तस्यैव भागे मणिमौक्तिकाढ्यं षड्वर्गशुद्धः कनकोद्भवं च।।

(*Vridh Yavan Jatak,* Ch-34, Vers-21)

If Venus occupies the 10th house in the sign of exaltation, the native takes up a popular and well liked profession.

If Venus obtains exalted *navamsa,* the native trades in Diamonds & Pearls.

If Venus occupies the $10^{th}$ in beneficial *vargas*, the native trades in gold.

**Unsuccesful vocations:**

नीचाश्रयस्थः भृगुजः खसंस्थः कर्म प्रसूते वनिताश्रितं च।
तस्यैव भागेऽल्पसुखं नितान्तं पापस्य वर्गे गुरुदुःखजं च।।

(*Vridh Yavan Jatak,* Ch-34, Vers-22)

If Venus occupies the $10^{th}$ house in the sign of debilitation, the native takes up a job requiring contacts with women.

If Venus occupies the $10^{th}$ in debilitated *navamsa*, the person is engaged in difficult and ardous work giving him sorrow.

If Venus occupies the $10^{th}$ house in evil *vargas*, the native performs troublesome and fruitless works.

मित्राश्रयस्थो भृगुजोऽम्बरस्थः करोति कर्म प्रभुतासमेतम्।
तस्यैव भागे निजबन्धुजातं वर्गोत्तमस्थो बहुगौरवाढ्यम्।।

(*Vridh Yavan Jatak,* Ch-34, Vers-23)

If Venus in the $10^{th}$ joins his friendly sign, the native joins a profession with authority and power.

If Venus occupies the $10^{th}$ house and obtains friendly *navamsa*, the native engages in business with the help of his brothers.

If Venus falls in *vargottam navamsa*, the native takes on business of dignity and pride.

शत्र्वाश्रयस्थो भृगुजोऽम्बरस्थः कर्म प्रसूते विरजं नृशंसम्।
तस्यैव भागे बहुचिन्तयाढ्यं मूलत्रिकोणे ऽनृतसंयुतं च।।

(*Vridh Yavan Jatak,* Ch-34, Vers-24)

If Venus occupies the inimical sign in the $10^{th}$ house, the native performs cruel jobs

If Venus occupies the $10^{th}$ house in inimical *navamsa*, the native performs works giving much anxiety.

If Venus in the $10^{th}$ house joins his *Mooltrikona* sign, the native takes up the works based on lies.

## Nature of Venus

माणिक्यनागाश्वसुवर्णमूलात्तक्रौदनक्षारगुणक्रयेण ।
लोभेन बध्वाः सुरभिक्रयेण जातो जनो जीवति भार्गवांशे ।।

(*Jyotish Tattwam,* Ch-23, Vers-133)

In *navamsa* of Venus, livelihood is through gems, *Haati Daant*, horses, gold, rice, salt, favour of women, purchase of cows and talents.

## 1.8 Results of Saturn in the Tenth House

**Gentle or harried profesions:**

तुङ्गाश्रितः सूर्यसुतोऽम्बरस्थः कर्म प्रसूते ऽतिमृदुस्थिरं च ।
तस्यैव भागे बहुशिल्पजं च षड्वर्गशुद्धः प्रियसाध्वसं च ।।

(*Vridh Yavan Jatak,* Ch-34, Vers-25)

If Saturn occupies the $10^{th}$ house in the sign of exaltation, the native's vocation is permanent, soft and tender.

If Saturn obtains exalted *navamsa* in the $10^{th}$ house, the native engages in an employment associated with art, craft and sculpting.

If Saturn occupies the $10^{th}$ in beneficial *vargas*, the native's job is harried and anxious.

नीचाश्रितः सूर्यसुतोऽम्बरस्थः कर्म प्रसूते द्विजद्रोहजातम् ।
तस्यैव भागे नृपसेवजं च पापस्य वर्गे सनृशंसरूपम् ।।

(*Vridh Yavan Jatak,* Ch-34, Vers-26)

If Saturn occupies the $10^{th}$ house in the sign of debilitation, the native revolts against Bahmins.

If Saturn occupies the $10^{th}$ in debilitated *navamsa*, the native works for the king (Government).

If Saturn occupies the 10th house in evil *vargas*, the native performs gruesome works.

मित्राश्रितो भास्करजश्च स्वस्थः करोति कर्म प्रभुताविहीनम् ।
तस्यैव भागे नृपसेवजं च वर्गोत्तमस्थो मृगया समेतम् ।।

(*Vridh Yavan Jatak,* Ch-34, Vers-27)

If Saturn in the 10th joins his friendly sign, the native engages in a profession devoid of authority, influence or power.

If Saturn obtains friendly *navamsa*, the native takes up a government job.

If Saturn joins the 10th house in *vargottam navamsa*, the native earns his livelihood through *Shikar.*

शत्र्वाश्रयस्थोऽर्कसुतोऽम्बरस्थः कर्म प्रसूते बहुकष्टजातम् ।
तस्यैव भागे परपैशुनोत्थं मूलत्रिकोणे भिषजोद्भवं च ।।

(*Vridh Yavan Jatak,* Ch-34, Vers-28)

If Saturn occupies the inimical sign in the 10th house, the native performs difficult and ardous jobs.

If Saturn occupies the 10th house in inimical *navamsa,* the native takes up the job criticizing and censuring others.

If Saturn in the 10th house joins his *Mooltrikona* sign, the native takes up medical profession etc

राज्यपदव्यापारमुद्रानृपमानराज्यपितृमहत्पदाप्तिपुण्याज्ञाकीर्ति-
वृष्टिप्रवृत्तिप्रवासकर्माजीवजानु पूर्त्यादिदशमाच्चिन्त्यम् ।।

(*Jatak Bhushanam,* Ch-12, Vers-8)

**Following should be delineated from the 10th house:**

Government job, trading currency, honour from government, gain of kingdom, father, acquiring high post, command, fame, rain, *Punya,* foreign travel, residence in foreign land, livelihood, occupation, knees, accomplishment of work.

## Nature of Saturn

मन्दांशके मार्गगमादिकेन मिथो विरोधोद्भवहेतुतोऽस्य।
वधादिकैः काष्ठमयैः सुनीचशिल्पैः प्रवृत्तिः श्रमभारवाहात्।।

(*Jyotish Tattwam,* Ch-23, Vers-134)

In the *navamsa* of Saturn, livelihood is through to & fro tavel, mutual disrespect and repulsion, murder etc, wood, lowly craft, labour and carrying burden.

## 1.9 Different Signs in the Tenth House

**Vargas of Aries in the tenth**

आरामपुत्र (बुद्धि) सेवाकृषिरसवणिगर्कदूतकार्येण।
जीवन्ति नरा नित्यं मेषगणे दशमराशिस्थे।।

(*Saravali,* Ch-32, Vers-66)

If *vargas* of Aries fall in the 10th house of the natal chart, the native earns his livelihood through garden, sons, intelligence, service, agriculture, sale of juice, trader or emissary.

**Vargas of Taurus in the tenth**

वृषभगणे दशमस्थे शकटचतुष्पदविहङ्गमृगजीवी।
धान्यादिसङ्ग्रहेण च जाङ्गलदेशे फलं प्रायः।।

(*Saravali,* Ch-32, Vers-67)

If *vargas* of Taurus fall in the 10th house of the natal chart, the native earns through vehicles, animals, birds, deers and accumulation of cereals, and generally this is advantageos in wild places.

**Vargas of Gemini in the tenth**

जलवणिजः सुसमृद्ध्या मुक्ताशङ्खप्रवालभाण्डैश्च।
लिपिगणितलेख्यजीवी नृमिथुनवर्गे दशमसंस्थे।।

(*Saravali,* Ch-32, Vers-68)

If *vargas* of Gemini fall in the 10th house of the natal chart, the native earns his livelihood through water, money i.e. interest, trading in pearl, coral, Conch shell, utensils, and calculation and talent of writing.

**_Vargas_ of Cancer in the tenth**

शस्त्राग्नियोनिपोषणमुक्तासंख्योपजीवनं चैव।
आखेटकवृत्त्या वा कर्किणि वर्गे च दशमस्थे।।

(*Saravali,* Ch-32, Vers-69)

If *vargas* of Cancer fall in the 10th house of the natal chart, the native earns his livelihood through arms, fire, prostitution, pearl, mathematics or hunting.

**Vargas of Leo in the tenth**

सन्नाहका मणीनां पाषाणस्वर्णरूप्यकूटांश्च।
कर्षणनिरता लेये गोजीवा धान्यवाणिजकाः।।

(*Saravali,* Ch-32, Vers-70)

If *vargas* of Leo fall in the 10th house of the natal chart, the native earns his livelihood through making jewellewry; trading in stones, gold, silver; agriculture, cows and buffaloes; and trading in cereals.

**Vargas of Virgo in the tenth**

शाकटिका मणिकारा हैरण्या गन्धविक्रये निपुणाः।
गान्धर्वशिल्पलेख्यैः कन्यावर्गे सदा विभवाः।।

(*Saravali,* Ch-32, Vers-71)

If *vargas* of Virgo fall in the 10th house of the natal chart, the native is a car mechanic, gold smith, *Jauhri,* expert in selling perfumes, and prospers as a singer, artist or a writer.

**Vargas of Libra in the tenth**

प्रायोज्यानुपदेशाद्धिरण्यपरिवर्तनाच्च मित्राय।
जायन्ते च मनुष्या नानाव्यवहारभागिनः सततम्।।

वाणिज्यविपणिजीवा गोजीवा महिषजीवाश्च।
नानापण्यसमृद्धाः सलिलोद्भवपण्यवृत्तयः ख्याताः।।

धनधान्यमूलवणिजः फलमूलकृषीबलाश्चैव।
जायन्ते घटवर्गे दशमस्थानस्थिते कलावृत्ताः।।

(*Saravali,* Ch-32, Vers 72-74)

If *Rashi* or *vargas* of Libra fall in the 10th house of the natal chart, the native earns his livelihood through commandsorder without any reason; change of gold for friend; by behaving differently; through trade, shop, cows or buffaloes; involved in trading of different things; famous trader of articles growing in water; money, cereals; production and sale of fruits and roots, and by using his artistic talents.

**Vargas of Scorpio in the tenth**

स्त्रीसम्पर्कजविभवा जायन्ते कर्षणानुतिरताश्च।
नित्योद्युक्ताश्चौराः पृथिवीपतिसेवकाः पापाः।।

देहचिकित्सानिरता लोहकरा जीविनोऽलिसंज्ञर्क्षे।
वर्गे नभस्तलगते धान्यानां चोपजीविनो नित्यम्।।

(*Saravali,* Ch-32, Vers 75-76)

If *vargas* of Scorpio fall in the 10th house of the natal chart, the native prospers through contact with ladies, is dedicated to agriculture, is enterprising in daily chores, is a thief, wrong doer, servant of a king, *Vaidya*, iron smith, and a trader in cereals.

**Vargas of Sagittarius in the tenth**

नृपसचिवदुर्गपालनगोजीवनवाजिकाष्ठशकुनैश्च ।
यन्त्रोपस्करगणितैर्जीवन्ति नराश्चिकित्सया धनुषः।।

(*Saravali,* Ch-32, Vers 77)

If *vargas* of Sagittarius fall in the 10th house of the natal chart, the native is minister of a king, guard of the fort, attends to cows and ox, earns through horses, wood, clothes, technical instruments, mathematics and medicine.

**Vargas of Capricorn in the tenth**

दशमे कुरङ्गवर्गे जलपण्यधनो भवेन्महाविभवः।
खट्वारामारोपणरसायनैर्वर्तते जातः ।।

(*Saravali,* Ch-32, Vers-78)

If *Rashi* of Capricorn falls in the 10th house or in the 10th maximum *vargas* of Capricorn are there, the native gets wealth through trade in water, bed, plantation of trees in the garden and chemicals.

**Vargas of Aquarius in the tenth**

शस्त्रदहनप्रभेदैश्चौर्येण च वर्तते खननवृत्त्या।
दशमे घटधरवर्गे भारवहस्कन्धबाहुबलात् ।।

(*Saravali,* Ch-32, Vers-79)

If *Rashi* of Aquarius falls in the 10th house, or in the 10th, maximum *vargas* of Aquarius are there, the native earns through arms, process of burning, as a thief, by digging in the ground, through the strength of his arms and shoulder, by carrying load etc.

**Vargas of Pisces in the tenth**

शस्त्रासात्सलिलाद्योनिप्रपोषणादश्वविक्रयाद्वाऽपि।
वर्गे मीनप्रभवे दशमस्थे जायते वृत्तिः ।।

(*Saravali,* Ch-32, Vers-80)

If *Rashi* of Pisces falls in the 10th house or in the 10th maximum *vargas* of Pisces are there, the native earns through arms, water, prostitution, and sale of horses.

## CHAPTER-2

# Propensities for Administrative Services

Indian Administrative Services are the most sought after services. They attract highest attention in the present age because of its many inherent advantages. Apart from being highest paid among the government servants they include officers who make the system run. They are the backbone of the administration of the country. During the change of political parties, running the state, it is the administrative servants who form the continuity. Any student, who is a little intelligent, definitely aspires for and at least once tries his luck in the civil services examinations. Apart from IAS proper, this civil service examination also includes other class one services as well.

The ascendant must be strong, as this is unquestionable for any successful vocation of high attributes. *Rashi* and *navamsa* both should be considered. The ascendant signifies the aptitude of the native as far as professional aspect is concerned.

The Sun and Moon are the royal planets, whereas Cancer and Leo are the royal signs. They are also treated as king and queen in the group of all planets. IAS is directly linked with the government throughout their service. So, these kingly planets have a prominent role to play in their birth charts. The Sun or Moon must be linked with the $10^{th}$, $9^{th}$, $8^{th}$, or the $1^{st}$ house, in one or the other way, as the case may be. The Sun or Moon must be placed there or may aspect these houses or may be associated with their lords. If it is not so, one will not be successful in IAS proper. Before proceeding further, we would like to lay emphasis on the fact that the $8^{th}$ house is the most misunderstood house even today. A general understanding has very strongly been inserted in our minds that the lords of 6th, 8th or 12th houses are bad. They spoil the house wherever they are posited. Those houses are also spoiled whose lords join 6th, 8th or 12th from the ascendant. This is absolutely wrong, at least the way in which we have adopted it.

The 6th house is 9th, if reckoned from the 10th house, and it is 10th, if counted from the 9th house. Thus, 6th house indicates fortunes of service like promotion, extension etc. Of course, the 6th house is an evil house as it indicates diseases, enemies, loans and the like but this can not be taken as malefic for all service matters also. For one to be in service, and not the business or otherwise, the sixth house should be related to the ascendant or the 10th house in any manner. The lord of the sixth may be placed in the ascendant or the 10th, or vice versa, or these lords may be conjoined together in any house or aspect each other. They may occupy each other's *navamsa* as well. For a govt. service, involvement of one of the royal signs, Cancer or Leo, or the influence of one of the luminaries over the combination of service would be there.

The 8th house is also mostly wrongly interpreted by majority of students. The lord of the 10th if joins the 8th, a general understanding will be there that the profession of the native will be very ordinary. But it is not so and he may even become the head of the department provided other factors are also favourable. This can very strongly be said, as we have frequently found the relation between the 10th and the 8th house in the birth charts of top executives, heads of the departments and IAS etc., but mostly in the service class persons.

The 8th house is 11th from the 10th house while 10th from the 11th house. The 11th house indicates sources of income, wealth and accomplishment of ambitions. So, the 8th house represents ambitions connected with service. This house also shows the nature of work, one will undertake as his profession. As the relation between *lagna* and 11th house is treated as auspicious for all matters, which come under the domain of *lagna*, similarly the relation between the $8^{th}$ and the $10^{th}$ houses should be regarded as auspicious for all the matters connected with the $10^{th}$ i.e. all service and professional matters. We can not ignore the $8^{th}$ house while deciding the vocation for anyone. The $10^{th}$ house signifies the work done by a native to earn money while the $8^{th}$ house denotes the earnings through that work. As the work and earnings from that are directly related, similarly the $10^{th}$ and the $8^{th}$ houses are strongly related. This should be borne in mind whenever analyzing any horoscope for deciding vocation or means of livelihood.

The $9^{th}$ and the $10^{th}$ houses from the *lagna* are most important. If the $9^{th}$ house is not strong that means his fortune is weak. Our sages have said *'Na Dhan Balam Na Paurusham, Bhagyati Phalti Sarvatra'*. One may be very knowledgeable but his merits remain unrecognized, if he is unlucky. The $9^{th}$ house must also be very strongly disposed for one's success in IAS. If the luminaries are connected with the $9^{th}$ house or its lord in any way, the native has chances to get success in IAS examinations, provided other factors for this are also present in the horoscope.

There must be a link between the $10^{th}$ and the $9^{th}$ house, which means that one's profession is supported by his fortune. Both of these houses must be strong.

(a) If luminaries occupy the $10^{th}$ house in association with their lords.

(b) If the Sun is exalted in the $9^{th}$ house and Moon in the $10^{th}$.

(c) If the $9^{th}$ lord occupies the $9^{th}$ and the $10^{th}$ lord occupies the $10^{th}$ e.g. the Sun in the $10^{th}$ and Moon in the $9^{th}$, for Scorpio ascendant.

(d) If there is mutual exchange between lords of $9^{th}$ and $10^{th}$ houses.

(e) If the $10^{th}$ lord joins $9^{th}$ in association with the $9^{th}$ lord, or vice versa.

(f) The $10^{th}$ and $9^{th}$ lords conjoin at a favourable place and aspect the $10^{th}$ and $9^{th}$ houses respectively, e.g. for Aries ascendant, Jupiter and Saturn, lords of $9^{th}$ and $10^{th}$, conjoin in *lagna*, from where they aspect their own houses $9^{th}$ and $10^{th}$.

(g) The $10^{th}$ and $9^{th}$ lords conjoin in $4^{th}$ or $5^{th}$ or even in the *lagna*.

(h) The $9^{th}$ and the $10^{th}$ lords aspect each other's house and also aspect mutually.

These are a few positions, which show that $9^{th}$ and $10^{th}$ houses are strong enough and one may get success in all India competition of civil services, provided other conditions are also present in the birth chart of the native aspiring for IAS.

Karmic Control Planets do play a vital role for one to be successful as an administrative officer. Mr. M.C. Jain has discovered Karmic control planets and has written a book on this subject. These are the planets that give results due to deeds of past life, good or bad. The dispositors of Rahu and Ketu are called the Karmic control planets.

For one's success in IAS, at least one of the Karmic control planets must be related with any of the luminary i.e. the Sun or Moon, either by conjunction or aspect. If it is not so, then it must be linked either with *lagna*, $10^{th}$ or the $9^{th}$ house, though in that case success will come after great difficulty. If Rahu or Ketu join the royal sign, Cancer or Leo, the Karmic control planet will itself be a luminary. That may tend one to become an IAS, if $9^{th}$, $8^{th}$ and the $10^{th}$ houses are disposed as discussed above.

Scholars and students of astrology will be surprised to know that Venus is one of the chief planets for becoming IAS. We have invariably found that Venus is conjoined with the Sun or Moon, or the $9^{th}$ and $10^{th}$ lords, in all IAS natives. Venus should join or aspect or own the $10^{th}$ or $9^{th}$ house or should be associated with the luminaries.

The reason appears to be very simple that IAS officers have all sorts of comforts and luxuries in life. They possess decent bungalows to live, cars to move and many servants to help them. They have all kinds of modern amenities and facilities at their command. The government provides these all to them. Therefore, Venus plays a vital role in the horoscopes of IAS natives.

We can **conclude** thus:

1. The 6th house should be related with the 10th or the ascendant, in any manner along with the influence of luminaries, for one to be in government service.
2. The10th and 9th houses should be strong or related to each other powerfully, with a strong *lagna*.
3. The 10th and 8th houses may be related to each other. If it is so, it should be considered an auspicious factor for success in IAS.
4. Role of luminaries must be seen. At least one of them, the Sun or Moon, may have a concern with the *lagna*, 10th, 9th or the 8th house.
5. Karmic Control planets must have a say with the luminaries or otherwise with the 9th or 10th lords.
6. Venus plays a vital role for administrative services. That should be related with the Sun, Moon, or with 9th or 10th lords.

Let us now verify the principles enumerated above with the help of some practical examples.

*Illustration : 2.1* **(AB)** *Horoscope No.: 1*

Date of birth : 02.05.1957 Time of birth : 12:38:00 hrs
Place of birth : Gorakhpur Lat 26:45:00 N Long 83:23:00E
Ayanamsa : 23:15:51 Sidereal Time : 03:21:16

| **Pln** | **Degree** | **Rasi** | **Nakshatra** | **Pad** |
|---|---|---|---|---|
| Asc | 1:34:35 | Leo | Magha | 1 |
| Sun | 18:20:56 | Ari | Bharani | 2 |
| Mon | 16:22:00 | Tau | Rohini | 2 |
| Mar | 5:15:51 | Gem | Mrigsira | 4 |

| | | | | |
|---|---|---|---|---|
| Mer (R/C) | 24:08:30 | Ari | Bharani | 4 |
| Jup (R) | 28:59:55 | Leo | U. Phalguni | 1 |
| Ven (C) | 22:58:44 | Ari | Bharani | 3 |
| Sat (R) | 19:50:33 | Sco | Jyestha | 1 |
| Rah | 26:18:50 | Lib | Visakha | 2 |
| Ket (C) | 26:18:50 | Ari | Bharani | 4 |

**Lagna Chart**

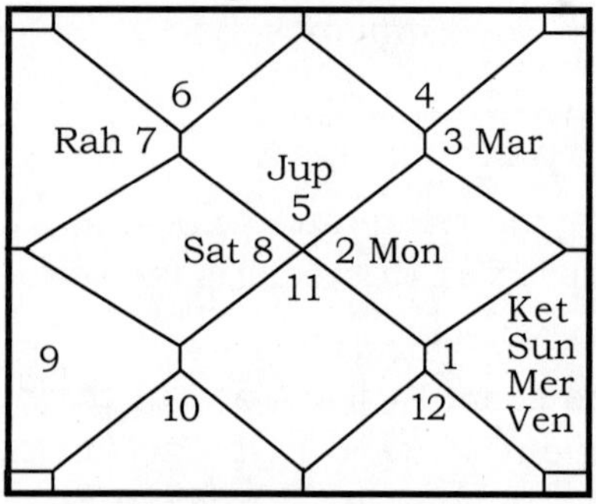


**Navamsa Chart**

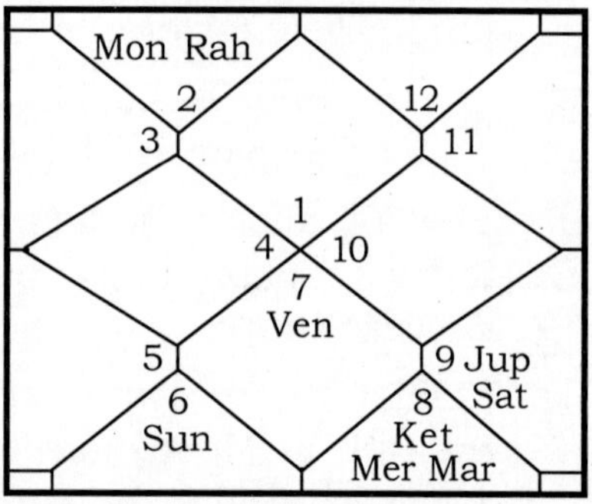


Balance of Vimsottari Dasa of **Mon 5Y 2M 21D**

This native had the second position in the IAS examination of 1980. Let us analyze this horoscope.

The 6th lord Saturn aspects the 10th house and luminary Moon is in the 10th. House. This confirms the govt. service.

**The10th house:** The exalted Moon has occupied the 10th house. The lord of the 10th, Venus, conjoins with *lagna* lord Sun and 11th lord Mercury in the 9th house.

**The 9th house:** The 9th house contains exalted Sun, in association with the 10th lord Venus and 11th lord Mercury i.e. the lords of *lagna*, 10th and 11th get conjoined in *Bhagya Bhavan* under the aspect of 8th lord Jupiter. The 11th house is the house of fulfillment of desires and earnings. The mutual exchange of the 11th and 9th lords is very auspicious.

**The Ascendant:** The 5th and 8th lord Jupiter joins the *lagna* in a friendly sign. The occupation of Jupiter in the *lagna* has bestowed the native a very handsome and attractive physique and gracious personality.

***Navamsa* Chart:** The *navamsa* chart is also equally important for the consideration of vocation. Here, the 10$^{th}$ lord Venus occupies own *navamsa*. Occupant of the 10$^{th}$ house Moon obtains *vargottam navamsa* and is 9$^{th}$ from the lord of *lagna*, the Sun. The 9$^{th}$ lord Mars also obtains own *navamsa* and *lagna* lord Sun is 11$^{th}$ from the 9$^{th}$ lord. The 8$^{th}$ lord Jupiter, who also happens to be the 5$^{th}$ lord, obtains own *navamsa*. The 9$^{th}$ and 10$^{th}$ houses are very well disposed in the *navamsa* chart as well, as both the lords conjoin in the 9$^{th}$ house and *lagna* lord is tenth from this combination.

**Karmic Control Planets:** Karmic control planets have an important role to play in each nativity. As told earlier, dispositors of Rahu and Ketu are called the Karmic control planets. In this chart, these are Venus and Mars. We have observed in most of the horoscopes of IAS officers that one of the Karmic control planets is associated with either of the luminaries. Here, Venus, who is the one karmic control planet, joins the Sun.

**Venus:** In our close observation of a number of cases, we have found that Venus is mostly related with 9$^{th}$ or the 10$^{th}$ house or with either of the luminaries. In this horoscope, Venus occupies the 9$^{th}$ house, as a lord of the 10$^{th}$, in association with one of the luminary, the Sun.

IAS officers have immense responsibilities but their lives are very comfortable and full of various kinds of luxuries. So, Venus is mostly associated with the luminaries or 9$^{th}$ or the 10$^{th}$ house.

*Illustration : 2.2* **(MJ)** *Horoscope No.: 2*

Date of birth : 14.03.1953 Time of birth : 14:10:00 hrs
Place of birth : Lucknow Lat 26:50:00 N Long 80:54:00E
Ayanamsa : 23:12:25 Sidereal Time : 01:30:16

| Pln | Degree | Rasi | Nakshatra | Pad |
|---|---|---|---|---|
| Asc | 7:43:31 | Can | Pushya | 2 |
| Sun | 0:16:06 | Pis | P. Bhadrapad | 4 |

| | | | | |
|---|---|---|---|---|
| Mon | 14:35:53 | Aqu | Satabhisha | 3 |
| Mar | 2:26:44 | Ari | Asvini | 1 |
| Mer (R/C) | 7:55:16 | Pis | U. Bhadrapad | 2 |
| Jup | 24:44:29 | Ari | Bharani | 4 |
| Ven | 6:39:23 | Ari | Asvini | 2 |
| Sat (R) | 2:56:22 | Lib | Chitra | 3 |
| Rah (R) | 18:36:06 | Cap | Sravna | 3 |
| Ket (R) | 18:36:06 | Can | Aslesha | 1 |

**Lagna Chart**

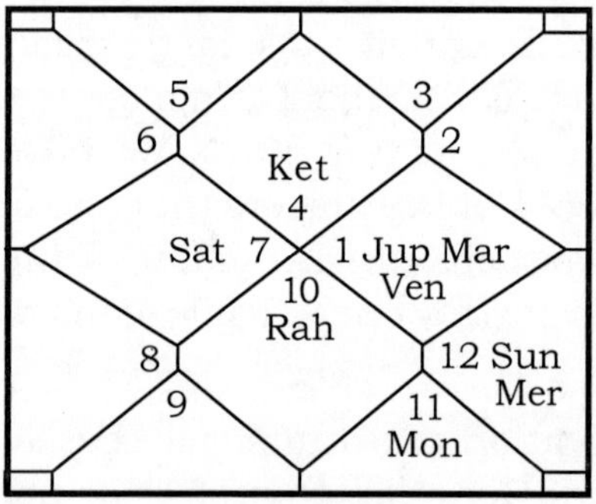


**Navamsa Chart**

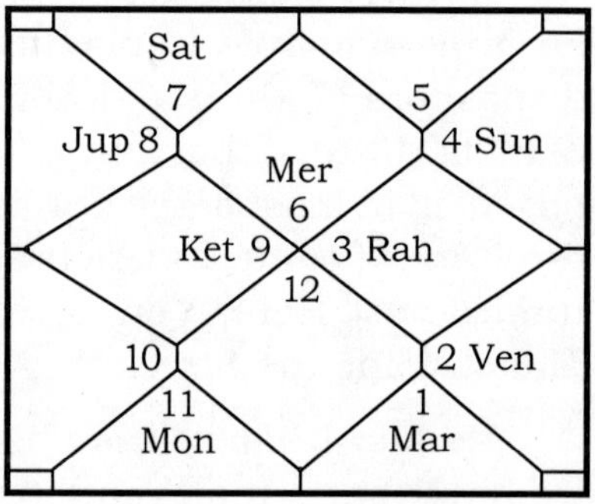


Balance of Vimsottari Dasa of **Rah 7Y 3M 15D**

This is the birth chart of a beautiful lady, who is a very successful IAS officer but could not prove herself to be a good and adjusting wife. She had a love marriage but the difference in their status created a big gap between them. She divorced her husband. Combination of Mars, Jupiter and Venus in mutual quadrants, and opposition of Mars and 7th lord Saturn may be noted for this. However, we are not concerned here with her marital aspect. Let us analyse the horoscope for her professional aspect.

The sixth lord Jupiter occupies the 10th house along with the lord of the 10th, Mars

**The 10th house:** The lord of 10th house joins the 10th itself, with the 9th lord Jupiter and 11th lord Venus. Conjunction of 9th, 10th and 11th lords in the 10th may be seen. Mars is a *Yogakaraka* for Cancer ascendant and forms

*Ruchhak Mahapurush Rajyoga.* This adds further strength.

**The 9th House:** The lord of the 9th house, Jupiter, is in conjunction with the 10th lord Mars in the 10th house.

**The 8th House:** The lord of the 8th house, Saturn, is exalted in the 4th house forming *Sasa Mahapurush Rajyoga* and aspects 9th, 10th, and 11th lords and the 10th house. Thus, the lords of 8th, 9th, 10th, and 11th are related with each other, either by association or by aspect. This again supports our contention that 8th house is no less important than 9th or the 10th house for administrative services.

**The Ascendant:** The lord of the ascendant, Moon, joins the 8th house and Ketu is posited there. The ascendant is not strong. This has caused poor health and kept her devoid of marital bliss.

**The Luminaries:** The Sun or Moon, or both, must be related to the concerned houses 8th, 9thor 10th or their lords. The Sun here occupies the 9th house while Moon is tenanted in the 8th.

**Karmic Control Planets:** Karmic control planets are Saturn and Moon in this chart. One of the Karmic control planets is Moon itself, a luminary. And Saturn aspects the 10th house.

***Navamsa* chart:** The lord of the 10th house, Mars, obtains *vargottam navamsa*. Ascendant lord Moon also falls in *vargottam* sign in the *navamsa* chart. Saturn also does so. The lord of the 4th and 11th Venus occupies its own *navamsa*. Mercury also falls in its own *navamsa* i.e. in its exaltation *navamsa*. Thus, the *navamsa* chart is very strong having three planets in *vargottam* and two in own *navamsa*s. The ascendant lord Moon is in the 11th from 10th lord Mars and 4th from 9th lord Jupiter and 5th from 8th lord Saturn. These positions of *lagna* lord must be studied for a powerful occupation.

**The Venus:** Venus occupies the 10th house with the 9th and 10th lords, Mars and Jupiter. This is a compulsory factor in the horoscopes of administrative officers.

*Illustration : 2.3* **(MS)** *Horoscope No.: 3*

Date of birth : 29.11.1960 Time of birth : 01:16:00 hrs
Place of birth : Bijnor Lat 29:22:00 N Long 78:09:00E
Ayanamsa : 23:18:32 Sidereal Time : 05:29:25

| **Pln** | **Degree** | **Rasi** | **Nakshatra** | **Pad** |
|---|---|---|---|---|
| Asc | 29:59:47 | Leo | U. Phalguni | 1 |
| Sun | 13:17:14 | Sco | Anuradha | 3 |
| Mon | 22:32:50 | Pis | Revati | 2 |
| Mar (R) | 24:52:51 | Gem | Punarvasu | 2 |
| Mer | 24:11:50 | Lib | Visakha | 2 |
| Jup | 13:16:53 | Sag | Moola | 4 |
| Ven | 22:55:00 | Sag | Purvasadha | 3 |
| Sat | 22:36:17 | Sag | Purvasadha | 3 |
| Rah (R) | 18:11:02 | Leo | P. Phalguni | 2 |
| Ket (R) | 18:11:02 | Aqu | Satabhisha | 4 |

**Lagna Chart**

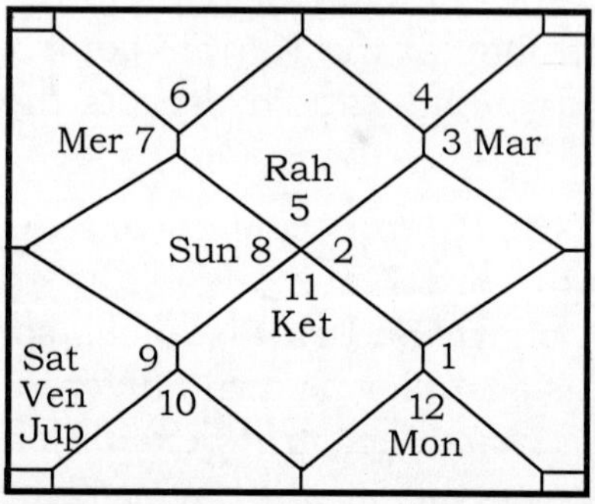


**Navamsa Chart**

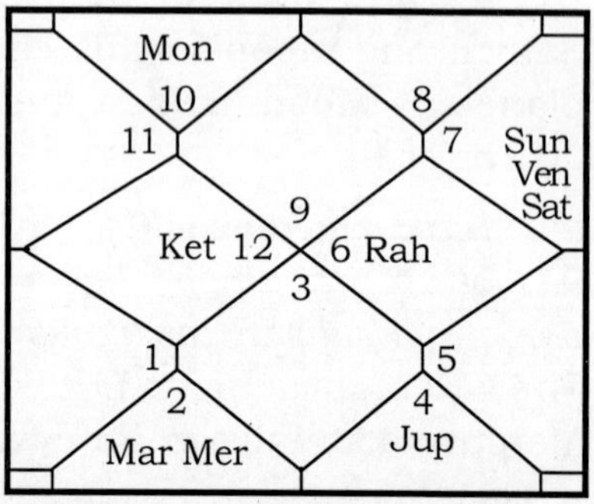


Balance of Vimsottari Dasa of **Mer 9Y 6M 0D**

This is the horoscope of the native who was selected against the class 1 post in the Railways after passing from B. Tech. from IIT, Kanpur. While serving there he prepared for IAS examinations and secured 17th position in India in 1986. Let us examine his horoscope.

The lords of the 6th and the 10th houses, Saturn and

Venus, are conjoined in the 5th house whose lord Jupiter obtains the *navamsa* of luminary Moon. Both, Saturn and Venus, are conjoined in the *navamsa* also, in association with Sun.

**The 10th House:** The lord of the 10th house, Venus, is situated in the 5th house. The lord of the 9th Mars joins 11th house. Thus, the lords of the 9th and 10th houses are under mutual aspect i.e. both influence each other.

**The 9th house:** The lord of the 9th house, Mars, joins the 11th, which is 7th from the position of the lord of the 10th house, Venus. The 9th and 10th houses are thus related with each other. The relationship between the 9th and 10th houses, either by exchange of their lords or the placement of the lord of the 9th in the 10th, with the 10th lord, or vice versa, or mutual aspect between the 9th and 10th lords or their conjunction at a beneficial place, is a very important factor for success in IAS examination.

**The 8th House:** The lord of the 8th house, Jupiter, conjoins with the 10th lord Venus in the 5th house and gets the aspect of the 9th lord Mars. Thus, the lords of the 8th, 9th and the 10th houses are related to each other in a triangle, by conjunction and aspect.

**The Luminaries:** The *lagna* lord Sun aspects the 10th house and Moon joins the 8th house i.e. the 10th and the 8th houses are influenced by the luminaries due to aspect and placement, respectively.

**The Ascendant:** The *lagna* lord Sun joins a quadrant and is hemmed between benefic planets like Jupiter, Venus and Mercury. The *lagna* receives the aspect of Jupiter. Thus, the *lagna* is quite powerful.

**The Karmic Control Planets:** The Sun and Saturn are Karmic control planets here. The Sun aspects the 10th house. As already said earlier, one of the Karmic control planets should either be a luminary itself or should conjoin or aspect any of the luminary.

**The *Navamsa* chart:** The lord of the 10th house, Venus,

obtains own *navamsa* in association with the exalted Saturn. The 8th house lord Jupiter is exalted. Of course, the 9th lord Mars is not very well disposed in the *navamsa* chart, which caused a few obstructions and the native had to do other services before finally joining the elite civil services.

**Moon chart:** Moon chart is very powerful in this horoscope. In the 10th house, from Moon, are placed Jupiter, Saturn and Venus, where Jupiter owns the 10th and Venus owns the 8th. The Sun joins the 9th house while 9th lord retrograde Mars is 7th from Jupiter having mutual aspect with the 10th house, as reckoned from Moon.

**Venus:** Venus also has an important role in the charts of the administrative officers. Here, Venus owns the 10th house and aspects the 9th lord Mars. If Venus is not related, either with 10th or 9th house or with any of the luminary, the concerned officers may not lead a comfortable life and will be short of luxuries etc.

*Illustration : 2.4* **(AKS)** *Horoscope No.: 4*

Date of birth : 15.04.1964 Time of birth : 18:04:00 hrs
Place of birth : Lucknow Lat 26:50:00 N Long 80:54:00E
Ayanamsa : 23:21:11 Sidereal Time : 07:32:24

| **Pln** | **Degree** | **Rasi** | **Nakshatra** | **Pad** |
|---|---|---|---|---|
| Asc | 27:13:20 | Vir | Chitra | 2 |
| Sun | 2:12:41 | Ari | Asvini | 1 |
| Mon | 13:41:34 | Tau | Rohini | 2 |
| Mar (C) | 19:50:42 | Pis | Revati | 1 |
| Mer | 18:04:12 | Ari | Bharani | 2 |
| Jup (C) | 7:25:21 | Ari | Asvini | 3 |
| Ven | 17:49:49 | Tau | Rohini | 3 |
| Sat | 8:50:34 | Aqu | Satabhisha | 1 |
| Rah (R) | 11:06:26 | Gem | Ardra | 2 |
| Ket (R) | 11:06:26 | Sag | Moola | 4 |

**Lagna Chart**

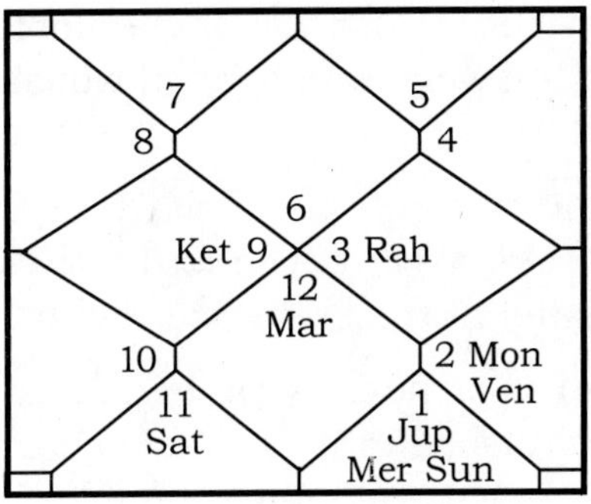


**Navamsa Chart**

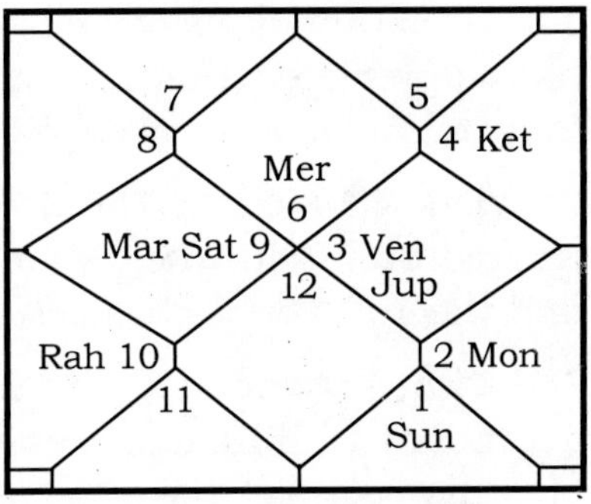


Balance of Vimsottari Dasa of **Mon 7Y 2M 23D**

This is the chart of a very intelligent young officer who had stood second in the civil services examination of 1986, in the very first attempt after completing the minimum required age. He also had a splendid academic record throughout his studies, where he always secured high rank. He got 19th position in the Joint Entrance Examination of IIT, and did M.Tech. from IIT, Kanpur in 1987, in second position. He had also qualified in the Indian Engineering Services in the second position. Apart from his academic abilities he also has interest and talent in fine arts and music.

Let us examine the birth chart of this brilliant young officer :

The sixth house is occupied by its own lord Saturn, who aspects the lord of the 10th house Mercury, placed in the 8th house, in association with Sun. We have invariably found that there is relationship of 6th and 10th and some luminary, in one or the other way, in case of govt. servants.

**The Tenth House:** The lord of the tenth house, Mercury, falls in the 8th house with exalted Sun, and obtains the exalted *navamsa* in *vargottam* ascendant, which indicates a very strong 10th house.

**The 9th House:** Moon is exalted in the 9th house, in

conjunction with the 9th lord Venus. Moon is the owner of 11th house and is associated with the 9th lord. Dr B. V. Raman has appreciated this combination very much in his book 'How to Judge a Horoscope-Vol. II'.

**The 8th House:** The 8th house has been joined by the exalted Sun, with the 10th lord Mercury i.e. the lords of 8th and the 10th houses are associated in the 8th house.

**The Ascendant:** The native is born with *vargottam* ascendant with its lord Mercury placed in it. In *Rashi* chart Mercury occupies the 8th house. Devakeralam mentions that a planet, if occupies own or exalted *navamsa*, will produce very auspicious results even if that occupies his debilitated sign in *Rashi* chart.

**The Luminaries:** The Sun is under *Vipreet Rajyoga* and is exalted in the 8th house. Moon is exalted in the 9th house. Thus, both the luminaries, the Sun and Moon, are exalted, synchronizing with the 8th and 9th house, respectively. The attention of the readers is invited towards the special characteristics of this chart. The Sun and Moon, both, obtain their signs of exaltation even in *navamsa* i.e. both the luminaries are very much powerful as both are exalted and obtain *vargottam* position. The *lagna* is also *vargottam.*

Thus, the study of this chart reveals how much important role the 8th house, in deciding administrative career, plays

**Karmic Control Planets (KCP):** Jupiter and Mercury are the Karmic Control Planets in this horoscope. One of the KCPs, Mercury, is associated with a luminary, Sun.

***Navamsa* chart:** The native is born in the *vargottam* ascendant. The 9th lord Venus occupies 10th in association with Jupiter. The *lagna* lord Mercury is in exalted *navamsa* and 4th from the 9th lord Venus. The 8th lord Mars and 9th lord Venus are under mutual aspect. However, the combination of Mars and Saturn in the 4th house is not good, for the aspects as apparent.

**Moon Chart:** From the Moon chart, Saturn is a

*yogakaraka* and joins the 10th house of its own. The Moon chart is encouraging as well.

Generally, it is seen that administrative officers, though have a lot of responsibilities, have a comfortable and luxurious life. Mostly all their materialistic ambitions are fulfilled. Venus denotes luxuries. So, mostly Venus is related with either of the luminaries, or the 9th or 10th house or their lords. In this horoscope, we find that Venus is associated with a luminary, Moon, and that too in the 9th house. The native will, therefore, live most luxuriously and will play in wealth (2nd lord Venus +11th lord Moon, in the 9th house, with 9th lord Venus). Both the luminaries are exalted. Therefore, the native is sure to shine and earn high merits of recognition with lasting fame and reputation.

*Illustration : 2.5* (**AKT**) *Horoscope No.: 5*

Date of birth : 09.07.1950 Time of birth : 04:00:00 hrs

Place of birth : Agra Lat 29:22:00 N Long 78:09:00E

Ayanamsa : 23:09:57 Sidereal Time : 22:47:48

| **Pln** | **Degree** | **Rasi** | **Nakshatra** | **Pad** |
|---|---|---|---|---|
| Asc | 3:12:08 | Gem | Mrigsira | 3 |
| Sun | 22:59:48 | Gem | Punarvasu | 1 |
| Mon | 12:52:50 | Ari | Asvini | 4 |
| Mar | 18:41:40 | Vir | Hasta | 3 |
| Mer (C) | 20:17:17 | Gem | Punarvasu | 1 |
| Jup (R) | 14:03:27 | Aqu | Satabhisha | 3 |
| Ven | 20:23:19 | Tau | Rohini | 4 |
| Sat | 21:50:15 | Leo | P. Phalguni | 3 |
| Rah (R) | 8:29:50 | Pis | U. Bhadrapad | 2 |
| Ket (R) | 8:29:50 | Vir | U. Phalguni | 4 |

**Lagna Chart**

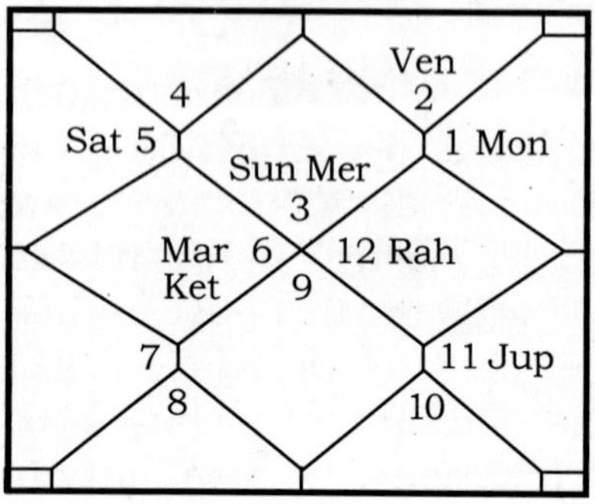


**Navamsa Chart**

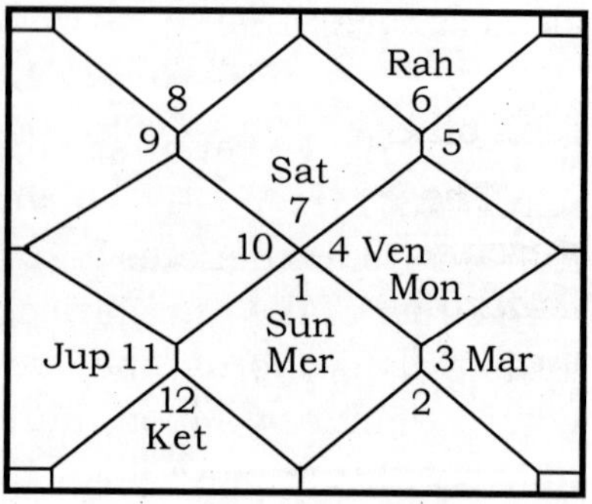


Balance of Vimsottari Dasa of **Ket 0Y 2M 25D**

The native is a very handsome, tall and smart person. His academic ability is also unique. He had broken all records of Agra College in B.Sc. and M. Sc. He was an outstanding student and received the award 'Topper among Toppers', and a gold medal from Mrs. Indira Gandhi, for breaking all the previous records. In the competition of civil services, he secured the first position.

Let us analyze his horoscope :

The 6th lord Mars aspects the 10th house and falls in the constellation of luminary, Moon.

**The 10th House:** The lord of the 10th house, Jupiter, occupies the 9th house and lord of 9th house, Saturn, is under mutual aspect with the 10th lord Jupiter. Moreover, Saturn aspects his own house i.e. the 9th. Jupiter is retrograde and obtains *vargottam navamsa.* Thus, the lord of the 10th house joins the 9th under retrograde motion and gets the aspect from 9th lord. This auspicious combination has made the native so meritorious and the topper of IAS examination.

**The 9th House:** The lord of the 9th joins the royal sign Leo and falls in the constellation *Purvaphalguni*, which is owned by Venus, and obtains the exaltation sign Libra in *navamsa* chart. Thus, the 9th lord Saturn is very powerful in *navamsa* chart, as for the *navamsa lagna*, Saturn is a *Yogakaraka* also.

**The 8th House:** Saturn is the lord of 8th house also and, as discussed above, it is under mutual aspect with the 10th lord Jupiter. Thus, the 10th, 9th, and 8th lords are related to each other.

**The Ascendant:** The ascendant contains the Sun and Mercury. Mercury is lord of the ascendant and has formed *Bhadrika Mahapurush Rajyoga* under a powerful aspect from Jupiter. Thus, the ascendant is quite powerful.

**The Luminaries:** The Sun joins *lagna*, in a friendly sign, with the *lagna* lord Mercury. In *navamsa* chart, the Sun is exalted and is well associated with *lagna* lord Mercury. The Moon owns the 2nd house and joins 11th in *Rashi* chart and obtains own *navamsa*, that too in the 10th house from *navamsa lagna*, in association with Venus. Thus, the luminaries lend their effect on the ascendant and the 10th house, and Venus is also related with one of them.

**Karmic Control Planet:** Mercury and Jupiter are Karmic control planets in this chart. Mercury is associated with one of the luminaries, the Sun, while the other Karmic control planet Jupiter aspects its own house, the 10th, and occupies the 9th.

**The Venus:** Here, Venus and Moon are very closely related. Both conjoin the 10th house from *navamsa lagna*. Venus joins his own sign Taurus and falls in the constellation of Moon. Venus also obtains the *navamsa* Cancer, ruled by Moon.

*Illustration : 2.6* **(RM)** *Horoscope No.: 6*

Date of birth : 13.09.1961 Time of birth : 21:32:00 hrs

Place of birth : Khurja Lat 28:15:00 N Long 77:51:00E

Ayanamsa : 23:19:09 Sidereal Time : 20:43:01

| Pln | Degree | Rasi | Nakshatra | Pad |
|---|---|---|---|---|
| Asc | 0:17:14 | Tau | Krittika | 2 |
| Sun | 27:17:44 | Leo | U. Phalguni | 1 |
| Mon | 7:00:42 | Lib | Svati | 1 |

| | | | | |
|---|---|---|---|---|
| Mar | 24:33:07 | Vir | Chitra | 1 |
| Mer | 19:40:53 | Vir | Hasta | 3 |
| Jup (R) | 4:09:36 | Cap | Uttarasadha | 3 |
| Ven | 24:37:26 | Can | Aslesha | 3 |
| Sat (R) | 0:04:47 | Cap | Uttarasadha | 2 |
| Rah (R) | 3:46:39 | Leo | Magha | 2 |
| Ket (R) | 3:46:39 | Aqu | Dhanishtha | 4 |

**Lagna Chart**

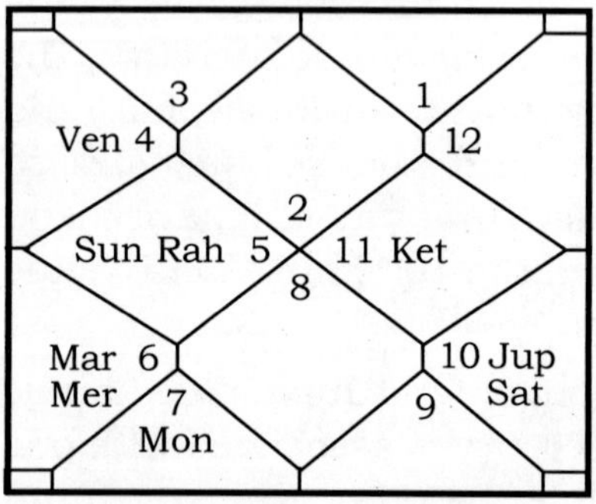


**Navamsa Chart**

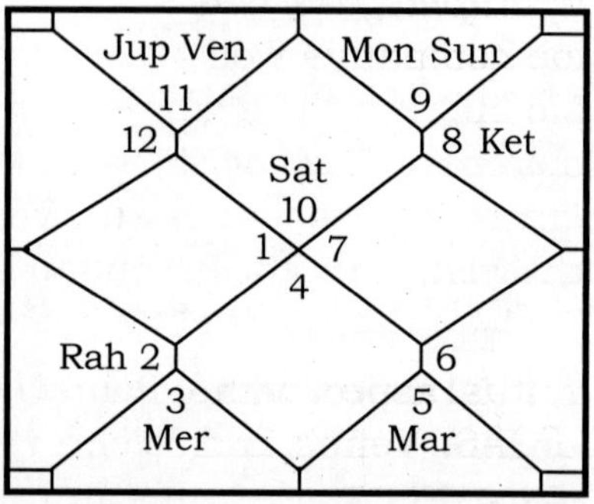


Balance of Vimsottari Dasa of **Rah 17Y 6M 12D**

The native has done B.E. from Roorkee University. Thereafter, he got success in IAS securing 100th position in 1986.

The 6th and 10th lords, Venus and Saturn, mutually aspect each other. The 6th lord Venus occupies the sign of Moon and Moon occupies the 6th house, while Sun also aspects the 10th house. The 10th lord Saturn also falls in the constellation of Sun. These all strongly indicate his profession to be a good govt. service.

**The 10th and 9th House:** The Saturn is a *Yogakaraka* for persons born in Libra ascendant, as it is the owner of 9th and 10th house. Here, Saturn occupies 9th house in the company of 8th and 11th lord Jupiter. Jupiter and Saturn, both, are retrograde, so have acquired much strength to improve luck and profession. The 10th house is receiving the aspect of royal planet, the Sun. The lord of *lagna* , Venus, occupies Moon's sign Cancer in the 3rd house, where the *lagna* lord Venus, the 9th and 10th lord Saturn and the 8th & 11th lord Jupiter are under mutual aspect. Thus, the ascendant, 8th, 9th, 10th, and 11th houses are related with each other. The lord of 9th and 10th Saturn obtains *vargottam navamsa.*

**Karmic Control Planets:** The Sun and Saturn are Karmic control planets here. One of them itself is a luminary while the other is the 10th lord.

**The Luminaries:** The Sun falls in own constellation *Uttaraphalguni,* own sign Leo and in Jupiter's *navamsa,* in the company of other royal planet Moon. The Sun aspects the 10th house. The lord of 9th and 10th house, Saturn, and the lord of 8th and 11th, Jupiter, fall in *Uttarasadha nakshatra,* which is owned by Sun. Thus, the 10th house is under the influence of Sun.

**The Venus:** The 10th lord Saturn (*vargottam*) is under mutual aspect with Venus, who is a planet of vital importance for IAS. Venus and Moon have a mutual exchange of their signs.

**The Ascendant:** The *lagna* and its lord Venus, both, are receiving the benefic aspect of Jupiter.

One important point to be noted in this chart is that the Saturn and Sun occupy their own signs, whereas Mercury is exalted. The 4th lord occupies the 4th house, 5th lord occupies the 5th house and the 9th lord occupies the 9th house. This is really a splendid and fortunate combination of planets.

*Illustration : 2.7* (**SCT**) *Horoscope No.: 7*

Date of birth : 05.02.1946 Time of birth : 11:16:00 hrs

Place of birth : Gorakhpur Lat 26:45:00 N Long 83:23:00E

Ayanamsa : 23:05:59 Sidereal Time : 20:18:39

| Pln | Degree | Rasi | Nakshatra | Pad |
|---|---|---|---|---|
| Asc | 22:39:02 | Ari | Bharani | 3 |
| Sun | 22:43:55 | Cap | Sravna | 4 |

| | | | | |
|---|---|---|---|---|
| Mon | 1:08:56 | Pis | P. Bhadrapad | 4 |
| Mar (R) | 22:48:08 | Gem | Punarvasu | 1 |
| Mer (C) | 18:26:07 | Cap | Sravna | 3 |
| Jup | 4:12:30 | Lib | Chitra | 4 |
| Ven (C) | 23:36:33 | Cap | Dhanishtha | 1 |
| Sat (R) | 26:27:49 | Gem | Punarvasu | 2 |
| Rah (R) | 5:43:21 | Gem | Mrigsira | 4 |
| Ket (R) | 5:43:21 | Sag | Moola | 2 |

**Lagna Chart** **Navamsa Chart**

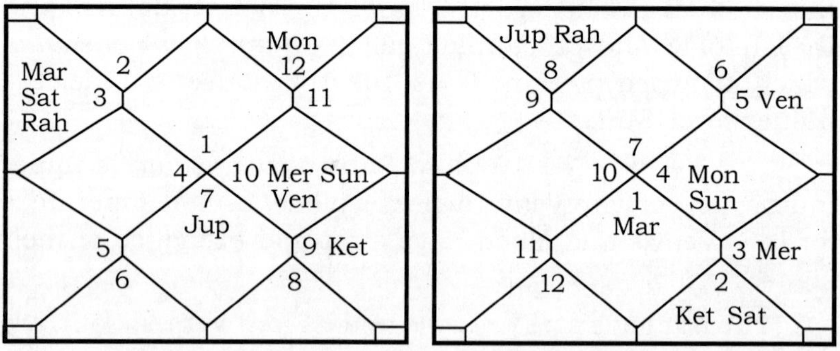


Balance of Vimsottari Dasa of **Jup 2Y 7M 13D**

The subject is a very senior IAS officer of U.P. Cadre. Let us find out the astrological reasons of his being so.

The 6th lord Mercury joins the 10th house in association with Sun. Moon aspects the 6th house, whereas the 6th lord Mercury falls in the constellation of Moon as well.

**The 10th and 9th houses:** The 10th lord Saturn is aspected by the 9th lord Jupiter and both are under mutual aspect in the *navamsa* chart. The 10th lord Saturn also falls in the constellation of 9th lord Jupiter i.e. in *Punarvasu nakshatra.*

**The 10th and 8th lords:** The 10th lord Saturn is associated with the 8th lord Mars. The 9th lord Jupiter also falls in the constellation as well as *navamsa* of Mars. Thus, the 10th and 8th lords are related to each other due to conjunction. The 8th lord Mars aspects the 9th and 10th lords both.

**The Ascendant:** The *lagna* lord Mars obtains own *navamsa* in Aries, as well as falls in own constellation *chitra.* The ascendant and its lord Mars, both, are aspected by *Bhagyadhipati* Jupiter.

**The luminaries:** The Sun occupies the ascendant and falls in the constellation of Moon i.e. *Sravna.* Moon falls in the *nakshatra* and sign of Jupiter. The Sun and Moon both are associated in Moon's *navamsa,* in the 10th house from the *navamsa lagna.*

**Karmic Control Planets:** Mercury and Jupiter are Karmic control planets here, and Mercury conjoins with a luminary, the Sun.

**The Venus:** The Venus and Sun are associated in the 10th house and obtain the *navamsa* of Sun.

The findings for IAS are fully applicable here. The best combination is there in the 10th house, as far as the *navamsa* chart is concerned. Both the royal planets, the Sun and Moon, are conjoined there. Mercury obtains own *vargottam navamsa.* The Moon and *lagnesh* Mars also fall in their own *navamsa.*

*Illustration : 2.8* (**AKG**) *Horoscope No.: 8*

Date of birth : 30.09.1955 Time of birth : 15:23:00 hrs
Place of birth : Dehradun Lat 30:19:00 N Long 78:03:00E
Ayanamsa : 23:14:36 Sidereal Time : 15:38:41

| **Pln** | **Degree** | **Rasi** | **Nakshatra** | **Pad** |
|---|---|---|---|---|
| Asc | 18:29:22 | Cap | Sravna | 3 |
| Sun | 13:13:14 | Vir | Hasta | 1 |
| Mon | 25:23:58 | Aqu | P Bhadrapad | 2 |
| Mar (C) | 28:24:27 | Leo | U Phalguni | 1 |
| Mer | 5:18:55 | Lib | Chitra | 4 |
| Jup | 29:47:58 | Can | Aslesha | 4 |
| Ven (C) | 21:02:02 | Vir | Hasta | 4 |
| Sat | 25:13:12 | Lib | Visakha | 2 |

| | | | | |
|---|---|---|---|---|
| Rah (R) | 27:05:55 | Sco | Jyestha | 4 |
| Ket (R) | 27:05:55 | Tau | Mrigsira | 2 |

**Lagna Chart**

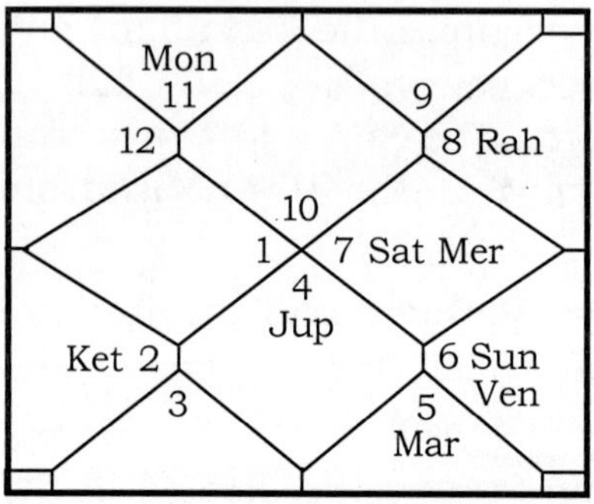


**Navamsa Chart**

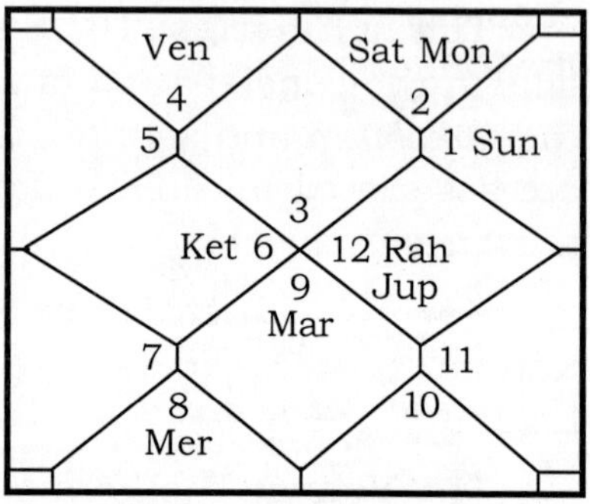


Balance of Vimsottari Dasa of **Jup 9Y 6M 7D**

The native competed in IAS in the very first attempt and secured fourth position in India. He had a very shining academic career. Configuration of planets in his birth chart is also equally shining.

The sixth lord Mercury joins the 10th house and the 10th lord Venus obtains the *navamsa* of Moon and conjoins with Sun in the *Rashi* chart.

**The 9th and 10th Houses:** The lord of the 9th house, Mercury, is posited in the 10th house, while the lord of the 10th house, Venus, joins the 9th in the company of a royal planet, the Sun. This is treated as the best combination for IAS, if there is a mutual exchange between the lords of the 9th and the 10th houses, as is in the present case here.

**The 8th and the 10th House:** The lord of the 8th house, Sun, and the lord of the 10th house, Venus, conjoin in the 9th house. Thus, the 8th, 9th and 10th houses are interlinked.

**The Ascendant:** The lord of the ascendant, Saturn, is exalted in the 10th house in association with the 9th lord Mercury. The ascendant is receiving the benefic aspect of exalted Jupiter

**The Luminaries:** Those who have exalted Sun and Moon

either in *Rashi* or in *navamsa* chart, have high merits in competition, as well as in their professional career. In this horoscope, the Sun and Moon, both, obtain their exaltation sign in *navamsa* chart. The ascendant also falls in the constellation of Moon i.e. Sravna. The Sun conjoins with the lord of $10^{th}$ house, Venus.

**Karmic Control Planets:** Mars and Venus are the Karmic control planets for this nativity. Venus is associated with a luminary, the Sun while the other, Mars, is aspected by Moon.

**The Venus:** Venus is itself the ruler of the $10^{th}$ house and conjoins with a luminary, the Sun, which is a positive factor for the success in IAS. If other conditions are fulfilled but Venus has nothing to do, either with the luminaries or with the 10th, $9^{th}$, or $8^{th}$ lord, one will hardly be successful in IAS proper. Any service that is linked with high quality of comforts and facilities will decidedly have the influence of Venus on the $10^{th}$, $9^{th}$, or $8^{th}$ house or their lords or on the *Karakas.* The luminaries may be treated as the significators for IAS services.

**The *navamsa* chart:** The lord of the $10^{th}$ house, Venus, falls in Moon's *navamsa* while Moon is exalted and is conjoined with the *lagna* lord Saturn in *navamsa*. The Sun and Moon, both, are exalted here while exalted Jupiter in *Rashi* obtains own *navamsa*. Jupiter, Sun and Moon are splendid in this birth chart.

*Illustration : 2.9* **(JPS)** *Horoscope No.: 9*

Date of birth : 21.06.1936 Time of birth : 05:15:00 hrs

Place of birth : Basti Lat 26:48:00 N Long 82:44:00E

Ayanamsa : 22:58:28 Sidereal Time : 23:11:55

| Pln | Degree | Rasi | Nakshatra | Pad |
|---|---|---|---|---|
| Asc | 7:36:28 | Gem | Ardra | 1 |
| Sun | 6:26:38 | Gem | Mrigsira | 4 |
| Mon | 29:03:15 | Gem | Punarvasu | 3 |
| Mar (C) | 3:42:05 | Gem | Mrigsira | 4 |

| Mer | 15:07:59 | Tau | Rohini | 2 |
|---|---|---|---|---|
| Jup (R) | 25:17:04 | Sco | Jyestha | 3 |
| Ven (C) | 4:07:55 | Gem | Mrigsira | 4 |
| Sat | 29:25:13 | Aqu | P Bhadrapad | 3 |
| Rah | 10:29:39 | Sag | Moola | 4 |
| Ket (C) | 10:29:39 | Gem | Ardra | 2 |

**Lagna Chart**

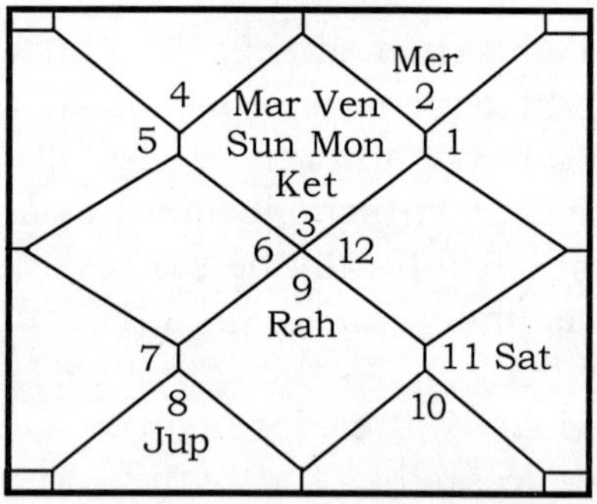


**Navamsa Chart**

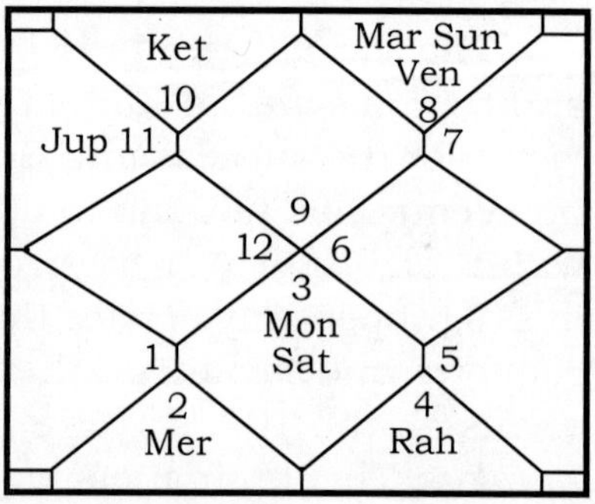


Balance of Vimsottari Dasa of **Jup 5Y 1M 18D**

The native was an IAS officer from U.P. cadre and retired from a very senior position in the central govt.

The 10th lord Jupiter occupies the 6th house, while the 6th lord Mars conjoins with luminaries, Sun and Moon, in the ascendant.

**The 9th and the 10th House:** The lord of the 10th house, Jupiter, occupies the 6th and aspects the 10th house, while the 9th lord Saturn is posited in the 9th itself, from where it lends aspect over the 10th lord Jupiter. In *navamsa*, the 10th lord Jupiter aspects the 9th lord Saturn. The 9th lord Saturn falls in the constellation of Jupiter, *Poorva Bhadrapada*, while the 10th lord Jupiter occupies the sign of 9th lord Saturn in *navamsa*.

**The 10th and 8th House:** The 8th lord Saturn occupies 9th and falls in the constellation of the 10th lord Jupiter.

**The Ascendant:** The ascendant is very powerful as it

contains the luminaries, in addition to Venus, Mars and Ketu. The lord of the ascendant, Mercury, obtains *vargottam navamsa*. Moon also does so. Thus the *lagna* is quite powerful though there is mutual exchange between the lords of ascendant and the 12th lord, Mercury and Venus.

**The Luminaries:** Both the luminaries conjoin in the ascendant. The Moon is associated with the 9th lord Saturn in the *navamsa* chart. The Sun aspects the *lagna* lord Mercury.

**Karmic Control Planets:** Jupiter and Mercury are the Karmic control planets in this horoscope. The Sun aspects Mercury in *navamsa* chart.

Here, we find that there is no direct relationship between Karmic control planets and the luminaries in the *Rashi* chart but both the luminaries conjoin with Ketu in the *lagna*. Dispositors of Rahu and Ketu are the Karmic control planets, so the conjunction of Sun and Moon with Rahu or Ketu means that luminaries are related with Karmic control planets, in a way directly.

**The Venus:** Venus falls in the *lagna*, in association with the significators Sun and Moon.

***Navamsa:*** The lord of 10th house, Jupiter, falls in the *navamsa* of 9th lord Saturn, and the *lagna* lord Mercury is 10th from there. This is auspicious.

Having understood the basics, we will now take up few complicated horoscopes where it is a bit difficult to judge that the native would become an IAS officer.

*Illustration : 2.10* **(AB)** *Horoscope No.: 10*

Date of birth : 02.11.1959 Time of birth : 20:30:00 hrs
Place of birth : Allahabad Lat 25:27:00 N Long 81:50:00E
Ayanamsa : 23:17:44 Sidereal Time : 23:11:53

| Pln | Degree | Rasi | Nakshatra | Pad |
|---|---|---|---|---|
| Asc | 6:35:42 | Gem | Mrigsira | 4 |
| Sun | 16:08:41 | Lib | Svati | 3 |

| | | | | |
|---|---|---|---|---|
| Mon | 9:49:30 | Sco | Anuradha | 2 |
| Mar (D) | 15:01:08 | Lib | Svati | 3 |
| Mer | 9:30:48 | Sco | Anuradha | 2 |
| Jup | 12:15:43 | Sco | Anuradha | 3 |
| Ven | 29:51:30 | Leo | U Phalguni | 1 |
| Sat | 9:48:33 | Sag | Moola | 3 |
| Rah (R) | 10:14:59 | Vir | Hasta | 1 |
| Ket (R) | 10:14:59 | Pis | U Bhadrapad | 3 |

**Lagna Chart**

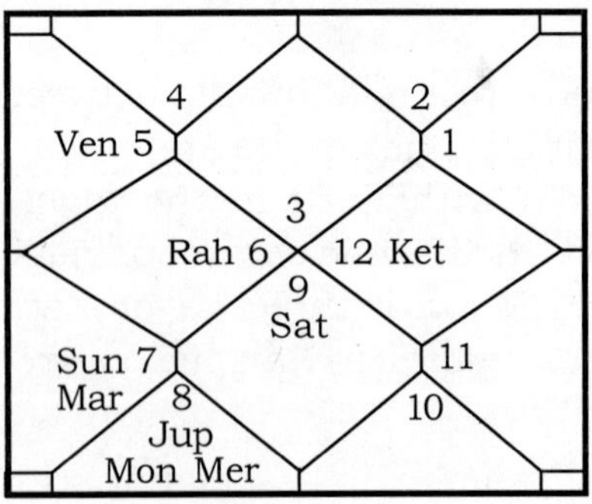


**Navamsa Chart**

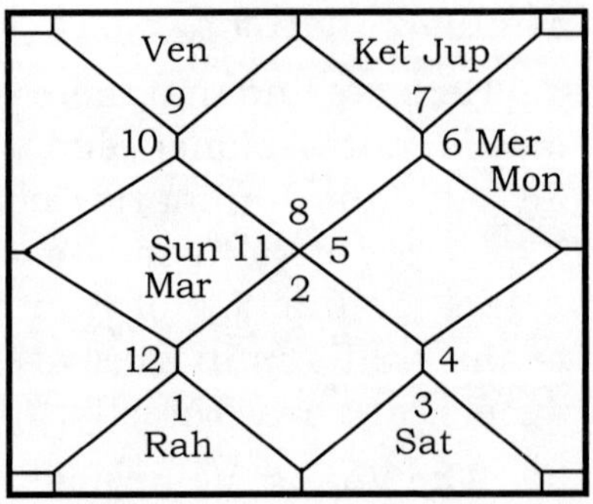


Balance of Vimsottari Dasa of **Sat 9Y 8M 30D**

Daughter of a chief engineer, the native of this chart was selected for allied services in the first attempt and got success in IAS proper in her second attempt. Her husband is an engineer. Difference in the professional levels of both brought them to the edge of separation.

The 10th lord Jupiter occupies the 6th house in association with ascendant lord Mercury and the 2nd lord luminary Moon. The 6th lord joins Sun in the 5th house. Relationship between 6th & 10th house in any way and the influence of either of the luminaries on the 6th, 10th or the ascendant confirms the govt. service of the native.

**The 10th and the 9th House:** Lord of the 10th house, Jupiter, occupies the 6th house and aspects the 10th. The Jupiter is conjoined with the luminary, Moon, and *lagnesh*

Mercury, and falls in the constellation of $9^{th}$ and $8^{th}$ lord Saturn. The lord of the $9^{th}$ house, Saturn, aspects the $9^{th}$ house and the *lagna*. In *navamsa* chart, the lord of the $10^{th}$, Jupiter, occupies the *navamsa* of Venus and aspects the $9^{th}$ lord Saturn.

**The $10^{th}$ and $8^{th}$ House:** Saturn is the lord of the $8^{th}$ house also, so the above is applicable for the $8^{th}$ house as well.

**The Ascendant:** The ascendant lord Mercury obtains the exalted sign in *navamsa*, in the $10^{th}$ from the *navamsa lagna* and in association with Moon. In *Rashi* chart *lagnadhipati* Mercury joins $6^{th}$ house with Moon and Jupiter. Thus, a luminary and the $10^{th}$ lord influence the *lagnesh.*

**Karmic Control Planets:** Mercury and Jupiter are Karmic control planets. Moon is conjoined with both of them and the combination of Jupiter, Mercury and Moon falls in the $6^{th}$ house. Mr. M. C. Jain has written in his book 'Karmic Control Planets' that, if both conjoin, there is no *Rajyoga* more powerful than this.

Here, both the Karmic control planets are related with the $10^{th}$ house and a luminary Moon that is a strong indicator of royal service like IAS. The Moon falls in *Anuradha* i.e. the constellation of the $9^{th}$ lord Saturn. So does Jupiter also.

**The Venus:** Venus aspects the $9^{th}$ house and falls in the sign, as well as *navamsa*, of the Sun.

In this horoscope, the conjunction of Moon and both the Karmic control planets in the same sign is mainly responsible for her success in IAS otherwise the chart is not very powerful. If both the Karmic control planets are placed $7^{th}$ from each other and the luminary, and the $10^{th}$ or the $9^{th}$ house has nothing to do with them or this conjunction is there, one will be successful in IAS but a careful judgment is necessary.

*Illustration : 2.11* **(SM)** *Horoscope No.: 11*

| | | | |
|---|---|---|---|
| Date of birth | : 08.09.1938 | Time of birth : | 11:30:00 hrs |
| Place of birth | : Lucknow | Lat 26:50:00 N | Long 80:54:00E |
| Ayanamsa | : 23:00:16 | Sidereal Time : | 10:30:10 |

| **Pln** | **Degree** | **Rasi** | **Nakshatra** | **Pad** |
|---|---|---|---|---|
| Asc | 6:09:25 | Sco | Anuradha | 1 |
| Sun | 21:55:19 | Leo | P Phalguni | 3 |
| Mon | 3:39:44 | Aqu | Dhanishtha | 4 |
| Mar (C) | 7:14:59 | Leo | Magha | 3 |
| Mer | 6:05:59 | Leo | Magha | 2 |
| Jup (R) | 1:59:20 | Aqu | Dhanishtha | 3 |
| Ven | 8:09:56 | Lib | Svati | 1 |
| Sat (R) | 23:47:26 | Pis | Revati | 3 |
| Rah (R) | 27:01:35 | Lib | Visakha | 3 |
| Ket (R) | 27:01:35 | Ari | Krittika | 1 |

**Lagna Chart**

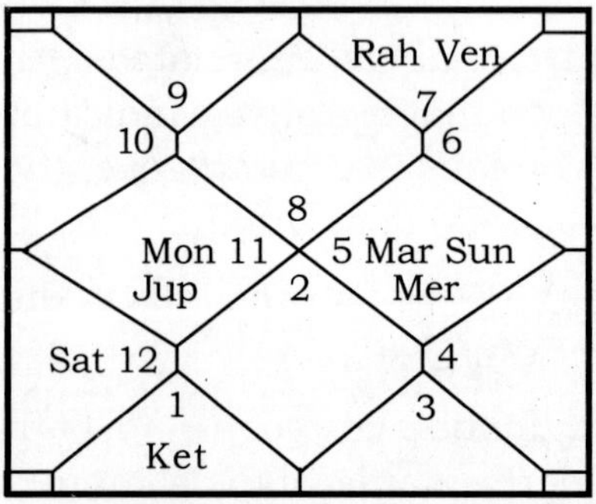


**Navamsa Chart**

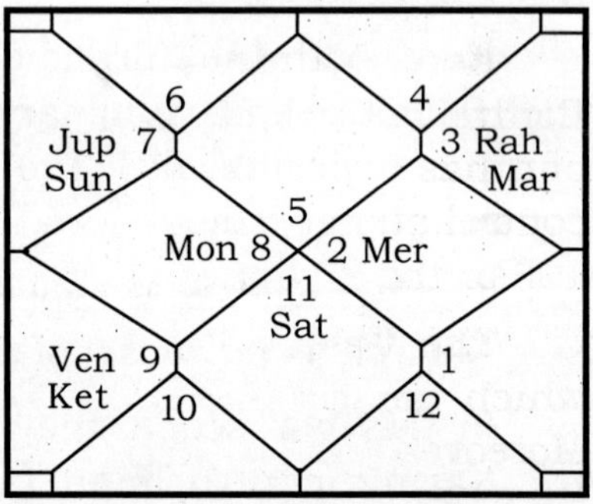


Balance of Vimsottari Dasa of **Mar 1Y 6M 28D**

The native retired as a commissioner in the U.P. Govt. and his horoscope is an ideal example for the study of the combinations of top civil services of India.

The 6th lord Mars occupies the 10th house, in the sign of luminary Sun, and is also conjoined with Sun there. Moon also aspects the 10th house in *Rashi* and *navamsa* both.

**The 9$^{th}$ and the 10$^{th}$ House:** The lord of the 10$^{th}$ house is Sun and he is posited in the 10$^{th}$ house. The 9$^{th}$ lord Moon occupies the 4$^{th}$ and is under mutual aspect with the Sun. Thus, the 9$^{th}$ and 10$^{th}$ lords are luminaries and they are aspecting each other, influencing the 10$^{th}$ house strongly and beneficially.

**The 8$^{th}$ and the 10$^{th}$ House:** The lord of 8$^{th}$ house is Mercury and joins the 10$^{th}$ house, in the company of 10$^{th}$ lord luminary Sun i.e. the lords of 8$^{th}$ and 10$^{th}$ are conjoined together under the beneficial aspect of 9$^{th}$ lord Moon and 5$^{th}$ lord Jupiter. This is a powerful combination for administrative services.

**The Ascendant:** The lord of the ascendant, Mars, is associated with the 10$^{th}$ lord Sun and 8$^{th}$ & 11$^{th}$ lord Mercury, in the 10$^{th}$ house. The 9$^{th}$ lord Moon aspects the Sun. The mutual aspect of Jupiter, from the 4th house, has further strengthened this favorable and powerful combination.

**The Luminaries:** Both the luminaries, the Sun and the Moon, have an auspicious mutual aspect, corresponding to the 9$^{th}$ and the 10$^{th}$ house.

**Karmic Control Planets:** Mars and Venus are Karmic Control planets here. Mars conjoins with the 10$^{th}$ lord Sun and has a mutual aspect with the 9$^{th}$ lord Moon. Karmic control planet has an important role to play in respect to 10$^{th}$ or the 9$^{th}$ house, or otherwise with luminaries.

**The Venus:** The 10$^{th}$ lord Sun obtains 21° 52' of Leo, which falls in the constellation *Pubba* ruled by Venus. Moreover, the 10$^{th}$ lord from *navamsa lagna* is Venus itself. Here, Venus is Karmic control planet also.

This is a powerful horoscope and having a background anyone could easily say that the native would become an IAS officer. However, the approach should be systematic and concept should be clear.

Ahead are the few horoscopes where the combinations of IAS are present but abrupt judgment of vocation will not give the correct results.

*Illustration : 2.12* **(RKM)** *Horoscope No.: 12*

Date of birth : 08.08.1949 Time of birth : 05:38:00 hrs
Place of birth : Muzaffarnagar Lat 29:28:00 N Long 77:42:00E
Ayanamsa : 23:09:06 Sidereal Time : 02:23:30

| **Pln** | **Degree** | **Rasi** | **Nakshatra** | **Pad** |
|---|---|---|---|---|
| Asc | 20:06:25 | Can | Aslesha | 2 |
| Sun | 21:57:45 | Can | Aslesha | 2 |
| Mon | 12:28:45 | Cap | Sravna | 1 |
| Mar | 17:21:35 | Gem | Ardra | 4 |
| Mer (C) | 4:21:29 | Leo | Magha | 2 |
| Jup (R) | 1:47:36 | Cap | Uttarasadha | 2 |
| Ven | 21:47:03 | Leo | P Phalguni | 3 |
| Sat | 13:15:39 | Leo | Magha | 4 |
| Rah (R) | 25:35:05 | Pis | Revati | 3 |
| Ket (R) | 25:35:05 | Vir | Chitra | 1 |

**Lagna Chart**

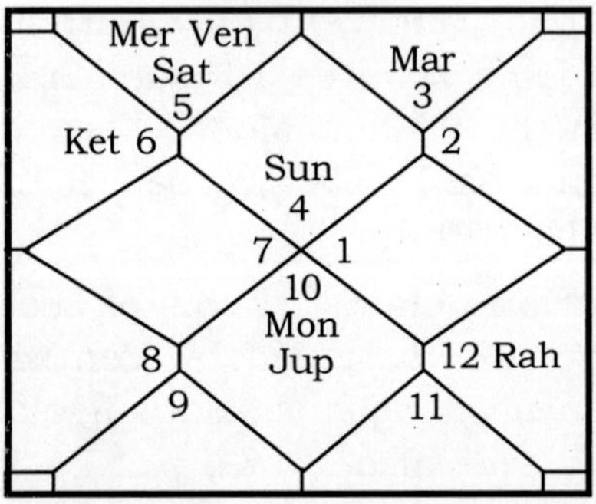


**Navamsa Chart**

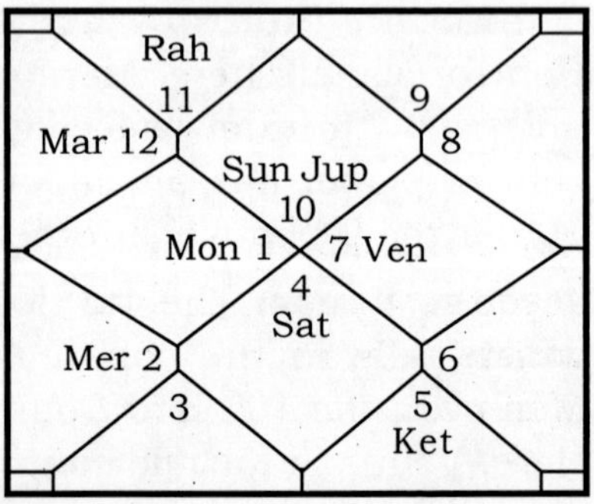


Balance of Vimsottari Dasa of **Mon 8Y 1M 20D**

This is a complicated case for the study of the combinations of IAS. Let's analyze.

The 10th lord Mars aspects the 6th house and its lord Jupiter, who is placed in the 7th house, in conjunction with Moon and gets the aspect of Sun.

**The 10th and 9th House:** The lord of the 9th house, Jupiter, is associated with Moon and is aspected by Sun. Thus, the 9th lord is under a powerful influence of the royal planets.

The 10th lord Mars joins the 12th house and apparently does not seem to have any relation with the 9th lord. But Mars has a relation with the 9th lord Jupiter. Mars has an aspect over Jupiter and falls in the constellation *Punarvasu,* ruled by Jupiter. In addition to this, Mars falls in *navamsa* of Jupiter, while the 9th lord Jupiter obtains *vargottam navamsa.*

**The 10th and 8th House:** In this case, the opposition of the Sun and Moon in respect of the 10th house makes one think if the native could become an IAS. The lord of the 8th house, Saturn, aspects his own house 8th, falls in royal sign Leo and royal *navamsa* Cancer. In *navamsa* chart, the 8th lord Saturn is receiving the joint aspect of 9th lord Jupiter and the Sun.

**The Ascendant:** The *lagna* Cancer is joined by one of the royal planets, the Sun and aspected by another royal planet, the Moon. Moreover *Bhagyadhipati* Jupiter's aspect on to them strengthens the combination. The joint influence of the Sun and the Moon on 10th, 9th, and *lagna* tends one to go in IAS. The *lagna* lord Moon falls in own constellation *Sravna* and in the *navamsa* of *Yogakaraka* 10th lord Mars.

**The Luminaries:** One of the luminaries must influence the 9th or the 10th house or their lords. Here, the Moon is associated with 9th lord Jupiter who falls in *Uttarashada* constellation ruled by the Sun. Moreover, the 9th lord Jupiter is in *vargottam navamsa,* in association with the Sun.

**Karmic Control Planets:** Jupiter and Mercury are the Karmic control planets. Jupiter joins the luminary Moon, while Mercury is associated with the 8th lord Saturn.

**The Venus:** Venus falls in own constellation *Pubba* and joins own *navamsa,* in the 10th from the *navamsa lagna.* Venus conjoins with the 8th lord Saturn in *Rashi* chart while receives the aspect of *lagna* lord Moon in the *navamsa* chart.

Thus, we see that all the combinations, as appended

above, as the essential factors for becoming an IAS officer, are present here. In such cases, first of all the *lagna* reveals the desired results.

A few charts ahead are discussed in short.

*Illustration : 2.13* **(MK)** *Horoscope No.: 13*

Date of birth : 24.11.1946 Time of birth : 06:30:00 hrs
Place of birth : Hissar Lat 29:10:00 N Long 75:45:00E
Ayanamsa : 23:06:37 Sidereal Time : 10:12:34

| **Pln** | **Degree** | **Rasi** | **Nakshatra** | **Pad** |
|---|---|---|---|---|
| Asc | 1:22:55 | Sco | Visakha | 4 |
| Sun | 8:02:11 | Sco | Anuradha | 2 |
| Mon (C) | 11:28:24 | Sco | Anuradha | 3 |
| Mar (C) | 19:26:30 | Sco | Jyestha | 1 |
| Mer (R/C) | 2:38:52 | Sco | Visakha | 4 |
| Jup | 19:42:54 | Lib | Svati | 4 |
| Ven (R) | 28:05:29 | Lib | Visakha | 3 |
| Sat (R) | 15:46:07 | Can | Pushya | 4 |
| Rah (R) | 18:38:04 | Tau | Rohini | 3 |
| Ket (R/C) | 18:38:04 | Sco | Jyestha | 1 |

**Lagna Chart**

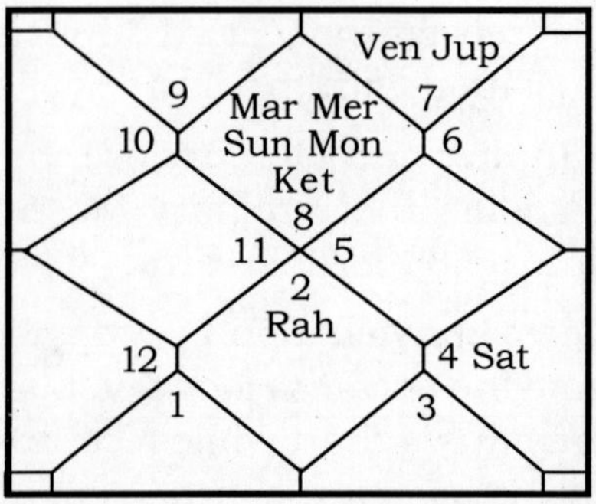


**Navamsa Chart**

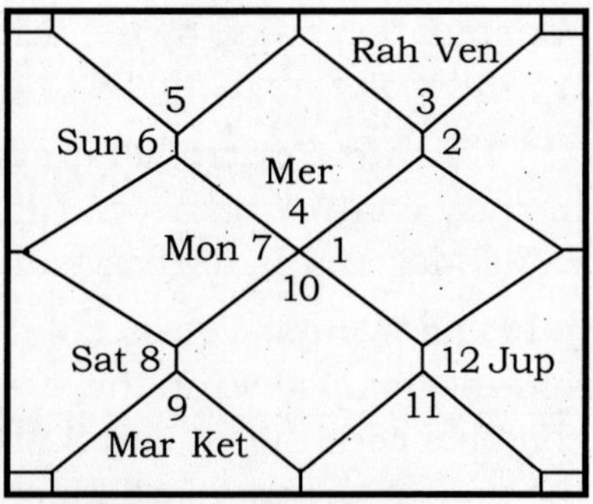


Balance of Vimsottari Dasa of **Sat 7Y 4M 24D**

The 6th & the 10th lords, Mars and Sun, are conjoined in the ascendant, in association with Moon. Moon also aspects the 10th house in *navamsa*. Involvement of 6th & 10th along with influence of luminary is clear indication of native joining the government service.

The lords of the 10th, 9th, 8th and the ascendant, the Sun, Moon, Mercury and Mars are conjoined in *lagna*, which is itself a very strong combination for IAS services. The luminaries have a vital role here as both are associated in the *lagna*. Karmic control planet Mars is also in their company. The 9th lord, as well as one of the luminaries the Moon, fall in the *navamsa* of Venus. Thus, all the desired combinations for IAS are present in this horoscope.

*Illustration : 2.14* **(SKA)** *Horoscope No.: 14*

Date of birth : 25.01.1959 Time of birth : 21:15:00 hrs

Place of birth : Delhi Lat 28:39:00 N Long 77:13:00E

Ayanamsa : 23:17:13 Sidereal Time : 05:10:40

| **Pln** | **Degree** | **Rasi** | **Nakshatra** | **Pad** |
|---|---|---|---|---|
| Asc | 25:51:23 | Leo | P Phalguni | 4 |
| Sun | 11:38:44 | Cap | Sravna | 1 |
| Mon | 22:09:14 | Can | Aslesha | 2 |
| Mar | 0:27:20 | Tau | Krittika | 2 |
| Mer (C) | 28:47:53 | Sag | Uttarasadha | 1 |
| Jup | 4:44:04 | Sco | Anuradha | 1 |
| Ven | 29:38:57 | Cap | Dhanishtha | 2 |
| Sat | 8:56:56 | Sag | Moola | 3 |
| Rah (R) | 22:25:45 | Vir | Hasta | 4 |
| Ket (R) | 22:25:45 | Pis | Revati | 2 |

**Lagna Chart**

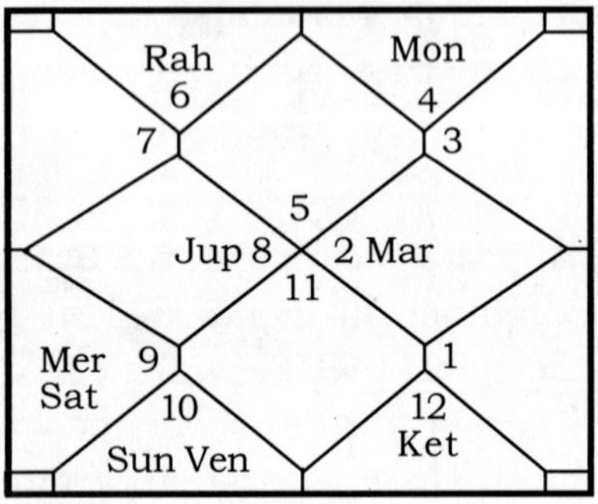


**Navamsa Chart**

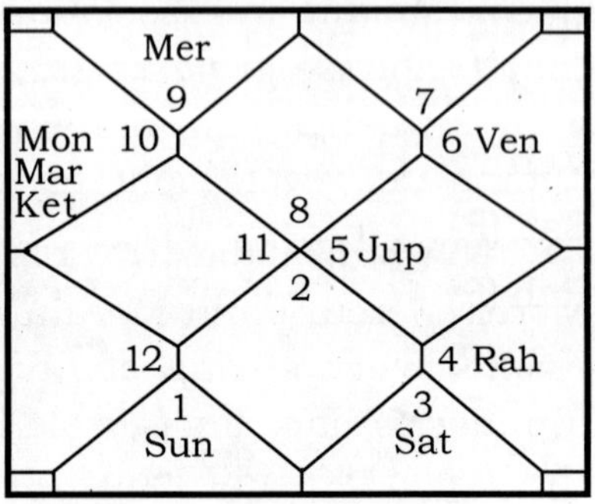


Balance of Vimsottari Dasa of **Mer 10Y 0M 1D**

The native was born in Leo ascendant whose lord Sun conjoins with the 10th lord Venus in the 6th house. The lord of the 9th house, Mars, joins the 10th while the 8th lord Jupiter aspects it as well as the 8th house. The 10th lord Venus is aspected by the luminary, the Moon, and conjoins with luminary, the Sun. Karmic control planets are Mercury and Jupiter. Jupiter has a mutual aspect with the 9th lord Mars and also lends his aspect over the 10th house.

*Lagna* lord Sun obtains the sign of its exaltation. The 9th lord Mars also does so, and conjoins with Moon in *navamsa*. Venus influences both the luminaries. Thus, the horoscope reveals that the native was destined to become an IAS, as all the essential combinations are present here.

*Illustration : 2.15* **(ST)** *Horoscope No.: 15*

Date of birth : 27.06.1958 Time of birth : 07:45:00 hrs

Place of birth : Gorakhpur Lat 26:45:00 N Long 83:23:00E

Ayanamsa : 23:16:46 Sidereal Time : 02:07:17

| Pln | Degree | Rasi | Nakshatra | Pad |
|---|---|---|---|---|
| Asc | 15:34:02 | Can | Pushya | 4 |
| Sun | 11:39:36 | Gem | Ardra | 2 |
| Mon | 17:13:15 | Lib | Svati | 4 |

| | | | | |
|---|---|---|---|---|
| Mar | 20:39:37 | Pis | Revati | 2 |
| Mer (C) | 21:36:01 | Gem | Punarvasu | 1 |
| Jup | 28:34:22 | Vir | Chitra | 2 |
| Ven | 6:52:20 | Tau | Krittika | 4 |
| Sat (R) | 28:11:11 | Sco | Jyestha | 4 |
| Rah (R) | 5:54:55 | Lib | Chitra | 4 |
| Ket (R) | 5:54:55 | Ari | Asvini | 2 |

**Lagna Chart**

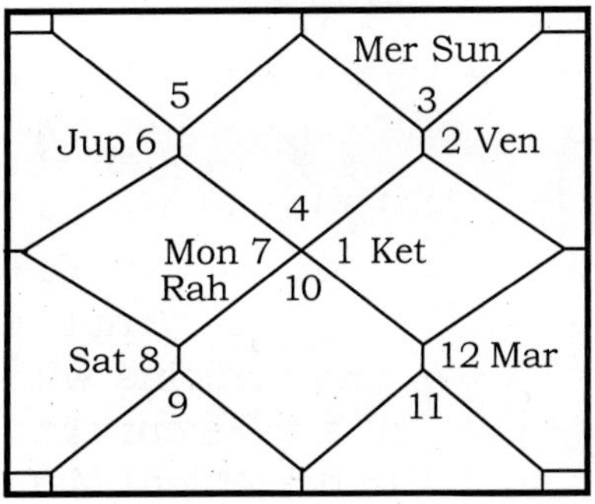


**Navamsa Chart**

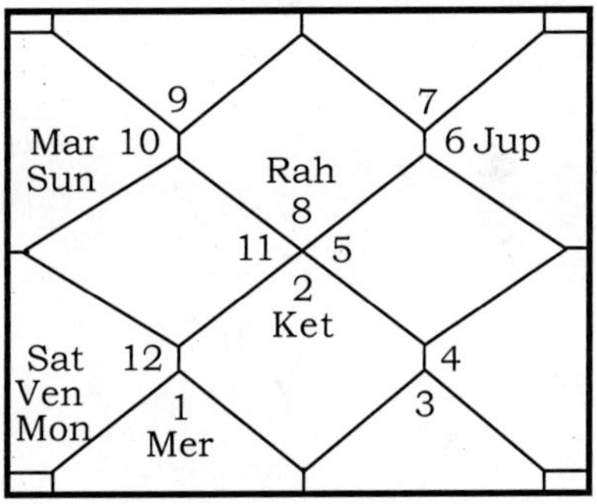


Balance of Vimsottari Dasa of **Rah 3Y 9M 0D**

The lord of the 6th house, Jupiter, aspects the 10th lord Mars, and Jupiter also falls in the constellation of Mars. Moon owns the ascendant and aspects the 10th house. The 10th lord Mars conjoins Sun in the *navamsa.*

The native competed in IAS in his very first attempt. The lord of the 10th house, in his birth chart, joins the 9th house and the lord of the 9th, Jupiter, has an aspect over 9th house. The 9th and the 10th lords are under mutual aspect as well. The 8th lord Saturn falls in the sign of the 10th lord Mars and aspects the 11th house, as well as its lord Venus. The 8th lord Saturn obtains the *navamsa* of the 9th lord and conjoins with the royal planet Moon, as well as Venus, in *navamsa.* The *lagna* lord Moon aspects the 10th house. Both the Karmic control planets, Mars and Venus, are associated with luminaries in *navamsa.*

*Illustration : 2.16* (**SPC**) *Horoscope No.: 16*

Date of birth : 28.09.1950 Time of birth : 13:04:00 hrs
Place of birth : Delhi Lat 28:39:00 N Long 77:13:00E
Ayanamsa : 23:10:08 Sidereal Time : 13:08:55

| Pln | Degree | Rasi | Nakshatra | Pad |
|---|---|---|---|---|
| Asc | 10:05:14 | Sag | Moola | 4 |
| Sun | 11:26:17 | Vir | Hasta | 1 |
| Mon | 5:31:49 | Ari | Asvini | 2 |
| Mar | 8:33:44 | Sco | Anuradha | 2 |
| Mer | 25:03:19 | Leo | P Phalguni | 4 |
| Jup (R) | 5:31:37 | Aqu | Dhanishtha | 4 |
| Ven | 29:26:50 | Leo | U Phalguni | 1 |
| Sat (C) | 1:01:49 | Vir | U Phalguni | 2 |
| Rah (R) | 5:19:01 | Pis | U Bhadrapad | 1 |
| Ket (R/C) | 5:19:01 | Vir | U Phalguni | 3 |

**Lagna Chart**

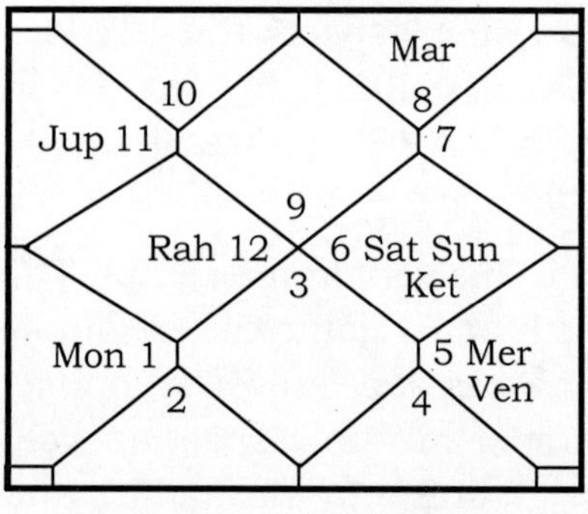


**Navamsa Chart**

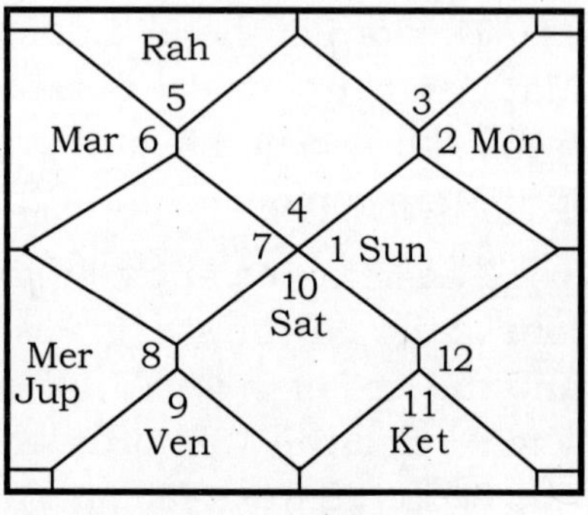


Balance of Vimsottari Dasa of **Ket 4Y 1M 4D**

The native is born under a very specific combination for IAS. The 6th and the 10th lords, Venus and Mercury, conjoin in the 9th house, in the sign of Sun. Sun occupies the 10th house. The 6th lord also falls in the constellation of Sun.

Mutual exchange of lords of 9th, the Sun, and the 10th, Mercury, is present in this chart. The 10th lord Mercury is associated with Venus under the mutual aspect with the *lagna* lord Jupiter.

The lord of the 8th house, Moon, and that of the 9th house, Sun, both are exalted in *navamsa* chart, in the 10th and 11th house from the *navamsa lagna.*

Mercury and Jupiter are Karmic control planets and both are conjoined in the *navamsa* chart and are aspected by luminary Moon. In *Rashi* chart both the Karmic control planets are under mutual aspect, where one conjoins with the lord of 10th and the other aspects it. Thus, all the necessary factors, as per our findings, are present in this birth chart.

*Illustration : 2.17* (**DT**) *Horoscope No.: 17*

Date of birth : 26.01.1941 Time of birth : 11:35:00 hrs

Place of birth : Varanasi Lat 25:20:00 N Long 83:00:00E

Ayanamsa : 23:02:05 Sidereal Time : 19:57:34

| **Pln** | **Degree** | **Rasi** | **Nakshatra** | **Pad** |
|---|---|---|---|---|
| Asc | 15:44:32 | Ari | Bharani | 1 |
| Sun | 12:52:43 | Cap | Sravna | 1 |
| Mon | 28:01:21 | Sag | Uttarasadha | 1 |
| Mar | 21:27:13 | Sco | Jyestha | 2 |
| Mer (C) | 22:56:52 | Cap | Sravna | 4 |
| Jup | 13:48:04 | Ari | Bharani | 1 |
| Ven | 22:24:04 | Sag | Purvasadha | 3 |
| Sat | 15:07:11 | Ari | Bharani | 1 |
| Rah (R) | 10:31:06 | Vir | Hasta | 1 |
| Ket (R) | 10:31:06 | Pis | U Bhadrapad | 3 |

**Lagna Chart**

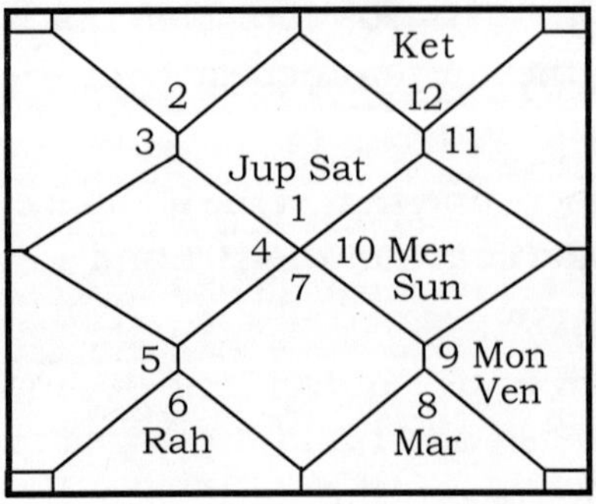


**Navamsa Chart**

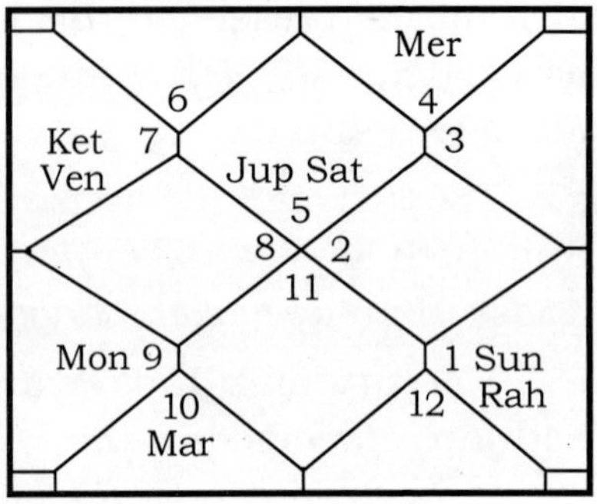


Balance of Vimsottari Dasa of **Sun 5Y 4M 20D**

This horoscope is of a very top civil servant. Following combinations may be noted, which are very powerful for success in IAS.

1. The $6^{th}$ lord Mercury falls in the $10^{th}$ house in conjunction with Sun. Mercury also falls in the constellation of Moon, another luminary. This confirms his govt. service.

2. The lord of the $9^{th}$, Jupiter, and $10^{th}$, Saturn, are conjoined in the *lagna*.

3. The $9^{th}$ and the $10^{th}$ houses are occupied by the royal planets, the Moon and the Sun, respectively.

4. The $5^{th}$ lord Sun occupies the $10^{th}$ while the $4^{th}$ lord Moon occupies the $9^{th}$.

5. The $10^{th}$ lord Saturn aspects the $10^{th}$ house, whereas the $9^{th}$ lord Jupiter aspects the $9^{th}$.

6. The *lagna* lord Mars joins the $8^{th}$ in own sign Scorpio. This position should never be treated inauspicious for learning or profession. Dr. B.V. Raman has clearly mentioned in his famous work 'How to judge a Horoscope' vol. 1 in chapter 4 that the *Lagna*dhipati's position in the $8^{th}$ house made the native a very learned man.

7. The Sun obtains the sign of his exaltation in *navamsa* and that too in $9^{th}$, a triangle.
8. The $9^{th}$ and the $10^{th}$ lords, Jupiter and Saturn, conjoin in the *navamsa lagna.*
9. The Moon obtains *vargottam navamsa* in the sign of Jupiter, the $9^{th}$ lord.
10. The $8^{th}$ and the *lagna* lord Mars obtains exaltation sign in *navamsa.*
11. Venus conjoins with the luminary Moon in the $9^{th}$ house and is also under mutual aspect with the Sun in *navamsa.*
12. Karmic control planets, Mercury and Jupiter, are placed in the $10^{th}$ and *lagna*, respectively.
13. The Karmic control planet, Mercury, is placed in the $10^{th}$ house in association with the luminary Sun, while the other one i.e. Jupiter conjoins with the $10^{th}$ lord Saturn.

Thus, we see that the horoscope is most powerful for success in IAS. This native had secured first position in the competition at the age of 22 years in his very first attempt. Here, I would like to draw the attention of the readers towards the lord of *lagna* in the $8^{th}$ house. This may affect the health but it is not at all inauspicious for profession, education or wealth etc. Had the *lagna* been weak, according to a general understanding of the *lagna* lord in the $8^{th}$ house, how the native would have touched the apex of administrative services? Similarly, the lords of the $9^{th}$ and the $10^{th}$ houses in the $8^{th}$ are not inauspicious, as we have already explained earlier. Of course, the link between the $8^{th}$ and the $10^{th}$ houses signifies one's earnings through service where many persons work under his control.

*Illustration : 2.18* (**GPS**) *Horoscope No.: 18*

Date of birth : 11.02.1944 Time of birth : 00:33:00 hrs
Place of birth : Ballia Lat 25:45:00 N Long 84:09:00E
Ayanamsa : 23:04:22 Sidereal Time : 08:58:25

| **Pln** | **Degree** | **Rasi** | **Nakshatra** | **Pad** |
|---|---|---|---|---|
| Asc | 16:39:02 | Lib | Svati | 3 |
| Sun | 27:49:10 | Cap | Dhanishtha | 2 |
| Mon | 14:15:47 | Leo | P Phalguni | 1 |
| Mar | 17:12:30 | Tau | Rohini | 3 |
| Mer | 4:26:46 | Cap | Uttarasadha | 3 |
| Jup (R) | 29:09:43 | Can | Aslesha | 4 |
| Ven | 23:31:35 | Sag | Purvasadha | 4 |
| Sat (R) | 26:41:53 | Tau | Mrigsira | 2 |
| Rah (R) | 13:38:35 | Can | Pushya | 4 |
| Ket (R/C) | 13:38:35 | Cap | Sravna | 2 |

**Lagna Chart**

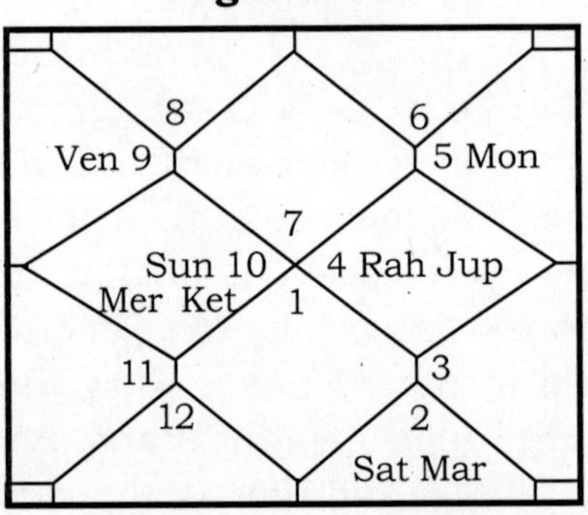


**Navamsa Chart**

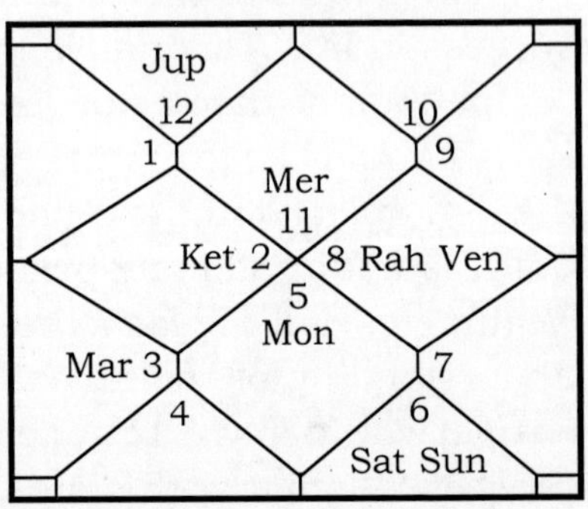


Balance of Vimsottari Dasa of **Ven 18Y 7M 8D**

This horoscope belongs to the person who topped not only in IAS but also in all other competitions for which he appeared. He has held very important and powerful positions in bureaucracy

1. The 6th lord Jupiter occupies the 10th house in the sign

of Moon and also gets the aspect of Sun from the 4$^{th}$ house. The 10$^{th}$ lord Moon is placed in the sign of Sun and obtains the *navamsa* of Sun. This clearly shows his means of livelihood through govt. service.

2. The lord of the 9$^{th}$ house, Moon, joins the 10$^{th}$ in Leo with *vargottam navamsa* position.
3. Jupiter is exalted in the 9$^{th}$ house as an owner of a triangle, the 5$^{th}$ house, and this exalted Jupiter mutually aspects the 10$^{th}$ lord Sun.
4. Jupiter aspects *lagna* and 5$^{th}$ house also.
5. The 8$^{th}$ lord Mercury and 10$^{th}$ lord Sun conjoin in the 3$^{rd}$ house.
6. The *lagna* lord Mars aspects the *lagna*.
7. In *navamsa* chart, Jupiter obtains his own *navamsa* synchronizing with the 9$^{th}$ house, from the *navamsa lagna*.
8. Venus conjoins with the 10$^{th}$ lord Sun and aspects the 9$^{th}$ house. The 8$^{th}$ lord Mercury also joins Venus.
9. Karmic control planets are Moon and Saturn and Moon herself occupies the 10$^{th}$ house.

Thus, all what is needed in a horoscope to be successful in IAS, is present in this birth chart. For Scorpio natives, exalted Jupiter and the Sun and/or Moon in the 10$^{th}$ is a very strong combination for IAS, provided other factors also support.

*Illustration : 2.19* **(AM)** *Horoscope No.: 19*

Date of birth : 13.12.1964 Time of birth : 02:30:00 hrs
Place of birth : Cuttack Lat 27:09:00 N Long 83:58:00E
Ayanamsa : 23:21:45 Sidereal Time : 08:02:13

| Pln | Degree | Rasi | Nakshatra | Pad |
|---|---|---|---|---|
| Asc | 3:43:17 | Lib | Chitra | 4 |
| Sun | 27:31:43 | Sco | Jyestha | 4 |

| | | | | |
|---|---|---|---|---|
| Mon | 4:53:43 | Pis | U Bhadrapad | 1 |
| Mar | 23:54:15 | Leo | P Phalguni | 4 |
| Mer (R) | 10:20:23 | Sag | Moola | 4 |
| Jup (R) | 24:06:49 | Ari | Bharani | 4 |
| Ven | 28:39:36 | Lib | Visakha | 3 |
| Sat | 6:24:14 | Aqu | Dhanishtha | 4 |
| Rah (R) | 29:39:18 | Tau | Mrigsira | 2 |
| Ket (R/D) | 29:39:18 | Sco | Jyestha | 4 |

**Lagna Chart**

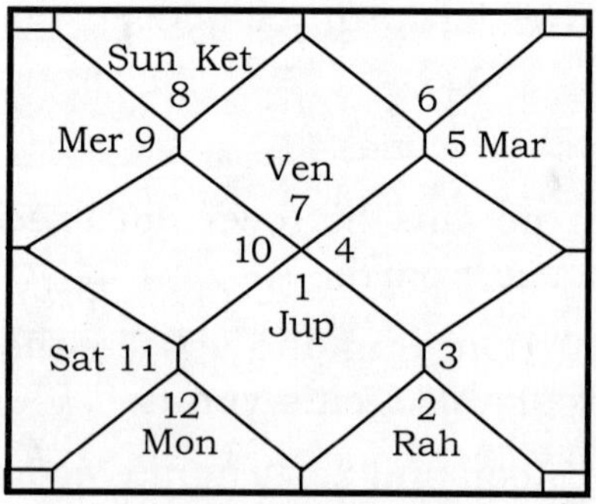


**Navamsa Chart**

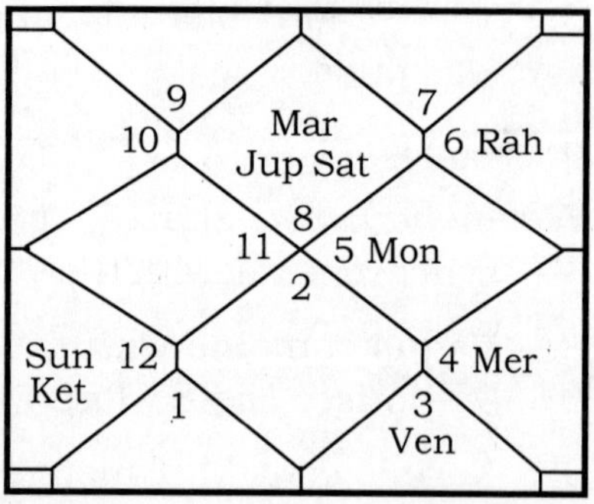


Balance of Vimsottari Dasa of **Sat 16Y 9M 8D**

This is the horoscope of a senior IAS officer who got selected in civil services in the batch of 1988. He was allotted Tamil Nadu cadre where he worked in several positions of eminence. He has been DM of Billupuram in Pondicherry, and so many other places. About 10 years back he was shifted to New Delhi where he worked as PS to cabinet ministers of coal, Railways and Health. Presently he is Commissioner of Sugar in Chennai. He got married to one of the most beautiful girl of her times. He is blessed with two charming daughters.

Let us analyze his horoscope from the point of his profession and try to verify our observations.

- The 10th lord Moon, in the birth chart of the native, joins the sixth house, which indicates means of his livelihood to be through service, and mostly govt. service as Moon is a luminary. Moreover, this 10th lord Moon obtains the *navamsa* of another luminary the Sun, which further confirms the service to be a good govt. service.

- The 9th lord Mercury aspects the 9th house and joins the *navamsa* of the 10th lord Moon i. e. Cancer. The 8th lord Venus occupies the ascendant, in own sign Libra, giving rise to *Malvya Mahapurush Rajyoga.* Venus also obtains the *navamsa* of 9th lord Mercury.
- Both the Karmic control planets, Mars and Venus, are well placed in the horoscope in friendly and own sign. Mars obtains own *navamsa*. Thus, there is relationship between 8th, 9th, and 10th houses.

One of the Karmic control planets should occupy or be associated with 9th, 10th or the ascendant. Here, Venus joins the ascendant and Mars aspects the 10th lord.

Position of Sun and Moon should also be taken into account. Here, the lord of the 11th house, Sun, falls in the sign of one KCP and aspects the 8th house while Moon obtains the *navamsa* of Sun.

Thus, these combinations are so well disposed in the horoscope of the native which leave no scope of doubt of his getting into the top most civil services.

*Illustration : 2.20* (**RKM**) *Horoscope No.: 20*

Date of birth : 19.07.1953 Time of birth : 05:23:00 hrs
Place of birth : Muzaffarnagar Lat 29:28:00 N Long 77:42:00E
Ayanamsa : 23:12:44 Sidereal Time : 0:49:44

| Pln | Degree | Rasi | Nakshatra | Pad |
|---|---|---|---|---|
| Asc | 0:10:33 | Can | Punarvasu | 4 |
| Sun | 2:48:38 | Can | Punarvasu | 4 |
| Mon | 0:31:56 | Lib | Chitra | 3 |
| Mar (C) | 29:46:11 | Gem | Punarvasu | 3 |

| | | | | |
|---|---|---|---|---|
| Mer (R/C) | 13:07:45 | Can | Pushya | 3 |
| Jup | 22:43:25 | Tau | Rohini | 4 |
| Ven | 19:03:01 | Tau | Rohini | 3 |
| Sat | 27:51:45 | Vir | Chitra | 2 |
| Rah (S) | 10:06:25 | Cap | Sravna | 1 |
| Ket (S) | 10:06:25 | Can | Pushya | 3 |

**Lagna Chart**

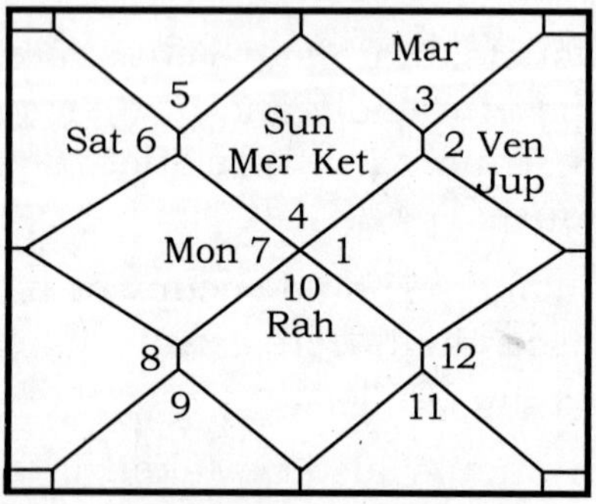


**Navamsa Chart**

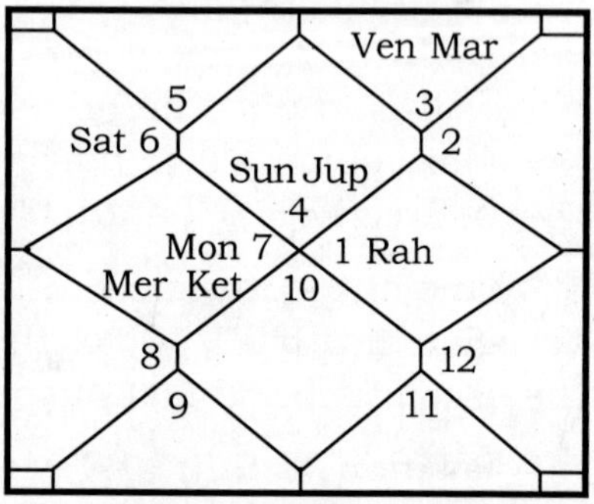


Balance of Vimsottari Dasa of **Mar 3Y 2M 19D**

The birth chart belongs to a very senior, as well as one of the most controversial, IAS officer of U. P. cadre. Because of his power of maneuvering and obsequiousness to his political masters he managed to stay put in 'green' departments most of time in his career. He joined the service in July 1976 and was posted as DM of Badaun, Nainital and Commissioner of Agra at different points of time. He was also Special Housing Secretary. He was married on 8.12.1978 and is blessed with one son and one daughter. During certain adverse vibrations of his birth chart he was incriminated in a major case having large political connotation. He was then suspended; even the proceedings for his dismissal had started.

Let us look at the astrological aspect of this individual who has seen many ups, as well as many downs, in his career.

- The 6th lord Jupiter obtains the *navamsa* of a luminary,

Moon, in association with another luminary Sun.

- The lord of the 8th house, Saturn, aspects the 9th house whereas the lord of the 9th house, Jupiter, aspects the 8th lord Saturn.
- *Yogakaraka* 10th lord Mars joins the ascendant in the sign of a luminary, Moon and in association with another luminary, Sun and 3rd lord Mercury.
- Karmic control planets are Moon and Saturn who aspect the 9th and 10th house, respectively.
- The 9th lord Jupiter obtains the *navamsa* of luminary Moon, along with Sun, whereas Moon who is also the ascendant lord, obtains *vargottam navamsa.*
- The 10th lord Mars obtains *vargottam navamsa.* The 8th lord Saturn also obtains *vargottam navamsa.*

Sun is afflicted, being on the axis of nodes, and both the Karmic control planets, Saturn and Moon, are not very well disposed. They are inimical too. Therefore, he suffered suspension and termination during the *Dasa-Bhukti* of Saturn-Moon.

*Illustration : 2.21* **(IPA)** *Horoscope No.: 21*

Date of birth : 21.11.1940 Time of birth : 19:01:00 hrs

Place of birth : Bareilly Lat 28:20:00 N Long 79:24:00E

Ayanamsa : 23:01:54 Sidereal Time : 22:50:11

| **Pln** | **Degree** | **Rasi** | **Nakshatra** | **Pad** |
|---|---|---|---|---|
| Asc | 3:19:57 | Gem | Mrigsira | 3 |
| Sun | 6:04:15 | Sco | Anuradha | 1 |
| Mon | 21:51:36 | Can | Aslesha | 2 |
| Mar | 7:31:23 | Lib | Svati | 1 |
| Mer | 19:01:50 | Lib | Svati | 4 |
| Jup (R) | 15:11:06 | Ari | Bharani | 1 |
| Ven | 0:54:10 | Lib | Chitra | 3 |

| | | | | |
|---|---|---|---|---|
| Sat (R) | 16:53:07 | Ari | Bharani | 2 |
| Rah (R) | 16:42:11 | Vir | Hasta | 3 |
| Ket (R) | 16:42:11 | Pis | Revati | 1 |

**Lagna Chart**

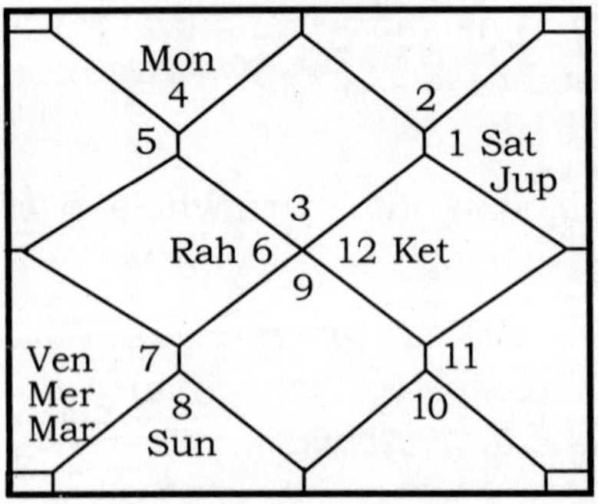


**Navamsa Chart**

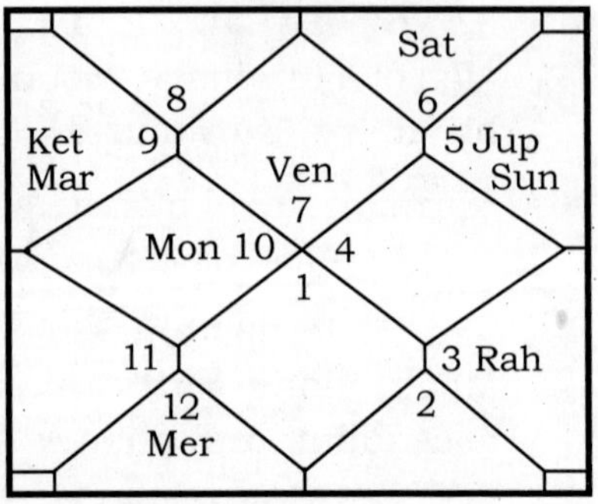


Balance of Vimsottari Dasa of **Mer 10Y 4M 16D**

This very senior IAS officer worked in various positions during his career where he earned accolades for his administrative acumen. He was also once Commissioner of Lucknow. He rose to the position of Chief Secretary and retired from service on 30.11.1999. The native, in addition to his administrative ability, is also proficient at composing poem and making marvelous paintings. His paintings used to be cynosures of all critics and used to sell in lakhs. His poems won may awards.

- The 10th lord Jupiter obtains the *navamsa* of Sun, Leo, in association with Sun, whereas the 6th lord Mars obtains the *navamsa* of Jupiter, the 10th lord. This configuration confirms service and that too a government one.
- The 9th and the 10th lords, Saturn and Jupiter, are conjoined in the 11th house. Saturn, being the 8th lord too, also aspects the 8th house.
- Both the Karmic control planets, Mercury and Jupiter, are aspecting each other. They are in *Samsaptak* position which is very good. Mercury and Jupiter are lords of all the *Kendras* and thus all lords of *Kendra* are opposite each other.

- The lord of ascendant, Mercury, aspects the 8th lord Saturn and the 10th lord Jupiter. Thus, there is good relationship between ascendant, 10th and the 8th house. We have been emphasizing the role of the 8th house in administrative services since long.
- The 5th lord Venus obtains own *navamsa* and is *vargottam*. Sun obtains own *navamsa* whereas Moon obtains the *navamsa* of 9th lord Saturn. Sun falls in constellation of 9th lord Saturn whereas Moon falls in the constellation of lord of *lagna*.
- The lord of the ascendant, Mercury, joins the 5th house in association with the 5th lord Venus. This has given the native creative ability and his poems and art have made him popular and prominent.

*Illustration : 2.22* (**SKA**) *Horoscope No.: 22*

Date of birth : 06.09.1950 Time of birth : 01:10:00 hrs

Place of birth : Delhi Lat 28:39:00 N Long 77:13:00E

Ayanamsa : 23:10:06 Sidereal Time : 23:46:13

| **Pln** | **Degree** | **Rasi** | **Nakshatra** | **Pad** |
|---|---|---|---|---|
| Asc | 16:03:51 | Gem | Ardra | 3 |
| Sun | 19:29:22 | Leo | P Phalguni | 2 |
| Mon | 3:10:12 | Gem | Mrigsira | 3 |
| Mar | 23:17:58 | Lib | Visakha | 1 |
| Mer (R) | 9:05:10 | Vir | U Phalguni | 4 |
| Jup (R) | 7:56:57 | Aqu | Satabhisha | 1 |
| Ven | 1:35:33 | Leo | Magha | 1 |
| Sat (C) | 28:13:46 | Leo | U Phalguni | 1 |
| Rah (R) | 5:21:18 | Pis | U Bhadrapad | 1 |
| Ket (R) | 5:21:18 | Vir | U Phalguni | 3 |

**Lagna Chart**

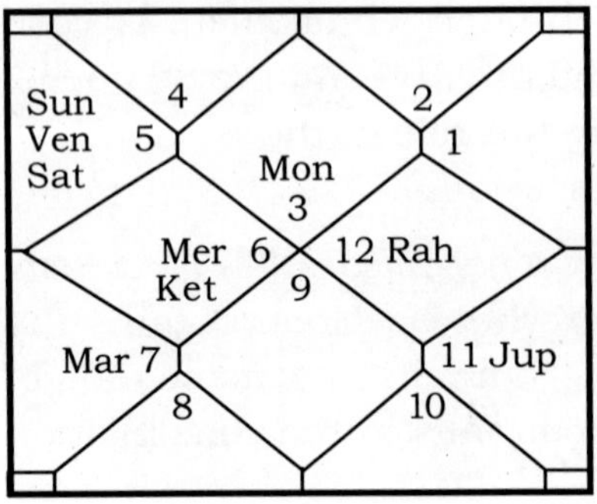


**Navamsa Chart**

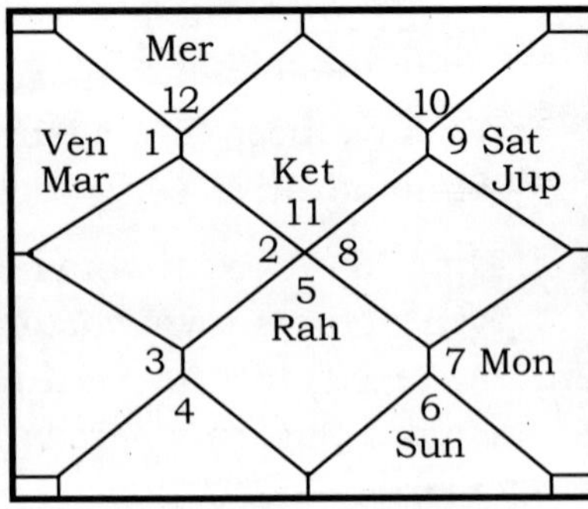


Balance of Vimsottari Dasa of **Mar 1Y 10M 0D**

This is the birth chart of a very senior officer of Principal Secretary rank in Uttar Pradesh. During the change of governments he had to suffer because of change in the political milieu.

- The lord of the 10th house, Jupiter, aspects the 6th lord Mars, placed in the 5th house. Jupiter mutually aspects the luminary Sun.
- Lord of the 10th house, Jupiter, occupies the 9th house aspecting the ascendant, 3rd and the 5th houses. Aspect between the 10th lord Jupiter and the 8th & 9th lord Saturn is very auspicious one, for getting a class one civil service.
- The 8th & 9th lord Saturn and the 10th lord Jupiter obtain the *navamsa* of 10th lord Jupiter.
- Ascendant lord Mercury joins the 4th house in exaltation, aspects the 10th house and falls in the constellation of Sun.
- Sun, Saturn and Venus fall in the sign of Sun, Leo.
- Karmic control planets are Mercury and Jupiter. Mercury aspects the 10th house while Jupiter falls in the 9th house, aspecting the 9th lord.

*Illustration : 2.23* **(HR)** *Horoscope No.: 23*

Date of birth : 25.02.1964 Time of birth : 17:30:00 hrs
Place of birth : Delhi Lat 28:39:00 N Long 77:13:00E
Ayanamsa : 23:21:06 Sidereal Time : 03:26:26

| **Pln** | **Degree** | **Rasi** | **Nakshatra** | **Pad** |
|---|---|---|---|---|
| Asc | 3:05:56 | Leo | Magha | 1 |
| Sun | 12:33:54 | Aqu | Satabhisha | 2 |
| Mon | 16:56:25 | Can | Aslesha | 1 |
| Mar (D) | 10:44:41 | Aqu | Satabhisha | 2 |
| Mer (C) | 29:07:08 | Cap | Dhanishtha | 2 |
| Jup | 26:00:55 | Pis | Revati | 3 |
| Ven | 23:55:48 | Pis | Revati | 3 |
| Sat (C) | 3:28:07 | Aqu | Dhanishtha | 4 |
| Rah (R) | 16:27:51 | Gem | Ardra | 3 |
| Ket (R) | 16:27:51 | Sag | Purvasadha | 1 |

**Lagna Chart**

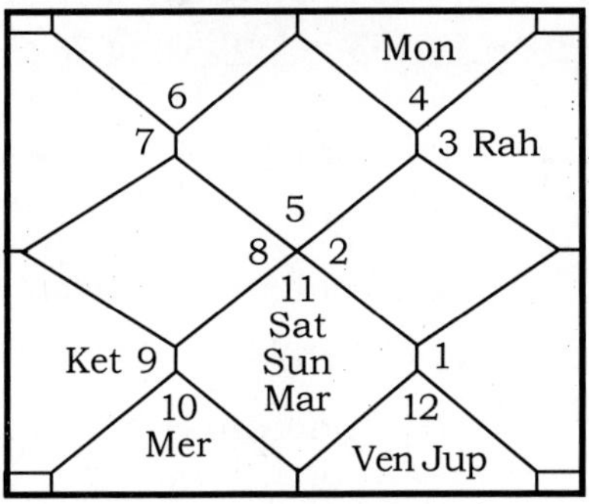


**Navamsa Chart**

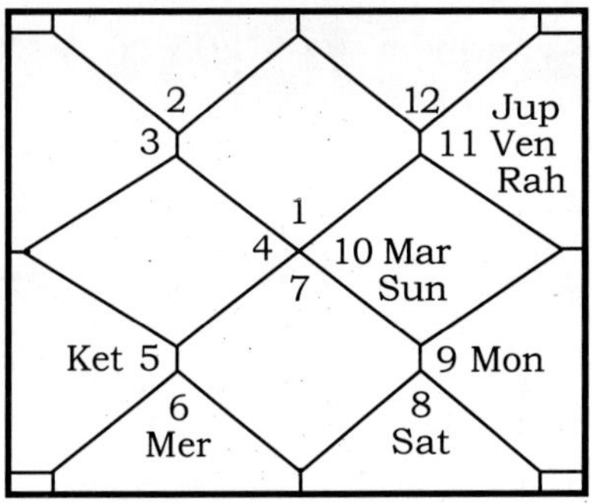


Balance of Vimsottari Dasa of **Mer 16Y 7M 24D**

The native of this birth chart is a senior IAS officer of UP cadre and recently has been Principal Secretary Home in the UP secretariat. His wife is also senior officer in the Ministry of Education, New Delhi.

Following combinations in his birth chart may be taken note of:

- The 10th lord Venus and 8th lord Jupiter obtain the *navamsa* of 6th lord Saturn.
- The 6th lord Saturn and ascendant lord Sun are conjoined in the 7th house and lend aspect over ascendant. This combination is important for entering into a govt. service.
- The ascendant lord Sun obtains the *navamsa* of 6th lord Saturn, and is associated with 9th lord Mars.
- 9th and 4th lord *Yogakaraka* Mars aspects the 10th house and is associated with ascendant lord Sun and 6th lord Saturn.
- Karmic control planets are Mercury and Jupiter. Jupiter conjoins with the 10th lord Venus in the 8th house.

*Illustration : 2.24* (**DDM**) *Horoscope No.: 24*

Date of birth : 15.09.1942 Time of birth : 23:31:00 hrs

Place of birth : Amethi Lat 26:09:00 N Long 81:48:00E

Ayanamsa : 23:03:16 Sidereal Time : 22:04:18

| **Pln** | **Degree** | **Rasi** | **Nakshatra** | **Pad** |
|---|---|---|---|---|
| Asc | 21:06:10 | Tau | Rohini | 4 |
| Sun | 29:09:36 | Leo | U Phalguni | 1 |
| Mon | 2:51:56 | Sco | Visakha | 4 |
| Mar (C) | 5:50:09 | Vir | U Phalguni | 3 |
| Mer | 25:42:48 | Vir | Chitra | 1 |
| Jup | 27:13:15 | Gem | Punarvasu | 3 |
| Ven | 13:14:45 | Leo | Magha | 4 |
| Sat | 19:23:09 | Tau | Rohini | 3 |
| Rah (R) | 11:08:12 | Leo | Magha | 4 |
| Ket (R) | 11:08:12 | Aqu | Satabhisha | 2 |

**Lagna Chart**

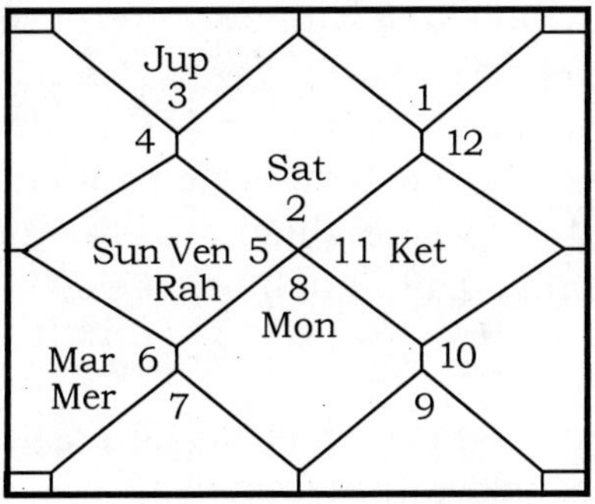


**Navamsa Chart**

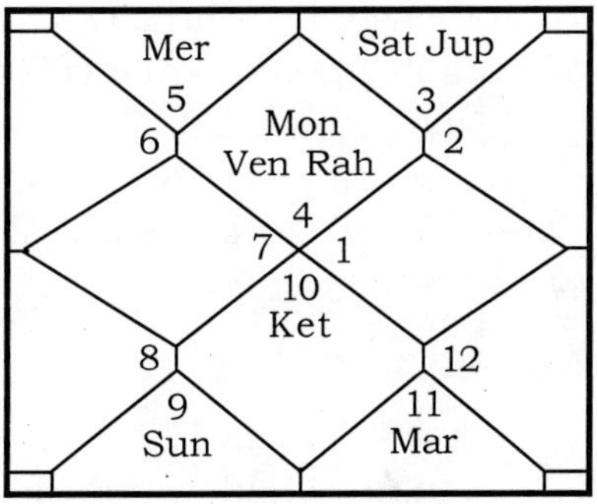


Balance of Vimsottari Dasa of **Jup 0Y 6M 22D**

- The 6th and ascendant lord, Venus, occupies the 4th house, in the sign of Sun, aspecting the 10th. Venus, the 6th lord is associated with Sun. Sun obtains the *navamsa* of 8th lord Jupiter. Thus, native's govt. service can now be easily predicted, as per our observations enumerated earlier.
- The 8th lord Jupiter aspects the 8th and the 10th, and also the 6th house.
- The 9th and 10th lord *Yogakaraka* Saturn occupies the ascendant, aspecting the 10th.
- The 9th & 10th lord Saturn and the 8th lord Jupiter conjoin in the *navamsa.*
- Karmic control planets are Sun and Saturn and both aspect the 10th house and influence the ascendant (One KCP occupies the ascendant and the other is associated with its lord).
- In *navamsa* chart, 10th lord Mars falls in the 8th house and is aspected by the 9th lord Jupiter. 8th lord Saturn aspects the 9th lord and is associated with the 9th lord in *navamsa.*

## 2.1 Combinations for Allied Services

The examination conducted by Union Public Service Commission recruits officers for Indian Administrative

Service as well as for some allied services. These are also class one services having somewhat same glamour but these officers are posted in specific departments of Govt. of India such as Income tax, Railways, Information service, Audit and Accounts service etc. Indian Police Service and Indian Forest Service officers are allotted to states like IAS. Let us see what combinations get the natives to such services.

## 2.2 INCOME TAX

The $8^{th}$ is the $11^{th}$ from the $10^{th}$; therefore it should be taken into consideration if the native is destined to enter into Revenue Service. The $12^{th}$ house is also important because it deals with losses through raids etc and penalty due to taxation, expenditure, payments etc.

The $6^{th}$ house deals with service as well as court cases; therefore for revenue services all the *trik* houses must have a concern with the vocation of the native. Jupiter is the significator of tax; therefore it should also be examined.

*Illustration : 2.25* (**DS**) *Horoscope No.: 25*

Date of birth : 17.01.1954 Time of birth : 16:35:00 hrs

Place of birth : Karnal Lat 29:41:00 N Long 76:59:00E

Ayanamsa : 23:13:11 Sidereal Time : 23:58:16

| **Pln** | **Degree** | **Rasi** | **Nakshatra** | **Pad** |
|---|---|---|---|---|
| Asc | 19:10:44 | Gem | Ardra | 4 |
| Sun | 3:35:43 | Cap | Uttarasadha | 3 |
| Mon | 13:31:55 | Gem | Ardra | 3 |
| Mar | 23:25:46 | Lib | Visakha | 2 |
| Mer (D) | 5:20:04 | Cap | Uttarasadha | 3 |
| Jup (R) | 24:09:08 | Tau | Mrigsira | 1 |
| Ven (C) | 0:35:11 | Cap | Uttarasadha | 2 |
| Sat | 15:18:59 | Lib | Svati | 3 |
| Rah (D) | 0:47:14 | Cap | Uttarasadha | 2 |
| Ket | 0:47:14 | Can | Punarvasu | 4 |

**Lagna Chart**

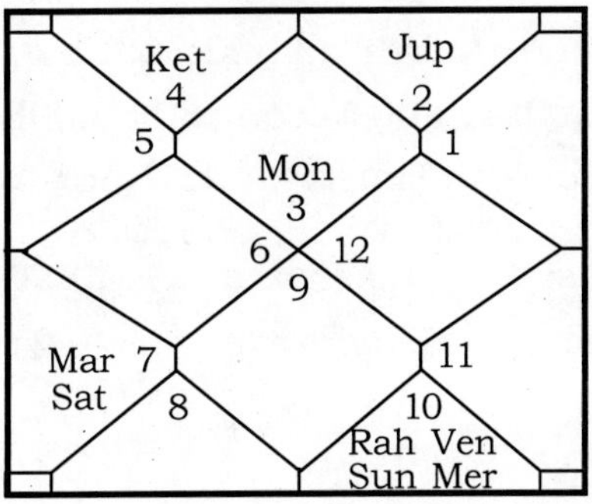


**Navamsa Chart**

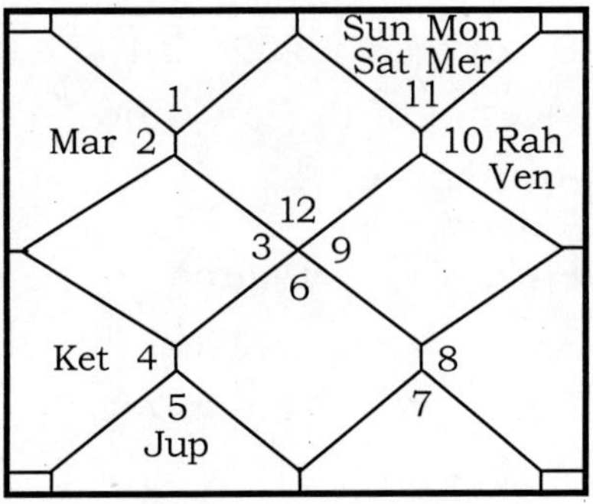


Balance of Vimsottari Dasa of **Rah 8Y 8M 23D**

This is the birth chart of a senior commissioner of Income Tax posted in financial capital of India. He is a very well known astrologer as well.

- The native was born in Gemini ascendant. The 10th lord Jupiter falls in the constellation of 6th lord Mars and obtains the *navamsa* of Sun i.e. Leo, which indicates govt. service.

- The 6th lord and 11th lord Mars also aspects the 10th lord Jupiter, ascendant lord Mercury and other planets in the 8th house.

- The lord of the 10th house, Jupiter, falls in the 12th house whereas the ascendant & 4th lord Mercury, 12th lord Venus and 3rd lord Sun fall in the 8th house along with Rahu. These four important planets are 11th from the 10th house and are aspected by the 10th lord Jupiter and 11th and 6th lord Mars. Thus, the involvement of the house of income is there in many ways.

- Karmic control planets are Saturn and Moon. Moon occupies the ascendant and both Saturn and Moon are conjoined in the *navamsa* chart, under the aspect of the 10th lord Jupiter.

*Illustration : 2.26* (**AC**) *Horoscope No.: 26*

Date of birth : 02.12.1962 Time of birth : 23:00:00 hrs
Place of birth : Lucknow Lat 26:50:00 N Long 80:54:00E
Ayanamsa : 23:20:04 Sidereal Time : 03:37:55

| **Pln** | **Degree** | **Rasi** | **Nakshatra** | **Pad** |
|---|---|---|---|---|
| Asc | 5:09:41 | Leo | Magha | 2 |
| Sun | 16:43:37 | Sco | Jyestha | 1 |
| Mon | 21:42:06 | Cap | Sravna | 4 |
| Mar | 28:14:45 | Can | Aslesha | 4 |
| Mer (C) | 20:48:17 | Sco | Jyestha | 2 |
| Jup | 11:24:58 | Aqu | Satabhisha | 2 |
| Ven (R) | 18:53:33 | Lib | Svati | 4 |
| Sat | 13:45:58 | Cap | Sravna | 2 |
| Rah | 7:33:07 | Can | Pushya | 2 |
| Ket | 7:33:07 | Cap | Uttarasadha | 4 |

**Lagna Chart**

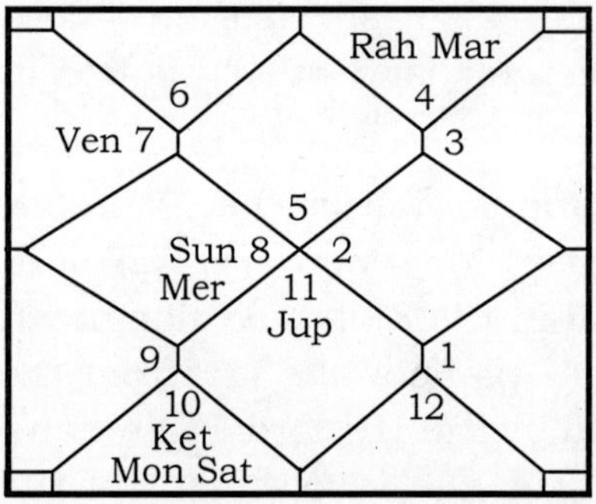


**Navamsa Chart**

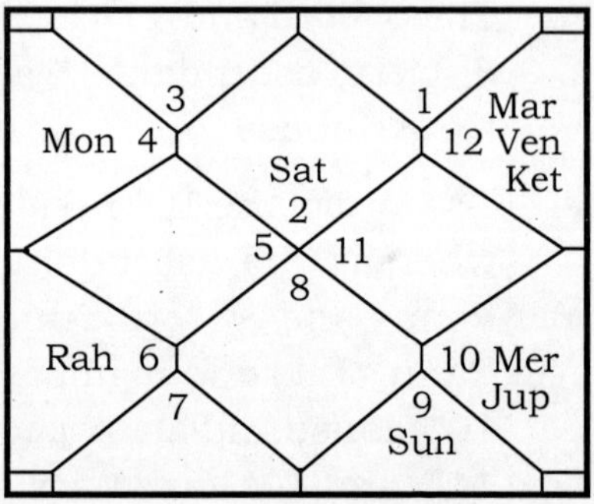


Balance of Vimsottari Dasa of **Mon 1Y 2M 20D**

This is the birth chart of a lady additional commissioner of Income tax whose husband is also in the same service.

- The 6th lord Saturn obtains the *navamsa* of 10th lord Venus.

- The 12th lord Moon, a luminary and 6th lord Saturn are associated with each other in the 6th house which indicates govt. service.
- The 10th lord Venus occupies the 3rd house in own sign and is aspected by the 8th lord Jupiter. Thus, the 10th lord is under the influence of 8th lord.
- The 10th lord Venus obtains the *navamsa* of Jupiter as well. Moon obtains own *navamsa* i.e. of 12th lord. Saturn's aspect on the 10th lord i .e. Venus is also one of the strong points.
- Karmic control planets, Saturn and Moon, are conjoined in the 6th house.

*Illustration : 2.27* (**DC**) *Horoscope No.: 27*

Date of birth : 22.03.1961 Time of birth : 21:15:00 hrs

Place of birth : Ranchi Lat 23:22:00 N Long 85:20:00E

Ayanamsa : 23:18:47 Sidereal Time : 09:25:57

| **Pln** | **Degree** | **Rasi** | **Nakshatra** | **Pad** |
|---|---|---|---|---|
| Asc | 23:09:49 | Lib | Visakha | 1 |
| Sun | 8:28:25 | Pis | U Bhadrapad | 2 |
| Mon | 22:03:31 | Tau | Rohini | 4 |
| Mar | 16:23:41 | Gem | Ardra | 3 |
| Mer | 10:50:40 | Aqu | Satabhisha | 2 |
| Jup | 7:57:41 | Cap | Uttarasadha | 4 |
| Ven (R) | 5:42:54 | Ari | Asvini | 2 |
| Sat | 4:43:41 | Cap | Uttarasadha | 3 |
| Rah (R) | 12:35:13 | Leo | Magha | 4 |
| Ket (R) | 12:35:13 | Aqu | Satabhisha | 2 |

**Lagna Chart**

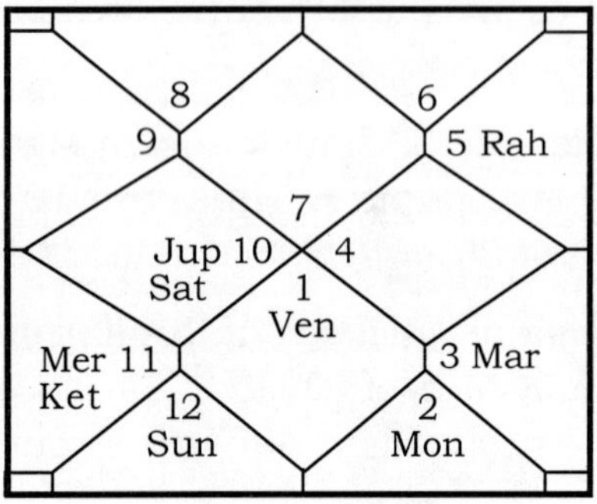


**Navamsa Chart**

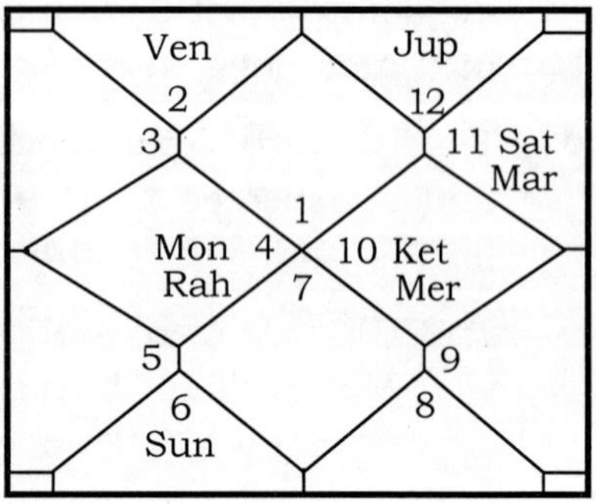


Balance of Vimsottari Dasa of **Mon 0Y 11M 14D**

This is the birth chart of the husband of above native who is also an officer of Indian Revenue Service, presently posted as commissioner of Income tax in Mumbai.

Let us note the combinations in his chart:

- The native is born in Libra ascendant at 23:09:49. The $6^{th}$ lord Jupiter lends aspect over the $10^{th}$ house and also the $10^{th}$ lord. Jupiter falls in the constellation of Sun. Sun occupies the $6^{th}$ house as well. This, thus, indicates the govt. service.
- The $10^{th}$ lord Moon occupies the $8^{th}$ house in exaltation under the aspect from the $6^{th}$ lord Jupiter.
- Ascendant is strong as its lord Venus aspects the ascendant and obtains own *navamsa*.
- Lord of the $12^{th}$ house, Mercury, is posited in the $5^{th}$ house, which is $10^{th}$ from the $10^{th}$ lord Moon.
- Moreover, the $10^{th}$ lord Moon and the $6^{th}$ lord Jupiter, both, obtain their own *navamsa*.
- Moon receives the aspect of Jupiter in the *navamsa* chart as well.
- Karmic control planets are Saturn and Sun. Saturn aspects the $10^{th}$ house and the ascendant, and Sun occupies the sixth house.

The combinations, as enumerated by us, for govt. service, as also for civil service and that too in the field of Income Tax i.e. Revenue Service are clearly present.

*Illustration : 2.28* (**BPS**) *Horoscope No.: 28*

Date of birth : 16.03.1960 Time of birth : 13:45:00 hrs

Place of birth : Deoria Lat 26:31:00 N Long 83:48:00E

Ayanamsa : 23:18:02 Sidereal Time : 01:25:53

| **Pln** | **Degree** | **Rasi** | **Nakshatra** | **Pad** |
|---|---|---|---|---|
| Asc | 6:33:49 | Can | Pushya | 1 |
| Sun | 2:27:16 | Pis | P Bhadrapad | 4 |
| Mon | 10:33:36 | Lib | Svati | 2 |
| Mar | 23:39:51 | Cap | Dhanishtha | 1 |
| Mer (R/C) | 21:59:22 | Aqu | P Bhadrapad | 1 |
| Jup | 8:28:34 | Sag | Moola | 3 |
| Ven | 7:01:29 | Aqu | Satabhisha | 1 |
| Sat | 23:42:22 | Sag | Purvasadha | 4 |
| Rah | 1:14:47 | Vir | U Phalguni | 2 |
| Ket (D) | 1:14:47 | Pis | P Bhadrapad | 4 |

**Lagna Chart**

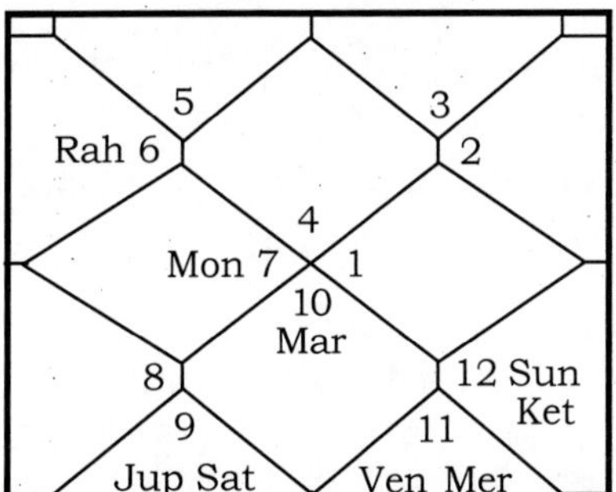


**Navamsa Chart**

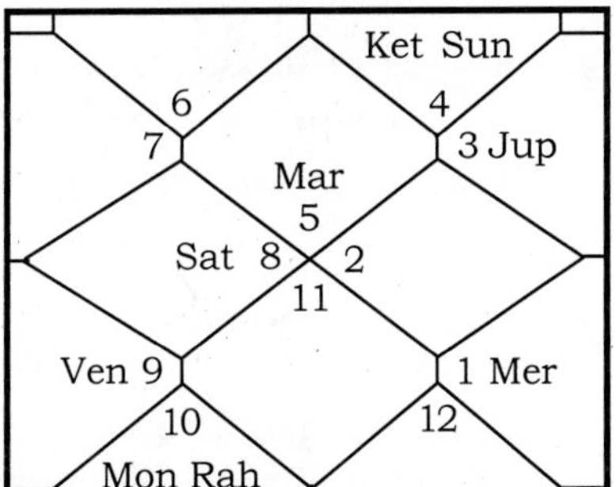


Balance of Vimsottari Dasa of **Rah 12Y 8M 28D**

The native also is a very senior member of Indian

Revenue Service and is posted as commissioner of Income Tax.

Relevant combinations in his birth chart can be spelt out as below:

- The native is born in Cancer ascendant, lord of which is a luminary Moon.
- The $10^{th}$ lord Mars occupies the $7^{th}$ house in exaltation, from where it aspects the $10^{th}$ house. Mars obtains the *navamsa* of Sun, thus confirming the govt. service.
- The $8^{th}$ lord Saturn and the $9^{th}$ lord Jupiter are conjoined in the $6^{th}$ house.
- The $10^{th}$ house is aspected by the $9^{th}$ lord, as well by its own lord.
- Jupiter, significator for revenue service, aspects the $10^{th}$ and the $12^{th}$ house, as also the $2^{nd}$ house.
- *Karaka* or the significator for civil services, Venus, joins the $8^{th}$ house. *Karaka* should be involved either with $8^{th}$, $9^{th}$ or the $10^{th}$.
- If reckoned from the $10^{th}$ house, lord of $3^{rd}$ and sixth Mercury occupies the $11^{th}$.
- *Dhankaraka* Jupiter obtains the *navamsa* of the $12^{th}$ lord Mercury and $12^{th}$ lord Mercury falls in the constellation of Jupiter
- The $8^{th}$ lord Saturn falls in the sign of Jupiter and obtains the *navamsa* of $10^{th}$ lord Mars.
- Karmic control planets are Mercury and Jupiter. Jupiter aspects the $10^{th}$ house and Mercury falls in the $8^{th}$ house.
- The $10^{th}$ house is aspected by the ascendant lord Moon, as well as by $6^{th}$ and $9^{th}$ lord Jupiter confirming good govt. service.

## 2.3 AUDIT AND ACCOUNTS SERVICE

For Audit and accounts services involvement of Mercury and Jupiter should be there. Jupiter and Mercury are the significator of wealth and accounts. Therefore, apart from the other important combinations for a govt. service and success in civil service or IAS, involvement of Jupiter and Mercury, with the professional aspect of the native, may take him to Audit and Accounts services.

*Illustration : 2.29* (**KNR**) *Horoscope No.: 29*

Date of birth : 12.10.1931 Time of birth : 07:54:00 hrs
Place of birth : Masullapatnam Lat 26:44:00 N Long 79:24:00E
Ayanamsa : 22:54:12 Sidereal Time : 09:00:25

| **Pln** | **Degree** | **Rasi** | **Nakshatra** | **Pad** |
|---|---|---|---|---|
| Asc | 16:58:25 | Lib | Svati | 4 |
| Sun | 24:53:47 | Vir | Chitra | 1 |
| Mon (C) | 2:45:04 | Lib | Chitra | 3 |
| Mar | 24:01:57 | Lib | Visakha | 2 |
| Mer (C) | 20:04:45 | Vir | Hasta | 4 |
| Jup | 24:42:44 | Can | Aslesha | 3 |
| Ven (C) | 3:54:21 | Lib | Chitra | 4 |
| Sat | 24:04:50 | Sag | Purvasadha | 4 |
| Rah (R) | 12:37:58 | Pis | U Bhadrapad | 3 |
| Ket (R/C) | 12:37:58 | Vir | Hasta | 1 |

**Lagna Chart**

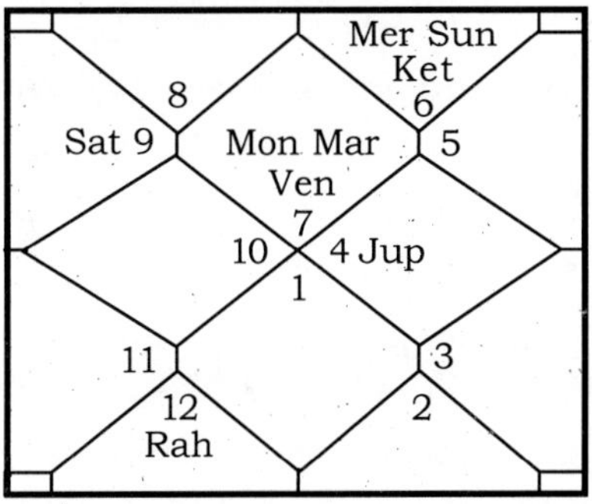


**Navamsa Chart**

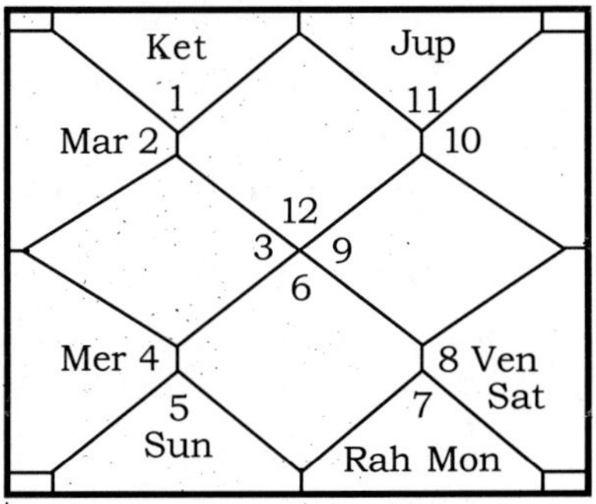


Balance of Vimsottari Dasa of **Mar 2Y 0M 20D**

This horoscope belongs to one of the retired CAG, the top officer of the Indian Audit and Accounts Service. The native is also a very bright star in the firmament of astrology. A keen, methodical research scholar of astrology, he is a prolific writer too, on various subjects of this science. Having written a large no. of research articles and a number of books, he is still receptive to new ideas and researches in the field of astrology.

Let us look at the planetary combinations for his professional achievements:

- The 6th lord Jupiter occupies the 10th house in exaltation.
- The 8th lord Venus occupies the ascendant, in association with the 10th lord Moon
- The 9th lord Mercury is posited in the 12th house, in association with 11th lord Sun.
- 9th lord Mercury obtains the *navamsa* of the 10th lord Moon
- Jupiter, Mercury and Sun aspect the 6th house, which is a clear indication for Audit and accounts services.
- Karmic control planets are Mercury and Jupiter. Jupiter occupies the 10th house and both aspect the 6th house.
- The 9th lord Mercury falls in the constellation *Hasta,* whose lord is Moon, the owner of the 10th house, while the occupant of the 10th house, Jupiter, falls in the constellation of Mercury, owner of the 9th house.

These combinations are splendid for success in civil service and Jupiter and Mercury's involvement in the professional aspect took him to IAAS.

## 2.4 INDIAN POLICE SERVICE

We have studied a number of horoscopes of personnel in police services and have found that there must be some involvement of Mars in the houses and planets responsible for profession of the native. In addition, the 6th house, as it indicates crime and court cases etc. should also be involved.

Combinations for civil service should also be there additionally, to bring the person to the Indian Police Service:

*Illustration : 2.30* (**YKM**) *Horoscope No.: 30*

Date of birth : 28.07.1944 Time of birth : 05:40:00 hrs
Place of birth : Dehradun Lat 30:19:00 N Long 78:03:00E
Ayanamsa : 23:04:43 Sidereal Time : 0:44:13

| **Pln** | **Degree** | **Rasi** | **Nakshatra** | **Pad** |
|---|---|---|---|---|
| Asc | 29:31:19 | Gem | Punarvasu | 3 |
| Sun | 11:40:05 | Can | Pushya | 3 |
| Mon | 5:51:40 | Lib | Svati | 1 |
| Mar | 16:40:42 | Leo | P Phalguni | 2 |
| Mer | 5:26:48 | Leo | Magha | 2 |
| Jup | 7:18:54 | Leo | Magha | 3 |
| Ven (C) | 20:10:48 | Can | Aslesha | 2 |
| Sat | 11:40:55 | Gem | Ardra | 2 |
| Rah (C) | 4:34:51 | Can | Pushya | 1 |
| Ket | 4:34:51 | Cap | Uttarasadha | 3 |

**Lagna Chart**

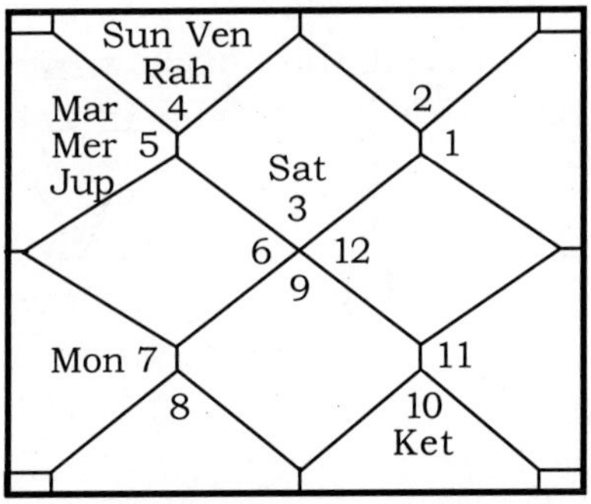


**Navamsa Chart**

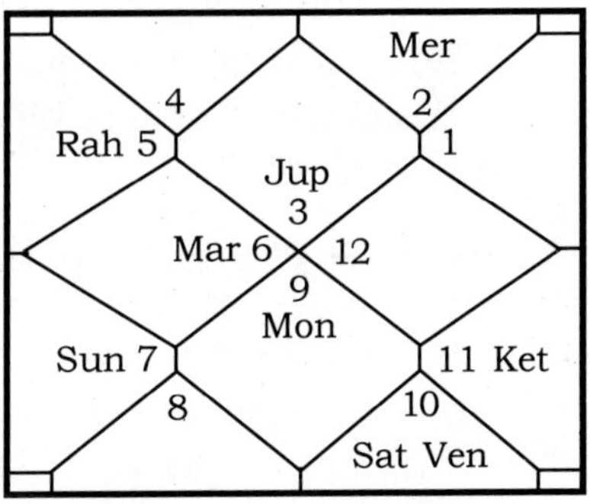


Balance of Vimsottari Dasa of **Rah 17Y 8M 25D**

This is the horoscope of an IPS officer of UP cadre, who retired from the post of director General few years back. This courageous officer had earned a name in the department, for bravery.

Planetary combinations in his birth chart are as below:

- The 6th lord Mars occupies the sign of Sun, Leo in the 3rd house along with the 10th lord Jupiter. The 6th lord Mars also aspects the 6th & the 10th house. This proves the native's govt. service. The lord of ascendant, Mercury, also joins the combination of 6th and 10th lords.
- The 8th lord Saturn occupies the ascendant.
- The 10th lord Jupiter aspects the 9th house while the 8th & 9th lord Saturn aspects the 10th house, as well as the 10th lord Jupiter.
- Ascendant lord is also under the influence of Mars, as it is conjoined with Mars in the 3rd house and also obtains the *navamsa* of Mars.
- Karmic control planets are Moon and Saturn. Saturn aspects the 10th house and 10th lord.
- 10th lord Jupiter falls in the constellation of Ketu occupant of the 8th house and falls in the constellation of ascendant lord Mercury.

Thus, there is good relationship between 8th, 10, and ascendant and overwhelming influence of Mars over the 6th, 9th, 10th and ascendant, which has made him a brilliant and dashing IPS officer.

## 2.5 INDIAN FOREST SERVICE

Indian Forest service is an elite service of officers managing our forest wealth and forest reserves. Involvement of Saturn, Sun and Mars must be there. These planets should have a concern with 10th, 6th or the 8th house. Sun indicates forests, wood, while Saturn would indicate earth, soil and Mars indicates vast areas of land, as also policing involved in the forests.

*Illustration : 2.31* (**USS**) *Horoscope No.: 31*

Date of birth : 16.07.1955 Time of birth : 02:10:00 hrs
Place of birth : Chhapra Lat 25:47:00 N Long 84:47:00E
Ayanamsa : 23:14:27 Sidereal Time : 21:50:48

| **Pln** | **Degree** | **Rasi** | **Nakshatra** | **Pad** |
|---|---|---|---|---|
| Asc | 17:20:15 | Tau | Rohini | 3 |
| Sun | 29:19:48 | Gem | Punarvasu | 3 |
| Mon | 9:09:05 | Tau | Krittika | 4 |
| Mar (C) | 9:37:18 | Can | Pushya | 2 |
| Mer | 9:43:24 | Gem | Ardra | 1 |
| Jup | 13:35:07 | Can | Pushya | 4 |
| Ven | 16:21:19 | Gem | Ardra | 3 |
| Sat (R) | 21:16:11 | Lib | Visakha | 1 |
| Rah | 3:05:23 | Sag | Moola | 1 |
| Ket | 3:05:23 | Gem | Mrigsira | 3 |

**Lagna Chart**

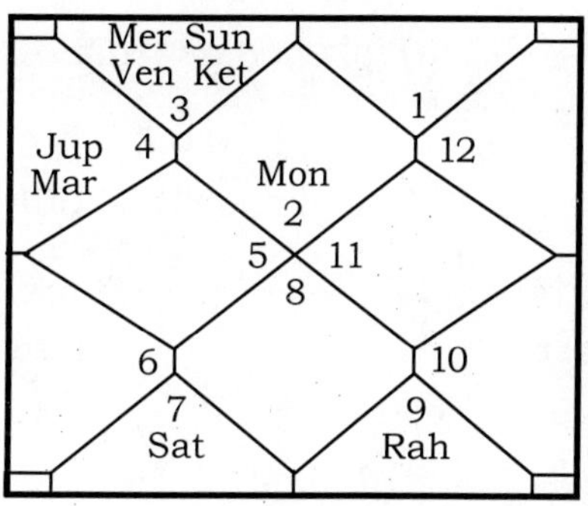


**Navamsa Chart**

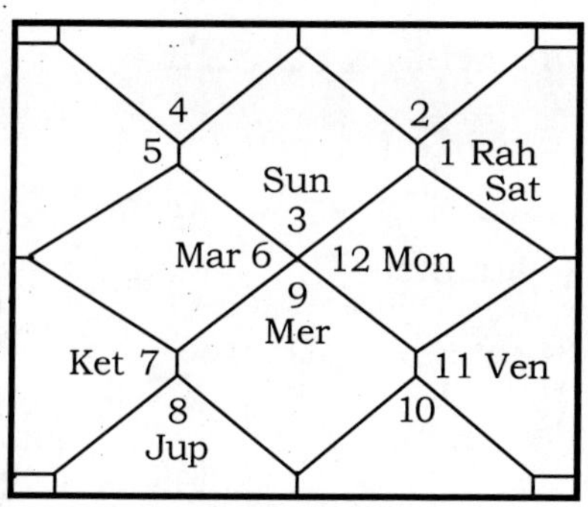


Balance of Vimsottari Dasa of **Sun 0Y 4M 17D**

This is the birth chart of a conservator of forest of UP cadre. He is also connected with one of the top political family of the country. He is very tall, smart, and handsome, and have a dashing personality. For last one year or so he is in hot waters in his professional matters.

- The 10th lord Saturn is placed in the 6th house.
- Mars aspects the tenth house as well as the tenth lord Saturn.
- The 8th lord Jupiter aspects the 9th house while the 9th lord Saturn aspects the 8th house and 8th lord Jupiter.
- The 10th lord Saturn obtains the *navamsa* of Mars and the 10th house is aspected by Mars as well.
- Ascendant lord Venus is in the *navamsa* of 10th lord Satrun, which is *Karaka* for forest service.
- The ascendant lord is associated with Sun while the ascendant is occupied by the other luminary Moon.

## 2.6 RAILWAYS IN CIVIL SERVICES

For being connected with the department of railways, one should have good influence of Saturn, Venus and Moon on the planetary configuration responsible for one's vocation. 9th house being the house of journey and the 12th house also should have some connection.

*Illustration : 2.32* (**KD**) *Horoscope No.: 32*

Date of birth : 04.09.1961 Time of birth : 00:02:00 hrs
Place of birth : Lucknow Lat 26:50:00 N Long 80:54:00E
Ayanamsa : 23:19:08 Sidereal Time : 22:46:12

| **Pln** | **Degree** | **Rasi** | **Nakshatra** | **Pad** |
|---|---|---|---|---|
| Asc | 1:19:02 | Gem | Mrigsira | 3 |
| Sun | 17:40:47 | Leo | P Phalguni | 2 |
| Mon | 8:28:12 | Gem | Ardra | 1 |
| Mar | 18:04:21 | Vir | Hasta | 3 |
| Mer | 4:49:35 | Vir | U Phalguni | 3 |
| Jup (R) | 4:38:01 | Cap | Uttarasadha | 3 |
| Ven | 12:48:17 | Can | Pushya | 3 |
| Sat (R) | 0:22:51 | Cap | Uttarasadha | 2 |

| | | | | |
|---|---|---|---|---|
| Rah (C) | 3:53:45 | Leo | Magha | 2 |
| Ket | 3:53:45 | Aqu | Dhanishtha | 4 |

**Lagna Chart**

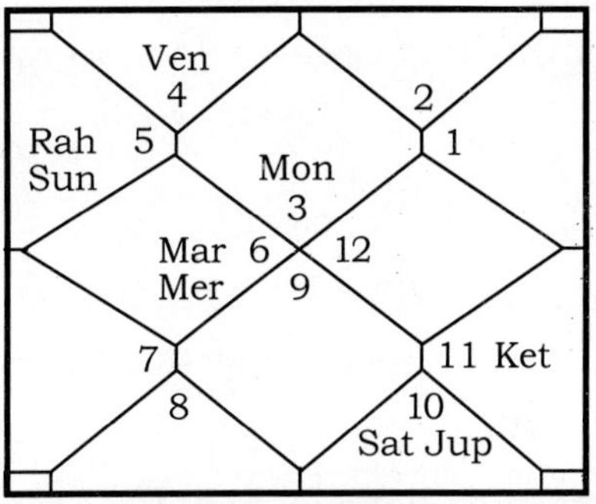


**Navamsa Chart**

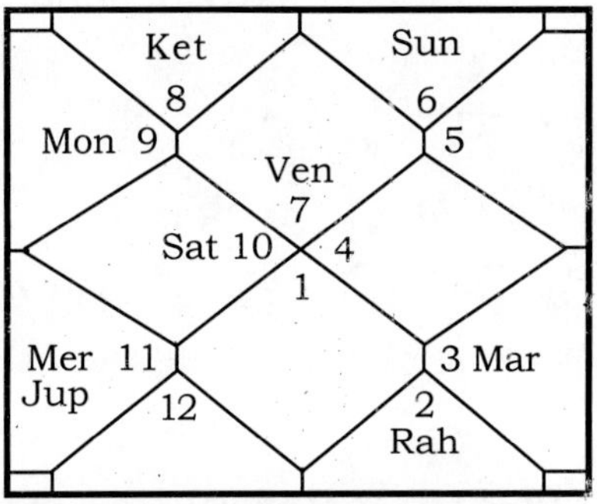


Balance of Vimsottari Dasa of **Rah 15Y 6M 23D**

This horoscope belongs to a dynamic lady officer in the Indian Railways Traffic Service. Some of the dynamism of this lady had been subdued due to her unsatisfactory marital life. Let us look into her horoscope from professional angle:

- The 6th lord Mars aspects the 10th house and falls in the constellation of a luminary, Moon. Mars is also associated with the ascendant lord Mercury
- The 10th lord Jupiter falls in the constellation of Sun. Both these points confirm the govt. service.
- The 9th and 10th lords, Saturn and Jupiter, are conjoined in the 8th house and are aspected by the 12th lord Venus.
- Moon occupies the ascendant.
- The 10th lord Jupiter obtains the *navamsa* of Saturn as well as the sign of Saturn. Saturn, the 8th & 9th lord, obtains *vargottam navamsa*. Thus, the effect of Saturn can clearly be seen.
- Moon obtains the *navamsa* of 10th lord Jupiter.
- Venus occupies the sign of *Karaka* Moon and obtains own *navamsa*.
- Venus gets the aspect of 10th lord Jupiter and the 9th & 8th lord Saturn.

- Karmic control planets are Sun and Saturn. Sun aspects the 9th house and Saturn aspects the 10th house

Thus, the involvement of 9th and the 12th houses and influence of Saturn, Moon and Venus, apart from the combination for civil services, brought her in the service in the department of Railways.

*Illustration : 2.33* **(KMT)** *Horoscope No.: 33*

Date of birth : 22.12.1960 Time of birth : 02:30:00 hrs

Place of birth : Gorakhpur Lat 26:45:00 N Long 83:23:00E

Ayanamsa : 23:18:36 Sidereal Time : 8:35:14

| **Pln** | **Degree** | **Rasi** | **Nakshatra** | **Pad** |
|---|---|---|---|---|
| Asc | 11:05:14 | Lib | Svati | 2 |
| Sun | 6:42:47 | Sag | Moola | 3 |
| Mon | 24:43:52 | Cap | Dhanishtha | 1 |
| Mar (R) | 18:47:47 | Gem | Ardra | 4 |
| Mer (C) | 28:13:08 | Sco | Jyestha | 4 |
| Jup | 18:26:14 | Sag | Purvasadha | 2 |
| Ven | 20:15:42 | Cap | Sravna | 4 |
| Sat | 25:05:49 | Sag | Purvasadha | 4 |
| Rah (R) | 15:19:12 | Leo | P Phalguni | 1 |
| Ket (R) | 15:19:12 | Aqu | Satabhisha | 3 |

**Lagna Chart**

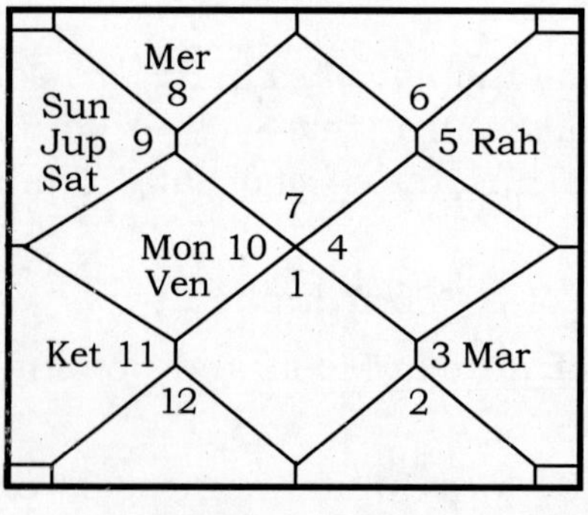


**Navamsa Chart**

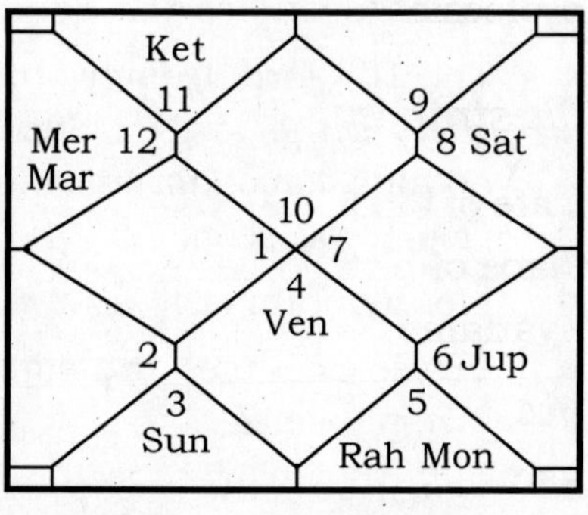


Balance of Vimsottari Dasa of **Mar 6Y 3M 5D**

The native is a senior officer in the Ministry of railways and had joined the service through civil service exams. He had been posted in Lucknow when he met us for astrological consultation.

- Sixth lord Jupiter is associated with Sun.
- Tenth lord Moon obtains the *navamsa* of Sun. Both these confirm govt. service.
- The 10th lord Moon falls in the sign of Saturn and is associated with the 8th lord Venus in the 4th house.8th and 10th lords, both, aspect the 10th house.
- 9th and 12th lord Mercury joins the 2nd house, from where it lends aspect over the 8th house.
- *Yogakaraka* Saturn and 3rd and 6th lord Jupiter, along with Sun, aspect the 9th house.
- The 9th lord Mercury obtains the *navamsa* of Jupiter and aspects the 10th lord Moon.

## 2.7 INFORMATION SERVICE

Indian Information Service is the cadre of officers controlling and managing press, news in electronic media, films and publicity of govt. of India. They are truly speaking spokespersons of govt. of the day.

There should be involvement and influence of Jupiter, Mercury and the 3rd house over the configuration indicating professional aspect.

*Illustration : 2.34* **(VKG)** *Horoscope No.: 34*

Date of birth : 27.09.1965 Time of birth : 19:26:00 hrs
Place of birth : Allahabad Lat 25:27:00 N Long 81:50:00E
Ayanamsa : 23:22:26 Sidereal Time : 19:47:56

| Pln | Degree | Rasi | Nakshatra | Pad |
|---|---|---|---|---|
| Asc | 12:27:46 | Ari | Asvini | 4 |
| Sun | 10:52:04 | Vir | Hasta | 1 |

| | | | | |
|---|---|---|---|---|
| Mon | 13:00:07 | Lib | Svati | 2 |
| Mar | 1:55:55 | Sco | Visakha | 4 |
| Mer (D) | 10:50:58 | Vir | Hasta | 1 |
| Jup | 7:08:17 | Gem | Ardra | 1 |
| Ven | 22:41:12 | Lib | Visakha | 1 |
| Sat (R) | 18:54:22 | Aqu | Satabhisha | 4 |
| Rah (R) | 13:05:15 | Tau | Rohini | 1 |
| Ket (R) | 13:05:15 | Sco | Anuradha | 3 |

**Lagna Chart**

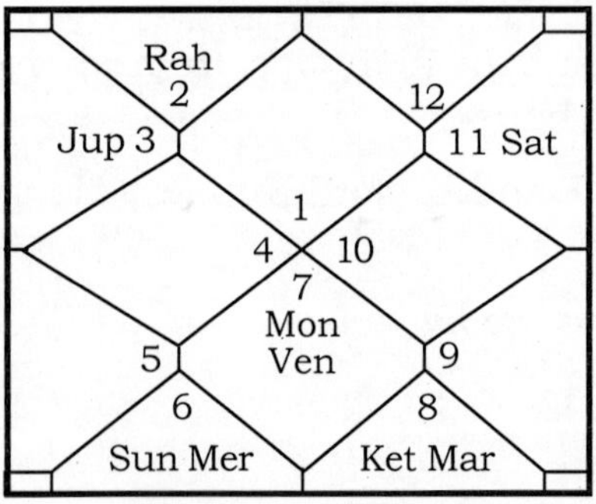


**Navamsa Chart**

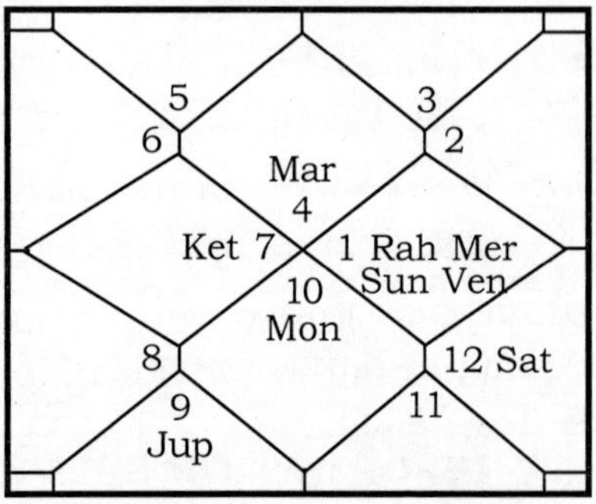


Balance of Vimsottari Dasa of **Rah 9Y 5M 11D**

This is the birth chart of a young, dynamic and very intelligent officer who heads Press Information Bureau as its Director in one of the capitals. This native is basically an engineer and had got in his written examinations of civil services such high marks that would be envied by others, but because of his marks in the interview he could not get the position in IAS mains and was allotted Indian Information Service. Destiny played its trick.

Let us see what the destiny had for him?

- The $10^{th}$ lord Saturn occupies the $11^{th}$ house, from where it aspects the $8^{th}$ house as well as its lord Mars placed therein.
- The $6^{th}$ lord Mercury occupies $6^{th}$ itself along with Sun.
- The $6^{th}$ lord Mercury is associated with Sun in *navamsa* as well.

- The 9th lord Jupiter aspects the 9th house and the 10th lord Saturn, and joins the 3rd house in the sign of Mercury.
- 10th lord Saturn obtains the *navamsa* of the 9th lord Jupiter while Jupiter obtains own *navamsa*.
- Karmic control planets are Mars and Venus. Mars occupies the 8th house and Venus aspects the ascendant. Venus also obtains the *navamsa* of 1st & 8th lord Mars.

As such involvement of the 3rd house, Jupiter and also Mercury can be very well seen, which brought him into this service.

## Conclusion

We have discussed various conjunctions and placements of planets for success in IAS. At times combinations can easily be judged but in a few horoscopes a deep analysis may be required to reach at the correct judgement.

The luminaries, the Sun and the Moon, must be given importance for consideration of administrative career. These are the royal planets and are said to be the king and queen. So, these planets will certainly be involved wherever administration is there. This is the reason that the luminaries play a vital role in political career also. But no profession should be decided on the basis of a single planet or combination, otherwise wrong conclusions would be drawn. The Sun also plays a prominent role in the horoscope of persons who are dealing in medicines such as doctors, physicians, surgeons etc., so only by seeing Sun in the 10th house in a favorable position one should not think that the native would be successful in IAS. Similarly, the Moon also signifies various professions. Therefore, a careful application of the rules regarding luminaries should be made. The Sun and the Moon should be treated as the main significators for IAS.

The sub significator for IAS is Venus. As the administrative services include all kinds of comforts, luxuries, vehicles, bungalows, servants etc., Venus who controls all this must be given the importance of sub-*Karaka* for IAS. In most of the cases, Venus either joins a luminary or the 9th or the 10th lord. If all other factors are present and Venus doesn't influence either luminaries or the 9th or the 10th lords, one should see if Venus joins 8th lord or *lagna*, or the royal planets fall in the *navamsa* or constellation of Venus. This is one of the essential factors for becoming an IAS officer.

The 9th and 10th lords must be favourably placed or the exalted planets or the luminaries should occupy these houses. The lords of the 9th and the 10th may have a mutual exchange of houses or one's lord should be in the other house with the other's lord. These planets may conjoin with each other, aspect their houses or aspect houses of each other. The lord of the 9th may be in the 10th and 10th lord in the 4th having mutual aspect; or the 10th lord may be in the 10th and 9th lord in the 4th; or the 5th lord may be in the 9th in exalted position and the 9th and 10th lords in the 5th etc. There can be dozens of such combinations which will make a sound and favourable relationship between the 10th and the 9th houses. *Navamsa* chart should also be considered like *Rashi* chart in addition to *navamsa* position of concerning planets.

The 8th house being 11th from 10th and 10th from 11th signifies the income from profession. The 10th shows the *Karma,* which one does, in a particular profession while the 8th shows the income that will come after doing that work as denoted by the 10th house. For the persons who are in service the 8th house is very important. Even the exchange of the lords of the 8th and the 10th or the 9th is not inauspicious. On the other hand it is auspicious and a favourable combination for a successful career. Many persons work under his control. The 11th house, of course, represents income in general. In the horoscope of persons who are engaged in independent occupation, the 11th house has a prominent role. If the 9th, 10th, and 8th houses are related with each other, it is good fro the prospects of service.

The *lagna* must be strong, which is essential for any successful profession. The Karmic control planets have also much to do with the 9th or the 10th lords or luminaries. The dispositors of Rahu and Ketu are called Karmic control planets. One of them should join either the luminaries or otherwise the lord of the 9th or the 10th house. There is no yoga better than the conjunction of both the karmic control planets and even their opposition or mutual aspect between them.

On the basis of these findings we have discussed about one and a half dozen horoscopes of IAS officers showing the presence of all these factors in various ways under different kinds of placement. These findings have been reached after extensive study of about fifty horoscopes of IAS officers. The horoscopes containing similar combinations have not been repeated in the illustrations.

●

# Chapter-3

# Determinants of Medical Profession

One of the noblest profession is the profession of a doctor, the healer. Doctors are regarded next to God. It is the power and knowledge of reducing the pain or the sufferings of the human beings that elevates them to the echelon of God. In some western countries people used to tell it with pride if they happen to be the neighbor of a doctor. However, there are some ethics to follow while practicing medicine. It is not for money alone that a doctor should work. Some avaricious medical professionals, who do all sorts of unethical work, bring bad name to the profession in general. It is true that we should not see in the same light much nobler persons of the profession.

Let us see, what the planetary combinations responsible for the medical profession are. Let us first look at the planets involved.

## The Planets

**The Sun:** The Sun is the main significator of medical vocation. The Sun gives us energy and is most essential for life. As the rays of Sun are extremely essential for the normal functioning of heart, Sun governs heart and life as well. The person who deals in a profession of saving the life and to keep one healthy is a doctor or a medical practitioner. His profession is governed by Sun. It is true that Sun rules over many other professions also like dealing in wool, wood grain, gold, politics etc. Therefore, while determining one's profession we have to judge several other factors and only after that the conclusion should be drawn.

**The Mars :** Mars is also quite important for the profession of doctors because Mars deals with fire, blood, muscles, cuts, wounds, burns, injuries, accidents, operations etc. which are commonly observed in the medical profession. However, Mars indicates many other vocations too such as army, construction work, dealing in minerals, stones or metals etc.

**The Jupiter :** Jupiter gives a correct judgement regarding any walk of life. Jupiter has the power of healing and cure. It also indicates herbs. So, Jupiter has a great significance in the profession of medicine. Some other occupations signified by Jupiter are lawyers, judges, teachers, brokers, consultants, preachers, ministers etc.

Mainly these three planets have a vital role to play for charting out the medical vocation. But Saturn being the significator of old age, debility, chronic disease, pains etc., is also important. Ketu and Venus have also some significance but much importance may not be given to them all the time.

## The Signs

**Leo :** Leo has a special property for medical line, drugs and chemicals. Leo is a utopian royal sign. Leo prominent natives reach very high in jobs. They have power and are authoritative. This sign also rules stock exchange, investment business, jewelry, gold etc. The persons who have Leo in their $10^{th}$ house or *lagna*, along with other factors, are more inclined towards the medical career.

**Scorpio :** This is a mystic sign. It signifies nurses, chemists, doctors, explorers, geographers, barbers, astrologers etc. People born in Scorpio ascendant or this sign falling in their $10^{th}$ or the $5^{th}$ house are found to have deep interest in medicines. This is also true particularly for the Scorpio natives as other two signs representing medical career i.e. Pisces and Leo fall in $5^{th}$ and $10^{th}$ house respectively. In our analysis, about 50% doctors are born under Scorpio ascendant.

**Pisces :** This sign rules doctors, surgeons, nurses, monks, jailers, prison workers, sanatorium workers etc. Work involving imagination suites these natives. Though both the signs ruled by Jupiter i.e. Sagittarius and Pisces have their prominent roles in medical profession but Pisces has certainly much greater importance than what Sagittarius has.

## Planetary combinations for Medical Profession

The tenth house is mainly dealt for profession but in determining the vocation, the ascendant is equally important for the professional attitude. In the profession of medical personnel, the bent of mind is also one of the essential factors to judge. Therefore, the $5^{th}$ house should be analyzed. Generally, we find that Mars in the $5^{th}$ creates interest in Biology, operations, medicines etc.

Following are the two most essential factors for one, to earn his livelihood by medical profession. If both these combinations are present in any nativity, one is destined to select medical career either by establishing a hospital, nursing home, chemist shop, or by doing private practice or joining the government as a doctor.

1. If the Sun joins the $10^{th}$ or the $5^{th}$ house, preferably receiving the aspect of or conjoined with Mars.
   - ❖ Lord of $5^{th}$ Mars or Jupiter, if tenanted in the $10^{th}$ with Sun.
   - ❖ Lord of $10^{th}$ Jupiter or Sun, if posited in the $5^{th}$ with Mars.
   - ❖ Lord of $5^{th}$ in the $10^{th}$ with Sun and /or Mars.
   - ❖ Lord of $10^{th}$ in the $5^{th}$ with Mars and /or Jupiter.
2. Aspect or placement of Mars in the $5^{th}$ house particularly synchronizing with the signs Leo, Scorpio and Pisces.
   - ❖ If, either of Mars or Jupiter owns $5^{th}$ house and is aspected by the other.

- ❖ If, either of Mars or Jupiter is tenanted in the 5th house. If planet placed in the 5th is aspected by or conjoined with them that tends more to steer the native towards the medical field.
- ❖ If Mars, Sun, Jupiter or any two of them are placed in the 5th or the 10th house.

  Apart from these two important combinations there are few other combinations, which are more often found in the horoscopes of the natives connected with the medical field. Some of them are as below:

3. The Saturn is placed in the sign of Venus, or Venus and Saturn aspect each other by opposition or both of these conjoin.
4. Combination of no. 1 and 2 above.

   At least two planets from among the Sun, Mars and Jupiter should influence or be connected with the 5th or the 10th houses or their lords, either by ownership or by aspect or by conjunction or by exchange of houses.
5. The 6th, 8th and the 12th houses are the evil houses indicating various diseases, afflictions and troubles. The duty of a doctor or function of medicines is to cure the diseases and the one who deals in it must be having a connection of these houses with that of profession or with the Karaka of that profession. So, the lords of *Trikas* (6, 8, and 12) should influence the 10th house or the Sun.
   - ❖ The Sun if owns any of the 6th, 8th or 12th houses and joins the 10th or aspects the 10th lord or conjoins with them.
   - ❖ The lords of 6th, 8th, or 12th houses are positioned in the 10th or aspect the lord of the 10th.
6. In the horoscopes of many successful medical practitioners, Saturn is found exalted and mostly it aspects Jupiter (so Jupiter is either exalted or in Sagittarius or Aries).

7. *Lagna* has also a great significance in deciding the aptitude of the native. The $10^{th}$ house represents *Karma* and the $8^{th}$, the nature of duties. Therefore, if these houses are tenanted by the concerning planets i.e. the Sun, Mars or Jupiter, one is likely to take up medicine as his occupation.

Mere framing of rules is not sufficient; their practical application is also equally important. There is no single rule in astrology that could be applied in all the horoscopes verbatim. While analyzing the horoscopes with proper application of rules, due prudence at one's command must also be used. We hasten to add that apparently the horoscope of a native may not show the prevalence of the rules enshrined above, but a deep and concentrated study will show the relation and relevance of the rules, if the native thrives on medical profession.

Sri Gopesh Kumar Ojha opines that Virgo, Scorpio and Pisces are the prominent signs in the horoscopes of medical persons. Following degrees of various signs have also something to do with the medical profession.

| | |
|---|---|
| $4^0$ or $26^0$ to 30' | of Cancer and Capricorn |
| $4^0$ | of Aries and Libra |
| $22^0$ | of Virgo and Pisces |
| $18^0$ to $22^0$ | of Leo and Aquarius |
| $14^0$ | of Taurus and Scorpio |
| $12^0$ | of Gemini and Sagittarius |

*Illustration : 3.1* **(BS)** *Horoscope No.: 35*

Date of birth : 19.06.1955 Time of birth : 12:41:00 hrs

Place of birth : Jhansi Lat 25:27:00 N Long 78:34:00E

Ayanamsa : 23:14:22 Sidereal Time : 6:12:13

| **Pln** | **Degree** | **Rasi** | **Nakshatra** | **Pad** |
|---|---|---|---|---|
| Asc | 9:31:10 | Vir | U Phalguni | 4 |
| Sun | 4:00:05 | Gem | Mrigsira | 4 |

| Mon | 21:34:36 | Tau | Rohini | 4 |
|---|---|---|---|---|
| Mar | 22:32:43 | Gem | Punarvasu | 1 |
| Mer (R/C) | 29:26:48 | Tau | Mrigsira | 2 |
| Jup | 8:00:18 | Can | Pushya | 2 |
| Ven | 13:58:20 | Tau | Rohini | 2 |
| Sat (R) | 21:58:10 | Lib | Visakha | 1 |
| Rah | 3:09:05 | Sag | Moola | 1 |
| Ket (C) | 3:09:05 | Gem | Mrigsira | 3 |

**Lagna Chart**

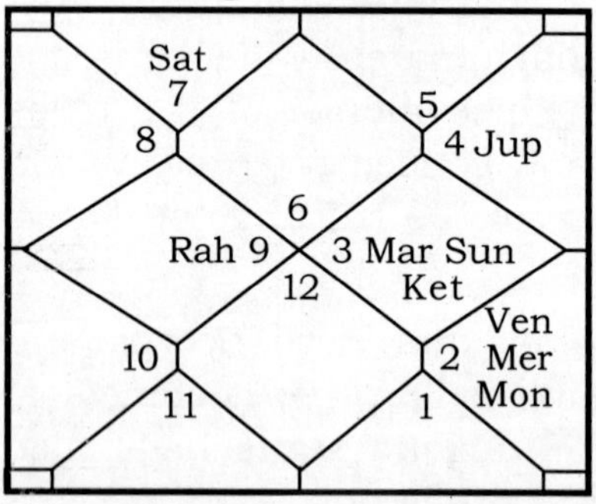


**Navamsa Chart**

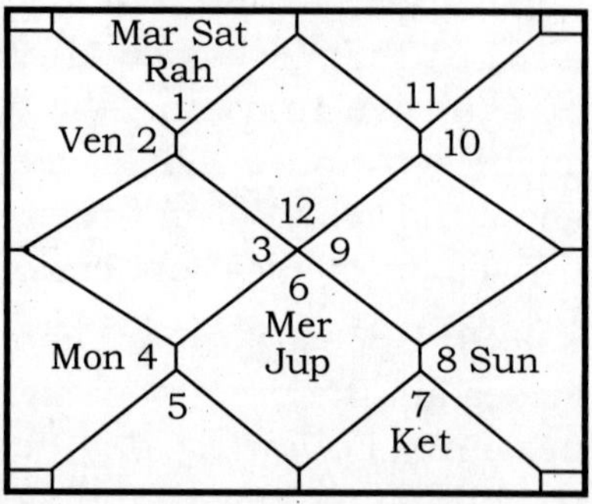


Balance of Vimsottari Dasa of **Mon 1Y 3M 24D**

This is the horoscope of a very successful and popular private practitioner of Lucknow.

- Conjunction of the significator of medical profession i.e. the Sun with Mars in the 10th house has made him a doctor as per rule no.1.
- Lord of the 8th house, Mars, and that of 12th, the Sun, are conjoined in 10th as per rule no. 5, indicating successful medical career.
- Jupiter and Saturn are exalted as per rule no. 6 and
- Saturn joins the sign of Venus, Libra, as per rule no. 3.
- In rule 2, we note that Jupiter or Mars should influence the 5th house. Here, both of them are aspecting the 5th house.
- As per rule no. 4, Mars and Sun influence the 10th house

due to their placement. Therefore, the entire factors essential for a doctor are present in this horoscope.

Apart from these combinations, there are following vital points indicating that the person will reach to a very high position successfully.

1. Three planets, Jupiter, Moon and Saturn, are exalted while one i.e. Venus is in own sign.
2. Lord of the 9th Venus and 10th Mercury conjoin in the 9th house along with the lord of the 11th house, the exalted Moon.
3. Lord of 5th Saturn and 10th Mercury are retrograde.
4. Venus obtains *vargottam navamsa* while Moon that of her own.
5. Two occupants of the 10th house i.e. the Sun and Ketu fall in *Mrigsira* constellation of Mars while Mars falls in the constellation of Jupiter, *Punarvasu*.
6. Lord of the 5th house, Saturn, also falls in the constellation of Jupiter.
7. Occupants of the 10th house, the Sun and Mars, fall in *navamsa* of Mars.

These are the factors which indicate very strongly that the native will become a famous physician. This is a perfect example horoscope of a doctor but it does not mean that all these combinations will be found in the horoscopes of all doctors.

*Illustration : 3.2* (**PD**) *Horoscope No.: 36*

Date of birth : 17.10.1957 Time of birth : 13:15:00 hrs

Place of birth : Muzaffarnagar Lat 29:28:00 N Long 77:42:00E

Ayanamsa : 23:16:13 Sidereal Time : 14:37:59

| **Pln** | **Degree** | **Rasi** | **Nakshatra** | **Pad** |
|---|---|---|---|---|
| Asc | 1:39:44 | Cap | Uttarasadha | 2 |
| Sun | 0:24:06 | Lib | Chitra | 3 |
| Mon | 10:04:33 | Can | Pushya | 3 |

| | | | | |
|---|---|---|---|---|
| Mar (C) | 21:48:01 | Vir | Hasta | 4 |
| Mer (C) | 25:37:39 | Vir | Chitra | 1 |
| Jup (C) | 21:23:32 | Vir | Hasta | 4 |
| Ven | 15:00:02 | Sco | Anuradha | 4 |
| Sat | 17:43:13 | Sco | Jyestha | 1 |
| Rah (R) | 17:28:06 | Lib | Svati | 4 |
| Ket (R) | 17:28:06 | Ari | Bharani | 2 |

**Lagna Chart**

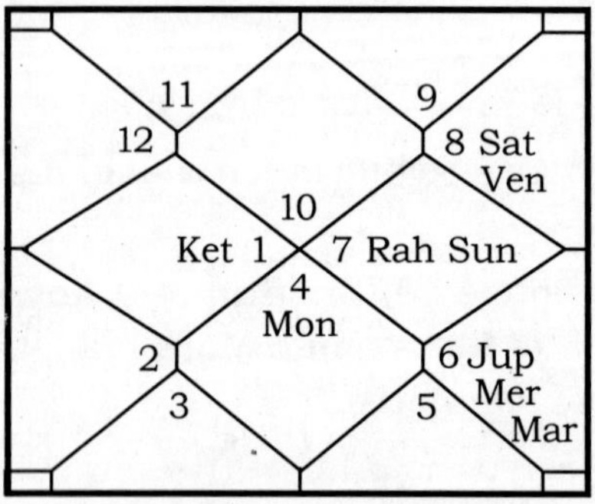


**Navamsa Chart**

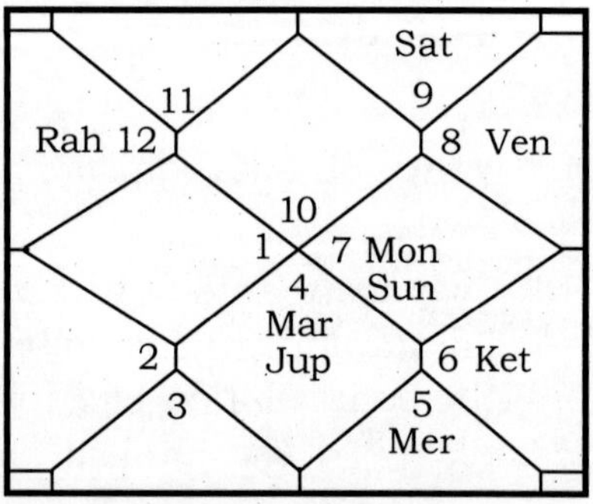


Balance of Vimsottari Dasa of **Sat 9Y 4M 21D**

This is the horoscope of a lady doctor who had been to many foreign countries.

- As per rule no. 1, the presence of Sun and Rahu can be noted in the 10th house, which has directed the native to medical career. She is a famous gynaecologist.
- As per rule no. 2, Jupiter is aspecting the 5th house and Mars is associated with him. Both are aspecting Pisces.
- As per rule no.3, Saturn is conjoined with Venus as lord of the ascendant and the 5th house.
- As per rule no. 5, the lord of the 8th house, Sun, joins the 10th.
- As per rule no. 4, the Sun falls in the constellation of Mars, *Chitra*, in the 10th house and obtains *vargottam navamsa*. Conjunction of Moon and Sun in the 10th house, from the *navamsa* ascendant, is being aspected by Mars.

*Navamsadhipati* of the lord of the 10th house is Mars. Lord of the 10th is Venus. The Sun is debilitated in the sign of Venus in the 10th house and lord of the 5th house, Venus, obtains *vargottam navamsa*, having an aspect over 5th. Due to the prominence of Venus on the 5th and the 10th house, she became a gynaecologist though she very much wanted to become a general surgeon.

*Illustration : 3.3* **(MM)** *Horoscope No.: 37*

Date of birth : 06.10.1954 Time of birth : 12:52:00 hrs

Place of birth : Meerut Lat 29:00:00 N Long 77:42:00E

Ayanamsa : 23:13:46 Sidereal Time : 13:30:28

| **Pln** | **Degree** | **Rasi** | **Nakshatra** | **Pad** |
|---|---|---|---|---|
| Asc | 14:55:38 | Sag | Purvasadha | 1 |
| Sun | 19:16:43 | Vir | Hasta | 3 |
| Mon | 1:44:17 | Cap | Uttarasadha | 2 |
| Mar | 27:18:56 | Sag | Uttarasadha | 1 |
| Mer | 14:39:49 | Lib | Svati | 3 |
| Jup | 4:00:49 | Can | Pushya | 1 |
| Ven | 0:31:06 | Sco | Visakha | 4 |
| Sat | 15:21:41 | Lib | Svati | 3 |
| Rah (R) | 16:46:50 | Sag | Purvasadha | 2 |
| Ket (R) | 16:46:50 | Gem | Ardra | 4 |

**Lagna Chart**

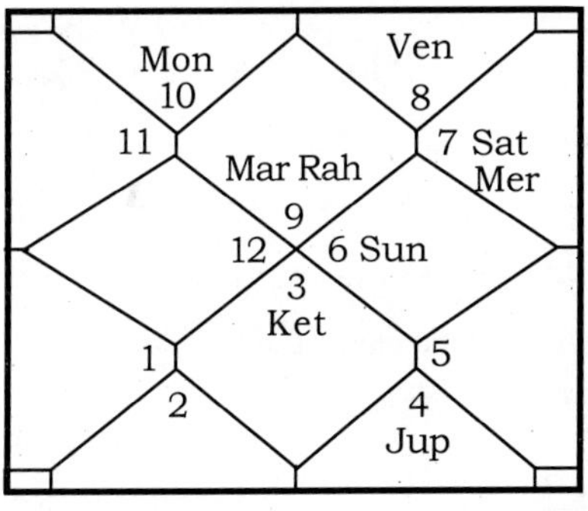


**Navamsa Chart**

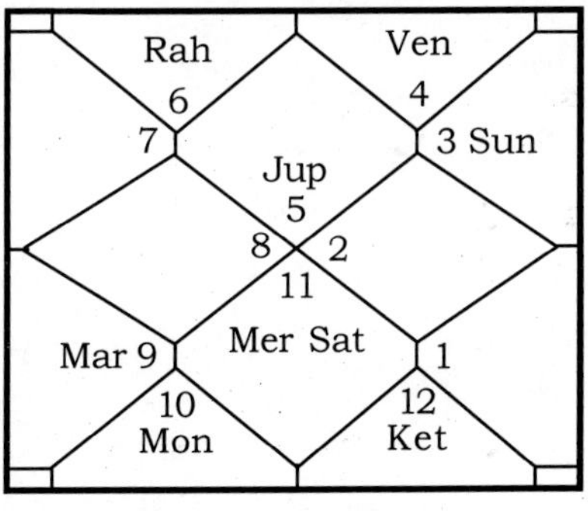


Balance of Vimsottari Dasa of **Sun 3Y 8M 18D**

She is very beautiful lady doctor serving in the Paediatrics department of Kanpur Medical College. Her interest in higher studies and academics led her to join teaching side after acquiring her postgraduate degrees.

- As per rule no.1, the placement of Sun in the 10th, as the lord of the 9th house, should be noted.
- The Sun, Mars and Jupiter are aspecting Pisces. Generally, we have found that Pisces plays a vital role in the horoscopes of medical men.
- As per rule no. 2, lord of the 5th house, Mars, is aspecting the lord of *lagna* and 4th, Jupiter.
- As per rule no. 3, Saturn joins the sign of Venus, Libra, and as per rule 6 Saturn and Jupiter both are exalted.
- Also note that *vargottam* Mars in the 5th is receiving the aspect of Sun and Jupiter. Lord of the 8th house, Moon, also obtains *vargottam navamsa*.
- As per rule no. 7, *lagna*, the 10th and the 8th houses have the influence of Mars, Sun and Jupiter respectively, indicating that she will become a medical practitioner.

*Illustration : 3.4* **(PG)** *Horoscope No.: 38*

Date of birth : 30.03.1966 Time of birth : 21:55:00 hrs
Place of birth : Allahabad Lat 25:27:00 N Long 81:50:00E
Ayanamsa : 23:22:52 Sidereal Time : 10:22:46

| **Pln** | **Degree** | **Rasi** | **Nakshatra** | **Pad** |
|---|---|---|---|---|
| Asc | 4:43:55 | Sco | Anuradha | 1 |
| Sun | 16:08:00 | Pis | U Bhadrapad | 4 |
| Mon | 26:42:22 | Gem | Punarvasu | 3 |
| Mar (C) | 22:53:31 | Pis | Revati | 2 |
| Mer (R) | 0:18:28 | Pis | P Bhadrapad | 4 |
| Jup | 0:47:56 | Gem | Mrigsira | 3 |
| Ven | 29:56:24 | Cap | Dhanishtha | 2 |

| | | | | |
|---|---|---|---|---|
| Sat | 28:54:23 | Aqu | P Bhadrapad | 3 |
| Rah (R) | 3:07:30 | Tau | Krittika | 2 |
| Ket (R) | 3:07:30 | Sco | Visakha | 4 |

**Lagna Chart**

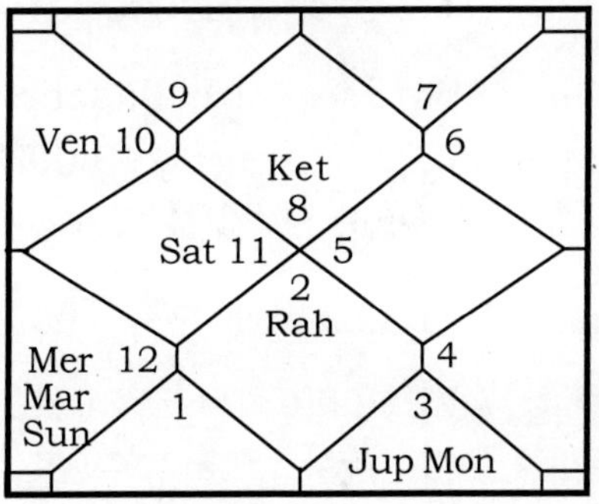


**Navamsa Chart**

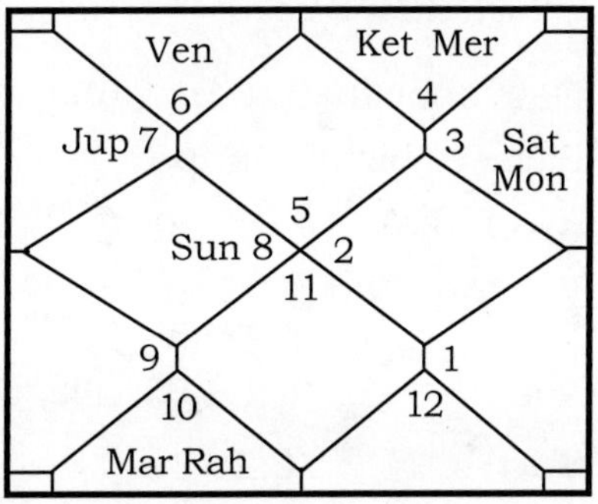


Balance of Vimsottari Dasa of **Jup 7Y 11M 13D**

This is chart of a dental surgeon whose father is an engineer and one of our close family friends.

- Presence of Mars and the Sun in Pisces in the 5th house, in any horoscope, tends one towards the study of medical subjects. Here, in this chart lord of the 10th house is Sun, who conjoins with the 6th lord Mars, in the 5th house, in the sign Pisces, as per rule no.1.
- Mars is placed in the 5th house and is aspecting the 5th lord Jupiter (2).
- Saturn and Venus are also in close proximity and their distance is less than $30^0$ (3).
- Rule no. 4 & 5 are also applicable as the Sun, who is lord of the 10th house, is joined by 6th and 8th lords, Mars and Mercury.
- As per rule no. 7, *lagna*, the 10th and the 8th houses have been influenced by Mars and Sun, Sun and Mars, & Jupiter and Mars respectively. The lord of the 10th house, the Sun, obtains the *navamsa* of Mars assuring success in the medical field.

So, if the lord of the 10th house, the Sun, is placed in the 5th in conjunction with Mars or the 5th lord Mars is placed in the 10th with Sun, one is most likely to take medicine as his career.

*Illustration : 3.5* *Horoscope No.: 39*

Date of birth : 10.01.1953 Time of birth : 10:40:00 hrs
Place of birth : Kanpur Lat 26:27:00 N Long 80:19:00E
Ayanamsa : 23:12:16 Sidereal Time : 17:48:59

| **Pln** | **Degree** | **Rasi** | **Nakshatra** | **Pad** |
|---|---|---|---|---|
| Asc | 2:58:05 | Pis | P Bhadrapad | 4 |
| Sun | 26:28:18 | Sag | Purvasadha | 4 |
| Mon | 17:02:46 | Lib | Svati | 4 |
| Mar | 14:44:33 | Aqu | Satabhisha | 3 |
| Mer | 12:15:01 | Sag | Moola | 4 |
| Jup | 17:48:47 | Ari | Bharani | 2 |
| Ven | 12:09:37 | Aqu | Satabhisha | 2 |
| Sat | 3:30:22 | Lib | Chitra | 4 |
| Rah (R) | 19:22:50 | Cap | Sravna | 3 |
| Ket (R) | 19:22:50 | Can | Aslesha | 1 |

**Lagna Chart**

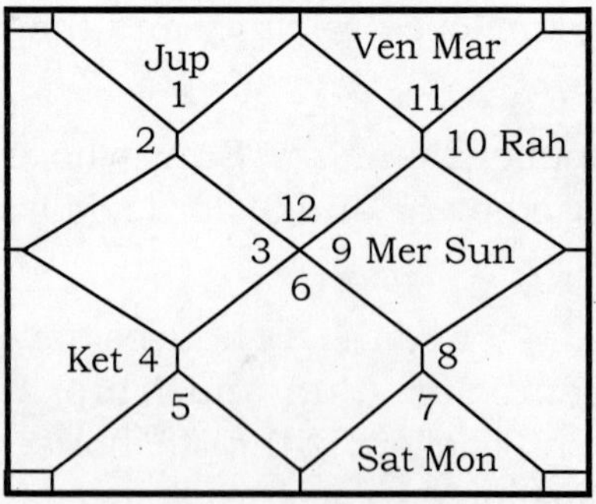


**Navamsa Chart**

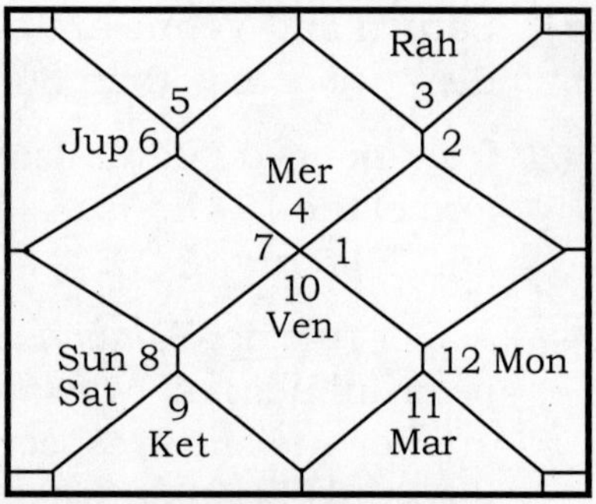


Balance of Vimsottari Dasa of **Rah 3Y 11M 25D**

This is the horoscope of an erudite physician, who, in addition to being in the medical profession, is also deeply inclined towards spiritualism. He is a great disciple of Sri Shri Ram Sharma Acharya. But he is also an unfortunate person who has suffered on many fronts of life. He got married in the family of millionaires but his family life is full of disharmony and discord. On 17th of Dec. in 1984 he met with a great tragedy when a strong cracker burst in his hands resulting in the loss of palm.

In this horoscope following combinations are to be noted:

- The Sun occupies the 10th house in the sign of Jupiter, as per 1 & 4.
- Further, Jupiter aspects the Sun.
- As per rule 3 & 6, Saturn occupies the sign of Venus, Libra, and Venus occupies the sign of Saturn, Aquarius.
- As per 5, lord of 6th the Sun, in the 10th is receiving the aspect of 12th lord Saturn, who is tenanted in the 8th.
- The 5th lord Moon is also being aspected by Jupiter.

*Illustration : 3.6* (**RCA**) *Horoscope No.: 40*

Date of birth : 30.03.1956 Time of birth : 22:30:00 hrs
Place of birth : Gorakhpur Lat 26:45:00 N Long 83:23:00E
Ayanamsa : 23:15:01 Sidereal Time : 11:05:44

| **Pln** | **Degree** | **Rasi** | **Nakshatra** | **Pad** |
|---|---|---|---|---|
| Asc | 13:35:39 | Sco | Anuradha | 4 |
| Sun | 16:42:58 | Pis | Revati | 1 |
| Mon | 6:46:47 | Sco | Anuradha | 2 |
| Mar | 26:54:13 | Sag | Uttarasadha | 1 |
| Mer (C) | 10:08:05 | Pis | U Bhadrapad | 3 |
| Jup (R) | 28:43:58 | Can | Aslesha | 4 |
| Ven | 1:56:40 | Tau | Krittika | 2 |

| Sat (R) | 9:16:42 | Sco | Anuradha | 2 |
|---|---|---|---|---|
| Rah (R) | 16:37:38 | Sco | Anuradha | 4 |
| Ket (R) | 16:37:38 | Tau | Rohini | 2 |

**Lagna Chart**

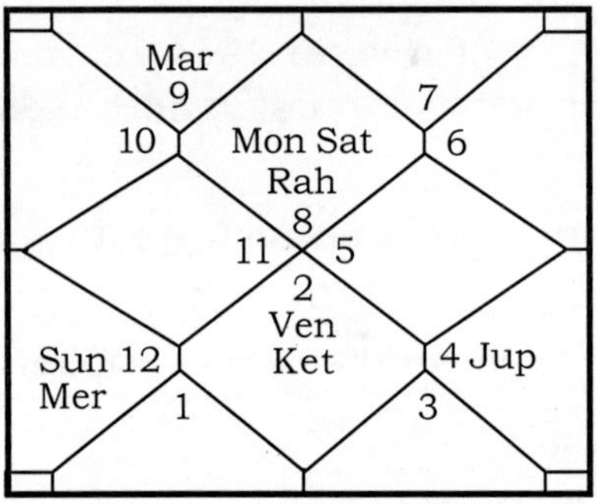


**Navamsa Chart**

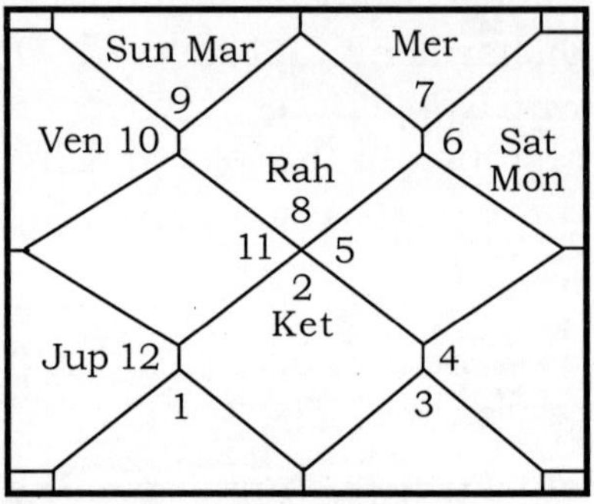


Balance of Vimsottari Dasa of **Sat 14Y 1M 2D**

The horoscope belongs to an ambitious doctor, who after graduating from medical college joined the Central Health service on a class one post in the year1981. After few years, he took study leave to complete his post graduation in Psychiatry. Having completed his PG he left the service after few years, to settle for private practice in an industrial city near Delhi. He is presently having a roaring practice. Let us look into the combinations in his birth chart:

- Lord of 10th, the Sun occupies the 5th house, receiving the aspect of Jupiter and Mars (1, 2, 4).
- Mars aspects Jupiter in the 9th house and obtains the *navamsa* of Jupiter as well
- Venus and Saturn are under mutual aspect (3).
- Lord of 10th, the Sun is in conjunction with 8th lord Mercury, receiving the aspect of 6th lord Mars (5).
- Jupiter is exalted and aspects Saturn (6).
- Jupiter obtains own *navamsa* and aspects Saturn in *navamsa* too.

- The 10[th] lord Sun and the 6[th] lord Mars acquire the *navamsa* of Jupiter

All these combinations took him to the medical profession.

*Illustration : 3.7* *Horoscope No.: 41*

Date of birth : 10.01.1953 Time of birth : 00:35:00 hrs
Place of birth : Allahabad Lat 25:27:00 N Long 81:50:00E
Ayanamsa : 23:12:16 Sidereal Time : 7:48:23

| Pln | Degree | Rasi | Nakshatra | Pad |
|---|---|---|---|---|
| Asc | 1:09:16 | Lib | Chitra | 3 |
| Sun | 26:02:36 | Sag | Purvasadha | 4 |
| Mon | 11:41:36 | Lib | Svati | 2 |
| Mar | 14:25:09 | Aqu | Satabhisha | 3 |
| Mer | 11:37:03 | Sag | Moola | 4 |
| Jup | 17:48:23 | Ari | Bharani | 2 |
| Ven | 11:41:19 | Aqu | Satabhisha | 2 |
| Sat | 3:29:14 | Lib | Chitra | 4 |
| Rah (R) | 19:23:51 | Cap | Sravna | 3 |
| Ket (R) | 19:23:51 | Can | Aslesha | 1 |

**Lagna Chart**

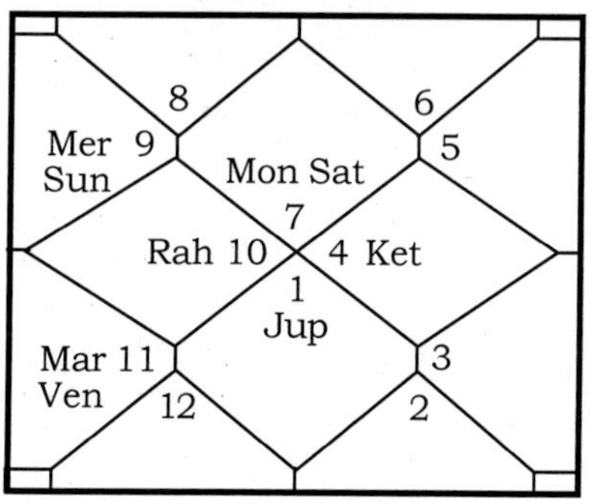


**Navamsa Chart**

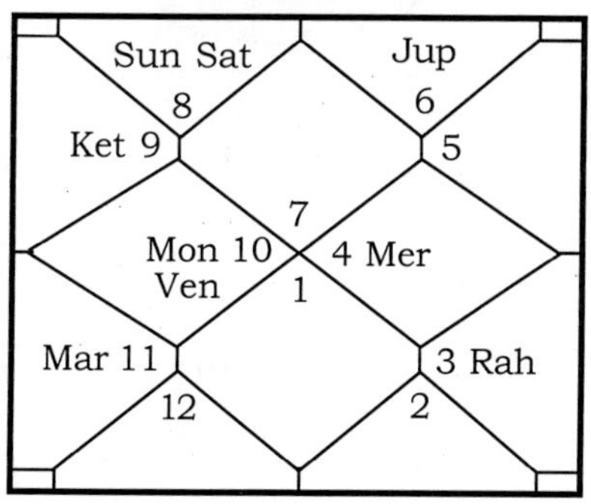


Balance of Vimsottari Dasa of **Rah 11Y 2M 17D**

This is an interesting chart with a difference. Such horoscopes must be studied at priority for the determination of medical profession.

- The 5th house is tenanted by Mars (2).
- Saturn is exalted i.e. placed in the sign of Venus and is aspected by Jupiter (3) & (6).
- Jupiter is aspecting 5th lord Saturn and the *karaka*, the Sun, and also the lord of tenth house, the Moon (4).
- The 10th lord Moon conjoins with Saturn, the 5th lord and obtains the *navamsa* of Saturn as well, in conjunction with the 8th lord Venus.
- Lord of 6th Jupiter aspects 10th and 5th lords, Moon and Saturn, respectively.
- Sun is aspected by the 5th lord Saturn & the 6th lord Jupiter, conjoins with 12th lord Mercury and obtains the *navamsa* of Mars in conjunction with Saturn.

*Illustration : 3.8* *Horoscope No.: 42*

Date of birth : 14.09.1952 Time of birth : 10:35:00 hrs
Place of birth : Ghazipur Lat 25:36:00 N Long 83:36:00E
Ayanamsa : 23:11:58 Sidereal Time : 10:11:52

| **Pln** | **Degree** | **Rasi** | **Nakshatra** | **Pad** |
|---|---|---|---|---|
| Asc | 2:30:09 | Sco | Visakha | 4 |
| Sun | 28:06:58 | Leo | U Phalguni | 1 |
| Mon | 2:35:00 | Can | Punarvasu | 4 |
| Mar | 17:41:22 | Sco | Jyestha | 1 |
| Mer (C) | 18:57:43 | Leo | P Phalguni | 2 |
| Jup (R) | 27:45:31 | Ari | Krittika | 1 |
| Ven | 20:10:29 | Vir | Hasta | 4 |
| Sat | 21:29:48 | Vir | Hasta | 4 |
| Rah | 28:09:30 | Cap | Dhanishtha | 2 |
| Ket | 28:09:30 | Can | Aslesha | 4 |

**Lagna Chart**

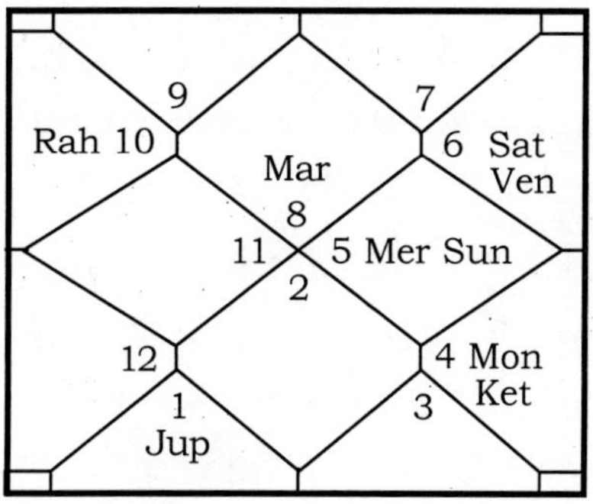


**Navamsa Chart**

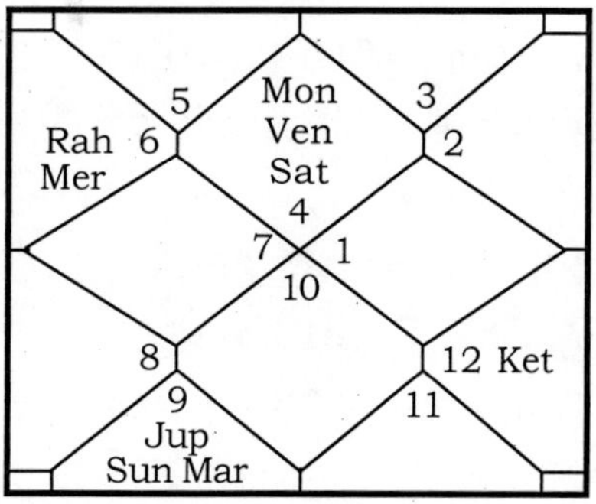


Balance of Vimsottari Dasa of **Jup 0Y 10M 24D**

The doctor of this birth chart is a senior officer in the state government medical and health service. He was chief medical superintendent of a district hospital and will soon be promoted to the senior post in the headquarters. Combinations in his horoscope can be noted as under:

- The ruler of 10th house, the Sun is placed in own sign (1).
- Aspect of 5th lord Jupiter is also there on 10th house and on the Sun (4).
- Sun, Mars and Jupiter are conjoined in *navamsa* of Jupiter.
- Saturn and Venus are in conjunction (3).
- Mars in own sign in ascendant and the Sun in own sign in 10th, latter under the aspect of 8th lord Jupiter is the clear indication of medical career (7).
- Lord of 8th Mercury conjoins tenth lord Sun (5).
- *Karmadhipati* and *Bhagyadhipati* have joined their own sign, which made the native to rise very high in medical profession.

The combinations enumerated as above are sufficient to indicate the medical profession.

*Illustration : 3.9* *Horoscope No.: 43*

Date of birth : 23.10.1955 Time of birth : 20:00:00 hrs
Place of birth : Lucknow Lat 26:50:00 N Long 80:54:00E
Ayanamsa : 23:14:39 Sidereal Time : 21:58:31

| Pln | Degree | Rasi | Nakshatra | Pad |
|---|---|---|---|---|
| Asc | 19:49:42 | Tau | Rohini | 3 |
| Sun | 6:09:55 | Lib | Chitra | 4 |
| Mon | 2:13:21 | Cap | Uttarasadha | 2 |
| Mar | 13:14:59 | Vir | Hasta | 1 |
| Mer | 19:58:34 | Vir | Hasta | 3 |
| Jup | 3:43:34 | Leo | Magha | 2 |
| Ven | 19:56:46 | Lib | Svati | 4 |
| Sat | 27:41:55 | Lib | Visakha | 3 |
| Rah (S) | 25:18:02 | Sco | Jyestha | 3 |
| Ket (S) | 25:18:02 | Tau | Mrigsira | 1 |

**Lagna Chart**

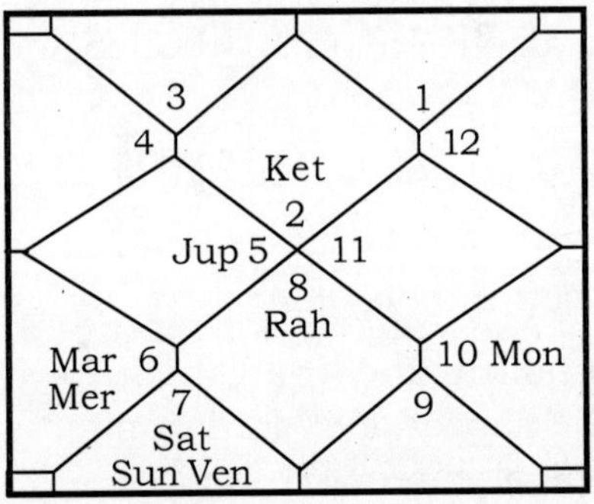


**Navamsa Chart**

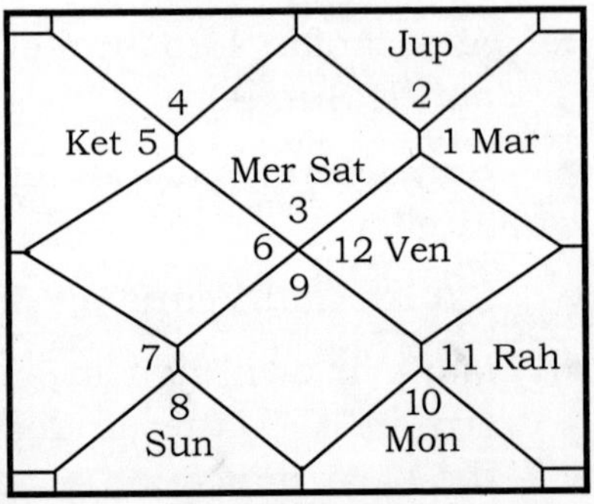


Balance of Vimsottari Dasa of **Sun 3Y 5M 30D**

The beautiful and sweet natured lady doctor is presently the Head of the department of Gynaecology in a state medical college. Having risen from humble circumstances, she is a well known name in the city and the state too. Relevant combinations are:

- Mars joins the 5th house and conjoins with the lord of 5th house, Mercury.
- The Sun is associated with the lord of the 10th house, Saturn, and the ascendant lord Venus in the 6th house, influencing both and intending towards Medical field (1, 5).
- Saturn and Sun are conjoined together in Libra (3.6).
- Saturn occupies the sign of Venus and conjoins with Venus.
- Jupiter aspects the 10th house being placed in the sign Leo.
- Mars in 5th and the Sun with the lord of 10th (5) signify a successful medical profession throughout life.
- The 12th house is aspected by Mars, Saturn, Sun and Jupiter and the 6th house also gets the aspect of Mars, Jupiter and Saturn.

  Combinations of medical line are also pronounced by Moon Chart equally.
- In the Moon chart, the 8th lord Sun is placed in the 10th house, with the lord of the 10th and the lord of the ascendant.
- Mars occupies the 9th house with the 6th lord Mercury.
- Jupiter occupies the 8th house in Leo, aspecting the 5th house

Great influence of Venus over the 10th house and Sun, both in the *Rashi* chart and Moon chart and exaltation of Venus in the *navamsa* gave her the branch of Gynaecology.

*Illustration : 3.10* *Horoscope No.: 44*

Date of birth : 13.09.1950 Time of birth : 03:10:00 hrs

Place of birth : Bijnor Lat 29:22:00 N Long 78:09:00E

Ayanamsa : 23:10:06 Sidereal Time : 2:17:53

| Pln | Degree | Rasi | Nakshatra | Pad |
|---|---|---|---|---|
| Asc | 18:51:47 | Can | Aslesha | 1 |
| Sun | 26:22:26 | Leo | P Phalguni | 4 |

| | | | | |
|---|---|---|---|---|
| Mon (C) | 6:21:06 | Vir | U Phalguni | 3 |
| Mar | 28:00:27 | Lib | Visakha | 3 |
| Mer (R/C) | 5:07:54 | Vir | U Phalguni | 3 |
| Jup (R) | 7:05:04 | Aqu | Satabhisha | 1 |
| Ven | 10:20:00 | Leo | Magha | 4 |
| Sat (D) | 29:06:40 | Leo | U Phalguni | 1 |
| Rah | 5:15:03 | Pis | U Bhadrapad | 1 |
| Ket (C) | 5:15:03 | Vir | U Phalguni | 3 |

**Lagna Chart**

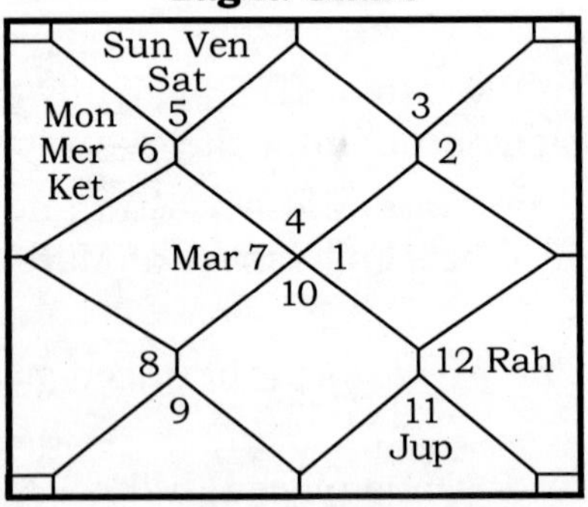


**Navamsa Chart**

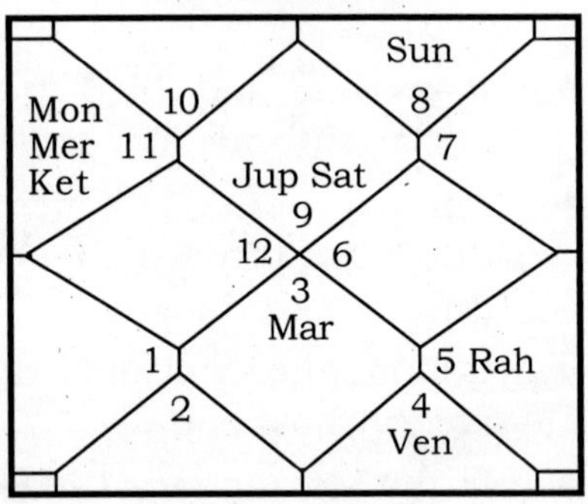


Balance of Vimsottari Dasa of **Sun 1Y 7M 21D**

This is the horoscope of the spouse of above. He is an E.N.T. surgeon.

- The lord of the 5th house, Mars, aspects the 10th house(2).
- Jupiter aspects the significator of medical career, the Sun, as well as the lord of 5th and 10th house, Mars (4).
- Saturn conjoins with Venus in Leo (3).
- Sun obtains the *navamsa* of the 10th lord Mars.
- Ascendant lord Moon falls in the constellation of Sun and gains the *navamsa* of 8th lord Saturn.
- Jupiter is lord of 6th and aspects Sun & Mars, from the 8th house (5).

This is indicating a bright medical career, particularly due to aspect of *Yogakaraka* Mars on the 10th house and Jupiter being in triangle, in respect to Mars.

*Illustration : 3.11* *Horoscope No.: 45*

Date of birth : 04.03.1953 Time of birth : 08:00:00 hrs
Place of birth : Gorakhpur Lat 26:45:00 N Long 83:23:00E
Ayanamsa : 23:12:23 Sidereal Time : 18:49:46

| **Pln** | **Degree** | **Rasi** | **Nakshatra** | **Pad** |
|---|---|---|---|---|
| Asc | 24:00:29 | Pis | Revati | 3 |
| Sun | 20:01:04 | Aqu | P Bhadrapad | 1 |
| Mon | 26:09:40 | Vir | Chitra | 1 |
| Mar | 24:51:46 | Pis | Revati | 3 |
| Mer | 7:52:33 | Pis | U Bhadrapad | 2 |
| Jup | 22:57:46 | Ari | Bharani | 3 |
| Ven | 1:49:43 | Ari | Asvini | 1 |
| Sat (R) | 3:28:08 | Lib | Chitra | 4 |
| Rah (R) | 18:46:34 | Cap | Sravna | 3 |
| Ket (R) | 18:46:34 | Can | Aslesha | 1 |

**Lagna Chart**

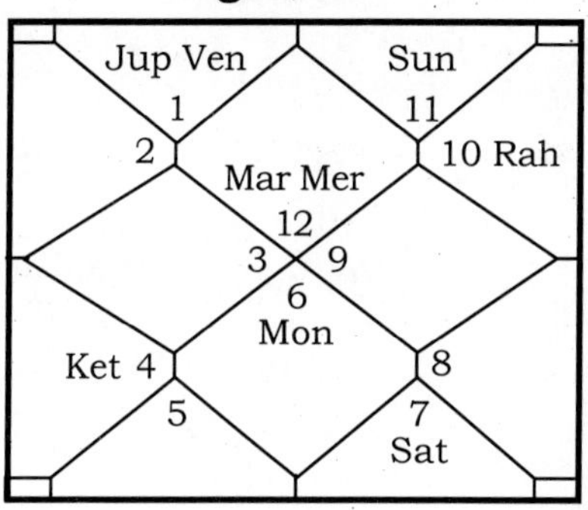


**Navamsa Chart**

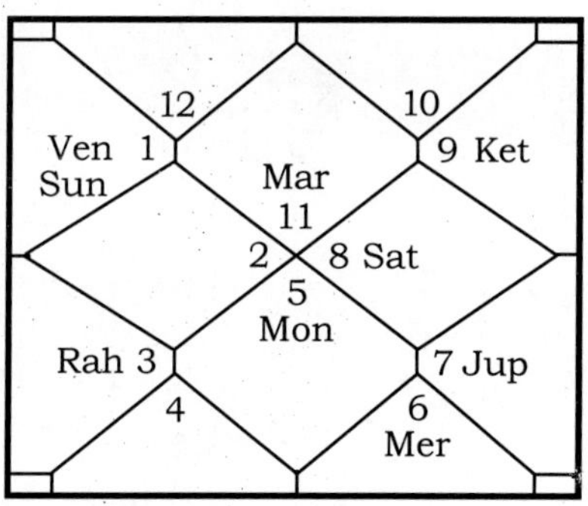


Balance of Vimsottari Dasa of **Mar 5Y 6M 5D**

In this horoscope, the combination of medical career are not quite clear though the native has received M.D. and is very well doing in a Government service. Let us examine the horoscope to understand the combinations, which impelled the native to join medical field.

- Lord of 5th house, Moon, receives the aspect of Mars (2).
- Jupiter aspects tenth house by being placed in the sign of Mars, while Mars aspects the 5th lord Moon by being placed in the sign of Jupiter (4).
- Saturn is exalted and also aspected by Venus and Jupiter (5).
- Sun obtains the *navamsa* of Mars, falls in the constellation of Jupiter and aspects the 10th lord Jupiter in the *navamsa* chart.
- The 5th lord Moon acquires the *navamsa* of Sun.
- Mars and Jupiter influence *lagna* by placement and ownership (Also influence 8th by aspect and 10th by ownership and aspect respectively (7), indicating the native to go in medical line.

*Illustration : 3.12* *Horoscope No.: 46*

Date of birth : 25.03.1932 Time of birth : 23:05:00 hrs
Place of birth : Nagora Lat 10:49:00 N Long 79:50:00E
Ayanamsa : 22:54:38 Sidereal Time : 11:06:11

| Pln | Degree | Rasi | Nakshatra | Pad |
|---|---|---|---|---|
| Asc | 20:30:45 | Sco | Jyestha | 2 |
| Sun | 11:56:54 | Pis | U Bhadrapad | 3 |
| Mon | 26:59:37 | Lib | Visakha | 3 |
| Mar (C) | 0:24:21 | Pis | P Bhadrapad | 4 |
| Mer | 0:08:03 | Ari | Asvini | 1 |
| Jup (R) | 19:59:45 | Can | Aslesha | 1 |
| Ven | 25:56:12 | Ari | Bharani | 4 |
| Sat | 9:53:11 | Cap | Uttarasadha | 4 |
| Rah (R/C) | 3:10:21 | Pis | P Bhadrapad | 4 |
| Ket (R) | 3:10:21 | Vir | U Phalguni | 2 |

**Lagna Chart**

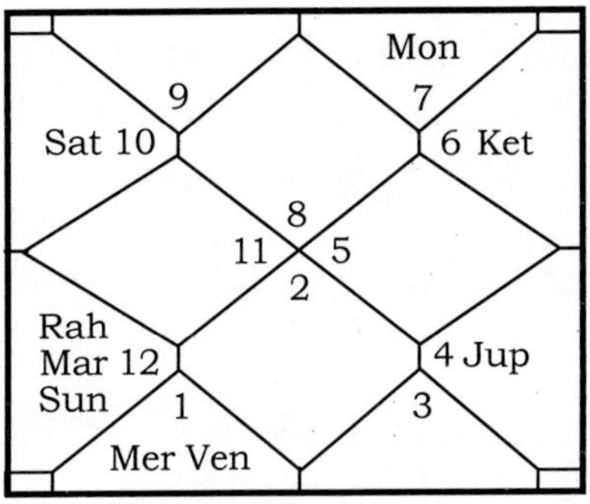


**Navamsa Chart**

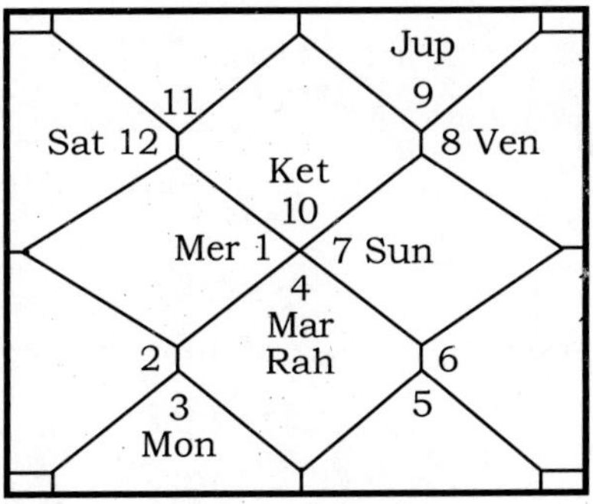


Balance of Vimsottari Dasa of **Jup 7Y 7M 8D**

This is the horoscope of a Chief Medical officer of the District Hospital. The native is M.B.B.S., Dip. in Orthopedic Surgery and M.S. in Orthopedics.

- The lord of the 10th house, the Sun is tenanted in 5th house in association with the *Lagna* lord Mars.
- The combination takes place in Pisces, the sign owned by Jupiter.
- Leo falls in 10th house (1) & (2).
- Jupiter is also aspecting Mars and the Sun in the 5th house.
- Moreover, Jupiter is lord of the 5th house (4).
- Lords of 8th, Mercury and 6th, Mars are conjoined with the lord of the 10th house, the Sun (5).
- Jupiter is exalted and Saturn occupies its own sign, Capricorn. Both are aspecting each other (6).
- *Lagna*, 8th and 10th houses are also influenced by Mars.

So, having such a prominent placement of planets forming the combinations of medical vocation, the native was destined to pursue the medical profession.

*Illustration : 3.13* | *Horoscope No.: 47*

Date of birth : 08.09.1927 Time of birth : 11:08:00 hrs
Place of birth : Lucknow Lat 26:50:00 N Long 80:54:00E
Ayanamsa : 22:50:32 Sidereal Time : 10:06:47

| Pln | Degree | Rasi | Nakshatra | Pad |
|---|---|---|---|---|
| Asc | 1:18:07 | Sco | Visakha | 4 |
| Sun | 21:44:02 | Leo | P Phalguni | 3 |
| Mon | 7:02:21 | Cap | Uttarasadha | 4 |
| Mar (C) | 5:37:54 | Vir | U Phalguni | 3 |
| Mer (C) | 26:49:32 | Leo | U Phalguni | 1 |
| Jup (R) | 7:31:27 | Pis | U Bhadrapad | 2 |
| Ven (R/C) | 25:42:54 | Leo | P Phalguni | 4 |
| Sat | 9:04:18 | Sco | Anuradha | 2 |
| Rah (R) | 1:34:37 | Gem | Mrigsira | 3 |
| Ket (R) | 1:34:37 | Sag | Moola | 1 |

**Lagna Chart**

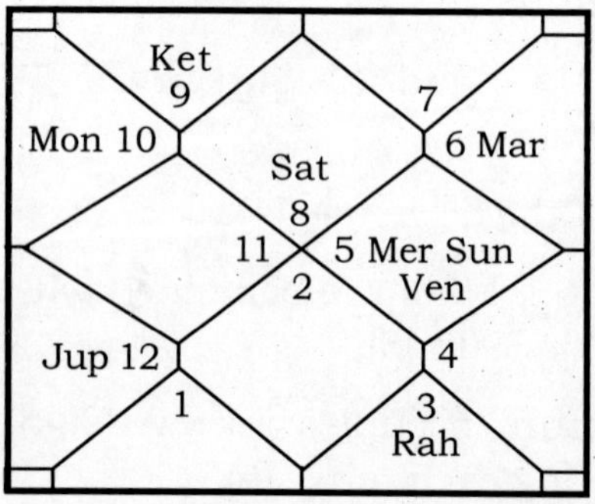


**Navamsa Chart**

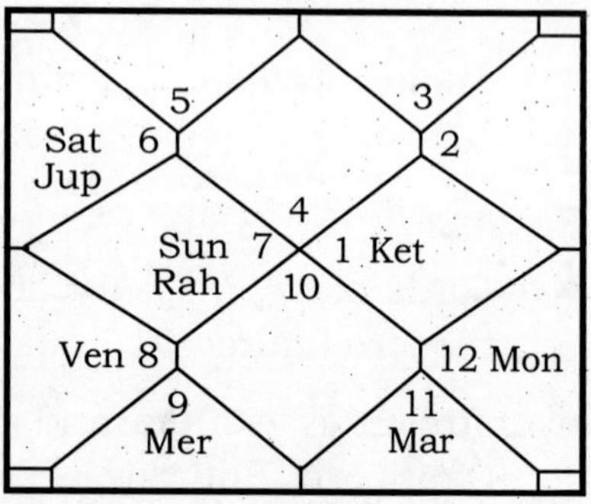


Balance of Vimsottari Dasa of **Sun 1Y 3M 30D**

This is the horoscope of the most prominent, popular and capable Private Medical Practitioner of Lucknow of his times. He was very honest and used to pay heaviest income tax in the city.

Conjunction of Mars and Venus in the 11th house has given him immense wealth, particularly owing to the aspect of benefic Jupiter (*Dhanesh*) over the 11th house and planets placed therein.

- Sun's placement in own sign in the 10th house has made him so successful and renowned in Medical profession (1) & (2).
- Jupiter occupies his own 5th house.
- The 5th lord Jupiter aspects the ascendant lord Mars.
- Mars aspects the 5th house as well as the 6th house of its own.
- Lord of the 8th house, Mercury, joins Sun in the 10th house (5).
- Jupiter aspects the 9th house and Moon also aspects the 9th house of her own. Jupiter and Moon mutually aspect in the *navamsa* chart also. Effect of both the triangles on the 9th house has made the doctor very fortunate and has bestowed profound capability, intelligence and intuition. He has achieved 95% success in the medical field though his qualification is nothing more than M.B.B.S. He has acquired maximum recognition in the Lucknow City for his generosity as well.

*Illustration : 3.14* *Horoscope No.: 48*

Date of birth : 19.05.1949 Time of birth : 22:20:00 hrs
Place of birth : Jaunpur Lat 25:44:00 N Long 82:41:00E
Ayanamsa : 23:08:52 Sidereal Time : 14:08:50

| **Pln** | **Degree** | **Rasi** | **Nakshatra** | **Pad** |
|---|---|---|---|---|
| Asc | 26:12:27 | Sag | Purvasadha | 4 |
| Sun | 5:12:27 | Tau | Krittika | 3 |
| Mon | 4:01:27 | Aqu | Dhanishtha | 4 |
| Mar (C) | 21:23:56 | Ari | Bharani | 3 |
| Mer | 23:36:45 | Tau | Mrigsira | 1 |

| | | | | |
|---|---|---|---|---|
| Jup | 9:01:24 | Cap | Uttarasadha | 4 |
| Ven (C) | 13:50:27 | Tau | Rohini | 2 |
| Sat | 6:27:32 | Leo | Magha | 2 |
| Rah (R) | 2:02:19 | Ari | Asvini | 1 |
| Ket (R) | 2:02:19 | Lib | Chitra | 3 |

**Lagna Chart**

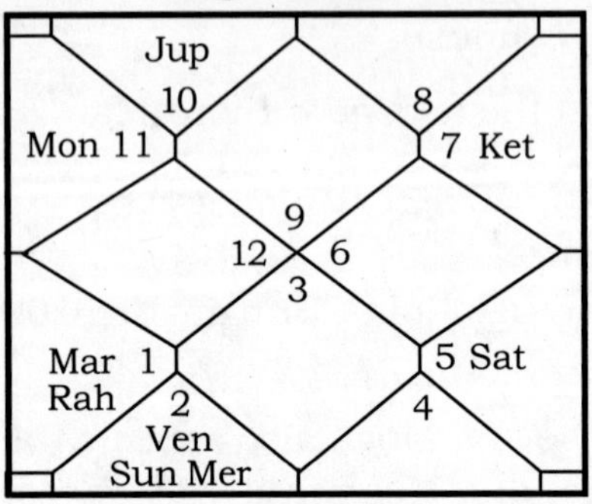


**Navamsa Chart**

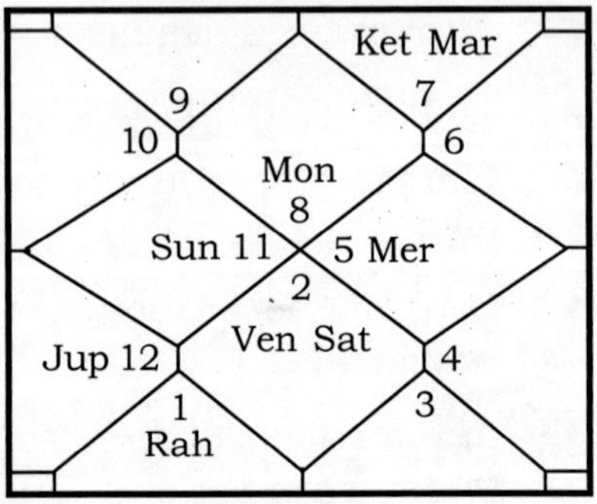


Balance of Vimsottari Dasa of **Mar 1Y 4M 19D**

The native is a popular doctor at a district headquarters. He was in state govt. service, as well as doing private practice.

- Presence of Mars, the lord of 5th house, can be very well seen in the 5th house. (1,2). Jupiter aspects the lord of the 10th house and Sun.
- The 10th lord Mercury joins 6th (5) in association with Sun.
- Lord of 12th, Mars falls in the constellation of 6th lord Venus and the 8th lord Moon falls in the constellation of 5th & 12th lord Mars.
- Jupiter has also to do in the combination. Being *lagna* lord, he is aspecting the 10th house and the lord of 10th house as well.

So, 5th and 10th houses are under the influence of Sun, Mars and Jupiter. As a result, these combinations impelled the native to join medical career, in which he has attained prominent success as a Child specialist.

*Illustration : 3.15* *Horoscope No.: 49*

Date of birth : 08.03.1949 Time of birth : 11:41:00 hrs
Place of birth: Allahabad Lat 25:27:00 N Long 81:50:00E
Ayanamsa : 23:08:42 Sidereal Time : 22:40:49

| **Pln** | **Degree** | **Rasi** | **Nakshatra** | **Pad** |
|---|---|---|---|---|
| Asc | 29:30:22 | Tau | Mrigsira | 2 |
| Sun | 24:12:39 | Aqu | P Bhadrapad | 2 |
| Mon | 26:55:12 | Tau | Mrigsira | 2 |
| Mar (D) | 26:10:34 | Aqu | P Bhadrapad | 2 |
| Mer | 28:27:11 | Cap | Dhanishtha | 2 |
| Jup | 1:32:23 | Cap | Uttarasadha | 2 |
| Ven | 14:09:24 | Aqu | Satabhisha | 3 |
| Sat (R) | 8:30:03 | Leo | Magha | 3 |
| Rah (R) | 3:14:30 | Ari | Asvini | 1 |
| Ket (R) | 3:14:30 | Lib | Chitra | 3 |

**Lagna Chart**

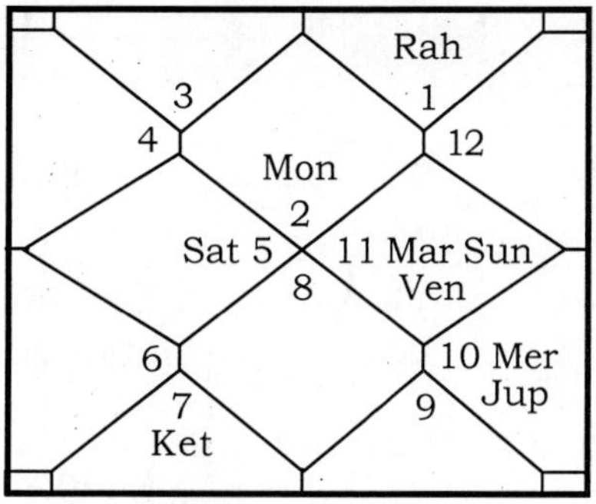


**Navamsa Chart**

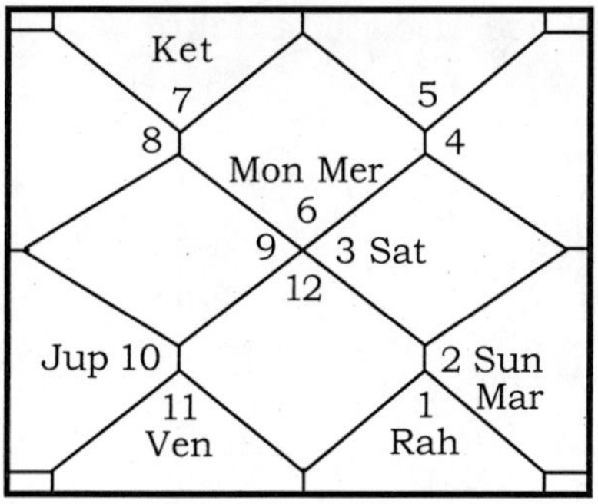


Balance of Vimsottari Dasa of **Mar 5Y 1M 12D**

This is the birth chart of the most popular neuro-physician of the city. He has been a very senior member of the faculty of the Medical University.

- There is conjunction of Sun and Mars in the 10th house.

- Both Sun and Mars aspect the 10th lord Saturn.
- Jupiter aspects the ascendant and the 5th house.
- The 6th lord Venus occupies the 10th house in conjunction with Sun and Mars.
- Both, Mars and Jupiter, aspect the 5th house.
- Saturn and Venus aspect each other.
- Jupiter, the 8th lord falls in the constellation of Sun while Mars and Sun fall in the constellation of Jupiter.

Thus, there is involvement and influence of all the relevant planets Sun, Mars and Jupiter and the 10th, 5th, 6th, 8th & 12th houses. These planetary combinations are responsible for his medical profession. Aspect of 9th lord and *Yogakaraka* Saturn over the 10th house and the ascendant, and conjunction of Karmic control planets, Mars and Venus, in the 10th house have made his career brilliant and have given him much name, fame and prosperity.

*Illustration : 3.16* *Horoscope No.: 50*

Date of birth : 15.12.1958 Time of birth : 22:55:00 hrs
Place of birth : Lucknow Lat 26:50:00 N Long 80:54:00E
Ayanamsa : 23:17:06 Sidereal Time : 4:24:26

| Pln | Degree | Rasi | Nakshatra | Pad |
|---|---|---|---|---|
| Asc | 15:32:50 | Leo | P Phalguni | 1 |
| Sun | 29:57:34 | Sco | Jyestha | 4 |
| Mon | 4:10:01 | Aqu | Dhanishtha | 4 |
| Mar (R) | 23:25:56 | Ari | Bharani | 4 |
| Mer (R) | 17:47:00 | Sco | Jyestha | 1 |
| Jup | 27:32:20 | Lib | Visakha | 3 |
| Ven (C) | 8:18:40 | Sag | Moola | 3 |
| Sat (C) | 4:16:03 | Sag | Moola | 2 |
| Rah (R) | 26:38:52 | Vir | Chitra | 1 |
| Ket (R) | 26:38:52 | Pis | Revati | 3 |

**Lagna Chart**

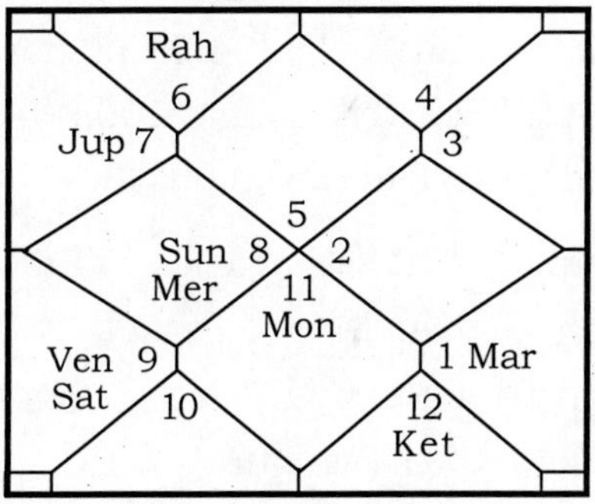


**Navamsa Chart**

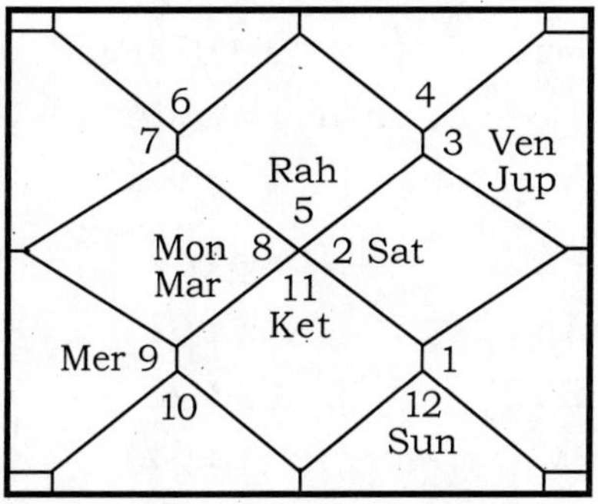


Balance of Vimsottari Dasa of **Mar 1Y 3M 22D**

This is the birth chart of a practicing cardiologist. He is quite popular among his patients.

- The lord of the 10th house, Venus, joins the 5th house in the sign of Jupiter, who also owns the 8th house. Venus is associated with the 6th lord Saturn in the *Rashi* and with 8th lord Jupiter in *navamsa.*
- Sun aspects the 10th house.
- Jupiter owns the 5th house and 5th lord Jupiter is aspected by Mars.
- Venus and Saturn conjoin in the 5th house.

  In this particular case, Moon chart makes the things more obvious.
- In the Moon chart, Aquarius falls in the *lagna* and the 6th lord Moon is placed here.
- Sun occupies the 10th house in Scorpio in conjunction with the 5th lord Mercury.
- Tenth lord Mars is aspected by Jupiter and Mars aspects the 10th house.
- Jupiter aspects the 5th house also, in addition to the ascendant.

As such both, Moon chart and the Rashi chart, corroborate our view point.

*Illustration : 3.17* *Horoscope No.: 51*

Date of birth : 20.07.1950 Time of birth : 04:21:00 hrs
Place of birth : Calcutta Lat 27:30:00 N Long 81:00:00E
Ayanamsa : 23:09:59 Sidereal Time : 0:03:38

| **Pln** | **Degree** | **Rasi** | **Nakshatra** | **Pad** |
|---|---|---|---|---|
| Asc | 19:20:01 | Gem | Ardra | 4 |
| Sun | 3:30:20 | Can | Pushya | 1 |
| Mon | 1:18:27 | Vir | U Phalguni | 2 |
| Mar | 24:24:58 | Vir | Chitra | 1 |
| Mer (C) | 13:21:33 | Can | Pushya | 4 |
| Jup (R) | 13:26:56 | Aqu | Satabhisha | 3 |
| Ven | 3:29:46 | Gem | Mrigsira | 4 |
| Sat | 22:49:27 | Leo | P Phalguni | 3 |
| Rah (S) | 7:11:46 | Pis | U Bhadrapad | 2 |
| Ket (S) | 7:11:46 | Vir | U Phalguni | 4 |

**Lagna Chart**

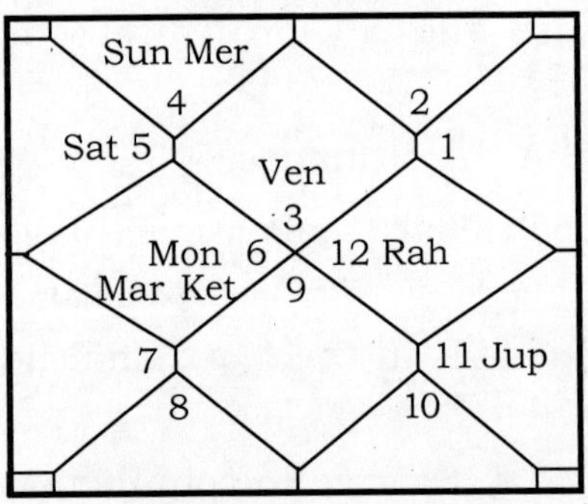


**Navamsa Chart**

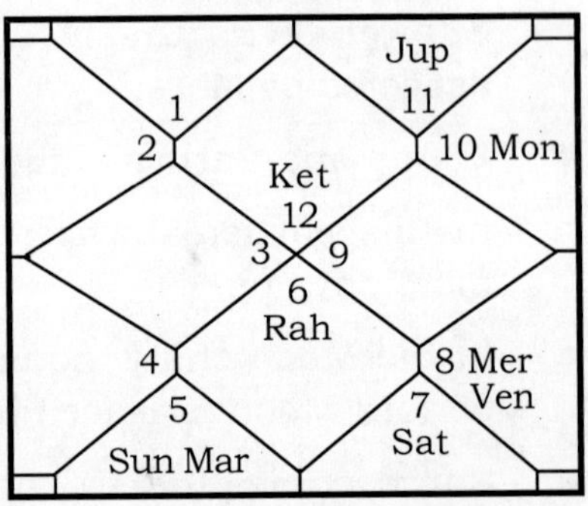


Balance of Vimsottari Dasa of **Sun 3Y 10M 28D**

This is the birth chart of the wife of the native of horoscope no. 49. She has a well established practice of her own. Her birth chart is little complex.

- She is born in Gemini ascendant with $5^{th}$ lord Venus placed therein. The $5^{th}$ lord Venus falls in the constellation of Mars.

- The 10th house is owned by Jupiter who occupies the 9th house.
- Mars owns the 6th house and aspects the 10th house.
- Sun and Mars conjoin in the *navamsa* chart in the sign Leo.
- Saturn, the 8th lord occupies the sign of Sun and *navamsa* of its exaltation. Saturn mutually aspects the 10th lord Jupiter.
- *Lagna* is aspected by Jupiter and *lagna* lord Mercury conjoins with Sun and obtains the *navamsa* of Mars.

*Illustration : 3.18* *Horoscope No.: 52*

Date of birth : 15.03.1957 Time of birth : 16:10:00 hrs
Place of birth : Lucknow Lat 26:50:00 N Long 80:54:00E
Ayanamsa : 23:15:47 Sidereal Time : 3:28:40

| Pln | Degree | Rasi | Nakshatra | Pad |
|---|---|---|---|---|
| Asc | 3:11:17 | Leo | Magha | 1 |
| Sun | 1:19:33 | Pis | P Bhadrapad | 4 |
| Mon | 22:05:41 | Leo | P Phalguni | 3 |
| Mar | 5:11:46 | Tau | Krittika | 3 |
| Mer (C) | 26:18:11 | Aqu | P Bhadrapad | 2 |
| Jup (R) | 3:55:13 | Vir | U Phalguni | 3 |
| Ven (C) | 23:40:07 | Aqu | P Bhadrapad | 2 |
| Sat | 20:59:01 | Sco | Jyestha | 2 |
| Rah (R) | 28:04:46 | Lib | Visakha | 3 |
| Ket (R) | 28:04:46 | Ari | Krittika | 1 |

**Lagna Chart**

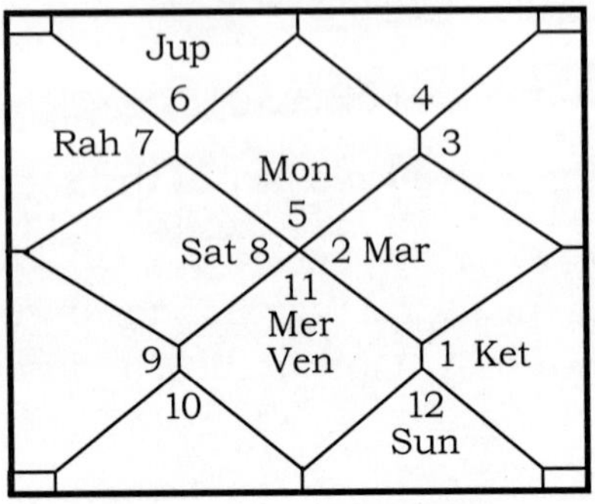


**Navamsa Chart**

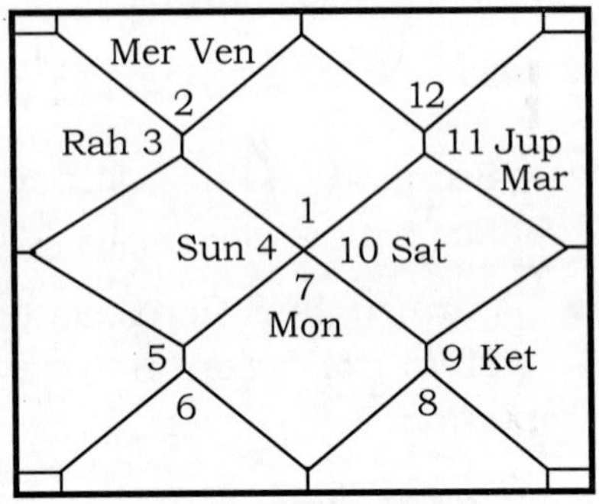


Balance of Vimsottari Dasa of **Ven 6Y 10M 8D**

This is the horoscope of a qualified homeopathic lady doctor who has acquired much recognition in her career.

- Mars is positioned in $10^{th}$ house and aspects $5^{th}$ (2).
- Jupiter aspects Mars in the $10^{th}$ house and the Sun in the $8^{th}$ house (4).
- Lord of $6^{th}$ house, Saturn, aspects the $10^{th}$ house and Mars who occupies $10^{th}$ (5).

These combinations made the girl a private homeopathic medical Practitioner.

Many more such illustrations of successful medical practitioners, Doctors, Surgeons, Medical Shop Keepers and the Doctors who are running their own hospital or nursing homes can be produced to ensure the relevance of the combinations and reliability of the findings.

The crux of the above study is that Jupiter, Sun and Mars have decisive role to play in pursuing the medical studies. Each and every illustration (of practical horoscope) in this article, (astro-) logically elucidates some final determinants related with the Medical avocation. Thus, the $5^{th}$ and $10^{th}$ houses achieve greater significance over others and the combinations, which bring the other houses in determinative ambit, are the $6^{th}$, $8^{th}$ and $12^{th}$. Sun, Mars, Jupiter are the significators. Blending of these will make the final denouement.

●

Chapter-4

# Planetary Combinations for Engineers

"The most difficult and at the same time the most important in the analysis of a horoscope is the determination of one's occupation or profession. In fact the number of avocations is so vast that it looks almost impossible to ascertain with any degree of accuracy, the nature of one's profession, writes Dr. B.V. Raman in the editorial of September, 1971 issue of "The Astrological Magazine."

Determination of exact career or profession is a very skilful task. A most sublime and useful science, astrology can indicate tendencies of avocation and can help parents to correctly guide their children, to choose a suitable line of education from the very beginning of their academic career. One swims faster, with least resistance and obstructions, with the flow of the river. On the other hand, if he tries to swim against the current, his speed will be slower; distance covered will be less and labour more. Similarly, if the education of the child is according to the nature of his profession, he will get absolute success in his career. An occupation wrongly chosen or thrust upon anyone, by parents or others, will never yield the person a prosperous career.

Everyone is ambitious and has a desire to become a doctor, an engineer, an I.A.S. officer, a lawyer, an industrialist or the like. For an I.A.S. officer, a very strong ninth and tenth house, and a mutual exchange of lords of ninth and tenth houses with beneficial and powerful aspects is essential. For a medical career, a strong Sun is needed in the alignment of tenth house or its lord. Sun's connection with Mars or Saturn, can make one a Surgeon or a doctor in the government service respectively. There are so many factors, which are responsible and must be essentially taken into consideration for a proper judgement of one's career. For all this, a keen analysis of birth chart is needed.

It's easy to justify events once they have occurred or the nature of profession already being practiced but it is tough to predict this before hand. This is the actual utility of practical astrology. Usually the avocation is judged with the help of tenth house, lord of tenth house, *navamsa* occupied by the lord of tenth house, constellation in which the lord of tenth house falls from *lagna* and Moon, whichever is stronger. We opine that, apart from tenth house, *lagna* and eighth house must also be considered for finding out career or means of livelihood. Mr. Kannan has dealt with this, in length, in his article "Vocation from the Eighth House" in the annual number of 'The Astrological Magazine' of 1963 and also in the September, 1971 issue under the caption "Some Guidelines for determining profession". In this connection our view is that the main *Rashi* chart or birth chart should reveal the nature of profession in general, without going into details of calculations. *Navamsa* chart, constellations occupied by planets, the strongest planet and the like should only be considered for finding other smaller and precise details or for the confirmation of the facts revealed by the birth chart or *Rashi* chart. In these pages, we will deal with the horoscope of engineers only. Dr. Raman has mentioned in his great, unique and unparalleled work "How To Judge a Horoscope–Vol. II" that in the study of tenth house, Mercury, Mars and Saturn play important roles in the horoscope of engineers and are responsible for engineering profession.

Before proceeding onwards we should know about the nature of profession of an engineer. An engineer is one who is involved in the practical application of technology, designing and construction work of public utility; he should be capable of planning and should be adept in skills of construction, designs and supervision. For all this, an engineer must possess intelligence.

An engineer deals with steel, wire, metals, electric

wires, cement, bricks, earth and machines etc. A few of these are represented by Mars e.g. bricks, machines, stones, and some are represented by Saturn e.g. Earth, cement, steel, etc. Raw material for bricks is Earth, for cement stone and for machines it is steel. This means, that for engineering, Mars and Saturn are inter-related and both are equally important. Mercury represents skill and intelligence, without which one is an incomplete engineer.

For successful engineers, unaffected Mars, Mercury and Saturn play prominent roles. The influences of these planets are highlighted when they come under the favourable influences of benefics like Jupiter. In horoscopes where Venus is also significantly related with career, along with Saturn, Mercury and Mars, the native will be more successful as a designer. That means he will be capable of exhibiting his skills both in the design office and the field but if Mars is weak he will not be that much successful in the field i.e. in practical construction work. Engineers, who have, in their birth chart, a weak Mars and strong Venus, in reference to their vocation, may be successful in Project Division and Circles, where mainly the design or planning is undertaken.

These engineers who have very strong Mars are very bold, courageous, active, self-reliant and hard working and possess good administrative qualities. While those who have predominance of Saturn, (they) are not self-reliant and do not take any risk. They always try to thrust their responsibilities over others and at times they are known as coward and mean. But even then they are very laborious and do not trust others much but want to see or do most of the things themselves.

However, the following guide lines may give clues for the determination of engineering profession.

1. ***Lagna:*** *Lagna* shows the general aptitude or mental inclination of the native and must have influence of Mars, Mercury or Saturn by occupation, ownership or aspect. That means, that either the sign in which the *lagna* falls should be ruled by Mars or Mercury or Saturn;

or either of these planets should aspect *lagna* or *lagnadhipati*; or the lord of the ascendant should be placed in the signs ruled by them; or either of these planets should be positioned in the ascendant.

2. **Tenth House:** Tenth house represents *Karma* and this must be connected with Mars, Mercury or Saturn by aspect, ownership or occupation.
3. **Eighth House:** Eighth house plays quite an important role in deciding avocation of the native. This will be proved below with the help of dozens of illustrations. Eighth house shows career that will be taken up by the native and this house should also be influenced by the vibrations of Saturn, Mercury and Mars by placement, lordship or aspect.
4. To find out the exact nature of the job and for successful and rising career Venus and Jupiter's role in a horoscope should also be judged and these should be treated as supporting significators for the profession of engineers.
5. Apart from Saturn, role of the $6^{th}$ house can not be overlooked. In fact, the $6^{th}$ house indicates service. Lord of the $10^{th}$, if placed in the $6^{th}$ or vice versa, one earns through service. Similarly, if the ascendant has a concern with the $6^{th}$ lord, the subject will enter into service. If the lord of *lagna* & $6^{th}$ house or the lord of $10^{th}$ & $6^{th}$ house or all the three influence each other, either by way of conjunction or aspect, one will earn through service. If the luminaries are also involved with these lords, in one or the other way, the native will get a govt. service.

Almost all engineering graduates seek a good service though this is not necessary for those, who have studied medicine or law. For engineers, the most common way is service and Saturn represent service. Therefore, Saturn also plays an important role in the horoscope of engineers (because mostly they join services).

We will now discuss a number of birth charts of engineers.

The considerations regarding determination of occupation should be made from *lagna* or Moon whichever is stronger. This is quite simple. We are required to judge 1st, 8th and 10th houses with the influences of Mars, Mercury and Saturn in reference to these houses. *Navamsa* and constellation occupied by planets may be used for further confirmation of the avocation, or in case of any confusion in finding out the nature of profession, *navamsa* chart and asterisms of concerning planets may be taken into account.

We are giving some horoscope here for illustration of engineering profession in regard to above principle:

*Illustration : 4.1* **(AKH)** *Horoscope No.: 53*

Date of birth : 13.11.1941 Time of birth : 02:20:00 hrs

Place of birth : Allahabad Lat 25:27:00 N Long 81:50:00E

Ayanamsa : 23:02:37 Sidereal Time : 5:43:41

| **Pln** | **Degree** | **Rasi** | **Nakshatra** | **Pad** |
|---|---|---|---|---|
| Asc | 3:16:16 | Vir | U Phalguni | 2 |
| Sun | 27:02:31 | Lib | Visakha | 3 |
| Mon | 4:57:31 | Leo | Magha | 2 |
| Mar | 18:04:18 | Pis | Revati | 1 |
| Mer | 8:00:38 | Lib | Svati | 1 |
| Jup (R) | 26:34:31 | Tau | Mrigsira | 1 |
| Ven | 13:54:12 | Sag | Purvasadha | 1 |
| Sat (R) | 2:25:13 | Tau | Krittika | 2 |
| Rah | 27:48:48 | Leo | U Phalguni | 1 |
| Ket | 27:48:48 | Aqu | P Bhadrapad | 3 |

**Lagna Chart**

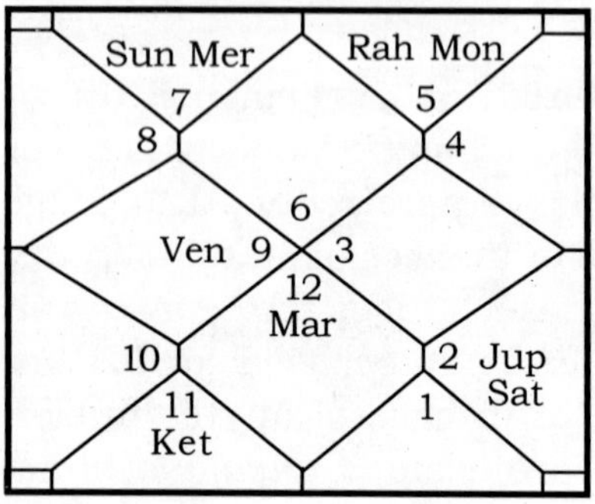


**Navamsa Chart**

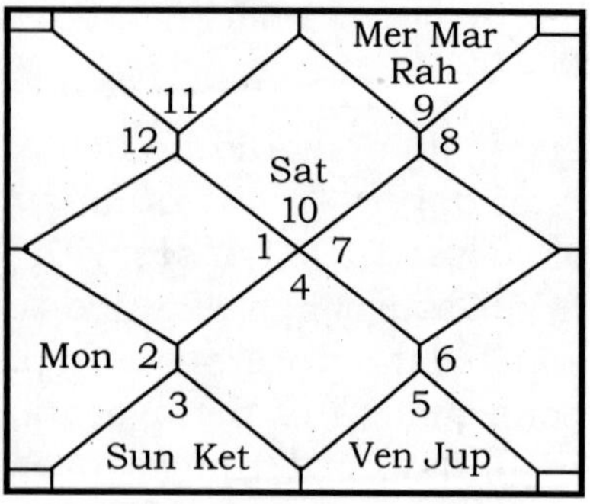


Balance of Vimsottari Dasa of **Ket 4Y 4M 23D**

The native of this birth chart is an electrical engineer who retired as member of UP Power Corporation. He is pursuing the study of Astrology after retirement.

- He was born in Virgo ascendant, which falls in Capricorn *navamsa*. We have observed that Saturn, Mercury and Mars play an important role in making one engineer, if the 10$^{th}$, 8$^{th}$, 6$^{th}$ and ascendant are under the influence of these planets.

  In the case of this native, following planetary placements are to be noted:

- The 10$^{th}$ and ascendant lord Mercury and the 8$^{th}$ lord Mars both influence the 10$^{th}$ house. Mercury is the lord of the 10$^{th}$ house and Mars aspects the10$^{th}$ house. Both Mercury and Mars, obtain the *navamsa* of Mars.
- The 10$^{th}$ lord Mercury falls in Rahu's constellation *Svati*, which shows that the native would be an electrical engineer. Electricity can not be seen but it can be experienced. Similarly, Rahu and Ketu are not visible, so placement of the 10$^{th}$ lord in the constellation of Rahu indicates that the native will be an electrical engineer.
- The 6$^{th}$ lord Saturn joins the 9$^{th}$ house and aspects the 6$^{th}$ house and obtains own *navamsa*. This shows earnings through service only.

- There is mutual exchange of houses between the 4th lord Jupiter and the 9th lord Venus giving rise to *Maharaja Yoga.* This *Rajyoga* elevated the native to the top most position in his career.
- Jupiter and Venus both obtain the *navamsa* of Sun, and Moon aspects the 6th house, which further confirms the livelihood through govt. service.

*Illustration : 4.2* (**NCG**) *Horoscope No.: 54*

Date of birth : 21.10.1940 Time of birth : 17:02:17 hrs
Place of birth : Muzaffarnagar Lat 29:28:00 N Long 77:42:00E
Ayanamsa : 23:01:50 Sidereal Time : 18:42:07

| **Pln** | **Degree** | **Rasi** | **Nakshatra** | **Pad** |
|---|---|---|---|---|
| Asc | 22:04:26 | Pis | Revati | 2 |
| Sun | 4:53:23 | Lib | Chitra | 4 |
| Mon | 1:51:03 | Gem | Mrigsira | 3 |
| Mar | 17:13:43 | Vir | Hasta | 3 |
| Mer | 29:12:18 | Lib | Visakha | 3 |
| Jup (R) | 19:16:11 | Ari | Bharani | 2 |
| Ven | 23:42:28 | Leo | P Phalguni | 4 |
| Sat (R) | 19:20:08 | Ari | Bharani | 2 |
| Rah (R) | 17:58:21 | Vir | Hasta | 3 |
| Ket (R) | 17:58:21 | Pis | Revati | 1 |

**Lagna Chart**

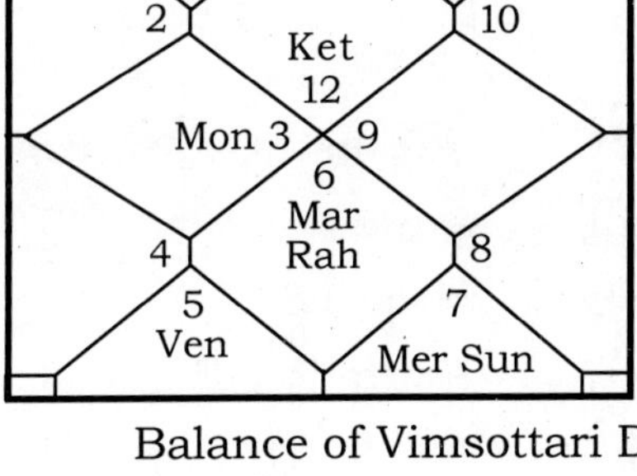


**Navamsa Chart**

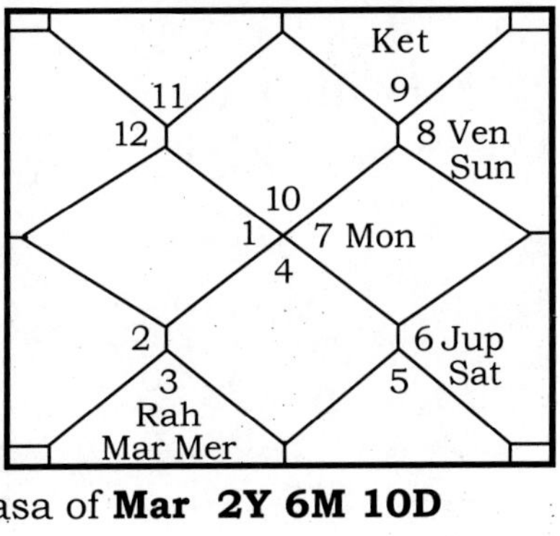


Balance of Vimsottari Dasa of **Mar 2Y 6M 10D**

The native retired as Chief Engineer (Civil) in the Public Works Department. He was topper of Thompson College of Engineering, Roorkee. He worked in various other departments after retirement as consultant.

- The native was born in Pisces ascendant. The lord of the ascendant and the $10^{th}$ Jupiter falls in the $2^{nd}$ house in Aries and aspects the $10^{th}$ house of its own.
- The $10^{th}$ lord Jupiter obtains the *navamsa* of Mercury along with $11^{th}$ lord Saturn.
- The $6^{th}$ lord Sun is associated with Mercury in the $8^{th}$ house and obtains the *navamsa* of $9^{th}$ lord Mars.
- The $5^{th}$ lord Moon falls in the $4^{th}$ house in Gemini, ruled by Mercury, and obtains the *navamsa* of $2^{nd}$ & $9^{th}$ lord Mars. Moon, who is under the influence of Mars and Mercury both, has an aspect over the $10^{th}$ house.
- Thus, the $10^{th}$ house is aspected by the $10^{th}$ lord Jupiter, $5^{th}$ lord Moon and the $9^{th}$ lord Mars. The $11^{th}$ lord Saturn and the ascendant and the $10^{th}$ lord Jupiter are posited under mutual aspect with the $6^{th}$ lord Sun and $4^{th}$ & $7^{th}$ lord Mercury, corresponding with the $2^{nd}$ and the $8^{th}$ house.

Therefore, there is strong indication that the native will rise as a civil engineer.

*Illustration : 4.3* **(HKT)** *Horoscope No.: 55*

Date of birth : 17.06.1913 Time of birth : 06:13:00 hrs
Place of birth : Bareilly Lat 28:20:00 N Long 79:24:00E
Ayanamsa : 22:38:54 Sidereal Time : 23:39:17

| Pln | Degree | Rasi | Nakshatra | Pad |
|---|---|---|---|---|
| Asc | 14:53:16 | Gem | Ardra | 3 |
| Sun | 2:33:50 | Gem | Mrigsira | 3 |
| Mon | 11:23:50 | Sco | Anuradha | 3 |
| Mar | 7:21:14 | Ari | Asvini | 3 |

| Mer | 19:17:14 | Gem | Ardra | 4 |
|---|---|---|---|---|
| Jup (R) | 22:35:10 | Sag | Purvasadha | 3 |
| Ven | 18:12:08 | Ari | Bharani | 2 |
| Sat (C) | 17:15:58 | Tau | Rohini | 3 |
| Rah (R) | 6:33:53 | Pis | U Bhadrapad | 1 |
| Ket (R) | 6:33:53 | Vir | U Phalguni | 3 |

**Lagna Chart**

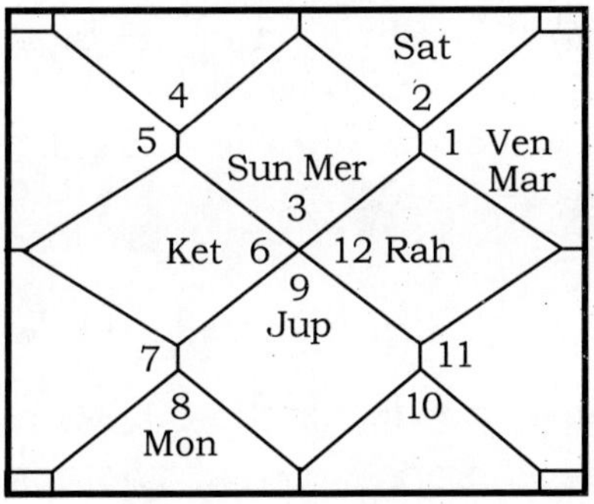


**Navamsa Chart**

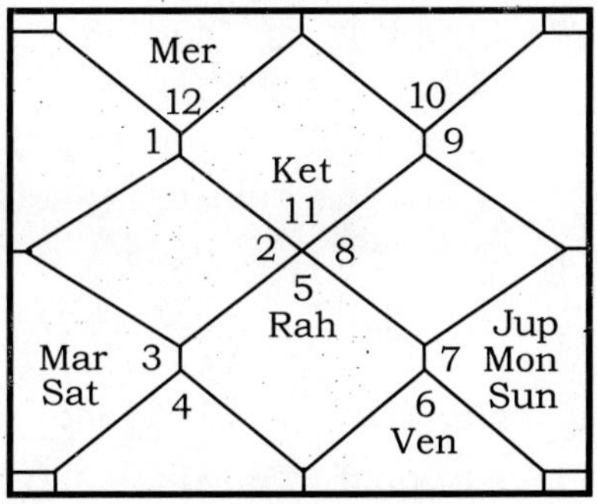


Balance of Vimsottari Dasa of **Sat 7Y 6M 3D**

The native retired as an Executive engineer in PWD. He did many reforms and improvements in the department. He is remembered for founding an Association of subordinate engineers. He received many awards, accolades and admirations for his outstanding performance. He was basically a civil engineer.

- He was born in Gemini ascendant with the ascendant lord Mercury and the 3rd lord Sun placed in the ascendant itself. The lord of the 10th house Jupiter falls in the 7th house and aspects the 6th lord Mars, the 5th & 12th lord Venus, in addition to the ascendant and the 10th lord Mercury and 3rd lord Sun. This signifies the govt. service.
- The 9th lord Saturn aspects the 9th house of its own and the 2nd house and lord thereof, Moon. This made the native fortunate and prosperous.

- The lord of the 6th and 11th house, Mars, aspects the 2nd house and 2nd lord Moon. Thus, the 2nd house and the 2nd lord Moon are under the aspect of both Mars and Saturn.
- Moon falls in Saturn's constellation *Anuradha* and sign Scorpio. Thus, there is strong influence of Saturn and Mars over the 2nd lord Moon.
- The lord of 8th and 9th house, Saturn, and the 6th lord Mars obtain the *navamsa* of ascendant and 4th lord Mercury. The 10th lord Jupiter and Mercury aspect each other. Thus, there is powerful justification in the birth chart that the native would serve in a govt. department as a civil engineer. Joint effect of Mars and Saturn indicates civil engineering.

*Illustration : 4.4* **(GKT)** *Horoscope No.: 56*

Date of birth : 21.02.1928 Time of birth : 06:39:00 hrs

Place of birth : Bareilly Lat 28:20:00 N Long 79:24:00E

Ayanamsa : 22:50:57 Sidereal Time : 16:25:31

| **Pln** | **Degree** | **Rasi** | **Nakshatra** | **Pad** |
|---|---|---|---|---|
| Asc | 4:31:43 | Aqu | Dhanishtha | 4 |
| Sun | 8:19:10 | Aqu | Satabhisha | 1 |
| Mon (C) | 3:39:05 | Aqu | Dhanishtha | 4 |
| Mar | 1:41:45 | Cap | Uttarasadha | 2 |
| Mer (R/C) | 15:29:06 | Aqu | Satabhisha | 3 |
| Jup | 12:59:44 | Pis | U Bhadrapad | 3 |
| Ven | 5:09:24 | Cap | Uttarasadha | 3 |
| Sat | 25:10:17 | Sco | Jyestha | 3 |
| Rah (R) | 22:42:50 | Tau | Rohini | 4 |
| Ket (R) | 22:42:50 | Sco | Jyestha | 2 |

**Lagna Chart**

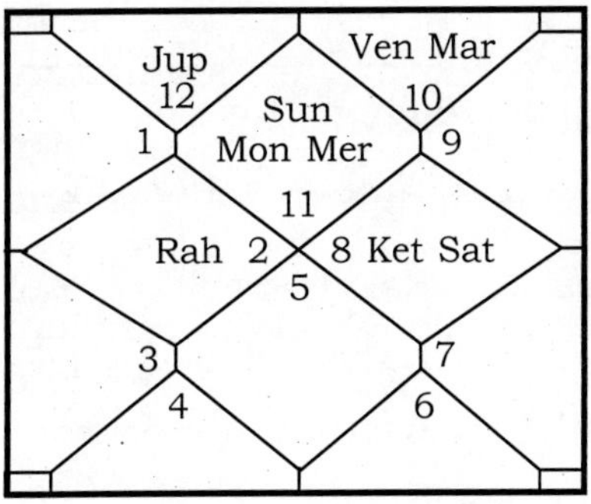


**Navamsa Chart**

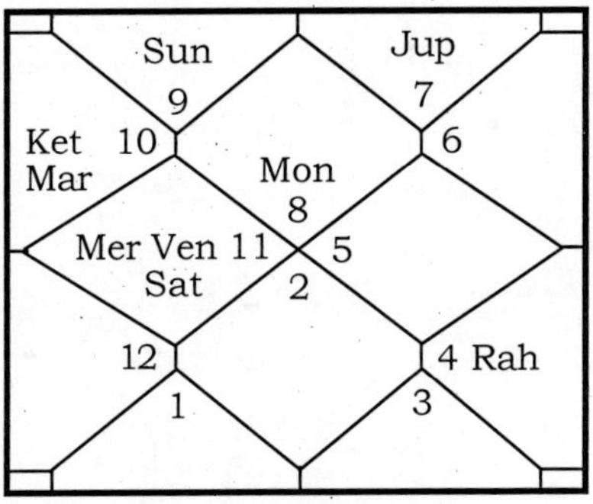


Balance of Vimsottari Dasa of **Mar 1Y 6M 30D**

The native joined U.P. Nirman Nigam as an Assistant Engineer and rose to the top most position. He retired as the Managing Director of Jal Nigam. He was basically a civil engineer.

- The native was born in Aquarius ascendant with Sun, Moon and Mercury placed therein. Lord of the ascendant, Saturn, is posited in the 10th house in the sign of Mars, Scorpio.
- The lord of the 6th house, Moon, and that of the 8th house Mercury are associated in the ascendant with Sun, which strongly shows top govt. service and the position of the head of the department.
- The lord of the 10th house, Mars, is exalted in the 12th house and aspects the 6th and 7th house including its aspect on its own 3rd house.
- The lord of the 11th and 2nd Jupiter falls in own sign Pisces, in the 2nd house, and lends its favourable aspect over the 6th, 7th and the 10th house.
- Saturn, Mercury and Mars obtain Saturn's *navamsa*, whereas the 6th lord Moon obtains the *navamsa* of Mars, who is the lord of the 10th house.

Thus, the best and powerful combinations are there in his birth chart and these indicate that the profession of the native will be an engineer in a govt. organization.

*Illustration : 4.5* (**VNR**) *Horoscope No.: 57*

Date of birth : 18.04.1933 Time of birth : 00:40:00 hrs

Place of birth : Bijnor Lat 29:22:00 N Long 78:09:00E

Ayanamsa : 22:55:37 Sidereal Time : 14:04:26

| Pln | Degree | Rasi | Nakshatra | Pad |
|---|---|---|---|---|
| Asc | 23:21:16 | Sag | Purvasadha | 4 |
| Sun | 4:22:52 | Ari | Asvini | 2 |
| Mon | 12:15:26 | Cap. | Sravna | 1 |
| Mar | 8:07:40 | Leo | Magha | 3 |
| Mer | 7:12:17 | Pis | U Bhadrapad | 2 |
| Jup (R) | 21:08:23 | Leo | P Phalguni | 3 |
| Ven (D) | 3:22:14 | Ari | Asvini | 2 |
| Sat | 22:13:06 | Cap | Sravna | 4 |
| Rah | 13:32:32 | Aqu | Satabhisha | 3 |
| Ket | 13:32:32 | Leo | P Phalguni | 1 |

**Lagna Chart** **Navamsa Chart**

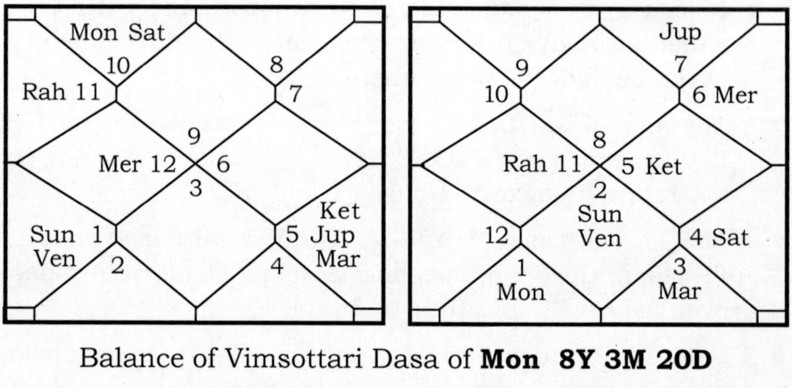


Balance of Vimsottari Dasa of **Mon 8Y 3M 20D**

The birth chart belongs to a Chairman of UPSEB, who is man of extraordinary merits and caliber. His knowledge knew no bounds and his acumen was admirable.

- The native was born in Sagittarius ascendant. The lord

of the ascendant Jupiter and that of the 5th house, Mars are associated in the 9th house in Leo.

- The 10th lord Mercury occupies the 4th house and aspects the 10th house. Mercury also receives the aspect of 5th lord Mars.
- The 8th lord Moon is conjoined with the 2nd & the 3rd lord Saturn in the 2nd house. Moon and Saturn, both aspect the 8th house.
- Saturn aspects the 10th lord Mercury in addition to the 8th house.
- Sun is exalted in the 5th house and receives the powerful and favourable aspect of Jupiter.
- The 9th lord Sun is conjoined with the 6th lord Venus and both are aspected by the ascendant lord Jupiter.
- Thus, the ascendant lord Jupiter aspects the 9th lord Sun, the 6th lord Venus and the ascendant. The 10th lord Mercury aspects the 10th and is aspected by the 2nd lord Saturn. Saturn and 3rd lord Moon are associated with each other and jointly aspect the 8th house. These combinations are quite strong to make the native an engineer, getting a govt. job and rising to the height of Chairman i. e. the Head of the Department.

*Illustration : 4.6* (**GPS**) *Horoscope No.: 58*

Date of birth : 14.08.1935 Time of birth : 16:28:00 hrs

Place of birth : Bulandshahr Lat 28:30:00 N Long 77:49:00E

Ayanamsa : 22:57:45 Sidereal Time : 13:37:00

| **Pln** | **Degree** | **Rasi** | **Nakshatra** | **Pad** |
|---|---|---|---|---|
| Asc | 17:02:18 | Sag | Purvasadha | 2 |
| Sun | 27:45:33 | Can | Aslesha | 4 |
| Mon | 26:42:53 | Cap | Dhanishtha | 2 |
| Mar | 15:59:06 | Lib | Svati | 3 |
| Mer (C) | 2:22:51 | Leo | Magha | 1 |

| | | | | |
|---|---|---|---|---|
| Jup | 22:07:06 | Lib | Visakha | 1 |
| Ven | 29:33:37 | Leo | U Phalguni | 1 |
| Sat (R) | 15:06:52 | Aqu | Satabhisha | 3 |
| Rah (R) | 28:57:48 | Sag | Uttarasadha | 1 |
| Ket (R) | 28:57:48 | Gem | Punarvasu | 3 |

**Lagna Chart**

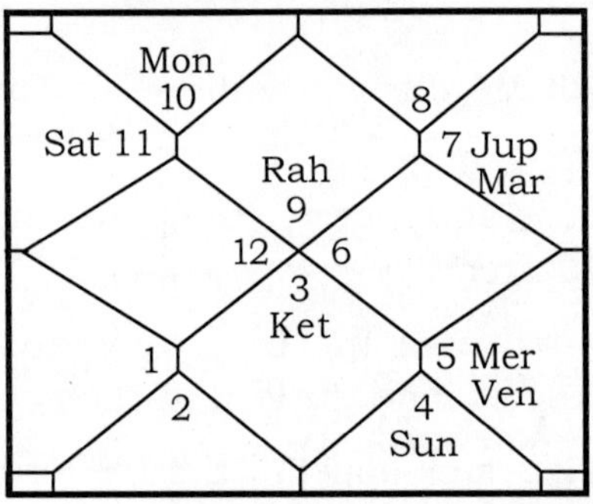


**Navamsa Chart**

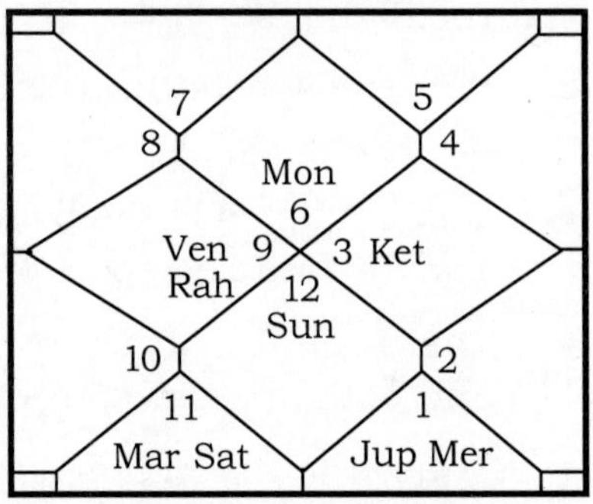


Balance of Vimsottari Dasa of **Mar 5Y 2M 21D**

The native retired as Chief engineer from UP State Electricity board. Following combinations may be noted:

- The native was born in Sagittarius ascendant. Lord of the *lagna* Jupiter occupies the 11th house in conjunction with 5th & 12th lord Mars.
- The 6th lord Venus and the 10th lord Mercury conjoin in the 9th house in sign Leo and are aspected by Saturn. 6th lord Venus falls in the constellation of Sun. These combinations confirm the govt. service.
- Tenth lord Mercury obtains the *navamsa* of Mars while Mars obtains the *navamsa* of Saturn. Ascendant lord Jupiter also obtains the *navamsa* of Mars.
- The 9th lord Sun falls in the constellation of Mercury, *Aslesha*, while the 8th lord Moon falls in the constellation *Dhanishtha*, ruled by Mars.
- Saturn aspects the 5th house, the 9th house and also the 6th & 10th lords, Venus and Mercury.

Thus, there is enough influence of Saturn, Mercury and Mars over the ascendant, 10th, 8th and 5th to indicate the engineering career. Relationship between 6th and the 10th and influence of Sun confirms the service in a govt. department.

*Illustration : 4.7* (**SKS**) *Horoscope No.: 59*

Date of birth : 25.11.1930 Time of birth : 00:40:00 hrs

Place of birth : Orai Lat 29:22:00 N Long 78:09:00E

Ayanamsa : 22:53:23 Sidereal Time : 4:34:40

| Pln | Degree | Rasi | Nakshatra | Pad |
|---|---|---|---|---|
| Asc | 18:28:08 | Leo | P Phalguni | 2 |
| Sun | 8:54:16 | Sco | Anuradha | 2 |
| Mon | 0:52:49 | Cap | Uttarasadha | 2 |
| Mar | 20:36:00 | Can | Aslesha | 2 |
| Mer (C) | 18:49:30 | Sco | Jyestha | 1 |
| Jup (R) | 27:09:48 | Gem | Punarvasu | 3 |
| Ven (R/C) | 5:36:47 | Sco | Anuradha | 1 |
| Sat | 16:38:45 | Sag | Purvasadha | 1 |
| Rah (R) | 0:04:39 | Ari | Asvini | 1 |
| Ket (R) | 0:04:39 | Lib | Chitra | 3 |

**Lagna Chart**

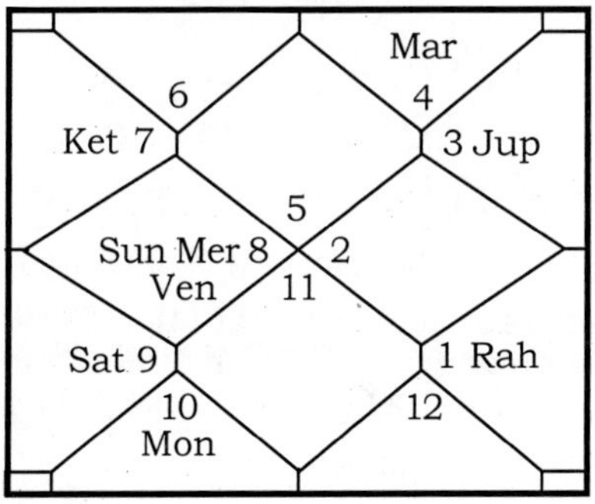


**Navamsa Chart**

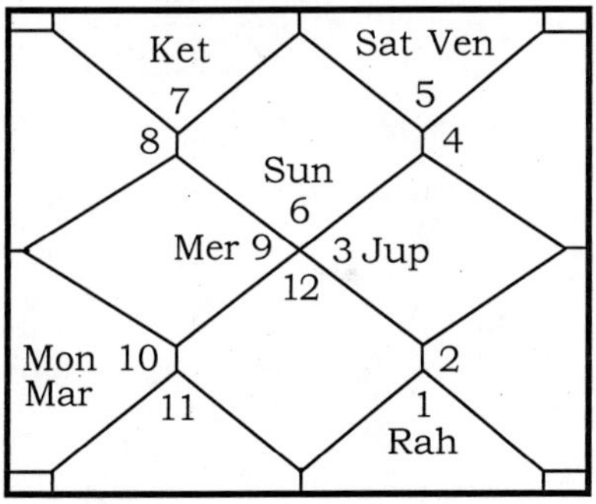


Balance of Vimsottari Dasa of **Sun 4Y 1M 7D**

The native retired as the chief engineer from the Jal Nigam in Uttar Pradesh.

- The ascendant falls in the sign Leo, whose lord Sun occupies the 4th house in the sign of Mars, Scorpio, in association with the 2nd &11th lord Mercury and the 10th lord Venus. Sun, Mercury and Venus aspect the 10th house.
- Ascendant lord Sun falls in the constellation of Saturn and obtains the *navamsa* of Mercury.
- The 6th lord Saturn falls in the constellation of 10th lord Venus and occupies the sign of 5th & 8th lord Jupiter, in the 5th house. The 6th and 10th lords, Saturn and Venus, are conjoined in the *navamsa* of Sun.
- The 10th lord Venus occupies the sign Scorpio, owned by Mars and falls in the constellation *Anuradha*, owned by Saturn. Venus obtains the *navamsa* of ascendant lord Sun.
- The 9th lord Mars is posited in the 12th house in Cancer, owned by Moon while Moon gets the sign and *navamsa* of Saturn, under the aspect of Mars in *Rashi* and in association with Mars in *navamsa* chart. Mars falls in the constellation of Mercury.

Thus, here also, influence of Mars, Saturn and Mercury and also Jupiter is very clear, which led the native into the engineering career. Also, the clear relationship between 6th & the 10th, superimposed with the influence of Sun, makes the govt. service very obvious.

*Illustration : 4.8* **(SCR)** *Horoscope No.: 60*

Date of birth : 21.09.1946 Time of birth : 12:05:00 hrs
Place of birth : Dibai Lat 28:13:00 N Long 78:15:00E
Ayanamsa : 23:06:29 Sidereal Time : 11:46:10

| Pln | Degree | Rasi | Nakshatra | Pad |
|---|---|---|---|---|
| Asc | 21:49:02 | Sco | Jyestha | 2 |
| Sun | 4:33:45 | Vir | U Phalguni | 3 |

| | | | | |
|---|---|---|---|---|
| Mon | 13:26:47 | Can | Pushya | 4 |
| Mar | 4:35:36 | Lib | Chitra | 4 |
| Mer (C) | 9:50:30 | Vir | U Phalguni | 4 |
| Jup | 6:03:06 | Lib | Chitra | 4 |
| Ven | 20:03:34 | Lib | Visakha | 1 |
| Sat | 12:38:25 | Can | Pushya | 3 |
| Rah (R) | 22:06:04 | Tau | Rohini | 4 |
| Ket (R) | 22:06:04 | Sco | Jyestha | 2 |

**Lagna Chart**

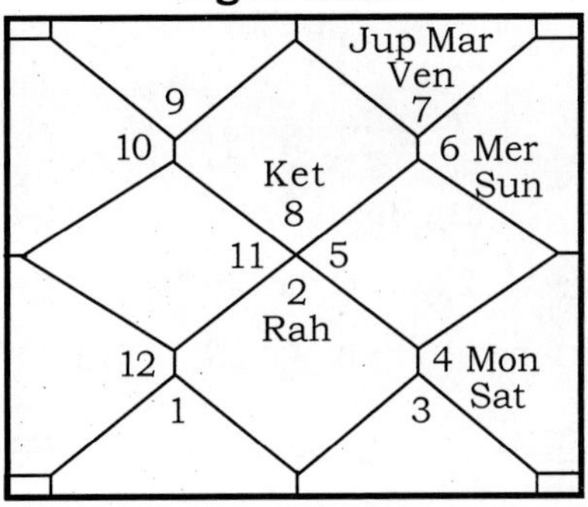


**Navamsa Chart**

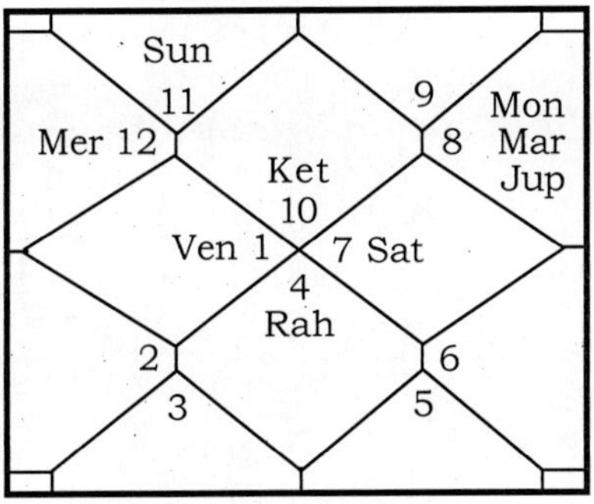


Balance of Vimsottari Dasa of **Sat 4Y 7M 1D**

The native of this birth chart is an electrical engineer, who retired from the post of Chief Engineer from UP State Electricity Board. He was known for his strict discipline.

- The ascendant is Scorpio, sign ruled by Mars, who falls in the $12^{th}$ house, in association with $5^{th}$ lord Jupiter and $7^{th}$ lord Venus. Mars falls in own constellation, *Chitra* and obtains own *navamsa*, in association with Jupiter and $9^{th}$ lord Moon.
- The tenth lord Sun joins the sign of Mercury, Virgo in association with Mercury. Sun obtains the *navamsa* of Saturn, is aspected by Saturn and falls in own constellation, *U. Phalguni.*
- The $9^{th}$ lord Moon joins the ninth house in conjunction with Saturn. Moon obtains the *navamsa* of Mars in

association with Mars and falls in the *nakshatra* of Saturn.

- The 5th lord Jupiter falls in the constellation and *navamsa* of Mars and is associated with Mars in the 12th house.
- The 8th lord Mercury conjoins with 10th lord Sun, aspects the 5th house and obtains the *navamsa* of Jupiter, the 5th lord. Jupiter aspects the 8th house.

Thus, the influence of Saturn, Mars and Mercury over the relevant houses, as enumerated earlier, is quite obvious, which made the native an engineer.

*Illustration : 4.9* **(ANB)** *Horoscope No.: 61*

Date of birth : 10.04.1920 Time of birth : 06:44:00 hrs

Place of birth : Ajmer Lat 26:29:00 N Long 74:40:00E

Ayanamsa : 22:44:49 Sidereal Time : 19:24:32

| Pln | Degree | Rasi | Nakshatra | Pad |
|---|---|---|---|---|
| Asc | 5:59:41 | Ari | Asvini | 2 |
| Sun | 27:07:23 | Pis | Revati | 4 |
| Mon | 10:36:52 | Sag | Moola | 4 |
| Mar (R) | 12:09:10 | Lib | Svati | 2 |
| Mer | 1:02:44 | Pis | P Bhadrapad | 4 |
| Jup | 15:24:45 | Can | Pushya | 4 |
| Ven | 4:45:08 | Pis | U Bhadrapad | 1 |
| Sat (R) | 12:41:27 | Leo | Magha | 4 |
| Rah | 23:03:09 | Lib | Visakha | 1 |
| Ket | 23:03:09 | Ari | Bharani | 3 |

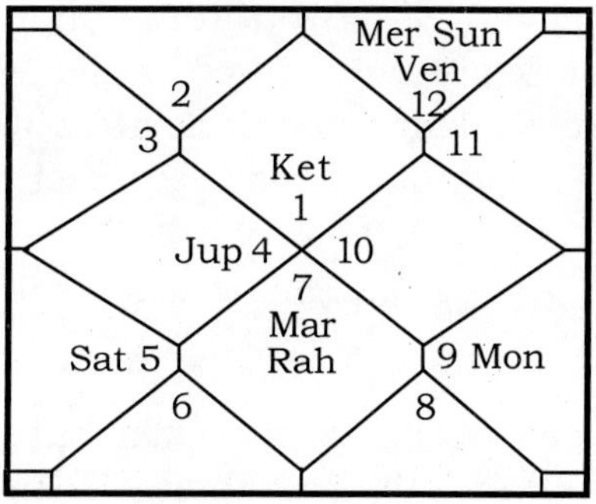


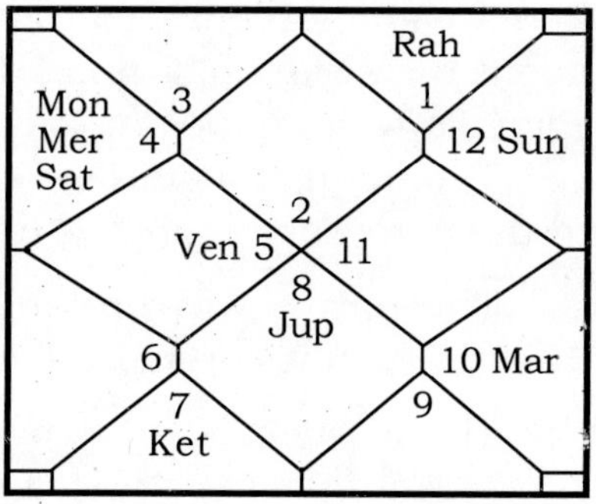


Balance of Vimsottari Dasa of **Ket 1Y 5M 3D**

This is the horoscope of a very successful and fortunate engineer, who rose up to the position of the Chairman of Uttar Pradesh Rajya Vidyut Parishad and at present he is employed by the Govt. of United States of America at a very important post. Now, let us examine his birth chart regarding the nature of occupation.

- Mars is the owner of the ascendant and also aspects that. Mars obtains the *navamsa* of Saturn, under mutual aspect with Saturn and Mercury in the *navamsa* chart
- Mars aspects tenth house and lord of tenth house Saturn aspects Mars, the *lagna* lord. Jupiter, the 9th lord, aspects the 10th house.
- Eighth house is owned by Mars and is aspected by Jupiter. Lord of eighth, Mars also receives the aspects of Saturn, the lord of tenth house, and obtains the *navamsa* of exaltation.
- Lords of 6th and 10th, Mercury and Saturn, obtain the same *navamsa* of Moon, in association with luminary Moon. The 6th lord Mercury falls in the constellation of 9th lord Jupiter.
- *Karaka* planet Mercury receives the beneficial aspects of exalted Jupiter. Eighth and tenth houses are also benefited by receiving the aspect of Jupiter.

There are many *Rajyogas* in this birth chart. Though, here we are not much concerned with *Yogas* but to mention about the *sloka* no. 2 and 10 of Chapter No. IV of *Bhavarth Ratnakar* will not be out of context, which are translated by Dr. B. V. Raman as under. These combinations are present in the horoscope of the native.

The native will undoubtedly be extremely happy if Jupiter occupies or aspects fourth house / / "2" / /.

The learned in astrology say that a person will have *Bhagyavardhan Yoga* if lord of 4th and 9th interchange their houses. / / "10" / /

Again in Chapter VIII on page no. 137 of *Bhavartha Ratnakar* by Dr. B.V. Raman, it is mentioned that the person will be fortunate in respect of that *Bhava* whose *Karaka* is substituted in the 12th from ascendant. / / "6" / /

Lord of the tenth house in fifth, lord of the 4th in 9th and lord of ninth in the fourth house, and aspect of *lagna* lord over 10th & *lagna* are quite fortunate *yogas*. So, merely by luck he could reach this height and he is the only chairman of U.P.S.E.B. who had spotless career.

*Illustration : 4.10* (**JNM**) *Horoscope No.: 62*

Date of birth : 29.07.1907 Time of birth : 03:18:00 hrs

Place of birth : Lucknow Lat 26:50:00 N Long 80:54:00E

Ayanamsa : 22:33:43 Sidereal Time : 23:33:14

| Pln | Degree | Rasi | Nakshatra | Pad |
|---|---|---|---|---|
| Asc | 12:52:08 | Gem | Ardra | 2 |
| Sun | 12:04:26 | Can | Pushya | 3 |
| Mon | 2:55:57 | Pis | P Bhadrapad | 4 |
| Mar (R) | 15:17:15 | Sag | Purvasadha | 1 |
| Mer (R/C) | 5:58:49 | Can | Pushya | 1 |
| Jup (C) | 2:50:59 | Can | Punarvasu | 4 |
| Ven | 28:58:52 | Gem | Punarvasu | 3 |

| | | | | |
|---|---|---|---|---|
| Sat (R) | 4:35:40 | Pis | U Bhadrapad | 1 |
| Rah (R/C) | 0:50:33 | Can | Punarvasu | 4 |
| Ket (R) | 0:50:33 | Cap | Uttarasadha | 2 |

**Lagna Chart** **Navamsa Chart**

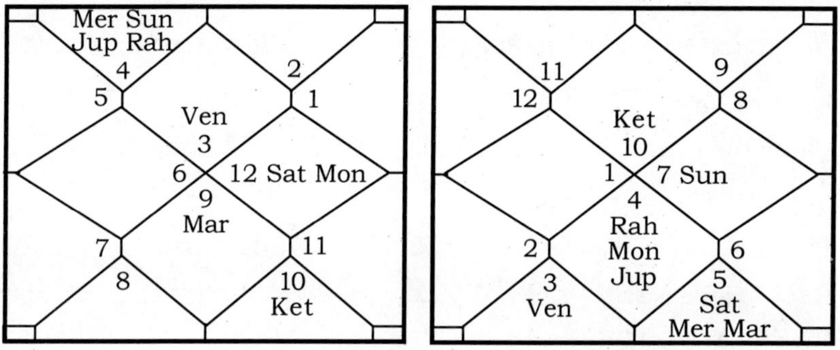


Balance of Vimsottari Dasa of **Jup 0Y 5M 23D**

This chart pertains to a chief engineer of the Irrigation Department of U.P. He was the most renowned Chief Engineer of his time. Let us see the professional side of this horoscope.

- Mars aspects the *lagna* and lord of *lagna* Mercury. The rising ascendant is Gemini, which is owned by Mercury. Therefore, the *lagna* has influences of Mars and Mercury.
- Saturn is placed in the tenth house. Mars aspects tenth house, lord of tenth house, Jupiter, and the planets placed in tenth house, Saturn and Moon.
- Eighth house is ruled by Saturn and is aspected by so many planets including Mercury and Jupiter. Mars aspects lord of eighth house Saturn.
- The 8th & 9th lord Saturn obtains the *navamsa* of Sun, in conjunction with Mars and Mercury.
- The 6th lord Mars aspects the 10th house and its lord Jupiter. The 10th lord Jupiter conjoins with Sun, while another luminary Moon occupies the 10th house. This combination ensures govt. service.

Thus, all the three houses are influenced by Mars, Saturn and Mercury. Jupiter aspects 8th and 10th and conjoins with *lagna* lord, therefore the native had a very smooth professional career. He was the Chief Engineer at that time when there used to be one Chief Engineer in a department.

*Illustration : 4.11* **(GPS)** *Horoscope No.: 63*

Date of birth : 27.12.1927 Time of birth : 22:10:00 hrs

Place of birth : Varanasi Lat 26:50:00 N Long 80:54:00E

Ayanamsa : 22:50:48 Sidereal Time : 4:24:17

| **Pln** | **Degree** | **Rasi** | **Nakshatra** | **Pad** |
|---|---|---|---|---|
| Asc | 15:50:39 | Leo | P Phalguni | 1 |
| Sun | 12:05:40 | Sag | Moola | 4 |
| Mon | 24:04:12 | Cap | Dhanishtha | 1 |
| Mar | 20:52:04 | Sco | Jyestha | 2 |
| Mer (C) | 4:59:35 | Sag | Moola | 2 |
| Jup | 3:08:26 | Pis | P Bhadrapad | 4 |
| Ven | 28:34:43 | Lib | Visakha | 3 |
| Sat | 20:10:08 | Sco | Jyestha | 2 |
| Rah (R) | 25:47:16 | Tau | Mrigsira | 1 |
| Ket (R) | 25:47:16 | Sco | Jyestha | 3 |

**Lagna Chart**

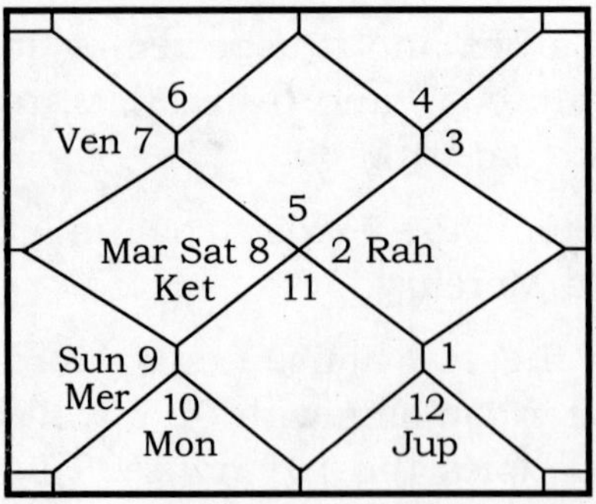


**Navamsa Chart**

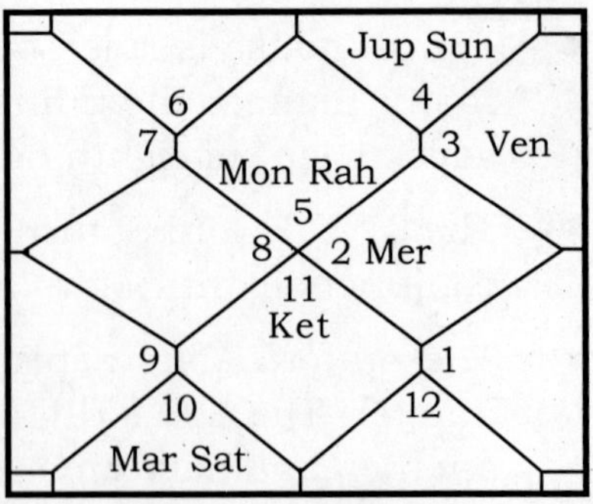


Balance of Vimsottari Dasa of **Mar 6Y 7M 10D**

This horoscope belongs to an additional Chief Engineer.

- The ascendant is Leo and the lord of the ascendant is Sun, a luminary, who joins Mercury in the 5th house. The ascendant is aspected by Saturn.
- The 6th lord Saturn aspects the 10th house and luminary Moon occupies the 6th house. These two points indicate the govt. service.
- Both, Saturn and Mars, aspect the 10th house and receive the aspect of the 8th & the 5th lord Jupiter.
- Jupiter occupies eighth house as an owner of the 8th house.
- Let us also see the position of *navamsa* and constellation. The lord of the tenth house, Venus, acquires *navamsa* of Mercury.
- Jupiter falls in its own constellation and obtains the *navamsa* of its exaltation, in conjunction with ascendant lord Sun.
- Mars and Saturn, both, fall in the constellation of Mercury and gain *navamsa* of Saturn.

Thus, in case of any confusion, *navamsa* and constellations may confirm the position.

*Illustration : 4.12* **(VPK)** *Horoscope No.: 64*

Date of birth : 29.02.1936 Time of birth : 02:05:00 hrs
Place of birth : Hoshiarpur Lat 31:30:00 N Long 75:59:00E
Ayanamsa : 22:58:13 Sidereal Time : 12:09:33

| **Pln** | **Degree** | **Rasi** | **Nakshatra** | **Pad** |
|---|---|---|---|---|
| Asc | 25:24:06 | Sco | Jyestha | 3 |
| Sun | 16:07:51 | Aqu | Satabhisha | 3 |
| Mon | 9:22:05 | Tau | Krittika | 4 |
| Mar | 12:09:21 | Pis | U Bhadrapad | 3 |
| Mer | 19:25:27 | Cap | Sravna | 3 |
| Jup | 28:51:13 | Sco | Jyestha | 4 |
| Ven | 15:13:10 | Cap | Sravna | 2 |

| Sat (C) | 19:23:33 | Aqu | Satabhisha | 4 |
|---|---|---|---|---|
| Rah (R) | 17:54:24 | Sag | Purvasadha | 2 |
| Ket (R) | 17:54:24 | Gem | Ardra | 4 |

**Lagna Chart**

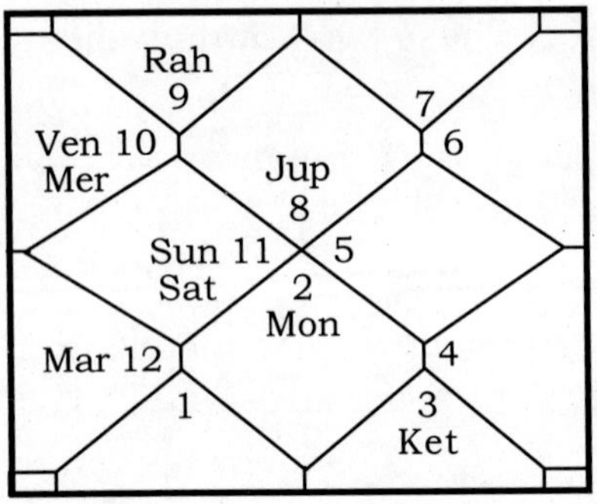


**Navamsa Chart**

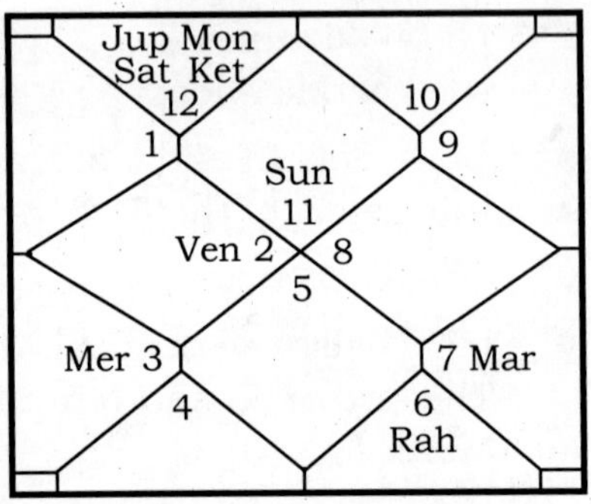


Balance of Vimsottari Dasa of **Sun 0Y 3M 12D**

The native is very gentle and helpful individual who has been in our close acquaintance for over three decades. He retired as a chief engineer.

- Ascendant is ruled by Mars and lord of *lagna* is aspected by Jupiter. Jupiter occupies ascendant and Saturn & 9th lord Moon aspect the ascendant & Jupiter placed therein. Mars falls in the constellation of Saturn.
- Lord of tenth house that is Sun, aspects the tenth house and he is in close proximity with Saturn, who also aspects tenth and conjoins with the lord of tenth house. The 10th lord Sun acquires the *vargottam navamsa* of Saturn. Both, Sun & Saturn, fall in the constellation of Rahu (The native was an electrical engineer).
- Mercury is lord of the 8th house. Mars aspects the 8th house. The 8th lord falls in the constellation of 9th lord Moon and obtains the *navamsa* of Mercury.

Thus, Mars, Saturn and Jupiter influence *lagna*; Saturn and Sun influence tenth and Mercury influences eighth house.

*Illustration : 4.13* (**SKM**) *Horoscope No.: 65*

Date of birth : 14.02.1925 Time of birth : 23:30:00 hrs
Place of birth : Allahabad Lat 25:27:00 N Long 81:50:00E
Ayanamsa : 22:48:28 Sidereal Time : 9:04:17

| Pln | Degree | Rasi | Nakshatra | Pad |
|---|---|---|---|---|
| Asc | 18:16:59 | Lib | Svati | 4 |
| Sun | 2:44:46 | Aqu | Dhanishtha | 3 |
| Mon | 11:43:22 | Lib | Svati | 2 |
| Mar | 13:10:44 | Ari | Asvini | 4 |
| Mer | 18:41:35 | Cap | Sravna | 3 |
| Jup | 20:04:10 | Sag | Purvasadha | 3 |
| Ven | 15:39:17 | Cap | Sravna | 2 |
| Sat | 21:27:28 | Lib | Visakha | 1 |
| Rah (R) | 20:47:34 | Can | Aslesha | 2 |
| Ket (R/C) | 20:47:34 | Cap | Sravna | 4 |

**Lagna Chart**

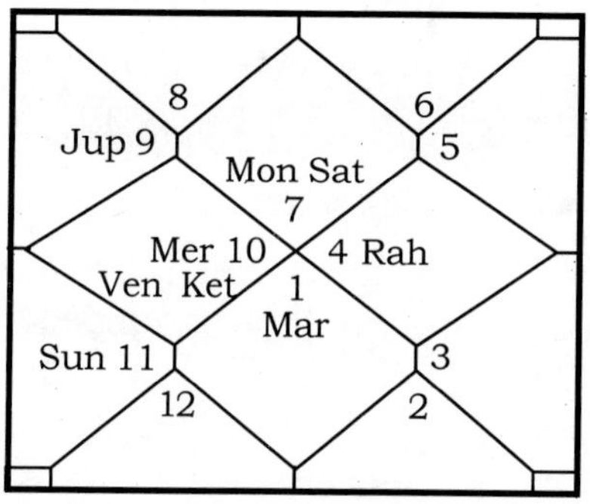


**Navamsa Chart**

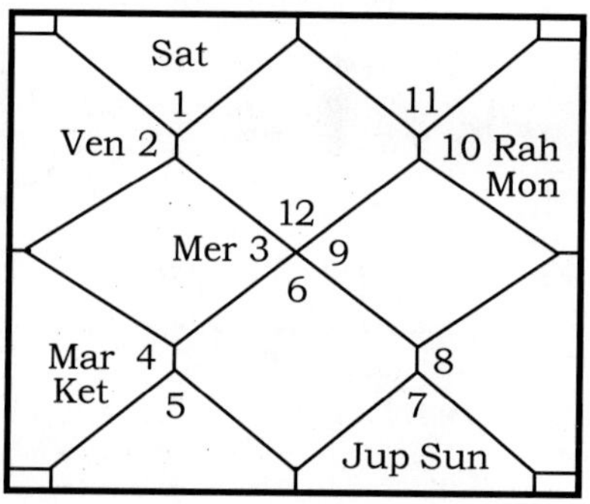


Balance of Vimsottari Dasa of **Rah 11Y 2M 2D**

The native was a Chief Engineer in U.P. Housing and Development Board. He was born in a very ordinary family.

- The ascendant is Libra. Exalted Saturn is placed in the ascendant and Mars aspects both, ascendant and Saturn. Ascendant lord Venus conjoins with Mercury in the sign owned by Saturn.

- Lord of tenth house, Moon, joins the *lagna* in association with Saturn and tenth house itself is receiving full aspects of Mars, Saturn and Mercury. Moon acquires the *navamsa* of Saturn while Mars obtains the *navamsa* of Moon.
- Eighth lord Venus is placed in the sign of Saturn and is associated with Mercury. Both aspect the 10th house. Venus falls in the constellation of 10th lord Moon.
- The 5th lord is Saturn, who aspects the 10th house. Saturn gains the *navamsa* of Mars.
- The 6th lord Jupiter occupies own sign, falls in the constellation of ascendant lord Venus and also obtains the *navamsa* of Venus, in conjunction with Sun.

Thus, Saturn and Mercury influence *lagna*, tenth and eighth house. This indicates engineering Career and also the govt. service.

*Illustration : 4.14* **(LDJ)** *Horoscope No.: 66*

Date of birth : 11.03.1932 Time of birth : 04:03:00 hrs
Place of birth : Hathras Lat 27:36:00 N Long 78:02:00E
Ayanamsa : 22:54:37 Sidereal Time : 14:58:39

| Pln | Degree | Rasi | Nakshatra | Pad |
|---|---|---|---|---|
| Asc | 8:38:58 | Cap | Uttarasadha | 4 |
| Sun | 27:14:39 | Aqu | P Bhadrapad | 3 |
| Mon | 6:42:12 | Ari | Asvini | 3 |
| Mar (C) | 18:47:27 | Aqu | Satabhisha | 4 |
| Mer (C) | 9:09:21 | Pis | U Bhadrapad | 2 |
| Jup (R) | 20:57:54 | Can | Aslesha | 2 |
| Ven | 9:13:31 | Ari | Asvini | 3 |
| Sat | 8:39:04 | Cap | Uttarasadha | 4 |
| Rah (C) | 3:09:50 | Pis | P Bhadrapad | 4 |
| Ket | 3:09:50 | Vir | U Phalguni | 2 |

**Lagna Chart**

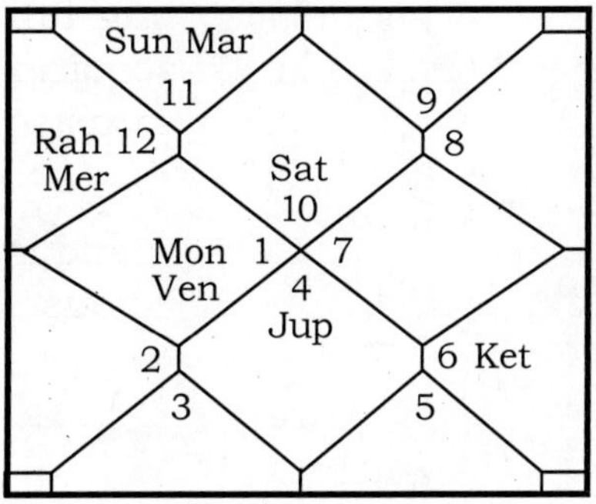


**Navamsa Chart**

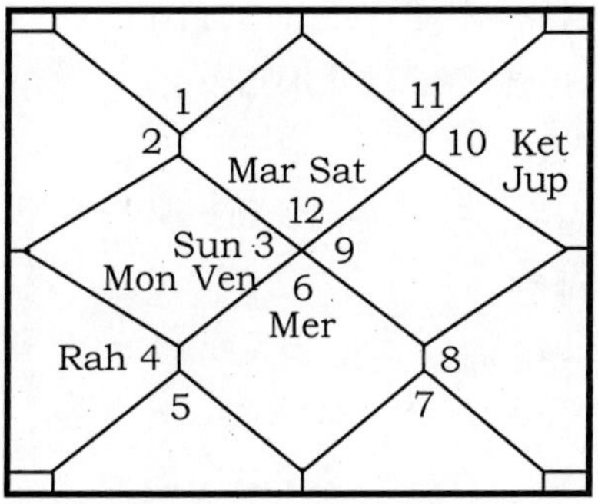


Balance of Vimsottari Dasa of **Ket 3Y 5M 23D**

The person was a Chief Engineer in the Hydel Department.

- The native was born in Aquarius ascendant. Lord of the ascendant occupies ascendant itself and aspects the $10^{th}$ house. Saturn and Jupiter mutually aspect each other. Saturn obtains the *navamsa* of Jupiter in association with Mars.
- Saturn aspects the tenth house, and the lord of $5^{th}$ & $10^{th}$ house Venus also aspects the tenth house. Venus obtains the *navamsa* of $6^{th}$ lord Mercury in association with luminaries.
- The $6^{th}$ & $9^{th}$ lord Mercury obtains own *navamsa* and Saturn's constellation.
- Lord of eighth house, Sun, is associated with Mars, in Saturn's sign and both aspect eighth house.

All these factors show engineering career and govt. service.

*Illustration : 4.15* (**KNS**) *Horoscope No.: 67*

Date of birth : 17.07.1918 Time of birth : 05:30:00 hrs
Place of birth : Lucknow Lat 26:50:00 N Long 80:54:00E
Ayanamsa : 22:43:27 Sidereal Time : 0:59:36

| Pln | Degree | Rasi | Nakshatra | Pad |
|---|---|---|---|---|
| Asc | 1:37:14 | Can | Punarvasu | 4 |
| Sun | 0:52:45 | Can | Punarvasu | 4 |
| Mon | 8:55:17 | Lib | Svati | 1 |
| Mar | 19:00:44 | Vir | Hasta | 3 |
| Mer | 20:53:36 | Can | Aslesha | 2 |
| Jup | 8:06:21 | Gem | Ardra | 1 |
| Ven | 28:01:58 | Tau | Mrigsira | 2 |
| Sat | 22:07:08 | Can | Aslesha | 2 |
| Rah | 29:10:09 | Sco | Jyestha | 4 |
| Ket | 29:10:09 | Tau | Mrigsira | 2 |

**Lagna Chart**

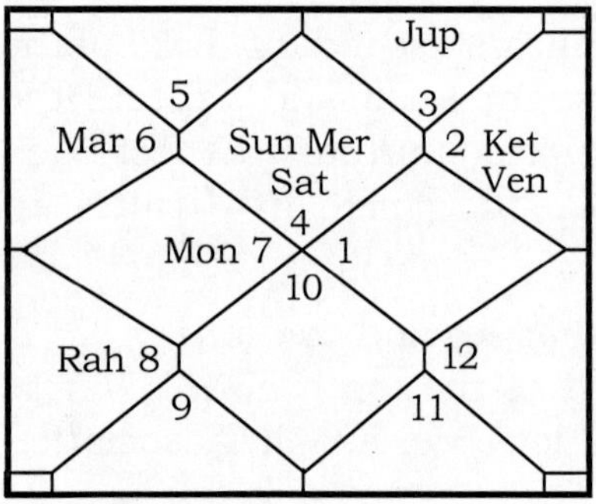


**Navamsa Chart**

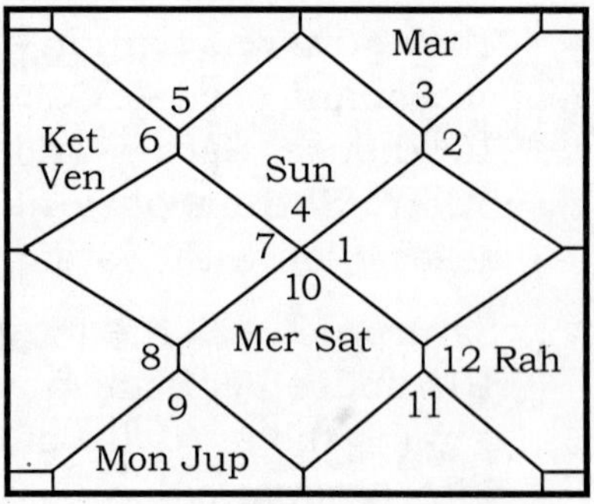


Balance of Vimsottari Dasa of **Rah 14Y 11M 14D**

This is also the horoscope of an engineer who worked as Chief Engineer for a considerably long period.

- Sun, Saturn and Mercury are placed in the ascendant and lord of the ascendant, Moon, gets aspect of Jupiter. Moon also acquires the *navamsa* of Jupiter, in association with Jupiter, under aspect of Mars (in the *navamsa*).
- Lord of fifth & tenth house, Mars, is placed in the 3rd house, in the sign of Mercury, from where Mars aspects the 10th house of its own, as well as the 9th house and the 6th. Tenth house also gets the aspect of Saturn.

Fifth & tenth lord Mars also obtains the *navamsa* of Mercury.

- The 8th lord Saturn joins the *lagna* in conjunction with Sun & Mercury, aspects the tenth house and obtains his own *navamsa* in association with Mercury. Saturn also falls in the constellation of Mercury.

It is seen here that there is an effect of Saturn and Mercury on *lagna* and eighth house, and Mars, Saturn and Mercury on the tenth, which reveals that he would have a successful career but on account of weak lord of tenth (Mars joins the inimical sign & *navamsa*, without any beneficial aspect) his career was not smooth.

*Illustration : 4.16* (**PNG**) *Horoscope No.: 68*

Date of birth : 04.06.1925 Time of birth : 01:30:00 hrs

Place of birth : Sitapur Lat 25:11:00 N Long 80:52:00E

Ayanamsa : 22:48:41 Sidereal Time : 18:10:29

| **Pln** | **Degree** | **Rasi** | **Nakshatra** | **Pad** |
|---|---|---|---|---|
| Asc | 10:46:41 | Pis | U Bhadrapad | 3 |
| Sun | 19:52:43 | Tau | Rohini | 3 |
| Mon | 8:07:58 | Lib | Svati | 1 |
| Mar | 22:57:25 | Gem | Punarvasu | 1 |
| Mer | 2:03:05 | Tau | Krittika | 2 |
| Jup (R) | 28:48:06 | Sag | Uttarasadha | 1 |
| Ven | 0:44:15 | Gem | Mrigsira | 3 |
| Sat (R) | 15:56:00 | Lib | Svati | 3 |
| Rah (R) | 13:16:21 | Can | Pushya | 3 |
| Ket (R) | 13:16:21 | Cap | Sravna | 1 |

**Lagna Chart**

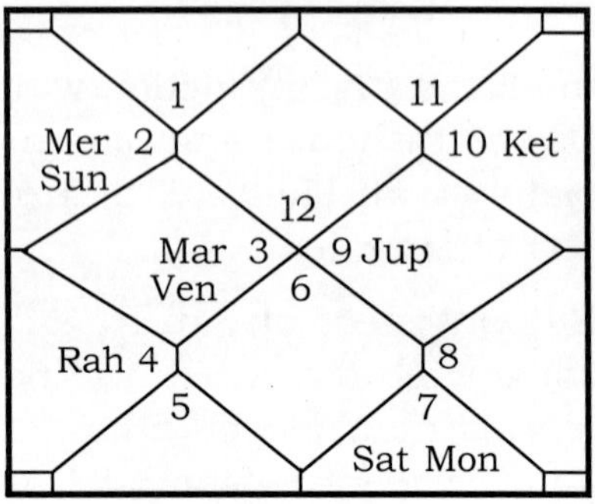


**Navamsa Chart**

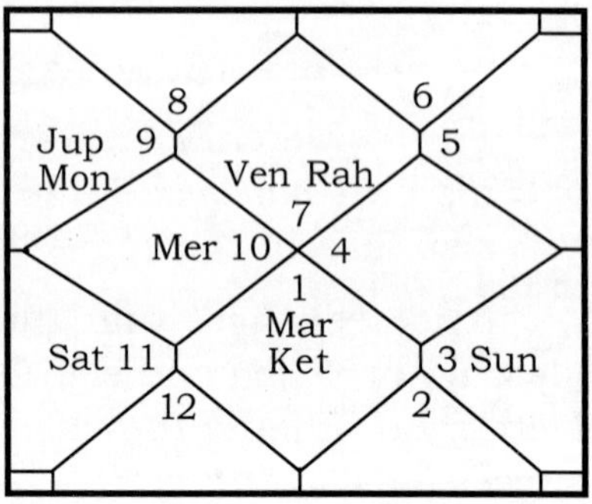


Balance of Vimsottari Dasa of **Rah 16Y 0M 7D**

He was a superintending engineer.

The native was born in Pisces ascendant. The lord of the $10^{th}$ & ascendant, Jupiter, occupies the $10^{th}$ house, falls in the constellation of $6^{th}$ lord Sun and obtains own *navamsa* i.e. is *vargottam.*

Both, Mars and Saturn, aspect the tenth house, and its lord thereof.

The $9^{th}$ lord Mars occupies Gemini, which is a sign of Mercury and falls in the constellation of $10^{th}$ lord Jupiter.

The $8^{th}$ lord Venus also occupies the sign of Mercury, in conjunction with Mars. Venus also falls in the constellation of Mars.

The $6^{th}$ house is aspected by $10^{th}$ lord Jupiter. Jupiter falls in the constellation of Sun, thus confirming the govt. service.

Thus, we have seen in all the horoscopes above that Mars, Saturn and Mercury play important roles in determining an engineering occupation. The houses which are to be judged along with the influences of these planets are ascendant, tenth and eighth. These houses must be connected with Mars, Mercury or Saturn, either by placement or ownership or aspect or conjunction. If these influences will be strong and afflictions less, one will be a more successful engineer. If indications of these planets are feeble in regard to $1^{st}$, $8^{th}$ and $10^{th}$ houses, with other afflictions in the horoscope, the native would become an engineer but will not rise very high in his career. He may become a Junior Engineer or Sub-Engineer in the beginning and may or may not be promoted thereafter, depending on the other factors of his horoscope.

However, Mars and Mercury are more prominent in Mechanical Engineers' horoscope, while Saturn and Mars are stronger in the horoscope of Civil Engineers. Saturn, Mars and Mercury have almost equal roles in the horoscope of Electrical Engineers.

Venus is found to be connected with other planetary indications in the horoscope of Architects or Design Engineers. Jupiter also plays an important role, if its vibrations are received by Mars, Mercury or Saturn and $1^{st}$, $8^{th}$ and $10^{th}$ house. Jupiter indicates science. Engineering is also a science of technology; therefore Jupiter's position in reference to above, strengthens planetary influences already present.

One should be quite honest and careful in judgement of vocation and in case of any doubt or confusion *navamsa* chart or constellations may be referred for further confirmation of the occupation which the native will undertake. Accurate prediction of one's profession can help him to take up an occupation which suits him best and ensures professional fulfillment and satisfaction.

## Chapter-5

# Teaching : An Honourable Profession

Out of so many occupations, teaching is one of the most honorable one. A teacher commands much respect in the society. Good teachers are remembered by their students throughout their life for their growth due to the strong foundation made by the teachers. A teacher on the other hand also has enormous responsibility, substantial onus of improving & imparting the knowledge to his students and carving out their future, as best as possible.

Teacher ought to have, in addition to good knowledge, an aptitude for it. While studying number of horoscopes for ferreting out the indications for the profession of teaching, we found that Jupiter and Mercury, planets known for intelligence and knowledge, should have good influence over the triangles. Influence of these planets over the 10$^{th}$ or the ascendant would be further better.

Let us analyze some birth charts:

*Illustration : 5.1* (**RM**) *Horoscope No.: 69*

Date of birth : 28.03.1968 Time of birth : 01:48:00 hrs

Place of birth : Lucknow Lat 26:50:00 N Long 80:54:00E

Ayanamsa : 23:24:42 Sidereal Time : 14:02:53

| **Pln** | **Degree** | **Rasi** | **Nakshatra** | **Pad** |
|---|---|---|---|---|
| Asc | 23:52:07 | Sag | Purvasadha | 4 |
| Sun | 13:48:45 | Pis | U Bhadrapad | 4 |
| Mon | 1:18:23 | Pis | P Bhadrapad | 4 |
| Mar | 6:28:57 | Ari | Asvini | 2 |
| Mer | 20:15:48 | Aqu | P Bhadrapad | 1 |

| | | | | |
|---|---|---|---|---|
| Jup (R) | 3:23:08 | Leo | Magha | 2 |
| Ven | 21:43:32 | Aqu | P Bhadrapad | 1 |
| Sat (C) | 20:54:40 | Pis | Revati | 2 |
| Rah (R/C) | 25:09:43 | Pis | Revati | 3 |
| Ket (R) | 25:09:43 | Vir | Chitra | 1 |

**Lagna Chart**

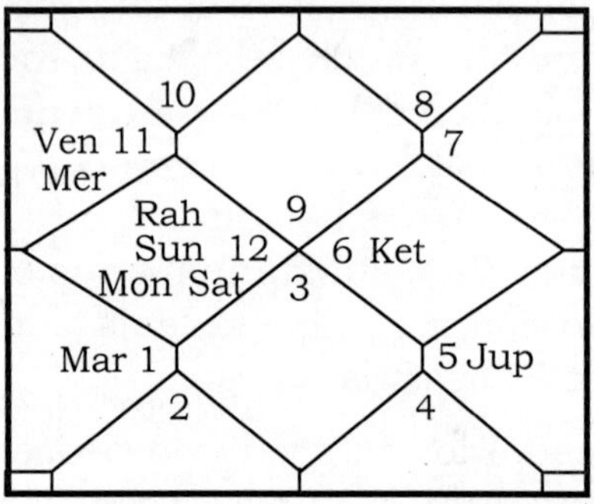


**Navamsa Chart**

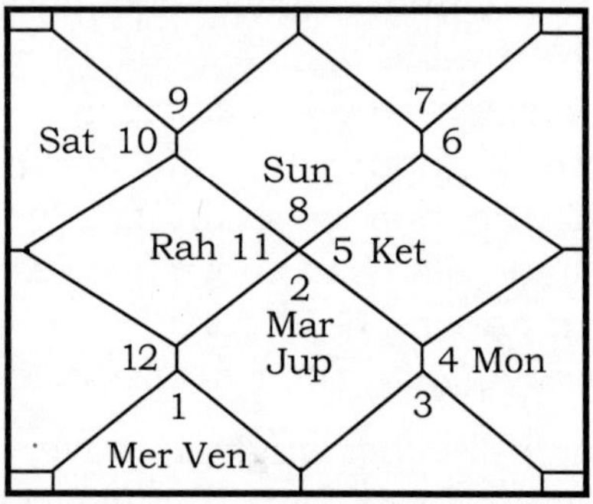


Balance of Vimsottari Dasa of **Jup 2Y 5M 5D**

The native has the honour of his name being included in the Guinness Book of World Records as he has obtained 18 professional degrees with all outstanding qualifications and that too within a record period of only three and a half year. He is teaching in Indian Institute of Management for last many years. Following planetary combinations are present in his birth chart, which are important to make him a professor in IIM.

The lord of the 10th house, Mercury, and the lord of the ascendant, Jupiter have a mutual aspect with each other, corresponding to the 3rd and the 9th house.

Moon falls in the fourth house. The fourth house governs qualification and educational degrees, certificates of acquired education. Moon joins the fourth house, identical to Jupiterian sign Pisces. Moon falls in *Poorvabhadrapad* constellation, which is also ruled by Jupiter. This clearly signifies that the native has an exceptional interest in the study of various branches of knowledge and acquiring educational qualifications as much as possible.

Placement of Mars in the 5th house provides strong determination, mental inclination and aptitude. Here, Mars owns and occupies the 5th house and receives the most benefic and extremely auspicious aspect of the ascendant and 4th lord Jupiter, who is tenanted in the 9th house. Thus, 5th and ascendant lords, Mars and Jupiter, are triangular from each other.

Three benefics Jupiter, Mercury and Venus are very well placed in the 9th and the 3rd house and have mutual aspect on each other. The 10th lord Mercury and the 6th lord Venus are closely conjoined in the 3rd house and fall in Jupiter's constellation *Poorva Bhadrapada.* This shows profession of a teacher who acquired extremely high educational qualifications.

The 4th house rules over the educational qualifications, certificates and degree etc. Both the luminaries, the Sun and Moon, aspect the 10th house and are associated with Rahu and Saturn in the fourth house in Jupiter's sign Pisces. Moreover, Saturn and Rahu fall in the constellation of *Revati,* the constellation of Mercury, who is the *Karaka* for Knowledge, wisdom and sharpness of mind etc.

Both Karmic control planets, Jupiter and Mercury, occupy 9th and 3rd house and they are *Samsaptak* from each other.

Ketu is posited in the 10th house in Virgo sign, ruled by Mercury. Rahu is placed in the 4th house in Pisces, ruled by Jupiter. The second house should also be taken into consideration while judging the profession.

In this chart, lord of the second house, Saturn, falls in the 4th house in Jupiter's sign Pisces and Mercury's *nakshatra Revati.* Saturn obtains *vargottam navamsa* and its aspect on the 6th and the 10th house has compelled the native to earn his livelihood through service only.

Conjunction of the 6th lord Venus with the 10th lord Mercury, with the favourable aspect of the ascendant lord Jupiter, has further strengthened the livelihood through service. It means that if the native takes up business as his main vocation, he will receive serious setbacks due to heavy losses.

*Illustration : 5.2* **(BKM)** *Horoscope No.: 70*

Date of birth : 06.11.1951 Time of birth : 19:59:00 hrs

Place of birth : Farrukhabad Lat 27:23:00 N Long 79:35:00E

Ayanamsa : 23:11:09 Sidereal Time : 22:47:19

| **Pln** | **Degree** | **Rasi** | **Nakshatra** | **Pad** |
|---|---|---|---|---|
| Asc | 2:00:06 | Gem | Mrigsira | 3 |
| Sun | 20:1:03 | Lib | Visakha | 1 |
| Mon | 24:13:08 | Cap | Dhanishtha | 1 |
| Mar | 26:31:00 | Leo | P Phalguni | 4 |
| Mer | 4:25:51 | Sco | Anuradha | 1 |
| Jup (R) | 12:00:22 | Pis | U Bhadrapad | 3 |
| Ven | 3:46:04 | Vir | U Phalguni | 3 |
| Sat | 16:50:06 | Vir | Hasta | 3 |
| Rah (R) | 14:10:36 | Aqu | Satabhisha | 3 |
| Ket (R) | 14:10:36 | Leo | P Phalguni | 1 |

**Lagna Chart**

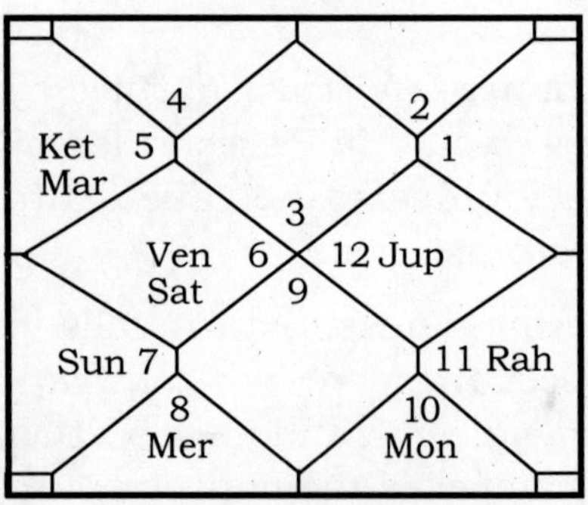


**Navamsa Chart**

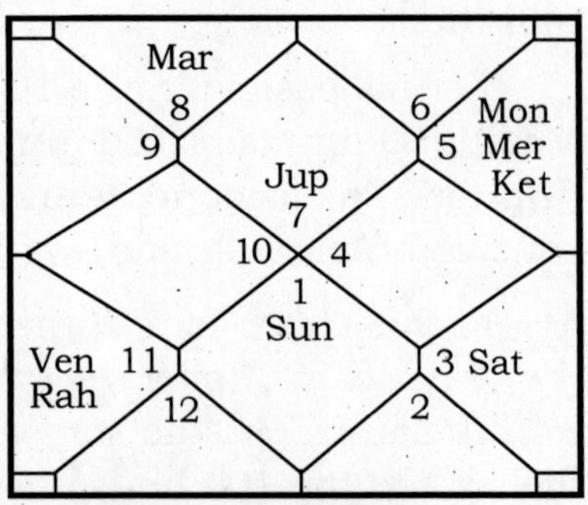


Balance of Vimsottari Dasa of **Mar 6Y 6M 12D**

The native is a very intelligent person who has been a topper of IIT during his times. He is teaching Mechanical Engineering and is Head of the department in HBTI Kanpur.

- Jupiter occupies the 10th house of its own i. e. in the sign Pisces.
- The tenth lord Jupiter falls in the constellation of Saturn, the 9th lord.
- The 9th lord Saturn aspects the tenth house and the tenth lord.
- The ascendant lord, Mercury occupies the 6th house and thus receives the aspect of Jupiter, the tenth lord, Saturn, the ninth lord and Mars, the eleventh & the sixth lord. Sixth lord Mars aspects the tenth house. This relationship between ascendant, 6th and the tenth confirms his livelihood through service.
- The fifth lord Venus occupies the sign of Mercury and is aspected by Jupiter.
- The ninth lord Saturn and the fifth lord Venus (both triangle lords) occupy the fourth house under mutual aspect of tenth lord Jupiter.
- The ninth lord Saturn obtains the *navamsa* of Mercury and tenth lord Jupiter obtains the *navamsa* of fifth lord Venus.

Thus, there is significant influence of Mercury and Jupiter over the triangles and also the tenth house, giving him the teaching profession

*Illustration : 5.3* **(CSD)** *Horoscope No.: 71*

Date of birth : 09.12.1954 Time of birth : 14:45:00 hrs

Place of birth : Rampur Lat 28:48:00 N Long 79:03:00E

Ayanamsa : 23:13:55 Sidereal Time : 19:41:31

| **Pln** | **Degree** | **Rasi** | **Nakshatra** | **Pad** |
|---|---|---|---|---|
| Asc | 11:51:07 | Ari | Asvini | 4 |
| Sun | 23:32:05 | Sco | Jyestha | 3 |

| Mon | 14:18:55 | Tau | Rohini | 2 |
|---|---|---|---|---|
| Mar | 10:22:22 | Aqu | Satabhisha | 2 |
| Mer (C) | 14:39:26 | Sco | Anuradha | 4 |
| Jup (R) | 5:53:45 | Can | Pushya | 1 |
| Ven | 21:40:18 | Lib | Visakha | 1 |
| Sat | 22:50:59 | Lib | Visakha | 1 |
| Rah (R) | 12:23:14 | Sag | Moola | 4 |
| Ket (R) | 12:23:14 | Gem | Ardra | 2 |

**Lagna Chart**

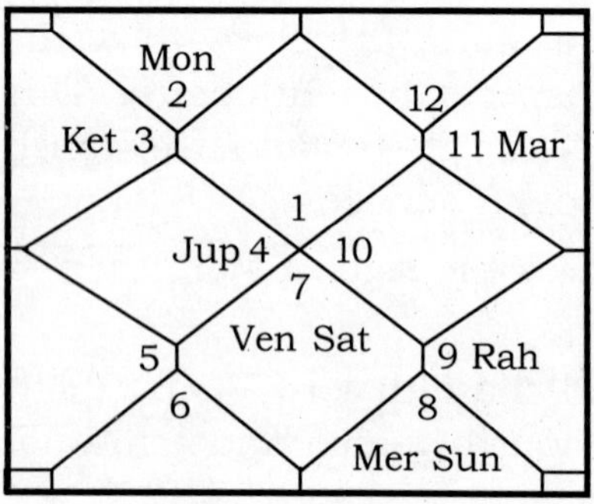


**Navamsa Chart**

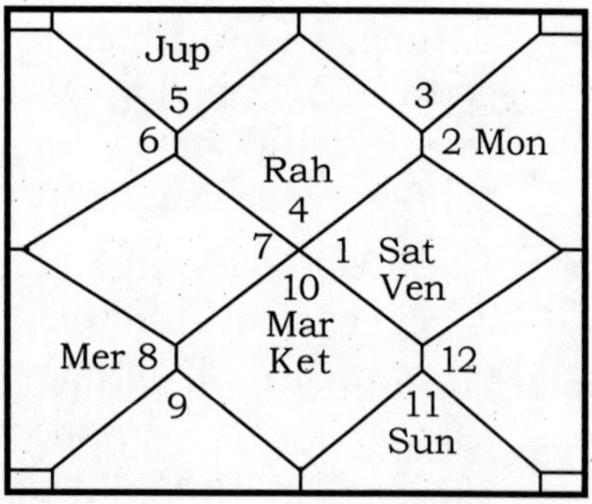


Balance of Vimsottari Dasa of **Mon 6Y 9M 4D**

The native is a professor of Geology in the University of Delhi. Let us analyze his birth chart from the point of profession.

- The tenth lord Saturn occupies the seventh house, in exaltation, with the lord of the seventh Venus. Thus, both *Sash* and *Malvya Mahapurush Rajyogas* are formed, giving the native high position, name, fame and honour.
- The ninth lord Jupiter occupies the fourth house aspecting the tenth house, and the tenth lord Saturn aspects the ninth house, as well as the ninth lord Jupiter.
- The ninth lord Jupiter falls in the constellation of tenth lord Saturn, while the tenth lord Saturn falls in the constellation of ninth lord Jupiter. Thus, there is mutual

exchange of constellations between ninth and tenth lords. This splendid relationship between the ninth and the tenth house is creating a great *Rajyoga* and has given the native immense name, fame and recognition all over the globe, in addition to abundant wealth.

- The fifth lord is associated with Mercury and the fifth lord Sun falls in the constellation *Jyestha*, ruled by Mercury.
- Mercury falls in the constellation of tenth lord Saturn.
- The fifth lord and Mercury are aspected by Jupiter.

The influence of Jupiter and Mercury over the tenth house and also the fifth house has resulted in academics and teaching to be his profession.

*Illustration : 5.4* **(PKG)** *Horoscope No.: 72*

Date of birth : 12.06.1942 Time of birth : 20:00:00 hrs

Place of birth : Lucknow Lat 26:50:00 N Long 80:54:00E

Ayanamsa : 23:03:04 Sidereal Time : 13:14:44

| **Pln** | **Degree** | **Rasi** | **Nakshatra** | **Pad** |
|---|---|---|---|---|
| Asc | 12:32:00 | Sag | Moola | 4 |
| Sun | 27:55:28 | Tau | Mrigsira | 2 |
| Mon | 14:02:12 | Tau | Rohini | 2 |
| Mar | 5:59:08 | Can | Pushya | 1 |
| Mer (R/D) | 28:19:29 | Tau | Mrigsira | 2 |
| Jup (C) | 7:26:22 | Gem | Ardra | 1 |
| Ven | 19:06:24 | Ari | Bharani | 2 |
| Sat | 11:25:13 | Tau | Rohini | 1 |
| Rah (R) | 14:33:04 | Leo | P Phalguni | 1 |
| Ket (R) | 14:33:04 | Aqu | Satabhisha | 3 |

**Lagna Chart**

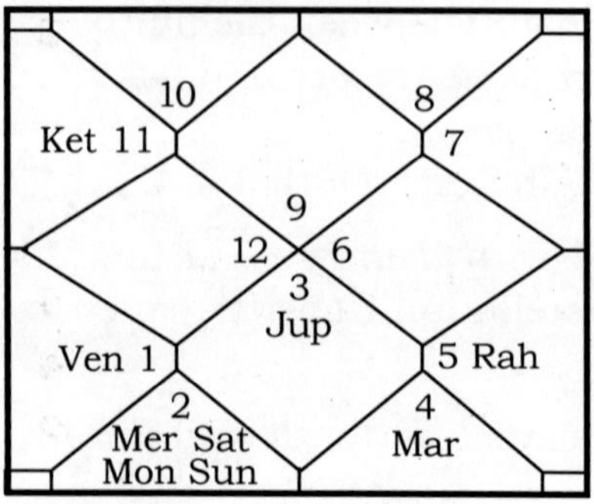


**Navamsa Chart**

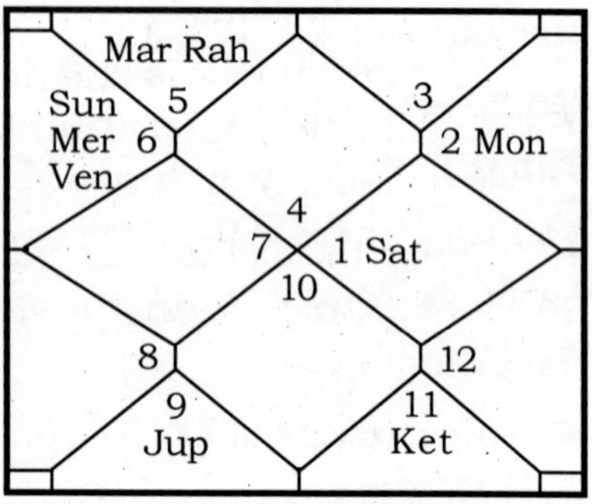


Balance of Vimsottari Dasa of **Mon 6Y 11M 20D**

The native was a professor of History in the University of Lucknow. Let us look into the planetary combinations in his birth chart.

- The tenth lord Mercury occupies the sixth house, in association with ninth lord Sun. The sixth lord Venus obtains the *navamsa* of Mercury, along with Sun and Mercury.
- Jupiter as the ascendant lord aspects the ascendant and occupies the sign of Mercury. Jupiter obtains own *navamsa.*
- Tenth lord Mercury falls in the constellation of fifth lord Mars.

Influence of Mercury and Jupiter over the ascendant, tenth and fifth strongly indicates his teaching profession.

*Illustration : 5.5* (**VSM**) *Horoscope No.: 73*

Date of birth : 23.01.1926 Time of birth : 10:20:00 hrs

Place of birth : Lucknow Lat 26:50:00 N Long 80:54:00E

Ayanamsa : 22:49:13 Sidereal Time : 18:09:06

| **Pln** | **Degree** | **Rasi** | **Nakshatra** | **Pad** |
|---|---|---|---|---|
| Asc | 10:22:01 | Pis | U Bhadrapad | 3 |
| Sun | 9:37:19 | Cap | Uttarasadha | 4 |

| | | | | |
|---|---|---|---|---|
| Mon | 6:36:21 | Tau | Krittika | 3 |
| Mar | 25:17:15 | Sco | Jyestha | 3 |
| Mer | 24:21:50 | Sag | Purvasadha | 4 |
| Jup (D) | 11:12:37 | Cap | Sravna | 1 |
| Ven (R) | 2:40:20 | Aqu | Dhanishtha | 3 |
| Sat | 1:47:31 | Sco | Visakha | 4 |
| Rah | 2:38:24 | Can | Punarvasu | 4 |
| Ket (C) | 2:38:24 | Cap | Uttarasadha | 2 |

**Lagna Chart**

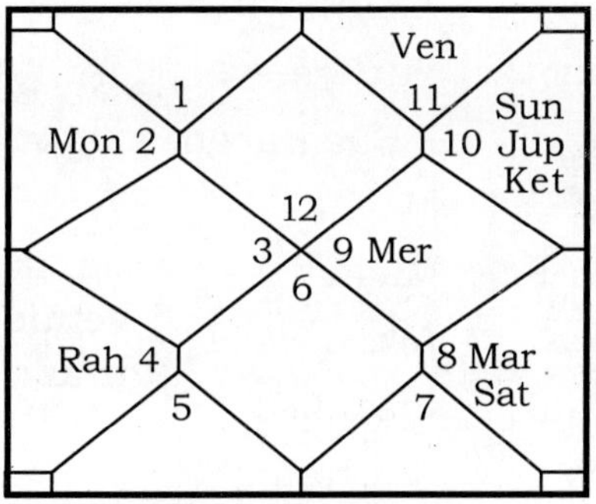


**Navamsa Chart**

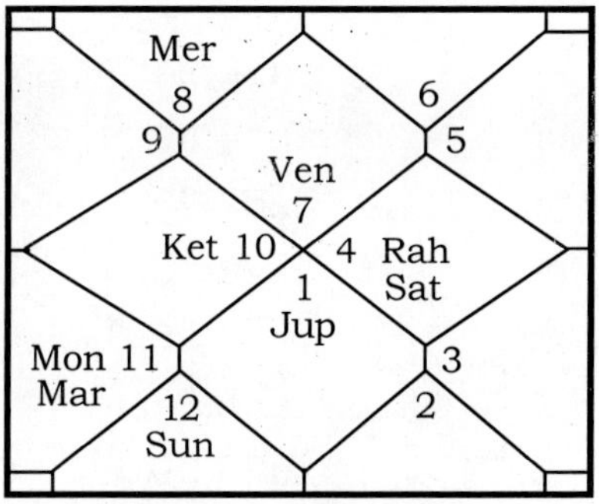


Balance of Vimsottari Dasa of **Sun 1Y 6M 10D**

The native is a scholar of Chemistry and was teaching in a University, where he was elevated to the post of Head of the department.

- Mercury is placed in the tenth house.
- Ascendant & tenth lord Jupiter occupies the eleventh house aspecting the fifth house.
- The ninth lord Mars occupies the ninth house itself.
- Saturn, placed in the ninth house, falls in the constellation of Jupiter, the tenth lord.
- Mars, placed in the ninth house obtains the *navamsa* of Mercury.
- The fifth lord Moon and the ninth lord Mars aspect each other.

- Both ninth and the tenth lords, Mars and Jupiter, aspect the fifth lord Moon.

*Illustration : 5.6* (**MM**) *Horoscope No.: 74*

Date of birth : 06.08.1956 Time of birth : 03:34:00 hrs
Place of birth : Allahabad Lat 25:27:00 N Long 81:50:00E
Ayanamsa : 23:15:19 Sidereal Time : 0:29:01

| **Pln** | **Degree** | **Rasi** | **Nakshatra** | **Pad** |
|---|---|---|---|---|
| Asc | 23:50:44 | Gem | Punarvasu | 2 |
| Sun | 20:09:43 | Can | Aslesha | 2 |
| Mon (C) | 12:12:24 | Can | Pushya | 3 |
| Mar | 0:14:50 | Pis | P Bhadrapad | 4 |
| Mer | 6:57:22 | Leo | Magha | 3 |
| Jup | 12:28:05 | Leo | Magha | 4 |
| Ven | 7:42:40 | Gem | Ardra | 1 |
| Sat | 2:56:29 | Sco | Visakha | 4 |
| Rah (R) | 12:33:39 | Sco | Anuradha | 3 |
| Ket (R) | 12:33:39 | Tau | Rohini | 1 |

**Lagna Chart**

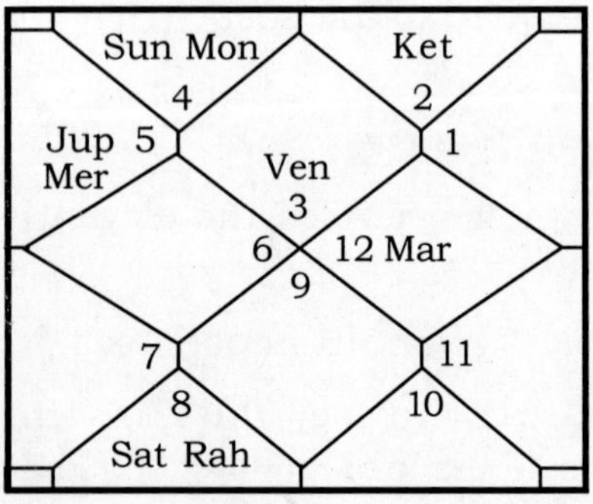


**Navamsa Chart**

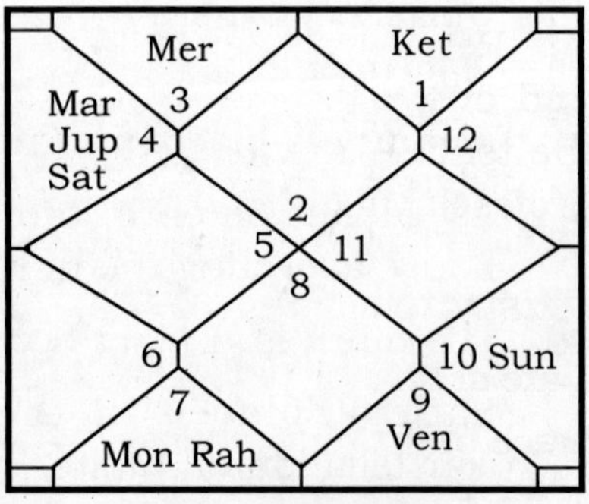


Balance of Vimsottari Dasa of **Sat 6Y 4M 8D**

This intelligent lady is a very popular teacher for the last 23 years. Let us verify our observations in her birth chart.

- The ascendant is Gemini, owned by Mercury.
- The tenth lord Jupiter combines with Mercury, also the ascendant lord, in the 3rd house, thus aspecting the ninth house. Even this combination would indicate her teaching profession.
- The sixth lord Mars occupies the tenth house indicating service.
- The ninth lord Saturn aspects the tenth lord Jupiter, while the tenth lord Jupiter aspects the ninth house and the ninth lord.
- Ninth lord Saturn falls in the constellation of tenth lord Jupiter.
- Both ninth and tenth lords, Saturn and Jupiter conjoin in *navamsa.*
- Tenth lord Jupiter is exalted in *navamsa.*
- Fifth lord Venus occupies the ascendant, in the sign of Mercury, which is aspected by Mars, placed in the tenth house in Jupiter's sign Pisces. Fifth lord obtains the *navamsa* of Jupiter.
- Occupant of the tenth house Mars falls in Jupiter's constellation.

Relationship between sixth and tenth gave her service and overwhelming influence of Jupiter and Mercury over the tenth, ascendant and triangles has made teaching her profession.

*Illustration : 5.7* (**SIHJ**) *Horoscope No.: 75*

Date of birth : 04.09.1969 Time of birth : 00:30:00 hrs

Place of birth : Bombay Lat 18:58:00 N Long 72:50:00E

Ayanamsa : 23:26:03 Sidereal Time : 22:42:16

| Pln | Degree | Rasi | Nakshatra | Pad |
|---|---|---|---|---|
| Asc | 26:25:59 | Tau | Mrigsira | 1 |
| Sun | 17:38:49 | Leo | P Phalguni | 2 |

| | | | | |
|---|---|---|---|---|
| Mon | 18:35:03 | Tau | Rohini | 3 |
| Mar | 26:26:19 | Sco | Jyestha | 3 |
| Mer | 14:40:52 | Vir | Hasta | 2 |
| Jup | 15:19:25 | Vir | Hasta | 2 |
| Ven | 13:17:32 | Can | Pushya | 3 |
| Sat (R) | 15:21:12 | Ari | Bharani | 1 |
| Rah | 27:48:16 | Aqu | P Bhadrapad | 3 |
| Ket (C) | 27:48:16 | Leo | U Phalguni | 1 |

**Lagna Chart**

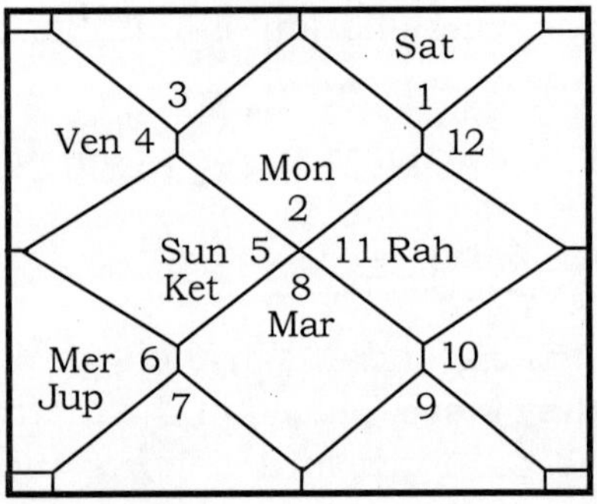


**Navamsa Chart**

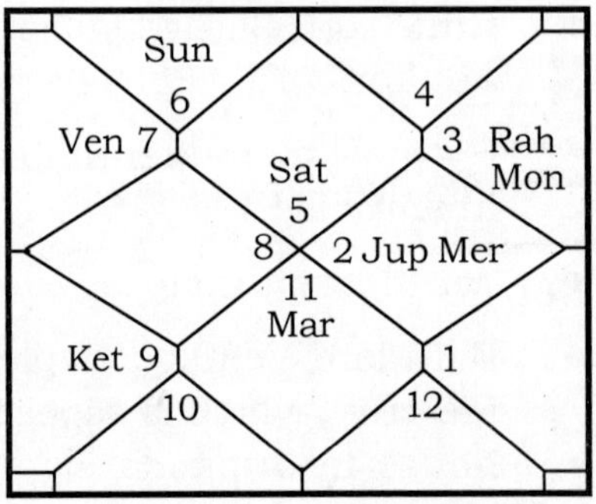


Balance of Vimsottari Dasa of **Mon 3Y 6M 22D**

This native is a teacher of a junior college. In addition to that he runs an institute of his own.

- The sixth lord Venus falls in the constellation of *yogakaraka* and ninth & tenth lord Saturn, while tenth lord Saturn falls in the constellation of 6th lord Venus.
- Mercury and Jupiter are conjoined in the fifth house, in the sign of Mercury.
- Jupiter and Mercury are conjoined in the *navamsa* as well, in the *navamsa* of ascendant lord Venus.
- Ninth & Tenth lord Saturn occupies the 12th house, from where it aspects the ninth house.
- Mars falls in constellation of Mercury and aspects the ascendant, as also the tenth house.

*Illustration : 5.8* (**SV**) *Horoscope No.: 76*

Date of birth : 10.09.1956 Time of birth : 07:54:00 hrs
Place of birth : Jaipur Lat 26:53:00 N Long 75:50:00E
Ayanamsa : 23:15:23 Sidereal Time : 06:43:43

| **Pln** | **Degree** | **Rasi** | **Nakshatra** | **Pad** |
|---|---|---|---|---|
| Asc | 16:30:06 | Vir | Hasta | 2 |
| Sun | 24:05:42 | Leo | P Phalguni | 4 |
| Mon | 2:20:16 | Sco | Visakha | 4 |
| Mar (R) | 25:06:57 | Aqu | P Bhadrapad | 2 |
| Mer | 18:19:40 | Vir | Hasta | 3 |
| Jup (C) | 20:00:21 | Leo | P Phalguni | 3 |
| Ven | 8:29:06 | Can | Pushya | 2 |
| Sat | 4:15:29 | Sco | Anuradha | 1 |
| Rah (R) | 8:40:07 | Sco | Anuradha | 2 |
| Ket (R) | 8:40:07 | Tau | Krittika | 4 |

**Lagna Chart**

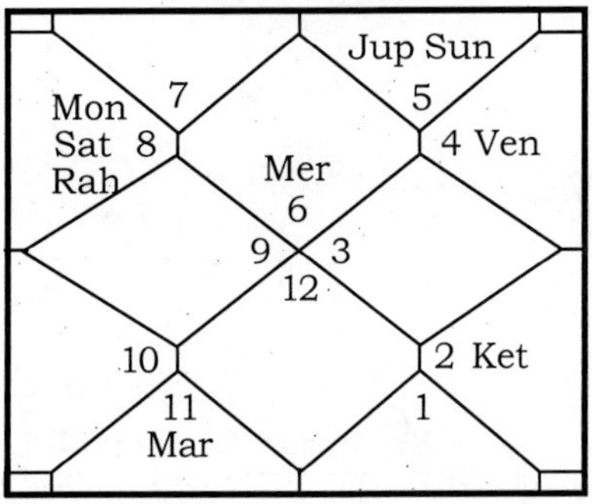


**Navamsa Chart**

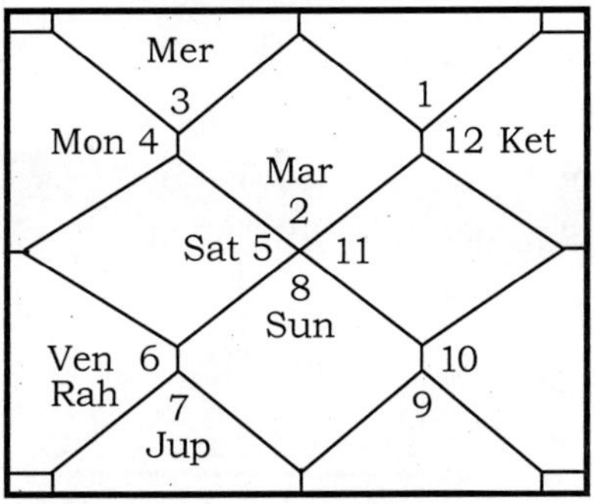


Balance of Vimsottari Dasa of **Jup 1Y 2M 10D**

This is the birth chart of a lady teacher, who is the vice principal of a Govt. Girls College in Rajasthan. The native is very intelligent and elegant, and also diligent and dexterous.

- The ascendant is Virgo, ruled by Mercury.
- Mercury also occupies the ascendant and obtains own *navamsa*.
- Ninth lord Venus obtains the *navamsa* of Mercury. Tenth

lord Mercury obtains own *navamsa* i. e. Mercury.

- The fifth and sixth lord Saturn aspects the ninth house, and also Jupiter.

The ascendant, ninth and the tenth house, all are under the influence of Mercury. Jupiter also aspects the tenth lord Mercury in *navamsa*. This all made her profession to be teaching.

*Illustration : 5.9* **(PT)** *Horoscope No.: 77*

Date of birth : 24.08.1963 Time of birth : 00:00:00 hrs
Place of birth : Lucknow Lat 26:50:00 N Long 80:54:00E
Ayanamsa : 23:20:41 Sidereal Time : 21:47:19

| **Pln** | **Degree** | **Rasi** | **Nakshatra** | **Pad** |
|---|---|---|---|---|
| Asc | 17:03:50 | Tau | Rohini | 3 |
| Sun | 6:33:21 | Leo | Magha | 2 |
| Mon | 28:04:12 | Vir | Chitra | 2 |
| Mar | 23:50:03 | Vir | Chitra | 1 |
| Mer | 3:50:46 | Vir | U Phalguni | 3 |
| Jup (R) | 25:48:26 | Pis | Revati | 3 |
| Ven (D) | 4:49:56 | Leo | Magha | 2 |
| Sat (R) | 25:37:54 | Cap | Dhanishtha | 1 |
| Rah (R) | 26:19:46 | Gem | Punarvasu | 2 |
| Ket (R) | 26:19:46 | Sag | Purvasadha | 4 |

**Lagna Chart**

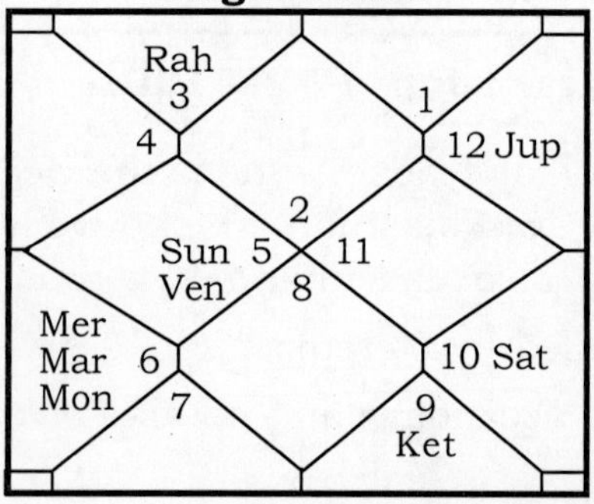


**Navamsa Chart**

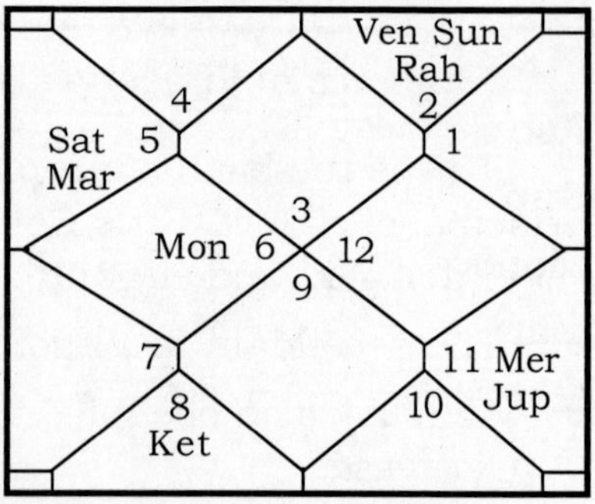


Balance of Vimsottari Dasa of **Mar 4Y 6M 4D**

This is the birth chart of a native who has music as the subject of teaching. He is working in a prominent chain of schools at Lucknow.

- Jupiter aspects the fifth house.
- Jupiter also falls in the constellation of Mercury, the fifth lord.
- The sixth lord Venus occupies the 4th house and aspects the tenth house.
- The 9th & 10th lord Saturn aspects Jupiter and the sixth house.
- Mercury is occupying its own sign in the fifth house.
- The ninth lord Saturn is placed in the ninth house itself, in its own sign.
- Mercury obtains the *navamsa* of Saturn, the tenth lord and conjoins with Jupiter in *navamsa.*

Thus, the influence of Mercury and Jupiter over the relevant houses indicates his profession of teaching. Well placed Venus in the fourth, aspecting the 10th house, made music to be his subject of study and vocation.

*Illustration : 5.10* (**ST**) *Horoscope No.: 78*

Date of birth : 24.01.1941 Time of birth : 03:35:00 hrs
Place of birth : Agra Lat 27:09:00 N Long 78:00:00E
Ayanamsa : 23:02:04 Sidereal Time : 11:28:22

| **Pln** | **Degree** | **Rasi** | **Nakshatra** | **Pad** |
|---|---|---|---|---|
| Asc | 18:31:36 | Sco | Jyestha | 1 |
| Sun | 10:30:21 | Cap | Sravna | 1 |
| Mon | 26:02:24 | Sco | Jyestha | 3 |
| Mar | 19:52:08 | Sco | Jyestha | 1 |
| Mer (C) | 18:54:17 | Cap | Sravna | 3 |
| Jup | 13:36:28 | Ari | Bharani | 1 |
| Ven | 19:29:07 | Sag | Purvasadha | 2 |

| | | | | |
|---|---|---|---|---|
| Sat | 15:03:08 | Ari | Bharani | 1 |
| Rah (R) | 10:52:49 | Vir | Hasta | 1 |
| Ket (R) | 10:52:49 | Pis | U Bhadrapad | 3 |

**Lagna Chart**

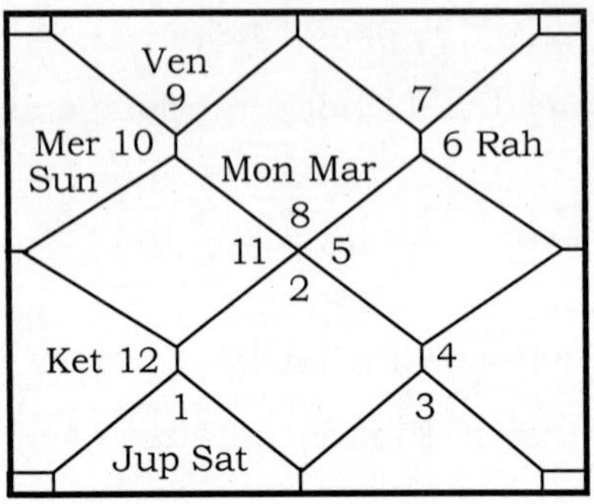


**Navamsa Chart**

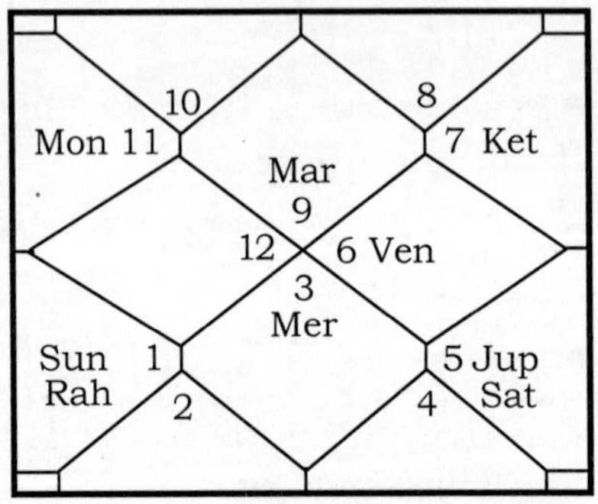


Balance of Vimsottari Dasa of **Mer 5Y 0M 17D**

The native was a teacher in a degree college from where he retired few years back.

- The fifth lord Jupiter occupies the 6th house, from where it aspects the tenth house.
- The tenth lord Sun is associated with Mercury and aspects the ninth house
- Tenth lord Sun falls in the constellation of Moon, the ninth lord, and ninth lord Moon falls in the constellation of Mercury.
- Ascendant & sixth lord Mars falls in the constellation of Mercury.
- Mercury falls in the constellation of ninth lord Moon
- Jupiter obtains the *navamsa* of tenth lord Sun.
- Jupiter aspects the 9th lord Moon in *navamsa.*
- Ninth & ascendant lords, Moon and Mars, are conjoined in the ascendant.

*Illustration : 5.11* (**DCG**) *Horoscope No.: 79*

Date of birth : 05.05.1944 Time of birth : 03:30:00 hrs
Place of birth : Mathura Lat 27:28:00 N Long 77:41:00E
Ayanamsa : 23:04:30 Sidereal Time : 17:01:13

| **Pln** | **Degree** | **Rasi** | **Nakshatra** | **Pad** |
|---|---|---|---|---|
| Asc | 16:28:49 | Aqu | Satabhisha | 3 |
| Sun | 21:10:17 | Ari | Bharani | 3 |
| Mon | 11:36:54 | Vir | Hasta | 1 |
| Mar | 26:52:43 | Gem | Punarvasu | 3 |
| Mer (R/C) | 17:42:34 | Ari | Bharani | 2 |
| Jup | 24:40:54 | Can | Aslesha | 3 |
| Ven | 6:52:10 | Ari | Asvini | 3 |
| Sat | 1:12:01 | Gem | Mrigsira | 3 |
| Rah (R) | 8:05:23 | Can | Pushya | 2 |
| Ket (R) | 8:05:23 | Cap | Uttarasadha | 4 |

**Lagna Chart**

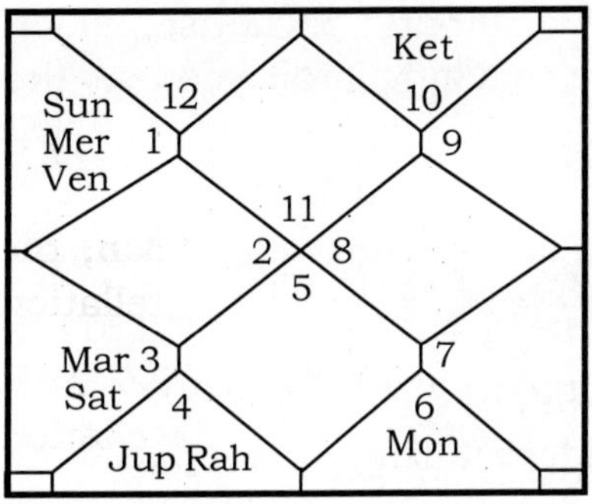


**Navamsa Chart**

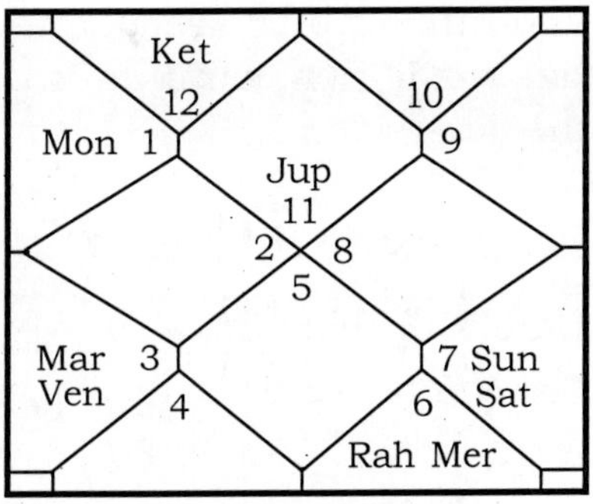


Balance of Vimsottari Dasa of **Mon 8Y 9M 14D**

The native of the birth chart is a very senior doctor of world fame. She is the first pediatric surgeon of the country. Having been associated with one or the other medical institute, all her career, she was always a teacher, in addition to being a surgeon. As professor of eminence she headed the departments and the institutes. She is presently the vice chancellor of a medical University.

Let us try to see the combinations for a teacher in her horoscope:

- The 5th house falls in Gemini whose lord is Mercury.
- Jupiter occupies the 6th house, from where it aspects the 10th house.
- Tenth lord Mars falls in the sign of Mercury, in association with ascendant lord Saturn.
- The 9th lord Venus is associated with Mercury and both aspect the 9th house.
- Ninth lord Venus obtains the *navamsa* of Mercury.
- Tenth lord Mars falls in the constellation of Jupiter and obtains the *navamsa* of Mercury. As such 9th & 10th lords, Mars and Venus, are conjoined in *navamsa*, in Mercury's sign.

We are not discussing the combinations for her medical line but have only tried to demonstrate the effect of Mercury and Jupiter over ascendant, 9th, 10th and 5th house, which has made her continue in the teaching profession in the medical side.

*Illustration : 5.12* (**KKD**) *Horoscope No.: 80*

Date of birth : 13.11.1926 Time of birth : 01:47:00 hrs
Place of birth : Sitapur Lat 27:33:00 N Long 80:40:00E
Ayanamsa : 22:49:50 Sidereal Time : 05:04:29

| **Pln** | **Degree** | **Rasi** | **Nakshatra** | **Pad** |
|---|---|---|---|---|
| Asc | 24:50:51 | Leo | P Phalguni | 4 |
| Sun | 26:52:04 | Lib | Visakha | 3 |
| Mon | 25:22:42 | Cap | Dhanishtha | 1 |
| Mar (R) | 15:34:51 | Ari | Bharani | 1 |
| Mer | 18:00:55 | Sco | Jyestha | 1 |

| | | | | |
|---|---|---|---|---|
| Jup | 25:54:53 | Cap | Dhanishtha | 1 |
| Ven (D) | 24:42:50 | Lib | Visakha | 2 |
| Sat (C) | 4:46:54 | Sco | Anuradha | 1 |
| Rah (R) | 15:33:19 | Gem | Ardra | 3 |
| Ket (R) | 15:33:19 | Sag | Purvasadha | 1 |

**Lagna Chart** **Navamsa Chart**

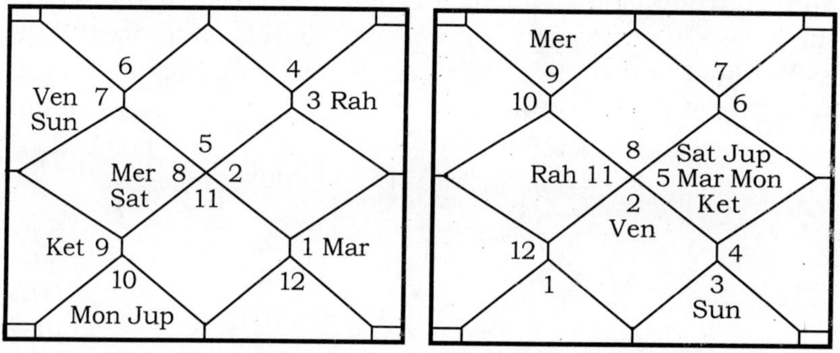


Balance of Vimsottari Dasa of **Mar 5Y 11M 3D**

This octogenarian native was professor of English in the University of Lucknow. He was a strict disciplinarian in his time.

- The lords of the ascendant and the 10th, Sun and Venus fall in the constellation of Jupiter, *Visakha*.
- Both Mercury and Jupiter aspect the 10th house.
- The ascendant lord Sun acquires the *navamsa* of Mercury.
- The 5th lord is Jupiter who obtains the *navamsa* of *lagna* lord Sun.
- Both, the 9th house and 9th lord Mars, get the aspect of ascendant lord & 10th lord, Sun and Venus.
- The 6th lord Saturn aspects the 10th house and obtains the *navamsa* of Sun, which confirms the govt. service.
- Jupiter falls in the constellation of 9th lord Mars.

Thus, there is considerable influence of Jupiter and Mercury over the triangles and the $10^{th}$ house.

All these illustrations should be sufficient enough to corroborate our view point regarding the planetary combinations for the respectable profession of teaching. Jupiter and Mercury are the planets of wisdom, knowledge, intellect and intelligence. The $5^{th}$ house shows the attitude and aptitude of the native. Influence of these planets over the house of profession and also on triangles and ascendant will indicate this career. More and more influence of Jupiter and Mercury on other planets and houses will further augment the proposition.

•

# CHAPTER-6

# Third House and Journalism

Journalism is one of the most dignified professions, which may be undertaken by the intelligent, sharp, dynamic, dashing, bold and fearless persons, who have an intense desire to serve the humanity and country in their own way. Though some petty journalists sometime give bad name to the profession by their unsavory deeds, still journalism gets its due recognition in the society. Mercury rules over the intelligence and Mars bestows boldness and courage. Therefore, the joint influence of Mercury and Mars on the concerning houses of occupation, makes one a versatile journalist. Jupiter should also be taken into account as it gives knowledge, sincerity and nobility, which are essential factors for the profession of journalism. Mercury and Mars are the prime significators and Jupiter is a supporting significator for journalism.

Third house must be strong and should be under the influence of the significator, Mercury or Mars or both. In fact, the third house rules over the communication and information. Mercury rules over the courage, interpretation, sensation, whereas Mars rules over the courage, fearlessness and boldness. The tenth house and its lord must be under the influence of Mercury, Mars or Jupiter. The lord of the tenth house should obtain *navamsa* of Mercury or Mars or otherwise should fall in the constellation of either of these.

The second house and Jupiter generally show the source of income. Many astrologers predict profession from the second house and Venus. However, Jupiter is the supporting significator for journalism. Following observations may be noted as important factor for the profession of journalism.

- Mars or Mercury or both should join either the ascendant, the third or the tenth house.
- Mars and Mercury should have an influence over each other in one or the other way. Mercury may obtain *navamsa* or constellation of Mars and vice-versa.
- Jupiter must influence third, sixth, second, eleventh or the tenth house and Mercury or Mars.
- The third house must be well disposed and should be under the influence of Mercury, Mars or Jupiter or any two or all.

We will now justify our view points and observations with the help of a few of practical nativities.

*Illustration : 6.1* **(RNG)** *Horoscope No.: 81*

Date of birth : 18.04.1904 Time of birth : 07:00:00 hrs
Place of birth : Kashipur Lat 19:22:00 N Long 83:11:00E
Ayanamsa : 22:31:11 Sidereal Time : 20:42:57

| Pln | Degree | Rasi | Nakshatra | Pad |
|---|---|---|---|---|
| Asc | 27:05:27 | Ari | Krittika | 1 |
| Sun | 5:04:10 | Ari | Asvini | 2 |
| Mon | 0:22:03 | Tau | Krittika | 2 |
| Mar (C) | 15:49:06 | Ari | Bharani | 1 |
| Mer | 24:28:47 | Ari | Bharani | 4 |
| Jup | 18:59:36 | Pis | Revati | 1 |
| Ven | 13:30:32 | Pis | U Bhadrapad | 4 |
| Sat | 26:57:31 | Cap | Dhanishtha | 2 |
| Rah (R) | 4:39:48 | Vir | U Phalguni | 3 |
| Ket (R) | 4:39:48 | Pis | U Bhadrapad | 1 |

**Lagna Chart**

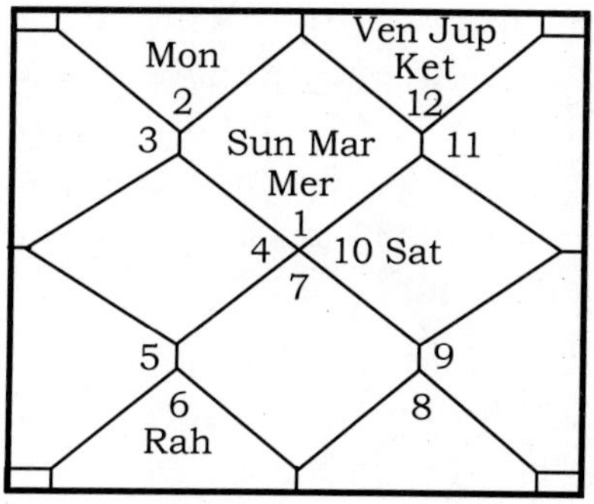


**Navamsa Chart**

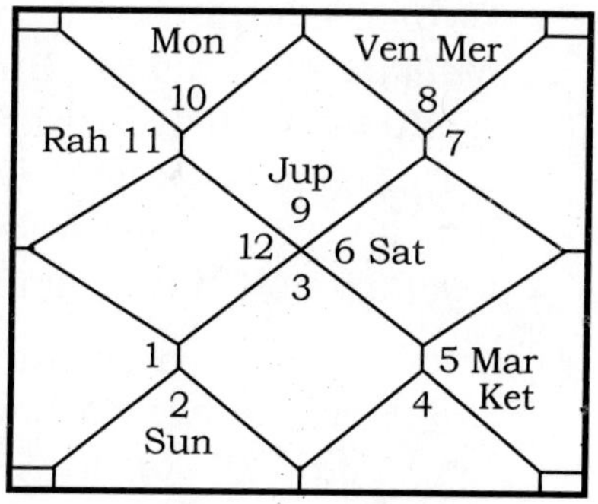


Balance of Vimsottari Dasa of **Sun 4Y 4M 0D**

Mr. Ram Nath Goenka was the Chief Editor and proprietor of Indian Express group. He came to India at the time of partition with Rs. 9.00 only. He rose so high within thirty years that top most leaders like, Mrs. Indira Gandhi, were scared of him. She applied all her power to demolish Indian Express Group. Mr. Ram Nath Goenka had enough courage and decided to fight with the Prime Minister. Ultimately, he got the success due to his unparalleled talent, capability and merits. He was one of the most successful journalists of our country and his name will remain immortal due to his extra-ordinary capability to fight.

1. He was born in Aries Ascendant, which falls in the *navamsa* of Jupiter. Lord of the ascendant, Mars joins the ascendant giving rise to *Ruchchak Mahapurusha Rajyoga.*

2. Lord of the third and the sixth house, Mercury, and the lord of the ascendant, Mars, are associated with each other in ascendant. This is a very powerful combination for a dynamic, dashing, bold and courageous journalist. Conjunction of the fifth lord Sun with Mars and Mercury, in the ascendant itself, has given rise to a *Rajyoga* and has added fuel in the fire. That means, it has given strength to the astrological justification of his being a journalist of international fame, reputation and honour.

3. Lord of the tenth house, Saturn, falls in own sign Capricorn in the tenth house and forms *Sasa Mahapurush Rajyoga.* But the most encouraging part of it is that the tenth lord Saturn obtains the navamsa of Mercury and straight way justifies the profession of journalism. Saturn falls in *Dhanishtha* constellation, ruled by one of the significator Mars.

4. Another significator Jupiter owns the ninth house and occupies the twelfth house. Jupiter falls in own sign Pisces and in *Revati* constellation ruled by Mercury. However, Jupiter obtains own *navamsa.* This is an additional factor for the profession of journalism.

5. Mr. Ram Nath Goenka enjoyed extra-ordinary success, fame, honour and wealth. He had many *Rajyogas* in his birth chart including *Ruchchak* and *Sasa Mahapurush Rajyoga.* He had exalted luminaries i.e. the Sun and Moon are exalted in the ascendant and the second house. Venus is exalted in the twelfth house as the lord of the second and seventh house. Jupiter was posited in own sign Pisces and obtained own *navamsa* Sagittarius as the lord of the house of fortune. Thus, all planets, excluding nodes, are either exalted or fall in their own sign. The most important significator Mercury obtains *navamsa* of Mars, who happens to be another significator of journalism.

These planetary combinations have made Mr. Ram Nath Goenka a journalist of worldwide fame, who survived successfully even after a serious fight with Mrs. Indira Gandhi, Prime Minister of his time. He laid the foundation of Indian Express Group.

*Illustration : 6.2* (**AS**) *Horoscope No.: 82*

Date of birth : 02.11.1941 Time of birth : 09:00:00 hrs
Place of birth : Jalandher Lat 28:39:00 N Long 77:13:00E
Ayanamsa : 23:02:36 Sidereal Time : 11:22:56

| Pln | Degree | Rasi | Nakshatra | Pad |
|---|---|---|---|---|
| Asc | 16:39:24 | Sco | Anuradha | 4 |
| Sun | 16:16:48 | Lib | Svati | 3 |
| Mon | 25:03:21 | Pis | Revati | 3 |
| Mar (R) | 18:28:46 | Pis | Revati | 1 |
| Mer (R) | 4:09:27 | Lib | Chitra | 4 |
| Jup (R) | 27:32:07 | Tau | Mrigsira | 2 |
| Ven | 2:15:11 | Sag | Moola | 1 |
| Sat (R) | 3:15:56 | Tau | Krittika | 2 |
| Rah (R) | 28:48:43 | Leo | U Phalguni | 1 |
| Ket (R) | 28:48:43 | Aqu | P Bhadrapad | 3 |

**Lagna Chart**

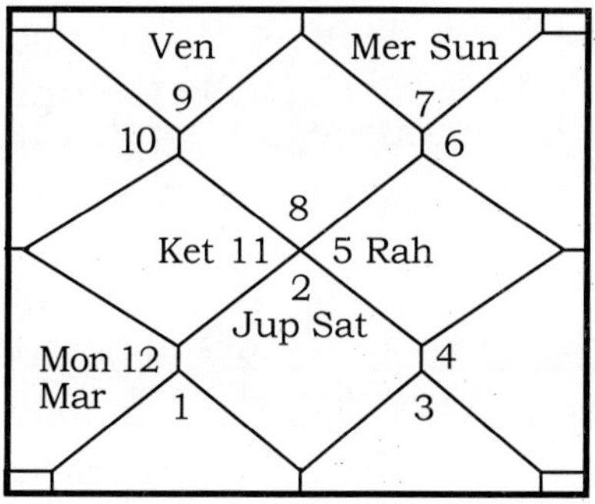


**Navamsa Chart**

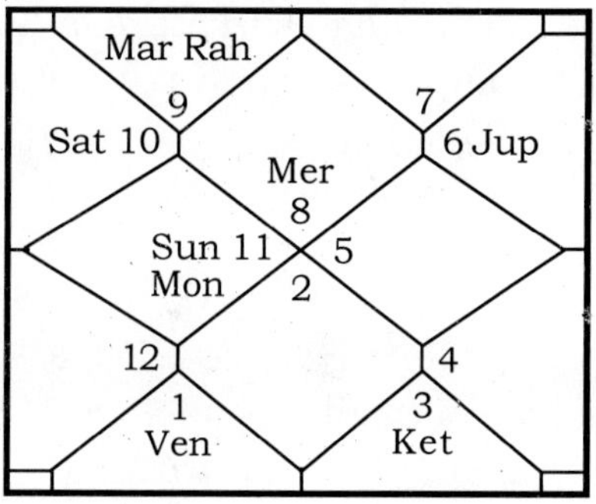


Balance of Vimsottari Dasa of **Mer 6Y 3M 19D**

The native of this horoscope Mr. Arun Shourie has been an economist with the World Bank, a consultant to the Planning Commission, India and Editor of the Indian Express, a leading newspaper. Following combinations are present in this horoscope for the enormous success of Mr. Arun Shourie in the field of journalism –

1. The native is born in Scorpio ascendant, whose lord Mars is associated with Moon in the fifth house. Mars lends its aspect over Sun and Mercury. Thus, Mercury is under the influence of Mars and Mercury obtains the *navamsa*

of Mars as well. In fact, blended influence of Mars and Mercury makes one a versatile, dynamic and dashing journalist. Courage and intelligence both are required in addition to interest in journalism and knowledge thereof. Mercury gives knowledge, experience and skill in journalism, whereas Mars bestows courage and boldness.

2. Lord of the second and fifth house, Jupiter, indicates profession and interest of the native. In fact, second house must be taken into consideration for the judgement of profession. The lord of second and fifth house, Jupiter, obtains the *navamsa* of Mercury and eleventh lord Mercury obtains the *navamsa* of Mars. Strong planetary combinations for success in journalism are present in this birth-chart.

3. The *lagna* lord Mars falls in Pisces sign, ruled by Jupiter and obtains Sagittarius *navamsa* ruled by Jupiter. Therefore, the native is a famous economist and journalist of India.

*Illustration : 6.3* (**SM**) *Horoscope No.: 83*

Date of birth : 14.08.1968 Time of birth : 23:55:00 hrs
Place of birth: Unnao Lat 26:32:00 N Long 80:30:00E
Ayanamsa : 23:25:04 Sidereal Time : 21:19:56

| **Pln** | **Degree** | **Rasi** | **Nakshatra** | **Pad** |
|---|---|---|---|---|
| Asc | 9:31:12 | Tau | Krittika | 4 |
| Sun | 28:34:29 | Can | Aslesha | 4 |
| Mon | 14:01:42 | Ari | Bharani | 1 |
| Mar (C) | 12:25:24 | Can | Pushya | 3 |
| Mer (C) | 6:04:00 | Leo | Magha | 2 |
| Jup | 17:33:06 | Leo | P Phalguni | 2 |
| Ven | 13:47:40 | Leo | P Phalguni | 1 |
| Sat (R) | 2:05:00 | Ari | Asvini | 1 |
| Rah | 17:15:47 | Pis | Revati | 1 |
| Ket | 17:15:47 | Vir | Hasta | 3 |

**Lagna Chart**

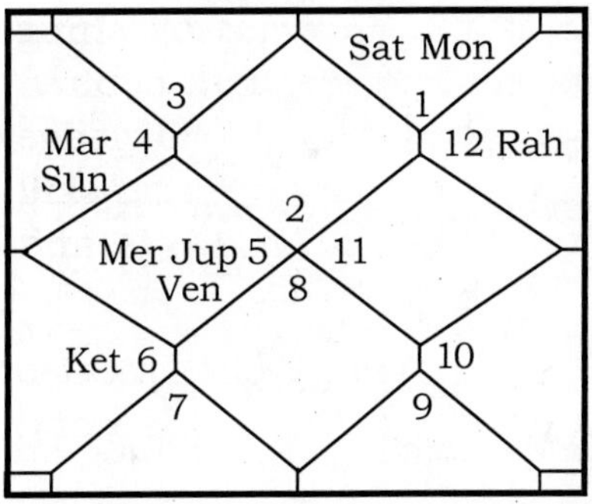


**Navamsa Chart**

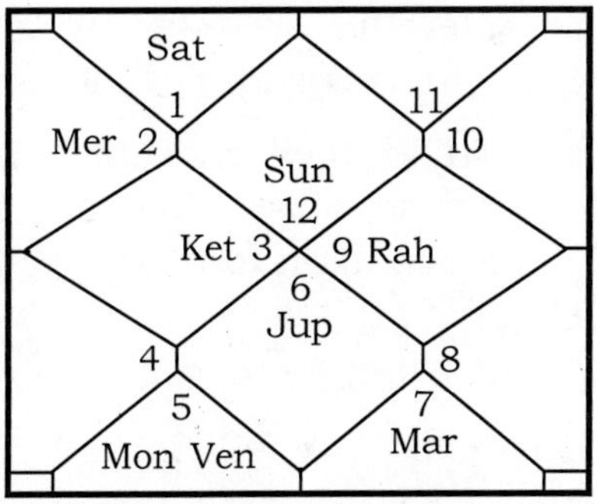


Balance of Vimsottari Dasa of **Ven 18Y 11M 14D**

This horoscope belongs to Chief Editor of Sahara Newspapers and various journals and magazines of Sahara. Following combinations are present in this horoscope –

1. The tenth house is aspected by Jupiter, Mercury and Venus. This is *Raj Lakshan* Yoga. Lord of tenth house, Saturn, is associated with Moon in Aries and is aspected by Jupiter. Moreover, Jupiter obtains the *navamsa* of Mercury. Thus, the eleventh lord Jupiter is under the influence of Venus, Mercury and the Sun. We have mentioned that joint influence of Jupiter, Mercury and Mars on the concerning houses makes one a successful journalist.

2. In this horoscope, the Sun and Mars occupy the third house. Here, Mars aspects the sixth, ninth and tenth house. The Sun falls in *Aslesha Nakshatra* ruled by Mercury. However, the tenth house is aspected by Mars, Mercury, Jupiter and Venus, which has made the native extremely successful and versatile journalist.

3. It may be noted that Mercury and Jupiter own the second and eleventh houses and both are conjoined with *lagna* lord Venus in the fourth house. Thus, the tenth house, which indicates the profession of the native, is under the influence of second lord Mercury, eleventh lord Jupiter, sixth lord Venus and the tenth lord Saturn. Mars falls in *Pushya Nakshatra* ruled by tenth lord Saturn.

However, eleventh lord Jupiter obtains the *navamsa* of Mercury and Mercury obtains the *navamsa* of Venus, who is the lord of the ascendant and the sixth house.

4. The joint effect of Mars, Mercury and Jupiter on the tenth house, *Rashi* chart and *navamsa* ensures profession of journalism to the native.

*Illustration : 6.4* (**SA**) *Horoscope No.: 84*

Date of birth : 25.09.1954 Time of birth : 17:00:00 hrs

Place of birth : Baghdad Lat 26:32:00 N Long 80:30:00E

Ayanamsa : 23:13:45 Sidereal Time : 17:06:59

| Pln | Degree | Rasi | Nakshatra | Pad |
|---|---|---|---|---|
| Asc | 18:29:56 | Aqu | Satabhisha | 4 |
| Sun | 8:37:51 | Vir | U Phalguni | 4 |
| Mon | 21:00:28 | Leo | P Phalguni | 3 |
| Mar | 21:05:40 | Sag | Purvasadha | 3 |
| Mer | 2:05:47 | Lib | Chitra | 3 |
| Jup | 2:33:36 | Can | Punarvasu | 4 |
| Ven | 23:01:53 | Lib | Visakha | 1 |
| Sat | 14:11:04 | Lib | Svati | 3 |
| Rah (R) | 17:58:52 | Sag | Purvasadha | 2 |
| Ket (R) | 17:58:52 | Gem | Ardra | 4 |

**Lagna Chart**

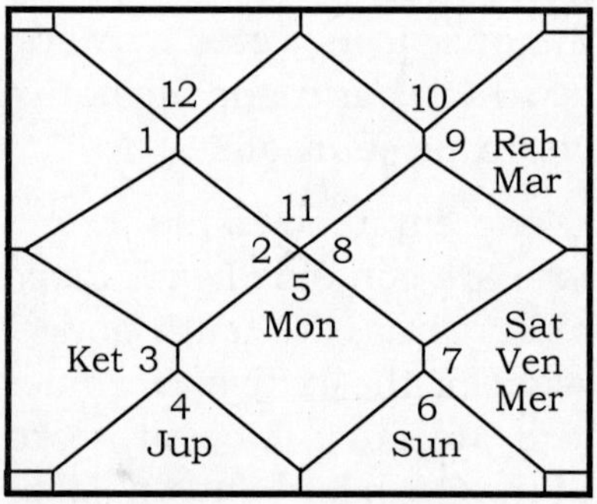


**Navamsa Chart**

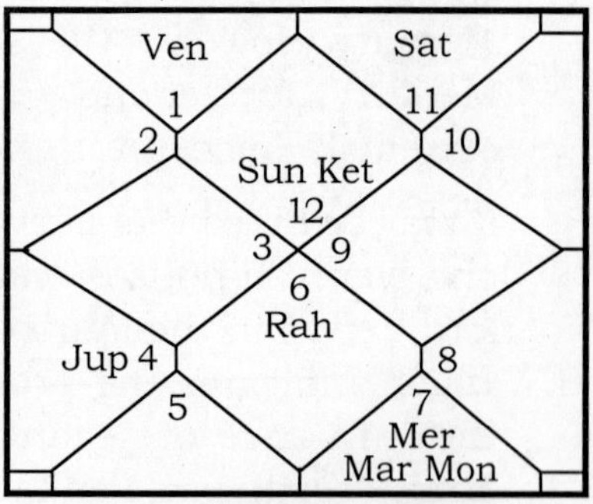


Balance of Vimsottari Dasa of **Ven 8Y 5M 26D**

She joined Hindustan Times as a correspondent and became bureau chief and then Editor with in a short span of time. Hindustan Times Group belongs to Birla. She was liked and appreciated by Mr. K.K. Birla a lot.

1. She is born in Aquarius ascendant. The fifth house is ruled by Mercury and is aspected by tenth lord Mars.
2. Sun and Saturn are the strongest planets in this horoscope. The Sun falls in Virgo and in own *nakshatra Uttaraphalguni* and obtains the *navamsa* of Jupiter.
3. The lord of second and eleventh house, Jupiter, falls in own *nakshatra Punarvasu* and obtains the *navamsa* of its exaltation.
4. Fifth lord Mercury falls in the constellation of *Chitra* ruled by Mars. Thus, the fifth house is under the influence of Mars and Mercury both.
5. Lord of ninth house Venus is associated with fifth lord Mercury and *lagna* lord Saturn. This is a strong *Rajyoga*, which resulted into her elevation and promotion speedily and quickly.
6. Third and sixth house should also be taken into account for the persons who earned their livelihood through journalism. The lord of the third house, Mars, aspects the fifth and sixth house.
7. Second and eleventh houses indicate source of income. For Aquarius ascendant, Jupiter is the lord of second and eleventh house. In this horoscope, Jupiter is posited in the sixth house in the sign of its exaltation, in own constellation *Punarvasu* and obtains *vargottam navamsa*. Position of Jupiter and Mercury has blessed her with wonderful writing skill, for which she has earned a high reputation. In fact, Jupiter is also one of the important planets to make one a journalist.
8. In this horoscope, the lord of second and eleventh house, Jupiter, aspects the tenth and second house. Exalted Jupiter in the sixth house has made her a famous journalist and a great thinker.

*Illustration : 6.5* (**PJ**) *Horoscope No.: 85*

Date of birth : 29.08.1970 Time of birth : 01:45:00 hrs
Place of birth : Yeotmal Lat 20:20:00 N Long 78:03:00E
Ayanamsa : 23:26:58 Sidereal Time : 23:53:43

| Pln | Degree | Rasi | Nakshatra | Pad |
|---|---|---|---|---|
| Asc | 13:31:34 | Gem | Ardra | 3 |
| Sun | 11:38:40 | Leo | Magha | 4 |
| Mon | 8:19:48 | Can | Pushya | 2 |
| Mar (C) | 3:08:16 | Leo | Magha | 1 |
| Mer | 4:27:26 | Vir | U Phalguni | 3 |
| Jup | 8:30:35 | Lib | Svati | 1 |
| Ven | 27:43:41 | Vir | Chitra | 2 |
| Sat | 29:07:58 | Ari | Krittika | 1 |
| Rah | 9:28:08 | Aqu | Satabhisha | 1 |
| Ket (D) | 9:28:08 | Leo | Magha | 3 |

**Lagna Chart**

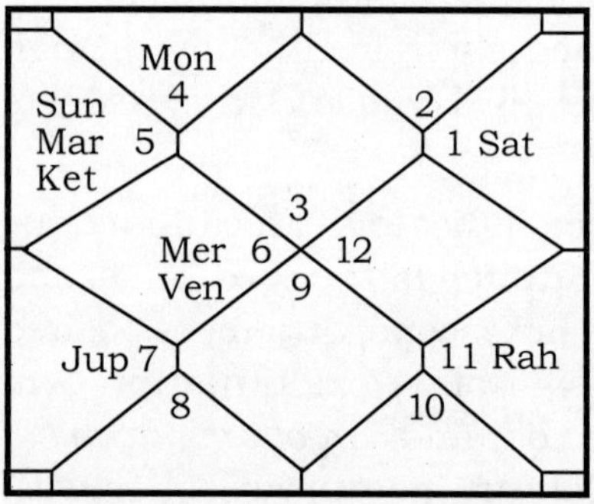


**Navamsa Chart**

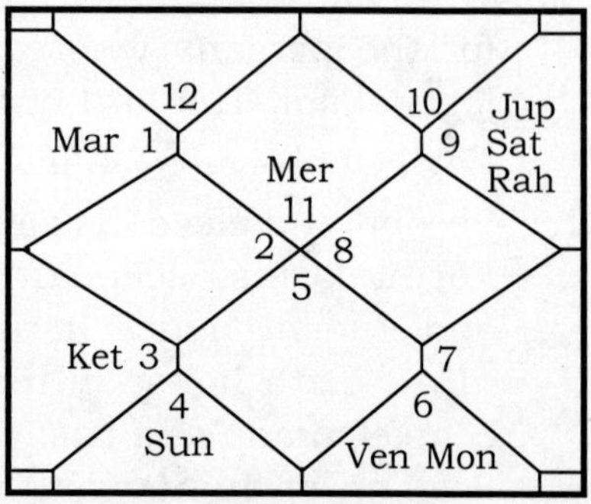


Balance of Vimsottari Dasa of **Sat 11Y 10M 16D**

The native is a bureau chief in Hindustan Times. Following combinations are present in this horoscope –

1. The lord of the tenth house, Jupiter, is posited in the fifth house with a mutual aspect with Saturn. Jupiter obtains own *navamsa*.

2. The second house indicates source of earning, which is occupied by its own lord Moon. Moon obtains the *navamsa* of Mercury.
3. The fifth lord Venus is associated with exalted Mercury in the fourth house. Both Mercury and Venus lend their aspect over the tenth house. Thus, the tenth house is under the influence of Jupiter, Mercury and Venus.
4. The lord of the second house, Moon, and that of the fifth house, Venus, obtain the *navamsa* of Mercury. Venus obtains *vargottam navamsa.*
5. In this horoscope, the third and sixth lords, Sun and Mars, are associated with each other in the third house with Ketu, which confirm that the native will enter into vocation of journalism.

*Illustration : 6.6* (**AS**) *Horoscope No.: 86*

Date of birth : 14.05.1971 Time of birth : 02:40:00 hrs

Place of birth : Mumbai Lat 18:58:00 N Long 72:50:00E

Ayanamsa : 23:27:35 Sidereal Time : 17:25:12

| **Pln** | **Degree** | **Rasi** | **Nakshatra** | **Pad** |
|---|---|---|---|---|
| Asc | 25:25:39 | Aqu | P Bhadrapad | 2 |
| Sun | 28:59:22 | Ari | Krittika | 1 |
| Mon | 9:15:56 | Sag | Moola | 3 |
| Mar | 11:34:05 | Cap | Sravna | 1 |
| Mer | 3:47:21 | Ari | Asvini | 2 |
| Jup (R) | 9:19:42 | Sco | Anuradha | 2 |
| Ven | 0:55:03 | Ari | Asvini | 1 |
| Sat (C) | 2:00:24 | Tau | Krittika | 2 |
| Rah (R) | 25:04:35 | Cap | Dhanishtha | 1 |
| Ket (R) | 25:04:35 | Can | Aslesha | 3 |

**Lagna Chart**

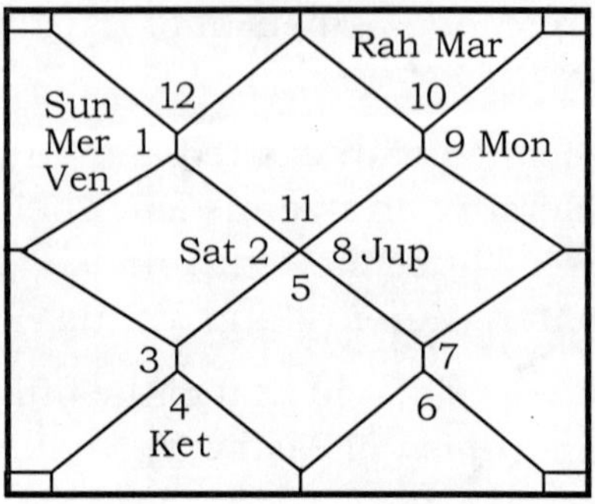


**Navamsa Chart**

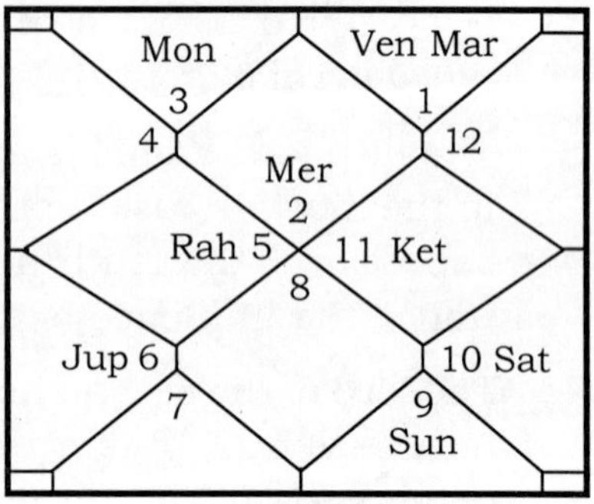


Balance of Vimsottari Dasa of **Ket 2Y 1M 19D**

She is a successful journalist, working in one of the most leading newspaper of India i.e. Times of India. Following combinations of a successful journalist are present in the horoscope of the subject –

1. She is born in Aquarius ascendant. Lord of the second house, Jupiter, joins the tenth house, identical with Martian sign Scorpio. Jupiter in tenth is under mutual aspect with *lagna* lord Saturn.

2. Fifth lord Mercury, fourth lord Venus and seventh lord Sun are associated with each other in the third house. The Sun is *atmakaraka* planet and is one of the strongest planets in this birth chart. *Atmakaraka* planet Sun, with Mercury and Venus, shows the occupation concerning journalism, especially because Sun obtains *navamsa* of Jupiter, the lord of second and eleventh house.

3. The lord of second and eleventh house, Jupiter, obtains the *navamsa* of Mercury i.e. Virgo.

4. Jupiter's aspect on the second and sixth house further confirms her occupation of working in a newspaper.

5. Exalted Mars in the twelfth house falls in Moon's constellation *Sravna* and lends its aspect over fifth lord Mercury. Therefore, the joint influence of Jupiter, Mars and Mercury has compelled her to become a journalist.

*Illustration : 6.7* (**AC**) *Horoscope No.: 87*

Date of birth : 22.03.1958 Time of birth : 22:40:00 hrs

Place of birth : Naihati Lat 22:54:00 N Long 88:26:00E

Ayanamsa : 23:16:33 Sidereal Time : 11:02:30

| **Pln** | **Degree** | **Rasi** | **Nakshatra** | **Pad** |
|---|---|---|---|---|
| Asc | 14:29:59 | Sco | Anuradha | 4 |
| Sun | 8:17:54 | Pis | U Bhadrapad | 2 |
| Mon | 3:13:01 | Ari | Asvini | 1 |
| Mar | 10:41:16 | Cap | Sravna | 1 |
| Mer | 24:59:13 | Pis | Revati | 3 |
| Jup (R) | 6:32:16 | Lib | Chitra | 4 |
| Ven | 23:16:50 | Cap | Sravna | 4 |
| Sat | 2:17:25 | Sag | Moola | 1 |
| Rah (R) | 8:07:03 | Lib | Svati | 1 |
| Ket (R) | 8:07:03 | Ari | Asvini | 3 |

**Lagna Chart**

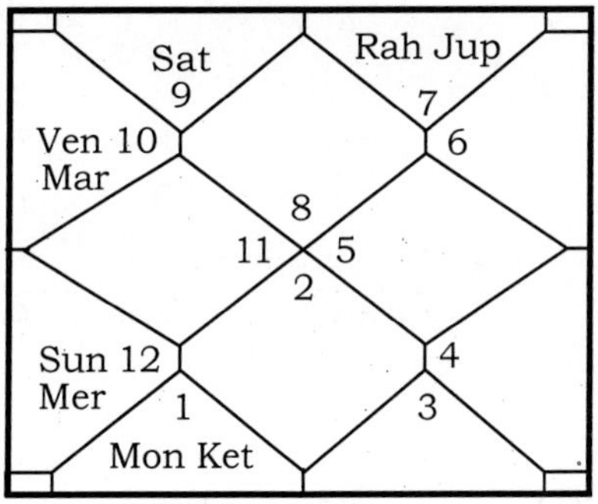


**Navamsa Chart**

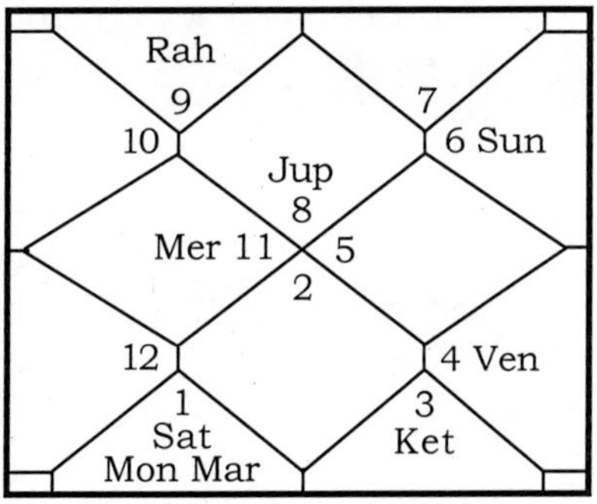


Balance of Vimsottari Dasa of **Ket 5Y 3M 22D**

The native was working as a senior correspondent in the 'Times of India' group. He worked in many other newspapers from time to time. The native is extremely short tempered. Therefore, he was forced to resign after a terrible and stormy argument with the Chief Editor of the paper.

He remained jobless for a few years. Ultimately, he compromised and joined another group at a smaller position. Following combinations are present in the birth chart of the native –

1. The lord of the tenth house, Sun, is conjoined with eleventh lord Mercury in the fifth house, which has resulted into an inclination towards journalism.
2. Lord of the ascendant, Mars, occupies the third house in association with the seventh lord Venus. Here, Mars aspects the sixth, ninth and the tenth house.
3. Lord of the fifth and second house, Jupiter, joins the twelfth house under retrograde motion. This disposition of Jupiter cannot be appreciated. However, Jupiter aspects the fourth, sixth and the eighth house and obtains *navamsa* of Mars, as the second and the fifth lord. This resulted into an occupation connected with journalism.
4. The lord of the tenth house, Sun, obtains *navamsa* of Mercury, which is a powerful indication of an occupation of a journalist.
5. Mercury, Jupiter and Mars are the significators for means of livelihood through journalism. Here, Mercury falls in own constellation *Revati* and is tenanted in Jupiter's sign Pisces. Jupiter is tenth from Mars. Jupiter and Mars both aspect the sixth house and ninth lord Moon.
6. Exalted Mars joins the tenth house in Moon Chart. The tenth lord Saturn falls in the ninth house in Jupiter's sign Sagittarius. Jupiter falls in *Chitra* constellation ruled by Mars. Mars and Jupiter both lend their aspect over Moon. Anyway, Moon and Jupiter both fall over the axis of Rahu and Ketu and all the four quadrants are vacant. Therefore, the native had to resign unceremoniously.

*Illustration : 6.8* **(TS)** *Horoscope No.: 88*

Date of birth : 07.02.1972 Time of birth : 07:24:00 hrs
Place of birth : Lucknow Lat 26:50:00 N Long 80:54:00E
Ayanamsa : 23:28:17 Sidereal Time : 16:22:48

| **Pln** | **Degree** | **Rasi** | **Nakshatra** | **Pad** |
|---|---|---|---|---|
| Asc | 3:34:44 | Aqu | Dhanishtha | 4 |
| Sun | 23:54:59 | Cap | Dhanishtha | 1 |
| Mon | 19:41:05 | Lib | Svati | 4 |
| Mar | 4:12:47 | Ari | Asvini | 2 |
| Mer (C) | 16:28:38 | Cap | Sravna | 2 |
| Jup | 6:34:40 | Sag | Moola | 2 |
| Ven | 2:31:50 | Pis | P Bhadrapad | 4 |
| Sat | 6:08:58 | Tau | Krittika | 3 |
| Rah (R/C) | 11:40:25 | Cap | Sravna | 1 |
| Ket (R) | 11:40:25 | Can | Pushya | 3 |

**Lagna Chart**

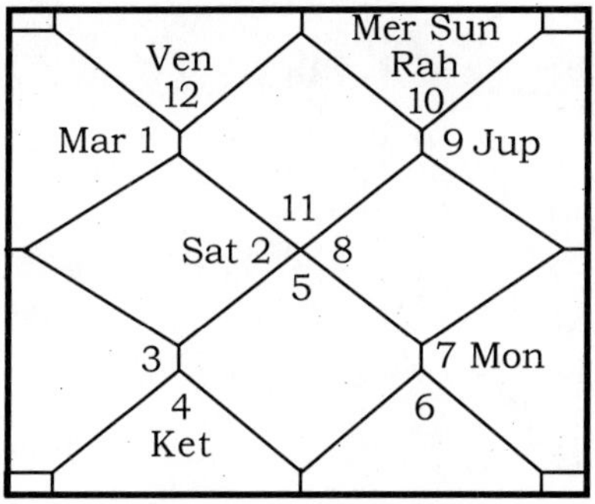


**Navamsa Chart**

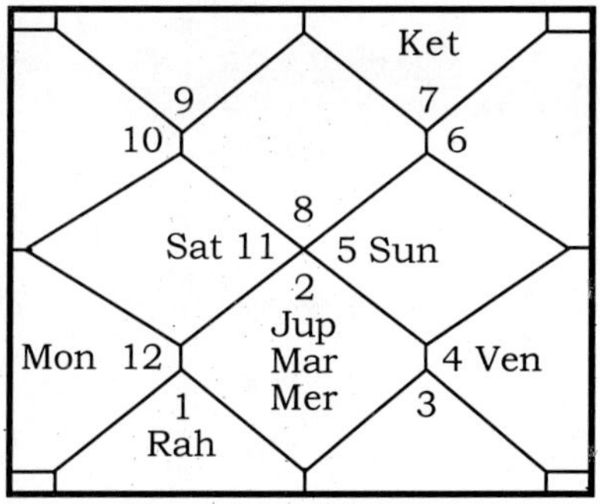


Balance of Vimsottari Dasa of **Rah 0Y 5M 3D**

The native is a famous and successful journalist who has worked in various newspapers of countrywide circulation. He had been looking after reputed monthly journals as well. Following combinations of a successful journalist are present in the horoscope of the subject –

1. Lord of tenth house Mars joins the third house of its own and aspects the tenth house.
2. The lord of second and eleventh house, Jupiter, joins the eleventh house of its own and aspects the tenth lord Mars.
3. The tenth house, ascendant and the sixth house are aspected by *lagna* lord Saturn. Mercury, Jupiter and Mars obtain the *navamsa* of *Yogakaraka* Venus and Venus occupies the second house. Thus, Jupiter, Mars and Mercury have influenced the profession of the native to a great extent and it singles out the profession of a journalist.

*Illustration : 6.9* (**BS**) *Horoscope No.: 89*

Date of birth : 01.09.1958 Time of birth : 12:35:00 hrs

Place of birth : Kanpur Lat 22:39:00 N Long 88:23:00E

Ayanamsa : 23:16:54 Sidereal Time : 11:38:18

| **Pln** | **Degree** | **Rasi** | **Nakshatra** | **Pad** |
|---|---|---|---|---|
| Asc | 22:28:16 | Sco | Jyestha | 2 |
| Sun | 15:03:29 | Leo | P Phalguni | 1 |
| Mon | 18:51:30 | Pis | Revati | 1 |
| Mar | 29:45:31 | Ari | Krittika | 1 |
| Mer (R) | 1:28:09 | Leo | Magha | 1 |
| Jup | 5:38:40 | Lib | Chitra | 4 |
| Ven | 26:34:44 | Can | Aslesha | 3 |
| Sat | 25:52:10 | Sco | Jyestha | 3 |
| Rah (R) | 29:40:35 | Vir | Chitra | 2 |
| Ket (R) | 29:40:35 | Pis | Revati | 4 |

**Lagna Chart**

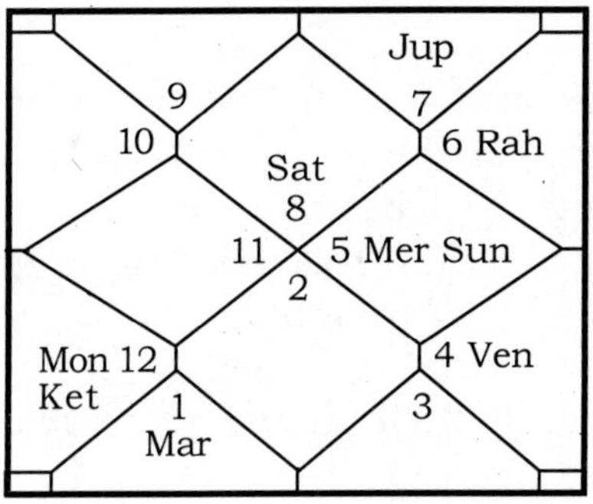


**Navamsa Chart**

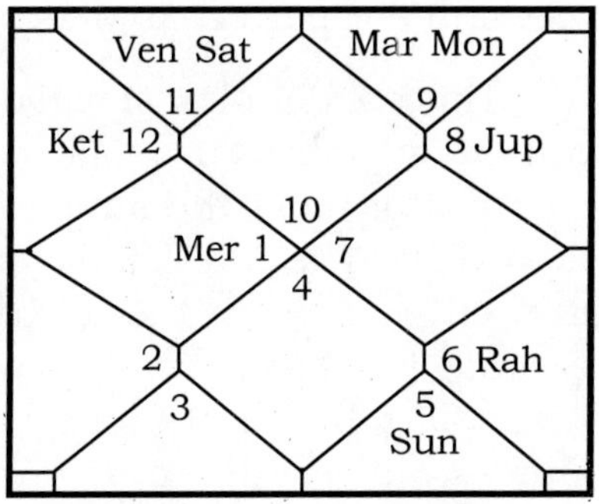


Balance of Vimsottari Dasa of **Mer 14Y 2M 14D**

The native is a Bureau Chief of a very well reputed Newspaper. He had been a Crime Reporter earlier. Following combinations of a successful journalist are present in the horoscope of the subject –

1. The native was born in Scorpio ascendant. The lord of the tenth house, Sun, falls in the tenth house of its own, in conjunction with eighth and eleventh lord Mercury. This combination of the Sun and Mercury is enough to make one a successful journalist. The Sun in the tenth in Leo is extremely powerful as it obtains *vargottam navamsa.*

2. Lord of the third and fourth house, Saturn, occupies the ascendant and lends its aspect over the tenth house, the Sun and Mercury. However, Saturn falls in own *navamsa* and falls in *Jyestha* constellation ruled by Mercury. Lord of the ascendant, Mars, and the lord of the second and the fifth house, Jupiter, have mutual aspect. Mars also aspects the ascendant and the third lord Saturn.

3. The ninth lord Moon falls in Jupiter's sign Pisces and Mercury's constellation *Revati* in the fifth house, which shows a keen interest towards journalism. Influence of the ascendant and the sixth lord by way of aspect over the ascendant, third lord Saturn, and second and the

fifth lord Jupiter compelled him to be one of the best crime reporter, as well.

These examples of famous journalists have confirmed our view point that Mars and Mercury are the prime significators and the supporting significator for journalism is Jupiter. The third house plays a vital role in addition to the tenth house in the birth charts of the natives, who are inclined to select journalism as their main vocation. However, if the sixth house, its' lord placed therein, are also involved, the subject will show his extreme and outstanding performance in the field of journalism. Such a native will be exceptionally sharp, bright, daring, dashing, intelligent and bold in whose horoscope third, sixth and tenth houses are under the influence of Mercury, Mars and Jupiter.

# CHAPTER-7

# Planetary Proposition for Actors

Film and Television are the biggest media of entertainment in our country at least. Film actors and actresses are successful, only if they are really talented and obtain perfection in the art of acting. There are many film artists, who will remain immortal for their extra ordinary performances in a few pictures. Who can forget Prithvi Raj Kapoor of Mugal-E-Azam, Dilip Kumar of Devadas, Devanand of Guide, Raj Kapoor of Mera Naam Joker, Meena Kumari of Paakeeja, and the like.

Film line was not considered decent, long ago. Persons of high society never liked to encourage their children to select film career in any way. But today it is not so. Boys and girls of all walks of life, who are talented and possess the art of acting, dancing or singing, are eager to go in films. There are many convenient ways today to become an actor or actress. One of the strong media is Television. Current period is an era of competition. There are number of channels, through which boys and girls can been selected for films on the basis of their performance and acting. If planets propose the individuals a career in films, they should be allowed and advised to join any reputed and decent institute of acting, singing or dancing, depending upon their interest and talent.

Let us study, what are the planetary propositions in the birth-chart, which tend one to act and provide talent and skill of acting.

1. Significators for the occupation of acting, in films or stage, are Venus, Moon and Mercury.
2. The $5^{th}$ and $3^{rd}$ houses are related with acting career, in

addition to the 10th and the 9th house. If the houses, or the lords of these houses are inter-related with each other in one or the other way, along with the effective role of significators on the concerning houses and their lords, one is bound to become successful in film line.

*Illustration : 7.1* (**DK**) *Horoscope No.: 90*

Date of birth : 11.12.1922 Time of birth : 23:15:00 hrs
Place of birth : Peshawar Lat 34:02:00 N Long 71:37:00E
Ayanamsa : 22:46:49 Sidereal Time : 3:50:04

| **Pln** | **Degree** | **Rasi** | **Nakshatra** | **Pad** |
|---|---|---|---|---|
| Asc | 9:58:08 | Leo | Magha | 3 |
| Sun | 26:08:19 | Sco | Jyestha | 3 |
| Mon | 26:42:55 | Leo | U Phalguni | 1 |
| Mar | 7:21:34 | Aqu | Satabhisha | 1 |
| Mer (C) | 28:53:05 | Sco | Jyestha | 4 |
| Jup | 16:49:21 | Lib | Svati | 4 |
| Ven (R) | 2:03:08 | Sco | Visakha | 4 |
| Sat | 25:16:52 | Vir | Chitra | 1 |
| Rah (R) | 3:01:13 | Vir | U Phalguni | 2 |
| Ket (R) | 3:01:13 | Pis | P Bhadrapad | 4 |

**Lagna Chart**

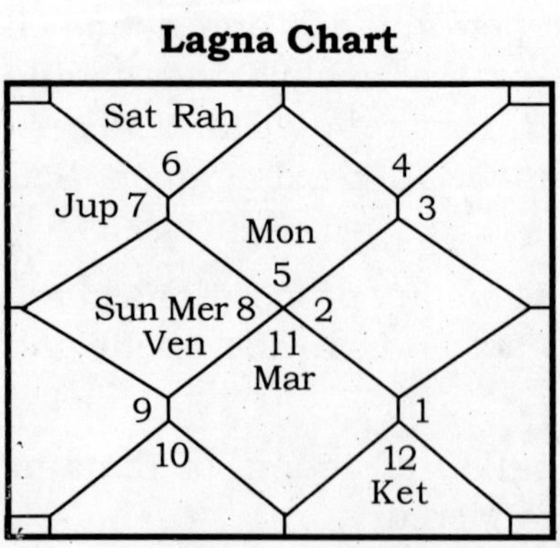


**Navamsa Chart**

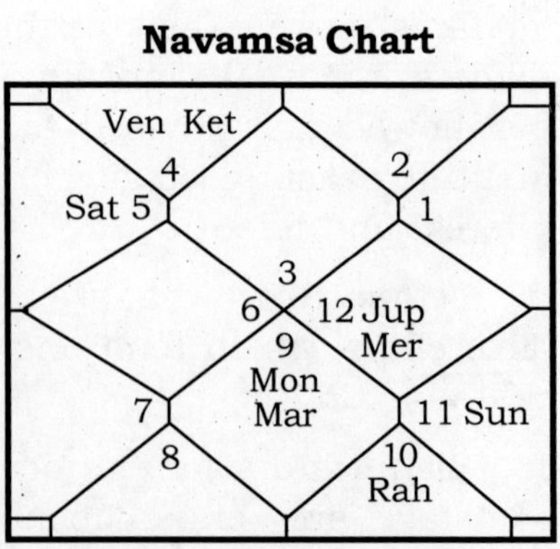


Balance of Vimsottari Dasa of **Sun 5Y 11M 22D**

Tragedy king Dilip Kumar is one of the most versatile and valued actor of repute. He is pride of our nation as far as Indian Film Industry is concerned. He was the costliest hero of his time. He won enormous honours, prizes, awards etc. for his unparallel acting talent, as the best actor. He is 86 years old at present and his contribution in films for more than 60 years, is priceless. He had been extremely careful for his roles in all his films and most of his films celebrated silver jubilee and golden jubilee. Devdas, Madhumati, Kohinoor, Jogan, Ganga Jamuna, Mugal-E-Azam, Dil Diya Dard Liya, Leader, Shakti, Bairag, Karma and Saudagar have been some of the most memorable and immortal films of Dilip Kumar.

## Planetary Combinations of the Birth chart of Dilip Kumar

1. Dilip Kumar was born in Leo ascendant with Moon therein.
2. The 5$^{th}$ lord Jupiter is posited in the 3$^{rd}$ house. Jupiter aspects the 9$^{th}$ house and 9$^{th}$ lord Mars.
3. Significators for film career, Mercury and Venus, aspect the 10$^{th}$ house. Venus own 10$^{th}$ and Mercury rules over the 2$^{nd}$ and 11$^{th}$ house. Thus, film career will be main means of livelihood, is quite evident.

Let us study and analyze the birth chart of the most popular actor Dilip Kumar with regard to his professional aspect.

### THE THIRD HOUSE

The 5$^{th}$ lord Jupiter occupies the 3$^{rd}$ house identical to Libra, which is ruled by Venus. This shows talent of acting. Jupiter obtains own *navamsa,* in association with significator Mercury, in the 10$^{th}$ house from *navamsa lagna.*

### THE FIFTH HOUSE

The 5$^{th}$ house is owned by the *Yogakaraka* Mars, who

aspects the $10^{th}$ house, & the ascendant. Mars is being aspected by Moon and Jupiter. This has provided immeasurable art and talent of acting in addition to immense fortune, because Mars is the second strongest planet in this horoscope. Aspect of Mars over the ascendant and Moon, has given Dilip Kumar youthful appearance, energy and long active life.

### THE TENTH HOUSE

The $10^{th}$ house, which is mainly dealt for professional progression is ruled and aspected by Venus, $9^{th}$ lord Mars, $2^{nd}$ and $11^{th}$ lord Mercury and the ascendant lord Sun. Thus, the $10^{th}$ house is very well disposed for film career.

### THE MOON

The $10^{th}$ lord Venus obtains *navamsa* of Moon, the significator. Moon is quite strong in *Shadabalas*. Placement of Moon in the ascendant has provided ability and art of changing the mood, exactly according to the role, in no time. Moon obtains *navamsa* of the $5^{th}$ lord Jupiter, which has blessed him with ability and intelligence of the selection of his role in films and has further strengthened the talent and art.

### THE MERCURY

Mercury is also a significator of film acting, provided influence of Venus and Moon is also there. Mercury is the lord of $2^{nd}$ and $11^{th}$ and it is posited in the $4^{th}$ house, with the $10^{th}$ lord Venus and ascendant lord, the Sun, and it lends its favourable aspect over the $10^{th}$ house. Moreover, Mercury falls in own constellation *Jyestha* and obtains *navamsa* of Jupiter. This shows that he will be bestowed with the amazing art of acting and that will be his prime vocation as well.

The $7^{th}$ lord Saturn occupies the $2^{nd}$ house, in association with Rahu, in a barren sign Virgo and is aspected by Mars as well. This delayed the marriage of Dilip Kumar and he was married at 44 years of age during the year 1966, with beauty queen Saira Bano. *Yogakaraka* Mars in the $7^{th}$

house gives much younger and very smart wife. Saira Bano was 22 years of age at the time of marriage. Mars obtains *navamsa* of Jupiter and is conjoined with Moon in *navamsa* chart, therefore Dilip Kumar was married with the most beautiful and young girl of her time.

*Illustration : 7.2* **(RK)** *Horoscope No.: 91*

Date of birth : 14.12.1924 Time of birth : 22:00:00 hrs
Place of birth : Peshawar Lat 34:02:00 N Long 71:37:00E
Ayanamsa : 22:48:19 Sidereal Time : 2:48:44

| **Pln** | **Degree** | **Rasi** | **Nakshatra** | **Pad** |
|---|---|---|---|---|
| Asc | 27:14:55 | Can | Aslesha | 4 |
| Sun | 29:37:54 | Sco | Jyestha | 4 |
| Mon | 6:20:33 | Can | Pushya | 1 |
| Mar | 4:21:39 | Pis | U Bhadrapad | 1 |
| Mer | 19:18:18 | Sag | Purvasadha | 2 |
| Jup (C) | 6:22:32 | Sag | Moola | 2 |
| Ven | 28:20:48 | Lib | Visakha | 3 |
| Sat | 17:40:44 | Lib | Svati | 4 |
| Rah (R) | 22:06:18 | Can | Aslesha | 2 |
| Ket (R) | 22:06:18 | Cap | Sravna | 4 |

**Lagna Chart**

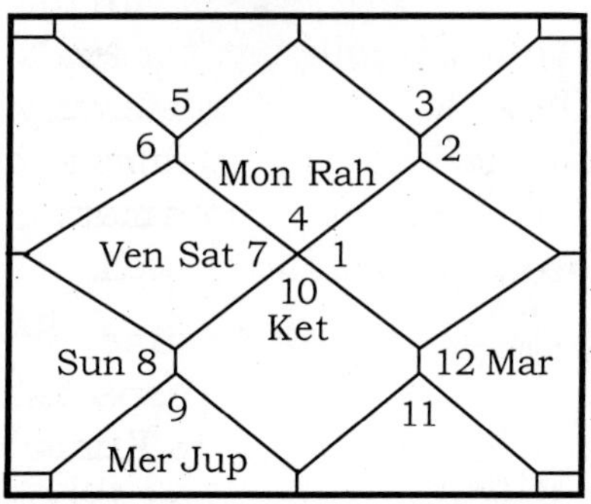


**Navamsa Chart**

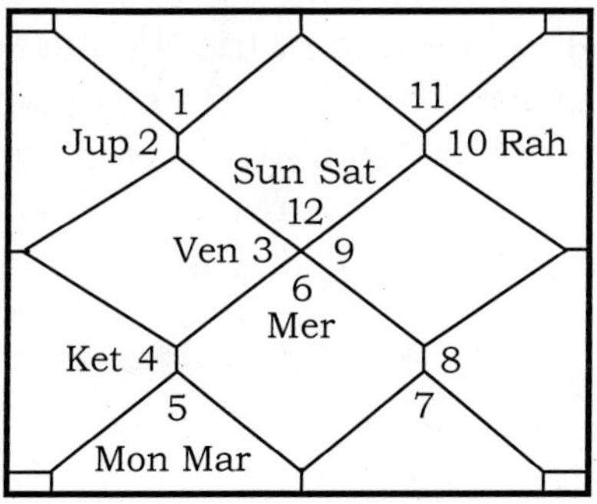


Balance of Vimsottari Dasa of **Sat 14Y 8M 16D**

Raj Kapoor did a lot for Indian films and film industry in various ways. He was a great showman of his time. Kapoor family and films have a strong bond with each other. This is the fourth generation of Kapoor's family, which is quite active in films. They have proved that without Kapoors, film industry remains incomplete. However, maximum credit should be given to Raj Kapoor, who was immensely talented and versatile actor, director and producer. A few of the films of Raj Kapoor have created history. These pictures are Shree 420, Awara, Jagte Raho, Sangam, Mera Naam Joker, Bobby, Dharam Karam etc.

Let's study the peculiar birth chart of everlasting showman Raj Kapoor.

## Planetary Combinations of the Birth chart of Raj Kapoor

1. Raj Kapoor was born in Cancer ascendant, with Moon and Rahu therein.
2. Saturn is exalted in the 4th house and is associated with *Swa-grahi* Venus. This combination of Saturn and Venus in the 4th house, in Libra has given rise to *Sasa* and *Malavya Mahapurusha Rajyogas.*
3. *Yogakaraka* Mars is placed in the 9th house, in a friendly sign Pisces, and aspects the 3rd and 4th house, as well as Saturn and Venus.
4. The lord of the 6th and 9th house, Jupiter, is posited in the 6th house of its own and aspects the 10th house. Thus, the 10th lord Mars occupies the 9th house and 9th lord Jupiter aspects the 10th house. Moreover, both Jupiter and Mars are in quadrant from each other.

**THE THIRD HOUSE**

The third house is a significator in the birth chart of film actors. Mercury is the lord of the 3rd house and occupies the 6th house, in association with Jupiter. Mercury obtains exalted *navamsa* and falls in the constellation of Venus i.e. *Poorvashadha*.

## THE FIFTH HOUSE

Fifth house controls talent, art, skill and intelligence. The 5th house is occupied by the 2nd lord Sun, who falls in *Jyestha* constellation, ruled by the significator Mercury. Sun obtains *navamsa* of the 9th lord Jupiter.

## THE TENTH HOUSE

The 10th house is aspected by Venus and Saturn along with Jupiter. Lord of the 10th house, Mars, occupies the 9th house and 9th lord Jupiter is 10th from the 10th lord Mars, as explained earlier. Mars obtains the *navamsa* of Sun, which is placed in the 5th house, in the sign of Mars.

## SIGNIFICATOR MOON

Moon controls Mood. A well disposed and strong Moon provides the intensive art and skill of switching over from one mood to another. Here, Moon's placement in own sign Cancer, in Leo *navamsa* provided unaccountable talent of acting to Raj Kapoor.

## SIGNIFICATOR VENUS

Venus is the significator of acting and its aspect over the 10th house shows occupation connected with films, especially because Venus obtains *navamsa* of Mercury, and falls in *Visakha* constellation, ruled by Jupiter.

Venus and Saturn exchange their properties, if both these planets influence each other. Kalidasa has written about the peculiar properties of the effect of Venus and Saturn in *Uttarakalamrit*. The effect of Saturn is very prominent in the birth chart e.g. Moon falls in Saturn's constellation *Pushya*. The 10th lord occupies Saturn's constellation *Uttara Bhadrapada*. Besides, Saturn and Moon are the strongest planets in this birth chart, as these obtain 1.54 and 1.47 *Shadabalas*. Saturn aspects ascendant lord Moon and the

10th house and is exalted in the fourth house. There are extremely favourable planetary combinations to become prominent, most successful, popular and meritorious film actor, director, producer etc. like the great showman of all times, Raj Kapoor.

*Illustration : 7.3* (**DA**) *Horoscope No.: 92*

Date of birth : 26.09.1923 Time of birth : 21:30:00 hrs
Place of birth : Gurdaspur Lat 22:12:00 N Long 85:23:00E
Ayanamsa : 22:47:24 Sidereal Time : 21:59:16

| **Pln** | **Degree** | **Rasi** | **Nakshatra** | **Pad** |
|---|---|---|---|---|
| Asc | 18:08:15 | Tau | Rohini | 3 |
| Sun | 9:44:16 | Vir | U Phalguni | 4 |
| Mon | 27:34:54 | Pis | Revati | 4 |
| Mar (C) | 23:30:35 | Leo | P Phalguni | 4 |
| Mer (R/C) | 15:00:02 | Vir | Hasta | 2 |
| Jup | 24:47:52 | Lib | Visakha | 2 |
| Ven (C) | 14:05:15 | Vir | Hasta | 2 |
| Sat | 27:45:10 | Vir | Chitra | 2 |
| Rah (R) | 18:43:33 | Leo | P Phalguni | 2 |
| Ket (R) | 18:43:33 | Aqu | Satabhisha | 4 |

**Lagna Chart**

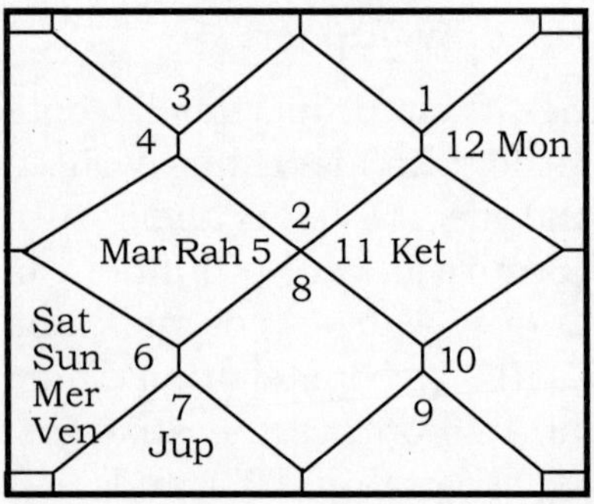


**Navamsa Chart**

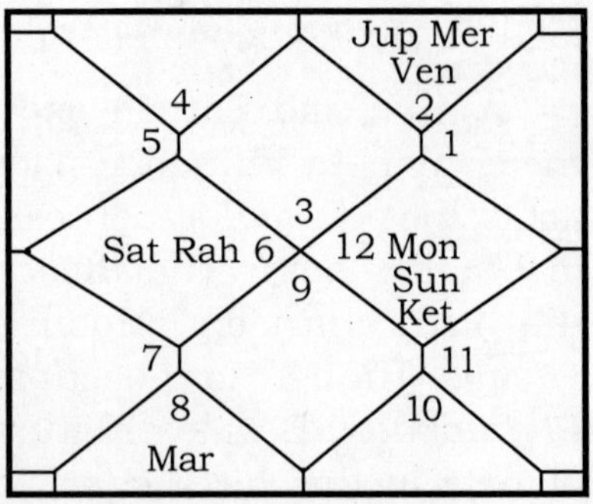


Balance of Vimsottari Dasa of **Mer 3Y 1M 0D**

Devanand needs no introduction as he is one of the top three top most pillars of the film industry of that era. Devanand, Dilip Kumar and Raj Kapoor were the three most popular, versatile, talented artist and actors. Devanand is an actor, director, producer etc. He made many historic films like Kala Bazaar, Humdum, Guide, Hare Rama Hare Krishna, Prem Pujari etc. He has made an unforgettable contribution in the history of films. He made 'Navketan Film Studios' in addition to many dozen successful silver jubilee hit films.

Devanand was born when Taurus ascendant was rising at 18° 8', which obtains *navamsa* of Gemini. The lord of the ascendant, Venus, the 9th and 10th lord *Yogakaraka* Saturn, and the 2nd and the 5th lord Mercury are associated with the 4th lord Sun in the 5th house. This, in itself, is a most powerful planetary combination for film career and extraordinary talent of acting. This shows intelligence for innovative creation, sharp vision and inclination towards making love etc.

The lord of the 3rd house, Moon, occupies the 11th house and aspects the 5th house. Moon is one of the most important significators, for bestowing acting skill, by changing the mood and switching over from one mood to another. Moon is the strongest planet in the birth chart and obtains 1.32 *Shadabalas.*

***Adhi Yoga:*** Jupiter, Venus and Mercury occupy the 6th, 7th and 8th house, as reckoned from Moon, and give rise to a powerful *Adhi Yoga,* which is most auspicious yoga and elevated Devanand to the top most position of his film career. He was liked and loved by almost all film goers, so much so, that many females committed suicide due to their uncontrollable liking for Dev Anand.

## Study of the Birth chart of Dev Anand

**THE THIRD HOUSE:**

Lord of the 3rd house, Moon, joins the 11th house, identical to Pisces sign and falls in the *Revati* constellation ruled by Mercury. Moon and Mercury both are the significators of film career. Moon lends its favourable aspect over the 5th house and obtains *vargottam navamsa*. Moreover, Moon receives the aspect of Mars, Mercury, Saturn, the Sun and the ascendant lord Venus. This planetary combination resulted into multifarious activities like acting, direction, production etc. This provided him multiple talent and intelligence to understand the demand and interests of the film goers.

## THE FIFTH HOUSE

The 5th house has important role to play with regards to one's merits, talent, ability, skill and intelligence etc. Devanand has been blessed with unfathomable innovative vision with regard to making films, and acting, along with production and direction. Placement of exalted Mercury, with the ascendant lord in the 5th house, is like the fragrance in the flower or fuel in the fire, which has further added the innovative ideas and sharpness of brain with immense intelligence and skill.

## THE TENTH HOUSE

The 10th house becomes extremely well disposed as its lord *Yogakaraka* Saturn joins the 5th house, in association with the 5th lord Mercury and the ascendant lord Venus. One becomes equal to a king, minister, M.P. or Chief of a big organization. This is one of the best possible combinations with regard to one's occupation and elevation. The 10th and the 5th house are strongly related with each other, which have elevated Devanand to enormous heights. The 10th lord Saturn obtains *navamsa* of Mercury and the 5th lord Mercury obtains *navamsa* of Venus along with Jupiter. Both luminaries, the Sun and Moon, obtain *navamsa* of 11th lord Jupiter. Mars obtains own *navamsa*, giving him a long stay in films.

## THE MERCURY

5th lord Mercury is exalted in the 5th house. Mercury

and Moon aspect each other. Mercury and Moon are the significators and have mutual exchange of constellation. Mercury falls in Moon's constellation *Hasta* and Moon falls in Mercury's constellation *Revati.* Moreover, Mercury is exalted in the $5^{th}$ and is placed together with the ascendant lord Venus, *Yogakaraka* $10^{th}$ lord Saturn and the $4^{th}$ lord Sun. Thus, the $5^{th}$ house and $5^{th}$ lord Mercury are very well disposed, distinctly showing an unparallel film career to Devanand.

## THE MOON

Moon lends its favourable aspect over the $5^{th}$ house and obtains *vargottam navamsa.* Moreover, Moon receives the aspect of Mars, Mercury, Saturn, the Sun and the ascendant lord Venus. This planetary combination resulted into multifarious activities like acting, direction, production etc. This provided him multiple talent and intelligence to understand the demand and interests of the film goers.

## VENUS

The lord of the ascendant and the $6^{th}$ house, Venus, falls in the $5^{th}$ house under debilitation, and obtains own *navamsa,* in association with the $5^{th}$ lord Mercury and $11^{th}$ lord Jupiter. This is a powerful and very well placed Venus, who is the chief significator of artistic talent for actors and actresses, singers and dancers. Venus falls in Moon's constellation *Hasta.* This is like 'golden feather in the crown' that all the three significators Venus, Moon and Mercury are influencing each other directly in *navamsa* chart, and *rashi* chart, along with mutual exchanges between their constellations.

These are the most important factors for making one an actor of the first row with regard to success talent, prosperity and popularity.

*Illustration : 7.4* **(AK)** *Horoscope No.: 93*

Date of birth : 13.10.1911 Time of birth : 14:55:00 hrs
Place of birth : Bhagalpur Lat 25:14:00 N Long 86:59:00E
Ayanamsa : 22:37:20 Sidereal Time : 16:36:14

| **Pln** | **Degree** | **Rasi** | **Nakshatra** | **Pad** |
|---|---|---|---|---|
| Asc | 9:16:27 | Aqu | Satabhisha | 1 |
| Sun | 26:17:57 | Vir | Chitra | 1 |
| Mon | 5:07:15 | Gem | Mrigsira | 4 |
| Mar | 18:09:38 | Tau | Rohini | 3 |
| Mer (C) | 18:46:17 | Vir | Hasta | 3 |
| Jup | 24:42:03 | Lib | Visakha | 2 |
| Ven | 21:34:52 | Leo | P Phalguni | 3 |
| Sat (R) | 26:12:56 | Ari | Bharani | 4 |
| Rah | 8:24:11 | Ari | Asvini | 3 |
| Ket (C) | 8:24:11 | Lib | Svati | 1 |

**Lagna Chart**

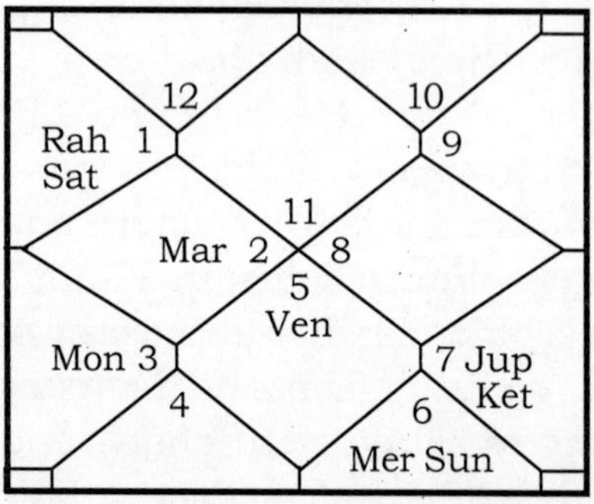


**Navamsa Chart**

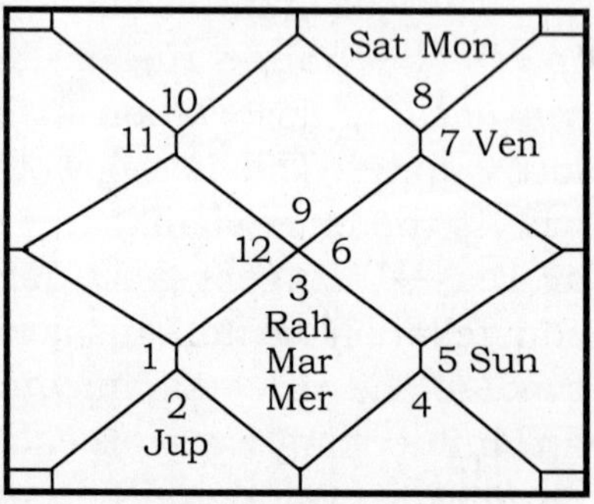


Balance of Vimsottari Dasa of **Mar 0Y 9M 22D**

Ashok Kumar was one of the multitalented actors of all times. He acted in many hundred films as Hero and character actor. His innumerable films celebrated silver jubilee. One of the famous pictures of Ashok Kumar 'Afsana' ran in one hall only, continuously for three years. He was always called *Sada Bahar* Hero, due to his active life, full of energy and enthusiasm. Following combinations may be studied.

## Study of the Birth chart of Ashok Kumar

### THE THIRD HOUSE

Ashok Kumar was born in Aquarius ascendant. The lord of the ascendant, Saturn, occupies the 3rd house. *Lagna* lord, if posited in the 3rd house or vice-versa, tends one to become an actor or actress.

### THE SIXTH HOUSE

The lord of the 6th house, Moon, joins the 5th house corresponding with Gemini sign. This indicates high degree of skill of acting and switching over from one mood to other very quickly. Mercury, Moon and Venus play significant role in the birth charts of actor and actresses, and other film artists, identical to the 3rd, 5th and 10th house particularly. Here, Moon is placed in the constellation of *Mrigsira*, ruled by the 10th lord Mars. This indicates that the native will earn his livelihood through an occupation, in which Moon and Mercury will have a prominent influence, like acting.

### THE TENTH HOUSE

The 10th lord Mars also owns the 3rd house and aspects the 10th. This provides enough strength to the 10th house. Moreover, Mars falls in Taurus, the sign ruled by Venus. Mars obtain the *navamsa* of the signaificator Mercury and falls in *Rohini nakshatra* ruled by Moon, which happens to be another *Karaka* for acting in films. Mercury provides intelligence and skill of acting, whereas Moon rules over the mental aptitude and inner ability of switching over the mood for acting in different roles.

### SIGNIFICATOR VENUS

Venus is a *Yogakaraka*, for Aquarius ascendant, and it falls in own constellation in *Poorvaphalguni*. Venus and

Moon are unusually strong in this birth chart having 1.39 and 1.47 *Shadabalas* respectively. Venus must be quite strong and well fortified for the success in film line as it is the major significator of film career. Venus obtains own *navamsa* and aspects the ascendant along with Jupiter. Thus, the ascendant is under the influence of Saturn, due to ownership, and Venus and Jupiter, due to their favourable and beneficial aspect over the ascendant.

## SIGNIFICATOR MERCURY

Mercury provides intelligence and art of acting. One cannot become a good and talented actor unless Mercury is strong and well disposed. Influence of Mercury over the 5$^{th}$ house, in one or the other way, is further good for meritorious acting. Here, Mercury owns the 5$^{th}$ house and is exalted in the 8$^{th}$ house in Virgo. This is just like to add fuel in the fire. The 5$^{th}$ lord Mercury falls in Moon's constellation *Hasta*. This shows extra-ordinary high talent and understanding of acting.

## SIGNIFICATOR MOON

The 6$^{th}$ lord Moon occupies the 5$^{th}$ house, identical to Gemini sign, ruled by Mercury. Thus, Moon joins the sign of Mercury and Mercury falls in the constellation of Moon, which gives intrinsic skill of acting and changing mood. Moon falls in *Mrigsira nakshatra* ruled by the 10$^{th}$ lord Mars, as well as obtains the *navamsa* of Mars, who is the lord of the 3$^{rd}$ and 10$^{th}$ house both.

Thus, Moon is most powerful indicator and significator in this birth chart showing that the native will have an occupation of a film actor and he will be extremely popular and successful. Aspect of *Yogakaraka* Venus and that of Jupiter, on the ascendant and ascendant lord Saturn, confirms a long and healthy life. Therefore, Ashok Kumar lived for around ninety years of age.

Above mentioned combinations and disposition of significators Venus, Mercury and Moon made Ashok Kumar highly meritorious, exceptionally popular and long lived film actor.

*Illustration : 7.5* **(HM)** *Horoscope No.: 94*

Date of birth : 16.10.1948 Time of birth : 00:31:00 hrs
Place of birth : Tiruchirapalli Lat 10:49:00 N Long 78:41:00E
Ayanamsa : 23:08:19 Sidereal Time : 1:52:35

| Pln | Degree | Rasi | Nakshatra | Pad |
|---|---|---|---|---|
| Asc | 6:50:59 | Can | Pushya | 2 |
| Sun | 29:11:17 | Vir | Chitra | 2 |
| Mon | 3:34:12 | Pis | U Bhadrapad | 1 |
| Mar | 5:49:43 | Sco | Anuradha | 1 |
| Mer (R/C) | 8:19:50 | Lib | Svati | 1 |
| Jup | 1:12:23 | Sag | Moola | 1 |
| Ven | 17:28:05 | Leo | P Phalguni | 2 |
| Sat | 9:46:01 | Leo | Magha | 3 |
| Rah (R) | 11:52:16 | Ari | Asvini | 4 |
| Ket (R/C) | 11:52:16 | Lib | Svati | 2 |

**Lagna Chart**

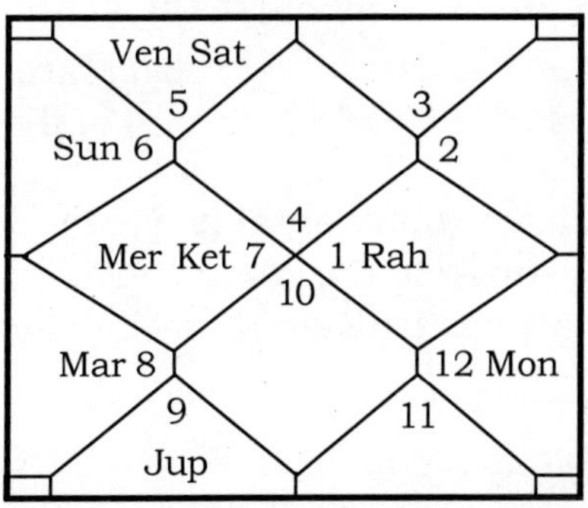


**Navamsa Chart**

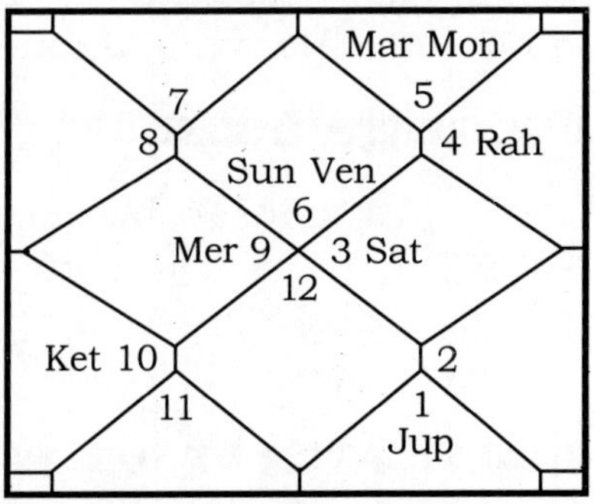


Balance of Vimsottari Dasa of **Sat 18Y 7M 28D**

Dream girl Hema Malini is still working in films in leading roles even at the age of 60 years. Her stay in films is perhaps the longest so far. She is always remembered for her box office hit films, like Sholey, Sharafat, Seeta aur Geeta, Sapno ka Saudagar, Dream Girl and Johny Mera Naam etc. Lately, her film Bagbaan created history of success due to her outstanding performance and appearance.

## Study of the Birth chart of Hema Malini

She was born in Cancer ascendant and Virgo *navamsa*. Lord of the ascendant, Moon, occupies the 9th house in Pisces. *Yogakaraka* Mars occupies the 5th house of its own. She was born on *Poornima*. Full Moon in the 9th house as *lagna* lord is extremely auspicious.

### THE THIRD HOUSE

The 3rd house is owned by Mercury, who is posited in the 4th house and aspects the 10th house. Placement of Mercury in Libra has blessed Hema Malini with acting talent. Mercury obtains *navamsa* of Jupiter. That has given her sobriety and simplicity in addition to good fortune.

### THE FIFTH HOUSE

*Yogakaraka* and 10th lord Mars is posited in the 5th house. This has blessed her with success in politics. She became a Member of Parliament, because the 10th house is under the influence of Mars and Jupiter.

### THE TENTH HOUSE

The 10th house is owned by Mars. Mars obtains *navamsa* of the Sun and falls in Saturn's constellation *Anuradha* and in own sign Scorpio. This is a powerful combination for political power.

### SIGNIFICATOR VENUS

The 4th and 11th houses are owned by Venus. Venus occupies the 2nd house and obtains *navamsa* of Mercury, which gives acting opportunities and talent. Venus is the strongest planet in this birth chart as it obtains 1.42

*Shadabalas.* Venus falls in own constellation *Poorvaphalguni* and falls in Leo owned by Sun. The Sun is the *Atmakaraka* and its placement in Virgo, under *Vargottam navamsa,* has given talent, skill and art of acting. *Atmakaraka* planet may also be the determinant of profession. Sun falls in *Chitra* constellation ruled by the 10th lord. This also inclines her to select film career.

## SIGNIFICATOR MOON

*Lagnadhipati* Moon is posited in the 9th house, in Pisces ruled by Jupiter. Jupiter and Moon are in mutual quadrant. Thus, an auspicious *Gajkesari Yoga* has been formed. Moon falls in Saturn's constellation and Saturn obtains *navamsa* of Mercury, which indirectly represents vocation having a concern with artistic talent.

*Navamsa* ascendant Virgo with Venus, and birth in Cancer ascendant with *lagna* lord Moon in Pisces justifies her beautiful appearance of a dream girl.

*Illustration: 7.6* (**Amitabh Bachchan**) *Horoscope No.: 95*

Date of birth : 11.10.1942 Time of birth : 16:00:00 hrs
Place of birth : Allahabad Lat 25:27:00 N Long 81:50:00E
Ayanamsa : 23:03:18 Sidereal Time : 16:14:42

| Pln | Degree | Rasi | Nakshatra | Pad |
|---|---|---|---|---|
| Asc | 1:55:45 | Aqu | Dhanishtha | 3 |
| Sun | 24:22:51 | Vir | Chitra | 1 |
| Mon | 10:18:36 | Lib | Svati | 2 |
| Mar (D) | 22:36:12 | Vir | Hasta | 4 |
| Mer (R/D) | 23:39:28 | Vir | Chitra | 1 |
| Jup | 0:32:15 | Can | Punarvasu | 4 |
| Ven (C) | 15:11:20 | Vir | Hasta | 2 |
| Sat (R) | 19:13:52 | Tau | Rohini | 3 |
| Rah (R) | 10:22:03 | Leo | Magha | 4 |
| Ket (R) | 10:22:03 | Aqu | Satabhisha | 2 |

**Lagna Chart**

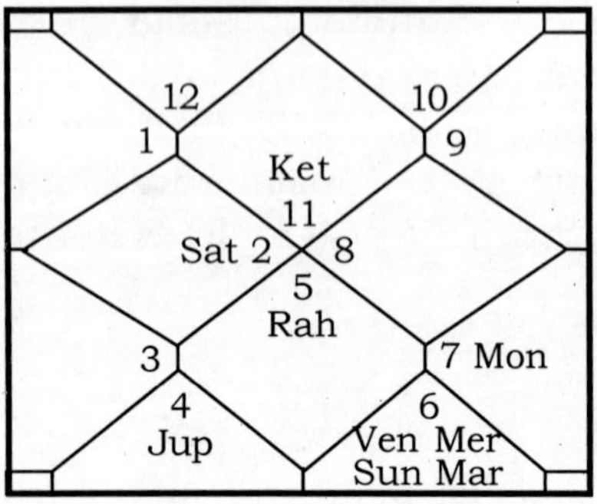


**Navamsa Chart**

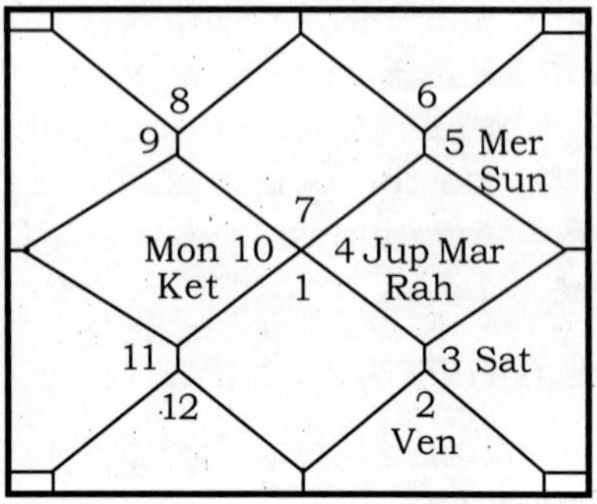


Balance of Vimsottari Dasa of **Rah 13Y 0M 29D**

Amitabh Bachchan has traveled a long way in film industry of India. He earned great respect and honour for the people of India in foreign countries and won innumerable awards, prizes and honours from time to time.

## Study of the Birth chart of Amitabh Bachchan

1. The lord of the 9th house, Venus, and that of the 10th house Mars, are conjoined in the 8th house, in Virgo sign ruled by Mercury. Thus, the joint effect of Mars, Venus and Mercury is present in this birth chart. Except 9th lord Venus, all planets, the Sun, Mars and Mercury are shifted in the 9th house. Thus, combination of four planets in the 9th house resulted into his great all-round success all over the world and made him extremely fortunate and rich person. We have mentioned at various places that the 8th house is most misunderstood house, especially with regard to all professional aspects. Importance and role of the 8th house has been dealt with, elsewhere.

2. The lord of the ascendant, Saturn, joins the fourth house and falls in *Rohini nakshatra* ruled by Venus and obtains *navamsa* of Mercury. Thus, the *lagna* lord Saturn is under the favourable influence of Venus, Moon and Mercury, and all of these are the significators of success in film line as an artist, actor or actress etc.

3. The lord of the $2^{nd}$ and $11^{th}$ house, Jupiter, is posited in the $6^{th}$ house in the sign of its exaltation. The $10^{th}$ house is aspected by *lagna* lord Saturn and $2^{nd}$ and $11^{th}$ lord (exalted) Jupiter, which shows that he will earn enormous wealth as a film artist. *Dhanadhipati* and *Dhanakaraka* Jupiter falls in own constellation *Punarvasu* and obtains *vargottam navamsa* as well.

4. The lord of the $10^{th}$ house, Mars, lord of the $2^{nd}$ and $11^{th}$ house, Jupiter, obtain *navamsa* of the significator Moon.

5. The $3^{rd}$ and $5^{th}$ houses have an important role to play, in addition to the $10^{th}$ house, in the birth chart of film actors. Here, the $3^{rd}$ lord Mars is posited in Virgo, the sign of Mercury and falls in the constellation of Moon, having an aspect over its own $3^{rd}$ house. Thus, the $3^{rd}$ house and its lord Mars are under the influence of Moon and Mercury, which has provided him great talent of art and acting.

6. $6^{th}$ lord Moon occupies the $9^{th}$ house in Libra and obtains the *navamsa* of the *lagna* lord Saturn and falls in *Svati* constellation ruled by Rahu.

7. $5^{th}$ lord Mercury is exalted in $8^{th}$ and is associated with $10^{th}$ lord Mars. Here, Mercury falls in the *Chitra* constellation ruled by Mars.

8. The Sun is *Atmakaraka* planet in this horoscope, which is posited in the $8^{th}$ house in Virgo and obtains the *navamsa* of its own i.e. Leo, in association with the $5^{th}$ lord Mercury. The Sun is the strongest planet in this birth chart, which has given interest and success in politics, in addition to his association with many politicians.

9. Major period of Saturn was running over Amitabh Bachchan from 10.11.1971, which was marvelous and outstanding. Thereafter, the $1^{st}$ part of the major period of Mercury for about 8 years and 6 months was a lean period for him but the later half of the major period of

Mercury proved exceptionally well, rather the best period of life. Any planet who owns two signs, gives the result of the first house, in which its sign falls, in the first half of the major period. Second half of the major period will give benefic or malefic results as per the position of the 2nd sign of the lord of the major period. In this horoscope, first half of the major period of Mercury, that is till 1999, had given the results of the 8th house and next half of the major period of Mercury gave the auspicious results of the 5th house from 1999 to 2007. However, major period of Mercury ended on 10.11.2007 and he is now passing through the major period of Ketu for next 7 years.

The above mentioned planetary combinations clearly indicate that the native is a very fortunate, talented and skilled artist of various divisions of film line such as acting, singing etc.

*Illustration : 7.7* **(SRK)** *Horoscope No.: 96*

Date of birth : 02.11.1965 Time of birth : 02:30:00 hrs

Place of birth : Delhi Lat 28:39:00 N Long 77:13:00E

Ayanamsa : 23:22:30 Sidereal Time : 4:52:37

| **Pln** | **Degree** | **Rasi** | **Nakshatra** | **Pad** |
|---|---|---|---|---|
| Asc | 21:48:23 | Leo | P Phalguni | 3 |
| Sun | 15:51:24 | Lib | Svati | 3 |
| Mon | 21:32:13 | Cap | Sravna | 4 |
| Mar | 27:19:30 | Sco | Jyestha | 4 |
| Mer | 6:06:50 | Sco | Anuradha | 1 |
| Jup (R) | 7:39:15 | Gem | Ardra | 1 |
| Ven | 2:24:27 | Sag | Moola | 1 |
| Sat (R) | 17:14:34 | Aqu | Satabhisha | 4 |
| Rah (R) | 11:36:02 | Tau | Rohini | 1 |
| Ket (R) | 11:36:02 | Sco | Anuradha | 3 |

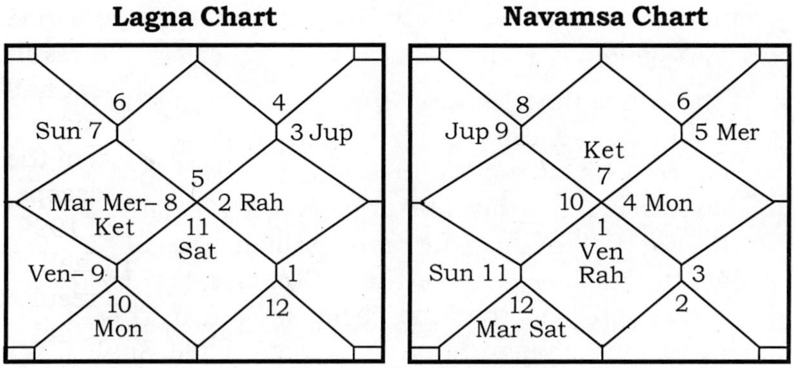


Balance of Vimsottari Dasa of **Mon 1Y 4M 5D**

Most successful and famous actor Shah Rukh Khan was born in Leo ascendant and Libra *navamsa*. Venus is the main significator of film career but Mercury cannot be overlooked. The lord of the 10th house, Venus, occupies the 5th house in Sagittarius and obtains the *navamsa* of Mars. This has given him great success in films.

1. *Yogakaraka Bhagyadhipati* Mars joins the 4th house of its own and gives rise to *Ruchaka Mahapurusha Rajyoga*. Mars and Mercury both lend their extremely beneficial aspect over the 10th house. This combination shows talent and ability with regard to his occupation.

2. Apart from the 10th house, 3rd and the 5th houses must also be examined for film career. This is most essential. The lord of the ascendant, Sun, occupies the 3rd house in Venus' sign Libra. Though the Sun is debilitated, yet it has provided the interest and aptitude of acting because the ascendant lord is related with the 3rd house.

3. The talent of changing the mood immediately for another scene comes under the control of Moon. Actors have an art of crying or laughing, according to requirement of the scene, and they are able to do it proficiently, if Moon is well fortified in the birth chart. In this birth chart, the 12th lord Moon falls in own constellation *Sravna* and obtains own *navamsa* Cancer. In fact, Moon is the

strongest planet in this birth chart, as it obtains 1.49 *shadabalas*.

4. The lord of the 5$^{th}$ house, Jupiter, is tenanted in the 11$^{th}$ house in Gemini, ruled by *Karaka* Mercury. Jupiter aspects its own 5$^{th}$ house and the 10$^{th}$ lord Venus. Jupiter is retrograde and obtains own *navamsa*. Jupiter lends his favourable aspect over the 3$^{rd}$ house, ascendant lord, lord of the 10$^{th}$ house Venus, the 7$^{th}$ house and the lord of the 7$^{th}$ house Saturn. This kind of marvelous configuration of planets made Shah Rukh Khan, so wealthy and costliest star of the present time. In fact in our research, we have established in '*Samriddhi Sutra*' that if the triangles from the 11$^{th}$ house, are strong and well disposed, in addition to the triangle places as reckoned from the 2$^{nd}$ house, one becomes extremely wealthy. In this birth chart, all favourable and strong combinations of a very wealthy person are present, apart from talent of acting, fame, success and prosperity.

5. Good fortune is also required for the success of this level. The 9$^{th}$ lord Mars, which is second strongest planet in this horoscope and forms *Ruchaka Mahapurusha Rajyoga,* is conjoined with *Dhanesh* and *Labhesh* Mercury. This is very powerful *Rajyoga* as well as *Dhana Yoga*.

Apart from *Ruchaka Mahapurush Rajyoga*, following encouraging combinations are also present in the birth chart :

*1.* *Sasa Mahapurusha Rajyoga* due to placement of Saturn in own sign Aquarius in the 7$^{th}$ house.

*2.* *Mahalakshmi Yoga* due to placement of the 9$^{th}$ lord Mars in own sign Scorpio in the 4$^{th}$ house.

*3.* *Vasumati Yoga, Parvata Yoga, Durdhara Yoga, Neech Bhang Rajyoga, Vipreet Rajyoga, Kahal Yoga, Kendra Trikona Rajyoga* etc.

*Illustration : 7.8* (**ARB**) *Horoscope No.: 97*

Date of birth : 01.11.1973 Time of birth : 12:16:00 hrs
Place of birth : Mangrol Lat 26:15:00 N Long 77:20:00E
Ayanamsa : 23:29:45 Sidereal Time : 14:36:59

| **Pln** | **Degree** | **Rasi** | **Nakshatra** | **Pad** |
|---|---|---|---|---|
| Asc | 2:53:38 | Cap | Uttarasadha | 2 |
| Sun | 15:12:39 | Lib | Svati | 3 |
| Mon | 23:35:46 | Sag | Purvasadha | 4 |
| Mar (R) | 5:47:16 | Ari | Asvini | 2 |
| Mer (R) | 2:51:43 | Sco | Visakha | 4 |
| Jup | 10:36:20 | Cap | Sravna | 1 |
| Ven | 1:52:17 | Sag | Moola | 1 |
| Sat (R) | 11:02:50 | Gem | Ardra | 2 |
| Rah | 6:18:26 | Sag | Moola | 2 |
| Ket | 6:18:26 | Gem | Mrigsira | 4 |

**Lagna Chart**

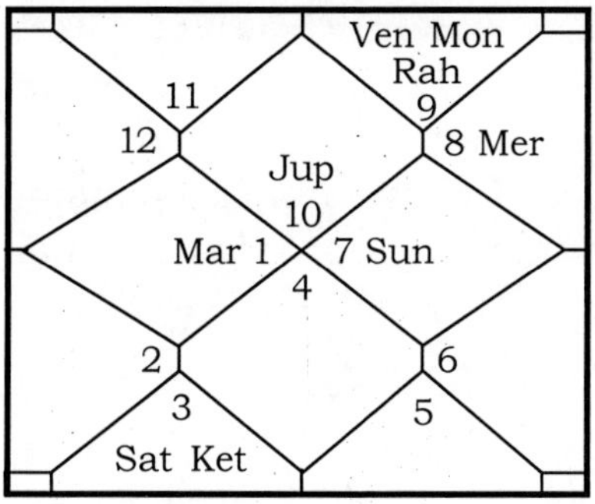


**Navamsa Chart**

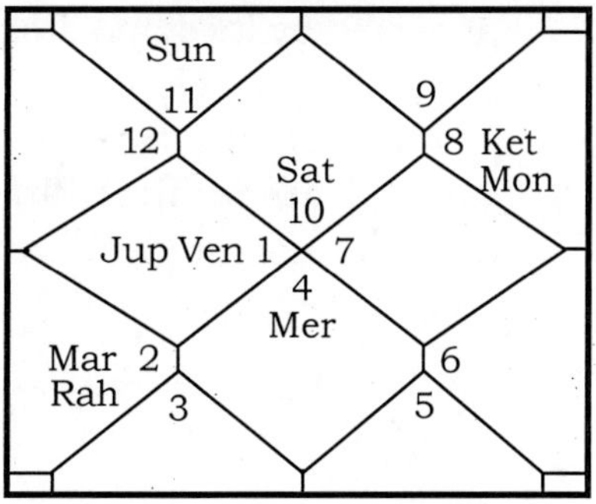


Balance of Vimsottari Dasa of **Ven 4Y 7M 8D**

Aishwarya Rai Bachchan his proud of being the most beautiful lady of the world, of her times, apart from winning the title of Miss World. She is one of the most famous actresses of the present time. She has acted in English films, too. She is fortunate to get married to Abhishek Bachchan even after involvement with so many other actors. She was married well in time, almost at appropriate age, in a most respectable and reputed Bachchan family. Following planetary proposition may be studied:

1. Lord of the 3rd house, Jupiter, occupies Capricorn ascendant, which is her rising sign. The ascendant obtains *Vargottam navamsa* with *lagna* lord Saturn in own *navamsa* Capricorn.

2. The lord of the 10th and 5th *Yogakaraka* Venus and the 7th lord Moon are placed together in the 12th house. Presence of Jupiter in the ascendant has blessed her with impressive overall physique and personality and expressive appearance.

3. Sun falls in the 10th house under debilitation, but there is cancellation of debilitation as well because the Sun obtains *Neech Bhanga Rajyoga.*

4. Jupiter and Venus both obtain *navamsa* of Mars, which made her high headed.

5. The 9th lord Mercury is posited in the 11th house and is aspected by its dispositor Mars. Mercury falls in Jupiter's constellation *Visakha* and obtains *navamsa* of Moon. Thus Mercury, who is the significator of wisdom and talent, is under the influence of Mars, Jupiter and Moon and that has made her extremely fortunate in almost all aspects of life.

6. Lord of the ascendant, Saturn, falls in the 6th house in Gemini, in Ardra constellation. Thus, Saturn falls in sign of Mercury and obtains own *navamsa*. This has further added talent of dance, acting etc.

7. Jupiter falls in Moon's constellation *Sravna*, the *Karaka* of success in films.

The above mentioned combinations have given her world wide fame. *Ruchaka Mahapurusha Rajyoga, Durdhara*

*Yoga, Vasumati yoga, Neech Bhanga Rajyoga* etc. are present in the birth chart.

We have discussed a few cases quite exhaustively to explain the planetary combinations for film actors and actresses. The third, the fifth and the tenth houses play significant role in their horoscopes. Venus, Moon and Mercury are the chief significators. These houses should have an influence of the significators to become a talented and successful film artist, actor, director, dancer, singer, lyric writer and the like.

Now, we will discuss the concerning planetary combinations of a few film actors, in brief.

*Illustration : 7.9* **(MK)** *Horoscope No.: 98*

Date of birth : 01.08.1932 Time of birth : 11:55:00 hrs

Place of birth : Mumbai Lat 18:58:00 N Long 72:50:00E

Ayanamsa : 22:55:00 Sidereal Time : 7:54:56

| **Pln** | **Degree** | **Rasi** | **Nakshatra** | **Pad** |
|---|---|---|---|---|
| Asc | 4:08:26 | Lib | Chitra | 4 |
| Sun | 15:51:03 | Can | Pushya | 4 |
| Mon | 1:50:46 | Can | Punarvasu | 4 |
| Mar | 4:42:01 | Gem | Mrigsira | 4 |
| Mer | 8:44:05 | Leo | Magha | 3 |
| Jup | 4:56:24 | Leo | Magha | 2 |
| Ven | 8:19:32 | Gem | Ardra | 1 |
| Sat (R) | 7:56:39 | Cap | Uttarasadha | 4 |
| Rah (R) | 24:40:52 | Aqu | P Bhadrapad | 2 |
| Ket (R) | 24:40:52 | Leo | P Phalguni | 4 |

**Lagna Chart**

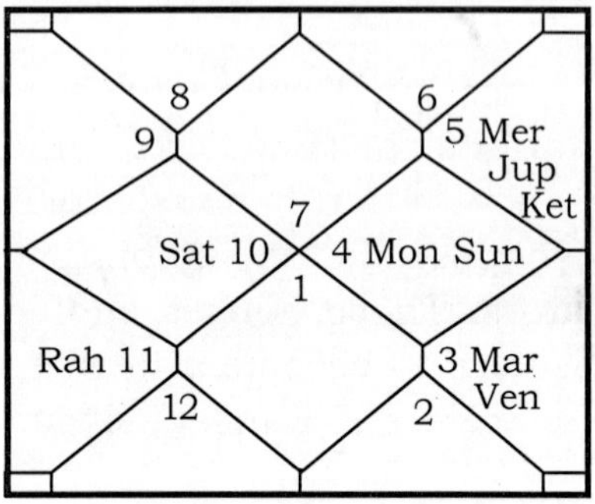


**Navamsa Chart**

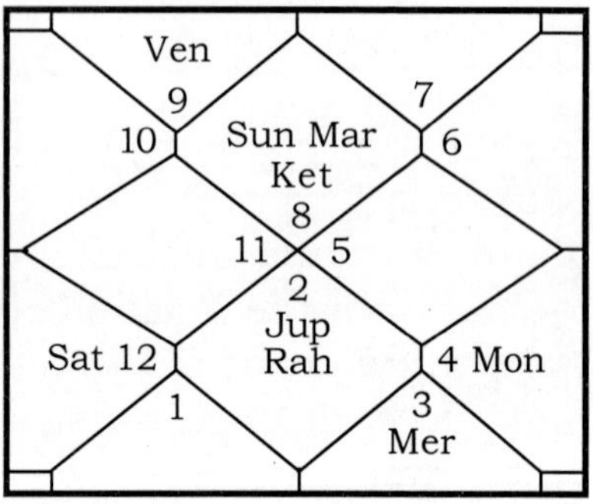


Balance of Vimsottari Dasa of **Jup 1Y 9M 12D**

Meena Kumari was born in Libra ascendant, which obtains *navamsa* of Scorpio.

*Yogakaraka* Saturn occupies the fourth house of its own giving rise to *Sasa Mahapurusha Rajyoga.* The 10th lord Moon is posited in the 10th house of its own and obtains *vargottam navamsa.* Moon falls in *Punarvasu* constellation, ruled by the 3rd lord Jupiter.

Lord of the 3rd house, Jupiter, and 9th lord Mercury are associated with each other. Both, Jupiter and Mercury, aspect the 5th house. The 10th house is occupied by both the luminaries, the Sun and Moon. Venus is one of the most important significator, who falls in the 9th house and owns the ascendant. Venus occupies the 9th house, identical to Gemini sign and obtains *navamsa* of the 3rd lord Jupiter and Jupiter obtains the *navamsa* of Venus. Thus, there is mutual exchange between the *navamsa* of the ascendant lord Venus and the 3rd lord Jupiter. This is the most powerful combination for success in films. These combinations made Meena Kumari the top most heroine of her time. She was called 'Tragedy queen' of Indian Film Industry.

*Illustration : 7.10* (**MS**) *Horoscope No.: 99*

Date of birth : 11.11.1936 Time of birth : 01:50:00 hrs

Place of birth : Calcutta Lat 22:30:00 N Long 88:20:00E

Ayanamsa : 22:58:46 Sidereal Time : 5:09:09

| **Pln** | **Degree** | **Rasi** | **Nakshatra** | **Pad** |
|---|---|---|---|---|
| Asc | 25:17:24 | Leo | P Phalguni | 4 |
| Sun | 25:16:28 | Lib | Visakha | 2 |
| Mon | 18:46:58 | Vir | Hasta | 3 |
| Mar | 4:44:55 | Vir | U Phalguni | 3 |
| Mer (C) | 20:44:09 | Lib | Visakha | 1 |
| Jup | 2:24:33 | Sag | Moola | 1 |
| Ven | 29:46:51 | Sco | Jyestha | 4 |
| Sat (R) | 22:51:57 | Aqu | P Bhadrapad | 1 |
| Rah (R) | 1:56:56 | Sag | Moola | 1 |
| Ket (R) | 1:56:56 | Gem | Mrigsira | 3 |

**Lagna Chart**

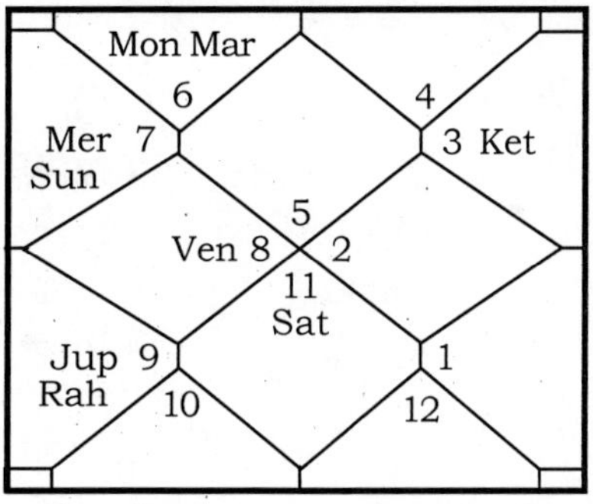


**Navamsa Chart**

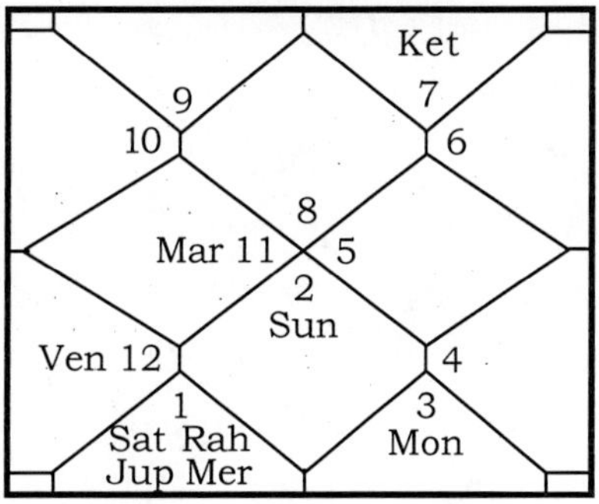


Balance of Vimsottari Dasa of **Mon 3Y 4M 29D**

She was born in Leo ascendant, which obtains *navamsa* of Scorpio. The lord of the ascendant, Sun, joins the 3rd house with Mercury, the *Karaka,* identical to Venus' sign Libra. This is the combination, which tends one towards film career and provides talent and the art of acting, dancing, singing etc.

Lord of the 10th and 3rd house, Venus, is posited in the 4th house and aspects the 10th house. Moreover, the 10th lord Venus obtains *navamsa* of its exaltation and falls in *Jyestha* constellation, ruled by the significator Mercury. Saturn is unusually strong in the 7th house in Aquarius and forms *Sasa Mashapurusha Rajyoga* and obtains 1.61 *Shadabalas*.

*Yogakaraka* Mars is associated with Moon in the 2nd house, which is 10th from the 5th and shows acting talent, as far as change and sharpness of mood is concerned. Moon obtains *navamsa* of Mercury, the lord of the 2nd and 11th house and significator of acting. Jupiter occupies the 5th house of its own and forms *Gajkeshari* and *Kalanidhi Yoga*. Many other *Yogas* such as *Obhaichari Yoga, Chandra-Mangal Yoga, Vasumati Yoga, Sasa Yoga* etc. are present in the birth chart, which resulted into great popularity, prosperity, name and fame etc. in addition to enormous acting skill.

*Illustration : 7.11* **(AP)** *Horoscope No.: 100*

Date of birth : Time of birth : hrs

Place of birth: Lat

Ayanamsa : Sidereal Time : 11:02:34

| **Pln** | **Degree** | **Rasi** | **Nakshatra** | **Pad** |
|---|---|---|---|---|
| Asc | 16:20:17 | Sco | Anuradha | 4 |
| Sun | 15:20:08 | Vir | Hasta | 2 |
| Mon | 13:05:22 | Gem | Ardra | 2 |
| Mar (D) | 16:34:46 | Vir | Hasta | 2 |
| Mer (R) | 2:11:16 | Lib | Chitra | 3 |
| Jup | 29:31:40 | Gem | Punarvasu | 3 |
| Ven | 3:45:12 | Vir | U Phalguni | 3 |
| Sat (R) | 19:25:25 | Tau | Rohini | 3 |
| Rah (R) | 10:40:22 | Leo | Magha | 4 |
| Ket (R) | 10:40:22 | Aqu | Satabhisha | 2 |

**Lagna Chart**

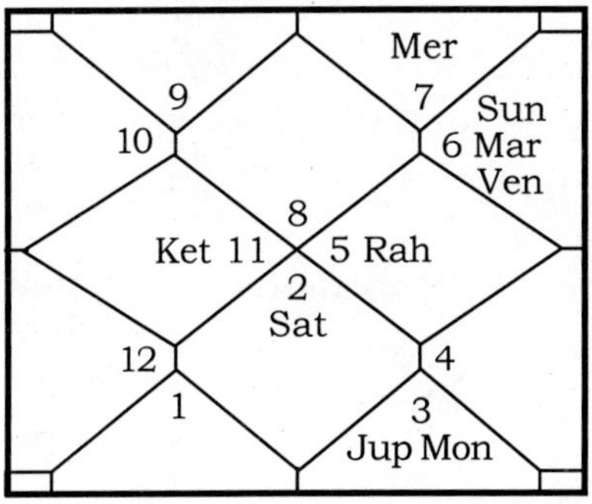


**Navamsa Chart**

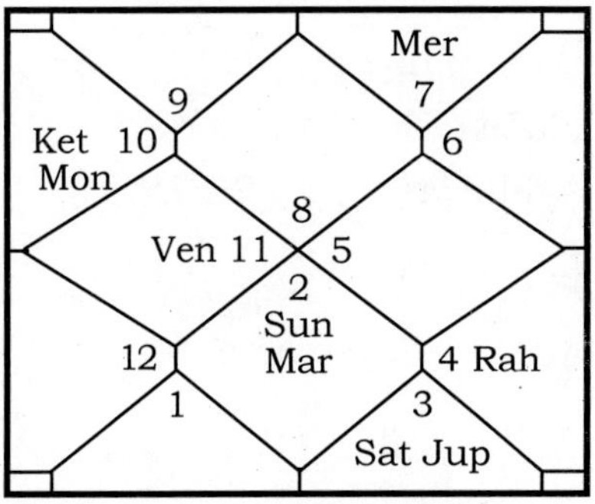


Balance of Vimsottari Dasa of **Rah 9Y 3M 28D**

Asha Parekh was born in Scorpio ascendant, which obtains *vargottam navamsa*. The lord of the ascendant Mars, and 7th lord Venus, are placed together with the 10th lord, the Sun, in the 11th house in Virgo, the sign of Mercury. These three planets the Sun, Venus and Mars lend their favourable aspect over the 5th house and provide acting, talent. The lord of the 3rd house, Saturn, joins the 7th in Taurus, the sign of the significator Venus.

The lord of the 2nd and 5th Jupiter is associated with the 9th lord Moon, in the sign of the significator Mercury. Thus, the *lagna* lord Mars, 10th lord Sun, 7th lord Venus and triangle lords, Moon and Jupiter, are in quadrant from each other, giving rise to auspicious *Yogas*.

The 10th lord Sun and the ascendant lord Mars obtain *navamsa* of the significator Venus, indicating vocation as an actress. The 3rd lord Saturn and the 5th lord Jupiter obtain *navamsa* of another significator Mercury giving her the art of acting. Mercury and Venus are the *Karakas* of vocation of acting, dancing, singing etc., who have mutual exchange of houses, which have given her the art of acting and earning through the same. The lord of the 3rd house, Saturn, falls in Taurus, and joins *Rohini* constellation, ruled by Moon, and obtains *navamsa* of Mercury. The 10th lord Sun and the ascendant lord Mars fall in the *navamsa* of Venus and strongly justify film career or a career of the world of light and glamour.

*Illustration : 7.12* (**Dharmendra**) *Horoscope No.: 101*

Date of birth : 08.12.1935 Time of birth : 06:00:00 hrs

Place of birth : Ludhiana Lat 30:56:00 N Long 75:52:00E

Ayanamsa : 22:57:59 Sidereal Time : 10:36:50

| **Pln** | **Degree** | **Rasi** | **Nakshatra** | **Pad** |
|---|---|---|---|---|
| Asc | 5:55:30 | Sco | Anuradha | 1 |
| Sun | 22:01:21 | Sco | Jyestha | 2 |
| Mon | 24:34:34 | Ari | Bharani | 4 |
| Mar | 7:40:39 | Cap | Uttarasadha | 4 |
| Mer (D) | 20:45:04 | Sco | Jyestha | 2 |
| Jup (C) | 13:27:41 | Sco | Anuradha | 4 |
| Ven | 6:22:43 | Lib | Chitra | 4 |
| Sat | 11:19:25 | Aqu | Satabhisha | 2 |
| Rah (R) | 20:05:27 | Sag | Purvasadha | 3 |
| Ket (R) | 20:05:27 | Gem | Punarvasu | 1 |

**Lagna Chart**

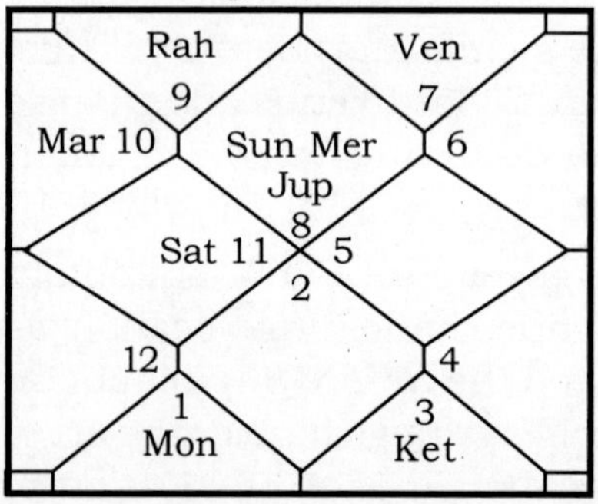


**Navamsa Chart**

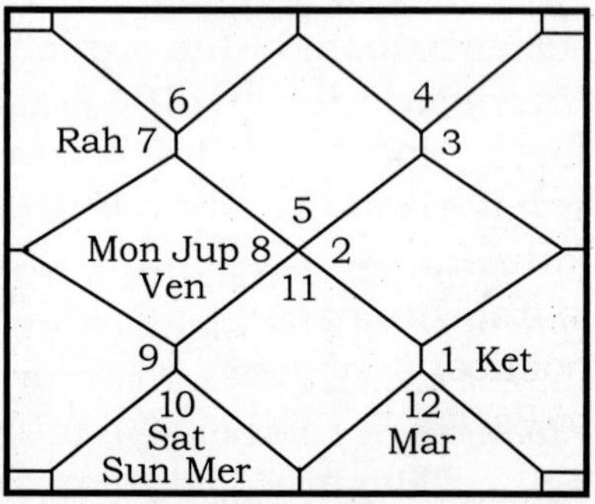


Balance of Vimsottari Dasa of **Ven 3Y 1M 19D**

Dharmendra is appreciated for his robust physique, proportionate limbs and impressive personality in film line. He acted in hundreds of films but unfortunately could not procure many awards. Satyakaam, Sholay, Phool Aur Patther, Mamta etc. were the most successful films, as far as acting part is concerned.

He was born in Scorpio ascendant with the 10th lord Sun, 11th lord Mercury and the 5th and 2nd lord Jupiter. This is a good planetary combination for attractive and impressive personality.

The 3rd house, if has a concern with the ascendant, and if Venus and Moon are well disposed, the native may have an occupation of acting. The lord of the ascendant, Mars, is exalted in the 3rd house and lends its favourable aspect over the 9th and 10th house, in addition to the 6th house and 9th lord Moon.

The 3rd and 4th lord Saturn occupies the 4th house, corresponding to Aquarius and forms *Sasa Mahapurusha Rajyoga.* Mars and Saturn, both, aspect Moon and Moon is the dispositor of Mars and falls in *Bharani* constellation, ruled by Venus. Moon and Venus both are the significators of the vocation of an actor or actress.

Venus joins the 12th house of its own and receives the aspect of the 9th lord Moon. Thus, the 9th lord Moon, ascendant lord Mars and the 7th lord Venus are in quadrant from each other, which have given rise to an auspicious yoga with regard to professional aspect. Both Karmic Control Planets, Jupiter and Mercury, are placed together in the ascendant. This is one of the strongest *Rajyoga* for success and prosperity. The 9th, 10th and the ascendant are very well fortified with the positive and powerful influence of Saturn, Mars, Jupiter, the Sun and Moon. That has resulted into political success as well. Dharmendra was elected Member of Parliament also.

*Illustration : 7.13* (**Rekha**) *Horoscope No.: 102*

Date of birth : 10.10.1954 Time of birth : 11:00:00 hrs

Place of birth : Madras Lat 13:05:00 N Long 80:18:00E

Ayanamsa : 23:13:47 Sidereal Time : 12:04:20

| **Pln** | **Degree** | **Rasi** | **Nakshatra** | **Pad** |
|---|---|---|---|---|
| Asc | 2:28:31 | Sag | Moola | 1 |
| Sun | 23:09:00 | Vir | Hasta | 4 |

| | | | | |
|---|---|---|---|---|
| Mon | 25:23:26 | Aqu | P Bhadrapad | 2 |
| Mar | 29:41:08 | Sag | Uttarasadha | 1 |
| Mer | 18:06:06 | Lib | Svati | 4 |
| Jup | 4:28:27 | Can | Pushya | 1 |
| Ven | 2:39:53 | Sco | Visakha | 4 |
| Sat | 15:48:16 | Lib | Svati | 3 |
| Rah (R) | 16:21:54 | Sag | Purvasadha | 1 |
| Ket (R) | 16:21:54 | Gem | Ardra | 3 |

**Lagna Chart**

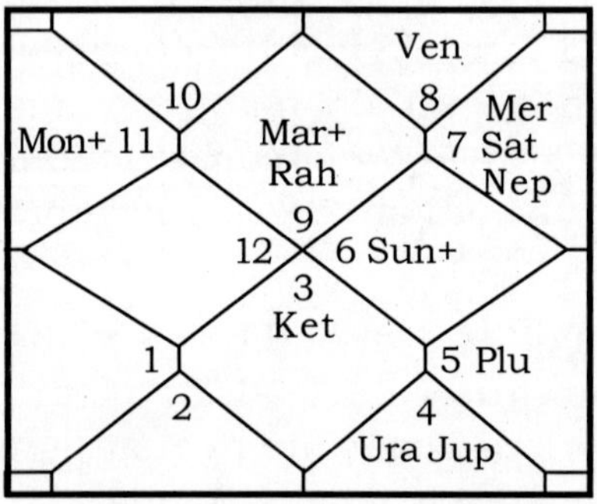


**Navamsa Chart**

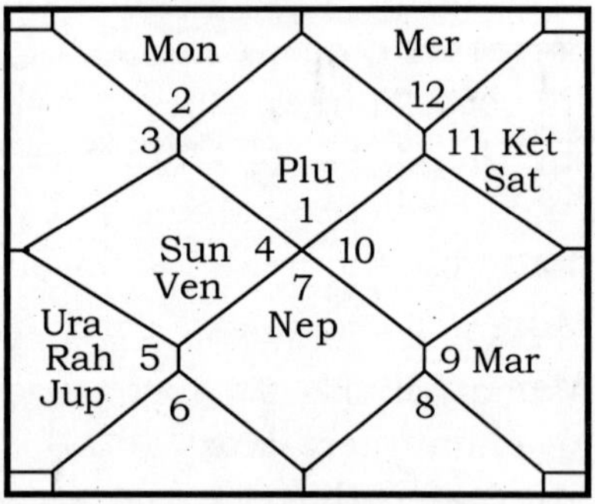


Balance of Vimsottari Dasa of **Jup 9Y 6M 11D**

Rekha was born in Sagittarius ascendant with Mars and Rahu therein. She is strong Mangli female and miserably suffered widowhood and other failures of many love affairs, though she was the most popular, prosperous and successful actress of her time.

Lord of the 3rd house, Saturn, occupies the 11th house identical to Libra, whose lord Venus obtains *navamsa* of the significator Moon. The lord of the 7th and 10th Mercury is also associated with 3rd lord Saturn, in Libra in 11th house. The 5th house, which controls talent, skill and art of acting, dancing, singing etc., receives the benefic aspect of 10th lord Mercury and 2nd and the 3rd lord Saturn. Lord of the 8th house, Moon, joins the 3rd house and obtains *navamsa* of Venus. Thus, there is mutual exchange of *navamsa* between both the significators, Venus and Moon. The lord of the ascendant

Jupiter is exalted in the 8th house and aspects Venus, and Venus falls in the constellation of Jupiter i.e. *Visakha.* Thus, the ascendant is also under the influence of significator Venus. Thus, all the significators i.e. Venus, Mercury and Moon are related with the 3rd, the 5th and the 10th house in one or the other way, giving top most film career to Rekha.

*Illustration : 7.14* (**Abhishek**) *Horoscope No.: 103*

Date of birth : 05.02.1976 Time of birth : 12:26:00 hrs

Place of birth : Bombay Lat 18:58:00 N Long 72:50:00E

Ayanamsa : 23:31:37 Sidereal Time : 20:45:36

| **Pln** | **Degree** | **Rasi** | **Nakshatra** | **Pad** |
|---|---|---|---|---|
| Asc | 26:38:48 | Ari | Bharani | 4 |
| Sun | 22:04:31 | Cap | Sravna | 4 |
| Mon | 18:08:12 | Pis | Revati | 1 |
| Mar | 22:36:33 | Tau | Rohini | 4 |
| Mer | 29:54:53 | Sag | Uttarasadha | 1 |
| Jup | 26:18:00 | Pis | Revati | 3 |
| Ven | 18:45:36 | Sag | Purvasadha | 2 |
| Sat (R) | 4:42:59 | Can | Pushya | 1 |
| Rah (R) | 23:38:12 | Lib | Visakha | 2 |
| Ket (R) | 23:38:12 | Ari | Bharani | 4 |

**Lagna Chart**

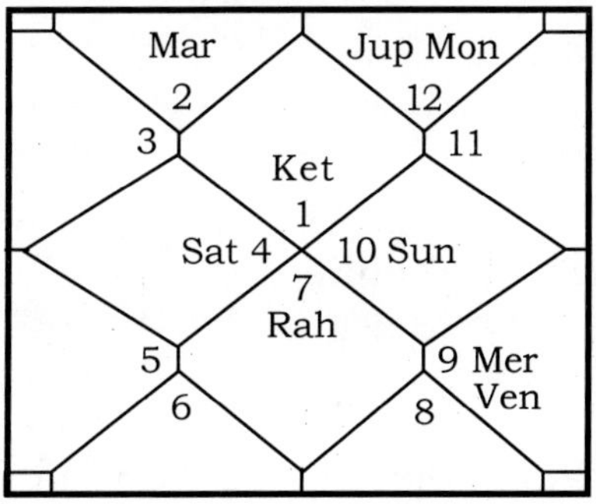


**Navamsa Chart**

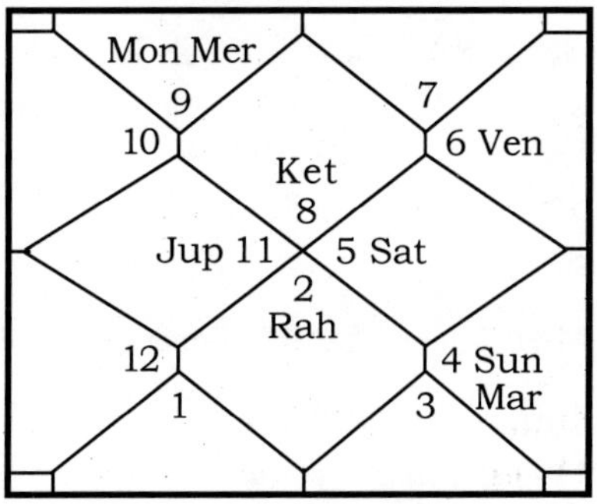


Balance of Vimsottari Dasa of **Mer 15Y 1M 15D**

Abhishek Bachchan was born in Aries ascendant, which obtains Scorpio *navamsa.*

Lord of the 5th house, Sun, occupies the 10th house in Capricorn. The lord of the 10th house, Saturn, aspects the 10th house and the 5th lord Sun. Lord of the 3rd house, Mercury, and the 2nd and 7th lord Venus are associated in the 9th house and lend their aspect over the 3rd house. *Lagna* lord Mars joins 2nd house in Taurus, ruled by Venus and Mars aspects the 3rd and 7th lord Mercury and Venus. The lord of 4th house Moon falls in *Revati* constellation ruled by the significator Mercury. The Sun and Mars obtain *navamsa* of the significator Moon. Venus, who is posited in the 9th house in Sagittarius, obtains the *navamsa* of another significator Mercury and Mercury obtains the *navamsa* of Jupiter. Venus falls in own *nakshatra Poorvashada.* Jupiter obtains the *Revati* constellation ruled by Mercury. Moon also falls in *Revati,* whereas the *lagna* lord Mars falls in Taurus, ruled by Venus and obtains *Rohini* constellation, ruled by Moon. Thus, the significators and the rulers of the concerning houses have an influence over each other, which has given great success and popularity to Abhishek Bachchan within a short span. He received the best actor award for 'Guru' for his outstanding performance.

*Illustration : 7.15* (**Nargis**) *Horoscope No.: 104*

Date of birth : 01.06.1929 Time of birth : 04:10:00 hrs
Place of birth : Calcutta Lat 22:30:00 N Long 88:20:00E
Ayanamsa : 22:52:02 Sidereal Time : 20:45:41

| **Pln** | **Degree** | **Rasi** | **Nakshatra** | **Pad** |
|---|---|---|---|---|
| Asc | 28:48:05 | Ari | Krittika | 1 |
| Sun | 17:04:04 | Tau | Rohini | 3 |
| Mon | 20:01:15 | Aqu | P Bhadrapad | 1 |
| Mar | 17:35:33 | Can | Aslesha | 1 |
| Mer (R) | 29:07:06 | Tau | Mrigsira | 2 |
| Jup | 4:27:24 | Tau | Krittika | 3 |

| | | | | |
|---|---|---|---|---|
| Ven | 5:34:25 | Ari | Asvini | 2 |
| Sat (R) | 5:39:09 | Sag | Moola | 2 |
| Rah | 28:15:40 | Ari | Krittika | 1 |
| Ket | 28:15:40 | Lib | Visakha | 3 |

**Lagna Chart**

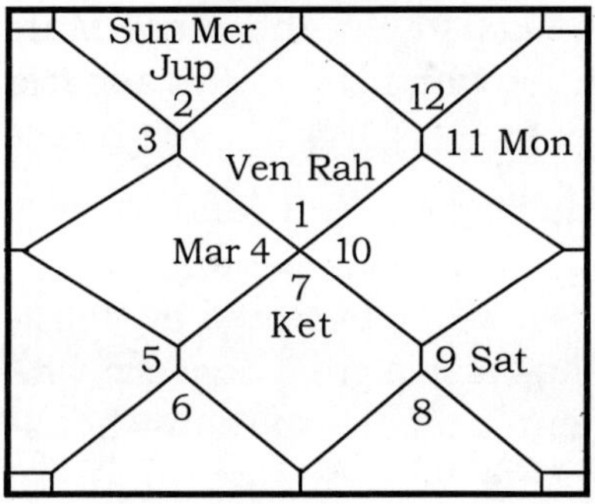


**Navamsa Chart**

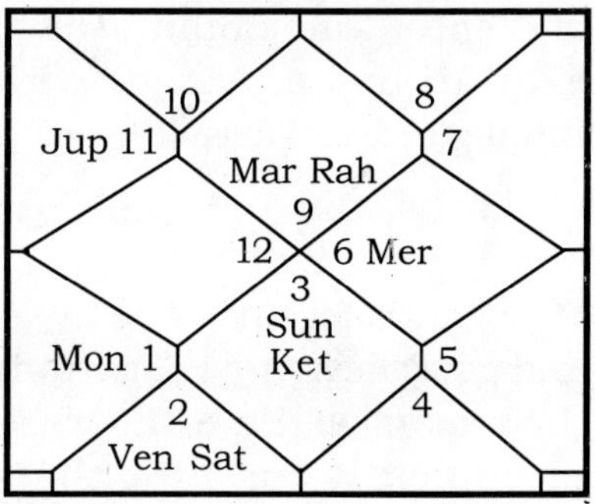


Balance of Vimsottari Dasa of **Jup 15Y 11M 21D**

Nargis was born in Aries ascendant with Venus therein. The lord of the 3rd house, Mercury, and 9th lord Jupiter are placed together in the 2nd house, with the Sun in Venus' sign Taurus. Lord of the 10th house, Saturn, and the 2nd and 7th lord Venus obtain the *navamsa* of Venus i.e. Taurus, indicating film career.

The 10th and 11th lord Saturn joins the 9th house and lends aspect over the 11th, 3rd and 6th house and on Moon as well.

The 5th lord Sun occupies the 2nd house, identical to Venusian sign Taurus, in association with 3rd lord Mercury and 9th lord Jupiter. The Sun falls in Moon's constellation *Rohini.* Moon, Venus and Mercury are the significators for the profession of the artists of films. Thus, the conjunction of the lords of both the triangles i.e. the Sun and Jupiter in the 2nd house is extremely auspicious with regard to prosperity & popularity, in addition to art and talent of acting. As the three planets fall in Taurus, which is owned by Venus, these planetary set up provided her extra-ordinary talent and true feeling of love. Who can forget Raj Kapoor and Nargis? Mars and Jupiter's aspect on the 10th house is splendid for film like occupation, as Mars falls in Moon's sign Cancer and Jupiter falls in Taurus, the sign of Venus.

The 3rd lord Mercury is *Atmakaraka*, therefore must be examined properly for profession. Mercury falls in the sign of Venus and obtains own *navamsa*, in the sign of its exaltation i.e. Virgo, which powerfully signifies her intelligence in activities of acting.

Thus, the 10th lord Saturn, 5th lord Sun, and 3rd lord Mercury are under the influence of the significators Venus, Moon and Mercury. The 2nd house, which is owned by Venus and governs source of earning, has also a great concern with the profession. Here, the placement of planets in the 2nd house prominently justifies that acting was her occupation. Everybody remembers outstanding performance and extraordinary talent of Nargis in the historical film 'Mother India' of Mehboob Khan.

*Illustration : 7.16* (**Madhubala**) *Horoscope No.: 105*

Date of birth : 14.02.1933 Time of birth : 06:55:00 hrs

Place of birth : Delhi Lat 28:39:00 N Long 77:13:00E

Ayanamsa : 22:55:30 Sidereal Time : 16:08:20

| **Pln** | **Degree** | **Rasi** | **Nakshatra** | **Pad** |
|---|---|---|---|---|
| Asc | 28:47:51 | Cap | Dhanishtha | 2 |
| Sun | 1:59:34 | Aqu | Dhanishtha | 3 |
| Mon | 15:56:07 | Vir | Hasta | 2 |
| Mar (R) | 23:38:00 | Leo | P Phalguni | 4 |
| Mer (C) | 6:47:31 | Aqu | Satabhisha | 1 |
| Jup (R) | 28:15:22 | Leo | U Phalguni | 1 |
| Ven | 15:20:30 | Cap | Sravna | 2 |
| Sat (C) | 16:18:00 | Cap | Sravna | 2 |
| Rah (C) | 14:48:16 | Aqu | Satabhisha | 3 |
| Ket | 14:48:16 | Leo | P Phalguni | 1 |

**Lagna Chart**

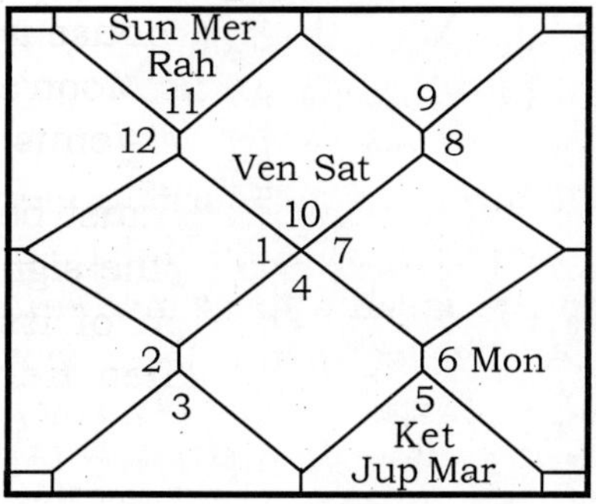


**Navamsa Chart**

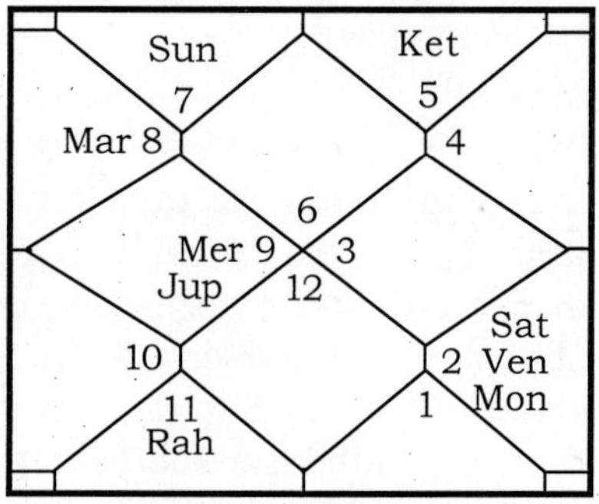


Balance of Vimsottari Dasa of **Mon 5Y 6M 17D**

Madhubala was born in Capricorn ascendant with *lagna* lord Saturn and *Yogakaraka* Venus placed therein. Here, Venus is the lord of the 5th and 10th house and joins the ascendant with ascendant lord. This is in itself very powerful combination for becoming a successful, famous, prosperous, popular and talented actress. Placement of Venus in the ascendant and in own *navamsa* Taurus blessed Madhubala with extraordinary charming and pretty appearance. She was so captivating, with extremely proportionate built and limbs, that even till today no actress could surpass her. She will always be remembered for outstanding performances, as well as extremely beautiful appearance.

Significator Moon joins the 9th house in own constellation *Hasta*. Moreover, Moon obtains *navamsa* of its exaltation and is associated with *lagna* lord Saturn and 10th lord Venus, in *navamsa* chart, which indicates the profession of an artist with regard to the world of glamour.

The lord of 11th, Mars is associated with 3rd lord Jupiter in the 8th house in Leo, and Mars falls in *Poorvaphalguni* constellation, ruled by Venus, and obtains own *navamsa*. Mars aspects the 11th house of its own, in addition to the 2nd and the 3rd house. We have learnt that 2nd and the 3rd houses are equally important for the judgement of profession along with the 10th house. Apart from the 2nd and 11th houses, the role of the 8th house is also significant for the examination of the professional progression and prosperity. These all planetary propositions may be studied in the birth chart of Madhubala.

The lord of the 2nd house, Venus, is associated with ascendant lord Saturn and obtains *navamsa* of Venus, indicating an occupation of Venus. Ascendant lord Saturn and significator Mercury receive the aspect of 3rd lord Jupiter and 11th lord Mars, which have contributed charm of attraction and impression over the facial appearance and speech i.e. in delivery of dialogues. The lord of the ascendant and 2nd house, Saturn, obtains *Sravna* constellation, ruled by the significator Moon. This has further strengthened the profession of an actress.

The lord of the 3rd Jupiter and that of the 6th and 9th house, Mercury, obtain *navamsa* of Jupiter, and Jupiter is retrograde in *Uttraphalguni* constellation of the Sun and provided Madhubala immense intelligence and sharpness of brain, apart from goodness and polite nature.

Thus, the significator Moon, Mercury and Venus influence the concerning houses quite distinctly and strongly and these combinations have elevated Madhubala, to the best and most beautiful, popular and extremely talented actress of her times.

*Illustration : 7.17* (**Smita Patil**) *Horoscope No.: 106*

Date of birth : 17.10.1955 Time of birth : 17:30:00 hrs

Place of birth : Pune Lat 18:34:00 N Long 73:58:00E

Ayanamsa : 23:14:38 Sidereal Time : 18:36:43

| **Pln** | **Degree** | **Rasi** | **Nakshatra** | **Pad** |
|---|---|---|---|---|
| Asc | 18:25:51 | Pis | Revati | 1 |
| Sun | 0:05:45 | Lib | Chitra | 3 |
| Mon | 19:28:44 | Lib | Svati | 4 |
| Mar | 9:20:09 | Vir | U Phalguni | 4 |
| Mer (R/C) | 22:29:20 | Vir | Hasta | 4 |
| Jup | 2:46:39 | Leo | Magha | 1 |
| Ven | 12:20:00 | Lib | Svati | 2 |
| Sat | 27:00:49 | Lib | Visakha | 3 |
| Rah (R) | 25:25:15 | Sco | Jyestha | 3 |
| Ket (R) | 25:25:15 | Tau | Mrigsira | 1 |

**Lagna Chart**

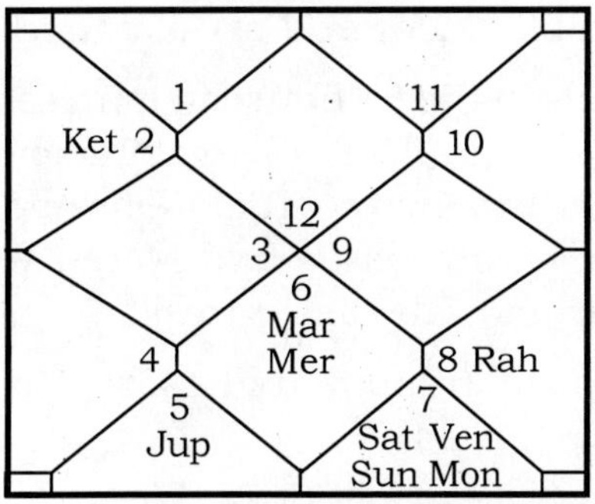


**Navamsa Chart**

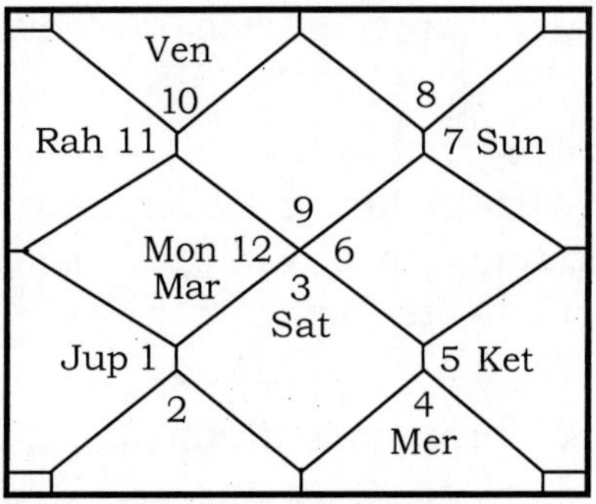


Balance of Vimsottari Dasa of **Rah 0Y 8M 13D**

Smita Patil was born in Pisces ascendant and obtains Sagittarius *navamsa*. We have observed that 8th house has a prominent role over profession. We can see that the 8th house is well disposed in the horoscopes of many persons of high walks of life including Amitabh Bachchan, Smita Patil etc. The 8th house is 11th from the 10th, the 10th from 11th and 2nd from the 7th and thus indicates professional prosperity, source of income and professional progression and advancements.

The lord of the 3rd house, Venus, joins the 8th house, identical to its own sign Libra. Lord of the 5th house, Moon, is also associated with Venus in the 8th house. Saturn is exalted in the 8th though the Sun is debilitated and is placed together with Venus, Moon and Saturn. This combination resulted into short span of life of Smita Patil but this combination also elevated her to one of the most successful and popular actress, especially of the art films. The 10th lord Jupiter aspects the 10th house. Mars and Saturn also have an aspect over the 10th house. Thus, the 10th house is under the influence of Jupiter, Mars and Saturn. Mercury is exalted in the 7th house in association with 9th lord Mars. Combination of Mars and Mercury in the 7th house is extremely adverse for marriage. She was like a second woman in the life of another hero and this cannot be appreciated. Mercury falls in the constellation of Moon and obtains the *navamsa* of Moon as well. Mercury is the significator for becoming actor or actress and its placement in the *nakshatra* and *navamsa* of Moon provided her unaccountable talent and art of acting.

The lord of the 5th house falls in the 8th house in inimical sign Libra with Venus, Saturn and Sun. This is a combination of death during delivery. Above mentioned combinations and strong Moon and Jupiter, along with Venus and Mercury, justify her being a very popular and talented actress.

With the help of so many illustrations and examples, we have made it quite clear that –

1. Apart from the 10th house, the 3rd and the 5th house must have a deep concern with the profession of the native, if she or he has to select film career.
2. Moon, Venus and Mercury are the chief significators. These planets must influence the concerning houses, either in *Rashi* chart or in *navamsa* or through the occupation of the concerning constellation.
3. Taurus, Gemini, Cancer, Virgo and Libra signs and *navamsa* should be examined in *Rashi* and *navamsa* chart both. The judgement should be made that the lord of which house is posited in these signs in *Rashi* and *navamsa* chart.
4. As we have repeatedly tried to invite the attention of readers that the 2nd and 11th house must also be examined for all kinds of profession as these indicate source of earning, whereas the 8th house indicates means of livelihood. We have contributed separate chapters on the role of the 2nd and 8th house in the judgement of one's occupation. All these houses should be looked into carefully in *Rashi*, *navamsa* and constellations, to find out one's means of livelihood. The results should be properly blended before reaching final judgement about profession. *Atmakaraka* planet also plays a prominent role in addition to the significators Moon, Venus and Mercury in the birth charts of film artists, actors, actresses, directors, singers and dancers etc.

●

## CHAPTER-8

# Stars Support Sports

In modern age, sports are a very huge source of earning. All famous and successful sportsmen, who play around the year in various parts of the globe are multimillionaires. If parents are well informed, by the genuine and dependable astrologer that their sons or daughters have a real talent of getting great success in sports, parents may give appropriate training of sports during the beginning of the career, as soon as the children step into their teenage. Let's know what combination of planets provide the talent of becoming sportsmen or sportswomen.

### Planetary Positions Indicating Success in Sports

A. **Mars:** Mars & Jupiter are the major significators for sports. Mars provides boldness, activeness, energy, fastness & courage to fight and defeat other co-players.

B. **Jupiter**: It makes one meritorious and talented in sport activities. Jupiter provides proper sense of judgment and keeps one under control to follow the rules and system of the game in a proper way. Jupiter, if well fortified, produces talent, ability, knowledge and art of playing games. Jupiter's influence tends one to specialize in some sport and to be perfect sportsman in the field of interest and inclination. Jupiter provides discipline.

C. **Mercury:** Though Mercury is not the significator of sports but it should be considered as the supporting significator, as Mercury rules over the intelligence and sharpness of brain. In absence of appropriate intelligence and proper timing, one can never be successful sportsperson. Mercury rules over the fertility and frequency of the brain, along with quick activities, fast reflex actions, cleverness, smartness, and swiftness etc.

D. **The lord of the 5th house** i.e. *Panchamadhipati***:** The 5th house rules over one's brain, brightness and decision making ability. Intelligence and art of application is very essential factor, while playing any of the games, and that comes under well fortified 5th house and its lord.

E. **The Third house:** The 3rd house governs independent decisions for action, bold activities and courage for the same. In any game, fearlessness and corresponding courage is very essential. Hesitant and shy persons can never make efforts and sincere endeavors to win over others, which is the foremost requirement of all sports and games. Thus, the 3rd house has a vital role and must be well disposed in the birth chart of the successful players.

F. **The Sixth house:** The 6th house rules over the enemies, competitors, opposition etc. The 6th house has also a deep concern with sport rivals. If the 6th house is strong and well disposed, one will win the game.

G. **The Tenth house:** When playing games becomes the source of earning then that is subjected to additional means of livelihood. The 10th house, its lord and planets placed therein play most prominent role in the judgment of the professional aspect of players.

H. **Sagittarius Sign:** Sagittarius sign indicates 'Bow', which is used to defeat enemy and opposition. Games are played so that one may defeat the opponents. Therefore, Sagittarius sign has a prominence over all other signs in the birth charts of sportspersons generally (though it is not essential in all cases).

Now, we will discuss a few birth charts of famous successful and popular spots persons, to illustrate our view point.

*Illustration : 8.1* **(PP)** *Horoscope No.: 107*

Date of birth : 10.06.1955 Time of birth : 03:27:00 hrs
Place of birth : Bangalore Lat 18:00:00 N Long 77:35:00E
Ayanamsa : 23:14:21 Sidereal Time : 20:17:17

| **Pln** | **Degree** | **Rasi** | **Nakshatra** | **Pad** |
|---|---|---|---|---|
| Asc | 17:01:03 | Ari | Bharani | 2 |
| Sun | 25:02:11 | Tau | Mrigsira | 1 |
| Mon | 12:34:06 | Cap | Sravna | 1 |
| Mar | 16:24:54 | Gem | Ardra | 3 |
| Mer (R/C) | 4:21:11 | Gem | Mrigsira | 4 |
| Jup | 6:09:53 | Can | Pushya | 1 |
| Ven | 2:34:55 | Tau | Krittika | 2 |
| Sat (R) | 22:27:12 | Lib | Visakha | 1 |
| Rah | 3:07:10 | Sag | Moola | 1 |
| Ket (C) | 3:07:10 | Gem | Mrigsira | 3 |

**Lagna Chart**

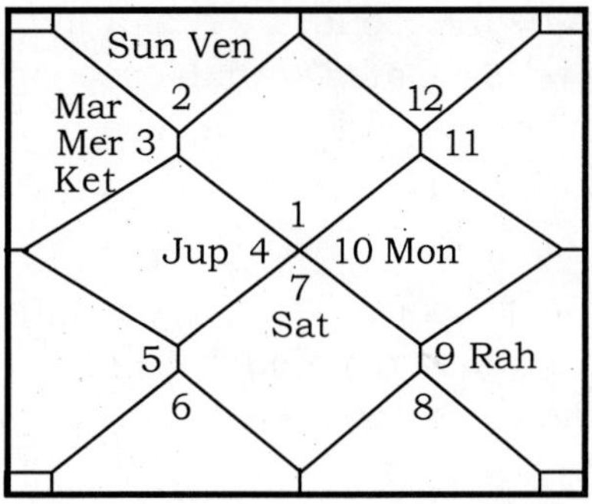


**Navamsa Chart**

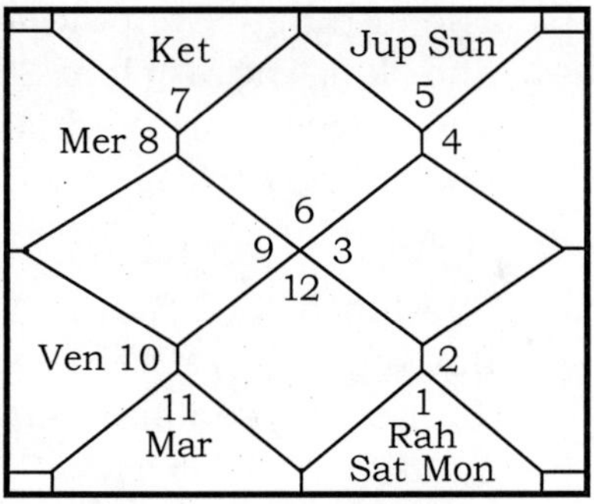


Balance of Vimsottari Dasa of **Mon 8Y 0M 26D**

Mr. Prakash Padukone is a very famous badminton player. Honorary degree of doctorate was conferred on him. He was also honoured in 1982 when he was honoured by Padmashree. During the year, 1972, he got Arjuna Award in sports for his outstanding performance in the games.

Sportsman of his caliber and talent, in the game of badminton, is a pride for our country.

## Planetary Combinations:

1. He was born in Aries ascendant with exalted Jupiter in the fourth house, giving rise to *Hamsa MahaPurusha Rajayoga*, and exalted Saturn in the seventh house, which has formed *Sasa MahaPurusha Rajayoga*. The fourth lord Moon occupies the $10^{th}$ house and forms powerful *Gajakesari yoga*.
2. Lord of the ascendant and *karaka* for sports, Mars, joins the third house with the third lord Mercury, in association with Ketu. This has provided him extraordinary skill, everlasting energy and stamina, unbeaten courage and a keen desire to defeat the sport partner and win the game.
3. Also, the lord of the sixth and third house is Mercury and its conjunction with ascendant lord Mars is certainly a blessing for any sportsperson, if it takes place in the third house particularly.
4. The fifth house should also be judged for merits, ability and skill. The fifth lord Sun is associated with the second and seventh lord Venus, in the second house. The Sun falls in the constellation *Mrigsira*, ruled by the *karaka* of sports, Mars.
5. The tenth lord Saturn, who is exalted in the seventh house, falls in *Visakha nakshatra* ruled by *karaka* Jupiter, and obtains *navamsa* of Mars as well, the other *karaka*.
6. Moon, who occupies the tenth house, obtains the *navamsa* of Mars in association with the $10^{th}$ lord Saturn. Moreover, Moon falls in own constellation *Sravana*. Thus, the tenth house is under the influence of Mars by aspect and *navamsa* lords, and Saturn due to ownership, and Moon due to placement. This is wonderful and most encouraging combination of this birth chart.

7. If reckoned from Moon, we find that Mars, Mercury and Ketu are there in the sixth house, exalted Jupiter in the seventh aspecting Moon, and exalted Saturn in the seventh aspecting the third lord Jupiter from Moon.

8. The tenth lord Saturn and the fifth lord, the Sun are the strongest planet in this birth chart. Saturn obtains 1.57 *shadabalas*, whereas the fifth lord Sun obtains 1.46 *shadabalas*. The ninth lord Jupiter obtains 1.53 *shadabalas*. The ninth lord and *Karaka* of children, Jupiter and the fifth lord Sun are very strong and very well placed. Therefore, the native is blessed with a daughter like Deepika Padukone who earned worldwide fame overnight after entering into films and immediately after her first release.

Above mentioned planetary combinations and configurations are responsible to make Mr. Prakash Padukone a world level badminton player along with great and wide fame, exceptional talent and skill in addition to fortune and finance.

*Illustration : 8.2* (**Dhyan Chand**) *Horoscope No.: 108*

Date of birth : 29.08.1905 Time of birth : 02:00:00 hrs
Place of birth : Allahabad Lat 25:27:00 N Long 81:50:00E
Ayanamsa : 22:32:14 Sidereal Time : 0:25:33

| **Pln** | **Degree** | **Rasi** | **Nakshatra** | **Pad** |
|---|---|---|---|---|
| Asc | 23:38:36 | Gem | Punarvasu | 2 |
| Sun | 12:17:37 | Leo | Magha | 4 |
| Mon | 19:37:34 | Can | Aslesha | 1 |
| Mar | 11:28:38 | Sco | Anuradha | 3 |
| Mer (R/D) | 14:40:24 | Leo | P Phalguni | 1 |
| Jup | 12:42:27 | Tau | Rohini | 1 |
| Ven | 2:50:31 | Can | Punarvasu | 4 |
| Sat (R) | 6:34:16 | Aqu | Dhanishtha | 4 |
| Rah (C) | 7:47:38 | Leo | Magha | 3 |
| Ket | 7:47:38 | Aqu | Satabhisha | 1 |

**Lagna Chart**

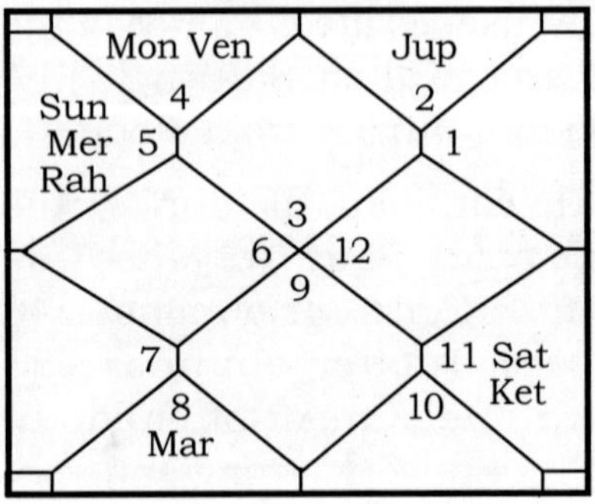


**Navamsa Chart**

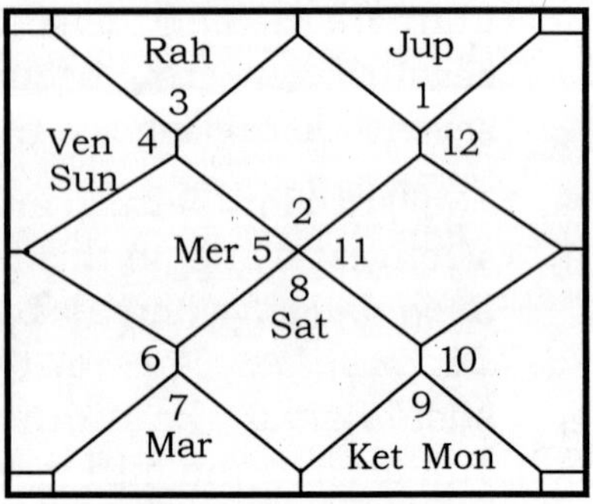


Balance of Vimsottari Dasa of **Mer 13Y 2M 21D**

Name of Dhyan Chand will remain immortal in international hockey. He was a great sportsman who rose to topmost height from a very low position. India won gold medals in Olympics during his time due to his extraordinary talent and fast game. Following planetary position may be noted in his birth chart-

## Planetary Combinations:

1. He was born in Gemini ascendant. All angles are vacant in his horoscope but the third and sixth houses, having a deep concern with sports, are very well disposed and are occupied by their own lords, the Sun and Mars respectively.

2. Dispositors of Rahu and Ketu are called Karmic control planets. If Rahu or Ketu is placed with its dispositor, that produces the best and very strong results. In this birth chart, Rahu and Ketu both are associated with their dispositors.

3. Sun and Saturn mutually aspect respectively, identical to the third and ninth house. Thus, the third house and its lord, the Sun, have become very strong and favourable. *Bhagyadhipati* Saturn and Ketu are conjoined in the ninth house, which is owned by Saturn itself that has provided immense fortune to the native. In absence of good fortune, simply the talents and merits are almost

useless because in that case, the native can not get suitable and appropriate opportunity to exhibit his talent. Thus, the third and ninth houses, in addition to the sixth house, are occupied by their own lords the Sun, Saturn and Mars. These are placed in mutual quadrant.

4. The tenth house is owned by Jupiter, who is posited in the 12th house. Jupiter obtains the *navamsa* of 6th and 11th lord Mars, showing income through sports.
5. Thus, all concerning planets for success in sports viz. Mars, the Sun, Jupiter, Saturn, Rahu and Ketu are placed in *Kendras* from each other. This is splendid, as three out of these occupy their own sign, in the respective and concerning houses.
6. The second house shows source of income. Here, the second lord Moon and the fifth lord Venus are placed together in the second house. Moon obtains Sagittarius *navamsa* and falls in Mercury's constellation *Aslesha*. Here, 5th lord Venus and Moon's constellation lord Mercury provided all essential intelligence and talent to Dhyan chand. Game is an art, which is blessed by the almighty to an individual from birth, and that can not come without the favourable influence of Venus and Mercury.

The above analysis clearly and distinctly justifies most magnificiecnt world level success of Dhyan Chand in Hockey.

*Illustration: 8.3* (**Sachin Tendulkar**) *Horoscope No.: 109*

Date of birth : 24.04.1973 Time of birth : 18:30:00 hrs
Place of birth : Mumbai Lat 18:58:00 N Long 72:50:00E
Ayanamsa : 23:29:18 Sidereal Time : 8:00:59

| **Pln** | **Degree** | **Rasi** | **Nakshatra** | **Pad** |
|---|---|---|---|---|
| Asc | 4:58:11 | Lib | Chitra | 4 |
| Sun | 10:42:50 | Ari | Asvini | 4 |

| | | | | |
|---|---|---|---|---|
| Mon | 27:19:00 | Sag | Uttarasadha | 1 |
| Mar | 26:51:52 | Cap | Dhanishtha | 2 |
| Mer | 17:04:02 | Pis | Revati | 1 |
| Jup | 16:37:08 | Cap | Sravna | 2 |
| Ven (C) | 14:32:21 | Ari | Bharani | 1 |
| Sat | 24:17:02 | Tau | Mrigsira | 1 |
| Rah | 16:33:43 | Sag | Purvasadha | 1 |
| Ket | 16:33:43 | Gem | Ardra | 3 |

**Lagna Chart**

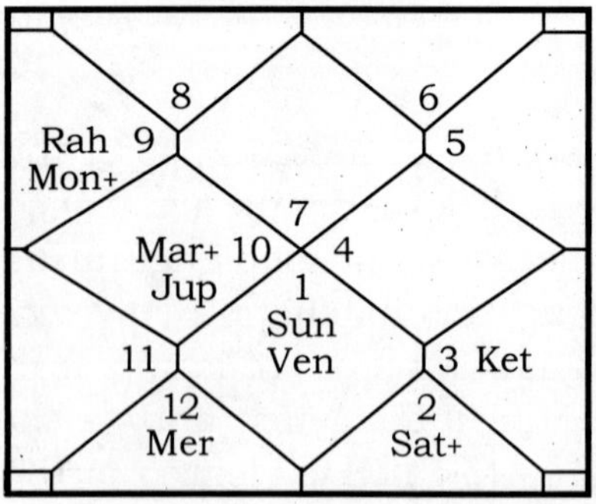


**Navamsa Chart**

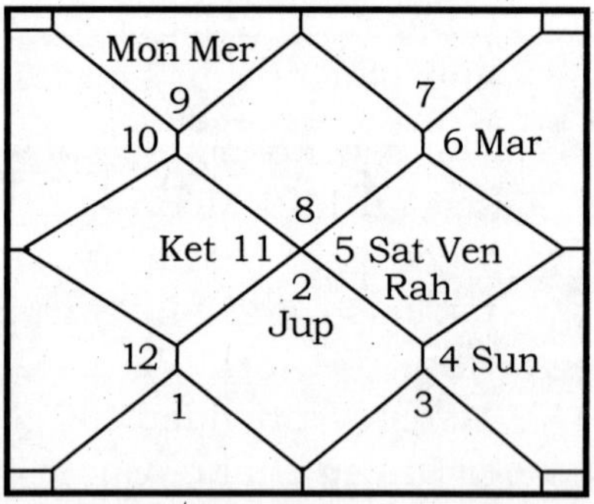


Balance of Vimsottari Dasa of **Sun 5Y 8M 14D**

Mr. Sachin Tendulkar has crossed almost all records of the game of cricket. He could not study much but he is a greatest aspiration and inspiration to all youths who play cricket. No. of books have been written on the extraordinary talent, exceptional success and outstanding performance of little master Sachin Tendulkar. What made him so successful that he earned worldwide fame, when he was just a teenager? This was the most auspicious and great moment of his birth, which elevated him to the level of sky, from the beginning till today. Following planetary placement may be noted -

## Planetary Combinations:

1. He was born in Libra ascendant, where lord Venus falls

in Aries, in the seventh house, and aspects the ascendant.

2. The lord of the tenth house, Moon, joins the third house and obtains *vargottam navamsa* in Sagittarius. In fact, Sagittarius is the ruling sign for sports, whereas Jupiter and Mars are the significators. The talent is provided by the fifth lord and Mercury. Therefore, only the combined study of all of these, with proper blending of their results and influence on the native, will reveal the degree of success of the native as a sportsperson. In this birth chart, Mars is exalted in the 4$^{th}$ house and is posited with the third and the sixth lord Jupiter, where Jupiter obtains *Neecha Bhanga Rajayoga* and Mars forms *Ruchaka Mahapurush Rajayoga.* Both, Mars and Jupiter, lend their aspect over the tenth house. This has given unparallel success to Sachin in sports.
3. The 11$^{th}$ lord Sun is exalted in the seventh and is placed together with ascendant lord Venus. Both join Aries, the sign of *karaka* Mars.
4. The 9$^{th}$ lord and *karaka* of wisdom, Mercury, is posited in the 6$^{th}$ house and gives rise to *Neecha Bhanga Rajayoga.* Placement of Mercury in the 6$^{th}$ house, in own constellation *Revati* and in Sagittarius *navamsa* has provided unbeaten talent and art of playing cricket to the Little Master Sachin.

*Illustration: 8.4* (**Pele**) *Horoscope No.: 110*

Date of birth : 23.10.1940 Time of birth : 20:00:00 hrs
Place of birth : Trescoracoes Lat 17:50:00 N Long 73:22:00E
Ayanamsa : 23:01:51 Sidereal Time : 21:30:53

| Pln | Degree | Rasi | Nakshatra | Pad |
|---|---|---|---|---|
| Asc | 8:21:24 | Tau | Krittika | 4 |
| Sun | 7:00:14 | Lib | Svati | 1 |
| Mon | 29:02:55 | Gem | Punarvasu | 3 |

| | | | | |
|---|---|---|---|---|
| Mar | 18:36:20 | Vir | Hasta | 3 |
| Mer | 1:06:04 | Sco | Visakha | 4 |
| Jup (R) | 18:59:42 | Ari | Bharani | 2 |
| Ven | 26:11:26 | Leo | P Phalguni | 4 |
| Sat (R) | 19:10:17 | Ari | Bharani | 2 |
| Rah (R) | 17:55:40 | Vir | Hasta | 3 |
| Ket (R) | 17:55:40 | Pis | Revati | 1 |

**Lagna Chart**

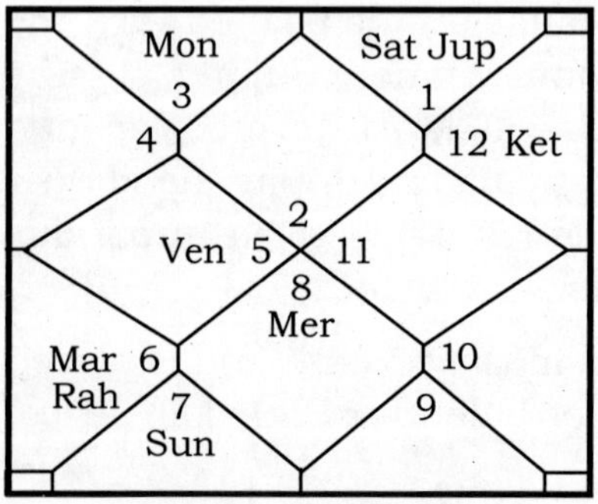


**Navamsa Chart**

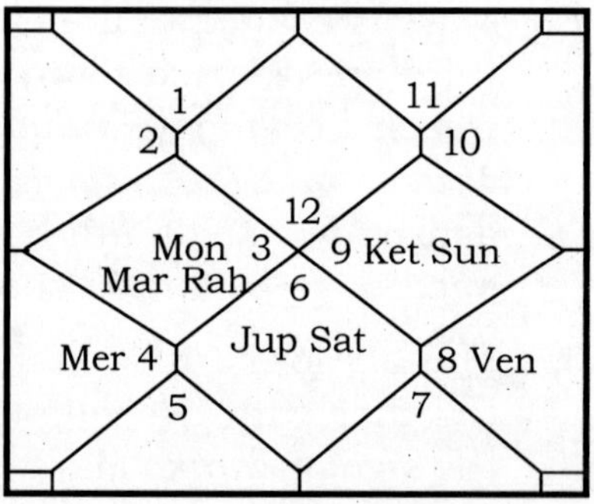


Balance of Vimsottari Dasa of **Jup 5Y 1M 21D**

Pele is a football player of worldwide fame and success. Let us analyze his birth chart with regard to his exceptionally talented sportsperson-

## Planetary Combinations:

1. Pele was born in Taurus ascendant. The lord of the 3rd house, Moon, falls in Gemini, in 2nd house, in *Punarvasu* constellation ruled by Jupiter. Moon obtains *vargottam navamsa* and receives the aspect of 9th and 10th lord *Yogakaraka* Saturn. This combination provides enough strength to the 3rd house and its lord Moon.

2. The 6th house is occupied by the 4th lord Sun and is aspected by the significator Jupiter. There is a mutual exchange between the 6th lord Venus and the 4th lord, Venus is also the *lagna* lord. This has enhanced the

strength of the 6th lord Venus and it obtains 1.52 *shadabala*, which has produced outstanding talent of a sportsperson.

3. There is a mutual exchange between the 7th lord Mars and 5th lord Mercury. This shows extreme fastness of the game of the native, in addition to sharpness and intelligence of the mind.

4. Jupiter and Mars are the main significators for sports, whereas the 5th lord and Mercury provide the intelligence, talent and art of playing the game. Here, the *karaka* Jupiter is associated with *Yogakaraka* Saturn in the 12th house and is aspected by its dispositor, as well as significator Mars, which has made Pele extremely talented player.

5. 10th lord Saturn and 11th lord Jupiter fall in Aries, in the 12th house, under the aspect of 10th and 7th lord Mars; and the Sun. Both, Jupiter and Saturn, obtain the *navamsa* of Mercury as well. This is also a powerful indication of earning money though sports, as well as possessing a high degree of caliber and talent of a player.

6. Jupiter aspects the 6th house, the Sun, who occupies the 6th house and the 6th lord Venus.

7. Lord of the 3rd house, Moon, joins the 2nd house in Gemini and falls in Jupiter's constellation *Punarvasu.* Jupiter is a significator of games specially when it is under the influence of Mars, identical to the 3rd or the 6th house. We hasten to add that the 3rd lord Moon in Gemini obtains *vargottam navamsa.*

8. Moon, Mars and Rahu obtain the *navamsa* of 5th lord Mercury, whereas *Yogakaraka* Saturn, who is the 9th and 10th lord, and Jupiter fall in the sign of Mars, Aries, and obtain the *navamsa* of Mercury as well. Even in *navamsa* chart, the ascendant and the 6th lord Venus obtain the *navamsa* of the significator Mars.

These are the strong indications for obtaining

extraordinary success, money, prosperity and popularity as a sportsman. Aspect of the 9th lord Saturn on the 9th house has made Pele extremely fortunate in the aspect of playing football and earning worldwide honour.

*Illustration: 8.5* (**Sunil Gavaskar**) *Horoscope No.: 111*

Date of birth : 10.07.1949 Time of birth : 20:42:00 hrs
Place of birth : Mumbai Lat 18:58:00 N Long 72:50:00E
Ayanamsa : 23:09:01 Sidereal Time : 15:16:11

| **Pln** | **Degree** | **Rasi** | **Nakshatra** | **Pad** |
|---|---|---|---|---|
| Asc | 17:09:45 | Cap | Sravna | 3 |
| Sun | 24:51:15 | Gem | Punarvasu | 2 |
| Mon | 28:41:11 | Sag | Uttarasadha | 1 |
| Mar | 28:16:12 | Tau | Mrigsira | 2 |
| Mer | 7:41:20 | Gem | Ardra | 1 |
| Jup (R) | 5:21:02 | Cap | Uttarasadha | 3 |
| Ven | 17:23:09 | Can | Aslesha | 1 |
| Sat | 10:05:03 | Leo | Magha | 4 |
| Rah (R) | 28:22:00 | Pis | Revati | 4 |
| Ket (R) | 28:22:00 | Vir | Chitra | 2 |

**Lagna Chart**

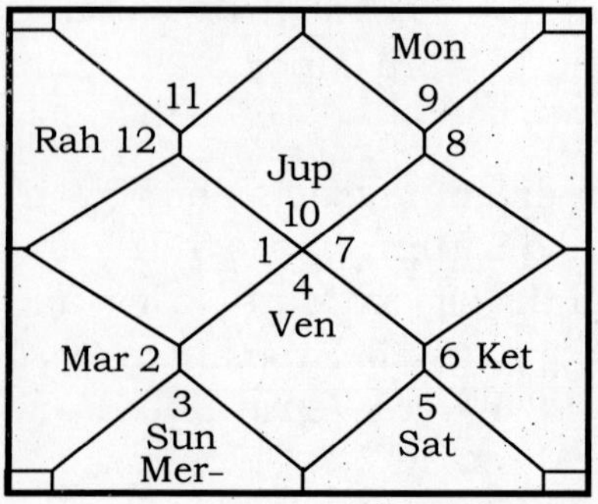


**Navamsa Chart**

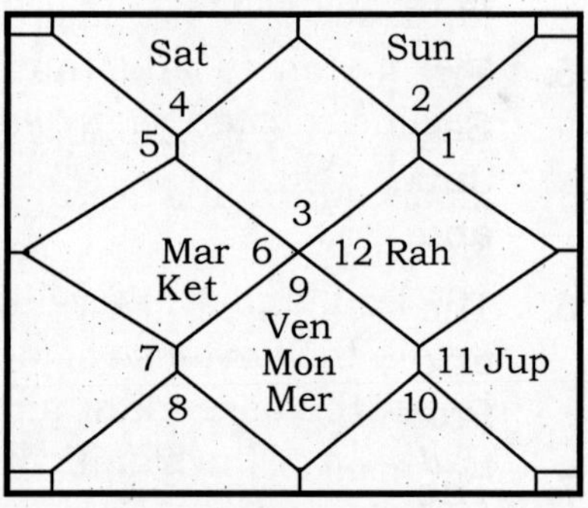


Balance of Vimsottari Dasa of **Sun 5Y 1M 2D**

The 3rd and the 6th house, if well disposed and powerful, can make the native a sportsperson if these houses are strong, their lords influence the 11th or 2nd house, the native will earn through sports.

## Planetary Combinations:

1. Rahu is posited in the 3rd house in Pisces and the 6th house is occupied by the 8th lord Sun and 6th and 9th lord Mercury. Thus, the 3rd and the 6th houses are well disposed and these are occupied by malefics Rahu and Sun.
2. The 5th house and Jupiter indicate intelligence, without which one can not become an international player. In this birth chart, the lord of the 5th house, Venus, falls in the 7th house and receives the favourable and benefic aspect of 3rd lord Jupiter, who occupies the ascendant.
3. The lord of 11th house, Mars, and that of the 2nd house, Saturn, aspect their own houses respectively, and have a mutual aspect with each other as well. This combination of the 2nd and 11th lords confirms huge earning through sports.
4. *Yogakaraka* i.e. 10th and 5th lord Venus falls in the constellation of the 6th lord Mercury i.e. *Aslesha* and Venus is aspected by the 3rd lord Jupiter, and Jupiter is placed in constellation of the Sun i.e. *Uttarashadha*, who is tenanted in the 6th house.
5. The 10th lord Venus obtains Jupiter's *navamsa* Sagittarius, which is the significator of sports. Moreover, Jupiter is the lord of the 3rd house and aspects the 10th and 11th lords, Venus and Mars, both.
6. The 6th and 9th lord Mercury, 7th lord Moon and the 5th and 10th lord Venus obtain Sagittarius *navamsa*. Prominence of Sagittarius does show success in sports.
7. The 7th lord Moon, who joins Sagittarius, obtains *vargottam navamsa*. Moon falls in Sun's constellation

*Uttarashadha* and receives the aspect of Mars, Sun and Mercury.

These factors very well signify Sunil Gavaskar's outstanding record and international success in cricket.

*Illustration: 8.6* (**P.T. Usha**) *Horoscope No.: 112*

Date of birth : 20.05.1965 Time of birth : 01:00:00 hrs

Place of birth : Calicut Lat 11:15:00 N Long 75:46:00E

Ayanamsa : 23:22:07 Sidereal Time : 16:22:06

| Pln | Degree | Rasi | Nakshatra | Pad |
|---|---|---|---|---|
| Asc | 7:54:13 | Aqu | Satabhisha | 1 |
| Sun | 5:12:51 | Tau | Krittika | 3 |
| Mon | 23:37:14 | Sag | Purvasadha | 4 |
| Mar | 20:08:55 | Leo | P Phalguni | 3 |
| Mer | 12:49:08 | Ari | Asvini | 4 |
| Jup (C) | 12:50:27 | Tau | Rohini | 1 |
| Ven (C) | 15:06:07 | Tau | Rohini | 2 |
| Sat | 22:35:44 | Aqu | P Bhadrapad | 1 |
| Rah | 20:21:52 | Tau | Rohini | 4 |
| Ket | 20:21:52 | Sco | Jyestha | 2 |

**Lagna Chart**

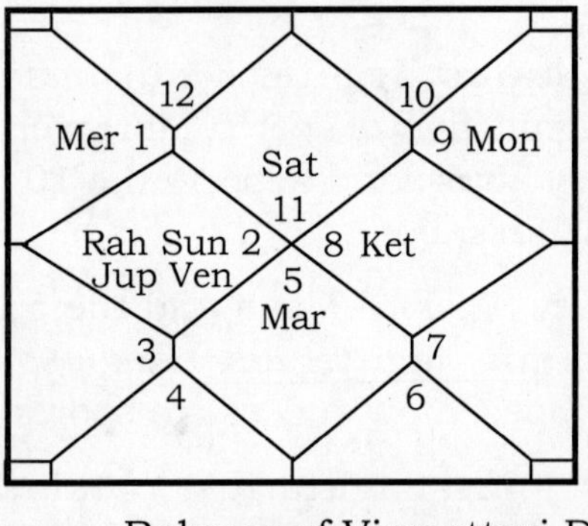


**Navamsa Chart**

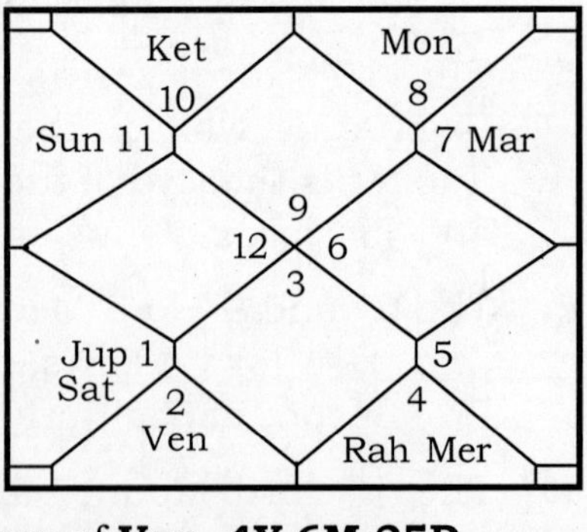


Balance of Vimsottari Dasa of **Ven 4Y 6M 25D**

Name of P.T. Usha needs no introduction except that she has won 101 medals as an athlete. She represented India in Olympics as well. She got Arjuna Award which is a matter of great pride for sportspersons. An honour of Doctorate has also been conferred on her.

## Planetary Combinations:

1. She was born in Aquarius ascendant with Saturn therein. Mercury is placed in the 3rd house, in Aries and is aspected by *lagna* lord Saturn. Thus, the 3rd house is well disposed. The lord of the 3rd house joins the 7th house, in Leo and has a mutual aspect with *lagna* lord Saturn. Thus, there is a mutual aspect between 3rd lord Mars and *lagna* lord Saturn, corresponding with the 7th house and the ascendant. This has strengthened the 3rd house with regard to prospects of sports.
2. Lord of the 6th house, Moon, joins the 11th house in Sagittarius. Moon falls in *Purvasadha nakshatra* ruled by *Yogakaraka* Venus and obtains the *navamsa* of the significator Mars.
3. The 10th house is owned by Mars and in aspected by Mars itself. 2nd and 11th lord Jupiter, *Yogakaraka* Venus, the 7th lord Sun also lend their favourable aspect over the 10th house. Therefore, the 10th house is well disposed and is under the influence of significators Jupiter and Mars.
4. *Yogakaraka* Venus obtains *vargottam navamsa* and falls in *Rohini* constellation, ruled by Moon, who is the 6th lord.
5. 11th and 2nd lord Jupiter obtains the *navamsa* of 3rd lord Mars. Thus, the 3rd and 6th houses are well disposed, in addition to the significators, Mars and Jupiter. She is fortunate enough as the 9th lord, *Yogakaraka* Venus, obtains *vargottam navamsa*. Venus and Mars, that is the 9th and the 10th lords, are strongest in this birth chart as these obtain 1.55 and 1.67 *shadabala*. The 10th house is

aspected by the 9th lord Venus and 10th lord Mars. Moreover, the karmic control planets, Venus and Mars, are in quadrant from each other and have strong influence over the 10th house by their favourable aspect.

These combinations of the birth chart of P.T. Usha have made her an athlete of worldwide fame.

*Illustration: 8.7* (**Steffi Graff**) *Horoscope No.: 113*

Date of birth : 14.06.1969 Time of birth : 23:30:00 hrs

Place of birth : Berlin Lat 52:32:00 N Long 13:24:00E

Ayanamsa : 23:25:49 Sidereal Time : 16:55:45

| Pln | Degree | Rasi | Nakshatra | Pad |
|---|---|---|---|---|
| Asc | 29:13:16 | Cap | Dhanishtha | 2 |
| Sun | 0:13:34 | Gem | Mrigsira | 3 |
| Mon (D) | 29:55:18 | Tau | Mrigsira | 2 |
| Mar (R) | 11:53:44 | Sco | Anuradha | 3 |
| Mer | 10:41:05 | Tau | Rohini | 1 |
| Jup | 3:25:25 | Vir | U Phalguni | 3 |
| Ven | 14:32:10 | Ari | Bharani | 1 |
| Sat | 11:53:05 | Ari | Asvini | 4 |
| Rah (R) | 2:31:45 | Pis | P Bhadrapad | 4 |
| Ket (R) | 2:31:45 | Vir | U Phalguni | 2 |

**Lagna Chart**

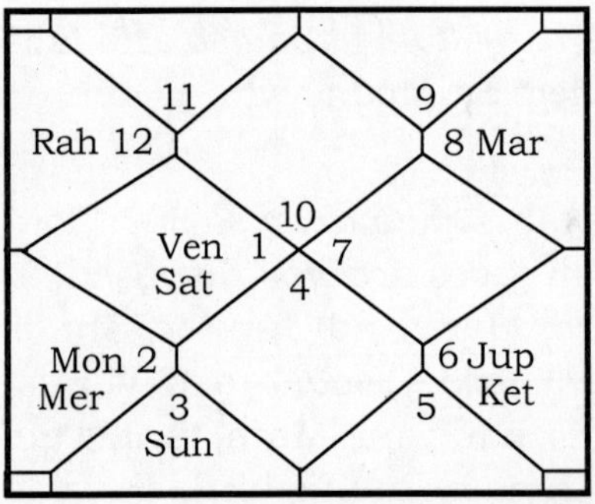


**Navamsa Chart**

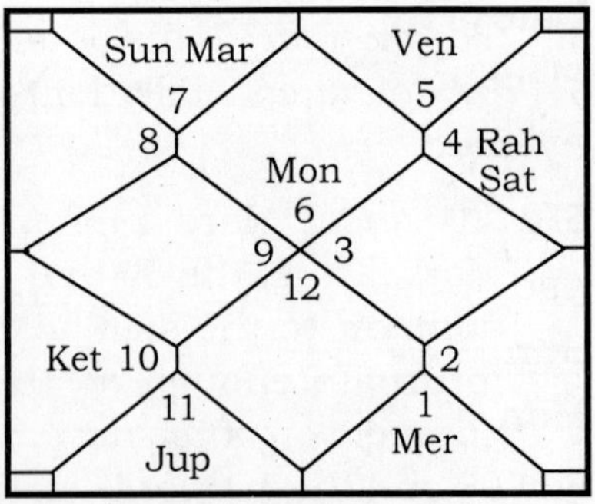


Balance of Vimsottari Dasa of **Mar 3Y 6M 15D**

The name of Steffi Graff is a strong landmark in the history of the game of tennis. She is one of the greatest female tennis players. There are many interesting and thought provoking planetary combinations, which justify her being a great tennis player.

## Planetary Combinations:

1. Rahu is posited in the 3rd house, whereas Sun joins the 6th. The signs involved are Jupiter and Mercury.
2. The 6th house and the Sun are aspected by Mars and Saturn both, which has made Steffi Graff world level tennis player.
3. Rahu is posited in the 3rd house and is aspected by 3rd lord Jupiter. Thus, the 3rd and 6th houses, signifying sports, are strong and well fortified.
4. The lord of 10th and 5th house *Yogakaraka* Venus joins *lagna* lord Saturn in the 4th house. Venus falls in own constellation *Bharani* and in the sign of Mars. Venus obtains the *navamsa* of Sun, who is posited in the 6th house. Thus, it shows that the game of tennis will be a source of earning for her. It may be noted that there is mutual exchange of the *navamsa* of Venus and Sun, showing professional success, name fame, honour and wealth.

*Illustration: 8.8* (**V. Anand**) *Horoscope No.: 114*

Date of birth : 11.12.1969 Time of birth : 12:00:00 hrs

Place of birth : Chennai Lat 13:05:00 N Long 80:18:00E

Ayanamsa : 23:26:17 Sidereal Time : 17:10:23

| **Pln** | **Degree** | **Rasi** | **Nakshatra** | **Pad** |
|---|---|---|---|---|
| Asc | 21:35:55 | Aqu | P Bhadrapad | 1 |
| Sun | 25:36:43 | Sco | Jyestha | 3 |
| Mon | 21:39:17 | Sag | Purvasadha | 3 |
| Mar | 3:20:10 | Aqu | Dhanishtha | 4 |
| Mer (C) | 9:11:25 | Sag | Moola | 3 |

| | | | | |
|---|---|---|---|---|
| Jup | 5:38:50 | Lib | Chitra | 4 |
| Ven | 14:56:06 | Sco | Anuradha | 4 |
| Sat (R) | 9:07:27 | Ari | Asvini | 3 |
| Rah (R) | 22:33:03 | Aqu | P Bhadrapad | 1 |
| Ket (R) | 22:33:03 | Leo | P Phalguni | 3 |

**Lagna Chart**

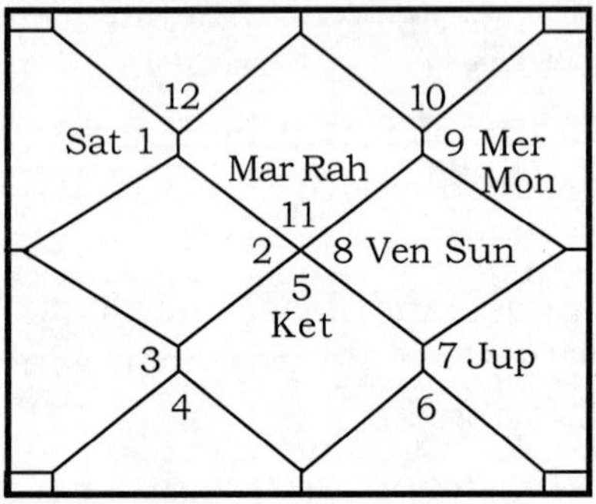


**Navamsa Chart**

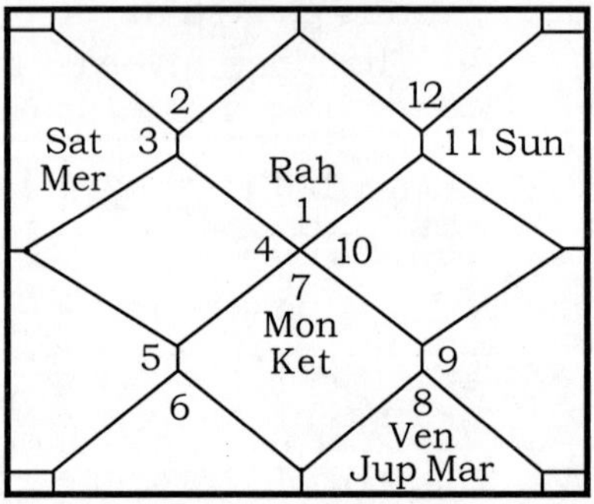


Balance of Vimsottari Dasa of **Ven 7Y 6M 6D**

The native of this birth chart, Vishwanathan Anand, is a chess grandmaster and the current world chess champion. It is evident that chess is a game of extreme intelligence and sharpness of brain and retentive memory. Therefore, the 5th lord and Mercury must have prominence in his horoscope. Following combinations are present in his birth chart to establish him a world renowned chess player:

## Planetary Combinations:

1. He was born in Aquarius ascendant with *Yogakaraka* Venus in the 10th house, which has elevated him to the top most position in his profession.
2. There is mutual exchange between the 3rd lord Mars and the ascendant lord Saturn. Thus, the 3rd house is very well fortified with *Neecha Bhanga Rajayoga* of Saturn.
3. 5th lord Mercury and 6th lord Moon are associated in Sagittarius (the sign representing success in sports).

Mercury and Moon both aspect the 5th house. This is a unique combination of super intelligence, sharpness, fertile brain and alert mind with creative activities and thinking. Generally, such nicely placed Mercury and Moon make one expert in mathematics, computer experts or analyst. Since in this birth chart this combination has a concern with the 5th and 6th house, therefore it makes one expert in games and sports where maximum intelligence, fertility of brain, sharpness of mind and extreme alertness is required. This has given him quick understanding of the skills of the game. Many times he is faster than computer.

4. The 11th and 2nd lord Jupiter is placed in the 9th house and aspects the ascendant, the ascendant lord Saturn, 10th lord Mars and the 5th house. This is splendid and signifies that he will be a champion of game like chess.
5. 5th house is signifying the skill of the game and is best disposed in this birth chart, because 5th lord Mercury, 11th and 2nd lord Jupiter, 6th lord Moon and *lagna* lord Saturn lend their favourable aspect over the 5th house.
6. Sagittarius sign, Moon and Mars are the main significators of sports in addition to the 3rd, 6th and 5th houses, as explained above.

These all planets and houses are nicely placed and have a deep concern in the birth chart of Mr. Vishwanathan Anand, which provide him extraordinary skill and art of playing the game of chess.

*Illustration: 8.9* (**Kapil Dev**) *Horoscope No.: 115*

Date of birth : 06.01.1959 Time of birth : 05:00:00 hrs

Place of birth : Chandigarh Lat 30:43:00 N Long 76:47:00E

Ayanamsa : 23:17:10 Sidereal Time : 11:36:21

| **Pln** | **Degree** | **Rasi** | **Nakshatra** | **Pad** |
|---|---|---|---|---|
| Asc | 18:18:55 | Sco | Jyestha | 1 |
| Sun | 21:36:29 | Sag | Purvasadha | 3 |

| | | | | |
|---|---|---|---|---|
| Mon | 8:15:04 | Sco | Anuradha | 2 |
| Mar | 24:59:02 | Ari | Bharani | 4 |
| Mer | 0:22:55 | Sag | Moola | 1 |
| Jup | 1:35:02 | Sco | Visakha | 4 |
| Ven | 4:59:58 | Cap | Uttarasadha | 3 |
| Sat (C) | 6:45:43 | Sag | Moola | 3 |
| Rah (R) | 24:56:22 | Vir | Chitra | 1 |
| Ket (R) | 24:56:22 | Pis | Revati | 3 |

**Lagna Chart**

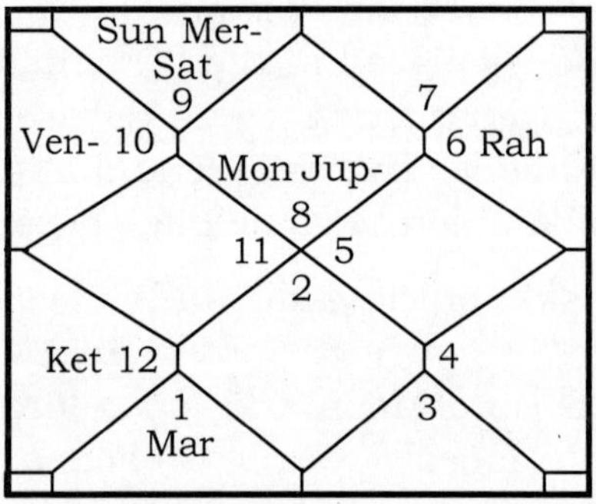


**Navamsa Chart**

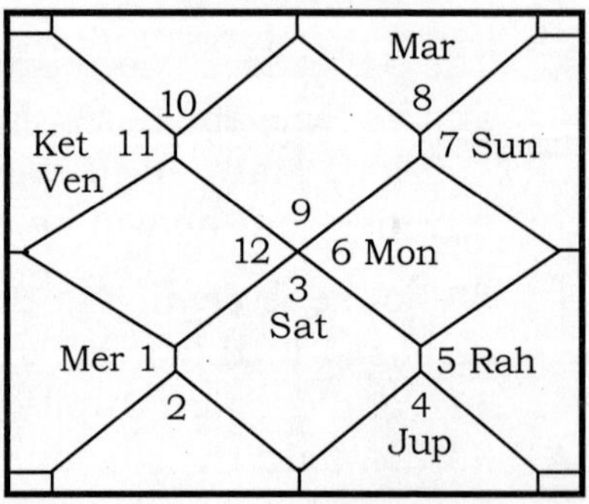


Balance of Vimsottari Dasa of **Sat 11Y 11M 27D**

Kapil Dev, the legendry cricket player, is also the pride of the country. He made many unbeaten records due to his fast and impressive game. He captained the world cup winning team of India. Let us study the planetary configurations which are responsible to elevate him so much that he earned international popularity and love. He had been an outstanding cricketer.

## Planetary Combinations:

1. Kapil Dev was born in Scorpio ascendant. The ruler of both the triangles, Jupiter and Moon, are conjoined in the ascendant itself, in their friendly sign Scorpio.
2. The lord of the ascendant, Mars, joins house of its own and aspects the ascendant. Thus, the ascendant is most

powerful, as it is occupied by lords of both the triangles and is aspected by its own lord Mars. Strong *lagna* shows equally successful, famous, and prosperous personality.

3. The 10$^{th}$ house governs profession. The 10$^{th}$ lord Sun falls in the 2$^{nd}$ house, in Sagittarius, in association with the 8$^{th}$ and 11$^{th}$ lord Mercury. Sagittarius sign signifies sports in general. The association of the 10$^{th}$ lord Sun and the 11$^{th}$ lord Mercury, in the 2$^{nd}$ house in Sagittarius, shows that sports and games will become the main source of earning of the native.

4. The 6$^{th}$ house plays a prominent role in the success in games and sports. The 6$^{th}$ and *lagna* lord Mars falls in own sign Aries, in the 6$^{th}$ house, and obtains own *navamsa* Scorpio. Mars falls in *Bharani nakshatra,* ruled by Venus, and Venus occupies the 3$^{rd}$ house, corresponding to Capricorn sign. In fact, the 3$^{rd}$ and 6$^{th}$ houses must be carefully analyzed for success in sports.

5. The 10$^{th}$ lord Sun and 3$^{rd}$ lord Saturn are placed together in the 2$^{nd}$ house, in Jupiter's sign Sagittarius. This is a very distinct combination, showing high degree of fame and enormous success, prosperity, and wealth, if the native takes up sports as his main occupation. In fact, at this level, sports have become a major source of earning and that should be termed as profession. Therefore, these players are called professional players.

We have taken the birth charts of most successful and world famous sportspersons to explain our view point and planetary combinations for various games.

Mars and Jupiter are the major significators of sport's skill and talent. Involvement of 10$^{th}$, 11$^{th}$ and 2$^{nd}$ house, in one or the other way, makes one to earn money through sports. So, sports become means of income, hence a profession as well. The most significant houses for success in sports are the 3$^{rd}$ and the 6$^{th}$. These should be well-disposed and strong, probably occupied by Mars, Mercury, Jupiter, Rahu or Ketu or Saturn. Prominence of Mercury will certainly be there in the birth charts, where extraordinary intelligence and skill is required such as the game of chess, badminton, tennis etc.

Sagittarius is one of the most significant sign, which is said to play a prominent role in the birth charts of sportsperson. However, we have our independent observation that without the God gifted skill and good luck one can never become a sportsperson of worldwide or country wide fame. So, the triangles must also be examined, in addition to the disposition of Mercury, to judge whether the native will become a successful and famous sportsperson.

●

CHAPTER-9

# Pointers to Police Personnels

Police service is not similar to other professions or services. Police is more responsible towards the nation as it protects the country and countrymen against the crime and helps in the maintenance of law and order. The persons in police are supposed to have a deep feeling of patriotism and responsibility towards the country. Police prevents citizens from breaking the rules of law. All these properties are covered by Mars and Jupiter. Law, patriotism and a feeling of responsibility towards the nation and the protection come under the influence of Jupiter, whereas role of police is indicated by Mars. Saturn and Mars are responsible for most of the crimes, therefore, both these planets are adversely but strongly placed in the birth charts of criminals like murderers, kidnappers, dacoits and smugglers. The duty of the police personnel is to stop crime and to inflict punishment on the violators of the law. This is covered by Mars.

We have observed that Mars and Jupiter play important role in determining the occupation of police service, but the role of Saturn can also not be overlooked. The joint influence of Mars, Jupiter and Saturn over the concerning houses of profession will tend the native to go to the police department.

The $6^{th}$ house indicates law and litigation, enmity, crime and fight etc. in addition to diseases, debts, destruction and the like. Therefore, the $6^{th}$ house does play a vital role in the judgement of career in police.

The $2^{nd}$ and $11^{th}$ houses are referred for wealth and income. These houses also have a lot to do in the judgement of source of income. It will not be out of place to mention that mostly the $10^{th}$ house is considered for all types of professions. It is decided generally by the planets placed in the 10$^{th}$ house, the lord of the 10$^{th}$ house and the *navamsa* occupied by the 10$^{th}$ lord, in addition to the planets having an aspect over the 10$^{th}$ house or its lord and the planets associated with these. Under our humble observation, we do not find it absolute. Second and 11$^{th}$ house should also be given due importance in the judgement of professional aspect of the native, in the same way as we do for the 10$^{th}$ house.

The role of the ascendant is most important as it indicates the aptitude of the native. If the profession is similar to the aptitude or inclination towards a particular job, one will be extremely successful in that particular profession. If Mars and Jupiter are conjoined in Leo ascendant, in addition to other indications of the concerning house, one will become a very famous, successful, popular, strict and tough police officer.

The role of Saturn is also equally important because it governs the citizenry of the nation. Saturn indicates masses and public in general. It also indicates government service. Police is one of the most important limbs of the government for maintenance of peace and harmony of the nation.

Thus, the 2$^{nd}$ and the 11$^{th}$ houses, in addition to the 10$^{th}$ house, should be under the influence of Mars, Jupiter and Saturn, either by occupation or by ownership of sign or *navamsa* or aspect. The 6$^{th}$ house must be related to either of these houses, in one or the other way.

The involvement of fiery signs in *Rashi* chart and *navamsa* is also essential. If the lords of 10$^{th}$, 2$^{nd}$ and 11$^{th}$ are placed in the sign or *navamsa* of Aries, Leo or Sagittarius, police services are strongly indicated, provided lords of concerning houses are Mars, Jupiter or Saturn or the lords of these houses join the signs ruled by the significators Mars, Jupiter and Saturn. Scorpio is not a fiery sign but is an owner of fiery and *Karaka* planet. So Scorpio should also be taken into consideration, in addition to fiery signs.

In fact, the Sun is a supporting *Karaka* of police services as it represents government, and police department is directly under the control of government and is endowed with the authority and power rendered by the government. Last but not the least, *Atmakaraka* planet should also be taken into account. The house owned by the *Atmakaraka* planet, and the *nakshatra* lord in which *Atmakaraka* planet falls, are of immense importance. *Atmakaraka* planet should always be considered as a supporting factor for the judgement of appropriate profession for the native. Thus, following factors, houses and planets should be analyzed.

| | | | |
|---|---|---|---|
| 1. | Ascendant | : | Aptitude, inclination, out look and ambition. |
| 2. | (a) The $10^{th}$ house | : | Professional aspects |
| | (b) The $2^{nd}$ house | : | The source of income |
| | (c) The $11^{th}$ house | : | Means of livelihood |
| | (d) The $9^{th}$ house | : | Fortune supporting the profession, income and other aspects of occupation and wealth. |
| 3. | The $6^{th}$ House | : | Litigation, crime, conflict, accidents, thefts, deceits, debts, loans, services, promotions, demotions, suspensions, extensions etc. |
| 4. | Significators | : | Mars, Jupiter, Saturn |
| 5. | Supporting significator | : | The Sun. |
| 6. | Concerning signs and *navamsa* | : | Aries, Leo, Scorpio and Sagittarius. |
| 7. | Concerning Constellations | : | *Krittika, Mrigsira, Punarvasu, Pushya, Uttraphalguni, Chitra, Visakha, Anuradha, Uttrasadha, Dhanishtha, Poorvabhadrapad* |
| 8. | For Government Services | : | Involvement of the Sun and Moon, identical to $1^{st}$ and $6^{th}$ or $10^{th}$ and $6^{th}$ or $1^{st}$ and $10^{th}$ or $1^{st}$, $6^{th}$ and $10^{th}$ house in one or the other way. |
| 9. | *Atmakaraka* Planet | : | (a) Sign, *navamsa* and constellation occupied by *Atmakaraka* planet. |

(b) Houses owned by *Atmakaraka* planet
(c) House, where *Atmakaraka* planet is posited.

Consideration of all above factors should be made sincerely and systematically, one by one, before finally reaching to any conclusion with regard to police services. In fact, not only for police services but all professions should be examined in the same way. The concerning houses, concerning sign, *navamsas* and *nakshatras* will be different, for various services.

All these factors will help us in making the correct judgement of the aptitude and profession for the service of police. We will now analyze a few practical cases.

*Illustration : 9.1* (**KPS Gill**) *Horoscope No.: 116*

Date of birth : 29.12.1934 Time of birth : 14:00:00 hrs
Place of birth : Lahore Lat 31:32:00 N Long 74:22:00E
Ayanamsa : 22:57:11 Sidereal Time : 19:55:53

| **Pln** | **Degree** | **Rasi** | **Nakshatra** | **Pad** |
|---|---|---|---|---|
| Asc | 17:59:07 | Ari | Bharani | 2 |
| Sun | 13:59:39 | Sag | Purvasadha | 1 |
| Mon | 16:58:43 | Vir | Hasta | 3 |
| Mar | 15:34:50 | Vir | Hasta | 2 |
| Mer (D) | 12:58:00 | Sag | Moola | 4 |
| Jup | 23:26:15 | Lib | Visakha | 2 |
| Ven (C) | 23:44:32 | Sag | Purvasadha | 4 |
| Sat | 1:47:24 | Aqu | Dhanishtha | 3 |
| Rah (R) | 8:26:00 | Cap | Uttarasadha | 4 |
| Ket (R) | 8:26:00 | Can | Pushya | 2 |

**Lagna Chart**

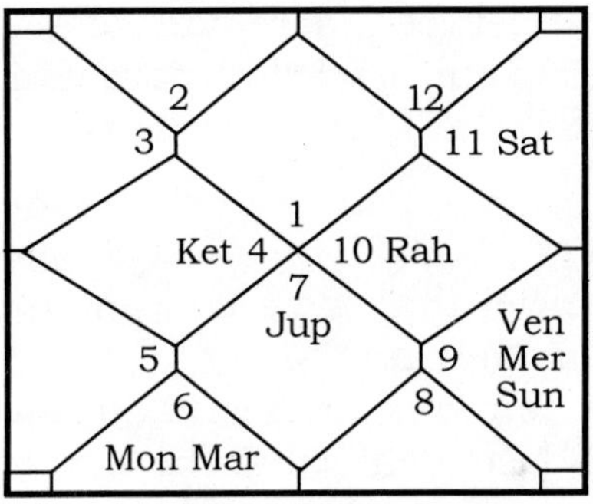


**Navamsa Chart**

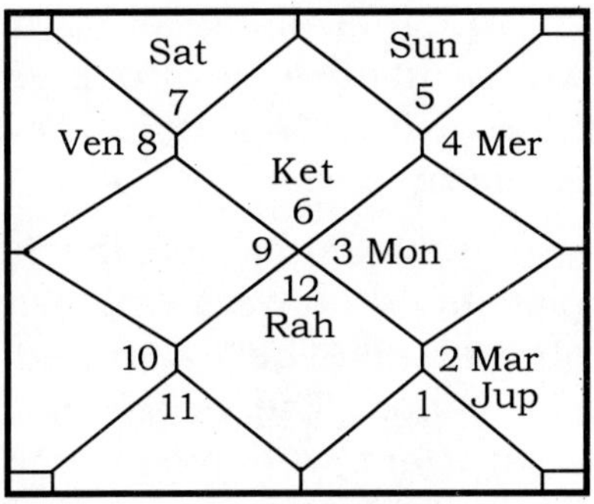


Balance of Vimsottari Dasa of **Mon 4Y 9M 5D**

K.P.S. Gill was Inspector General of Police. He was appointed Election Commissioner after retirement. He was born in Aries ascendant, which obtains *navamsa* of Mercury. Lord of the ascendant Mars is posited in the $6^{th}$ house and aspects the ascendant. In fact, the $6^{th}$ house rules over crimes. To rule out crime or to prevent it, it comes under the duties of police. Therefore, the $6^{th}$ house plays a prominent role in the birth charts of police personals. Besides this, the $6^{th}$ house rules over the means of livelihood through service. Involvement of the luminaries with the ascendant or the $10^{th}$ house or their lords, in *Rashi* or *navamsa* or asterisms, will result into government service. Here, the lord of the ascendant, Mars, occupies the $6^{th}$ house itself and falls in Moon's constellation *Hasta*, which justifies government police service.

The lord of the $3^{rd}$ and the $6^{th}$ house, Mercury, occupies the $9^{th}$ house, identical to Sagittarius sign. Jupiter, Mars and Saturn are the major significators of police services. The Sun is a supporting *Karaka* of police personnels. Here, the lord of the $6^{th}$ house, Mercury, is associated with the Sun and Venus in the $9^{th}$ house. The $6^{th}$ lord Mercury obtains Moon's *navamsa* Cancer and this again confirms and justifies government job.

Venus is *Atmakaraka* planet in this horoscope. Venus rules the $2^{nd}$ and the $7^{th}$ house and occupies the $9^{th}$ house in Sagittarius. Venus obtains *navamsa* of Mars and the ascendant lord Mars obtains *navamsa* of Venus. Thus, there is mutual exchange of *navamsa* between Mars and Venus, which justifies class one government service of police i.e. I.P.S., since Venus is the significator of administrative services as well.

In this horoscope, the Sun and Saturn are the strongest planets. We have mentioned earlier that the second house should also be examined for the judgement of one's occupation. The second house is owned by Venus in this birth chart, who joins the 9th house identical to the sign of Jupiter Sagittarius, and obtains *navamsa* of Mars. This shows that the native will be very successful and strong police person. The lord of the 10th house Saturn stays in own sign Aquarius in the 11th house. Saturn falls in *Dhanishtha* constellation ruled by Mars and obtains the *navamsa* of its exaltation. Saturn is the second strongest planet and obtains 1.44 *Shadabalas* and lends aspect over the 5th and the 8th house apart from the ascendant. The ascendant is, therefore, aspected by its lord Mars and the 10th lord Saturn. Thus, the ascendant is very strong and is under the powerful influence of Mars and Saturn, the *Karakas* of police services.

The *Atmakaraka* and the 2nd lord Venus obtains *navamsa* of Mars and falls in the sign of Jupiter corresponding with mutual exchange between Venus and Jupiter. Thus I.P.S. services are distinctly justified. The analysis may be made as given under:

| | **Sign** | **Nakshatra** | ***Navamsa*** |
|---|---|---|---|
| The 10th lord Saturn | Saturn | Mars | Venus |
| The 1st lord Mars | Mercury | Moon | Venus |
| The 6th lord Mercury | Jupiter | Ketu | Moon |
| The 2nd lord Venus | Jupiter | Jupiter | Mars |
| *Atmakaraka* Venus | Jupiter | Jupiter | Mars |
| The 11th lord Saturn | Saturn | Mars | Venus |
| The 9th lord Jupiter | Venus | Jupiter | Venus |

We find that Venus, Jupiter, Mars and Saturn play prominent role in the judgement of the profession and this indicates class one police service.

If Venus has also a concern with the professional aspect of the native, in addition to Mars, Jupiter and Saturn, one will be an IPS officer. In fact, Venus is the *karaka* of administrative or civil services, whereas Mars, Jupiter and Saturn signify police services. Mars indicates punishment for crime control over criminals, apart from looking after the rules and regulations regarding law and order, and authority. Jupiter signifies security, safety, protection of the countrymen. Jupiter also provides help assistance and benefits of the public. Jupiter rules over the welfare of all kinds. Saturn too is a *karaka* as it governs prosecution, punishment, rules, law and discipline etc.

The 6th house, the ascendant and the 10th house should be examined along with the 2nd, 11th and 9th houses and their lords. *Atmakaraka* planet and strongest planet prominently helps in the judgement of one's occupation.

We may hasten to add that the involvement of fiery signs Aries, Leo and Sagittarius should also be taken into consideration, in addition to Scorpio as it is ruled by the significator and the fiery planet Mars. In this birth chart, the Sun, Mercury and Venus fall in fiery signs and further justify police services of the native.

*Illustration : 9.2* (**Kiran Bedi**) *Horoscope No.: 117*

Date of birth : 09.06.1949 Time of birth : 14:10:00 hrs

Place of birth : Amritsar Lat 31:35:00 N Long 74:56:00E

Ayanamsa : 23:08:55 Sidereal Time : 6:49:17

| Pln | Degree | Rasi | Nakshatra | Pad |
|---|---|---|---|---|
| Asc | 17:26:44 | Vir | Hasta | 3 |
| Sun | 25:01:12 | Tau | Mrigsira | 1 |
| Mon | 4:37:31 | Sco | Anuradha | 1 |
| Mar | 6:21:57 | Tau | Krittika | 3 |
| Mer (R/C) | 17:02:16 | Tau | Rohini | 3 |
| Jup (R) | 8:24:52 | Cap | Uttarasadha | 4 |
| Ven | 9:11:32 | Gem | Ardra | 1 |
| Sat | 7:27:34 | Leo | Magha | 3 |

| Rah (R) | 1:21:21 | Ari | Asvini | 1 |
|---|---|---|---|---|
| Ket (R) | 1:21:21 | Lib | Chitra | 3 |

**Lagna Chart**

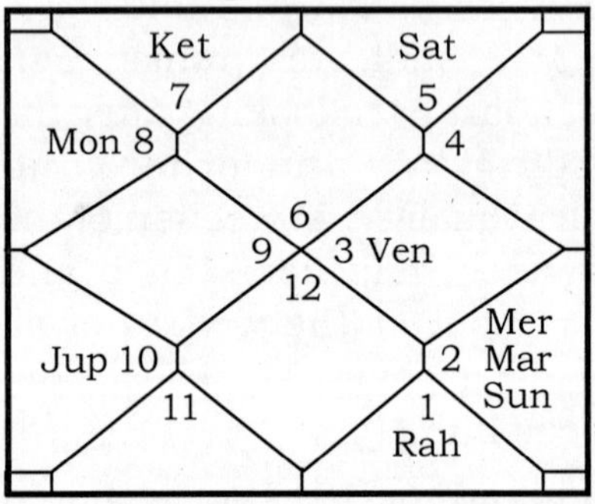


**Navamsa Chart**

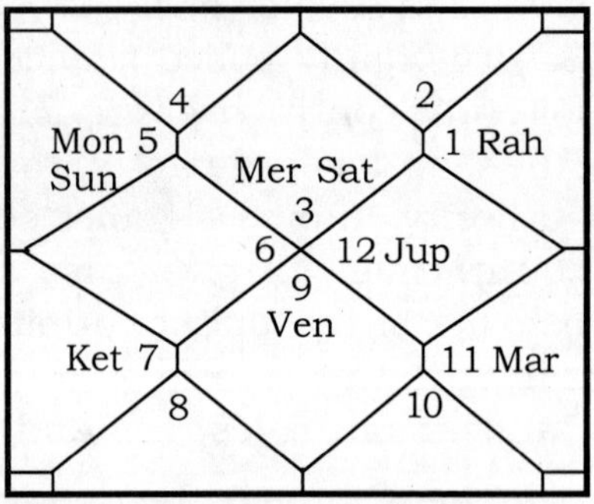


Balance of Vimsottari Dasa of **Sat 17Y 1M 27D**

First Indian lady I.P.S. Ms. Kiran Bedi is an immortal name in Police Department. She is known for her most dynamic, dashing, bold and extremely courageous personality. Our country is certainly proud of having Ms. Kiran Bedi as Director General of Police, who has established innumerable outstanding example of honesty and fearlessness. The analysis of the unique horoscope is as under:

In this case, Venus occupies the $10^{th}$ house identical to sign Gemini. The first significator of profession is Venus and the second is the lord of the $10^{th}$ house, Mercury. Now we see, whether any planet occupies the constellation of Venus. In this birth chart, there is no such planet. Then examine the *navamsa* occupied by the $10^{th}$ lord Mercury, and *navamsa* of the planet placed in the $10^{th}$ house i.e. Venus. Venus obtains Sagittarius *navamsa* and Mercury obtains own *navamsa* Gemini. This shows that the profession of the native may be connected with art, acting, dancing, singing or script writing.

Now examine the *Atmakaraka* planet, which is the Sun in this case. The Sun is posited in the $9^{th}$ house in Taurus, in *Mrigsira* ruled by Mars i.e. the Sun falls in Mars' constellation *Mrigsira*. The Sun and Mars are the strongest planets in this birth chart. The Sun obtains 1.87 *Shadabalas* and acquires own *navamsa*. This shows success in administrative field i.e. I.P.S. Exchange of the 9th lord, Venus, and 10th lord, Mercury, confirms civil or administrative services. Mars and Sun are associated with the 10th lord, Mercury, in the 9th house and further suggest success in police service.

The third step is the analysis of the 2nd house, which is owned by Venus in this case, who falls in the 10th house. Venus obtains *navamsa* of Jupiter and falls in Rahu's constellation *Ardra*. Rahu is tenanted in Aries ruled by Mars and obtains *vargottam navamsa*. It means that Venus is under the effects of Mercury, Jupiter, Rahu and Mars and that shows that the profession tends towards engineering or police.

Thereafter, the 11th house should be analyzed. The lord of the 11th, Moon, falls in Scorpio, ruled by Mars. Moon falls in the constellation *Anuradha*, ruled by Saturn and obtains *navamsa* of the Sun. This shows police services of high level.

Lastly, the judgement of the 9th house should be made. In this birth chart, the 9th house is occupied by Mercury, Mars and the Sun, which indicate police service and administration. There is mutual exchange of constellations between the Sun and Mars. The Sun falls in *Mrigshira* and Mars fall in *Kritika*, whereas Mercury falls in *Rohini*, whose ruler Moon occupies Scorpio. This also signifies police service of administrative level i.e. I.P.S. Mars obtains Saturn's *navamsa*; the Sun obtains own *navamsa* and Mercury obtains Gemini *navamsa*. The lord of the 9th house, Venus, falls in the 10th house and obtains *navamsa* of Jupiter and falls in *Ardra* constellation.

Thus, the Sun, Mars, Jupiter, Mercury and Venus have a profound concern with the occupation of the native. The strongest planet is the Sun, who obtains 1.87 *Shadabalas*. The 2nd strongest planet is Venus, who obtains 1.32 *Shadabalas* and 3rd strongest planet is Mars, who obtains 1.21 *Shadabalas* and then Jupiter obtains 1.1 *Shadabalas*. Mercury is weak as it obtains less than 0.1 *Shadabala*. Therefore, Mercury should be eliminated. Now the Sun,

Venus, Mars and Jupiter will decide the occupation of the native. We have explained in length, in a different chapter, that for administrative services, Venus, Sun and Moon are the significators. In this horoscope, Venus occupies the $10^{th}$ house; the Sun occupies the $9^{th}$ house and the Moon aspects the Sun and $10^{th}$ lord Mercury. Moreover, mutual exchange of the $9^{th}$ lord Venus and the $3^{rd}$ lord Mercury gives rise *Mahayoga* or *Maharaja Yoga*, which is one of the strongest planetary positions for administrative services. Overall, the horoscope strongly indicates Class-I administrative services.

Now, the remaining significators are the Sun, Mars and Jupiter, who are inter-related with each other as explained above. The influence of these planets strongly signifies police services. Now consider both i.e. administrative services and police services. Then, it will be quite clear that the native will be a successful, famous and strong IPS officer. In fact, this is the birth chart of Ms. Kiran Bedi, who has earned world wide reputation of a very strict IPS officer.

*Illustration : 9.3* (**ML**) *Horoscope No.: 118*

Date of birth : 13.01.1944 Time of birth : 15:36:00 hrs

Place of birth : Karnataka Lat 09:03:00 N Long 76:33:00E

Ayanamsa : 23:04:18 Sidereal Time : 21:39:00

| Pln | Degree | Rasi | Nakshatra | Pad |
|---|---|---|---|---|
| Asc | 7:15:00 | Tau | Krittika | 4 |
| Sun | 28:59:35 | Sag | Uttarasadha | 1 |
| Mon | 1:15:02 | Leo | Magha | 1 |
| Mar | 11:50:57 | Tau | Rohini | 1 |
| Mer (R/C) | 18:52:49 | Sag | Purvasadha | 2 |
| Jup (R) | 2:31:15 | Leo | Magha | 1 |
| Ven | 19:05:28 | Sco | Jyestha | 1 |
| Sat (R) | 27:54:32 | Tau | Mrigsira | 2 |
| Rah | 13:39:13 | Can | Pushya | 4 |
| Ket (C) | 13:39:13 | Cap | Sravna | 2 |

**Lagna Chart**

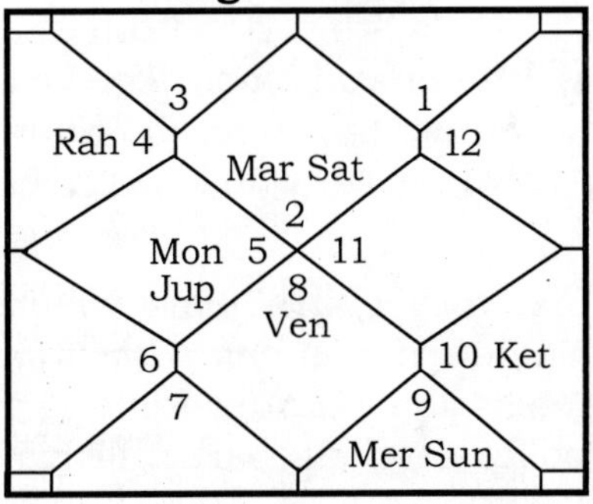


**Navamsa Chart**

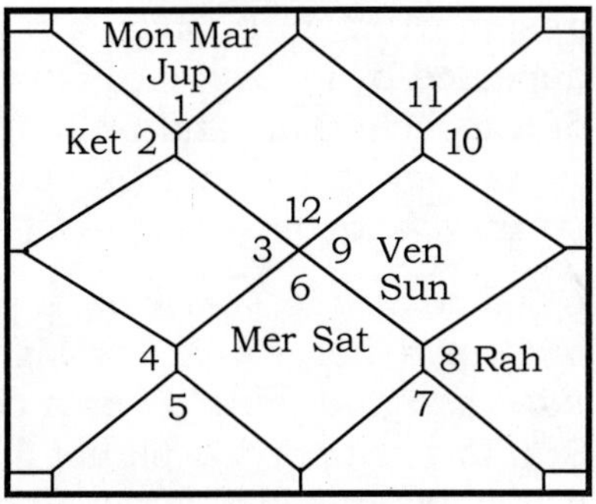


Balance of Vimsottari Dasa of **Ket 6Y 4M 3D**

The native retired as Director General of Police. Lastly, the enquiry of Madhumita murder case was made under him. He was born in Taurus ascendant with Mars and Saturn, therein. The ascendant must be examined, as it indicates aptitude inclination and outlook of the native. Presence of both the significators, Mars and Saturn, shows the tendency and ambition of going into police. The ascendant obtains *navamsa* of Jupiter, which does play a prominent role in the birth charts of police men as it covers protection, safety, security, help and rules of law as well.

Lord of the 10th house *Yogakaraka* Saturn falls in the ascendant, identical to *Mrigsira* constellation, ruled by Mars. Saturn is closely associated with Mars in the ascendant and aspects the *lagna* lord Venus, the 3rd house, the lord of the ascendant & the 6th Venus, which is tenanted in the 7th house in the sign of Mars, in Scorpio.

The 6th house governs crimes, criminals, conflicts, thefts, loans, debts, diseases, accidents, fights and service matters. Therefore, the involvement of the 6th house, if found prominent and strong, in addition to positive role of Mars, Saturn and Jupiter, one joins police services. In this birth chart, the lord of the 6th house, Venus, occupies sign of Mars, i.e. Scorpio and is aspected by Mars and Saturn, both significators, which is a strong indication of the position of a high and successful police personnel.

The 3rd lord Moon and 11th lord Jupiter are very well associated in the 4th house in Leo, and aspect the 10th house.

Both, Jupiter and Moon, obtain *navamsa* of Mars, in association with Mars as well. Thus, the 10th house is aspected by its own lord Saturn, Jupiter and Moon. The lord of the ascendant and 6th house, Venus, and the Sun obtain *navamsa* of the significator Jupiter, where the Sun falls under *vargottam navamsa.*

The Sun is *Atmakaraka* planet in this birth chart, which falls in a fiery Jupiter's sign Sagittarius under *vargottam navamsa* and joins its own constellation *Uttarashadha.* The Sun is a supporting planet for police services; particularly if it is class one civil service i.e. I.P.S.

Involvement of fiery signs, identical to the concerning planets and houses, also has a significant role. But Scorpio should also be included as its owner is the fiery planet Mars. Thus, Aries, Leo, Scorpio and Sagittarius signs, if influence Mars, Sun, Jupiter and Saturn in addition to the lords of the ascendant, the 6th and the 10th house, one will do extremely well in the police department.

In the horoscope, the 6th lord Venus and the 10th lord Saturn have a mutual aspect. Mars falls in Moon's constellation *Rohini* and aspects the ascendant and the 6th lord Venus, showing government service.

Five planets viz. Moon, Mars, Jupiter, Venus and the Sun obtain *navamsa* of fiery signs Aries and Sagittarius. Four planets viz. 3rd lord Moon, 8th and 11th lord Jupiter, the 4th lord Sun, 3rd and 5th lord Mercury are posited in fiery signs. The strongest planet, ascendant and the 6th lord Venus, falls in the sign Scorpio, ruled by the fiery significator Mars and is aspected by Mars and Saturn both, and obtains fiery *navamsa* Sagittarius. This is a powerful indication that the native will earn great name, fame and honour as an I.P.S. officer. He was bound to do government service due to the strong planetary set up in his birth chart.

*Illustration : 9.4* (**YKM**) *Horoscope No.: 119*

| | | | |
|---|---|---|---|
| Date of birth | : 26.07.1944 | Time of birth | : 05:44:00 hrs |
| Place of birth | : Dehradun | Lat 30:19:00 N | Long 78:03:00E |
| Ayanamsa | : 23:04:43 | Sidereal Time | : 0:40:20 |

| Pln | Degree | Rasi | Nakshatra | Pad |
|---|---|---|---|---|
| Asc | 28:41:49 | Gem | Punarvasu | 3 |
| Sun | 9:45:33 | Can | Pushya | 2 |
| Mon | 12:53:48 | Vir | Hasta | 1 |
| Mar | 15:26:22 | Leo | P Phalguni | 1 |
| Mer | 2:28:26 | Leo | Magha | 1 |
| Jup | 6:54:20 | Leo | Magha | 3 |
| Ven (C) | 17:43:11 | Can | Aslesha | 1 |
| Sat | 11:26:37 | Gem | Ardra | 2 |
| Rah (R/C) | 4:35:18 | Can | Pushya | 1 |
| Ket (R) | 4:35:18 | Cap | Uttarasadha | 3 |

**Lagna Chart**

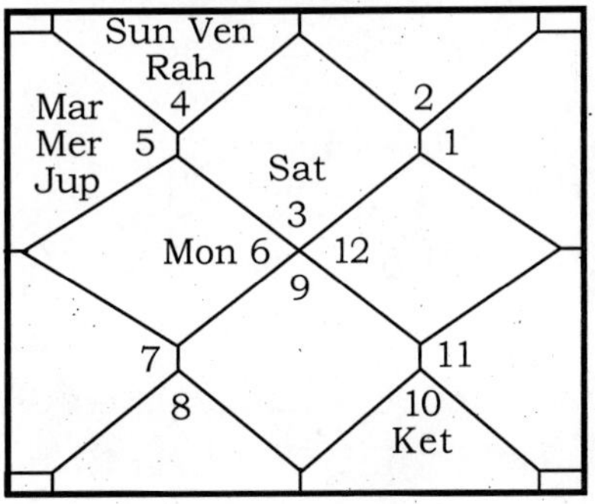


**Navamsa Chart**

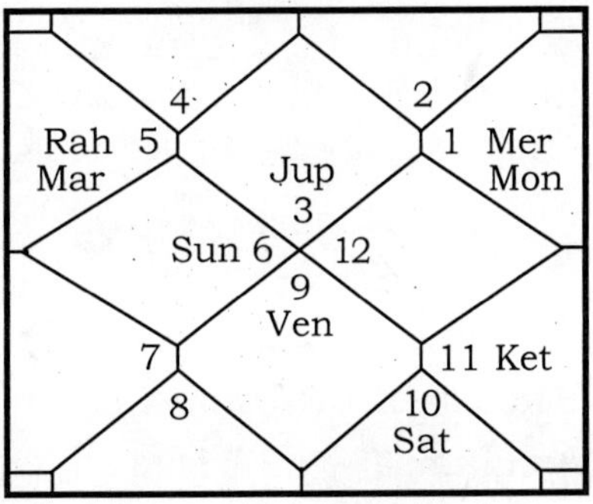


Balance of Vimsottari Dasa of **Mon 7Y 9M 28D**

The native retired as Director General of Police. Many times he was awarded for his brave and courageous actions.

He was born in Gemini ascendant, which obtains *vargottam navamsa*. Following factors in his horoscope may be noted:

(1) The 8th and 9th lord Saturn, who joins the ascendant aspects the 10th house and the lord Jupiter, whereas 10th lord Jupiter aspects the 9th house. This indicates class one service.

(2) The 6th lord Mars falls in Leo, in association with 10th lord Jupiter. Mars aspects the 6th, 9th and 10th houses.

This is a powerful indication of police services. Ascendant lord Mercury, 7th and 10th lord Jupiter, 6th and 11th lord Mars are associated in fiery signs Leo and all of these aspect the 9th house.

(3) The 2nd lord Moon obtains *navamsa* of Mars and 6th lord Mars obtains the *navamsa* of Sun, whereas the 9th lord and significator Saturn obtains own *navamsa.*

(4) *Atmakaraka* planet is Venus, who falls in Cancer in the *nakshatra* of ascendant lord and obtains fiery *navamsa* of Jupiter i. e. Sagittarius. This is a powerful indication for native entering into police services of class one cadre i.e. I.P.S. This indicates that the native was destined to become an I.P.S. officer. Ascendant lord Mercury falls in Leo in 3rd house and obtains *navamsa* of Mars.

Thus, the ascendant, the 6th and the 10th house are under the influence of the Sun, Saturn, Mars and Jupiter. These signify I.P.S. services, as explained above.

*Illustration : 9.5* **(MS)** *Horoscope No.: 120*

Date of birth : 26.01.1957 Time of birth : 09:10:00 hrs

Place of birth : Unnao Lat 26:32:00 N Long 80:30:00E

Ayanamsa : 23:15:42 Sidereal Time : 17:22:40

| **Pln** | **Degree** | **Rasi** | **Nakshatra** | **Pad** |
|---|---|---|---|---|
| Asc | 23:48:51 | Aqu | P Bhadrapad | 2 |
| Sun | 12:40:17 | Cap | Sravna | 1 |
| Mon | 20:34:22 | Sco | Jyestha | 2 |
| Mar | 5:15:21 | Ari | Asvini | 2 |
| Mer | 19:08:08 | Sag | Purvasadha | 2 |
| Jup (R) | 8:23:08 | Vir | U Phalguni | 4 |
| Ven | 23:22:01 | Sag | Purvasadha | 4 |
| Sat | 18:28:53 | Sco | Jyeshtha | 1 |
| Rah (R) | 3:12:51 | Sco | Visakha | 4 |
| Ket (R) | 3:12:51 | Tau | Krittika | 2 |

**Lagna Chart**

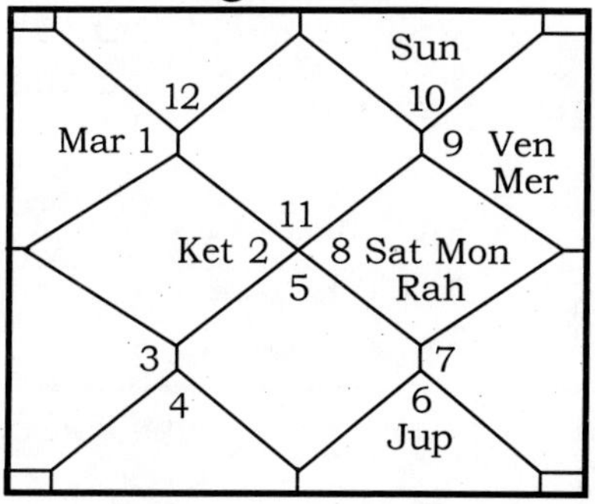


**Navamsa Chart**

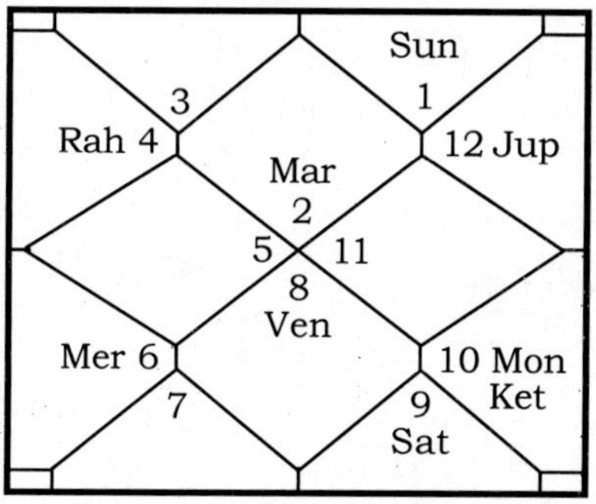


Balance of Vimsottari Dasa of **Mer 12Y 0M 7D**

This horoscope belongs to a female police officer, who is extremely beautiful, charming and captivating. She is known for outstanding beauty in U.P. Police. She discharges her duties most promptly, boldly, courageously and fearlessly.

She was born in Aquarius ascendant. Saturn, Moon and Rahu are posited in the 10$^{th}$ house, in Scorpio and are aspected by the 10$^{th}$ lord Mars. We have mentioned earlier that the involvement of 6$^{th}$ house or its lord is essential for police services. In this chart, the 6$^{th}$ lord Moon joins the 10$^{th}$ house in Scorpio and it also receives the aspect of the significator and the lord of 10$^{th}$ house Mars. This justifies the appointment in police department. Venus is *Atmakaraka* planet, who falls in Sagittarius, in own *nakshatra Poorvashada* and obtains *navamsa* of Mars. This further indicates service in the police department.

*Illustration : 9.6* (**DKS**) *Horoscope No.: 121*

Date of birth : 04.07.1950 Time of birth : 20:00:00 hrs
Place of birth : Aligarh Lat 10:49:00 N Long 78:41:00E
Ayanamsa : 23:09:56 Sidereal Time : 14:32:51

| Pln | Degree | Rasi | Nakshatra | Pad |
|---|---|---|---|---|
| Asc | 8:51:46 | Cap | Uttarasadha | 4 |
| Sun | 18:51:57 | Gem | Ardra | 4 |
| Mon | 20:09:54 | Aqu | P Bhadrapad | 1 |
| Mar | 16:34:09 | Vir | Hasta | 2 |

| | | | | |
|---|---|---|---|---|
| Mer (C) | 10:58:40 | Gem | Ardra | 2 |
| Jup (R) | 14:11:37 | Aqu | Satabhisha | 3 |
| Ven | 15:15:41 | Tau | Rohini | 2 |
| Sat | 21:29:15 | Leo | P Phalguni | 3 |
| Rah (R) | 8:32:51 | Pis | U Bhadrapad | 2 |
| Ket (R) | 8:32:51 | Vir | U Phalguni | 4 |

**Lagna Chart**

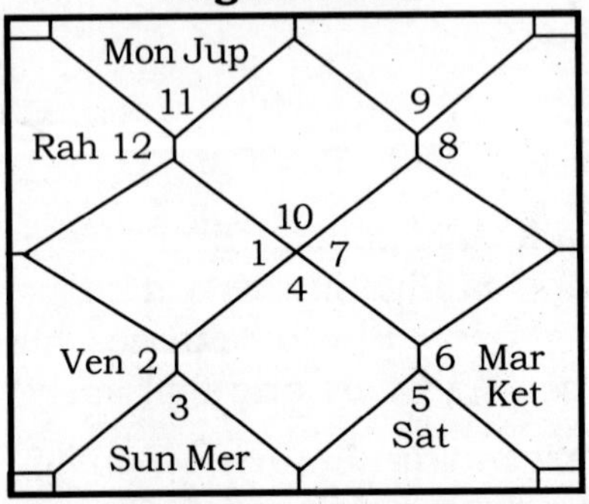


**Navamsa Chart**

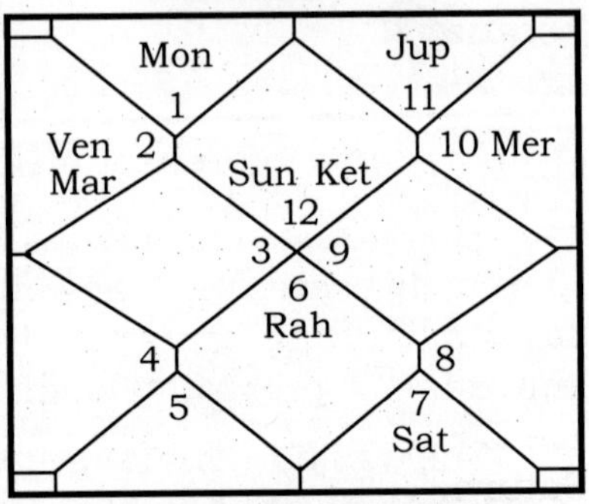


Balance of Vimsottari Dasa of **Jup 15Y 9M 19D**

This birth chart belongs to an Inspector General of Police. First of all let us examine the 10th house, whose lord *Yogakaraka* Venus falls in own sign Taurus, obtains *vargottam navamsa* and occupies *Rohini* constellation. This does not at all indicate police services.

Now let us find out the vocation of the native through the second house, which is occupied by Moon and Jupiter. The lord of the 2nd house, Saturn, joins the 8th house in Leo, which obtain *navamsa* of Venus. Thus, the 2nd house also does not reveal police service of the native.

The 11th and 9th houses should also be judged to pin point one's occupation in each and every birth chart. The lord of the 11th house, Mars, is placed in the 9th house, identical to Virgo sign. Mars obtains *navamsa* of Venus and falls in *Hasta* constellation. This is not an indication of police service. *Atmakaraka* planet is Saturn, which falls in Leo in 8th house corresponding with the *Poorvaphalguni* constellation of Venus. Saturn obtains *navamsa* of Venus as well. Thus, the role of Venus is most prominent with regard to examination of occupation. We have established that

Venus is the significator of Civil services and administration etc. apart from various articles and commodities concerning business. Venus is the strongest planet in this chart, as it gets 1.52 *Shadabalas*. But it does not justify police service. The native will be successful in administrative services. This is certainly a strong observation.

Now select the stronger between Moon and ascendant. Here, Moon chart should be taken into consideration because Moon is stronger than ascendant. The lord of the ascendant, Saturn, falls in the 8th house. With regard to Moon chart, the 10th house is owned by Mars, whose aspect is there over the 11th, 2nd and 3rd house. The Moon *lagna* is occupied by Jupiter and Moon, where Moon obtains *navamsa* of Mars i.e. Aries and Jupiter obtains *navamsa* of Saturn. In fact, Jupiter and Venus both obtain *vargottam navamsa*. The 2nd house is owned by Jupiter and aspected by Mars, whereas the 2nd lord Jupiter receives the aspect of Moon sign lord Saturn. Thus, the combination of Mars, Saturn, Jupiter and the Sun, in this birth chart, shows that the native will become an I.P.S. officer, who will not work in field and he will mostly look after the administrative aspect of police department.

*Illustration : 9.7* **(AD)** *Horoscope No.: 122*

Date of birth : 22.07.1975 Time of birth : 21:23:00 hrs
Place of birth : Allahabad Lat 25:27:00 N Long 81:50:00E
Ayanamsa : 23:31:11 Sidereal Time : 17:19:26

| **Pln** | **Degree** | **Rasi** | **Nakshatra** | **Pad** |
|---|---|---|---|---|
| Asc | 22:37:21 | Aqu | P Bhadrapad | 1 |
| Sun | 5:42:16 | Can | Pushya | 1 |
| Mon | 29:11:21 | Sag | Uttarasadha | 1 |
| Mar | 21:25:21 | Ari | Bharani | 3 |
| Mer (C) | 24:41:57 | Gem | Punarvasu | 2 |
| Jup | 0:18:57 | Ari | Asvini | 1 |
| Ven | 14:33:05 | Leo | P Phalguni | 1 |
| Sat (C) | 29:53:48 | Gem | Punarvasu | 3 |
| Rah (R) | 5:44:15 | Sco | Anuradha | 1 |
| Ket (R) | 5:44:15 | Tau | Krittika | 3 |

**Lagna Chart**

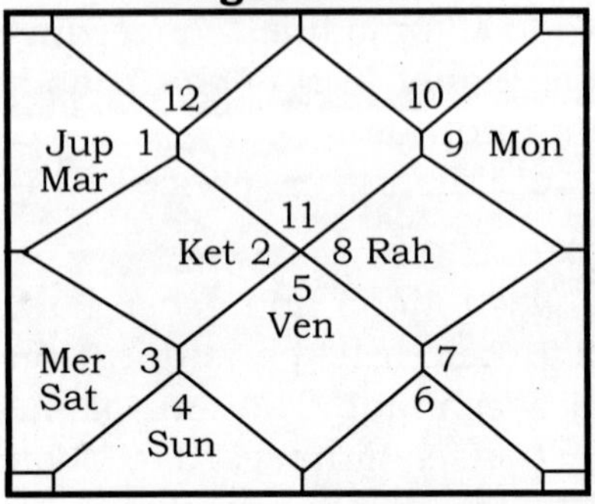


**Navamsa Chart**

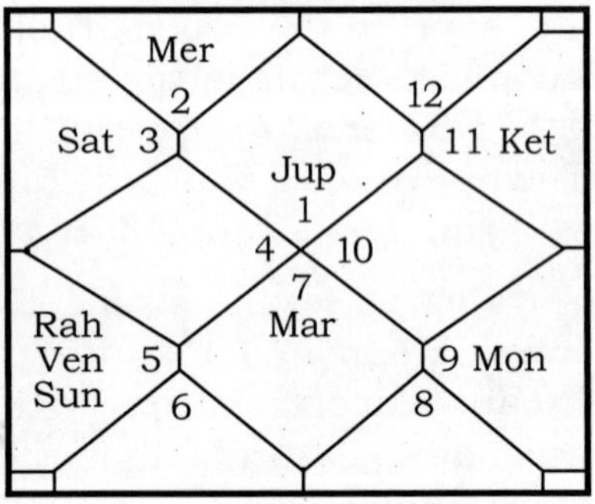


Balance of Vimsottari Dasa of **Sun 4Y 10M 11D**

The native is a Police Inspector and Station Officer. He has a very strong and impressive personality of a police man. The native was born in Aquarius ascendant, which obtains Aries *navamsa.*

The lord of the $10^{th}$ house, Mars, and that of the $2^{nd}$ and the $11^{th}$ house, Jupiter, are placed in the $3^{rd}$ house, in fiery sign of Mars i.e. Aries. The $10^{th}$ lord Mars aspects the $9^{th}$ house. The $11^{th}$ and $2^{nd}$ lord Jupiter obtains *navamsa* of Mars. These planetary combinations justify police service.

Saturn is *Atmakaraka* planet and the lord of the ascendant and obtains *vargottam navamsa.* Saturn falls in *Punarvasu* constellation of Jupiter, the ruler of $2^{nd}$ and $11^{th}$ house. Moreover, Saturn aspects the $2^{nd}$ and $11^{th}$ houses. Saturn also lends its aspect over the $6^{th}$ lord Moon, which obtains *vargottam navamsa* corresponding to Jupiter's sign Sagittarius. The Sun is the strongest planet in this birth chart as it obtains 1.48 *Shadabalas* and obtain own *navamsa.* The Sun is posited in *Pushya* constellation, ruled by Saturn. Thus, all houses, their lords and significators point towards an occupation related with the police department. The native has a bright future in police as the prominence of Mars, Saturn and Jupiter in the birth chart have made him extremely dynamic, dashing and brave.

*Illustration : 9.8* (**GS**) *Horoscope No.: 123*

Date of birth : 03.11.1949 Time of birth : 20:00:00 hrs
Place of birth : Maharajganj Lat 27:09:00 N Long 83:34:00E
Ayanamsa : 23:09:17 Sidereal Time : 22:54:20

| Pln | Degree | Rasi | Nakshatra | Pad |
|---|---|---|---|---|
| Asc | 3:33:03 | Gem | Mrigsira | 4 |
| Sun | 17:41:16 | Lib | Svati | 4 |
| Mon | 23:00:54 | Pis | Revati | 2 |
| Mar | 11:05:38 | Leo | Magha | 4 |
| Mer (C) | 6:32:24 | Lib | Chitra | 4 |
| Jup | 2:24:44 | Cap | Uttarasadha | 2 |
| Ven | 4:01:12 | Sag | Moola | 2 |
| Sat | 23:32:01 | Leo | P Phalguni | 4 |
| Rah (S) | 23:31:16 | Pis | Revati | 3 |
| Ket (S) | 23:31:16 | Vir | Chitra | 1 |

**Lagna Chart**

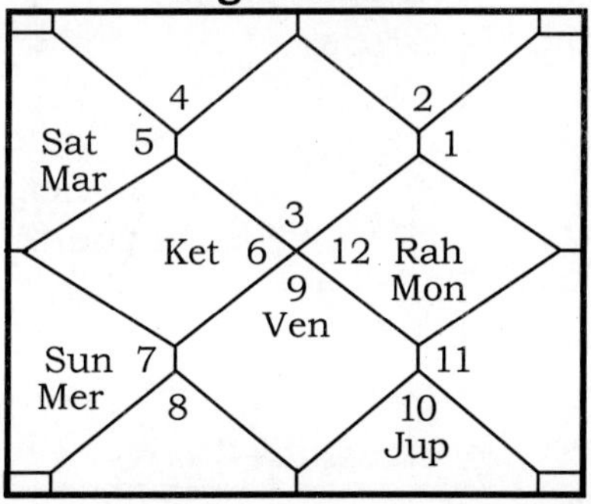


**Navamsa Chart**

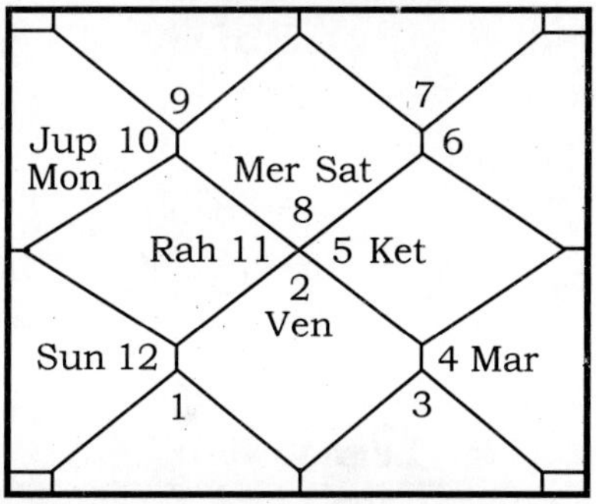


Balance of Vimsottari Dasa of **Mer 8Y 10M 26D**

The native is Senior Station Officer in Police department. Following combinations are present in this birth chart.

1. The 10th lord Jupiter joins Capricorn and obtains *vargottam navamsa*. Jupiter falls in Sun's constellation *Uttarashadha*.
2. The lord of the 6th and 11th house, Mars, is posited in the 3rd house in Leo, with the 9th lord Saturn and lends its aspect over the 6th as well as the 10th house. This strongly justifies the police service of the native.
3. Ascendant lord Mercury obtains *navamsa* of Mars and is associated with 9th lord Saturn, in Scorpio *navamsa*, indicating job connected with police.
4. *Atmakaraka* planet Saturn obtains *navamsa* of Mars. This

kind of planetary position is a strong pointer to police services as far as the aptitude, actions, activities, boldness, courage, stamina, fastness and vigilance is concerned for the security and safety of law and order.

*Illustration : 9.9* (**BRM**) *Horoscope No.: 124*

Date of birth : 04.11.1928 Time of birth : 04:29:00 hrs
Place of birth : Bareilly Lat 28:20:00 N Long 79:24:00E
Ayanamsa : 22:51:31 Sidereal Time : 7:08:24

| **Pln** | **Degree** | **Rasi** | **Nakshatra** | **Pad** |
|---|---|---|---|---|
| Asc | 22:13:15 | Vir | Hasta | 4 |
| Sun | 18:25:34 | Lib | Svati | 4 |
| Mon | 10:26:37 | Can | Pushya | 3 |
| Mar | 15:57:59 | Gem | Ardra | 3 |
| Mer | 1:11:35 | Lib | Chitra | 3 |
| Jup (R) | 11:41:34 | Ari | Asvini | 4 |
| Ven | 20:54:22 | Sco | Jyestha | 2 |
| Sat | 24:11:41 | Sco | Jyestha | 3 |
| Rah | 7:46:41 | Tau | Krittika | 4 |
| Ket | 7:46:41 | Sco | Anuradha | 2 |

**Lagna Chart**

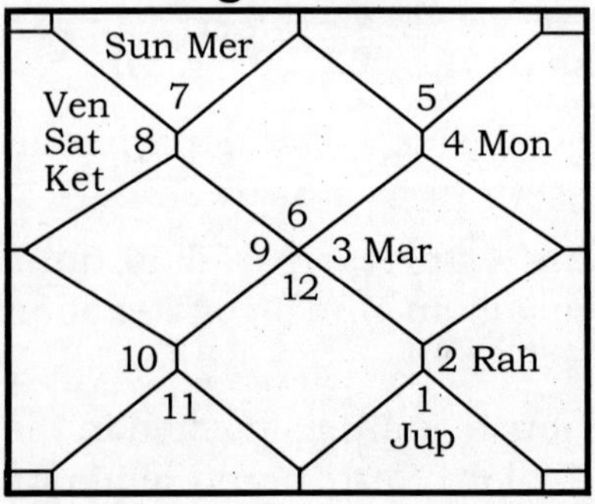


**Navamsa Chart**

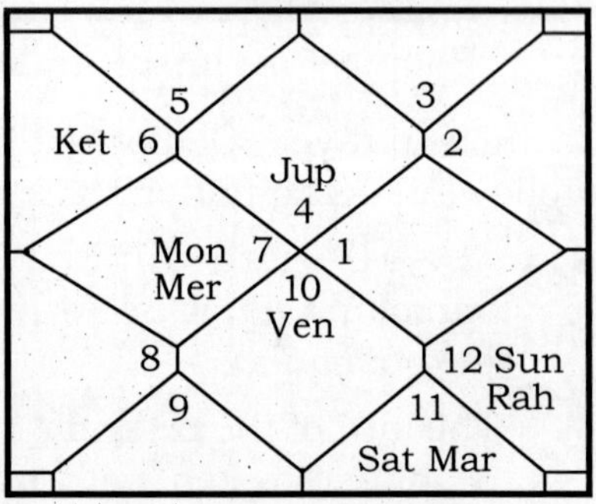


Balance of Vimsottari Dasa of **Sat 8Y 10M 12D**

The native was a very dynamic police officer. He was appointed as Sub-Inspector of Police but retired as Superintendent of Police. Mars is posited in the 10$^{th}$ house and aspects the ascendant, whereas significator Jupiter, 6$^{th}$ lord Saturn and the 9$^{th}$ lord Venus fall in Martian signs Aries and Scorpio.

Lord of the 10th house, Mercury, is in Libra and occupies the constellation of Mars i.e. Chitra. The 9th and the 2nd lord Venus, 5th and 6th lord Saturn and Ketu are posited in Scorpio. These are the dispositors of Mars and have an influence over the 10th house. Jupiter, who is also a significator, is posited in Aries, the sign of Mars and aspects the 2nd and the 4th house, the Sun and 10th lord Mercury. Thus, the 10th lord Mercury is under the influence of Mars, Jupiter and Venus. This shows that the native will earn money through police job.

Significators Mars and Saturn obtain *navamsa* of Saturn. Jupiter is posited in Mars' sign Aries and aspects the 10th lord Mercury and the Sun. The 5th and the 6th lord Saturn, who is also a significator, is *Atmakaraka* planet in this birth chart. Saturn joins Scorpio and obtains own *navamsa*. This confirms that the native will join police. The Saturn is strongest planet as well as *Atmakaraka*. Placement of Saturn in Scorpio, and in own *navamsa* Aquarius, strongly justifies the means of livelihood through police service partially. Placement of Mars in the 10th house and its association with Saturn in *navamsa* has further strengthened the combination of police job.

*Illustration : 9.10* (**USD**) *Horoscope No.: 125*

Date of birth : 18.09.1951 Time of birth : 06:15:12 hrs

Place of birth : Shimla Lat 28:30:00 N Long 77:49:00E

Ayanamsa : 23:11:03 Sidereal Time : 5:41:01

| Pln | Degree | Rasi | Nakshatra | Pad |
|---|---|---|---|---|
| Asc | 2:37:43 | Vir | U Phalguni | 2 |
| Sun | 1:07:10 | Vir | U Phalguni | 2 |
| Mon | 2:29:50 | Ari | Asvini | 1 |
| Mar | 26:15:33 | Can | Aslesha | 3 |
| Mer | 13:21:33 | Leo | P Phalguni | 1 |
| Jup (R) | 17:56:26 | Pis | Revati | 1 |
| Ven (R) | 9:54:45 | Leo | Magha | 3 |
| Sat (C) | 10:53:04 | Vir | Hasta | 1 |
| Rah (R) | 16:46:29 | Aqu | Satabhisha | 4 |
| Ket (R/C) | 16:46:29 | Leo | P Phalguni | 2 |

**Lagna Chart**

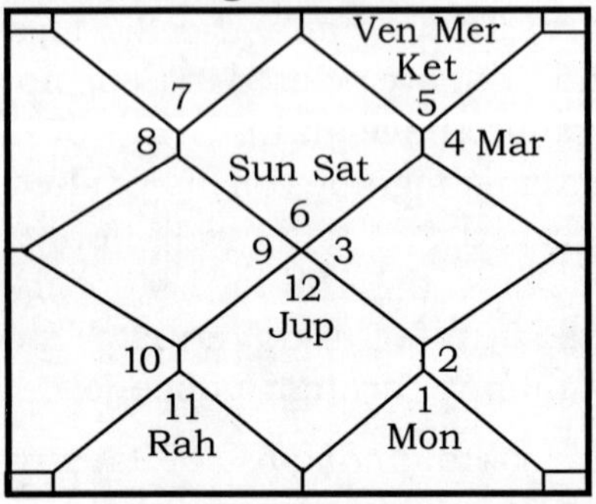


**Navamsa Chart**

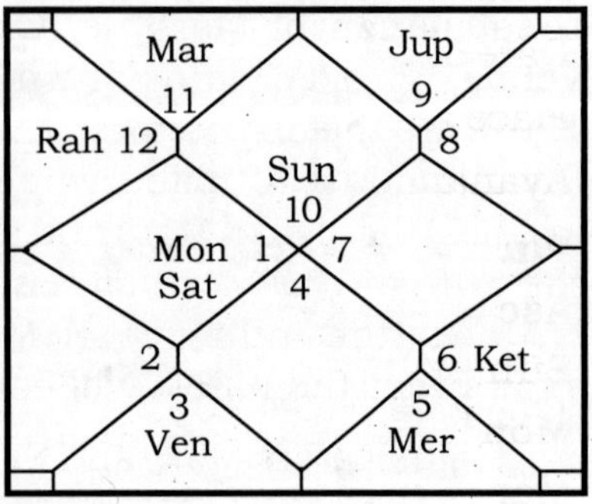


Balance of Vimsottari Dasa of **Ket 5Y 8M 8D**

The native is a very active, smart and famous police officer working as I.G. of Police. Professional aspect of the native may be judged as under:

1. The lord of the 10th house, Mercury, joins the 12th house in Leo under *vargottam navamsa.*
2. No planet is placed in the 10th house. It is only Saturn who lends its aspect over the 10th.
3. The 11th house is occupied by Mars and aspected by Jupiter.
4. The 11th lord Moon falls in the 8th house, in fiery sign Aries owned by Mars under *vargottam navamsa.* Thus, the 11th house is occupied by Mars and its lord Moon falls in the sign and *navamsa* of Mars.
5. The 6th lord Saturn, being placed in the *lagna*, aspects the 10th house and obtains *navamsa* of Mars.
6. The 10th lord Mercury, 3rd lord Mars and 2nd lord Venus jointly aspect the 6th house.
7. The 10th lord Mercury, the 11th lord Moon and the 2nd lord Venus all are placed in fiery signs i.e. Leo and Aries. Jupiter, Saturn, Moon and 10th lord Mercury obtain fiery *navamsa* i.e. Aries, Leo and Sagittarius.

Thus, we find that involvement of fiery signs and the role of Mars, Jupiter and Saturn in respect of the 10th, 11th and 2nd houses made the native a police officer, where the 6th house also has a specific importance.

*Illustration : 9.11* **(PCS)** *Horoscope No.: 126*

| | | | |
|---|---|---|---|
| Date of birth | : 24.02.1951 | Time of birth | : 13:53:00 hrs |
| Place of birth | : Ambala | Lat 30:19:00 N | Long 76:49:00E |
| Ayanamsa | : 23:10:32 | Sidereal Time : | 23:43:53 |

| Pln | Degree | Rasi | Nakshatra | Pad |
|---|---|---|---|---|
| Asc | 16:23:49 | Gem | Ardra | 3 |
| Sun | 11:44:29 | Aqu | Satabhisha | 2 |
| Mon | 12:06:08 | Vir | Hasta | 1 |
| Mar | 2:30:32 | Pis | P Bhadrapad | 4 |
| Mer (C) | 29:38:50 | Cap | Dhanishtha | 2 |
| Jup | 23:26:30 | Aqu | P Bhadrapad | 2 |
| Ven | 6:02:52 | Pis | U Bhadrapad | 1 |
| Sat (R) | 7:37:13 | Vir | U Phalguni | 4 |
| Rah (C) | 25:46:06 | Aqu | P Bhadrapad | 2 |
| Ket | 25:46:06 | Leo | P Phalguni | 4 |

**Lagna Chart**

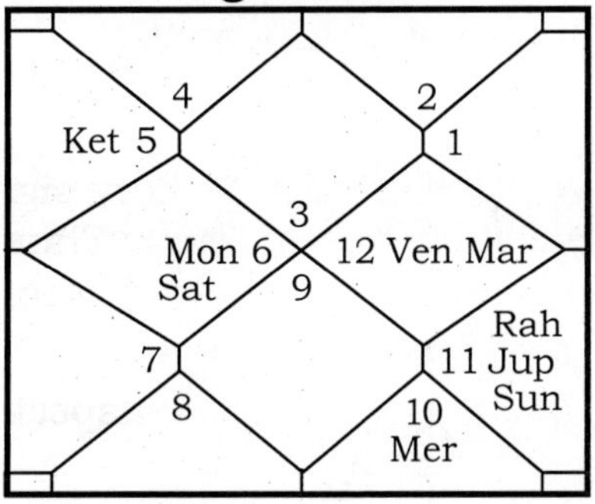


**Navamsa Chart**

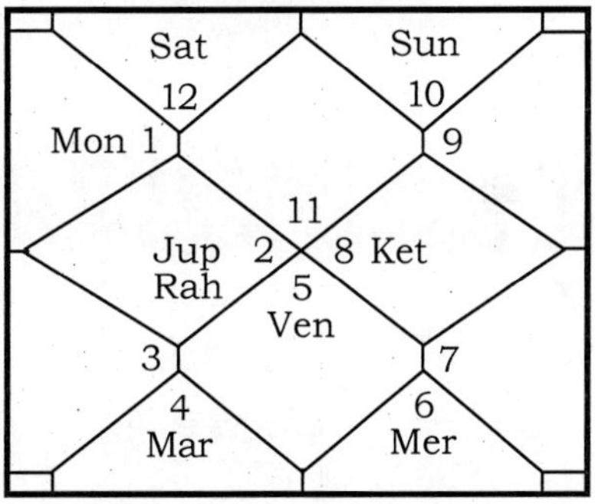


Balance of Vimsottari Dasa of **Mon 8Y 5M 2D**

The native, who is working as the I.G. of Police, was born under Gemini ascendant. The following are the combinations responsible for his joining the police service.

1. The 6th and 11th lord Mars is placed in the 10th house in Jupiter's sign Pisces.

2. The lord of the 2nd house, Moon, obtains the *navamsa* of Mars and also aspects the 10th house and Mars, who is placed in the 10th house.

3. There is mutual exchange of *navamsa* between the 6th and 11th lord Mars and 2nd lord Moon.
4. The *lagna* is aspected by Saturn and Mars both.
5. The 10th lord Jupiter is posited in the 9th house and 9th lord Saturn, who joins the 4th house, has an aspect over the 10th house and Mars over there.
6. The lord of the 2nd house, Moon, obtains the *navamsa* of a fiery sign Aries and Venus, who falls in the 10th house in association with Mars, in the sign of its exaltation, obtains a fiery *navamsa* Leo.

Thus, the lord of the 10th house Jupiter, lord of the 11th house Mars and the lord of the 2nd house Moon, all are related with the 10th house. Saturn, Mars and Jupiter aspect the ascendant. The 6th lord Mars is placed in the 10th house.

Various *Rajyogas* are also present in this birth chart as the lords of 5th and 9th, Venus and Saturn, are placed in 10th and 4th house, giving rise to strong professional aspect of the native. The native is a very successful and famous police officer of the State.

*Illustration : 9.12* **(SNC)** *Horoscope No.: 127*

Date of birth : 17.10.1950 Time of birth : 21:56:00 hrs

Place of birth : Kanpur Lat 26:27:00 N Long 80:19:00E

Ayanamsa : 23:10:10 Sidereal Time : 23:29:41

| **Pln** | **Degree** | **Rasi** | **Nakshatra** | **Pad** |
|---|---|---|---|---|
| Asc | 11:16:02 | Gem | Ardra | 2 |
| Sun | 0:33:41 | Lib | Chitra | 3 |
| Mon | 24:12:23 | Sag | Purvasadha | 4 |
| Mar | 22:21:37 | Sco | Jyeshtha | 2 |
| Mer (C) | 20:13:17 | Vir | Hasta | 4 |
| Jup (R) | 4:29:31 | Aqu | Dhanishtha | 4 |
| Ven (C) | 23:37:17 | Vir | Chitra | 1 |
| Sat | 3:21:35 | Vir | U Phalguni | 3 |
| Rah (R) | 4:57:44 | Pis | U Bhadrapad | 1 |
| Ket (R) | 4:57:44 | Vir | U Phalguni | 3 |

**Lagna Chart**

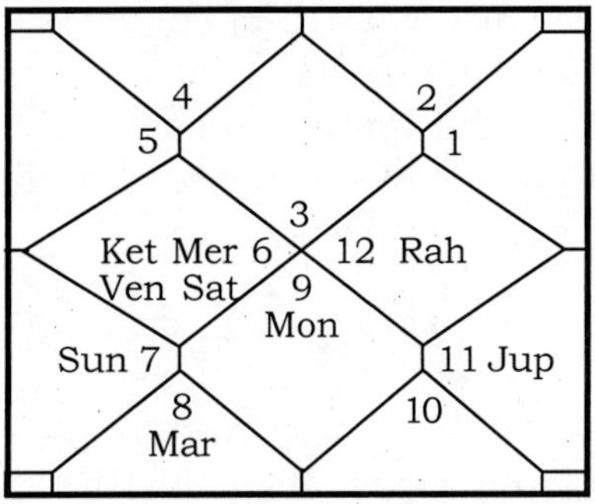


**Navamsa Chart**

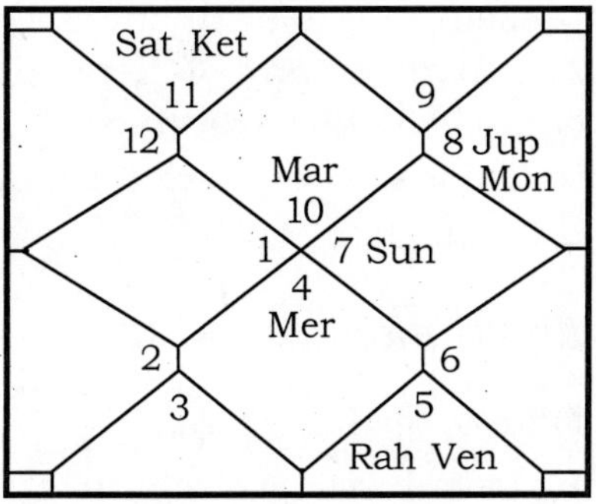


Balance of Vimsottari Dasa of **Ven 3Y 8M 8D**

The native is also working as an I.G. of Police. Following combinations may be noted:

1. The lord of the $10^{th}$ house, Jupiter, is posited in the $9^{th}$ and is aspected by $11^{th}$ and $6^{th}$ lord Mars.
2. The $10^{th}$ lord Jupiter obtains *navamsa* of Mars.
3. The lord of $6^{th}$ and $11^{th}$ house, Mars, obtains *navamsa* of its exaltation.
4. The lord of the $2^{nd}$ house, Moon, obtains the *navamsa* of Mars and is also associated with Jupiter in the *navamsa* chart.
5. The $10^{th}$ lord Jupiter falls in the $9^{th}$ house in the sign of Saturn, and $9^{th}$ lord Saturn has an aspect over the $10^{th}$ house. Saturn also obtains own *navamsa*.
6. Saturn and Mars both have an aspect over the *lagna*.
7. The lord of the $10^{th}$ house Jupiter, lord of the $9^{th}$ house Saturn, lord of the $11^{th}$ house Mars and the lord of the $2^{nd}$ house Moon aspect the *lagna*.
8. The $6^{th}$ and $11^{th}$ lord Mars is placed in the $6^{th}$ house, in its own sign Scorpio, from where it aspects the $10^{th}$ lord Jupiter.
9. The lord of the $2^{nd}$ house, Moon, falls in the fiery sign Sagittarius and obtains the *navamsa* of fiery planet Mars.

Thus, the conditions for becoming an IPS officer are present in this birth chart. He is working as IG of Police. But the involvement of fiery signs in *Rashi* and *navamsa* is comparatively less due to which the temperament of the native is not very strict. Many times he also suffered a lot on this account.

*Illustration : 9.13* (**JNS**) *Horoscope No.: 128*

Date of birth : 12.09.1966 Time of birth : 01:45:00 hrs

Place of birth : Azamgarh Lat 26:03:00 N Long 83:10:00E

Ayanamsa : 23:23:18 Sidereal Time : 1:09:16

| **Pln** | **Degree** | **Rasi** | **Nakshatra** | **Pad** |
|---|---|---|---|---|
| Asc | 2:42:16 | Can | Punarvasu | 4 |
| Sun | 25:14:41 | Leo | P Phalguni | 4 |
| Mon | 13:25:28 | Can | Pushya | 4 |
| Mar | 17:31:53 | Can | Aslesha | 1 |
| Mer (D) | 26:37:46 | Leo | P Phalguni | 4 |
| Jup | 4:01:55 | Can | Pushya | 1 |
| Ven | 10:08:32 | Leo | Magha | 4 |
| Sat (R) | 3:28:46 | Pis | U Bhadrapad | 1 |
| Rah (R) | 24:42:46 | Ari | Bharani | 4 |
| Ket (R) | 24:42:46 | Lib | Visakha | 2 |

**Lagna Chart**

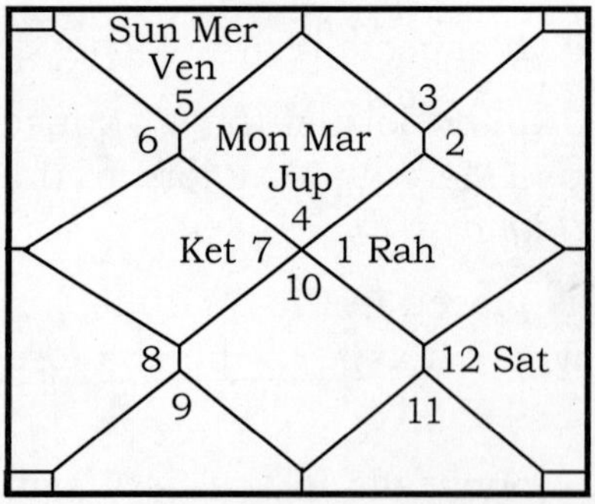


**Navamsa Chart**

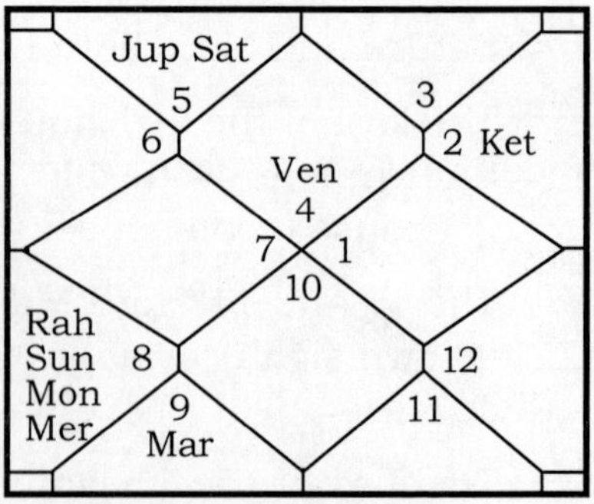


Balance of Vimsottari Dasa of **Sat 4Y 7M 13D**

The native is an IPS officer. The analytical judgement of his birth chart, in relation to his professional aspect, may be made as below:

1. The lord of the 10th house, Mars, is placed in the ascendant with the ascendant lord Moon and 6th and 9th lord Jupiter. The 10th lord Mars obtains the fiery *navamsa* of Jupiter, which is strong indication of entering into the police department.
2. The lord of the 2nd house is Sun, who is placed in own sign Leo, in the 2nd house itself, in association with the 11th lord Venus. Sun obtains Scorpio *navamsa.*
3. The 6th lord Jupiter, who is exalted in the ascendant, obtains the *navamsa* of Sun i.e. Leo. In *Rashi* chart, 6th and 10th lord, Jupiter and Mars are conjoined in the *lagna* with *Neechbhanga* of Mars, whereas in *navamsa* chart both fall in fiery *navamsa* and Jupiter aspects Mars, tending the native to join the police service.
4. In *Rashi* chart, Saturn aspects the 6th house and is aspected by the 6th lord Jupiter. Saturn also obtains Leo *navamsa.*
5. The lord of the 11th house, Venus, joins Sun in Leo, in the 2nd house. These are sufficient reasons for one entering into Police service.

*Illustration : 9.14* (**RPS**) *Horoscope No.: 129*

Date of birth : 15.07.1944 Time of birth : 09:00:00 hrs
Place of birth : Ballia Lat 25:45:00 N Long 84:09:00E
Ayanamsa : 23:04:41 Sidereal Time : 3:37:54

| **Pln** | **Degree** | **Rasi** | **Nakshatra** | **Pad** |
|---|---|---|---|---|
| Asc | 5:09:44 | Leo | Magha | 2 |
| Sun | 29:23:09 | Gem | Punarvasu | 3 |
| Mon | 28:08:54 | Ari | Krittika | 1 |
| Mar | 8:44:44 | Leo | Magha | 3 |

| Mer | 14:09:10 | Can | Pushya | 4 |
|---|---|---|---|---|
| Jup | 4:44:01 | Leo | Magha | 2 |
| Ven (C) | 4:20:32 | Can | Pushya | 1 |
| Sat | 10:06:32 | Gem | Ardra | 2 |
| Rah (R/C) | 4:35:39 | Can | Pushya | 1 |
| Ket (R) | 4:35:39 | Cap | Uttarasadha | 3 |

**Lagna Chart**

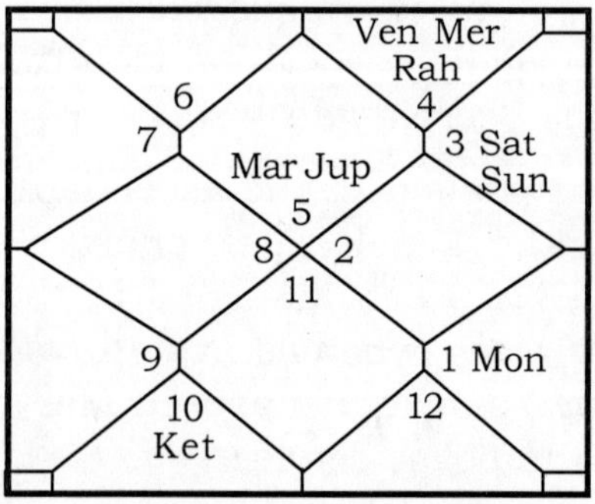


**Navamsa Chart**

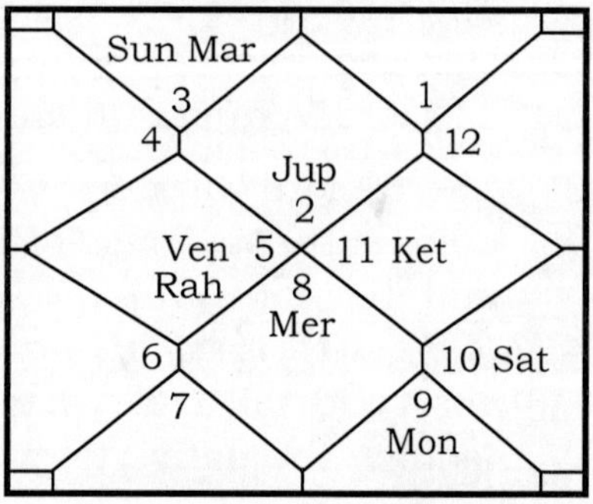


Balance of Vimsottari Dasa of **Sun 5Y 3M 30D**

The native was a dynamic police inspector who dealt with innumerable criminals in the most dashing and aggressive manner. He has a robust personality and has been a great terror to the offenders of law, who dreaded him wherever he had been posted.

1. The native was born in Leo ascendant with Mars and Jupiter.

2. The lord of the 10th house, Venus, is posited in the 12th from where it aspects the 6th house. Venus obtains the fiery *navamsa* of Sun i.e. Leo.

3. The 6th lord Saturn obtains Scorpio *navamsa*. Saturn is associated with Sun in the 11th house and aspects the *lagna* and Mars. Thus, the ascendant is under the influence of Mars, Saturn and Jupiter.

4. The lords of 2nd house, Mercury, and that of the 10th house, Venus, have an aspect over the 6th house.

5. The 2nd lord Mercury is placed in the 12th house over the axis of Rahu and Ketu under *Papakartari Yoga* formed due to the position of Mars and Saturn on either side of Mercury. Therefore, the native suffered a lot and could not be successful in IPS. He became Inspector of Police and has now been promoted as Deputy S.P.

*Illustration : 9.15* (**SS**) *Horoscope No.: 130*

Date of birth : 07.08.1957 Time of birth : 21:35:00 hrs

Place of birth : Varanasi Lat 25:20:00 N Long 83:00:00E

Ayanamsa : 23:16:06 Sidereal Time : 18:40:38

| **Pln** | **Degree** | **Rasi** | **Nakshatra** | **Pad** |
|---|---|---|---|---|
| Asc | 20:35:34 | Pis | Revati | 2 |
| Sun | 21:35:35 | Can | Aslesha | 2 |
| Mon | 19:27:43 | Sag | Puvasadha | 2 |
| Mar (C) | 6:22:44 | Leo | Magha | 2 |
| Mer | 18:15:54 | Leo | P Phalguni | 2 |
| Jup | 6:50:07 | Vir | U Phalguni | 4 |
| Ven | 21:52:48 | Leo | P Phalguni | 3 |
| Sat (R) | 14:25:43 | Sco | Anuradha | 4 |
| Rah (R) | 22:04:45 | Lib | Visakha | 1 |
| Ket (R) | 22:04:45 | Ari | Bharani | 3 |

**Lagna Chart**

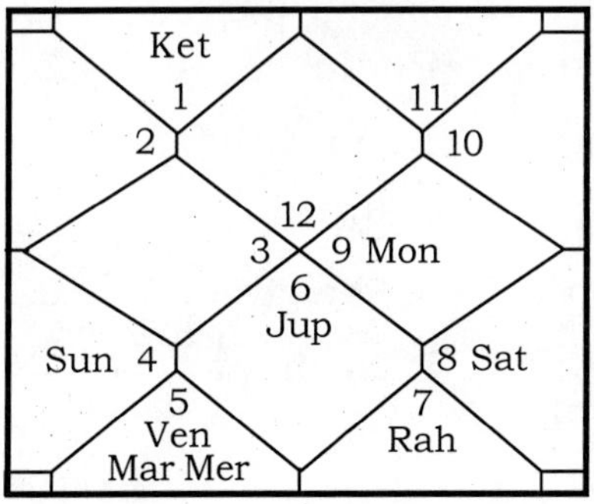


**Navamsa Chart**

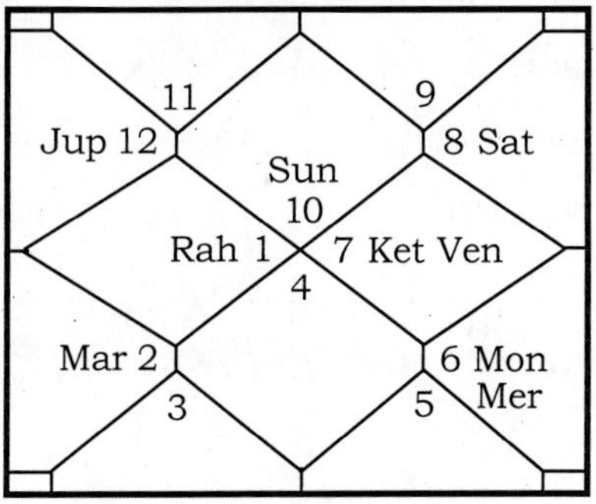


Balance of Vimsottari Dasa of **Ven 10Y 9M 20D**

The native is a Police Inspector. He was born under Pisces ascendant, whose ruler Jupiter is placed in the 7th house and aspects the ascendant and the 11th house. Moon falls in a fiery sign Sagittarius, in the 10th house. The lord of the 11th house, Saturn, falls in Scorpio, in the 9th house under *vargottam navamsa* and aspects the 11th and 6th house. The lord of the 2nd house, Mars, is placed in the 6th house, in a fiery sign Leo.

Thus, Mars in Leo in *Rashi* and Saturn in Sagittarius in *navamsa* aspect each other in *Rashi* chart as well as in *navamsa* chart. Malefics in the 6th house under the influence of Mars promote such kind of job.

*Illustration : 9.16* (**PKS**) *Horoscope No.: 131*

Date of birth : 08.01.1942 Time of birth : 19:50:00 hrs
Place of birth : Delhi Lat 28:39:00 N Long 77:13:00E
Ayanamsa : 23:02:46 Sidereal Time : 2:38:52

| **Pln** | **Degree** | **Rasi** | **Nakshatra** | **Pad** |
|---|---|---|---|---|
| Asc | 23:12:33 | Can | Aslesha | 2 |
| Sun | 24:38:26 | Sag | Purvasadha | 4 |
| Mon | 3:54:23 | Vir | U Phalguni | 3 |
| Mar | 5:19:55 | Ari | Asvini | 2 |
| Mer (C) | 5:13:47 | Cap | Uttarasadha | 3 |
| Jup (R) | 19:37:34 | Tau | Rohini | 3 |
| Ven | 27:45:01 | Cap | Dhanishtha | 2 |
| Sat (R) | 28:47:23 | Ari | Krittika | 1 |
| Rah | 22:05:44 | Leo | P Phalguni | 3 |
| Ket | 22:05:44 | Aqu | P Bhadrapad | 1 |

**Lagna Chart**

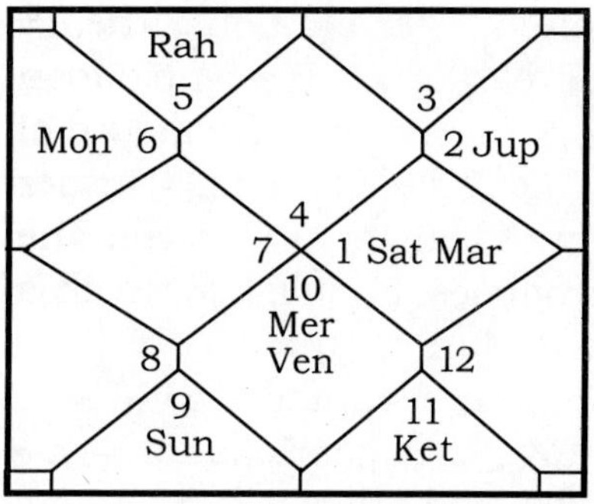


**Navamsa Chart**

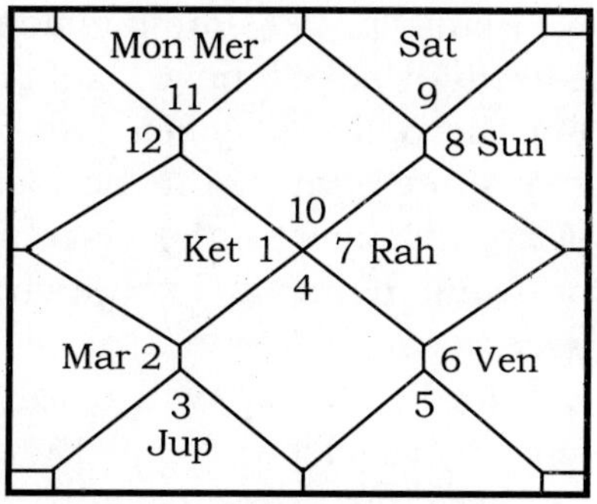


Balance of Vimsottari Dasa of **Sun 2Y 8M 27D**

The native is extremely energetic and most dynamic Police Commissioner. He is born in Cancer ascendant. The *Yogakaraka* Mars is posited in own fiery sign Aries in the 10th house and is associated with Saturn. The lord of the 2nd house, Sun, joins the 6th house in a fiery sign Sagittarius. The 6th lord Jupiter occupies the 11th house and aspects the 11th lord Venus, who falls in Capricorn i.e. the sign of Saturn. Saturn falls in a fiery *navamsa* and the 2nd lord Sun also obtains the *navamsa* of Mars. Venus falls in the constellation of Mars. Thus, the 2nd lord Sun, 10th lord Mars and 11th lord Venus fall in the fiery sign or *navamsa* or in the sign or constellation of Mars. Jupiter is also playing its role in the 11th house as 6th lord.

These combinations positively and powerfully indicate police job of an IPS officer.

After the examination and analysis of so many examples, we have found that Mars, Saturn and Jupiter are the major significators, whereas the Sun is the supporting significator. Venus does play a prominent role in the horoscopes of IPS and authorities above IPS, because Venus happens to be a significator for administrative and civil services.

Aries, Leo, Scorpio and Sagittarius signs are prominent in the horoscopes of police personnel.

The study of 2nd, 9th and 11th houses should be made, in

addition to the $10^{th}$ house, for all kinds of occupation. For a particular profession, consideration of certain houses is also essential, as we have explained earlier at different places. For the police services, the $6^{th}$ house must be related with the other concerning houses like $10^{th}$, $11^{th}$ or $2^{nd}$ house, either by aspect or by placement of planets or by ownership or owing to mutual exchange of houses. Such as, for Scorpio ascendant, placement of $6^{th}$ lord Mars in the $10^{th}$ and the $10^{th}$ lord in the $6^{th}$ will result into an occupation connected with police department. So many other combinations may be there in respect to the $6^{th}$ house and other houses having a concern over the profession. The study of *navamsa* chart and constellation is equally essential apart from the examination of *Atmakaraka* planet and the strongest planet of the horoscope. If Moon is much stronger than the ascendant, the occupation of the native should be analyzed from the Moon chart and not from the *Rashi* chart.

●

# CHAPTER-10

# Engagements in Banks and Planetary Equations

We cannot afford to ignore bank services, when we are discussing about the planetary set up for all kinds of professional engagements. Banks play a prominent role in running and maintaining the financial equilibrium of the country. There are various kinds of services in the bank. A few join in the capacity of officer, accountant or even manager, whereas many start their career as a clerk in the bank.

First of all, the horoscope of the native should be examined to know whether or not the bank services are indicated. If yes, the position of the 9$^{th}$ and the 10$^{th}$ house and their lords should be considered, in addition to the position of Sun. If these houses and Sun are well disposed, the native will join bank in the capacity of a senior officer, Manager, Accountant or so.

## THE 2$^{ND}$ HOUSE

The 2$^{nd}$ house rules over the accumulation or collection of money, which is the main object of the bank services. Therefore, the 2$^{nd}$ house must be taken into account for the judgement of success in bank services.

## THE 5$^{TH}$ HOUSE

Bank services require extreme concentration, intelligence, calculations, account keeping and maintenance of accounts etc., which come under the control of 5$^{th}$ house. The brain must be fertile and very active, in addition to the presence of mind. Therefore, the 5$^{th}$ house, and lord thereof, has a considerable concern with bank services provided it has an influence over the 10$^{th}$ house.

## THE 10<sup>TH</sup> HOUSE

The 10th house always plays a prominent role in the judgement of most appropriate and suitable business or service. Placement of Jupiter and Mercury in the 10th house will direct one towards the service in a bank or any financial institution or organization dealing with financial transactions, provided Jupiter or Mercury own the 2nd or 5th house, or are associated with the lord of the 10th house in one or the other way. Mutual exchange between the 2nd and the 10th lord, corresponding with Jupiter and Mercury, or their ruler ship, is the pointer to a bank professional. There are many such combinations, involving the role of Jupiter, Mercury, the 2nd and the 5th house in addition to the 10th house, which tend the individual to serve in any bank or finance company etc.

## THE JUPITER

Jupiter is *Dhanakaraka* and it is the most important significator of bank services. The ascendant or the 2nd lord Jupiter, if joins the 10th house, will indicate the service in bank.

## THE MERCURY

Mercury cannot be overlooked for bank personnel. Mercury has an important significance as far as accountancy, calculations, Computer operation, transaction and application of rules are concerned. In fact, Mercury symbolizes the 5th house. So, if Mercury is important for any job, the 5th house is equally important and should be analyzed properly along with Mercury.

## SUPPORTING SIGNIFICATOR VENUS

Venus is important for the judgement of administration and management. So, for direct appointment as a Class-I or Class-II officer in a bank, Venus must have a bearing over the profession of the native.

## SUPPORTING HOUSE, THE ELEVENTH

Eleventh house is studied for income and financial position. If the $11^{th}$ house is well disposed but the $2^{nd}$ house is not involved, or does not have any relation with the $10^{th}$ house and Jupiter, one will not be successful in bank. In fact, if the $11^{th}$ house and its lord are well fortified with the $10^{th}$ and $2^{nd}$ house, in addition to positive role of subsequent significators, Jupiter and Mercury, one will certainly join bank.

Now we will illustrate these planetary combinations in the birth charts of a few bank personnel.

*Illustration : 10.1* **(NM)** *Horoscope No.: 132*

Date of birth : 08.03.1957 Time of birth : 02:59:00 hrs

Place of birth : Lucknow Lat 26:50:00 N Long 80:54:00E

Ayanamsa : 23:15:46 Sidereal Time : 13:53:54

| **Pln** | **Degree** | **Rasi** | **Nakshatra** | **Pad** |
|---|---|---|---|---|
| Asc | 21:46:29 | Sag | Purvasadha | 3 |
| Sun | 23:47:34 | Aqu | P Bhadrapad | 2 |
| Mon | 4:15:15 | Tau | Krittika | 3 |
| Mar | 0:27:39 | Tau | Krittika | 2 |
| Mer (C) | 12:35:11 | Aqu | Satabhisha | 2 |
| Jup (R) | 4:53:06 | Vir | U Phalguni | 3 |
| Ven (C) | 14:15:48 | Aqu | Satabhisha | 3 |
| Sat | 20:49:42 | Sco | Jyestha | 2 |
| Rah | 28:47:10 | Lib | Visakha | 3 |
| Ket | 28:47:10 | Ari | Krittika | 1 |

**Lagna Chart**

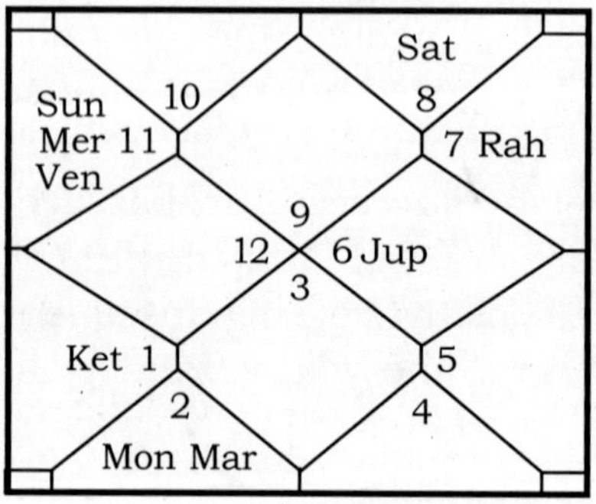


**Navamsa Chart**

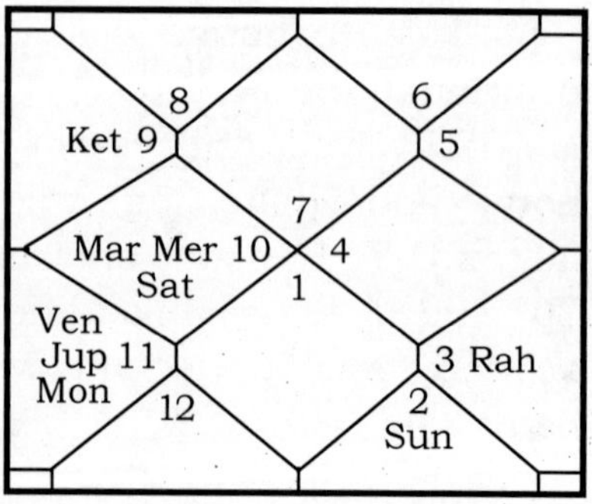


Balance of Vimsottari Dasa of **Sun 2Y 7M 0D**

She joined State Bank of India as a Probationary Officer after passing M.Sc. from Lucknow University. This charming young lady is now Chief Manager of a huge branch of State Bank of India. Following combinations may be noted, which make one successful in bank services.

1. She was born in Sagittarius ascendant, whose lord Jupiter is posited in the $10^{th}$ house in Virgo and aspects the $2^{nd}$ house, $4^{th}$ and $6^{th}$ house.

2. The lord of the $2^{nd}$ house, Saturn, also aspects the $2^{nd}$ house. Thus, the $2^{nd}$ house receives the aspect of the ascendant lord Jupiter and $2^{nd}$ lord Saturn, indicating her engagement in Bank.

3. Lord of the $9^{th}$ Sun, lord of the $10^{th}$ Mercury and lord of the $11^{th}$ Venus are closely associated in the $3^{rd}$ house and lend their auspicious aspect over the $9^{th}$ house.

4. The $5^{th}$ lord Mars, which joins the $6^{th}$ house, is aspected by the ascendant lord Jupiter and $2^{nd}$ lord Saturn, and Mars lends its own aspect over the $9^{th}$ house, the ascendant and $2^{nd}$ lord Saturn. Thus, the involvement of Jupiter, Mercury, and the $2^{nd}$ and $5^{th}$ house, in addition to $11^{th}$ lord Venus, in fixing up the occupation of the native, strongly indicate towards bank services.

5. *Atmakaraka* planet the Sun falls in *Purvabhadrapada* constellation ruled by Jupiter and tends her towards the service of teaching, bank or journalism. The Sun obtains *navamsa* of the 11th lord Venus. This shows a high administrative position in the bank. Therefore, the possibility of other occupations is ruled out.
6. The 7th and the 10th lord Mercury, the 5th lord Mars and the lord of the 2nd house, Saturn, obtain the *navamsa* of the 2nd lord Saturn. This kind of disposition confirms bank services quite logically and strongly.
7. There is mutual exchange of constellation between the Sun and Jupiter i.e. the 9th lord Sun and the ascendant lord Jupiter. Moreover, Jupiter obtains *navamsa* of the 2nd lord Saturn and aspects the 2nd house as well, giving an impression that the native will be quite successful and dynamic employee of a bank and will reach to the apex.

*Illustration: 10.2* (**GPM**) *Horoscope No.: 133*

Date of birth : 06.08.1961 Time of birth : 16:00:00 hrs
Place of birth : Jahanabad Lat 26:06:00 N Long 80:21:00E
Ayanamsa : 23:19:05 Sidereal Time : 12:50:18

| **Pln** | **Degree** | **Rasi** | **Nakshatra** | **Pad** |
|---|---|---|---|---|
| Asc | 6:57:52 | Sag | Moola | 3 |
| Sun | 20:23:26 | Can | Aslesha | 2 |
| Mon | 25:12:19 | Tau | Mrigsira | 1 |
| Mar | 0:00:52 | Vir | U Phalguni | 2 |
| Mer (C) | 11:27:35 | Can | Pushya | 3 |
| Jup (R) | 7:23:26 | Cap | Uttarasadha | 4 |
| Ven | 9:50:48 | Gem | Ardra | 1 |
| Sat (R) | 1:55:47 | Cap | Uttarasadha | 2 |
| Rah (R/C) | 3:57:19 | Leo | Magha | 2 |
| Ket (R) | 3:57:19 | Aqu | Dhanishtha | 4 |

**Lagna Chart**

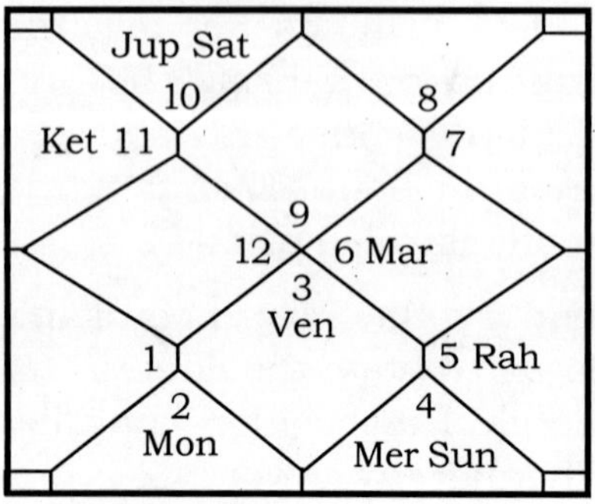


**Navamsa Chart**

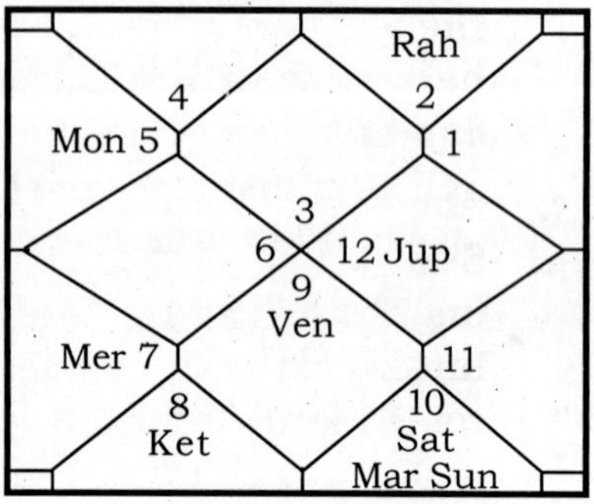


Balance of Vimsottari Dasa of **Mar 6Y 0M 6D**

The native was born in Sagittarius ascendant, which obtains *navamsa* of Gemini. Following combinations may be noted, which make one successful in bank services.

1. The lords of the ascendant, Jupiter, and that of 2nd house, Saturn, are placed together in the 2nd house, from where Jupiter aspects the 10th house, 10th lord Mercury and the 9th lord Sun. This indicates that the native will be successful, as a bank employee.

   **Rule – If the 2nd house and Jupiter influence the 10th house or its lord by conjunction or aspect, one will enter in Bank service.**

2. In this horoscope, ascendant lord, Jupiter, and lord of the 10th house, Mercury, have a mutual aspect. That justifies bank service of the subject.

3. Involvement of the 5th house and Mercury may also be taken into account for further confirmation. The ascendant lord Jupiter aspects the 5th lord Mars, who is placed in the 10th house. Thus, the placement of Jupiter in the 2nd house with the 2nd lord Saturn and its aspect over the 10th house and 10th lord Mercury, as well as on the 5th lord Mars, strongly justifies the livelihood of the native through service in the bank.

   He started his career as a clerk in U.B.I. and now the native is a Class-I officer in State Bank of Hyderabad at Mumbai.

**Rule – The 5th house, its lord and Mercury, if influence the 10th or 2nd house in one or the other way, the native is likely to join bank or any finance company or organization.**

4. *Atmakaraka* planet, the Moon, obtains the *navamsa* of Sun, who owns the 9th house and joins the 8th house under aspect from Jupiter. Moon occupies the 6th house under aspect from Jupiter, and falls in *Mrigsira*, the constellation of the 10th placed Mars.

5. The 10th lord Mercury obtains the *navamsa* of the 11th lord Venus, which occupies Gemini, the sign of Mercury. Moreover, 10th lord Mercury falls in *Pushya* constellation ruled by the 2nd lord Saturn. Thus, the 10th lord Mercury and *Atmakaraka* Moon are under the influence of the ascendant lord Jupiter, while both Jupiter and Saturn are conjoined in the 2nd house. These planetary configurations strongly ensure and justify the native being a bank servant.

*Illustration: 10.3* (**PKS**) *Horoscope No.: 134*

Date of birth : 13.05.1960 Time of birth : 22:50:00 hrs

Place of birth : Lucknow Lat 26:50:00 N Long 80:54:00E

Ayanamsa : 23:18:08 Sidereal Time : 14:09:27

| **Pln** | **Degree** | **Rasi** | **Nakshatra** | **Pad** |
|---|---|---|---|---|
| Asc | 25:38:10 | Sag | Purvasadha | 4 |
| Sun | 29:37:30 | Ari | Krittika | 1 |
| Mon | 4:30:06 | Sag | Moola | 2 |
| Mar | 8:32:20 | Pis | U Bhadrapad | 2 |
| Mer (C) | 24:55:20 | Ari | Bharani | 4 |
| Jup (R) | 9:27:41 | Sag | Moola | 3 |
| Ven | 18:50:51 | Ari | Bharani | 2 |
| Sat (R) | 24:55:04 | Sag | Purvasadha | 4 |
| Rah (R) | 29:22:01 | Leo | U Phalguni | 1 |
| Ket (R) | 29:22:01 | Aqu | P Bhadrapad | 3 |

**Lagna Chart**

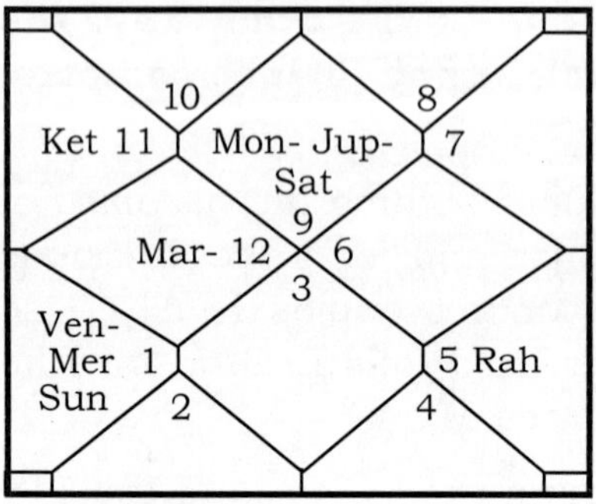


**Navamsa Chart**

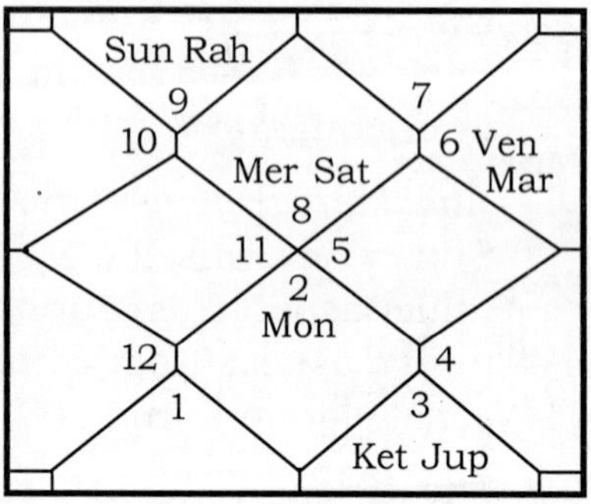


Balance of Vimsottari Dasa of **Ket 4Y 7M 19D**

The native started his career as a simple bank employee and gradually reached to the position of Chief Manager of Bank of Baroda. Following combinations may be noted, which make one successful in bank services.

1. The native was born in Sagittarius ascendant with the ascendant lord Jupiter, 2nd lord Saturn and the 8th lord Moon.
2. The 10th lord Mercury occupies the 5th house and the 5th lord Mars aspects the 10th house.
3. The 2nd lord Saturn and the 5th lord Mars, both aspect the 10th house, whereas Jupiter aspects the 10th lord Mercury and 11th lord Venus. Jupiter aspects the 9th lord the Sun, the 10th lord Mercury and the 11th lord Venus. Moreover, the *Atmakaraka* Sun obtains the *navamsa* of the *Dhankaraka* and the significator of bank service, Jupiter. The ascendant lord Jupiter and 11th lord Venus, both, obtain *navamsa* of Mercury. This has strengthened the combination of bank service to the native.

*Illustration: 10.4* (**AKS**) *Horoscope No.: 135*

| | | | |
|---|---|---|---|
| Date of birth | : 16.02.1949 | Time of birth : | 03:30:00 hrs |
| Place of birth | : Lucknow | Lat 26:50:00 N | Long 80:54:00E |
| Ayanamsa | : 23:08:40 | Sidereal Time : | 13:05:53 |

| Pln | Degree | Rasi | Nakshatra | Pad |
|---|---|---|---|---|
| Asc | 10:22:05 | Sag | Moola | 4 |
| Sun | 3:46:04 | Aqu | Dhanishtha | 4 |
| Mon | 9:30:24 | Vir | U Phalguni | 4 |
| Mar (C) | 10:08:45 | Aqu | Satabhisha | 2 |
| Mer | 11:27:43 | Cap | Sravna | 1 |
| Jup | 27:32:09 | Sag | Uttarasadha | 1 |
| Ven | 18:46:16 | Cap | Sravna | 3 |
| Sat (R) | 10:07:12 | Leo | Magha | 4 |
| Rah (R) | 4:16:21 | Ari | Asvini | 2 |
| Ket (R) | 4:16:21 | Lib | Chitra | 4 |

**Lagna Chart** **Navamsa Chart**

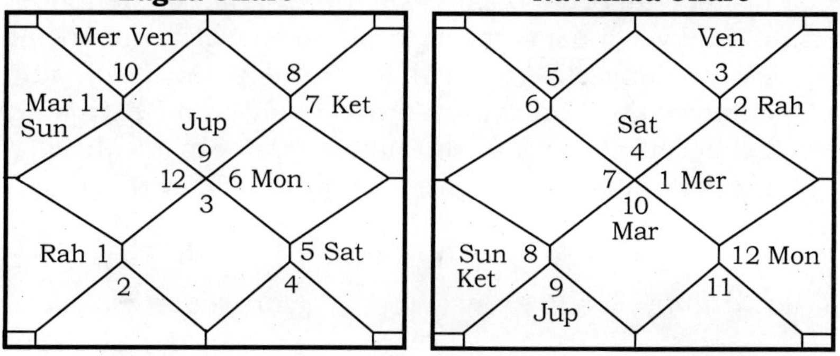


Balance of Vimsottari Dasa of **Sun 0Y 2M 20D**

This horoscope belongs to one of the most competent and proficient bank officer, who has been endowed with the heavy responsibility of installation of new branches of IDBI for at least at two dozen occasions. The native was born in Sagittarius sign with the placement of Jupiter therein. Following combinations may be noted, which make one successful in bank services.

1. Lord of the 10th house, Mercury, joins the 2nd house in association with 11th lord Venus. This combination is enough to advise bank services to the native.
2. Moon joins the 10th house in Virgo, whereas 2nd lord Saturn joins the 9th house in Leo.

3. The lord of the 5th house, Mars, is associated with 9th lord Sun and is aspected by the 2nd and 3rd lord Saturn. This is a marvelous combination for bank services.

4. The strongest planet is Jupiter, who obtains 1.38 *Shadabala* and it is *Atmakaraka* as well. Jupiter's placement in ascendant has given rise to *Hans Mahapurusha Rajyoga.* Besides this, Jupiter obtains *vargottam navamsa.* Jupiter falls in *Uttarashadha nakshatra* ruled by Sun.

5. There is mutual exchange between Sun and Saturn. Moreover, 5th lord Mars aspects the 10th house and Moon, who is placed in the 10th house. Moon also obtains the *navamsa* of Jupiter and strongly indicates bank services. Placement of Moon in *Poorvaphalguni* constellation, ruled by Venus, along with placement of Venus in the *Hasta* constellation, ruled by Moon, is a splendid combination for dynamic personality and extremely beneficial services of the native for the bank. In fact, involvement of Venus gives the cadre of Officer, Manager and other upper administrative grades.

*Illustration: 10.5* (**DS**) *Horoscope No.: 136*

Date of birth : 22.08.1972 Time of birth : 08:30:00 hrs

Place of birth : Kanpur Lat 26:27:00 N Long 80:19:00E

Ayanamsa : 23:28:46 Sidereal Time : 6:23:20

| **Pln** | **Degree** | **Rasi** | **Nakshatra** | **Pad** |
|---|---|---|---|---|
| Asc | 11:44:58 | Vir | Hasta | 1 |
| Sun | 5:38:04 | Leo | Magha | 2 |
| Mon | 2:53:00 | Cap | Uttarasadha | 2 |
| Mar (C) | 11:01:13 | Leo | Magha | 4 |
| Mer | 18:04:36 | Can | Aslesha | 1 |
| Jup (R) | 5:01:29 | Sag | Moola | 2 |
| Ven | 19:56:44 | Gem | Ardra | 4 |

| | | | | |
|---|---|---|---|---|
| Sat | 25:35:41 | Tau | Mrigsira | 1 |
| Rah (R) | 2:21:46 | Cap | Uttarasadha | 2 |
| Ket (R) | 2:21:46 | Can | Punarvasu | 4 |

**Lagna Chart**

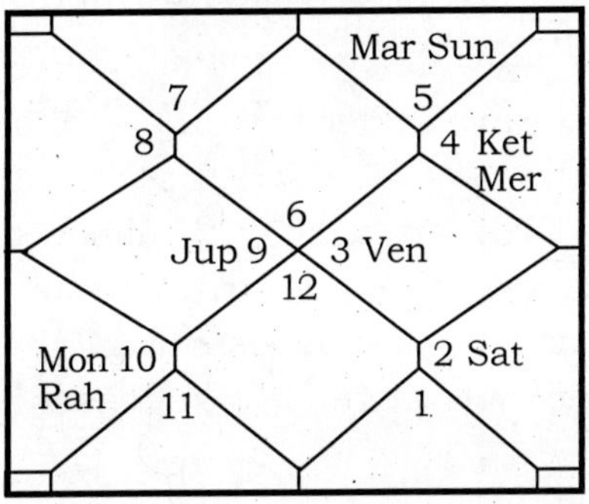


**Navamsa Chart**

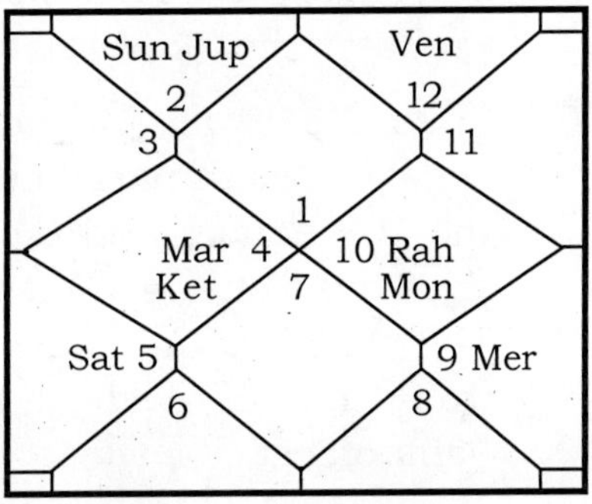


Balance of Vimsottari Dasa of **Sun 2Y 2M 13D**

She is the bank manager in Axis Bank. Earlier, she worked in I.D.B.I. and many other banks. She is extremely smart, talented and bright, as far as banking is concerned. She was born in Virgo ascendant. Following combinations may be noted, which make one successful in bank services.

1. The lord of the 2nd and 9th house, Venus, is placed in 10th house in Gemini and is aspected by Jupiter. This single combination is enough to advise the engagement in banks.

2. Here, the 10th and ascendant lord Mercury is placed in 11th house in Cancer, in own constellation *Aslesha*. Mercury lends its aspect over the 5th house and 11th lord Moon.

3. *Atmakaraka* planet, Saturn, is the lord of the 5th and 6th houses. Saturn joins the 9th house and aspects the 10th lord Mercury.

4. The lord of the ascendant and 10th Mercury obtains the *navamsa* of the main significator Jupiter, which clearly signifies that the native will do well to join bank as a Probationary Officer.

5. Venus owns the 2nd and 9th house and it is unusually strong as it obtains 1.68 *Shadabalas.* The lord of 2nd house is very well tenanted in the 10th house, corresponding with the sign Gemini ruled by Mercury. Moreover, 2nd lord Venus obtains *navamsa* of its exaltation i.e. *navamsa* of Jupiter.

6. Thus, the 9th and 10th houses are under the influence of significators Jupiter and Mercury. The 2nd, the 5th and the 10th houses and their lords are very well disposed and have a strong influence over the career of the native. The examination of the birth chart suggests that she would do very well and will be extremely successful bank officer.

*Illustration: 10.6* **(MA)** *Horoscope No.: 137*

Date of birth : 29.06.1975 Time of birth : 19:02:00 hrs

Place of birth : Chandausi Lat 28:06:00 N Long 77:50:00E

Ayanamsa : 23:31:07 Sidereal Time : 13:11:22

| **Pln** | **Degree** | **Rasi** | **Nakshatra** | **Pad** |
|---|---|---|---|---|
| Asc | 10:36:28 | Sag | Moola | 4 |
| Sun | 13:40:29 | Gem | Ardra | 3 |
| Mon | 20:23:14 | Aqu | P Bhadrapad | 1 |
| Mar | 5:20:25 | Ari | Asvini | 2 |
| Mer | 23:22:51 | Tau | Mrigsira | 1 |
| Jup | 27:53:25 | Pis | Revati | 4 |
| Ven | 28:34:07 | Can | Aslesha | 4 |
| Sat (C) | 26:54:46 | Gem | Punarvasu | 3 |
| Rah (R) | 6:48:36 | Sco | Anuradha | 2 |
| Ket (R) | 6:48:36 | Tau | Krittika | 4 |

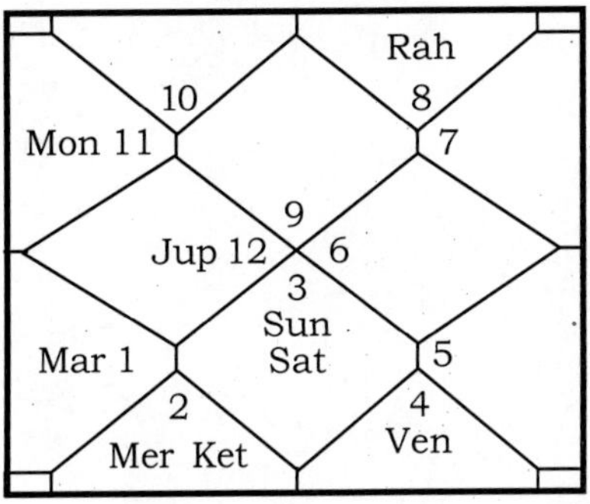


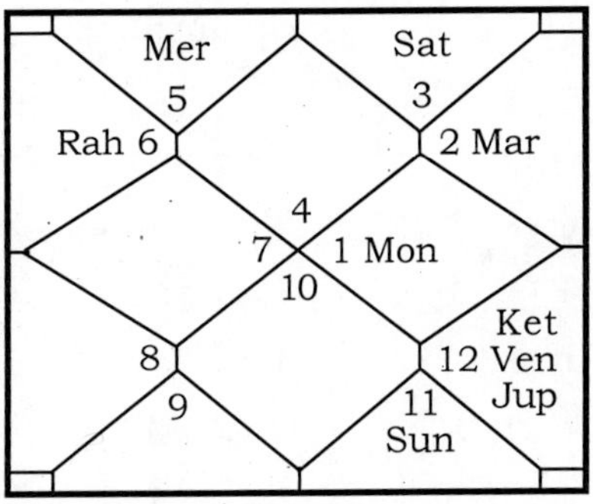


Balance of Vimsottari Dasa of **Jup 15Y 6M 12D**

The native is working as Assistant Manager in State Bank of India. He was born in Sagittarius ascendant, whose lord Jupiter occupies the 4th house of its own and aspects the 10th house. Following combinations may be noted, which make one successful in bank services.

1. The 10th lord Mercury is tenanted in the 6th house, in Taurus, ruled by the 11th lord Venus. In fact, Venus is *Atmakaraka* and very strong in this birth chart as it obtains *navamsa* of its exaltation, in association with the ascendant lord Jupiter and falls in *Aslesha* constellation ruled by the 10th lord Mercury. This configuration of planets inclines one to join bank service.

2. Lord of the 2nd house, Saturn, occupies the 7th house, identical to Gemini ruled by the 10th lord Mercury. Moreover, Saturn falls in Jupiter's constellation *Punarvasu* and obtains *vargottam navamsa* as well.

These combinations of the native's horoscope justify bank service to him.

*Illustration: 10.7* (**GSS**) *Horoscope No.: 138*

Date of birth : 20.08.1946 Time of birth : 03:15:00 hrs

Place of birth : Gangoli Ghat Lat 28:50:00 N Long 78:45:00E

Ayanamsa : 23:06:26 Sidereal Time : 0:50:33

| Pln | Degree | Rasi | Nakshatra | Pad |
|---|---|---|---|---|
| Asc | 0:10:09 | Can | Punarvasu | 4 |
| Sun | 3:10:15 | Leo | Magha | 1 |
| Mon | 1:13:52 | Tau | Krittika | 2 |
| Mar | 13:25:44 | Vir | Hasta | 2 |
| Mer | 14:44:10 | Can | Pushya | 4 |
| Jup | 0:09:35 | Lib | Chitra | 3 |
| Ven | 18:19:03 | Vir | Hasta | 3 |
| Sat | 9:03:47 | Can | Pushya | 2 |
| Rah (S) | 25:05:52 | Tau | Mrigsira | 1 |
| Ket (S) | 25:05:52 | Sco | Jyestha | 3 |

**Lagna Chart**

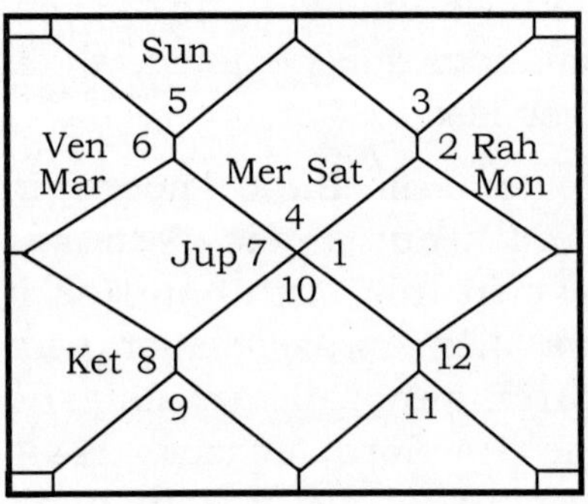


**Navamsa Chart**

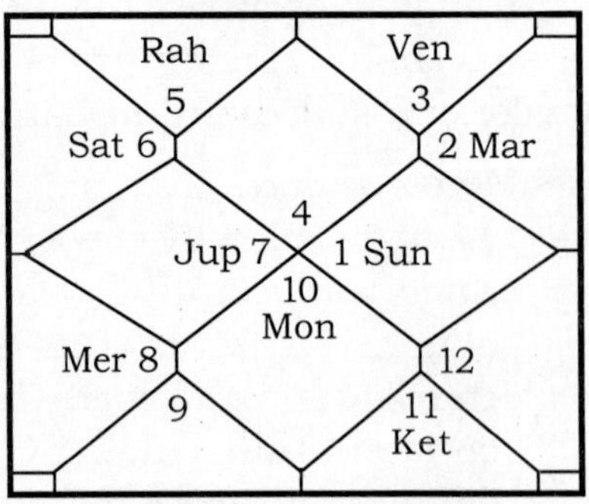


Balance of Vimsottari Dasa of **Sun 3Y 11M 10D**

The native is Regional Manager in State Bank of India and he is appreciated for his merits and talent. He was born in Cancer ascendant with *vargottam navamsa*. Following combinations may be noted, which make one successful in bank services.

1. The 6th and 9th lord Jupiter joins the 4th house and aspects the 10th house.

2. The lord of the 10th and the 5th *Yogakaraka* Mars is placed in the 3rd house in Virgo and lends very favourable aspect over the 10th house.

3. The 6th and 7th lord Saturn is associated with Mercury

in the ascendant. Thus, the 10th house is aspected by the 6th lord Jupiter, 7th lord Saturn and the 5th and 10th lord Mars. Thus, the 10th house is very well disposed and strong. Mercury obtains *navamsa* of the 10th lord Mars.

4. Significator Jupiter obtains *vargottam navamsa* in Libra ruled by the 11th lord Venus.
5. *Atmakaraka* planet Venus falls in Virgo and obtains *navamsa* of Mercury as well, indicating bank service to the native.
6. The Sun owns the 2nd house and is strongest planet in this horoscope. It obtains 1.72 *Shadabalas* and obtains the *navamsa* of its exaltation, corresponding with the sign of the 10th lord Mars.
7. Both Karmic Control Planets, Mars and Venus, are placed together in the 3rd house, in Virgo ruled by Mercury and both obtain *navamsa* of Taurus and Gemini respectively, justifying a recognized position of senior bank personnel.
8. If both the Karmic Control Planets are placed together in any birth chart, this is one of the most auspicious *Rajyoga*, as ascertained by Mr. M.C. Jain in his great work "Karmic Control Planets".

*Illustration: 10.8* (**GSS**) *Horoscope No.: 139*

Date of birth : 08.09.1952 Time of birth : 10:33:00 hrs

Place of birth : Moradabad Lat 28:50:00 N Long 78:45:00E

Ayanamsa : 23:11:57 Sidereal Time : 9:26:49

| **Pln** | **Degree** | **Rasi** | **Nakshatra** | **Pad** |
|---|---|---|---|---|
| Asc | 21:41:57 | Lib | Visakha | 1 |
| Sun | 22:16:42 | Leo | P Phalguni | 3 |
| Mon | 17:19:11 | Ari | Bharani | 2 |
| Mar | 13:50:16 | Sco | Anuradha | 4 |
| Mer | 8:00:50 | Leo | Magha | 3 |

| | | | | |
|---|---|---|---|---|
| Jup | 27:47:14 | Ari | Krittika | 1 |
| Ven | 12:47:21 | Vir | Hasta | 1 |
| Sat | 20:48:44 | Vir | Hasta | 4 |
| Rah (R) | 28:14:30 | Cap | Dhanishtha | 2 |
| Ket (R) | 28:14:30 | Can | Aslesha | 4 |

**Lagna Chart**

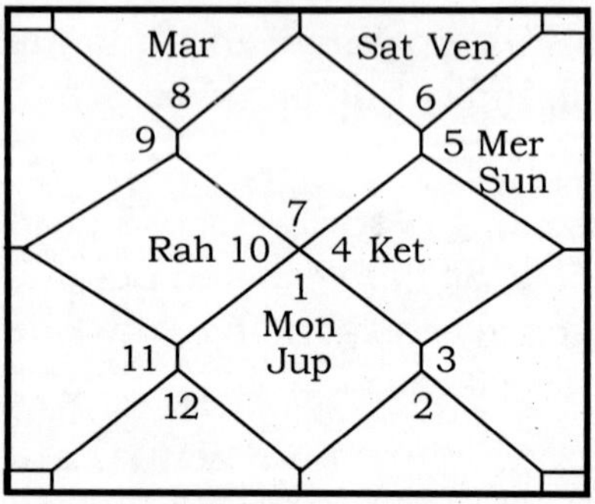


**Navamsa Chart**

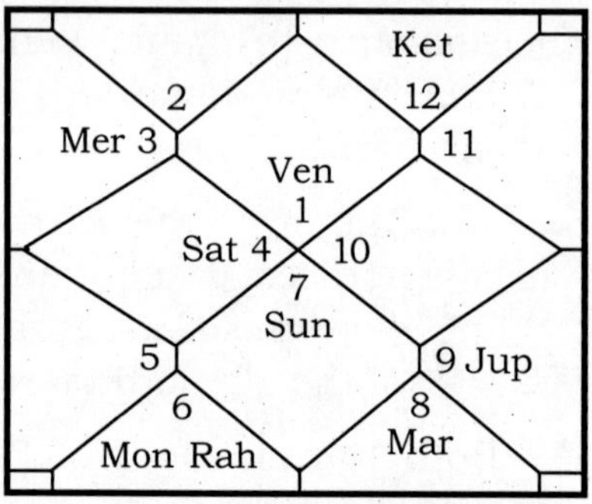


Balance of Vimsottari Dasa of **Ven 14Y 0M 7D**

The native is working in Reserve Bank of India as Manager. He was born in Libra ascendant, which falls in Aries *navamsa.* Following combinations may be noted, which make one successful in bank services.

1. The lord of the $10^{th}$ house, Moon, is associated with the $3^{rd}$ and $6^{th}$ lord Jupiter. Jupiter obtains own *navamsa,* whereas the $10^{th}$ lord Moon obtains the *navamsa* of the significator Mercury.

2. Jupiter is *Atmakaraka* planet and obtains own *navamsa* Sagittarius, which directs him towards any organization related with finance.

3. The strongest planet Sun (1.93 *Shadabalas*) occupies the $11^{th}$ house in own sign Leo, in association with the $9^{th}$ lord Mercury.

4. The lord of the $2^{nd}$ house, Mars, is tenanted in the $2^{nd}$ house of its own, obtains *vargottam navamsa* and falls in *Anuradha* constellation ruled by *Yogakaraka* Saturn, who is posited in Virgo with the ascendant lord Venus.

Thus, the ascendant and the 5th lords are combined in the 12th house in Virgo and justify the bank service to the native.

*Illustration: 10.9* (**KR**) *Horoscope No.: 140*

Date of birth : 10.01.1973 Time of birth : 18:40:00 hrs

Place of birth : Kanpur Lat 26:27:00 N Long 80:19:00E

Ayanamsa : 23:29:05 Sidereal Time : 1:50:54

| **Pln** | **Degree** | **Rasi** | **Nakshatra** | **Pad** |
|---|---|---|---|---|
| Asc | 11:43:50 | Can | Pushya | 3 |
| Sun | 26:41:09 | Sag | Uttarasadha | 1 |
| Mon | 5:30:07 | Pis | U Bhadrapad | 1 |
| Mar | 13:55:52 | Sco | Anuradha | 4 |
| Mer (C) | 15:33:57 | Sag | Purvasadha | 1 |
| Jup (D) | 26:33:38 | Sag | Purvasadha | 4 |
| Ven | 4:56:49 | Sag | Moola | 2 |
| Sat (R) | 21:11:51 | Tau | Rohini | 4 |
| Rah (R/C) | 23:18:33 | Sag | Purvasadha | 3 |
| Ket (R) | 23:18:33 | Gem | Punarvasu | 1 |

**Lagna Chart**

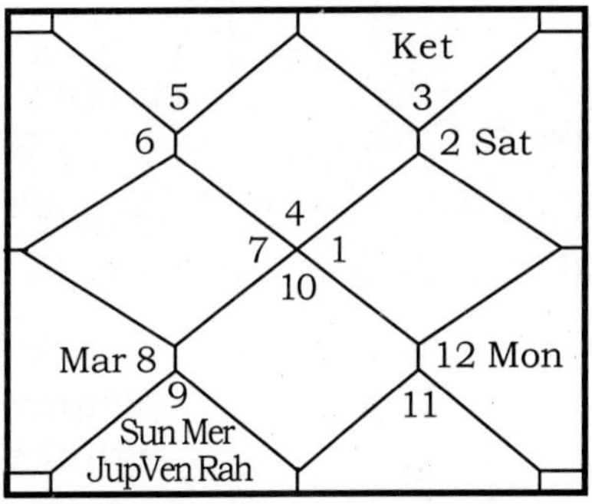


**Navamsa Chart**

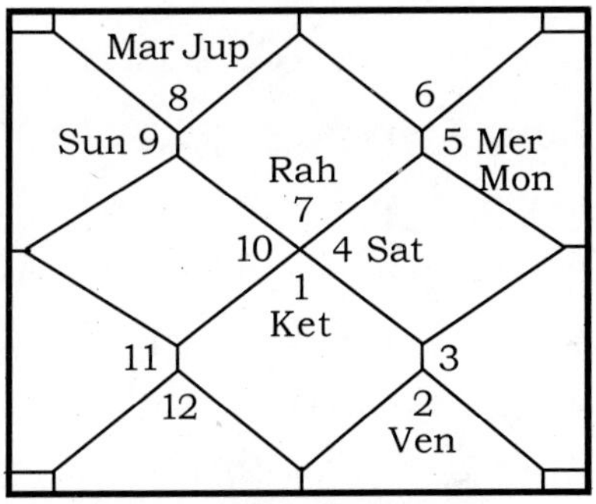


Balance of Vimsottari Dasa of **Sat 15Y 10M 27D**

The native is Manager in City Bank, at the moment. The native worked in many other banks earlier e.g. Para banking of Sahara India, The Times Bank, H.D.F.C. etc. He was born in Cancer ascendant. Following combinations may be noted, which make one successful in bank services.

1. The ascendant lord Moon joins the 9th house in Pisces. The 10th and the 5th lord *Yogakaraka* Mars falls in the 5th house of its own and obtains *vargottam navamsa*.
2. The lord of the 2nd house, Sun, obtains Sagittarius *navamsa* ruled by the significator Jupiter under *vargottam navamsa*. The 2nd lord Sun, who is *Atmakaraka* as well, is associated with significators, Jupiter and Mercury, in the 6th house, in Jupiter's sign Sagittarius.
3. The 11th lord Venus is also conjoined with Jupiter, Mercury and the Sun. Thus, the lords of 2nd & 11th, Sun and Venus, are placed together with the significators Jupiter and Mercury, whereas Jupiter lends its aspect over the 10th house.
4. Jupiter and Mars occupy the Scorpio *navamsa,* ruled by the 10th and 5th lord Mars. The 11th lord Venus obtains own *navamsa* Taurus. Venus owns the 11th house and falls in the 6th house in Jupiterian sign Sagittarius, in association with the 2nd lord Sun, Jupiter and Mercury. This indicates that the native will be engaged in high class bank services.

*Illustration: 10.10* **(MT)** *Horoscope No.: 141*

Date of birth : 20.12.1979 Time of birth : 22:40:00 hrs

Place of birth : Lucknow Lat 26:50:00 N Long 80:54:00E

Ayanamsa : 23:34:29 Sidereal Time : 4:28:22

| Pln | Degree | Rasi | Nakshatra | Pad |
|---|---|---|---|---|
| Asc | 16:01:07 | Leo | P Phalguni | 1 |
| Sun | 4:38:29 | Sag | Moola | 2 |
| Mon | 22:15:23 | Sag | Purvasadha | 3 |
| Mar | 17:51:58 | Leo | P Phalguni | 2 |
| Mer | 17:34:27 | Sco | Jyestha | 1 |
| Jup | 16:36:48 | Leo | P Phalguni | 1 |

| | | | | |
|---|---|---|---|---|
| Ven | 3:52:30 | Cap | Uttarasadha | 3 |
| Sat | 3:10:29 | Vir | U Phalguni | 2 |
| Rah (R) | 7:36:48 | Leo | Magha | 3 |
| Ket (R) | 7:36:48 | Aqu | Satabhisha | 1 |

**Lagna Chart**

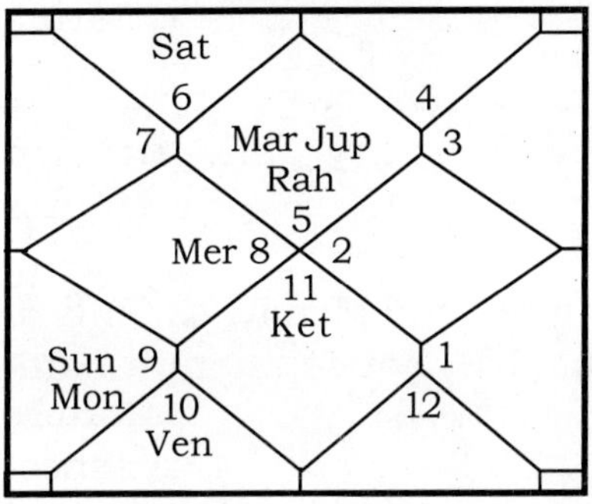


**Navamsa Chart**

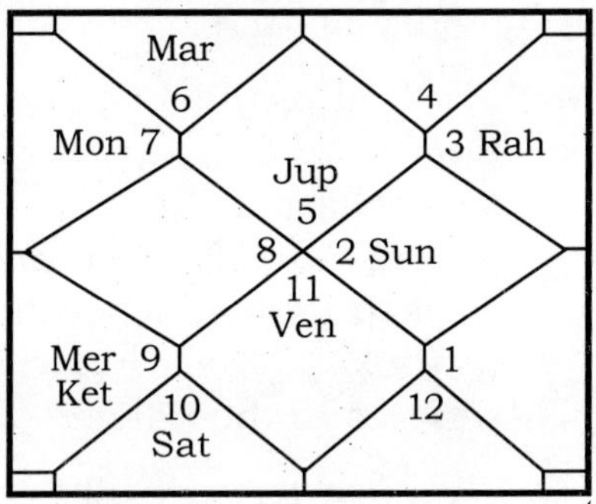


Balance of Vimsottari Dasa of **Ven 6Y 7M 11D**

This captivating and pretty girl is working in I.D.B.I. as Assistant Manager. She was born in Leo ascendant under *vargottam navamsa.* Following combinations may be noted, which make one successful in bank services.

1. The 5th lord Jupiter is placed in the ascendant with *Yogakaraka* Mars. Thus, the lords of the triangles, the 5th and the 9th, join the ascendant and give rise to a very important *Kendratrikona Rajyoga.*

2. The lord of the 11th and 2nd house, Mercury, occupies the 4th house and aspects the 10th house. The 10th lord Venus falls in the 6th house in *Uttarashadha* constellation, ruled by the ascendant lord Sun. It will not be out of place to mention that there is mutual exchange between the lords of the ascendant, Sun, and the 5th lord Jupiter, which is associated with the 9th lord *Yogakaraka* Mars. This is one of the strongest auspicious combinations for prosperity and happiness.

3. Moon is *Atmakaraka* planet, quite strong in *Shadabalas* and occupies the 5th house, corresponding with Sagittarius ruled by Jupiter. Moreover, Moon falls in the

constellation of Venus, *Purvashadha*, and obtains the *navamsa* of the 10th lord Venus too. Thus, the placement of Moon in Sagittarius, in the 5th house in *Purvasadha* constellation and Libra *navamsa*, distinctly indicates that she will acquire position of an officer in any financial organization, bank or the company dealing in money matters.

4. The lord of the 11th and the 2nd, Mercury, obtains the *navamsa* of Jupiter and Mercury falls in own constellation *Jyestha*, whereas the 5th lord Jupiter obtains *vargottam navamsa* along with the Leo ascendant. Thus, the prominence of Jupiter and Mercury, identical to the 2nd, the 5th and the 10th house, signify bank services to the native.

We have tried to illustrate a few cases of the bank personnel here to justify our view point and findings with regard to the natives, who are destined to serve in the bank or financial bodies. In fact, Jupiter and Mercury are the main significators and Venus is the supporting significator for the bank services. Besides the examination of the 10th house, the 2nd and the 5th must also be taken into consideration, along with the supporting 11th house. We have observed that Jupiter and the lord of 2nd house, when influence each other, either by conjunction or aspect, one secures services in a bank, provided the 5th house and Mercury also throw their positive effect over the 2nd and the10th house, their lords or Jupiter.

●

# CHAPTER-11

# Planets and Political Power

Desire for political power has always been at the top of professional achievements. Most of the successful persons of various engagements such as films, actors, actresses, industrialists, poets, journalists, writers, engineers, doctors, judges, advocates, civil servants and educational heads have always been the aspirants of political power, all over the world. Therefore, the strongest planetary combinations and *Rajyogas* must be present in the birth chart for political heights, prosperity, power and popularity. **It should be clear that the 9$^{th}$ house must be very strong in addition to *lagna*. One, having a strong 10$^{th}$ house but weak 9$^{th}$ house, can not attain much professional height.**

Even if one has a strong 9$^{th}$ but weak 10$^{th}$ house, he can touch the political heights, like Mr. Zail Singh, late President of India. If one has strong 10$^{th}$ and strong 9$^{th}$ house one will reach that position by way of his professional merits like Dr. Radhakrishanan. Both were the Presidents but there has been a lot of difference in their capabilities, wisdom, intelligence, actions and reputation in the society, as the general masses see it.

Following points are of great importance for the success in politics and to gain political power:

1. **The Ascendant**: The ascendant must be strong. It should be occupied by a benefic, *Yogakaraka*, 9$^{th}$ or 10$^{th}$ or 5$^{th}$ lord, or should be occupied by its own lord, and should be well aspected.

2. **The 9$^{th}$ house**: The 9$^{th}$ house must be very strong. It should be occupied by its own lord or by the lord of 4$^{th}$ or 10$^{th}$ house and by the lord of *lagna*. And the 9$^{th}$ lord

should also be well disposed in the 10th, 4th, 1st, or 9th house; and should be aspected by its own lord or the lord of 5th, 10th, 4th, or 1st house.

3. **The 10th house**: The 10th house must essentially be very strong. The lord of 10th should occupy 9th, 5th, or 4th house and should be well aspected. The planets placed in the 10th house should be strong and should own 9th, 5th, 1st or 4th house.

4. **The 9th and 10th lords:** should either exchange their signs or should be in mutual angle or triangle, or should be associated with each other. If these are not so placed and other combinations are favourable, one may get the political success/power but he will soon have to face political crisis or downfall.

5. **The luminaries**, the Sun and Moon, and also Mars do play a vital role in providing political power. The 1st, 9th, & 10th houses should be influenced by either of these, or all. This holds good even if the lords of 5th, 9th and 10th fall in the sign or *navamsa* of Sun, Moon or Mars. This is equally good if the Sun, Moon and Mars fall in the sign or *navamsa* of 5th, 9th, and 10th lords.

6. For a good fortune, 9th from 9th i.e. **5th** house should also be taken into consideration. If the 9th and 5th lords are in mutual angle or triangle, this will further promote the political fortune provided above mentioned combinations are also present in the chart.

7. **Karmic Control Planets (KCPs)** i.e. the dispositors of Rahu and Ketu play a very important role in each of the nativity. If both KCPs are placed together, this makes a very powerful *Rajyoga*. If both are in angle or triangle from each other that is also a *Rajyoga*, which promotes the career of the native. If KCP is conjoined with Rahu or Ketu **the strength of that planet to do good** gets enhanced. If both KCPs are in *Khadashtak* (6/8) or *dwidwadas* (2/12) from each other, the nativity becomes weak.

8. **Karakas**: The royal planets, Sun and Moon, play a prominent role in making one a successful politician and to confer on him power and quality of administration or rule. Mars indicates courage, boldness, frankness, confidence and patience. One can not become a leader or politician unless he has courage and ability to fight and struggle. Jupiter indicates reforms, help, and development, establishments to provide security, safety and to see the interest of the public and to take the nation on the right path. So, the Sun, Moon Mars and Jupiter should be well placed in *Rashi* and *navamsa*. Concerning lords should also be placed in their sign and *navamsa*.

9. It has been observed by us that the 8$^{th}$ house plays a prominent role in those engagements or occupations, which have a concern with masses. The 8$^{th}$ house is the 11$^{th}$ from the 10$^{th}$ and 10$^{th}$ from the 11$^{th}$. Generally, the placement of the 10$^{th}$ lord in the 8$^{th}$ house, and vice-versa, is considered bad for professional prosperity. We have made certain amendments in this rule that it is bad for professional aspect if the 10$^{th}$ lord is afflicted by malefics in the 8$^{th}$ house, or vice- versa. However, leaders and popular political personalities influence the masses and public. That is the reason that 8$^{th}$ house should be taken into consideration in the horoscope of political persons.

   It has been found that the leaders of masses, industrialists, who command and control thousands of employees, film actors, actresses and singers, dancers etc., who rule over the heart and emotions of the people, have specific planetary combination in their birth chart, where the 8$^{th}$ house or lord thereof, have an impact over the 10$^{th}$ house, or, vice-versa. If the 10$^{th}$ lord occupies the 8$^{th}$ house, or the 8$^{th}$ lord falls in the 10$^{th}$ house, the native will have to struggle a lot with regard to professional prosperity but he will unexpectedly rise and will command masses. Many people will either work under him or will like and obey him.

10. Rahu should be considered **supporting significator** for

the profession pertaining to power and politics. Placement of Rahu in the 10th house, or with the 10th lord, or with the significators, provides an aptitude and interest in politics.

**11.** *Upchaya* houses i.e. 3rd, 6th and 11th house also play a significant role in the horoscopes of leaders, ministers and politicians. The lords of these houses, if have a concern with the 10th house or its lord, the probability of entering into actual politics gets strengthened.

**12.** ***Atmakaraka* Planets** - The planet, which is placed at the maximum degree in any sign, is termed as *Atmakaraka* planet. The lord of the *navamsa* and the constellation occupied by the *Atmakaraka* planets gives a direction towards the means of earning livelihood. This is quite important for the confirmation and justification of the profession as examined in the birth chart of a native. This is a strong tool, which helps a lot in the judgement of the vocation and should never be ignored.

Thus, there are so many points to be taken into consideration for reaching to an ultimate conclusion whether the native will be successful in the field of politics i.e. he will become a successful politician, M.L.A., M.P., Minister, Chief Minister, Prime Minister and the like. These rules, as propounded here, should not be applied verbatim, but the application of these rules should be made quite intelligently and carefully to reach at the correct conclusion.

Let us study a few cases of top most politicians who were very successful, popular and earned worldwide fame.

*Illustration : 11.1* (**SC Bose**) *Horoscope No.: 142*

Date of birth : 23.01.1897 Time of birth : 12:29:00 hrs
Place of birth : Cuttack Lat 20:26:00 N Long 85:56:00E
Ayanamsa : 22:25:23 Sidereal Time : 20:40:27

| Pln | Degree | Rasi | Nakshatra | Pad |
|---|---|---|---|---|
| Asc | 26:55:12 | Ari | Krittika | 1 |
| Sun | 11:09:48 | Cap | Sravna | 1 |

| | | | | |
|---|---|---|---|---|
| Mon | 7:33:55 | Vir | U Phalguni | 4 |
| Mar | 19:26:28 | Tau | Rohini | 3 |
| Mer (R/D) | 9:35:33 | Cap | Uttarasadha | 4 |
| Jup (R) | 16:29:26 | Leo | P Phalguni | 1 |
| Ven | 26:19:41 | Aqu | P Bhadrapad | 2 |
| Sat | 6:38:22 | Sco | Anuradha | 1 |
| Rah (C) | 22:51:45 | Cap | Sravna | 4 |
| Ket | 22:51:45 | Can | Aslesha | 2 |

**Lagna Chart**

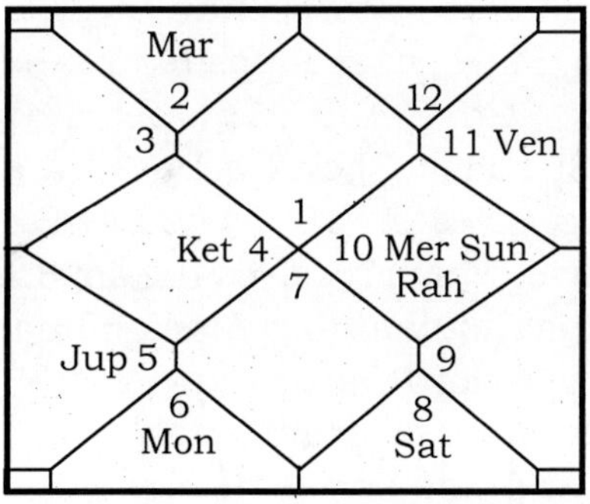


**Navamsa Chart**

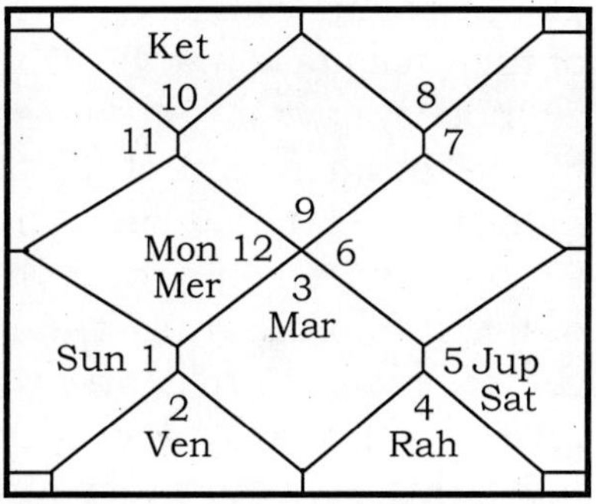


Balance of Vimsottari Dasa of **Sun 1Y 1M 4D**

Subhash Chandra Bose brought a great revolution in Indian politics to obtain independence. Some how, he had untimely death otherwise the shape of Indian politics would have been quite different.

He was born in Aries ascendant, which obtains Sagittarius *navamsa*. Both are fiery signs. The Sun joins the 10th house in association with Rahu in the 10th house. Lord of the 3rd and the 6th, Mercury, is conjoined with the Sun and Rahu, which has strengthened the combinations indicating successful politician.

The 8th house also plays an important role in deciding the professional prosperity and popularity of the native. It has been found that the leaders of masses, industrialists, who command and control thousands of employees, film actors, actresses and singers, dancers etc., who rule over the heart and emotions of the people, have specific planetary combination in their birth chart, where the $8^{th}$ house or lord thereof have an impact over the $10^{th}$ house or vice-versa. If the $10^{th}$ lord occupies the $8^{th}$ house or the $8^{th}$ lord falls in the $10^{th}$ house, the native will have to struggle a lot with regard to professional prosperity but he will unexpectedly rise and will command masses. Many people will either work under him or will like and obey him.

In the horoscope of Subhash Chandra Bose, the lord of the $10^{th}$ house, Saturn, falls in the $8^{th}$ house and aspects the $10^{th}$ house as well. Here, Saturn falls in Scorpio and the lord of the ascendant and $8^{th}$ house, Mars, who is posited in the $2^{nd}$ house, have a mutual aspect with Saturn. This resulted in the untimely end of life of Subhash Chandra Bose, in a plane crash. The $5^{th}$ lord Sun occupies the $10^{th}$, whereas the $9^{th}$ lord Jupiter joins the $5^{th}$ house, which receives the aspect of the $10^{th}$ lord Saturn and the ascendant lord Mars. Thus, the ascendant lord Mars, the $10^{th}$ lord Saturn and the $9^{th}$ lord Jupiter are placed in quadrant from each other indicating political prosperity and popularity.

***Atmakaraka* Planet** - Venus is *Atmakaraka* planet in this birth chart, which occupies the $11^{th}$ house identical to Saturn's sign Aquarius. Venus obtains own *navamsa* and owns the $2^{nd}$ and the $7^{th}$ house. This shows the acting talent of the native as well as class one service and administrative quality, which is true with Subhash Chandra Bose. Venus falls in *Purva Bhadrapada* constellation ruled by Jupiter. Venus and Jupiter have mutual aspect on each other.

**The $9^{th}$ and $10^{th}$ lord** - The $10^{th}$ lord Saturn and the $9^{th}$ lord Jupiter obtain *navamsa* of the Sun and the Sun obtains *navamsa* of its exaltation. This is a powerful indication of political activities and success.

**Significators** - The Sun, Moon, Mars and Jupiter are the major significators, which should influence the $9^{th}$ and the $10^{th}$ house, either by way of placement or conjunction, or aspect, or due to exchange of sign or *navamsa*. It is very much so in this birth chart as explained above.

**Supporting Significator**- Rahu is the supporting significator for occupations connected with politics. Here, Rahu joins the 10th house and it is associated with the Sun and Mercury in the 10th. This confirms the political success.

**Karmic Control Planet** – The dispositors of Rahu and Ketu are called Karmic Control Planets and have a great significance in building one's career. Here, Saturn and Moon are the Karmic Control Planets. Moon falls in Sun's constellation *Uttaraphalguni* and obtains *navamsa* of the significator Jupiter. Saturn owns the 10th, falls in the 8th in Scorpio, aspects the 10th and the 9th lord Jupiter and obtains *navamsa* of the significator Sun.

Thus, the birth chart of Subhash Chandra Bose is a model horoscope for showing political profession and progress along with political prosperity and popularity.

*Illustration : 11.2* (**B.B. Patel**) *Horoscope No.: 143*

Date of birth : 31.10.1875 Time of birth : 12:00:00 hrs
Place of birth : Nadiad Lat 22:42:00 N Long 72:55:00E
Ayanamsa : 22:07:19 Sidereal Time : 14:36:44

| **Pln** | **Degree** | **Rasi** | **Nakshatra** | **Pad** |
|---|---|---|---|---|
| Asc | 5:55:56 | Cap | Uttarasadha | 3 |
| Sun | 15:21:01 | Lib | Svati | 3 |
| Mon | 8:10:04 | Sco | Anuradha | 2 |
| Mar | 12:46:37 | Cap | Sravna | 1 |
| Mer (R/C) | 12:55:47 | Lib | Svati | 2 |
| Jup (C) | 18:58:43 | Lib | Svati | 4 |
| Ven (C) | 25:11:12 | Lib | Visakha | 2 |
| Sat | 27:19:36 | Cap | Dhanishtha | 2 |
| Rah (R) | 16:04:58 | Pis | U Bhadrapad | 4 |
| Ket (R) | 16:04:58 | Vir | Hasta | 2 |

**Lagna Chart**

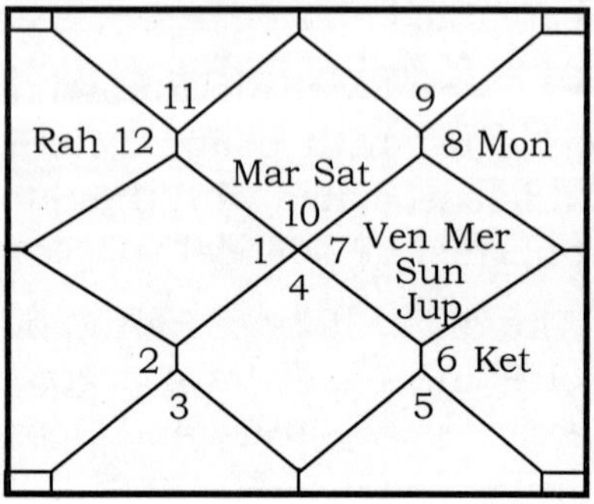


**Navamsa Chart**

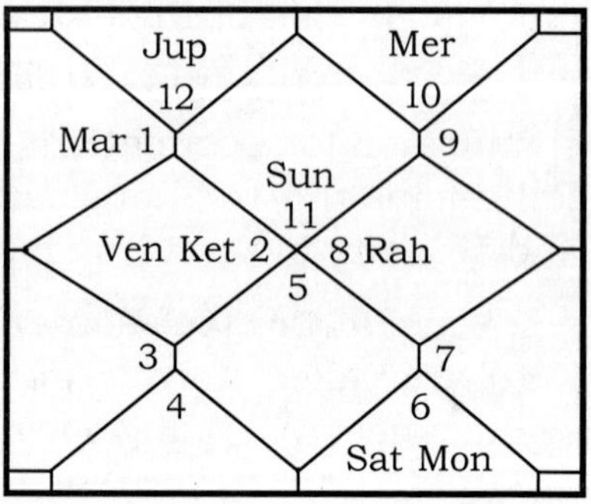


Balance of Vimsottari Dasa of **Sat 12Y 1M 9D**

Name of Sardar Ballabh Bhai Patel is immortal due to his various political activities, reforms and dynamic decisions. He was called 'Iron Man' of Indian Politics after independence.

He was born in Capricorn ascendant with Mars and Saturn. Mars is exalted in ascendant in Capricorn and is associated with Saturn, who is there in the ascendant in own sign Capricorn. This has given rise to *Sasa* and *Ruchhaka Mahapurusha Rajyoga.*

The Sun, Mercury, Venus and Jupiter are conjoined in the 10$^{th}$ house. Thus, many *Rajyogsa* are present in this birth chart including *Singhasan Yoga, Akhand Samrajya Yoga, Bharati Yoga, Parijaat Yoga, Vasumati Yoga, Anshawtar Yoga, Malvya Mahapurusha Rajyoga, Chaamar Yoga, Neech Bhanga Rajyoga, Rajyoga* formed by the conjunction of 9$^{th}$ and 10$^{th}$ lords in the 10$^{th}$ house, *Rajyoga* formed by the combination of the 5$^{th}$ and 9$^{th}$ lords in the 10$^{th}$ house and the like. Except Moon, all the six planets are very well posited in quadrants from the ascendant. Thus, this is one of a very strong horoscope as regards power and politics.

The ascendant lord Saturn, the *Atmakaraka* planet, joins own sign Capricorn and falls in *Dhanishtha* constellation ruled by Mars. The ascendant falls in *Uttarashadha* constellation ruled by the Sun and the Sun falls in the *navamsa* ascendant. Thus, the ascendant is under the strong influence of Saturn, the Sun and Mars. Moreover, Mars and Jupiter obtain own *navamsa* and both are in quadrant from each other, and from the ascendant as well. The Sun is the strongest planet in the birth chart as per *Shadabalas*, which is placed in the 10th house, indicating a prosperous political career and power. The combination of the 5th and the 10th lord Venus with the 9th lord Mercury makes one a Minister or equivalent as specified in classical works. The 9th and 10th lords must be strong for a successful politician. The Sun and Moon also play a vital role in the birth charts of powerful persons, who are active in politics. In this horoscope, the Sun is posited in the 10th house and Moon occupies the 11th as explained above.

Karmic Control Planets also have their own significance in the birth charts of famous, successful, powerful and wealthy natives. If both Karmic Control Planets, i.e. the dispositers of Rahu and Ketu, are associated with each other one of the strongest *Rajyoga* is constituted. In the horoscope of Sardar Ballabh Bhai Patel, both Karmic Control Planets, Jupiter and Mercury, are associated in the 10th house, with the Sun and 10th lord Venus. These combinations justifiy the most versatile, dynamic, dashing, bold and courageous personality of Sardar Ballabh Bhai Patel, who was the first Home Minister of India in the regime of Pt. Jawahar Lal Nehru.

*Illustration : 11.3* *Horoscope No.: 144*

Date of birth : 05.09.1888 Time of birth : 06:00:00 hrs
Place of birth : Tiruttani Lat 13:02:00 N Long 80:16:00E
Ayanamsa : 22:17:54 Sidereal Time : 4:58:14

| Pln | Degree | Rasi | Nakshatra | Pad |
|---|---|---|---|---|
| Asc | 22:26:57 | Leo | P Phalguni | 3 |
| Sun | 20:32:53 | Leo | P Phalguni | 3 |
| Mon | 5:19:47 | Leo | Magha | 2 |

| | | | | |
|---|---|---|---|---|
| Mar | 3:54:03 | Sco | Anuradha | 1 |
| Mer (C) | 1:08:50 | Vir | U Phalguni | 2 |
| Jup | 6:55:22 | Sco | Anuradha | 2 |
| Ven | 5:40:57 | Vir | U Phalguni | 3 |
| Sat | 22:02:57 | Can | Aslesha | 2 |
| Rah (R) | 7:32:51 | Can | Pushya | 2 |
| Ket (R) | 7:32:51 | Cap | Uttarasadha | 4 |

**Lagna Chart**

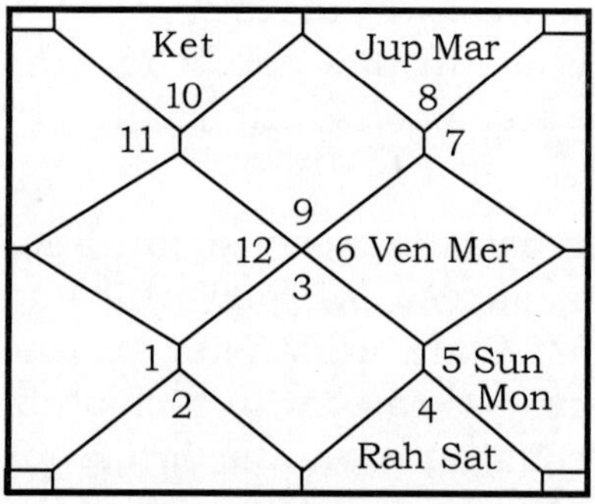


**Navamsa Chart**

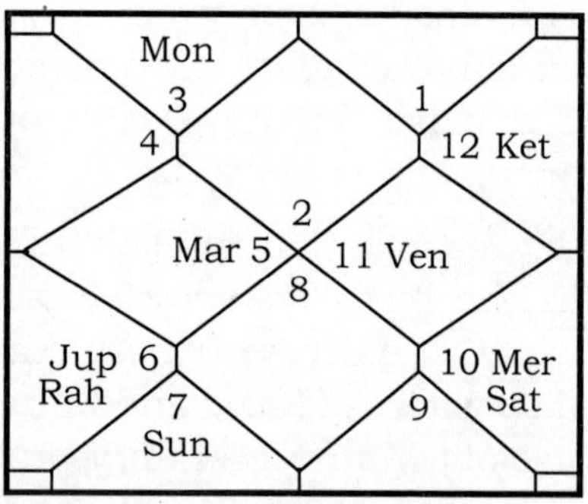


Balance of Vimsottari Dasa of **Ket 4Y 2M 12D**

Dr. Radhakrishnan was the first Vice President of Independent India. Later on, he became the second President of India from 13.05.1962 to 13.05.1967. He was recognized for his extra ordinary caliber and talent in the subject of Philosophy. He was a great statesman too. He had a high reputation around the world. Dr. Radhakrishnan wrote innumerable books and made the world famous translation of Srimad Bhagwat Geeta. He died on 17.05.1975.

Dr. Radhakrishnan was born in Sagittarius ascendant. The lord of the ascendant, Jupiter, falls in the 12th house in association with the 12th lord Mars. This has given him '*Moksha*'.

The lord of the 10th Mercury is exalted in the 10th house, in association with the 6th and 11th lord Venus. Mercury has formed *Bhadrika Mahapurusha Rajyoga*, whereas Venus obtains *Neech Bhanga Rajyoga*. Lord of the 9th, the Sun and the 8th lord Moon are placed together in the 9th house in the royal sign Leo.

The 8th house is occupied by the 2nd and the 3rd lord Saturn, identical to Moon's sign Cancer. Saturn receives the aspect of ascendant lord Jupiter. Thus, the 9th lord Sun falls in the 9th house and the 10th lord Mercury occupies the 10th house, in conjunction with 6th and 11th lord Venus. This indicates very high professional position.

The 5th lord Mars obtains *navamsa* of Sun and falls in own sign Scorpio. The 10th lord Mercury obtains *navamsa* of Saturn in association with Saturn. Saturn is *Atmakaraka* planet, who falls in royal sign Cancer and occupies the constellation of the 10th lord Mercury. Mercury and Venus are conjoined in the 10th house in Sun's constellation *Uttaraphalguni*. This indicates political future. Here, Moon is the stronger than the ascendant. Therefore, Moon Chart gives clearer picture.

**(Rectified time - S. Radhakrishnan)**

*Illustration: 11.3A* *Horoscope No.: 145*

Date of birth : 05.09.1888 Time of birth : 13:30:00 hrs

Place of birth : Tamilnadu Lat 22:39:00 N Long 88:23:00E

Ayanamsa : 22:17:54 Sidereal Time : 12:29:23

| Pln | Degree | Rasi | Nakshatra | Pad |
|---|---|---|---|---|
| Asc | 4:53:05 | Sag | Moola | 2 |
| Sun | 20:49:46 | Leo | P Phalguni | 3 |
| Mon (C) | 9:18:38 | Leo | Magha | 3 |
| Mar | 4:05:22 | Sco | Anuradha | 1 |
| Mer (C) | 1:38:57 | Vir | U Phalguni | 2 |
| Jup | 6:57:27 | Sco | Anuradha | 2 |
| Ven | 6:02:27 | Vir | U Phalguni | 3 |
| Sat | 22:05:01 | Can | Aslesha | 2 |

| | | | | |
|---|---|---|---|---|
| Rah (R) | 7:31:18 | Can | Pushya | 2 |
| Ket (R) | 7:31:18 | Cap | Uttarasadha | 4 |

**Lagna Chart**

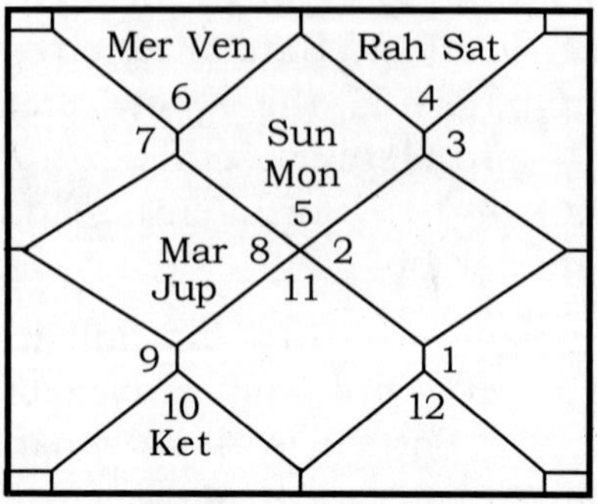


**Navamsa Chart**

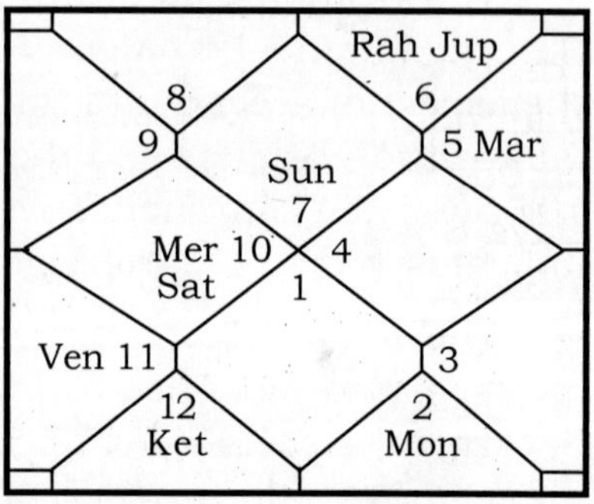


Balance of Vimsottari Dasa of **Ket 2Y 1M 10D**

He was born in Leo ascendant with Sun and Moon. Lord of the 10th house, Venus, joins the 2nd house in association with 2nd lord Mercury. Mars falls in the 4th house, identical to Scorpio, giving rise to *Ruchak Mahapurusha Rajyoga*. The 5th lord Jupiter and Mars are conjoined in the 4th house giving rise to *Guru-Mangal Yoga*. This is the combination of 9th and 5th lord in the 4th house. Both these planets, Mars and Jupiter, aspect the 10th house.

Saturn is *Atmakaraka* planet, which obtains own *navamsa* Capricorn and falls in *Aslesha Nakshatra* ruled by Mercury. Conjunction of Rahu and Saturn in the 12th house though is giving rise to *Vipreet Rajyoga* but cannot be appreciated for various reasons.

The Sun is the strongest planet in this birth chart, which is placed in *Poorvaphalguni nakshatra* ruled by the Sun. Therefore, there is mutual exchange between the *nakshatras* of the 10th lord Venus and the *lagna* lord Sun. The 5th and 9th lords, Jupiter and Mars, aspect the 10th house. This signifies the political future. The 9th lord Mars obtains *navamsa* of Sun, which is quite significant of a very high position in the political career.

Karmic Control Planets are Moon and Saturn, who are associated with the *lagna* lord Sun and Rahu, respectively, and that also indicates strong political career as discussed above.

There is a different school of thought, which confirms that the time of birth of Dr. Radhakrishnan was 13:30 hours on 05-09-1888. This time of birth has been rectified by Sri Daya Shanker, who is at present Commissioner of Income Tax and a great scholar of astrology. He is consulting Editor of the 'Times of Astrology' in Hindi and English. He has to his credit successful and absolutely correct forecasts about various events of the world, from time to time. We have high regards for Sri Daya Shanker and strongly believe that he is a true and great scholar of the sublime science of astrology. We would like to discuss the horoscope of Dr. Radhakrishnan on the basis of rectified time of birth, which is given below:

As per the rectified time Dr. Radhakrishnan was born on 05.09.1888 at 13:30 hours.

The Moon Chart is same as discussed above. The study of this horoscope has been made on the basis of Leo ascendant, when the time of birth taken is 6:00 hours instead of 13:30 hours. In both the cases, the horoscope of Dr. Radhakrishnan is extremely strong and indicates that he would become a great statesman of all times and he would enjoy the top most position of a politician like President or Vice President.

*Illustration : 11.4* **(J.L. Nehru)** *Horoscope No.: 146*

Date of birth : 14.11.1889 Time of birth : 23:30:00 hrs

Place of birth : Allahabad Lat 25:27:00 N Long 81:50:00E

Ayanamsa : 22:18:50 Sidereal Time : 3:06:07

| **Pln** | **Degree** | **Rasi** | **Nakshatra** | **Pad** |
|---|---|---|---|---|
| Asc | 28:52:14 | Can | Aslesha | 4 |
| Sun | 0:16:59 | Sco | Visakha | 4 |

| Mon | 18:06:12 | Can | Aslesha | 1 |
|---|---|---|---|---|
| Mar | 9:59:28 | Vir | U Phalguni | 4 |
| Mer (C) | 17:10:03 | Lib | Svati | 4 |
| Jup | 15:10:39 | Sag | Purvasadha | 1 |
| Ven | 7:22:40 | Lib | Svati | 1 |
| Sat | 10:47:43 | Leo | Magha | 4 |
| Rah | 11:27:12 | Gem | Ardra | 2 |
| Ket | 11:27:12 | Sag | Moola | 4 |

**Lagna Chart**

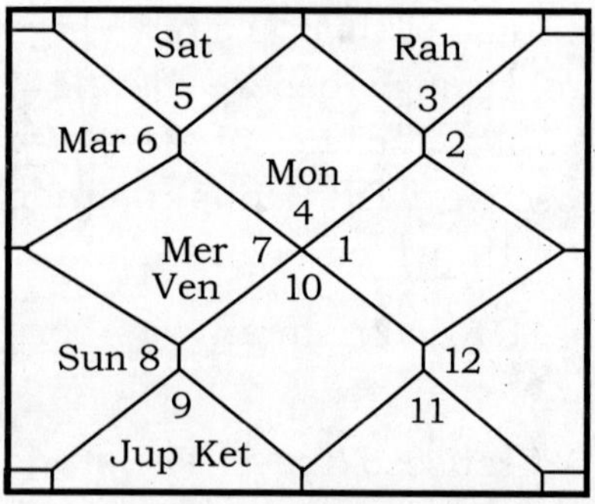


**Navamsa Chart**

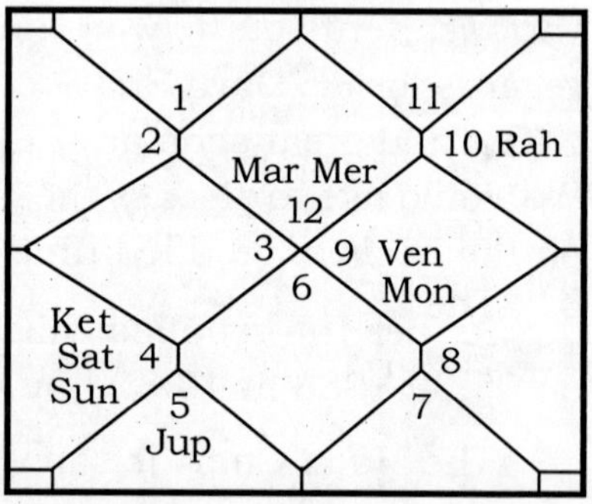


Balance of Vimsottari Dasa of **Mer 15Y 2M 0D**

Admired by children as dear chacha Nehru, Mr. Jawahar Lal Nehru was the beloved of masses of the country. He fought for freedom and served the nation as first PM of free India for 17 years. Very powerful combinations must be present in this horoscope for such a famous, successful, popular, prosperous, energetic, active and truthful PM who had an intellect of very high degree.

1. ***Lagna:*** *Lagna* lord Moon joins the *lagna* itself. Therefore, the *lagna* is quite strong. But the *lagna* is hemmed between malefics like Saturn and Rahu giving rise to formation of *Papakartari* Yoga. The malefic effects of the *Papakartari* yoga were that he faced innumerable problems throughout his life. The aspect of Jupiter over

Rahu and Saturn, both, has reduced the adversities of *Papakartari* yoga to an appreciable extent.

2. **Lord of the 10th house**: Lord of the 10th house, Mars, is a *Yogakaraka* for Cancer ascendant and Mars aspects its own house 10th, as well as 9th house and its lord Jupiter. The 9th lord Jupiter aspects the 10th house. Thus, the 10th house is quite strong and made Sri Nehru strong, bold, courageous, hard worker, self reliant, confident and successful.

3. **The 9th lord**: The 9th lord Jupiter is placed in the 6th house, which is 10th from 9th and 9th from 10th. The 9th lord Jupiter aspects the 10th house and obtains the *navamsa* of Sun.

4. The 9th lord Jupiter and 10th lord Mars are in quadrant from each other. These are 4th and 10th.

5. The second lord Sun falls in the 5th house, in the sign of Mars i.e. Scorpio, which provided him courage to fight and struggle with British. Sun obtains the *navamsa* of other luminary Moon, 9th lord Jupiter obtains the *navamsa* of Sun, and the *lagna* lord Moon obtains *navamsa* of Jupiter. This always tended him to help the mankind and to work for the prosperity of the nation.

6. KCPs are Jupiter and Mercury. Both are aspecting the 10th house, which has highly promoted the strength of the 10th house.

Thus this is a very powerful birth chart of the world famous politician Pt. Jawahar Lal Nehru because the *lagna*, the 10th house and its lord, the 9th house and its lord, the Sun, Moon, Mars and Jupiter are all very well placed. Other horoscopes should also be judged accordingly.

*Illustration : 11.5* (**M.K.Gandhi**) *Horoscope No.: 147*

Date of birth : 02.10.1869 Time of birth : 08:00:00 hrs
Place of birth : Porbandar Lat 21:40:00 N Long 69:40:00E
Ayanamsa : 22:02:03 Sidereal Time : 9:23:40

| Pln | Degree | Rasi | Nakshatra | Pad |
|---|---|---|---|---|
| Asc | 24:28:19 | Lib | Visakha | 2 |
| Sun | 16:57:13 | Vir | Hasta | 3 |
| Mon | 28:49:06 | Can | Aslesha | 4 |
| Mar | 26:24:30 | Lib | Visakha | 2 |
| Mer | 11:46:17 | Lib | Svati | 2 |
| Jup (R) | 28:08:03 | Ari | Krittika | 1 |
| Ven | 24:28:21 | Lib | Visakha | 2 |
| Sat | 20:19:57 | Sco | Jyestha | 2 |
| Rah (R) | 13:39:43 | Can | Pushya | 4 |
| Ket (R) | 13:39:43 | Cap | Sravana | 2 |

**Lagna Chart**

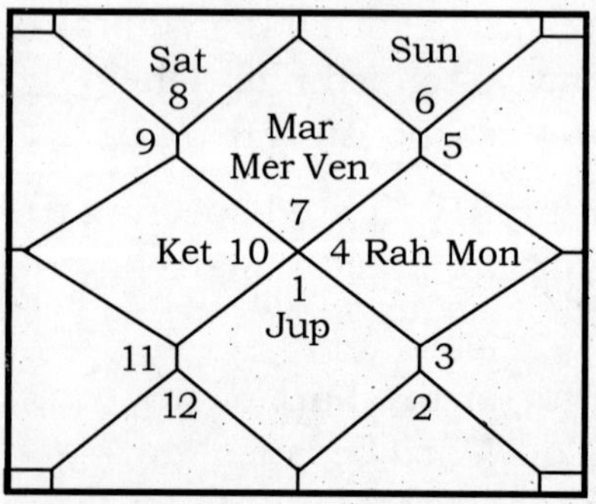


**Navamsa Chart**

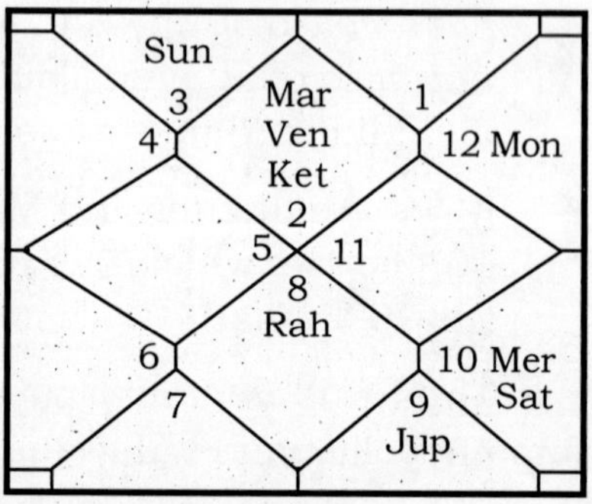


Balance of Vimsottari Dasa of **Mer 1Y 6M 2D**

The name of Mahatma Gandhi is immortal for his outstanding deeds and merits. He dedicated his life for the fight for the freedom of the country. He was a true son and sublime politician of India. Let us analyze his horoscope in respect of political prosperity and popularity:

1. ***Lagna:*** The lord of the *lagna*, Venus, occupies the *lagna,* in association with the 9th lord Mercury and 7th and 2nd lord Mars. The *lagna* lord Venus obtains own *navamsa.* Therefore, the *lagna* is quite strong. Mercury gave him a foresight, wisdom and art of conflict with Britishers. Venus in own sign Libra in the *lagna* blessed him with a long and active life, fame, honour, and popularity. Mars bestowed immense courage, patience, boldness and power to struggle. Mars is adverse, as it owns 2nd and 7th, for Libra *lagna,* and the joint aspect of Mars and Saturn on the 8th house resulted in his assassination.

2. **The 10th house**: The lord of the 10th house, Moon, falls in the 10th house itself, in Cancer, the royal sign, which is dealt for political success. Rahu in the 10th house also gives political success.

3. The *lagna* is hemmed between malefics, Saturn and Sun, giving rise to *Papakartari Yoga,* which kept him under struggle and tension throughout. The aspect of Jupiter over Saturn and Sun has reduced the adversities of *Papakartari yoga* to some extent.

4. The Sun—— The 11th lord Sun falls in the 12th house, and the lord of 3rd and 6th, Jupiter, aspects the Sun. Sun obtains the *navamsa* of 9th lord Mercury and that made him fortunate enough and gave the success in his undertakings.

6. Both Karmic control planets, Saturn and Moon, are in mutual triangle from each other, which is also a very prominent *Rajyoga,* especially when the signs of Mars and Moon are involved, the *Karaka* planets for political success.

These planetary combinations blessed Mahatma Gandhi with unaccountable political success, immortal name, honour, popularity, and dignity, and made him the father of the nation.

*Illustration: 11.6* (**George W. Bush**) *Horoscope No.: 148*

| | | | |
|---|---|---|---|
| Date of birth | : 06.07.1946 | Time of birth : | 07:26:00 hrs |
| Place of birth | : New Haven | Lat 41:18:00 N | Long 72:55:00E |
| Ayanamsa | : 23:06:19 | Sidereal Time : | 1:29:43 |

| **Pln** | **Degree** | **Rasi** | **Nakshatra** | **Pad** |
|---|---|---|---|---|
| Asc | 14:00:51 | Can | Pushya | 4 |
| Sun | 20:40:22 | Gem | Punarvasu | 1 |
| Mon | 23:35:35 | Vir | Chitra | 1 |
| Mar | 16:12:03 | Leo | P Phalguni | 1 |
| Mer | 16:43:17 | Can | Aslesha | 1 |
| Jup | 25:02:19 | Vir | Chitra | 1 |
| Ven | 28:23:17 | Can | Aslesha | 4 |
| Sat (C) | 3:23:56 | Can | Pushya | 1 |
| Rah (S) | 27:29:52 | Tau | Mrigsira | 2 |
| Ket (S) | 27:29:52 | Sco | Jyestha | 4 |

**Lagna Chart**

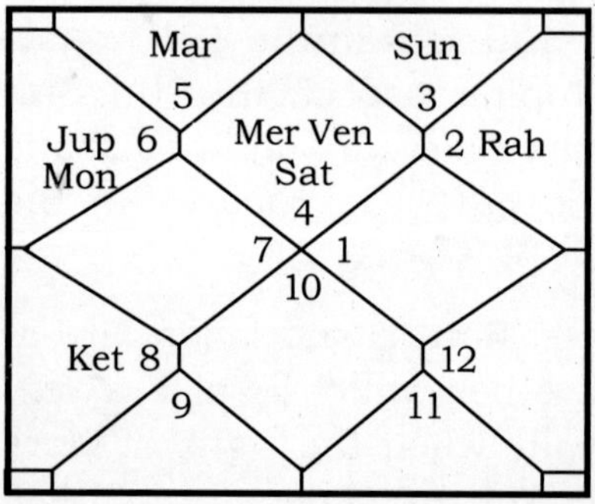


**Navamsa Chart**

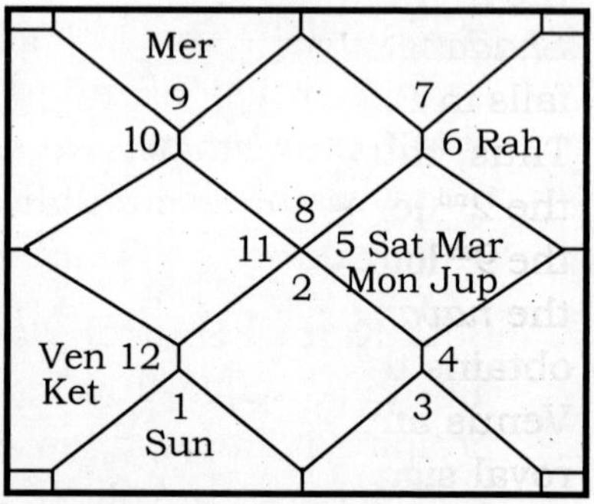


Balance of Vimsottari Dasa of **Mar 6Y 10M 11D**

President of U.S.A. Mr. George W. Bush was born in Cancer ascendant, which falls in Scorpio *navamsa*. The 7th and 8th lord Saturn is associated with 3rd lord Mercury and 11th lord Venus, in the ascendant. The 6th and 9th lord Jupiter is conjoined with the ascendant lord Moon in the 3rd house.

This has given him fame, prosperity and position. There is mutual exchange between 3rd lord Mercury and the ascendant lord Moon. *Yogakaraka* 10th lord Mars occupies the 2nd house in Leo and aspects the 5th and 9th houses. Thus, the 5th and 10th lord Mars and 9th lord Jupiter aspect the 9th house collectively. This combination has added immense potential in this birth chart.

Luminaries play a prominent role in the horoscope of politicians and men in power. The 10th lord *Yogakaraka* Mars, the 9th lord Jupiter, the 7th and 8th lord Saturn and the ascendant lord Moon obtain the *navamsa* of Sun, whereas the 5th and the 10th lord Mars obtains *vargottam navamsa*. Thus, this strongly justifies political career of George .W. Bush. The 4th and 11th lord Venus is *Atmakaraka* planet in this horoscope, which obtains *navamsa* of its exaltation and occupies the royal sign Cancer. Venus contains the effect of the 10th lord Mars as well because Mars is posited in *Purvaphalguni* constellation ruled by Venus.

The Sun does play most important role in the birth charts of Prime Minister or President etc. Here, the lord of the 2nd house, Sun, is the strongest planet, as it obtains 1.65 *Shadabalas* and acquires *navamsa* of its exaltation. The Sun falls in *Punarvasu* constellation, ruled by the 9th lord Jupiter. Thus, the 10th lord Mars is under the influence of Sun and the 2nd lord Sun is under the influence of Mars and Jupiter, the 9th lord. Moreover, Mars, Jupiter, Moon and Saturn obtain the *navamsa* of the Sun, whereas *Atmakaraka* planet Venus obtains the *navamsa* of its exaltation i.e. Jupiter's *navamsa*. Venus and Mars are Karmic Control Planets and fall in the royal signs Cancer and Leo, respectively. These planets are under the influence of Sun, Moon and Jupiter, which are the significators of political career.

There is formation of *Kaalsarp Yoga* in this horoscope, which we have discussed earlier in our famous book *"Kaalsarp Yoga: Shodh Sangyan"*. Thus, the ascendant, 9th, 10th, 5th and 6th house are ruled and influenced by the significators the Sun, Moon, Mars and Jupiter. The concerning houses are also under the influence of the 9th and 10th lords, Mars and Jupiter.

Karmic Control Planets, Mars and Venus, are also strengthening the combination of the top most political career of Mr. George W. Bush. However, in absence of *navamsa* chart and asterism and *Atmakaraka* planet Venus, one cannot draw the conclusion of his being the President of America.

*Illustration : 11.7* **(Bill Clinton)** *Horoscope No.: 149*

Date of birth : 19.08.1946 Time of birth : 05:00:00 hrs
Place of birth : Arkansas Lat 34:04:00 N Long 91:22:00E
Ayanamsa : 23:06:25 Sidereal Time : 2:43:19

| Pln | Degree | Rasi | Nakshatra | Pad |
|---|---|---|---|---|
| Asc | 25:50:30 | Can | Aslesha | 3 |
| Sun | 2:44:23 | Leo | Magha | 1 |
| Mon | 24:56:04 | Ari | Bharani | 4 |
| Mar | 13:08:38 | Vir | Hasta | 1 |
| Mer | 14:22:12 | Can | Pushya | 4 |
| Jup | 0:05:18 | Lib | Chitra | 3 |
| Ven | 17:50:24 | Vir | Hasta | 3 |
| Sat | 9:00:30 | Can | Pushya | 2 |
| Rah (R) | 25:06:00 | Tau | Mrigsira | 1 |
| Ket (R) | 25:06:00 | Sco | Jyestha | 3 |

**Lagna Chart**

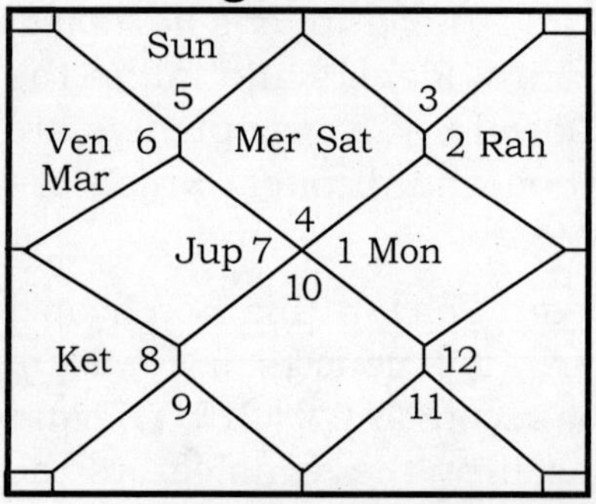


**Navamsa Chart**

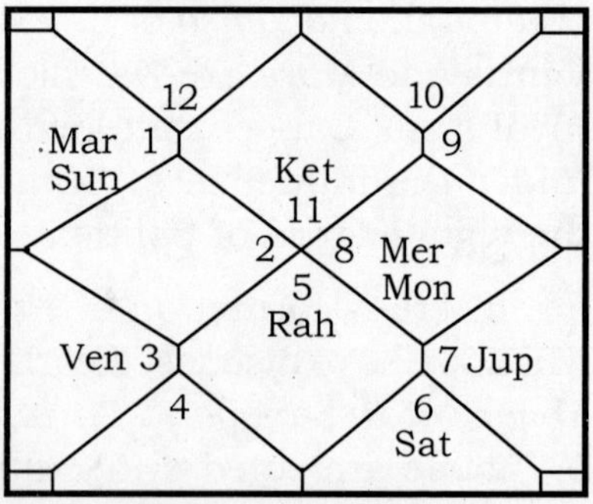


Balance of Vimsottari Dasa of **Ven 2Y 7M 5D**

Bill Clinton was 42nd President of U.S.A. He was 50th and 52nd Governor of Arkansas. He was the President of America from 20.01.1993 to 20.01.2001 i.e. for 8 years. Bill Clinton was born in Cancer ascendant with Mercury and Saturn placed therein. The lord of the ascendant, Moon, joins the 10th house in Aries and is aspected by the 10th and 5th lord *Yogakaraka* Mars. 9th lord Jupiter is posited in the 4th house and aspects the 10th house and *lagna* lord Moon. Thus, the 5th and 9th lords, Mars and Jupiter, both lend their favourable aspect over the 10th house, as well as the *lagna* lord Moon, who occupies the 10th house. Karmic Control Planets Venus and Mars are well associated in the 3rd house, where Venus obtains *Neech Bhanga Rajyoga*. This is a combination of 10th and 11th lords, and 4th and 5th lords as well, and it is also a conjunction of the Karmic Control Planets, Venus and Mars. Sun is posited in own sign Leo, in the 2nd house, who is the strongest planet in this horoscope as well, and obtains 1.92 *Shadabalas*.

Moon is the *Atmakaraka* planet, who is posited in 10th house in Aries and obtains the *navamsa* of Mars. The Sun obtains the *navamsa* of its exaltation and Mars obtain own *navamsa* Aries. Thus, all the concerning planets the Sun, Mars and Moon are very well placed, and justify the political position and President ship of U.S.A.

The 10th lord Mars falls in *Hasta nakshatra* ruled by the Moon, who is *Atmakaraka*. The 9th lord Jupiter falls in *Chitra nakshatra* ruled by the 10th lord Mars. Thus, the effect of the 9th and 10th lords on the 10th house and *Atmakaraka* Moon, with very strong Sun, confirms that the native would acquire the highest position of United States of America.

*Illustration : 11.8* (**Morarji Desai**) *Horoscope No.: 150*

Date of birth : 29.02.1896 Time of birth : 13:0:00 hrs
Place of birth : Valsad Lat 19:02:00 N Long 73:07:00E
Ayanamsa : 22:24:33 Sidereal Time : 23:34:34

| **Pln** | **Degree** | **Rasi** | **Nakshatra** | **Pad** |
|---|---|---|---|---|
| Asc | 9:38:49 | Gem | Ardra | 1 |
| Sun | 17:52:12 | Aqu | Satabhisha | 4 |
| Mon | 25:07:02 | Leo | P Phalguni | 4 |
| Mar | 5:14:35 | Cap | Uttarasadha | 3 |
| Mer | 21:16:36 | Cap | Sravna | 4 |
| Jup (R) | 7:39:04 | Can | Pushya | 2 |
| Ven | 14:34:17 | Cap | Sravna | 2 |
| Sat (R) | 26:41:31 | Lib | Visakha | 3 |
| Rah (R/C) | 11:11:51 | Aqu | Satabhisha | 2 |
| Ket (R) | 11:11:51 | Leo | Magha | 4 |

**Lagna Chart** **Navamsa Chart**

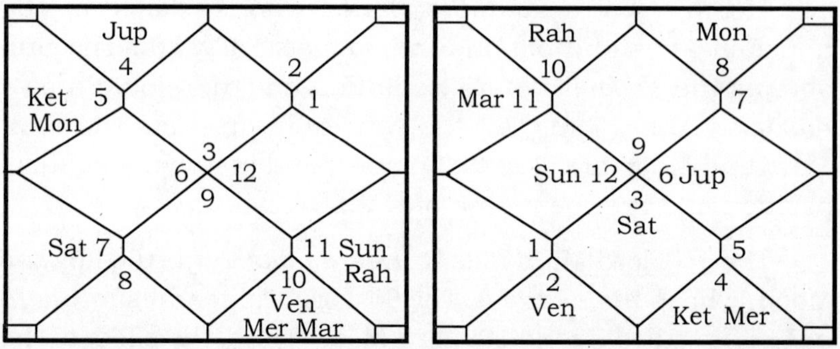


Balance of Vimsottari Dasa of **Ven 2Y 3M 27D**

Morarji Desai became the Prime Minister of India after the downfall of Mrs. Indira Gandhi in the year 1977. He was the minister of finance in the cabinet of Pt. Jawahar Lal Nehru. He always held very important portfolios and remained in power almost throughout his political career. His horoscope must confirm his political life. Let us analyze his birth chart:

**1.** ***Lagna*****:** There is no planet in *Kendra* and the *lagna* lord Mercury is also placed in the 8th house, in association with 11th and 6th lord Mars and 12th and 5th lord Venus. In the first sight it is difficult to say that the native of this chart would become the Prime Minister.

However, the lord of *lagna* Mercury falls in a friendly and movable sign Capricorn. Lord of 8th house, Saturn, falls in the sign of its exaltation, Libra. This indicates a very long life, and he lived for 99 years too. *Lagna* lord Mercury is aspected by exalted Jupiter, and Mercury in 8th house is associated with Mars and Venus. The *lagna* lord Mercury falls in royal sign Cancer in *navamsa*. Conjunction of *Lagnadhipati* Mercury and *Trikonadhipati* Venus, and the aspect of 7th and 10th lord Jupiter over these, has made the *lagna* strong.

**2. The 10th house:** The 10th lord Jupiter is posited in the 2nd house in the sign of its exaltation and aspects the 10th house. Here, Jupiter is retrograde, which made him very rich and industrialist as well. Jupiter falls in royal sign Cancer and receives the aspect of 9th lord Saturn.

**3. The 9th house:** The lord of the 9th house, Saturn, occupies the 5th house in Libra, the sign of its exaltation, and Saturn aspects the 10th lord Jupiter. Lord of the 3rd house, Sun, is placed in the 9th house, in conjunction with Rahu, and the 2nd lord Moon aspects Sun. Thus, the 9th house has been influenced by both the royal planets Sun and Moon.

**4. The 9th and 10th lords:** The lord of the 10th house, Jupiter, and lord of the 9th house, Saturn, both are placed in their signs of exaltation, Cancer and Libra, respectively, and both are in quadrant from each other.

**5. Karmic Control Planets:** Karmic Control planets are Sun and Saturn, and both are placed in triangle from each other. The strength of KCP gets enhanced if it is placed with its dispositor, Rahu and Ketu.

**6. Mars:** The lord of 11th and 6th, Mars, joins the 8th house in the sign of its exaltation and gives rise to *Vipreet Rajyoga*. Mars obtains the *navamsa* of 9th lord Saturn.

**7. Moon:** Moon falls in the royal sign Leo and obtains the *navamsa* of Mars, which indicates political career, courage, struggle, confidence, boldness and patience.

**8. The Sun:** The Sun is the dispositor of Moon and Ketu, and falls in the 9$^{th}$ house and obtains the *navamsa* of Jupiter, which gave him a feeling of real patriotism, help to mankind, desire, to make the country rich by applying beneficial and successful policies of finance and economy. This ability has been further multiplied due to Jupiter's aspect over the 10$^{th}$ house and placement of Jupiter in the *navamsa* of Mercury.

**9. The 4$^{th}$ and 9$^{th}$ house:** The lord of the 4$^{th}$ house, Mercury, and that of 9$^{th}$ Saturn are in mutual *Kendra*, giving rise to *Kahal Yoga*, and the lords of 4$^{th}$ and 5$^{th}$ house- Mercury and Venus- who are conjoined in the 8$^{th}$ house, have also given rise to *Rajyoga*. Venus and Saturn, who are the lords of both the triangles, are placed in mutual *Kendra*. These all are powerful combinations, which elevated Sri Morarji Desai to the level of PM of India. The combination of Mars and Mercury has somewhat reduced the potential of this horoscope due to which Morarji Desai could not continue long. The Sun and Moon, who are royal planets, are both eclipsed by Rahu and Ketu. Therefore, in spite of wisdom and capability, he faced many ups and downs and could not continue for long as PM. Much fame, honour and recognition of his achievements were definitely there but that was also eclipsed from time to time.

*Illustration : 11.9* (**Indira Gandhi**) *Horoscope No.: 151*

Date of birth : 19.11.1917 Time of birth : 23:33:55 hrs
Place of birth : Allahabad Lat 25:27:00 N Long 81:50:00E
Ayanamsa : 22:42:52 Sidereal Time : 3:24:00

| Pln | Degree | Rasi | Nakshatra | Pad |
|---|---|---|---|---|
| Asc | 2:23:37 | Leo | Magha | 1 |
| Sun | 4:08:27 | Sco | Anuradha | 1 |

| Mon | 5:48:06 | Cap | Uttarasadha | 3 |
|---|---|---|---|---|
| Mar | 16:22:58 | Leo | P Phalguni | 1 |
| Mer (C) | 13:15:12 | Sco | Anuradha | 3 |
| Jup (R) | 14:60:00 | Tau | Rohini | 2 |
| Ven | 21:01:19 | Sag | Purvasadha | 3 |
| Sat | 21:47:15 | Can | Aslesha | 2 |
| Rah | 9:18:39 | Sag | Moola | 3 |
| Ket | 9:18:39 | Gem | Ardra | 1 |

**Lagna Chart**

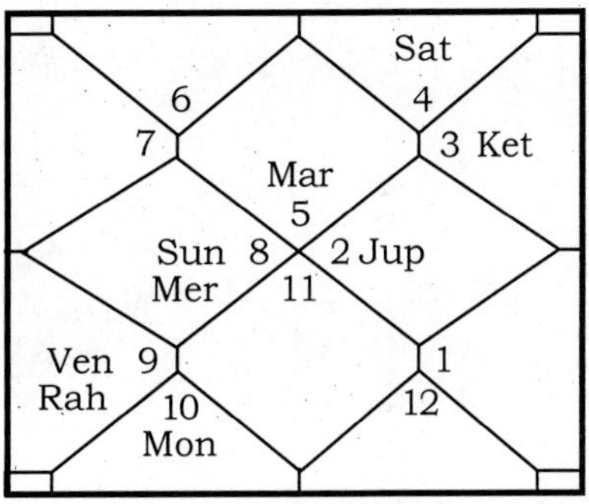


**Navamsa Chart**

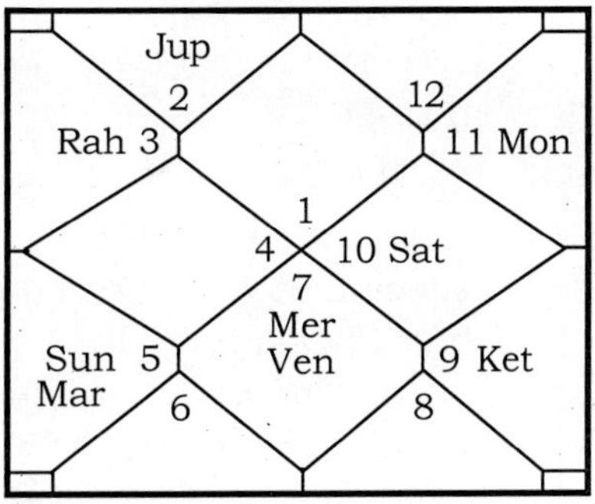


Balance of Vimsottari Dasa of **Sun 1Y 10M 20D**

It is believed that Mrs Indira Gandhi was born in Cancer ascendant. Dr. B.V. Raman also dealt her horoscope taking Cancer as her ascendant. But no prediction of any astrologer, including Dr. Raman, did come true. I wrote an article in P&F from Dec. 1983 to Feb. 1985, in series, "Indira Gandhi-an astrological profile" and established that she was born in Leo ascendant. The assassination of Mrs. Gandhi further proved her *lagna* as Leo, as Muntha of her 67th year falls in the 8th house. Mutual exchange of 5th and 10th lords makes one minister or PM and the son becomes the successor. It has been written in classics and in 'How to judge a horoscope' by Dr. B.V. Raman. This is possible only if *lagna* is Leo.

1. ***Lagna***: *Yogakaraka* Mars is placed in Leo *lagna*, which has certainly promoted the strength of *lagna*. The *lagna*

lord Sun is placed in the 4th house and the 4th lord Mars is posited in *lagna*, giving rise to *Vinimaya Parivartana Rajyoga.* The joint influence of Mars and Sun over the *lagna* of Mrs. Gandhi made her so strong, famous and successful, which has made history. Mrs. Gandhi was pride of India and she established her political superiority all over the world.

2. **The 10th house:** The 10th lord Venus is placed in the 5th house and the 5th lord Jupiter occupies the 10th house. This is mutual exchange of 5th and 10th lords, Jupiter and Venus, which is called *Maharaja Yoga.* Mutual exchange between 5th and 10th, 10th and 9th or 9th and 4th are very strong *Rajyogas.* Thus, the 10th house is very strong.
3. **The 9th house:** The lord of the 9th house, Mars, occupies *lagna*, the royal sign. Mars obtains *vargottam navamsa* in association with the *lagna* lord royal planet Sun. In *Rashi* chart, *lagna* lord Sun and *Yogakaraka* Mars have given rise to *Vinimaya Parivartana Rajyoga.* Lord of 9th house, Mars, also aspects the *lagna* lord Sun.
4. **The lord of 9th and 10th house:** The 10th lord Venus and 9th lord Mars are placed in triangle from each other.
5. **The 5th and 9th lords:** The lord of the 5th house, Jupiter, and lord of the 9th house, Mars, are in mutual quadrant from each other.
6. **Lord of *lagna* and 9th house:** The lord of *lagna*, Sun, and lord of 9th, Mars, have mutual exchange of signs and these are placed in quadrant from each other.

Following combinations may also be noted in this unique and splendid birth chart:

1. Mutual exchange between Sun and Mars and both in *Kendra* from each other.
2. Mutual exchange between Moon and Saturn and both are in *Kendra* from each other.
3. Mutual exchange between 5th and 10th lords, Jupiter and Venus.

4. There is no planet in own sign or the sign of exaltation or debilitation.
5. The *lagna* lord Sun, 10th lord Venus and 6th and 7th lord Saturn occupy their own *navamsa.*
6. Mercury falls in Saturn's constellation *Anuradha* and Saturn falls in Mercury's constellation *Aslesha,* i.e. there is mutual exchange of constellations of Mercury and Saturn.
7. There is mutual exchange in the constellations of Rahu and Ketu, who are placed in *Moola* and *Ardra Nakshatra* respectively.
8. The 9th lord Mars and 10th lord Venus are in triangle from each other.
9. 5th and 4th lords- Jupiter and Mars- are placed in *Kendra.*
10. The 10th house is under the influence of Venus, Jupiter, Sun and Mercury.
11. *Lagna* lord Sun falls in Mars' sign Scorpio and the 4th and 9th lord Mars falls in the royal sign Leo. Sun and Moon both obtain the *navamsa* of Sun.
12. Mars and Venus are placed in the constellation of 10th lord Venus. Jupiter and Moon are placed in the constellation of royal planets, Moon and Sun.

All these combinations and a very powerful Sun made Mrs. Indira Gandhi most successful and dominating PM of India for 17 years or so.

*Illustration : 11.10* **(L.K. Advani)** *Horoscope No.: 152*

Date of birth : 08.11.1927 Time of birth : 09:20:00 hrs
Place of birth : Hyderabad Lat 25:23:00 N Long 68:36:00E
Ayanamsa : 22:50:39 Sidereal Time : 11:29:47

| **Pln** | **Degree** | **Rasi** | **Nakshatra** | **Pad** |
|---|---|---|---|---|
| Asc | 19:49:19 | Sco | Jyestha | 1 |
| Sun | 21:53:58 | Lib | Visakha | 1 |

| | | | | |
|---|---|---|---|---|
| Mon | 6:00:56 | Ari | Asvini | 2 |
| Mar | 16:05:31 | Lib | Svati | 3 |
| Mer (R) | 26:42:45 | Lib | Visakha | 3 |
| Jup (R) | 0:59:46 | Pis | P. Bhadrapad | 4 |
| Ven | 5:53:58 | Vir | U. Phalguni | 3 |
| Sat | 14:23:28 | Sco | Anuradha | 4 |
| Rah (R) | 26:15:53 | Tau | Mrigsira | 1 |
| Ket (R) | 26:15:53 | Sco | Jyestha | 3 |

**Lagna Chart**

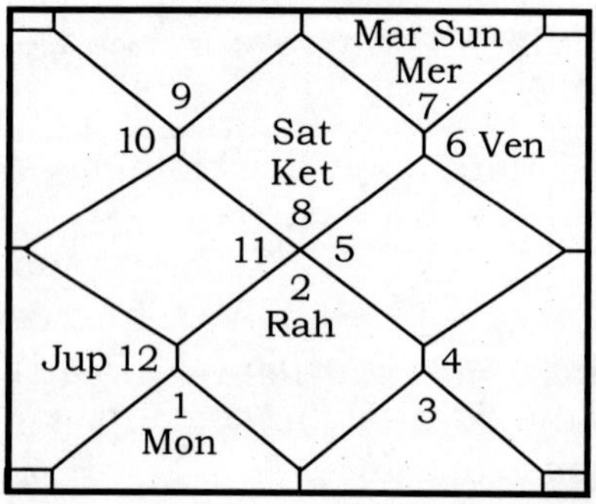


**Navamsa Chart**

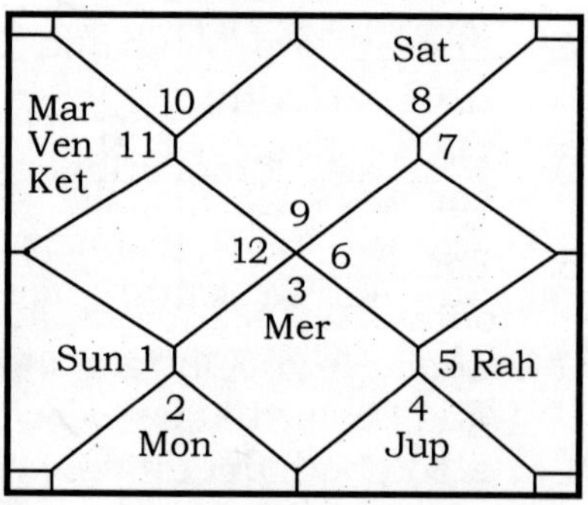


Balance of Vimsottari Dasa of **Ket 3Y 10M 3D**

Mr. L.K. Advani was chairman of Delhi Metropolitan office during the years 1966 to 1970. He became a national leader of BJP and became Minister of Information and Broadcasting from 1977 to 1979. He was the President of BJP from 1987 to 1991 and became the Union Home Minister in March 1998.

Let us analyze the horoscope of such a great leader, whose clean image and no non sense attitude are the hallmarks of his political success.

1. The 9th lord Moon placed in the 6th house, in Aries, obtains the *navamsa* of its exaltation. The 10th lord Sun falls in the 12th house in the *Rashi* chart and obtains *Neech Bhanga Rajyoga*. However, the Sun is shifted in the 11th house and Moon in the 5th in the Cuspal chart.

Sun obtains the *navamsa* of its exaltation. Both, the 10th lord Sun and 9th lord Moon are in mutual *Kendra*. This is essential factor a successful politician.

2. The lords of 4th and 5th houses, Saturn and Jupiter, are in mutual triangle. Saturn also receives the benefic aspect of Jupiter, which has provided him influential and powerful personality.
3. The *lagna* lord Mars occupies the 12th house with 10th lord Sun and 11th lord Mercury, and all the three planets are 7th from 9th lord Moon. The *lagna* lord Mars and 9th lord Moon are in mutual quadrant.
4. There is mutual exchange of signs between Mercury and Venus.
5. There is mutual exchange of *navamsa* between Saturn and Mars.
6. The 10th lord Sun, 9th lord Moon, and 5th lord Jupiter obtain *navamsa* of their exaltation. Mercury obtains own *navamsa*. Venus obtains *navamsa* of Saturn. This indicates powerful political prospects and absolute favour of fortune for promotion and elevation of *Karma.*
7. In Cuspal Chart, 9th lord Moon is placed in the 5th house. The 5th lord Jupiter and 4th lord Saturn are in triangle from each other. Venus in 10th in Leo is in *Samsaptak* position with 5th lord Jupiter. *Lagnesh* Mars and 10th lord Sun are conjoined in the 11th house and 9th lord Moon is 7th from there. Thus, 9th,10th, and *lagna* lords are in mutual *Kendra* and aspect each other in Cuspal chart
8. Karmic Control planets-Mars and Venus- are in *Dwidwadasa* position. This is adverse. This combination is responsible for his name being sullied in false charges of *'Hawala Kand'*. This may also bring about some most undesirable incidents in his life including serious or fatal accident.
9. The 10th lord Sun obtains *navamsa* of Mars, in the sign of its exaltation. Jupiter gets the *navamsa* of its exaltation i.e. the sign of Moon. Moon acquires its exalted *navamsa*

Taurus. Mars obtains *navamsa* of Saturn, whereas Saturn obtains the *navamsa* of Mars.

These four planets i.e. Sun, Moon, Mars and Jupiter are responsible for successful political career. The Sun, Mercury and Jupiter fall in constellation of Jupiter and Venus falls in constellation of Sun. Therefore, these planets are under the influence of Jupiter and Sun, which takes one towards political field.

*Illustration : 11.11* **(A.B.Vajpayee)** *Horoscope No.: 153*

Date of birth : 25.12.1924 Time of birth : 05:45:00 hrs

Place of birth : Gwalior Lat 26:12:00 N Long 78:09:00E

Ayanamsa : 22:48:21 Sidereal Time : 11:40:34

| **Pln** | **Degree** | **Rasi** | **Nakshatra** | **Pad** |
|---|---|---|---|---|
| Asc | 21:50:39 | Sco | Jyestha | 2 |
| Sun | 10:08:42 | Sag | Moola | 4 |
| Mon | 23:46:23 | Sco | Jyestha | 3 |
| Mar | 10:32:06 | Pis | U Bhadrapad | 3 |
| Mer (R/C) | 15:41:52 | Sag | Uttarasadha | 1 |
| Jup (D) | 8:44:27 | Sag | Moola | 3 |
| Ven | 11:08:29 | Sco | Anuradha | 3 |
| Sat | 18:39:31 | Lib | Svati | 4 |
| Rah (R) | 21:36:01 | Can | Aslesha | 2 |
| Ket (R) | 21:36:01 | Cap | Sravna | 4 |

**Lagna Chart**

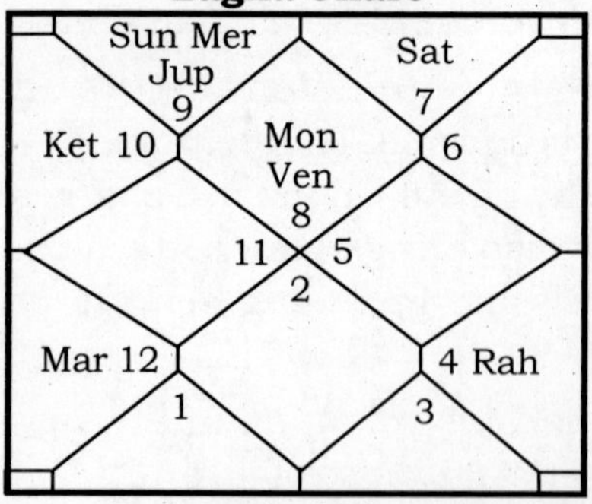


**Navamsa Chart**

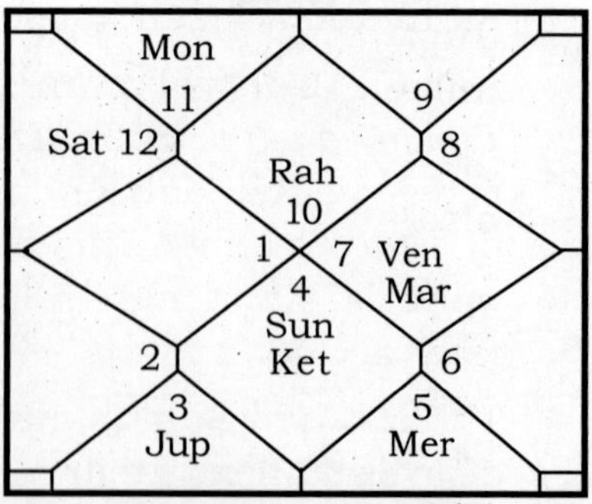


Balance of Vimsottari Dasa of **Mer 7Y 11M 08D**

Atal Behari Vajpayee is not only a charismatic leader but also a great statesman. Much of his political career passed with his being in opposition but there too he made an enviable place due to his oratory skills and great vision. He is one of those Prime Ministers who will be remembered for long.

Following combinations may be noted in his horoscope:

1. *Lagna* lord Mars is placed in the 5th house and 9th lord Moon is placed in *Lagna* in Scorpio with cancellation of debilitation. Thus 9th lord Moon in *lagna* and *lagna* lord Mars in 5th form *Kendra Trikona Rajyoga.*

2. The 10th lord Sun and the 9th lord Moon are placed in *Dwidwadasa* position, which is a negative point.

3. Lord of the 10th house, Sun and lord of *lagna,* Mars are placed in mutual quadrant.

4. Lord of 5th house, Jupiter and lord of 10th house, Sun are conjoined in the 2nd house, which shows political life.

5. Lord of 9th, Moon and lord of *lagna,* Mars are placed in triangle from each other.

6. *Lagna* lord Mars falls in Jupiter's sign Pisces. The 9th lord Moon falls in Martian sign Scorpio. The 10th lord sun also falls in Jupiter's sign Sagittarius. Jupiter also falls in its own sign, in association with 10th lord Sun. Thus, all Karaka planets- the Sun, Moon, Mars and Jupiter- are placed in each others sign and have influence over 9th, 10th, 1st and 5th houses.

7. Jupiter is not only associated with the 10th lord Sun but also aspects the 10th house, which has made Sri Vajpayee very balanced, polite and decent even in official matters.

8. Placement of Jupiter and Mercury in the 2nd house is a powerful *Rajyoga* as Mercury owns 11th and Jupiter owns 2nd house. Mercury and Jupiter are conjoined with 10th lord, which has made him popular, impressive and

influential. This combination makes one rich, powerful and very good orator, and Mr. Vajpayee's speech is too impressive and thought provoking.

9. The 10th lord Sun obtains *navamsa* of Moon and Sun is opposite Moon in the *navamsa* chart. This also shows political power.

10. Moon Venus combination in *Lagna* has kept him devoid of conjugal bliss.

11. The *lagna* is hemmed between malefics, like Saturn and Sun, giving rise to *Papakartari yoga* and that has made his life full of struggles.

These are important combinations, which made Mr. Vajpayee one of the most successful politician and charismatic leader.

*Illustration : 11.12* (**Arun Nehru**) *Horoscope No.: 154*

Date of birth : 25.05.1944 Time of birth : 18:30:00 hrs

Place of birth : Lucknow Lat 26:50:00 N Long 80:54:00E

Ayanamsa : 23:04:33 Sidereal Time : 9:35:24

| Pln | Degree | Rasi | Nakshatra | Pad |
|---|---|---|---|---|
| Asc | 24:19:28 | Lib | Visakha | 2 |
| Sun | 11:03:18 | Tau | Rohini | 1 |
| Mon | 20:47:38 | Gem | Punarvasu | 1 |
| Mar | 8:35:55 | Can | Pushya | 2 |
| Mer (C) | 17:10:04 | Ari | Bharani | 2 |
| Jup | 26:34:25 | Can | Aslesha | 3 |
| Ven | 2:11:07 | Tau | Krittika | 2 |
| Sat | 3:37:18 | Gem | Mrigsira | 4 |
| Rah (R) | 5:50:18 | Can | Pushya | 1 |
| Ket (R) | 5:50:18 | Cap | Uttarasadha | 3 |

**Lagna Chart**

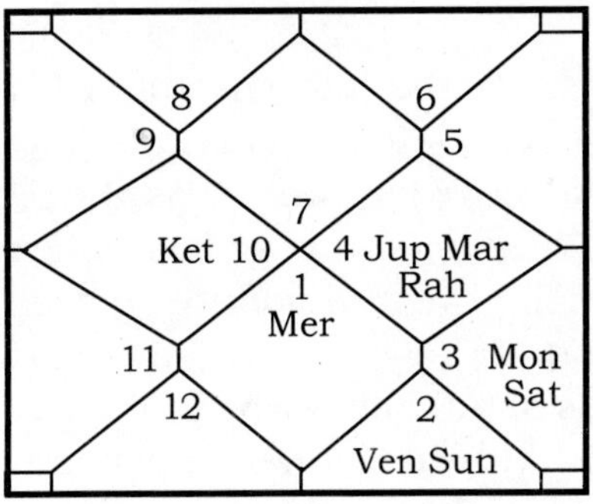


**Navamsa Chart**

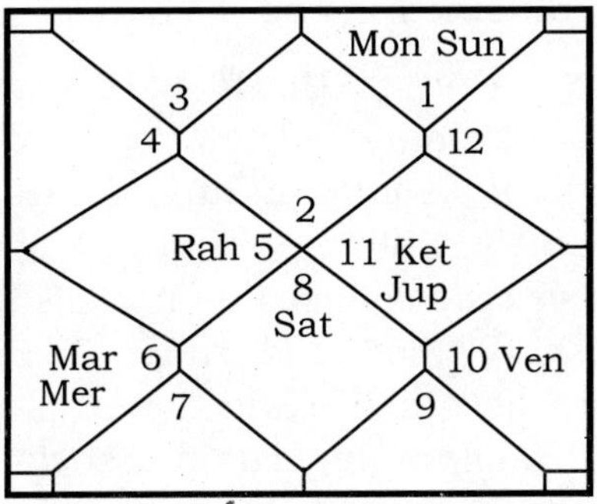


Balance of Vimsottari Dasa of **Jup 15Y 0M 17D**

Mr. Arun Nehru is an astute politician, a columnist and a psephologist. Having his family lineage in the Nehru clan, he was the grandson of Jawahar Lal Nehru's cousin Mr. Shyam Lal Nehru. Politics was not his original choice, as after studies he began his career in the corporate world. He rose to become the President of a group of companies where he was one of the first young corporate wizards to have climbed such heights. At the age of 37 he joined politics on the call of Mrs. Indira Gandhi. He was the chief strategist for Mr. Rajiv Gandhi and a minister in his government. He fell out with Rajiv Gandhi in 1984 and later joined hands with Mr. VP Singh. Presently he is politically more close to BJP.

Let us study his birth chart:

The ascendant is Libra, whose lord Venus falls in own sign Taurus in association with Sun. Venus falls in the constellation of Sun. *Lagna* is being aspected by the 9th lord Mercury and *Karaka* Mars.

The 9th house is occupied by the 10th lord Moon and the 4th & 5th lord Saturn. 9th lord Mercury joins the 7th house in the sign of Mars and obtains the *navamsa* of its exaltation, in association with Mars. Mercury also occupies the constellation of Venus, the *lagna* lord.

The 10th lord Moon joins the 9th house and 10th house is occupied by Mars and Jupiter.

Karmic control Planets are Moon and Saturn. Both are conjoined in the 9th house.

Houses 1st, 9th & 10th are under the influence of either of luminaries. The *lagna* lord is associated with and falls in the *nakshatra* of Sun. Moon is the 10th lord and joins the 9th house. Influence of Sun, Moon, Mars and Jupiter is all there over the concerning houses which gave him political power. The 9th house is under *Papakartarti* Yoga. As we have said earlier, the 9th and the 10th lords should either be in mutual triangle or angle or in association with each other for a steady and long political career. Here also, 9th & 10th lords are not so disposed, and also the 9th lord is the weakest planet in the birth chart having 1.01 *shadabala*. The native did not enjoy a long, gainful and successful political power. Exalted 3rd lord Jupiter in the 10th house has given him the intelligence and flair for writing and his one other important source of earning is from writing for the media.

*Illustration: 11.13*(**Benazir Bhutto**) *Horoscope No.: 155*

Date of birth : 21.06.1953 Time of birth : 20:15:00 hrs
Place of birth : Karachi Lat 24:53:00 N Long 67:00:00E
Ayanamsa : 23:12:39 Sidereal Time : 13:41:04

| **Pln** | **Degree** | **Rasi** | **Nakshatra** | **Pad** |
|---|---|---|---|---|
| Asc | 19:41:08 | Sag | Purvasadha | 2 |
| Sun | 6:43:08 | Gem | Ardra | 1 |
| Mon | 0:17:37 | Lib | Chitra | 3 |
| Mar (C) | 11:46:30 | Gem | Ardra | 2 |
| Mer | 1:16:01 | Can | Punarvasu | 4 |
| Jup | 16:47:54 | Tau | Rohini | 3 |
| Ven | 21:01:46 | Ari | Bharani | 3 |
| Sat (R) | 27:20:40 | Vir | Chitra | 2 |
| Rah (R) | 10:32:27 | Cap | Sravna | 1 |
| Ket (R) | 10:32:27 | Can | Pushya | 3 |

**Lagna Chart**

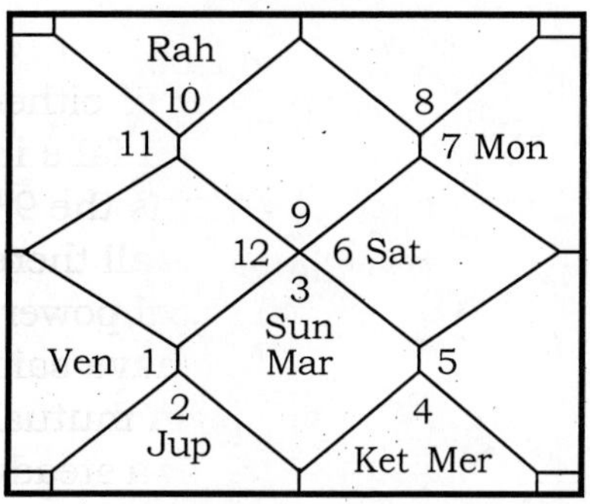


**Navamsa Chart**

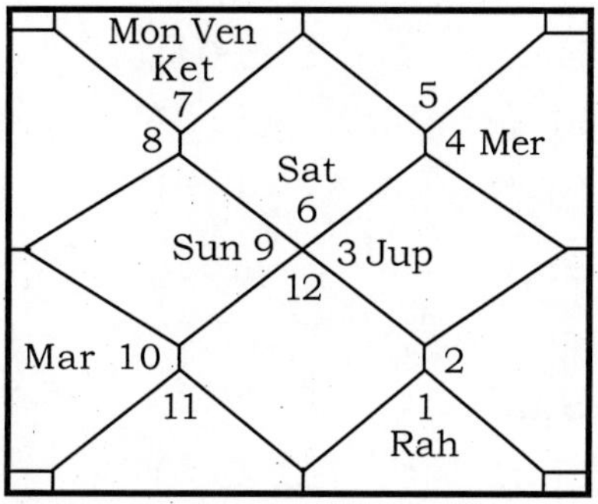


Balance of Vimsottari Dasa of **Mar 3Y 4M 4D**

Mrs. Bhutto was the eldest daughter of former Prime Minister of Pakistan Mr. Zulfikar Ali Bhutto, who had her most of the education of senior classes in United States and United Kingdom. Benazir chaired Pakistan Peoples Party and was the first woman elected to lead a Muslim state, having twice been Prime Minister of Pakistan.

The 9th and the 5th lords, Sun and Mars, are conjoined and are aspecting the ascendant. The ascendant lord joins the sign of Venus, who occupies the 5th house, and obtains the *navamsa* of 10th lord Mercury.

The 10th house is being aspected by the ascendant lord Jupiter and the 5th lord Mars. The 10th lord falls in the 8th house in the sign of luminary, and is *vargottam* in *navamsa*. Thus 9th, 10th and the *lagna* are quite strong and auspicious.

Both the luminaries, Sun and Moon, are connected with the 1st, 5th, 9th and 10th houses, in one or the other way.

Karmic control planets are Saturn and Moon, and join 10th and the 11th houses respectively. Saturn, who is *Atmakaraka* as well, is *vargottam* in *navamsa* and falls in the *nakshatra* of the 5th lord Mars. Thus, all the *karakas* are also well disposed and related with the concerned houses.

*Illustration: 11.14* (**Jagjivan Ram**) *Horoscope No.: 156*

Date of birth : 05.04.1908 Time of birth : 11:00:00 hrs
Place of birth : Ara Lat 25:34:00 N Long 84:40:00E
Ayanamsa : 22:34:15 Sidereal Time : 0:01:09

| **Pln** | **Degree** | **Rasi** | **Nakshatra** | **Pad** |
|---|---|---|---|---|
| Asc | 17:27:53 | Gem | Ardra | 4 |
| Sun | 22:27:47 | Pis | Revati | 2 |
| Mon | 13:23:01 | Tau | Rohini | 2 |
| Mar | 6:07:30 | Tau | Krittika | 3 |
| Mer | 26:18:27 | Aqu | P Bhadrapad | 2 |
| Jup | 11:02:39 | Can | Pushya | 3 |
| Ven | 6:43:43 | Tau | Krittika | 4 |
| Sat (C) | 9:29:21 | Pis | U Bhadrapad | 2 |
| Rah (R) | 16:21:21 | Gem | Ardra | 3 |
| Ket (R) | 16:21:21 | Sag | Purvasadha | 1 |

**Lagna Chart**

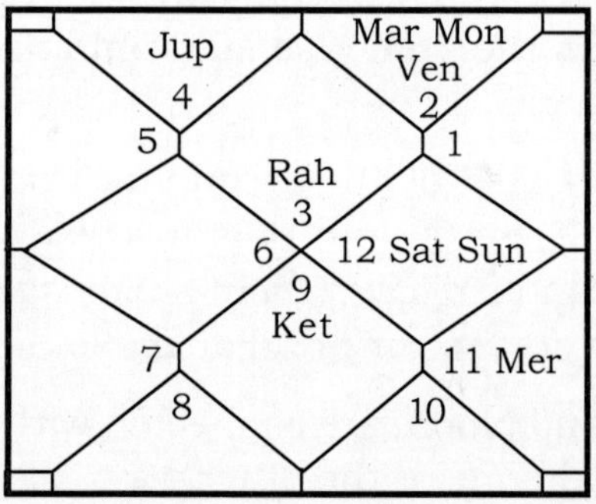


**Navamsa Chart**

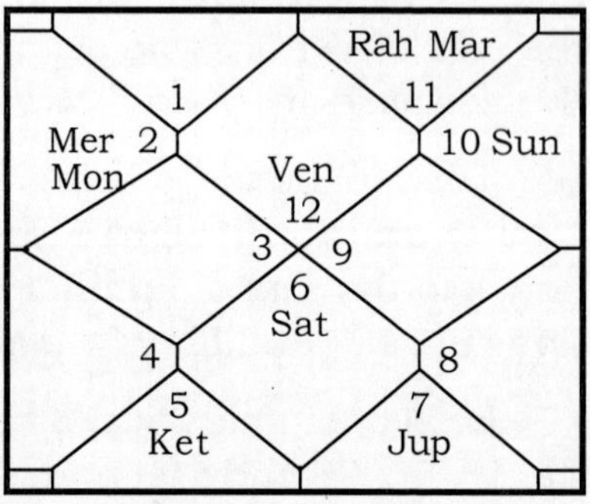


Balance of Vimsottari Dasa of **Mon 7Y 5M 16D**

Jagjivan Ram, known popularly as Babuji was a freedom fighter and a social reformer hailing from backward classes of Bihar. In 1946 he became the youngest minister in Jawahar Lal Nehru's provisional government. He served as a minister in Govt. of India with various portfolios for more than 40 years and also held the post of Deputy Prime Minister of India from March 23, 1977 to August 22, 1979.

His birth chart shows some splendid combinations as below:

1. The 10th house is occupied by the 9th lord Saturn and luminary Sun. The 10th lord Jupiter is exalted and aspects the 10th house. Jupiter falls in the constellation of the 9th lord Saturn. The Sun, who falls in the constellation of *lagna* lord Mercury and obtains the *navamsa* of 9th lord Saturn, being the strongest planet having 2.03 *shadabala*, occupies the 10th house.
2. The 9th lord occupies the 10th house and the 9th house is occupied by the *lagna* lord Mercury.
3. Karmic control planets are Jupiter and Mercury. Jupiter aspects the 10th house while Mercury is posited in the 9th house.
4. The 5th lord Venus, *karaka* Mars and Moon are aspected by the 9th lord Saturn. The 5th lord Venus, and Mars, fall in the *nakshatra* of Sun.
5. The 9th lord Saturn and the 10th lord Jupiter are placed in mutual triangle to each other (5/9).

*Illustration: 11.15* (**K.P. Tripathi**) *Horoscope No.: 157*

Date of birth : 04.09.1905 Time of birth : 03:00:00 hrs
Place of birth : Varanasi Lat 25:20:00 N Long 83:00:00E
Ayanamsa : 22:32:14 Sidereal Time : 1:49:22

| Pln | Degree | Rasi | Nakshatra | Pad |
|---|---|---|---|---|
| Asc | 11:55:48 | Can | Pushya | 3 |
| Sun | 18:08:25 | Leo | P Phalguni | 2 |
| Mon | 17:58:26 | Lib | Svati | 4 |
| Mar | 15:04:32 | Sco | Anuradha | 4 |
| Mer (R/C) | 9:36:19 | Leo | Magha | 3 |

| Jup | 13:11:03 | Tau | Rohini | 1 |
|---|---|---|---|---|
| Ven | 9:50:59 | Can | Pushya | 2 |
| Sat (R) | 6:07:22 | Aqu | Dhanishtha | 4 |
| Rah (R/C) | 7:43:49 | Leo | Magha | 3 |
| Ket (R) | 7:43:49 | Aqu | Satabhisha | 1 |

**Lagna Chart**

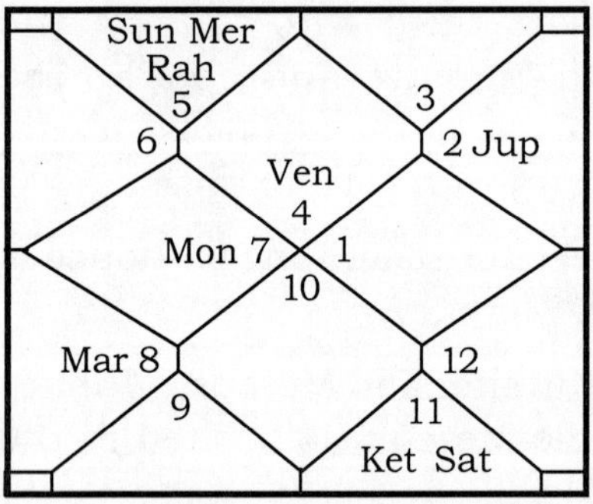


**Navamsa Chart**

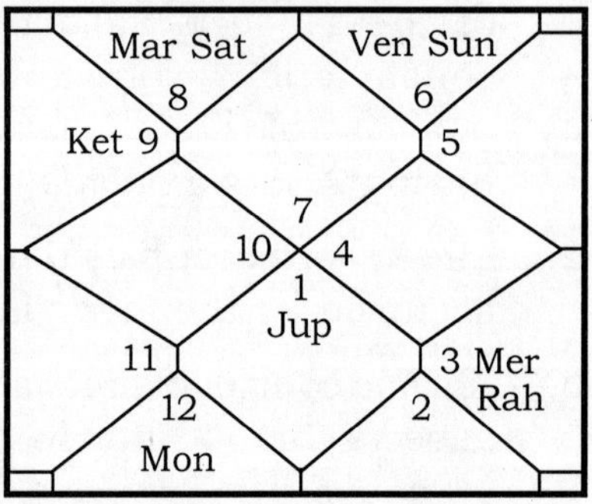


Balance of Vimsottari Dasa of **Rah 2Y 8M 24D**

Hailing from Varanasi, Kamalapati Tripathi was a very well known, popular and respected leader of Congress party from Uttar Pradesh. He was a freedom fighter too. He became the chief minister of U.P. and was later shifted to Centre where he served as Union Railway Minister.

Lat us study his birth chart to verify our point of view.

1. The ascendant is Cancer whose lord Moon occupies the 4th house and aspects the 10th house. 4th & 11th lord Venus occupies the *lagna*. No planet aspects the *lagna*.
2. The 10th house is aspected by the ascendant lord luminary Moon. 10th lord Mars occupies the 5th house in own sign Scorpio and is under mutual aspect with 9th lord Jupiter. Mars obtains *vargottam navamsa.*
3. The 9th lord Jupiter aspects the 10th lord Mars and the fifth house, and obtains the *navamsa* of Mars as well, aspecting the *lagna* in the *navamsa* chart.
4. Karmic control Planets are Sun and Saturn. Both aspect

each other and are placed with Rahu and Ketu. Saturn also aspects the 10th and the 5th house, and *Karaka* Mars.

5. 9th and 10th lords, Jupiter and Mars, are mutually in *Kendra,* which is very auspicious.
6. The 8th lord Saturn occupies the 8th house itself. Saturn aspects the 10th house, as well as the 10th lord Mars. Mars also aspects the 8th house and the 8th lord, placed therein.

We have said earlier that the involvement of 8th house and its relation with the 10th house or its lord is generally found in political personalities and other persons having influence over the masses. That's why, in addition to other combinations, that Kamlapati Tripathi was a recognized politician till his death.

*Illustration : 11.16* (**R.M. Lohia**) *Horoscope No.: 158*

Date of birth : 23.03.1910 Time of birth : 16:00:00 hrs
Place of birth: Akbarpur Lat 17:21:00 N Long 78:32:00E
Ayanamsa : 22:35:57 Sidereal Time : 3:44:17

| **Pln** | **Degree** | **Rasi** | **Nakshatra** | **Pad** |
|---|---|---|---|---|
| Asc | 5:10:35 | Leo | Magha | 2 |
| Sun | 9:19:12 | Pis | U Bhadrapad | 2 |
| Mon | 12:20:04 | Leo | Magha | 4 |
| Mar | 13:00:50 | Tau | Rohini | 1 |
| Mer (C) | 26:35:38 | Aqu | P Bhadrapad | 2 |
| Jup (R) | 18:03:22 | Vir | Hasta | 3 |
| Ven | 28:20:01 | Cap | Dhanishtha | 2 |
| Sat | 0:33:00 | Ari | Asvini | 1 |
| Rah (R) | 7:29:27 | Tau | Krittika | 4 |
| Ket (R) | 7:29:27 | Sco | Anuradha | 2 |

**Lagna Chart**

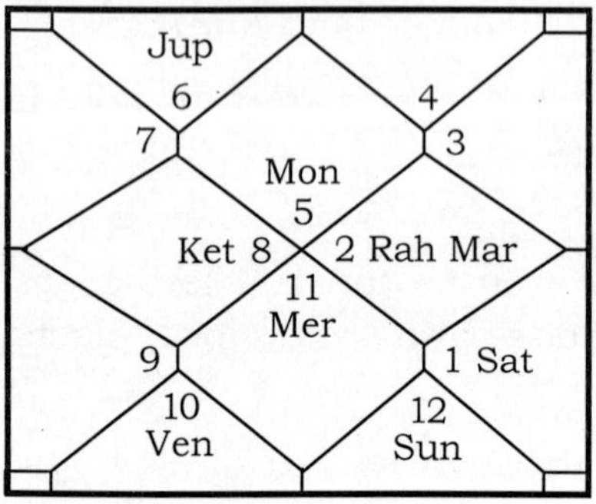


**Navamsa Chart**

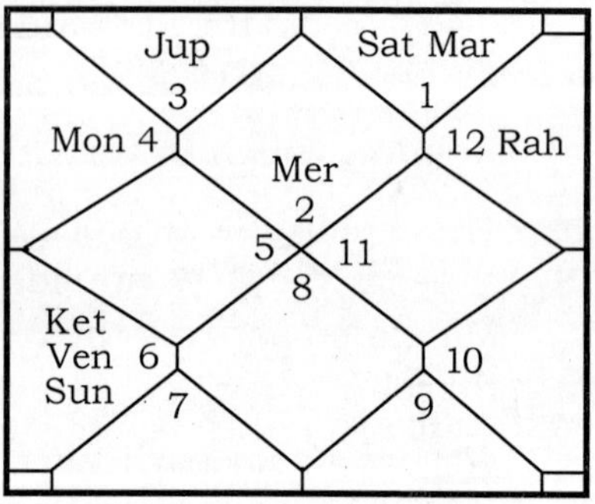


Balance of Vimsottari Dasa of **Ket 0Y 6M 8D**

Ram Manohar Lohia was a freedom fighter and a socialist political leader. He was born on 23.03.1910 in a village named Akbarpur in Faizabad district of U.P. in India.

Ram Manohar Lohia was born in Leo ascendant, with Moon placed therein. Rahu and *Yogakaraka* Mars join the 10th house. Saturn is posited in the 9th house in Aries and obtains *Neech Bhanga Rajyoga*. Jupiter aspects the 10th house, the 10th lord Venus and Mars and Rahu, who are placed in the 10th house. This indicates a strong leadership and the feeling and activity of nationality. Venus is *Atmakaraka* planet in this horoscope. Venus owns the 3rd and 10th house, joins the 6th house and falls in *Dhanishtha nakshatra* ruled by *Yogakaraka* Mars. Moon falls in Leo and obtains own *navamsa*.

Both the Karmic Control Planets, Venus and Mars, are triangular from each other and receive the aspect of the 5th lord Jupiter. Thus, planetary setup of this horoscope justifies that Ram Manohar Lohia was a great leader of his time. He was a freedom fighter and a nationalist.

•

# CHAPTER-12

# Determinants of Legal Profession

Judicial system is one of the most fundamental institutions of human society. As the concept of the social culture progressed, certain rules and regulations were established for the protection and betterment of the human beings. It is well known that persons have violated laws from time to time, since the days they were framed. In such situations the prime objective of the judicial system is to know the truth and deliver the justice. To serve this purpose, the most vital constituents are lawyers and judges. With the advancement of social organization, the system of law became so intricate that it requires much skill for the job of lawyers and judges.

Jupiter and Saturn are strongly related with the vocations of legal profession like judges, lawyers, advocates, counselors and barristers. Jupiter is the main significator of law as it binds us under certain rules and regulations. Jupiter is a law-loving planet, possesses a high conduct and observes all kinds of discipline. So, Jupiter is mainly the *Karaka* of law. Saturn is the planet of justice. As such, Saturn has a vital role in making one a legal professional. Mercury can not be overlooked, as it gives the power of argument and discussions. One becomes a good orator due to Mercury. Logical and analytical study of the cases can not be made if Mercury is not at a favourable place and has relation with either of the concerning houses.

Airy signs i.e. Gemini, Libra and Aquarius confer a good amount of ability as an orator and high degree of intelligence, talent, knowledge and immense power of expression. Libra is a sign of balance and, therefore an important sign out of these. The other important one is the fiery sign Sagittarius, which comes under the ruler ship of the significator Jupiter.

The 6th house denotes court, litigation and crime. The 10th house stands for profession. So, a relation between the 10th and the 6th, in addition to other indications, tends one to take up law as his profession.

A single planet should not be taken as a deciding factor for any vocation. In most of the cases, the lord of the 10th house is taken as a ruling planet for vocation. In other cases, the lord of *navamsa* occupied by the 10th lord is considered for this purpose, or otherwise the occupants of the 10th house. This is not sufficient. Suppose, Jupiter denotes one's occupation, what should one predict? Will he be an agriculturist or be in banking service or he will be successful in the field of education. Whether he will be a priest or an astrologer or a *Pandit* ? Will he be a social reformer of he may deal in medicines, herbs or so many other vocations that come under the ruler ship of Jupiter. Such kind of guidance will not be useful for the native if the astrologer can not pinpoint the vocation and kind of education indicated to the native. It should be properly judged before the commencement of professional education. Many people possessing very high capability of medical profession have been found working as a clerk. If the proper trade is not chosen, one will be unsuccessful in life. Generally, a strong ascendant and 10th house automatically tend one to go for the best suited job.

The ascendant, the 10th, the 6th and the 5th houses must be properly studied for lawyers, judges and other persons earning their livelihood through legal connection.

- The lord of the 10th house.
- The occupants of the 10th house.
- Lord of the *navamsa* occupied by the 10th lord.
- Planet aspecting the 10th.
- Planets and houses related with the 10th house or the 10th lord. For law, the 6th house must be related

with vocation, or with the 10th house, by one way or the other.

For the kind of intelligence and bent of mind, the 5th house should also be judged, for the persons dealing in law, as they must possess a particular kind of analytical brain and should have a good logical talent. Similarly, medical practitioners must have another kind of brain, which may help in making a right diagnosis.

We will be discussing here a few combinations for law personnel, which have been given at various places by different people. We will explain our findings for law people, after mentioning a few general observations of others, regarding this vocation.

Before that, we may add that the 5th house should also be judged for mental framework. If Jupiter is indicating law as a profession and Mars has anything to do with 5th house or influences Jupiter or 10th lord, one may become a lawyer in criminal branch. If Mercury and 8th or 11th house have a concern, one may become a lawyer in taxation. If Venus influences the concerning combination of law, one may deal in the advocacy of Rent control or property matters.

It will be worthwhile to repeat that first of all we will have to find out if Jupiter is really the indicator of profession in one's chart. Mostly the 10th lord, occupants of the 10th and the planets with the 10th lord or the *navamsa* lord occupied by the ruler of the 10th house is taken as the indicator of profession for a particular native. But this is not enough. The key planet for profession should be judged carefully. The planets that are with the lords of 11th and 8th house, or are conjoined with Mercury or Venus, have also their influence on one's occupation.

A few researchers opine that 2nd and 11th houses should also be judged, as these houses are related with money.

1. If Jupiter, Venus and the lord of 2nd house occupy their own or exaltation sign, one may earn through law.

2. If lord of 3rd and 6th is Jupiter and the 10th house is strong, and they are related with each other by one way or other, one may earn as an advocate, judge, and barrister. If Jupiter owns 5th or occupies own sign, under the aspect of Saturn, one becomes a lawyer or judge.
3. If Rahu and Mercury conjoin in the concerning houses of vocations, in addition to Jupiter as deciding factor, one may become a judge or advocate.
4. If Jupiter and Saturn are related with the 5th and 9th house, or if they occupy these houses, singly or jointly, or have an aspect over there, one will earn through law. He will become a very successful lawyer or judge. If Jupiter and Saturn occupy Aries, Gemini, Leo, Libra or Aquarius, one is more likely to earn through a profession of law.
5. If Jupiter and Saturn occupy 1st and 7th, or 2nd and 8th, or 3rd and 9th, or 5th and 11th, one will be earning through law. This combination is a strong indicator of professionals of law.
6. If Rahu, Moon are conjoined in any of the houses concerning vocation, one will be a diplomat. If the 7th lord occupies the 9th house, and the 9th lord occupies the 7th house, and these are in Jupiter or Saturn's sign, one becomes an advocate.
7. If 3rd, 6th and 11th houses contain signs ruled by evil planets and any of these houses have exalted planet, one will become a magistrate or a judge or a lawyer.

Let us see what are the important signs, planets or houses that play role in deciding law as vocation?

**Libra:** Libra is the sign of balance and governs the occupations in which balancing is required, in judging the situation. Where Libra is prominent and has a concern with one's occupation, one may select law as his profession. They can become good managers, consultants, lawyers, judges, solicitors, logicians and officers of law, diplomats and public relation officers.

Dr. B.V. Raman has noted in 'How to judge a horoscope' Vol.-II, while writing about Sagittarius in the XIV chapter that Saturn, Jupiter and Mercury would indicate lawyers, judges, advocates, magistrates and philosophers.

So, Libra and Sagittarius are the prominent signs, which have a concern with law personals.

What are the important planets which should be judged for the persons earning their means of livelihood through law?

**The Saturn:** Saturn is the planet of justice. This has been repeatedly written by Dr. B.V. Raman in 'How to judge a horoscope' Vol.-II in chapter XIV that Saturn, if occupies or owns the $10^{th}$ house, or falls in the sign of exaltation, Libra, one is likely to be a prominent lawyer or a judge. Saturn's exaltation sign, Libra, is a sign of balance. A planet governing one's vocation, falling in the sign of balance, will make one a lawyer or judge.

**The Jupiter :** Jupiter is the truth loving and a planet of honesty. Jupiter gives a good power of judgment and if, in a horoscope, Jupiter and Saturn are related, by one way or the other, in reference to the native's occupation, he will be very successful as a lawyer or judge. Jupiter should be treated as the *karaka* or significator of legal profession.

**The Mercury:** Mercury is a planet of logic and proofs. A good justice or advocate must possess a high intellect of understanding the truth behind any particular case and there must be a good logic before reaching any conclusion.

Concerning houses for the judgment of law personals should be as given below:-

**The $6^{th}$ house:** The sixth house rules over the court. Litigation is studied from the $6^{th}$ house. This is a house of crime, conflict, enmity, quarrels, differences and litigation. So, the $6^{th}$ house must have an important role in making one a justice or lawyer.

**The 10th house:** Planets, which occupy the 10th house or the owner of the 10th house, have certainly one of the most important role in judging one's vocation. The *navamsa* lord occupied by the lord of the 10th house is mostly taken as a key planet in the judgment of one's vocation.

**The 5th house :** One's intelligence, power of judgment, logical way of discussions and arguments are governed by the 5th house. The 4th and 2nd houses indicate one's education. One must have the preliminary qualification of law i.e. LL.B. before getting registered as lawyer in the court of law.

Following practical examples will make the understanding clear:

*Illustration : 12.1* (**RRM**) *Horoscope No.: 159*

Date of birth : 31.10.1929 Time of birth : 23:30:44 hrs

Place of birth : Banda Lat 25:28:00 N Long 80:20:00E

Ayanamsa : 22:52:24 Sidereal Time : 2:00:16

| Pln | Degree | Rasi | Nakshatra | Pad |
|---|---|---|---|---|
| Asc | 14:00:03 | Can | Pushya | 4 |
| Sun | 14:57:45 | Lib | Svati | 3 |
| Mon (C) | 6:01:51 | Lib | Chitra | 4 |
| Mar (C) | 24:30:33 | Lib | Visakha | 2 |
| Mer | 29:11:22 | Vir | Chitra | 2 |
| Jup (R) | 22:23:19 | Tau | Rohini | 4 |
| Ven | 21:24:52 | Vir | Hasta | 4 |
| Sat | 4:06:37 | Sag | Moola | 2 |
| Rah (S) | 19:21:38 | Ari | Bharani | 2 |
| Ket (S) | 19:21:38 | Lib | Svati | 4 |

**Lagna Chart**

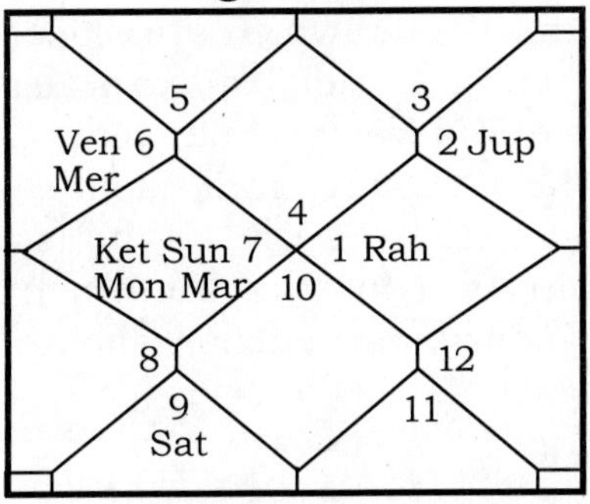


**Navamsa Chart**

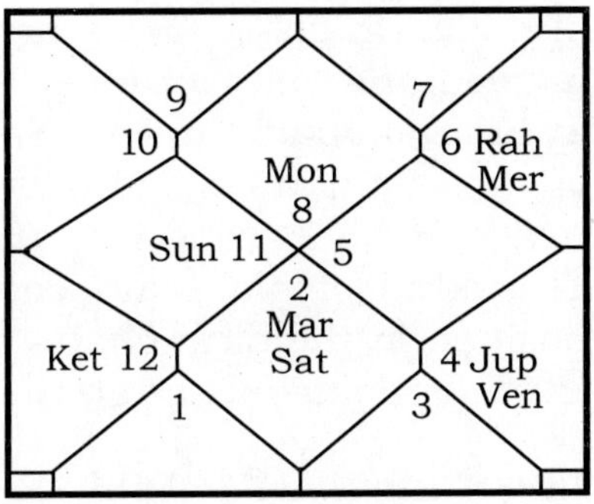


Balance of Vimsottari Dasa of **Mar 0Y 4M 0D**

This birth chart belongs to a judge of High Court. He passed whole of his career in law pursuits. He was famous for his sincere and honest working throughout his life.

He was born in Cancer ascendant, which obtains Scorpio *navamsa*. Libra plays an important role in the birth charts of law personals. In this birth chart, the lord of the 10th and 5th, the *yogakaraka* Mars falls in Libra, in the 4th house and aspects the 9th and the 6th lord Jupiter. Moreover, Mars falls in the *Visakha* constellation, ruled by Jupiter. Jupiter and Mercury and Saturn are the significators of persons engaged in working of law, either by the occupation of lawyer or judge.

Here, *Atmakaraka* planet is Mercury, who is exalted in the 3rd house. Mercury is associated with 11th lord Venus and is aspected by 6th and 9th lord Jupiter. Moreover, Mercury obtains *vargottam navamsa* and falls in *Chitra* constellation, ruled by the 10th and 5th lord Mars. This shows his interest as well as profession connected with law.

Involvement of the 6th house is also essential because it governs litigation, crime, accidents, diseases, fight, conflict, debts, enemies, rivals, opponents, competitors, win and defeat and various kinds of troubles. The 7th and 8th lord Saturn occupies the 6th house, identical to Sagittarius. Moreover, Saturn and the 10th lord Mars obtain *navamsa* of Venus. In fact, Venus is the supporting significator, since the sign Libra ruled by planet Venus symbolizes balance. This shows true judgment. Sagittarius and Libra have also a concern in the horoscopes of law personals. Strongest planets of this birth chart are Saturn and Venus, which are placed in quadrant from each other. Mercury, the *Atmakaraka* is also in mutual quadrant from Saturn and Venus. Four planets viz. the Sun, Moon, Mars and Ketu occupy Libra, identical to the 4th house, and lend their aspect over the 10th house. This kind of planetary combination finds a prominent position in the birth charts of judges, particularly who are there for doing justice on the basis of rules of law.

*Illustration : 12.2* (**RDS**) *Horoscope No.: 160*

Date of birth : 01.12.1949 Time of birth : 08:42:00 hrs
Place of birth : Lucknow Lat 26:50:00 N Long 80:54:00E
Ayanamsa : 23:09:21 Sidereal Time : 13:14:12

| **Pln** | **Degree** | **Rasi** | **Nakshatra** | **Pad** |
|---|---|---|---|---|
| Asc | 12:18:16 | Sag | Moola | 4 |
| Sun | 15:26:44 | Sco | Anuradha | 4 |
| Mon | 25:56:39 | Pis | Revati | 3 |
| Mar | 25:34:46 | Leo | P Phalguni | 4 |
| Mer (C) | 20:34:34 | Sco | Jyestha | 2 |
| Jup | 6:53:57 | Cap | Uttarasadha | 4 |
| Ven | 2:12:52 | Cap | Uttarasadha | 2 |
| Sat | 25:31:08 | Leo | P Phalguni | 4 |
| Rah (R) | 22:13:46 | Pis | Revati | 2 |
| Ket (R) | 22:13:46 | Vir | Hasta | 4 |

**Lagna Chart**

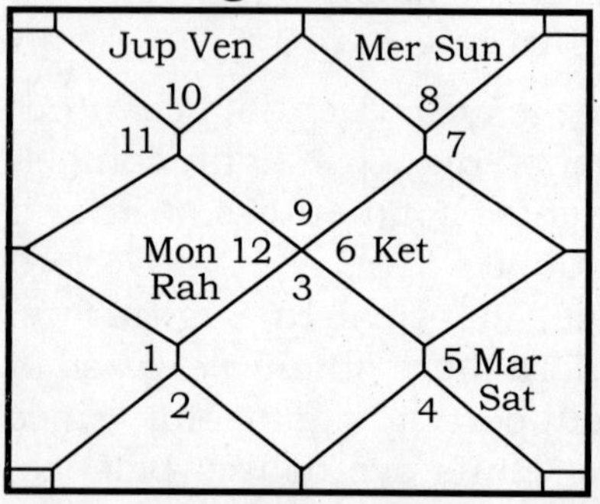


**Navamsa Chart**

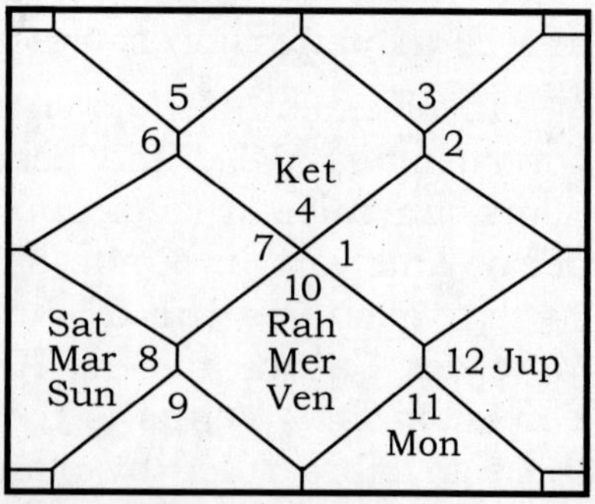


Balance of Vimsottari Dasa of **Mer 5Y 2M 1D**

The native was a judge of the civil court of law. Unfortunately dreaded disease Cancer was diagnosed to him, which resulted into an early end of his life.

The native was born in Sagittarius ascendant, whose lord Jupiter is posited in the 2nd house and aspects the 6th and the 10th house. Jupiter is quite strong planet here and obtains own *navamsa* Pisces. This is one of the points, for jobs connected with law.

Lord of the 10th house, Mercury, falls in own constellation *Jyeshtha* in the 12th house and aspects the 6th. The 6th lord Venus and the 10th lord Mercury both obtain *navamsa* of Saturn, the significator of law. Lord of the 6th house, Mars, and Saturn are placed together in the 9th house, identical to sign Leo and both obtain the *navamsa* of the 5th lord Mars i.e. Scorpio.

*Atmakaraka* planet Moon joins the 4th house in Pisces and obtains Aquarius *navamsa*. We have found that airy signs Gemini, Libra and Aquarius are prominent in the horoscopes of law personals, in addition to Sagittarius. The *Atmakaraka* Moon falls in Jupiter's sign Pisces, Mercury's constellation *Revati* and Saturn's *navamsa* Aquarius. This is a powerful indication for the native to become a justice, barrister or advocate etc.

*Illustration : 12.3* (**NP**) *Horoscope No.: 161*

Date of birth : 16.01.1920 Time of birth : 00:45:00 hrs

Place of birth : Lat 27:39:00 N Long 82:18:00E

Ayanamsa : 22:44:39 Sidereal Time : 8:19:58

| **Pln** | **Degree** | **Rasi** | **Nakshatra** | **Pad** |
|---|---|---|---|---|
| Asc | 8:06:24 | Lib | Svati | 1 |
| Sun | 1:37:07 | Cap | Uttarasadha | 2 |
| Mon | 2:06:56 | Sco | Visakha | 4 |
| Mar | 0:39:55 | Lib | Chitra | 3 |
| Mer (C) | 18:34:37 | Sag | Purvasadha | 2 |

| | | | | |
|---|---|---|---|---|
| Jup (R) | 22:45:34 | Can | Aslesha | 2 |
| Ven | 20:47:28 | Sco | Jyestha | 2 |
| Sat (R) | 18:26:15 | Leo | P Phalguni | 2 |
| Rah (R) | 0:12:25 | Sco | Visakha | 4 |
| Ket (R) | 0:12:25 | Tau | Krittika | 2 |

**Lagna Chart**

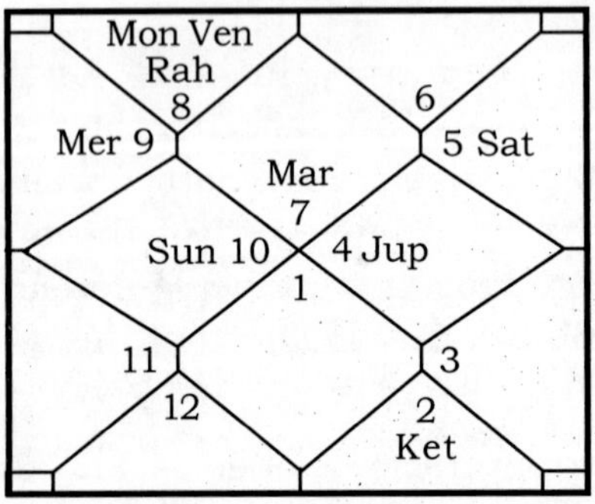


**Navamsa Chart**

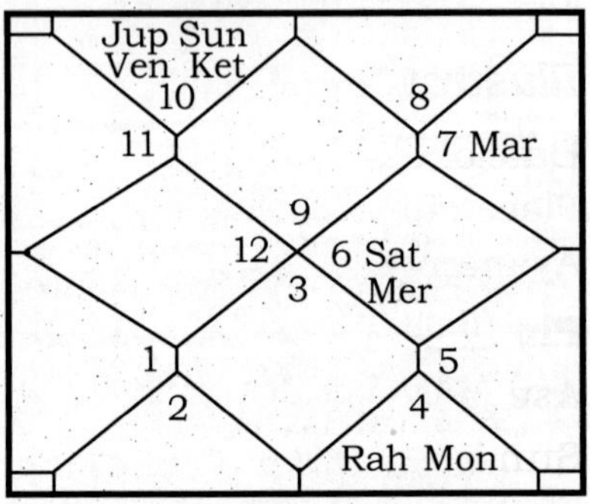


Balance of Vimsottari Dasa of **Jup 1Y 5M 16D**

This birth chart belongs to world famous advocate Nani Palkiwala who needs no introduction at all. He was born in Libra ascendant, the airy sign. The 3rd and the 6th lord, Jupiter, is exalted in the 10th and aspects the 6th house of its own, indicating serious inclination towards law.

The lord of the 10th house, Moon, is positioned in the 2nd house, in the constellation *Visakha,* ruled by the significator Jupiter. Thus, the 10th lord Moon falls in Jupiter's constellation and receives the aspect of Jupiter as well. Moon is also associated with the ascendant lord Venus, which is a powerful combination of a lawyer. Since this conjunction of the 10th lord Moon and the ascendant lord Venus took place in the Martian sign Scorpio, the native mostly dealt with the criminal cases. *Atmakarka* planet Jupiter falls in the 10th house, in Cancer, in *Aslesha* constellation ruled by the significator Mercury, and obtains the *navamsa* of the significator Saturn. This also confirms that the native will become a successful lawyer.

The lord of the 5th house *Yogakaraka* Saturn occupies the 11th house and aspects the ascendant, Mars, and the 5th and the 8th house. Saturn obtains the *navamsa* Virgo, ruled by the significator Mercury. Mars is the strongest planet and obtains sign of Venus under *vargottam navamsa*. The 9th lord and significator Mercury joins Sagittarius and obtains own or exaltation *navamsa*, which made him so famous and successful advocate.

*Illustration : 12.4* (**RJ**) *Horoscope No.: 162*

Date of birth : 14.09.1923 Time of birth : 16:12:00 hrs
Place of birth : Hyderabad Lat 17:22:00 N Long 78:26:00E
Ayanamsa : 22:47:23 Sidereal Time : 15:25:17

| Pln | Degree | Rasi | Nakshatra | Pad |
|---|---|---|---|---|
| Asc | 20:38:44 | Cap | Sravna | 4 |
| Sun | 27:47:40 | Leo | U Phalguni | 1 |
| Mon | 16:58:11 | Lib | Svati | 4 |
| Mar (C) | 15:44:16 | Leo | P Phalguni | 1 |
| Mer | 20:49:22 | Vir | Hasta | 4 |
| Jup | 22:38:41 | Lib | Visakha | 1 |
| Ven (D) | 28:52:17 | Leo | U Phalguni | 1 |
| Sat | 26:20:45 | Vir | Chitra | 1 |
| Rah (R/C) | 18:45:54 | Leo | P Phalguni | 2 |
| Ket (R) | 18:45:54 | Aqu | Satabhisha | 4 |

**Lagna Chart**

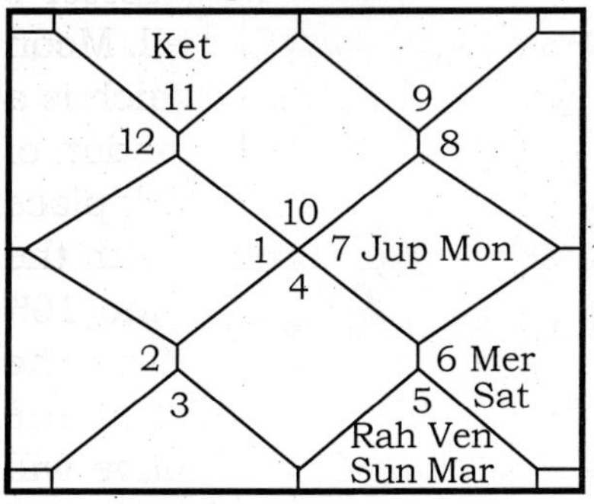


**Navamsa Chart**

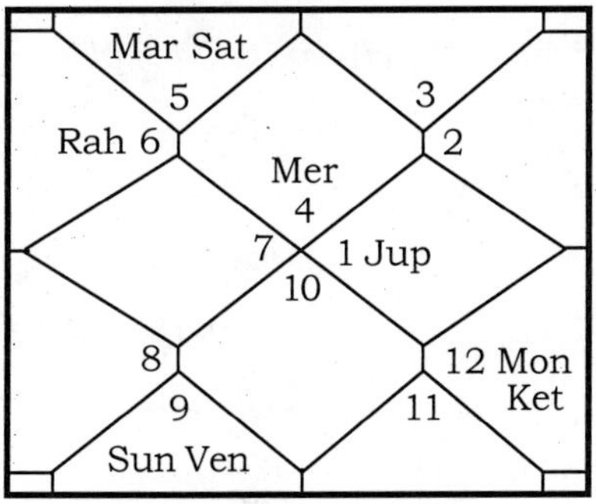


Balance of Vimsottari Dasa of **Rah 4Y 1M 2D**

World famous advocate Mr. Jethmalani needs no introduction. He was born in Capricorn ascendant. Jupiter and Moon occupy the 10th house. The 10th and 5th lord *Yogakaraka* Venus is posited in the 8th house in association with the Sun, Mars and Rahu. *Yogakaraka* Venus obtains *navamsa* of the significator Jupiter. The 6th lord Mercury is exalted and it is associated with ascendant lord Saturn in the 9th house. Moreover, Saturn aspects the 6th house and is associated with 6th lord Mercury. The 6th house has an influence of the significator Saturn, whereas the 10th house is tenanted by Jupiter and Moon. Thus, Jupiter, Saturn and Mercury are collectively indicating the legal profession to the native.

Moon, who is tenanted in the 10th house, obtains the *navamsa* of the significator Jupiter. Jupiter falls in own *nakshatra Visakha* and aspects the 2nd, 4th and the 6th house. Jupiter obtains the *navamsa* of Mars and Mars is associated with Rahu, Sun and Venus in Leo. This combination made the native the minister of law.

Venus is *Atmakaraka* planet and obtains the *navamsa* of Jupiter. This again signifies legal profession. The Sun is the strongest planet in the horoscope, which is posited in own sign Leo, in own constellation *Uttara Phalguni,* and obtains the *navamsa* of Jupiter i.e. Sagittarius, which distinctly justifies legal profession and law ministership to the native.

*Illustration : 12.5* **(LPN)** *Horoscope No.: 163*

Date of birth : 15.04.1908 Time of birth : 12:38:54 hrs

Place of birth : Kannauj Lat 27:04:00 N Long 79:55:00E

Ayanamsa : 22:34:16 Sidereal Time : 2:00:45

| **Pln** | **Degree** | **Rasi** | **Nakshatra** | **Pad** |
|---|---|---|---|---|
| Asc | 14:59:15 | Can | Pushya | 4 |
| Sun | 2:20:26 | Ari | Asvini | 1 |
| Mon | 15:36:56 | Vir | Hasta | 2 |
| Mar | 12:51:51 | Tau | Rohini | 1 |

| | | | | |
|---|---|---|---|---|
| Mer | 11:08:37 | Pis | U Bhadrapad | 3 |
| Jup | 11:22:55 | Can | Pushya | 3 |
| Ven | 17:28:30 | Tau | Rohini | 3 |
| Sat | 10:42:16 | Pis | U Bhadrapad | 3 |
| Rah (R) | 15:34:31 | Gem | Ardra | 3 |
| Ket (R) | 15:34:31 | Sag | Purvasadha | 1 |

**Lagna Chart**

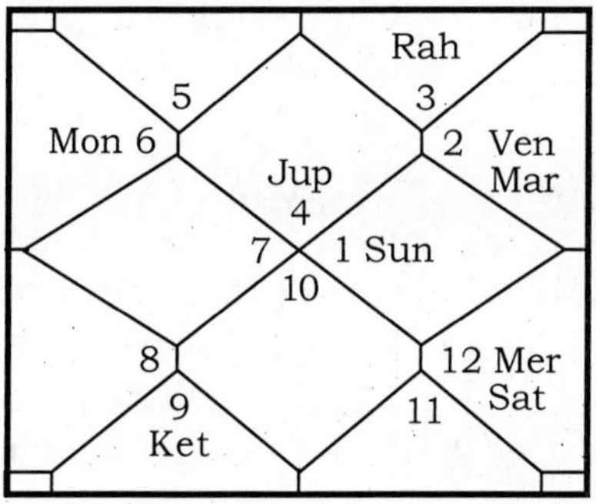


**Navamsa Chart**

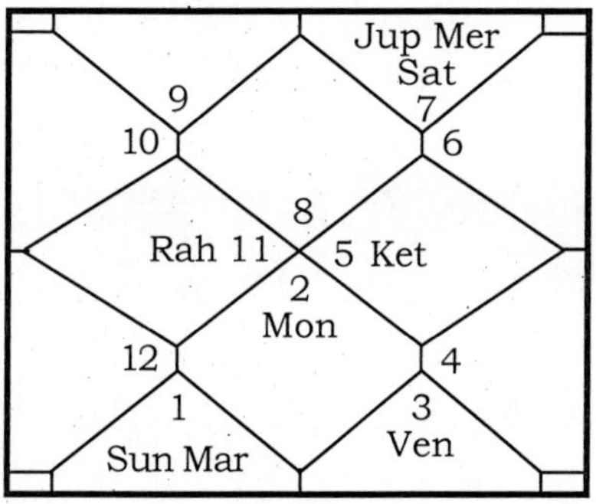


Balance of Vimsottari Dasa of **Mon 5Y 9M 13D**

The native was a great man of justice of his times. He was also bar-at-law. He played a key role in the judgment of various historical cases. He was born in Cancer ascendant with exalted Jupiter. The Sun is exalted in the 10th house and is extraordinary strong in *shadabala* as it obtains 2.26 *shadabalas*. Lord of the 10th house, *Yogakaraka* Mars is posited in Taurus and obtains own *navamsa*. Here, Mars is associated with Venus. Venus and Mars both are aspecting the 5th house.

The significator of legal professions are Jupiter, Mercury and Saturn and these obtain the *navamsa* of Venus, who is the supporting significator. This justifies prominently the profession of doing justice. In fact, Libra sign is the symbol of weighing device i.e. balancing machine. Therefore, Libra sign has its own significance for the persons who earn their livelihood through legal occupations. Libra sign is the sign of judgment, honesty and justice. Placement of all the three significators in Libra sign indicates that the native could be nothing less than a successful Judge.

Venus, the *Atmakaraka* planet is posited in the 11th house, own sign Taurus and obtains the Gemini *navamsa,* which is ruled by the significator Mercury. There is mutual exchange of *navamsa* between Venus and Mercury. Saturn and Mercury are closely associated in the 9th house in Jupiter's sign Pisces and Saturn's constellation *Uttara Bhadrapad*. Thus, these are strong indications in the horoscope of the native to become a law professional.

*Illustration : 12.6* (**RRA**) *Horoscope No.: 164*

Date of birth : 03.07.1959 Time of birth : 02:22:00 hrs
Place of birth : Raibareilly Lat 22:39:00 N Long 88:23:00E
Ayanamsa : 23:17:31 Sidereal Time : 21:26:06

| **Pln** | **Degree** | **Rasi** | **Nakshatra** | **Pad** |
|---|---|---|---|---|
| Asc | 9:22:07 | Tau | Krittika | 4 |
| Sun | 16:55:13 | Gem | Ardra | 4 |
| Mon | 11:02:35 | Tau | Rohini | 1 |
| Mar | 25:53:05 | Can | Aslesha | 3 |
| Mer | 12:16:11 | Can | Pushya | 3 |
| Jup (R) | 29:17:35 | Lib | Visakha | 3 |
| Ven | 1:57:14 | Leo | Magha | 1 |
| Sat (R) | 9:59:04 | Sag | Moola | 3 |
| Rah (R) | 15:17:04 | Vir | Hasta | 2 |
| Ket (R) | 15:17:04 | Pis | U Bhadrapad | 4 |

**Lagna Chart**

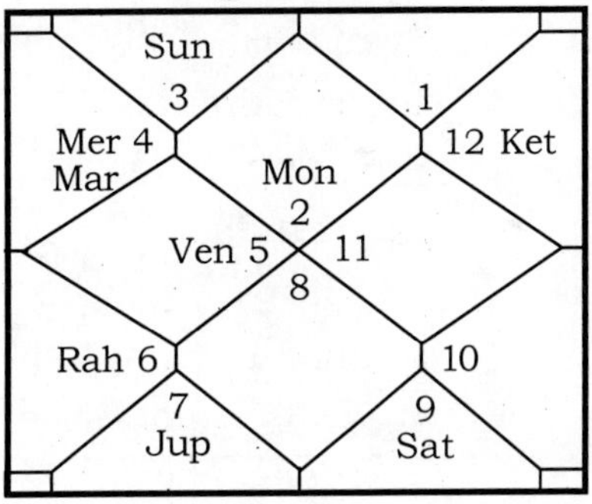


**Navamsa Chart**

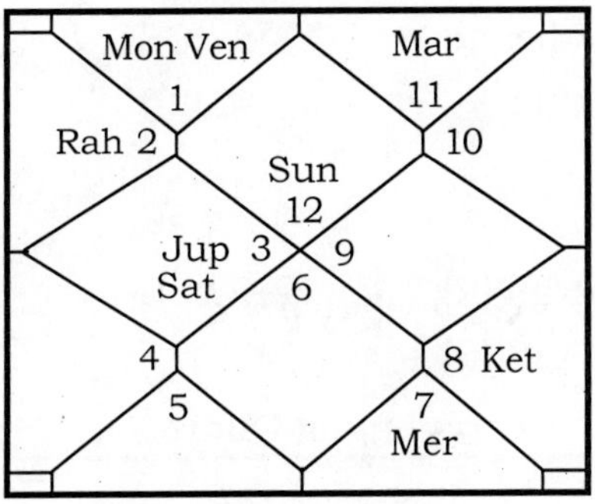


Balance of Vimsottari Dasa of **Mon 9Y 2M 18D**

The native is practicing in the High Court and is expected to be selected for the post of Judge within a short period. He was born in Taurus ascendant with the placement of Moon therein. The lord of the 9th and 10th house, Saturn, falls in the 8th house in Sagittarius. The 2nd and 5th lord Mercury occupies the 3rd house, identical to constellation of Saturn i.e. *Pushya*. Thus, the 9th and 10th lord Saturn, and 11th lord Jupiter obtain the *navamsa* of the significator Mercury. All the three significators play a vital role in the birth chart of the native and justify the legal profession.

The significator of justice, Jupiter, occupies the 6th house in Libra and aspects the 10th and 2nd house. Jupiter also happens to be the *Atmakaraka* planet and falls in own constellation *Visakha* and obtains the *navamsa* of Mercury, ensuring the legal profession to the native.

*Illustration : 12.7* *Horoscope No.: 165*

Date of birth : 14.10.1961 Time of birth : 13:58:00 hrs
Place of birth : Patna Lat 25:37:00 N Long 85:12:00E
Ayanamsa : 23:19:12 Sidereal Time : 15:39:24

| **Pln** | **Degree** | **Rasi** | **Nakshatra** | **Pad** |
|---|---|---|---|---|
| Asc | 20:51:19 | Cap | Sravna | 4 |
| Sun | 27:26:10 | Vir | Chitra | 2 |
| Mon | 21:35:35 | Sco | Jyestha | 2 |

| | | | | |
|---|---|---|---|---|
| Mar | 15:13:04 | Lib | Svati | 3 |
| Mer (R) | 13:57:08 | Lib | Svati | 3 |
| Jup | 4:41:20 | Cap | Uttarasadha | 3 |
| Ven | 2:01:14 | Vir | P Phalguni | 2 |
| Sat | 0:08:34 | Cap | Uttarasadha | 2 |
| Rah (R) | 2:09:06 | Leo | Magha | 1 |
| Ket (R) | 2:09:06 | Aqu | Dhanishtha | 3 |

**Lagna Chart**

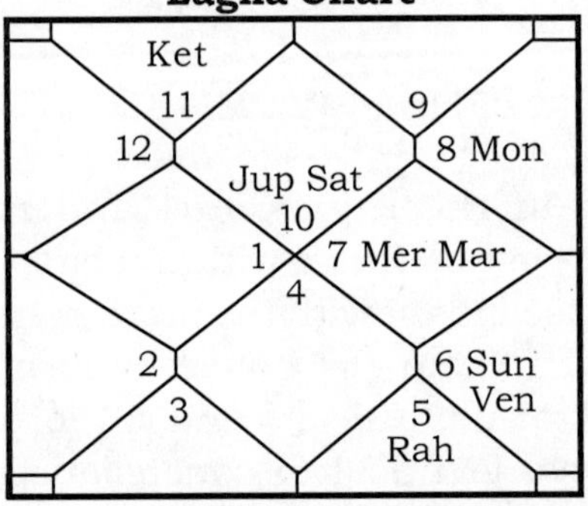


**Navamsa Chart**

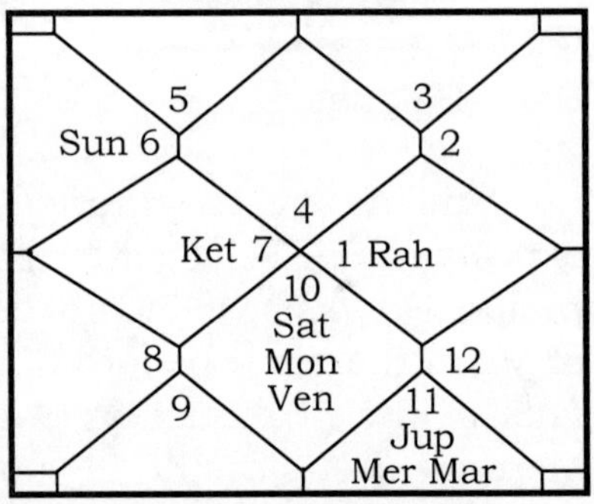


Balance of Vimsottari Dasa of **Mer 10Y 8M 19D**

The native is an established advocate of High Court. He is expected to become a Judge within a year or two. He was born in Capricorn ascendant with Jupiter and Saturn. Mars and Mercury occupy the 10th house, whereas the Sun and Venus are tenanted in the 9th house.

The ascendant lord Saturn aspects the 10th house, the 9th lord Mercury and the 11th lord Mars. Mars and Mercury both fall in Libra, in the 10th house and obtain the Aquarius *navamsa* ruled by Saturn. Aquarius, Libra and Gemini are the airy signs, which have significance with the law professionals. There is mutual exchange between 10th lord Venus and 9th lord Mercury, which confirms a high class professional position.

The ascendant lord Saturn, the 10th lord Venus and Moon obtain the *navamsa* of the significator Saturn. Venus is 5th and 10th lord and occupies the 9th house, in Virgo and it is associated with the *Atmakaraka* planet Sun. The Sun obtains *vargottam navamsa* in Virgo. Thus, *Atmakaraka* Sun and the 10th and 5th lord Venus are under the influence of the significator Mercury and Jupiter, whereas 6th lord Mercury is associated with 11th lord Mars and is aspected by the significator and 10th lord Saturn, which gives a clear picture of the livelihood of the native through legal occupation.

*Illustration : 12.8* **(KNS)** *Horoscope No.: 166*

Date of birth : 21.10.1924 Time of birth : 18:09:00 hrs
Place of birth : Allahabad Lat 25:27:00 N Long 81:50:00E
Ayanamsa : 22:48:12 Sidereal Time : 20:05:04

| Pln | Degree | Rasi | Nakshatra | Pad |
|---|---|---|---|---|
| Asc | 18:18:17 | Ari | Bharani | 2 |
| Sun | 5:02:03 | Lib | Chitra | 4 |
| Mon | 11:21:51 | Can | Pushya | 3 |
| Mar | 7:46:04 | Aqu | Satabhisha | 1 |
| Mer (C) | 1:55:21 | Lib | Chitra | 3 |
| Jup | 24:56:27 | Sco | Jyestha | 3 |
| Ven | 23:01:44 | Leo | P Phalguni | 3 |
| Sat (C) | 11:27:48 | Lib | Svati | 2 |
| Rah | 27:37:58 | Can | Aslesha | 4 |
| Ket | 27:37:58 | Cap | Dhanishtha | 2 |

**Lagna Chart**

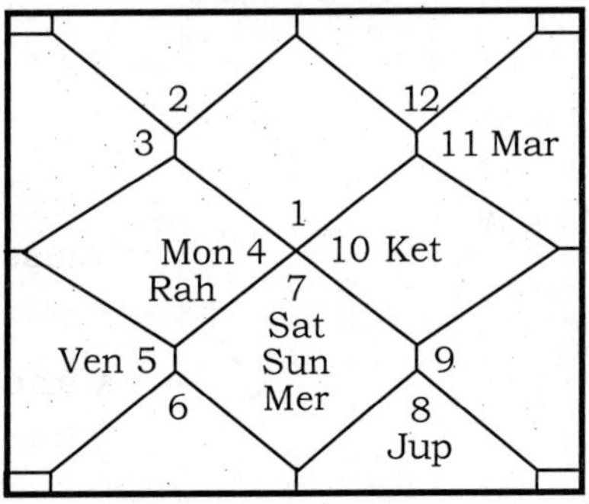


**Navamsa Chart**

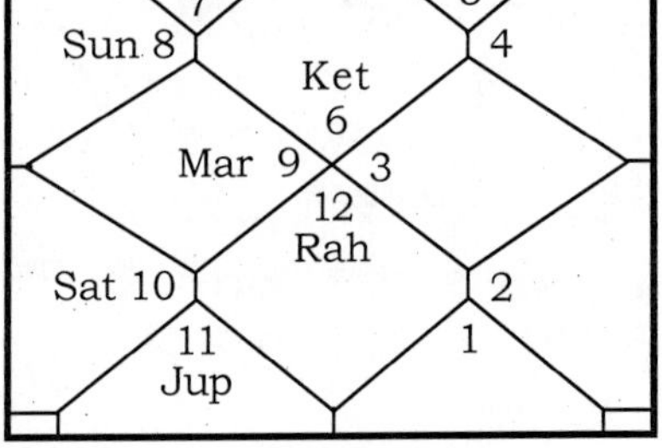


Balance of Vimsottari Dasa of **Sat 7Y 6M 20D**

This is the horoscope of a Supreme Court Justice who has acquired a great recognition for the clarity of his judgments and justice with the people.

Saturn, the planet of justice owns the $10^{th}$ and occupies his exaltation sign Libra i.e. a sign of balance. This means that the occupation of the native is concerned with law and balance of justice.

The $6^{th}$ lord Mercury, who gives an analytical intellect, falls in Libra, in association with the planet of justice i.e. Saturn.

The $5^{th}$ lord Sun is also associated with the intellectual planet Mercury and planet of justice Saturn. There is a mutual exchange of lords of the $7^{th}$ and the $5^{th}$ house i.e. Venus and the Sun, respectively.

The ascendant shows the aptitude of a person for his employment. The ascendant lord Mars occupies *navamsa* of Jupiter, the significator of law.

The ascendant is also aspected by Saturn, $6^{th}$ lord Mercury and the $5^{th}$ lord, the Sun. On the other hand, lord of ascendant Mars, who falls in Saturn's sign and Jupiter's *navamsa*, aspects Mercurial sign in the $6^{th}$ house.

For the proper analysis of the vocation, the *navamsa* chart must be judged along with *Rashi* Chart. Here, the lord of the $10^{th}$ Saturn, a planet indicating justice, obtains own *navamsa*. Ascendant lord Mars falls in Jupiter's *navamsa*. The $6^{th}$ lord Mercury obtains *vargottam navamsa*. In *navamsa* chart, Jupiter aspects the $10^{th}$ house while the $10^{th}$ lord Mercury is aspected by Saturn and Jupiter, both. On the other hand, Mercury has occupied a sign of balance, Libra, in *Rashi* and *Navamsa* both.

Thus, this horoscope powerfully indicates the judicial services and an analytical intellect of balancing his judgments.

*Illustration : 12.9* **(GPS)** *Horoscope No.: 167*

Date of birth : 21.11.1922 Time of birth : 13:52:00 hrs
Place of birth : Agra Lat 27:09:00 N Long 78:00:00E
Ayanamsa : 23:46:46 Sidereal Time : 17:32:13

| **Pln** | **Degree** | **Rasi** | **Nakshatra** | **Pad** |
|---|---|---|---|---|
| Asc | 27:30:31 | Aqu | P Bhadrapad | 3 |
| Sun | 5:28:11 | Sco | Anuradha | 1 |
| Mon | 6:32:56 | Sag | Moola | 2 |
| Mar | 22:30:50 | Cap | Sravna | 4 |
| Mer (C) | 26:44:19 | Lib | Visakha | 3 |
| Jup | 12:42:49 | Lib | Svati | 2 |
| Ven (R/C) | 11:44:09 | Sco | Anuradha | 3 |
| Sat | 23:25:23 | Vir | Chitra | 1 |
| Rah (R) | 4:58:38 | Vir | U Phalguni | 3 |
| Ket (R) | 4:58:38 | Pis | U Bhadrapad | 1 |

**Lagna Chart**

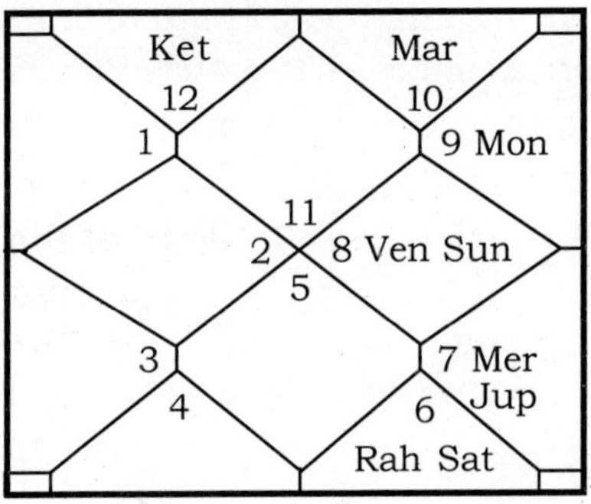


**Navamsa Chart**

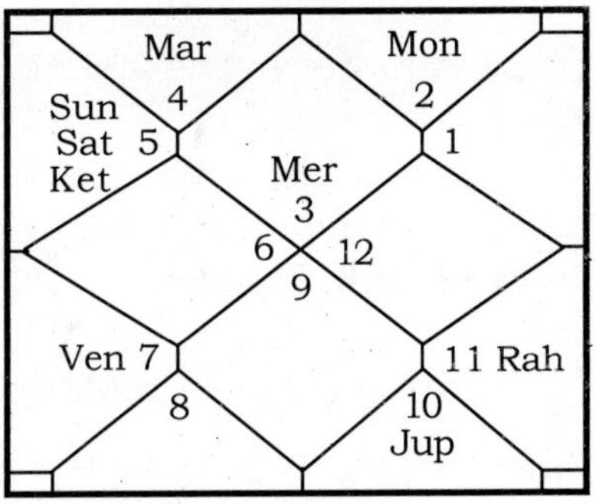


Balance of Vimsottari Dasa of **Ket 3Y 6M 22D**

This is the horoscope of a famous advocate of Rent Control. He was the President of Bar Association of Lucknow for almost a decade. He is a multimillionaire and owns dozens of palatial buildings.

Ascendant lord Saturn, the planet of justice falls in the

8th house in Virgo i.e. the sign of Mercury. Of course, the ascendant lord's position in the 8th house has given an unsound health to the native. The significator Jupiter falls in the sign of balance Libra, from where Jupiter lends his aspect over the ascendant.

*Yogakaraka* Venus and the Sun, owner of a quadrant, join the 10th house. This combination has provided enough strength to the 10th house. Saturn is also aspecting the 10th house.

The 6th house is aspected by the lord of the 10th house, Mars, while the 6th lord Moon joins the sign Sagittarius, the sign of significator, Jupiter.

The 5th house belongs to the planet of intelligence, Mercury. Saturn, Jupiter and Moon are aspecting the 5th house showing a very high degree of intellect and power of analyzing the truth deeply.

In *navamsa* chart, the significator Jupiter and the lord of the 10th house, Mars, are aspecting each other The planet of justice, Saturn, aspects the 6th lord Moon.

The 4th house, and Mars and Venus are related with property matters. The 4th lord Venus occupies the 10th. Venus is a *Yogakaraka* and joins own *navamsa* Libra. Venus falls in the sign Scorpio of Mars, in the 10th, and aspects her own 4th house. Therefore, the native dealt in the property matters and the Rent Control.

*Illustration : 12.10* **(SMA)** *Horoscope No.: 168*

Date of birth : 29.06.1946 Time of birth : 00:30:00 hrs

Place of birth : Rohtak Lat 28:54:00 N Long 76:38:00E

Ayanamsa : 23:06:30 Sidereal Time : 0:34:20

| Pln | Degree | Rasi | Nakshatra | Pad |
|---|---|---|---|---|
| Asc | 26:43:18 | Gem | Punarvasu | 3 |
| Sun | 11:55:55 | Vir | Hasta | 1 |
| Mon | 21:36:20 | Lib | Visakha | 1 |

| | | | | |
|---|---|---|---|---|
| Mar | 9:39:56 | Lib | Svati | 1 |
| Mer (C) | 22:35:04 | Vir | Hasta | 4 |
| Jup | 7:34:53 | Lib | Svati | 1 |
| Ven | 26:11:34 | Lib | Visakha | 2 |
| Sat | 13:19:40 | Can | Pushya | 3 |
| Rah (R) | 20:55:37 | Tau | Rohini | 4 |
| Ket (R) | 20:55:37 | Sco | Jyestha | 2 |

**Lagna Chart**

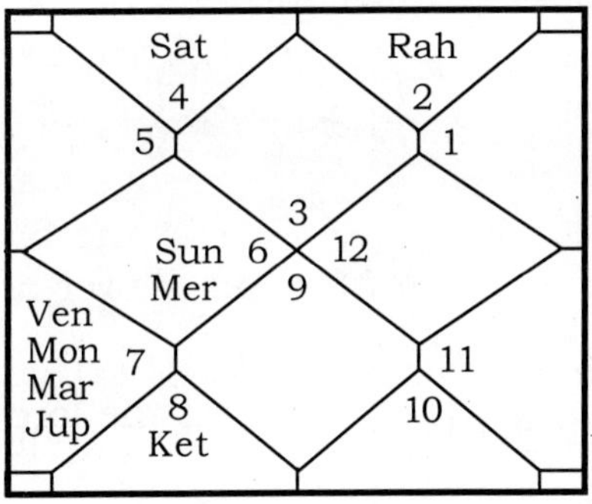


**Navamsa Chart**

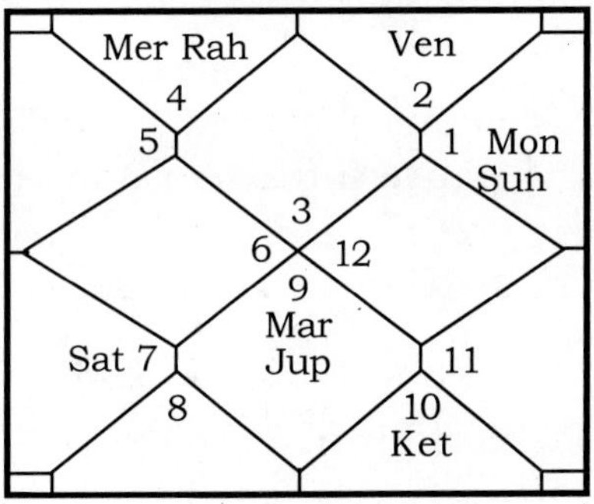


Balance of Vimsottari Dasa of **Jup 14Y 0M 26D**

The native is one of the senior most and richest lawyers of Taxation at Lucknow, possessing innumerable properties.

Ascendant lord Mercury is exalted in the 4th house and aspects the 10th house. The 10th lord and *karaka* Jupiter aspects ascendant, falls in Libra in the 5th house forming *Kendra Trikona Rajyoga.*

The 10th lord Jupiter falls in own *navamsa,* and joins 5th house in *Rashi* with the 5th and the 6th lords, Venus and Mars. Moon is also associated with these three, providing the native a high degree of intellect and a mind like a thinker of law.

Lord of the 6th, Mars, is associated with the 10th lord. The 6th house has a great concern with law and litigation. So, often 6th house is related with the 10th house, by way of conjunction of their lords or by aspect, or in so many other possible ways.

Presence of Jupiter in Libra has given the native ability to analyze the things correctly with justifications.

The 6th lord Mars and the 10th lord Jupiter obtain the *navamsa* Sagittarius. Sagittarius is a sign that covers law. In *Rashi* chart, Saturn aspects Mercury and in *navamsa* Saturn falls in the 6th house and aspects Mercury again.

In this chart, we see that Jupiter is playing a very important role. Therefore, the native is practicing in Income Tax. Jupiter also represents all kinds of taxes. 11th and 8th houses show the income by taxes and revenue etc.

So many planets in the 5th house, a few of which are also inimical to the sign Libra or with another one, have made the native intelligent and very clever.

*Illustration : 12.11* **(DK)** *Horoscope No.: 169*

Date of birth : 04.08.1951 Time of birth : 09:21:00 hrs
Place of birth : Bareilly Lat 28:20:00 N Long 79:24:00E
Ayanamsa : 23:10:57 Sidereal Time : 5:56:14

| Pln | Degree | Rasi | Nakshatra | Pad |
|---|---|---|---|---|
| Asc | 5:59:11 | Vir | U Phalguni | 3 |
| Sun | 17:47:37 | Can | Aslesha | 1 |
| Mon | 1:26:54 | Leo | Magha | 1 |
| Mar | 27:31:57 | Gem | Punarvasu | 3 |
| Mer | 15:03:45 | Leo | P Phalguni | 1 |
| Jup (S) | 20:59:50 | Pis | Revati | 2 |
| Ven | 23:37:31 | Leo | P Phalguni | 4 |
| Sat | 5:51:42 | Vir | U Phalguni | 3 |
| Rah (R) | 16:49:32 | Aqu | Satabhisha | 4 |
| Ket (R) | 16:49:32 | Leo | P Phalguni | 2 |

**Lagna Chart**

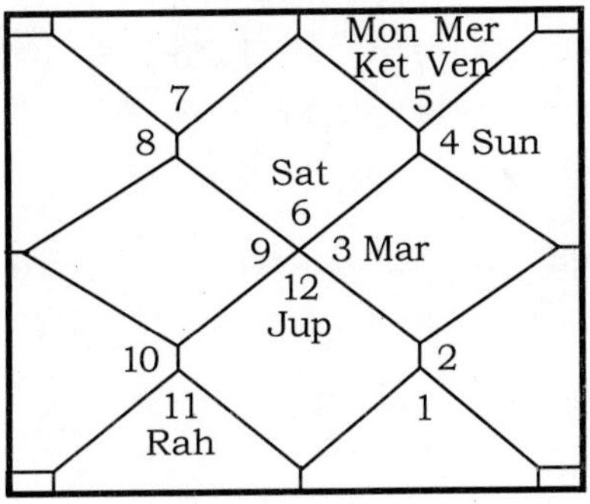


**Navamsa Chart**

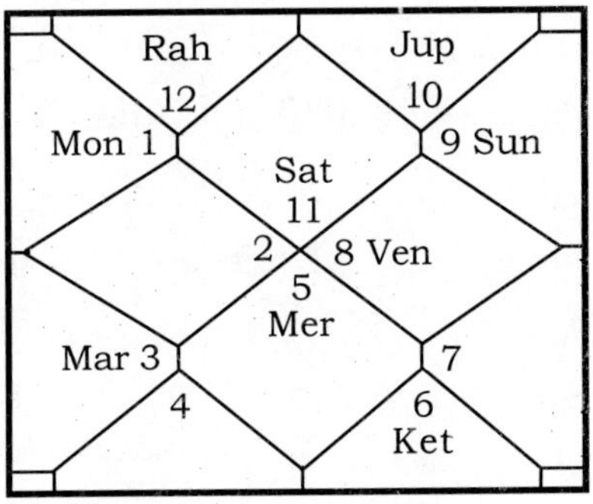


Balance of Vimsottari Dasa of **Ket 6Y 2M 26D**

This horoscope is also of an Income Tax practitioner. The native is extremely polite, gentle and kind-hearted. He has acquired great popularity and recognition for his merit. For number of people like us, he does the cases without any charge or fee.

The ascendant lord Mercury joins the 12$^{th}$ house along with Moon and Venus. The ascendant is a little weak this way. Saturn, the planet of justice occupies the ascendant and the significator of law, Jupiter aspects over there, making everything very clear. Saturn-Jupiter combination, involving the sign of Mercury or Venus, makes one an advocate provided this has concern with the 10$^{th}$ house.

The 10$^{th}$ lord Mercury obtains *vargottam navamsa* and aspects *navamsa* ascendant, 5$^{th}$ and 6$^{th}$ lord Saturn, who obtains own *navamsa* and aspects Mercury. Rather there is a mutual aspect between the planet of justice, Saturn and the planet of logic, Mercury, as far *navamsa* chart is concerned.

Saturn owns these houses and joins Virgo. The *karaka* Jupiter aspects Saturn. From another angle, the 5$^{th}$ and 6$^{th}$ lord joins the sign ruled by 10$^{th}$ lord Mercury and is aspected by the significator Jupiter.

*Illustration : 12.12* **(KK)** *Horoscope No.: 170*

Date of birth : 27.12.1947 Time of birth : 17:30:00 hrs
Place of birth : Lucknow Lat 26:50:00 N Long 80:54:00E
Ayanamsa : 23:07:36 Sidereal Time : 23:44:08

| **Pln** | **Degree** | **Rasi** | **Nakshatra** | **Pad** |
|---|---|---|---|---|
| Asc | 14:44:15 | Gem | Ardra | 3 |
| Sun | 11:45:56 | Sag | Moola | 4 |
| Mon | 6:49:57 | Gem | Ardra | 1 |
| Mar | 13:35:59 | Leo | P Phalguni | 1 |
| Mer (C) | 7:42:26 | Sag | Moola | 3 |
| Jup | 21:02:15 | Sco | Jyeshtha | 2 |
| Ven | 10:13:12 | Cap | Sravna | 1 |
| Sat (R) | 29:03:44 | Can | Aslesha | 4 |
| Rah (R) | 29:36:45 | Ari | Krittika | 1 |
| Ket (R) | 29:36:45 | Lib | Visakha | 3 |

**Lagna Chart**

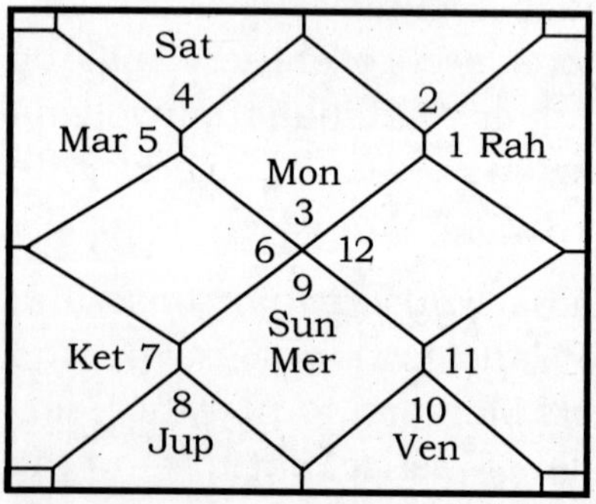


**Navamsa Chart**

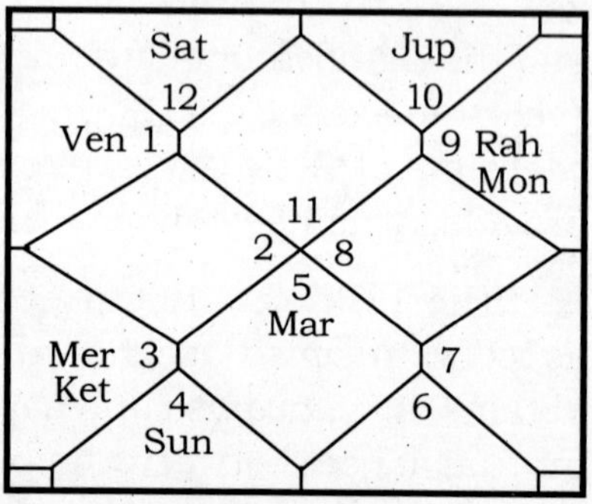


Balance of Vimsottari Dasa of **Rah 17Y 9M 9D**

The native is a successful Income Tax lawyer. He also deals in various other activities so as work to earn more and more money. The native works to be a multimillionaire overnight. Let us study his horoscope as far as his main profession of law is concerned.

The ascendant is Gemini, which is being aspected by its own lord Mercury. This has strengthened the ascendant. The ascendant lord Mercury occupies the sign Sagittarius i.e. that of the significator of law, Jupiter.

The lord of the $10^{th}$ house, Jupiter, occupies the $6^{th}$ house, denoting a profession concerning with law. Jupiter's aspect on the planet of justice, Saturn, and the $10^{th}$ house, has further confirmed it. Jupiter also falls in Saturn's *navamsa.*

The $6^{th}$ lord Mars occupies the $3^{rd}$ house, from where he aspects the $10^{th}$ house and the $10^{th}$ lord as well. Thus, the $10^{th}$ lord and the $10^{th}$ house are influenced by the $6^{th}$ lord Mars.

The $5^{th}$ lord, Venus, occupies the $8^{th}$ house, in the sign of Saturn. The $5^{th}$ house is occupied by Ketu, which has made the native fickle minded. The lord of $5^{th}$ house, Venus, is receiving the aspect of Saturn.

The $10^{th}$ lord Jupiter falls in Saturn's *navamsa,* while Saturn falls in Jupiter's *navamsa.* Mercury, the lord of the ascendant and $4^{th}$, falls in the $5^{th}$ house from *navamsa* ascendant, in own sign Gemini. Thus, there is a prominent role of Jupiter, Saturn and Mercury in deciding the means of livelihood in this horoscope. Therefore, native has chosen law as profession.

## Is there any role of Venus in determining Legal Profession?

We have said above that Jupiter is the significator of law, Saturn is a planet of Justice, and Mercury bestows logical thinking and the power of argument. So these are the planets playing prominent role in determining legal profession.

The ascendant shows the personality and aptitude towards a particular direction, the $10^{th}$ house governs vocation, the $6^{th}$ house rules court, litigation, disputes and judicial aspects and the $5^{th}$ house governs the power and intelligence or inclination of mind. So, these are main houses, which should be referred for determining law vocations.

Libra is sign of balance. Sagittarius is a law loving sign or a sign for justice and Gemini is a sign of thinking in a most logical way. So, these are the signs which have a strong concern with the law profession.

Dr. B.V. Raman has written in Chapter 14$^{th}$ of 'How to Judge a horoscope' Vol.-II that Venus represents counselors. Venus represents various other kinds of professions. So, it can not play a prominent role in making one a lawyer or so. But Venus is the ruler of Libra and Libra is a sign of balance, which is an important sign for law persons. Therefore, Venus also has a concern with law. Venus is a Guru of *Asuras*. Litigation or disputes etc, which come under the control of court law, can not be said *Satwik karma*. This may be nominated as *Asatwik* or *Tamsi Karmas* or *Neecha Karma*, which is expected to be done by *Asuras*. *Shukra* is the Guru of *Asuras*, so *Shukra* may have to play as justice on account of *Aasuri Karmas*. Perhaps this is the reason that at various places much importance has been given to Venus for the judgment of profession of law.

So, if Venus also influences the concerning houses, signs and planets, in addition to Jupiter, Saturn and Mercury, the legal profession will be a certainty.

In case no. 8, we see that Venus joins the 5$^{th}$ as 2$^{nd}$ lord and falls in own *navamsa* Libra.

In case no. 9, we see that Venus joins the 10$^{th}$ as a *Yogakaraka* and falls in own *navamsa* in Libra, in the 5$^{th}$ from *navamsa* ascendant.

In case no. 10, Venus owns 5$^{th}$ and is posited in the 5$^{th}$ with Jupiter, obtains own *navamsa* Taurus and aspects the 6$^{th}$ and Saturn.

In case no. 11, Venus is associated with the lord of the ascendant and the 10$^{th}$, Mercury, and aspects 6$^{th}$ house. In *navamsa* chart, Venus joins the 10$^{th}$ house under the aspect of Saturn.

In case no. 12, Venus owns 5th, and is posited in Capricorn under the mutual aspect with Saturn.

*Illustration: 12.13* (**Dr. R.Prasad**) *Horoscope No.: 171*

Date of birth : 03.12.1884 Time of birth : 08:45:00 hrs
Place of birth : Jirade Lat 25:33:00 N Long 77:29:00E
Ayanamsa : 22:15:02 Sidereal Time : 13:34:29

| **Pln** | **Degree** | **Rasi** | **Nakshatra** | **Pad** |
|---|---|---|---|---|
| Asc | 18:42:09 | Sag | Purvasadha | 2 |
| Sun | 19:11:08 | Sco | Jyestha | 1 |
| Mon | 24:19:03 | Tau | Mrigsira | 1 |
| Mar (C) | 5:57:30 | Sag | Moola | 2 |
| Mer | 4:28:58 | Sag | Moola | 2 |
| Jup | 13:04:22 | Leo | Magha | 4 |
| Ven | 12:58:30 | Lib | Svati | 2 |
| Sat (R) | 29:14:55 | Tau | Mrigsira | 2 |
| Rah (R) | 19:57:43 | Vir | Hasta | 3 |
| Ket (R) | 19:57:43 | Pis | Revati | 1 |

**Lagna Chart**

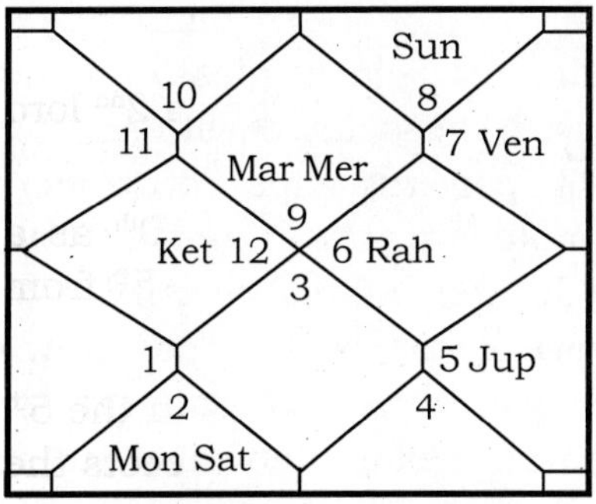


**Navamsa Chart**

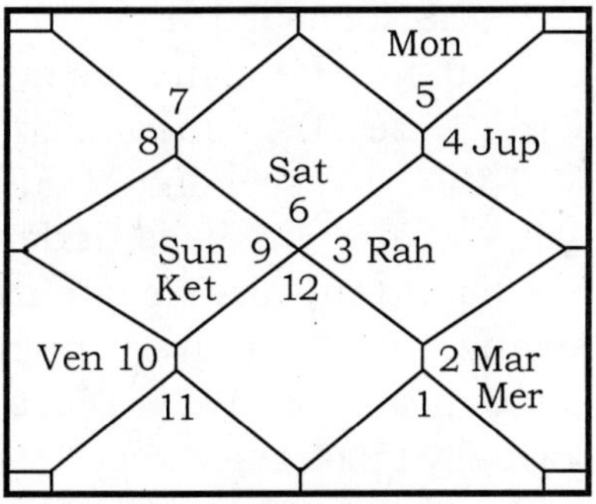


Balance of Vimsottari Dasa of **Mar 6Y 5M 24D**

This is the horoscope of the first President of India Dr. Rajendra Prasad. He was a legal practitioner before entering into politics. This is an extraordinary horoscope, which does not reflect in the first glance that the native will be the head of the country.

The ascendant falls in the sign Sagittarius, which is occupied by the 5th and the 10th lords, Mars and Mercury. Ascendant lord Jupiter aspects the ascendant. This is a strong *Rajyoga.*

Jupiter owns ascendant and 4th house, joins the 9th and aspects the ascendant, the 5th and the 3rd house. Moon is exalted and Venus occupies her own sign, Libra.

Let's see if the combinations of a successful lawyer are present in this horoscope-

The ascendant lord Jupiter falls in the 9th house. Mercury is posited in the ascendant as the 10th lord. The significator, Jupiter, aspects the ascendant.

The planet of logic and argument, Mercury, which occupies the ascendant, owns the 10th house. Jupiter aspects Mercury. This is an ideal combination for law professionals.

The exalted Moon is posited in the 6th house. The lord of the 6th house, Venus, occupies Libra, the sign of balance. Venus also throws her aspect over the 5th house.

The lord of the 5th house, Mars, joins Sagittarius ascendant, the sign which indicates legal profession. The lord of the 10th house, Mercury, is associated with the 5th lord Mars, in ascendant, under the powerful aspect of Jupiter. Thus, the 5th house is under the favourable influence of all the important planets such as Jupiter, Mars, Mercury, and Venus. This had given the native a very intellectual brain, deep power of thinking and weighing the judgments logically. 'Examinee is better than the examiner' was written by his examiner in his answer book.

Venus owns 6th, joins Libra in 11th and aspects the 5th house. Venus joins Saturn *navamsa* in 5th under mutual aspect with Jupiter from 11th.

*Illustration : 12.14* *Horoscope No.: 172*

Date of birth : 30.12.1907 Time of birth : 21:55:00 hrs
Place of birth : Bangalore Lat 13:00:00 N Long 77:35:00E
Ayanamsa : 22:34:03 Sidereal Time : 4:07:11

| **Pln** | **Degree** | **Rasi** | **Nakshatra** | **Pad** |
|---|---|---|---|---|
| Asc | 9:44:14 | Leo | Magha | 3 |
| Sun | 15:16:07 | Sag | Purvasadha | 1 |
| Mon | 18:07:33 | Lib | Svati | 4 |
| Mar | 29:20:39 | Aqu | P Bhadrapad | 3 |
| Mer (C) | 6:41:05 | Sag | Moola | 3 |
| Jup (R) | 19:38:07 | Can | Aslesha | 1 |
| Ven | 11:33:15 | Cap | Sravna | 1 |
| Sat | 29:13:20 | Aqu | P Bhadrapad | 3 |
| Rah (R) | 21:42:08 | Gem | Punarvasu | 1 |
| Ket (R/C) | 21:42:08 | Sag | Purvasadha | 3 |

**Lagna Chart**

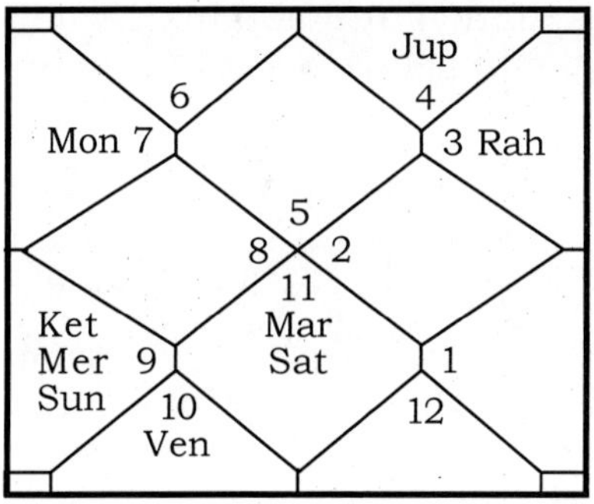


**Navamsa Chart**

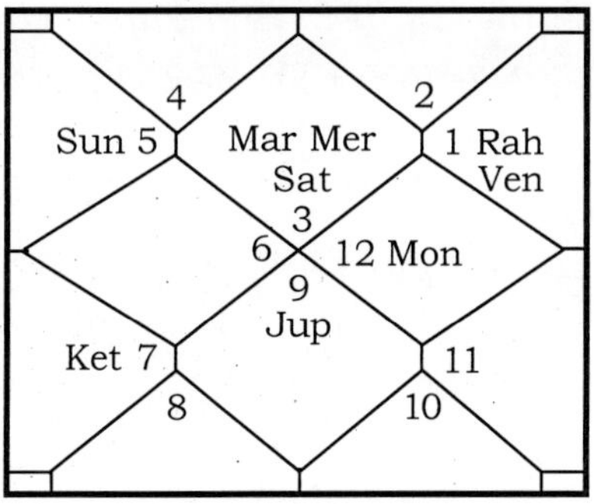


Balance of Vimsottari Dasa of **Rah 2Y 6M 11D**

This is the horoscope of a very brilliant jurist who started his profession as a lawyer and occupied the highest judicial office in the State.

The 10th house is Taurus aspected by Saturn. The 10th

lord Venus occupies the 6th house, which rules the judiciary, and is aspected by the exalted Jupiter.

The chart gains strength as the *Yogakaraka* Sun joins the 5th house, in association with 11th and 2nd lord Mercury. Sun obtains own *navamsa* as well. The 8th lord Jupiter occupies the 12th house, and the 12th lord Moon is posited in the 3rd house, in Libra. In *navamsa*, the 6th lord Saturn obtains the *navamsa* of Mercury, the 12th lord Moon obtains Jupiter's *navamsa.*

Ascendant lord, the Sun, is associated with Mercury, in Sagittarius, in the 5th house. The 10th lord Venus is posited in the 6th house, and the 5th lord Jupiter, who is the *Karaka* of law, also aspects the 10th lord Venus, signifying profession concerning with law.

The lord of the 6th house, Saturn, occupies Jupiter's constellation *P. Bhadrapad.* The significator Jupiter falls in own *navamsa..* Jupiter and Saturn, both, are under mutual aspect in *navamsa* chart.

Venus owns 10th, joins 6th in Saturn's sign and is aspected by *Karaka* Jupiter. *Atmakaraka* Mars falls in Aquarius in P. *Bhadrapad* constellation and obtains Gemini *navamsa,* which strongly justifies judiciary services.

*Illustration : 12.15* *Horoscope No.: 173*

Date of birth : 04.10.1895 Time of birth : 06:03:00 hrs
Place of birth : Bangalore Lat 13:00:00 N Long 77:35:00E
Ayanamsa : 22:24:09 Sidereal Time : 6:52:52

| **Pln** | **Degree** | **Rasi** | **Nakshatra** | **Pad** |
|---|---|---|---|---|
| Asc | 20:39:57 | Vir | Hasta | 4 |
| Sun | 18:08:50 | Vir | Hasta | 3 |
| Mon | 19:06:31 | Pis | Revati | 1 |
| Mar (D) | 20:32:27 | Vir | Hasta | 4 |
| Mer | 13:36:20 | Lib | Svati | 3 |

| | | | | |
|---|---|---|---|---|
| Jup | 12:35:35 | Can | Pushya | 3 |
| Ven (R) | 26:24:20 | Leo | P Phalguni | 4 |
| Sat | 14:06:48 | Lib | Svati | 3 |
| Rah (R) | 20:24:39 | Aqu | P Bhadrapad | 1 |
| Ket (R) | 20:24:39 | Leo | P Phalguni | 3 |

**Lagna Chart**

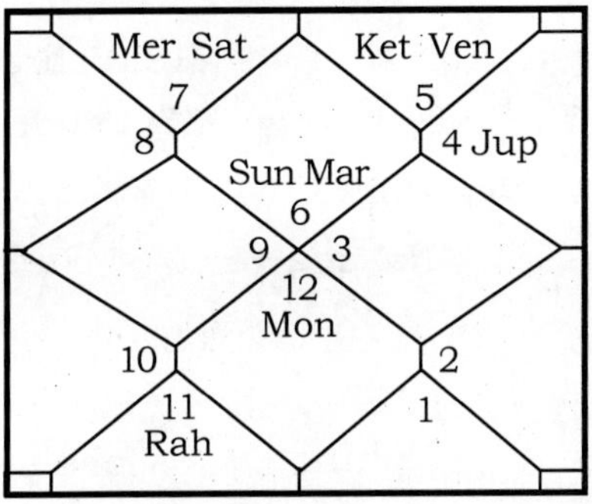


**Navamsa Chart**

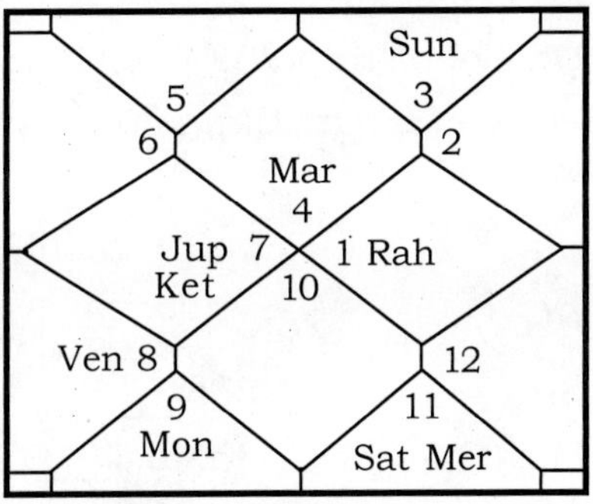


Balance of Vimsottari Dasa of **Mer 13Y 10M 19D**

This is birth chart of a High Court judge. Let us study the combinations responsible for bringing him into legal profession.

The ascendant is owned by Mercury, who joins the sign of balance Libra, in association with the planet of justice, Saturn.

The 10th lord Mercury and Saturn are conjoined in *navamsa* also as both occupy Saturn's *navamsa*.

The 6th lord is exalted in the 2nd house and is conjoined with the 10th lord Mercury i.e. 10th and 6th lords are placed together in the sign of balance, Libra. Saturn lends his aspect over the significator Jupiter. Saturn and Jupiter, both, are exalted.

The 5th lord Saturn is associated with the 10th lord Mercury in Libra. *Karaka* Jupiter aspects 5th and Moon, who is also a dispositor of Jupiter.

In the *navamsa* chart, the ascendant and the 10th lord Mercury is associated with 5th and 6th lord Saturn in the sign of Saturn, Aquarius. Jupiter obtains the *navamsa* of Libra, the sign of balance. So, Saturn, Mercury and Jupiter's influence on the concerning houses made the native a High Court judge.

*Illustration : 12.16* *Horoscope No.: 174*

Date of birth : 29.06.1924 Time of birth : 11:18:00 hrs
Place of birth : Bangalore Lat 13:00:00 N Long 77:35:00E
Ayanamsa : 22:47:59 Sidereal Time : 5:26:29

| Pln | Degree | Rasi | Nakshatra | Pad |
|---|---|---|---|---|
| Asc | 28:54:20 | Leo | U Phalguni | 1 |
| Sun | 14:23:04 | Gem | Ardra | 3 |
| Mon | 11:36:49 | Tau | Rohini | 1 |
| Mar | 8:37:13 | Aqu | Satabhisha | 1 |
| Mer (C) | 6:31:43 | Gem | Mrigsira | 4 |
| Jup (R) | 19:26:53 | Sco | Jyeshtha | 1 |
| Ven (R/C) | 17:57:49 | Gem | Ardra | 4 |
| Sat (S) | 2:49:02 | Lib | Chitra | 3 |
| Rah (R) | 1:12:51 | Leo | Magha | 1 |
| Ket (R) | 1:12:51 | Aqu | Dhanishtha | 3 |

**Lagna Chart**

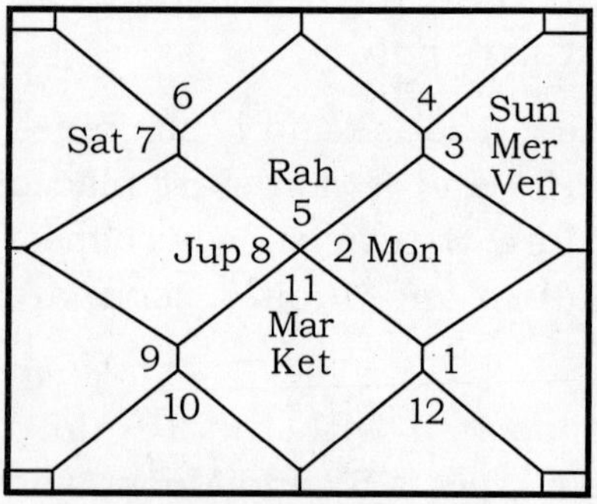


**Navamsa Chart**

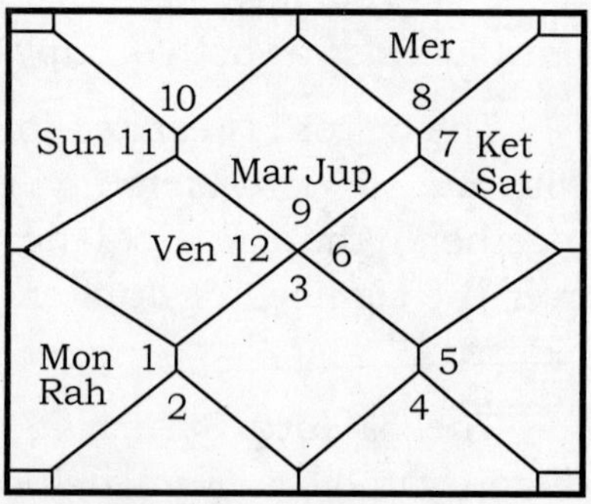


Balance of Vimsottari Dasa of **Mon 8Y 9M 14D**

This is the horoscope of a judicial officer.

The ascendant falls in sign Leo and the *navamsa* of Sagittarius. The ascendant lord Sun joins the 10th lord Venus and 2nd lord Mercury in the 11th house, in Gemini. The ascendant lord Sun obtains Saturn's *navamsa* Aquarius.

The 10th lord Venus joins the sign of Mercury and falls in the *navamsa* of Jupiter who is the main significator of Law. In *Rashi* chart, Jupiter aspects the 10th house.

The 6th lord Saturn joins his exaltation sign Libra, a sign of balance or also the sign owned by the 10th lord Venus.

The 5th house is owned by *Karaka* Jupiter, who joins the 4thhouse. Mercury, 10th lord Venus and the ascendant lord Sun lend their joint aspect over the 5th house, along with that of Saturn, from the 3rd house.

Ascendant falls in the amsa of Sagittarius with *karaka* Jupiter. Jupiter and the 10th lord Venus fall in the *navamsa* of Jupiter.

Venus owns the 10th, joins 11th, conjoins with the 2nd lord Mercury and ascendant lord, the Sun, and aspects the 5th. Venus falls in Jupiter's *navamsa.*

*Illustration : 12.17* *Horoscope No.: 175*

Date of birth : 21.11.1915 Time of birth : 07:30:00 hrs

Place of birth : Bangalore Lat 13:00:00 N Long 77:35:00E

Ayanamsa : 22:41:07 Sidereal Time : 11:06:18

| **Pln** | **Degree** | **Rasi** | **Nakshatra** | **Pad** |
|---|---|---|---|---|
| Asc | 19:54:44 | Sco | Jyestha | 1 |
| Sun | 4:59:24 | Sco | Anuradha | 1 |
| Mon | 27:49:40 | Ari | Krittika | 1 |
| Mar | 28:25:40 | Can | Aslesha | 4 |
| Mer (C) | 21:12:10 | Lib | Visakha | 1 |

| | | | | |
|---|---|---|---|---|
| Jup | 25:59:33 | Aqu | P Bhadrapad | 2 |
| Ven | 22:42:56 | Sco | Jyestha | 2 |
| Sat (R) | 23:22:08 | Gem | Punarvasu | 2 |
| Rah (R) | 18:26:04 | Cap | Sravna | 3 |
| Ket (R) | 18:26:04 | Can | Aslesha | 1 |

**Lagna Chart** **Navamsa Chart**

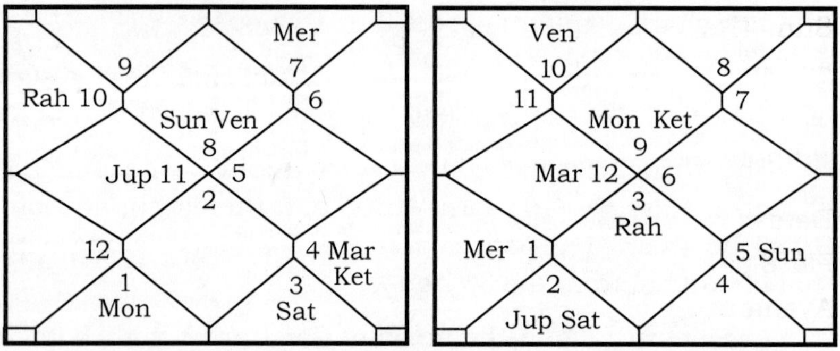


Balance of Vimsottari Dasa of **Sun 5Y 5M 22D**

This is the horoscope of a Civil Judge.

The ascendant falls in the *navamsa* of Jupiter. The 10th lord Sun joins the ascendant, in association with Venus. The lord of the ascendant, Mars, joins Jupiter's navamsa i.e. ascendant and its lord are under the influence of Jupiter, who is the *Karaka* of law profession.

The significator of law, Jupiter, and the planet of justice, Saturn, both are aspecting the 10th house.

Mars owns the 6th house. There is a mutual exchange of houses between 6th lord Mars and the 9th lord Moon.

The 5th lord Jupiter joins 4th and aspects 10th. The 4th lord Saturn also aspects the 5th house. Mercury does not show a prominent role in this horoscope regarding houses of vocation except that Mercury falls in the 5th from *navamsa* ascendant as an owner of 10th house.

In *navamsa* chart, Mercury owns $10^{th}$ and joins $5^{th}$; Jupiter rules ascendant and aspects the $10^{th}$ house and the $6^{th}$ lord Venus.

Since Mercury does not play any prominent role here, the native could not rise so much in his professional sphere and could only become a civil judge.

Venus joins ascendant, in association with the $10^{th}$ lord Sun. The $2^{nd}$ and $5^{th}$ lord, Jupiter, aspects the $10^{th}$ house, and Mercury and Saturn.

*Illustration : 12.18* *Horoscope No.: 176*

Date of birth : 17.12.1893 Time of birth : 08:02:00 hrs
Place of birth : Bangalore Lat 13:00:00 N Long 77:35:00E
Ayanamsa : 22:22:29 Sidereal Time : 13:45:51

| **Pln** | **Degree** | **Rasi** | **Nakshatra** | **Pad** |
|---|---|---|---|---|
| Asc | 27:07:14 | Sag | Uttarasadha | 1 |
| Sun | 3:04:29 | Sag | Moola | 1 |
| Mon | 11:19:50 | Pis | U Bhadrapad | 3 |
| Mar | 27:30:36 | Lib | Visakha | 3 |
| Mer | 11:56:31 | Sco | Anuradha | 3 |
| Jup (R) | 0:30:05 | Tau | Krittika | 2 |
| Ven | 19:56:20 | Cap | Sravna | 3 |
| Sat | 0:51:53 | Lib | Chitra | 3 |
| Rah (S) | 24:41:05 | Pis | Revati | 3 |
| Ket (S) | 24:41:05 | Vir | Chitra | 1 |

**Lagna Chart**

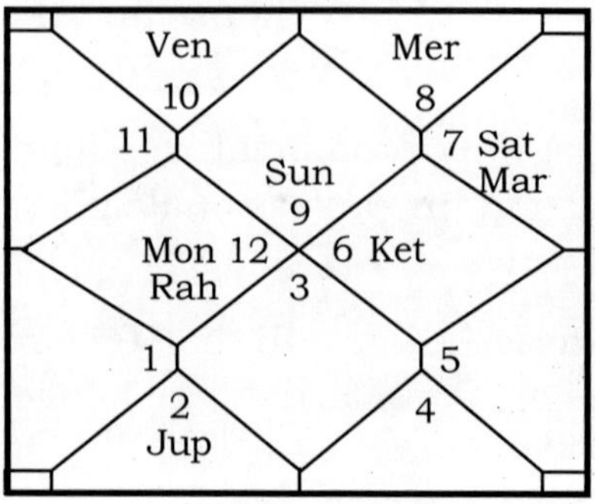


**Navamsa Chart**

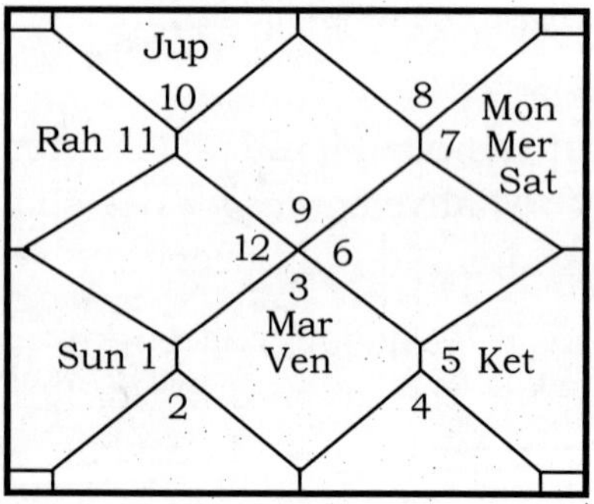


Balance of Vimsottari Dasa of **Sat 7Y 7M 7D**

The native is a High Court Judge.

The ascendant is Sagittarius whose lord Jupiter falls in the 6th house aspecting the 10th house and the 10th lord Mercury. The ascendant is *vargottam* and receives Saturn's aspect.

The 10th lord Mercury is under the mutual aspect with Jupiter, in reference to the 6th house. *Karaka* Jupiter aspects the 10th house and the 10th lord Mercury.

The 5th lord Mars has joined exalted Saturn in the 11th house. Both, Saturn and Mars, are aspecting the 5th house. The 5th lord Mars is aspecting the 6th lord Venus and the 5th and 6th houses.

The ascendant and exalted Saturn obtain *vargottam navamsa. Vargottam* and exalted Saturn's aspect on the ascendant and the 5th house gives a personality having a strong judicious outlook.

Venus and the lord of the 2nd house, Saturn, have mutual exchange of houses, 2nd and 11th influencing the 5th and the 6th houses.

## Conclusion :

To conclude all this we would like to say that Saturn and Jupiter both play most prominent role in bringing one in the legal profession. The $10^{th}$ and $6^{th}$ houses should be duly considered. There must be a relation of one with other for the greater success in the field of law.

Mercury is a planet of logic while the $5^{th}$ house denotes the way of one's thinking or the inclination of brain and intelligence. So, Mercury and the $5^{th}$ house should have an important role to play with the concerning planets and houses.

If Venus is related with the above combination, or it influences the ascendant, $5^{th}$, $6^{th}$ or $10^{th}$ house or lords thereof, one's going to the profession of law becomes cent percent sure.

Libra, Sagittarius and Gemini are the signs, which have their important say in deciding legal profession. Libra is a sign of balance and Sagittarius is for justice.

The ascendant must be taken into account for the judgment of the aptitude of the native.

If a careful judgment and a serious study for the determination of vocation is made, one will not err in judgment of profession if it is through law or a legal profession, should one remember the above findings for determining the legal profession.

It is ascertained that Jupiter, Saturn and Mercury are the major significators of the legal occupation and Venus should be considered as supporting significator. The $5^{th}$ and $6^{th}$ house must have a concern with the $10^{th}$ house or the ascendant, in one way or the other. If the $10^{th}$, $5^{th}$ and $6^{th}$ houses are under the influence of significator Jupiter, Saturn and Mercury, the legal profession will be the occupation of the native. If the significators are related with $10^{th}$ house or its lord, one will opt law as his means of livelihood. These houses or the concerning planets, if correspond with airy signs Gemini, Libra and Aquarius, the profession connected with law will more strongly be pronounced. Sagittarius and Libra signs also have a deep concern with law professionals in their horoscopes. *Atmakaraka* planets should never be ignored during the examination of most appropriate profession of the native.

If someone asks whether the legal profession will be appropriate for the native? it is very easy to reply on the basis of above planetary configurations. But it is a tough exercise to predict that only the legal profession will suit to the native. It is so because many professions and occupations come under the ruler ship of single planet. Only the clear conception about the distinction of the planetary configuration for various professions, along with thorough experience of thousands of horoscopes, can make one perfect in finding out most appropriate profession for the native. We have explained the art of the judgment of exact, most appropriate and suitable occupation for the native elsewhere, and that will be of immense benefit for the readers.

•

## Chapter-13

# Engagement of Chartered Accountant

Chartered Accountancy is a high educational qualification and it is not a designation or post. A Chartered Accountant can work in Banks, industries, in any financial institutions or otherwise he may work as consultant or lawyer. There are number of Chartered Accountants, who are working as Income Tax as consultant. Even then, we feel that the qualification of Chartered Accountant is a tough and very important one. The native, who has acquired the qualification of Chartered Accountant, is sure to have bright future prospects and extremely handsome income through the same. If the horoscope of a subject indicates the education of accounts, one should decide to go for Chartered Accountancy instead of engineering, legal or medical profession.

Mercury must be strong in the birth chart and should influence the $10^{th}$, $2^{nd}$ or $5^{th}$ house, in one way or the other. This is so because Mercury makes one talented in the art of planning and organizing. It gives a methodical way of working under specific system, rules and regulations. Strong and well-disposed Mercury means high degree of intelligence, sharpness of brain, logical way of planning, thinking, working and conversation. It gives ability of deep analysis and synthesis, so well placed Mercury is the foremost requirement for one, who is inclined to go for Chartered Accountancy.

Jupiter is also an essential planet, who plays a prominent role in making one Chartered Accountant but it should jointly influence the concerning houses along with Mercury. Jupiter is a thinker, philosopher and scientist. A well-disposed Jupiter bestows honesty, truthfulness, and sincerity and makes one talented to work most systematically, without any diplomacy and manipulations. However, Mercury may give the art of manipulations etc., which becomes essential, at times, in shaping out the projects and plans in a specific manner. Joint influence of Mercury and Jupiter, on each other, or on the $10^{th}$ and $5^{th}$, or $2^{nd}$ and $10^{th}$, or $11^{th}$ and $5^{th}$, or $2^{nd}$ and $5^{th}$, or $10^{th}$ and $11^{th}$, or $2^{nd}$ and $11^{th}$ can make one successful Chartered Accountant, provided the effect of Mars is also there in building the career of the native.

It has also been observed that airy signs i.e. Gemini, Libra and Aquarius are more likely to direct the native towards the education of Chartered Accountancy. Such native should plan to acquire the qualification of Chartered Accountant as that will be the most appropriate and suitable qualification for his occupation. He will earn his livelihood owing to his this educational qualification of Chartered Accountant either by working in Banks, Income Tax, Sales Tax, legal profession, auditor or as consultant.

*Illustration : 13.1* **(SKG)** *Horoscope No.: 177*

Date of birth : 16.11.1945 Time of birth : 01:17:34 hrs

Place of birth : Saharanpur Lat 29:58:00 N Long 77:33:00E

Ayanamsa : 23:05:45 Sidereal Time : 4:35:54

| **Pln** | **Degree** | **Rasi** | **Nakshatra** | **Pad** |
|---|---|---|---|---|
| Asc | 18:37:06 | Leo | P Phalguni | 2 |
| Sun | 0:00:13 | Sco | Visakha | 4 |
| Mon | 6:31:33 | Pis | U Bhadrapad | 1 |
| Mar | 7:51:54 | Can | Pushya | 2 |
| Mer | 22:09:16 | Sco | Jyestha | 2 |
| Jup | 24:15:57 | Vir | Chitra | 1 |
| Ven | 11:19:03 | Lib | Svati | 2 |

| | | | | |
|---|---|---|---|---|
| Sat (R) | 1:43:32 | Can | Punarvasu | 4 |
| Rah (R) | 7:31:20 | Gem | Ardra | 1 |
| Ket (R) | 7:31:20 | Sag | Moola | 3 |

**Lagna Chart**

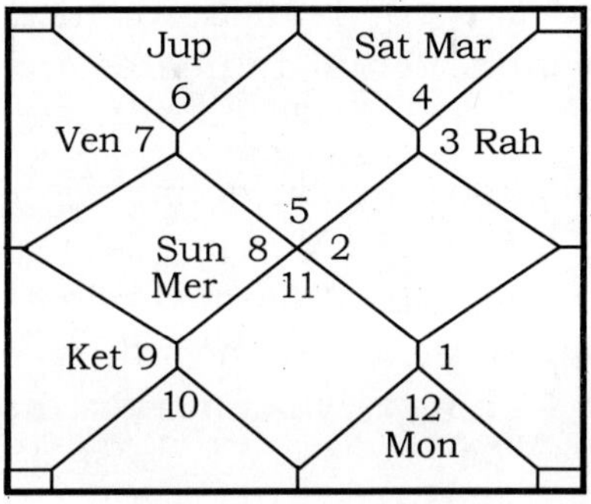


**Navamsa Chart**

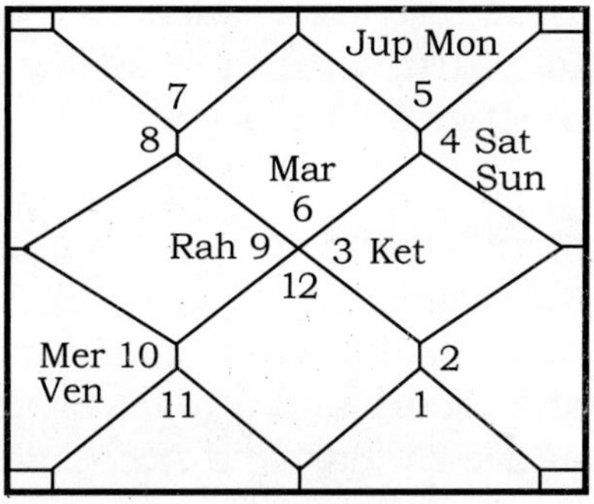


Balance of Vimsottari Dasa of **Sat 14Y 5M 12D**

The native is a reputed and competent Chartered Accountant, who is at present engaged in the practice of Income Tax at Allahabad. He has solved various complicated cases of Income Tax quite successfully and competently.

The native was born in Leo ascendant. The 10th house is owned by Venus, who joins its own signs Libra, in the third house. The fifth lord Jupiter is posited in 2nd house in Virgo, ruled by Mercury and aspects the 10th house. Mercury also lends its aspects over the 10th house. Thus, the 10th house is aspected by Jupiter, Mercury and ascendant lord Sun, whereas the 9th house is aspected by the 10th lord Venus. This indicates the job having a concern with the qualification of Chartered Accountant. We have mentioned earlier in the Chapter of "Legal Profession" that the involvement of the 5th and 6th house will be present in the horoscope of practicing advocates. Here, the 6th lord Saturn is associated with *Yogakaraka* Mars in the 12th house. 6th Lord Saturn aspects the 5th lord Jupiter and *Yogakaraka* Mars aspects the 10th lord Venus. The 9th house is aspected by the 6th lord Saturn and 10th lord Venus. This is a positive combination for a legal profession.

In this horoscope, Jupiter is *Atmakaraka* planet, who falls in the sign of Mercury and obtains the *navamsa* of the Sun. $10^{th}$ lord Venus is the strongest planet in this birth chart as it obtains 1.28 *Shadabalas* and falls in own sign Libra. Venus is posited in the *navamsa* of Saturn, which owns the $6^{th}$ house. Thus, the involvement of $6^{th}$, $5^{th}$ and $10^{th}$ houses, identical to Saturn, Jupiter, Mercury and Venus indicates the practice of Law.

The $4^{th}$ house signifies educational qualification, where Mercury and Sun are placed in Scorpio. Mercury falls in own constellation *Jyestha*, whereas Sun falls in Jupiter's constellation *Visakha*. This is a clear picture of the influence of Mercury and Jupiter on the $4^{th}$ house, which makes the native a Chartered Accountant.

*Illustration : 13.2* (**SKA**) *Horoscope No.: 178*

Date of birth : 15.08.1954 Time of birth : 22:13:00 hrs
Place of birth : Lucknow Lat 26:50:00 N Long 80:54:00E
Ayanamsa : 23:13:41 Sidereal Time : 19:40:48

| **Pln** | **Degree** | **Rasi** | **Nakshatra** | **Pad** |
|---|---|---|---|---|
| Asc | 10:52:19 | Ari | Asvini | 4 |
| Sun | 29:04:36 | Can | Aslesha | 4 |
| Mon | 15:16:49 | Aqu | Satabhisha | 3 |
| Mar | 4:20:56 | Sag | Moola | 2 |
| Mer (C) | 22:34:27 | Can | Aslesha | 2 |
| Jup | 25:14:53 | Gem | Punarvasu | 2 |
| Ven | 13:59:38 | Vir | Hasta | 2 |
| Sat | 10:41:38 | Lib | Svati | 2 |
| Rah (R) | 21:03:52 | Sag | Purvasadha | 3 |
| Ket (R) | 21:03:52 | Gem | Punarvasu | 1 |

**Lagna Chart**

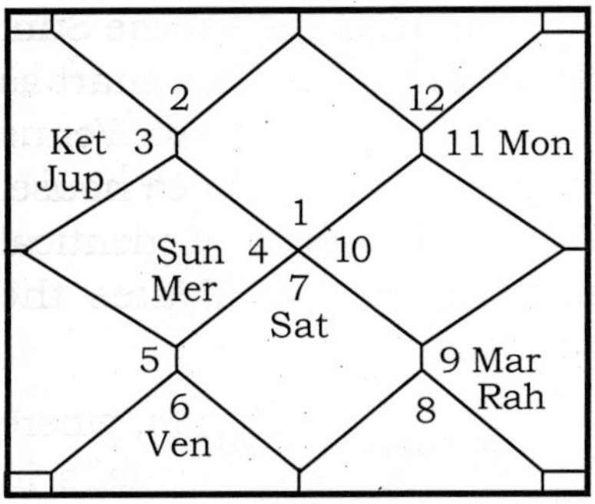


**Navamsa Chart**

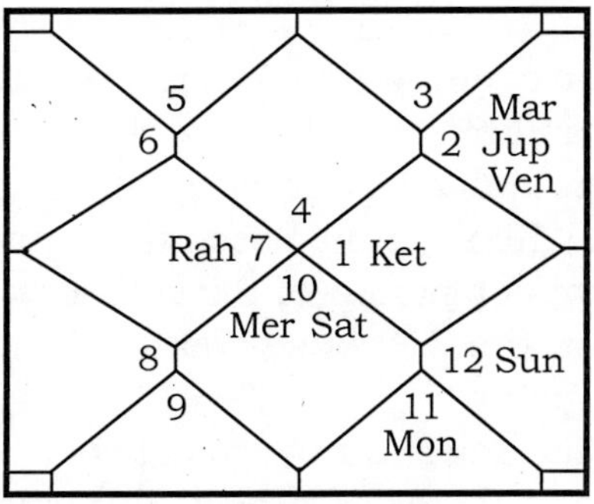


Balance of Vimsottari Dasa of **Rah 6Y 4M 13D**

The native is a very senior Chartered Accountant and Director of Finance in U.P. Power Corporation. He had been Finance Controller in various government departments earlier. The native is extremely noble, gentle and honest officer and he possesses high degree of intellect and fertile brain. He finds out the appropriate solution of various complicated problems of accounts very easily and quickly. The native is loved, liked and appreciated by one and all owing to his cooperative nature and friendly behavior.

The native is born in Aries ascendant. Lord of the 10$^{th}$ and 11$^{th}$ house, Saturn, is exalted in the 7$^{th}$ house and obtains own *navamsa.* 9$^{th}$ lord Jupiter falls in Gemini in 3$^{rd}$ house and aspects the 9$^{th}$ house of its own and ascendant lord Mars as well.

The Sun is *Atmakaraka* planet and it is quite strong in *shadabalas* as it obtains 1.41 *Shadabalas.* The Sun falls in 4$^{th}$ house with Mercury in *Aslesha nakshatra,* ruled by Mercury. Moreover, Sun obtains *navamsa* of Jupiter and it clearly shows the joint effect of Mercury and Jupiter over the 4$^{th}$ house, which shows that the native will acquire the qualification of Chartered Accountant. It will not be out of place to mention that the 4$^{th}$ house rules over the educational qualification of the native, whereas the 5$^{th}$ house controls the intelligence, memory, brightness, fertility of brain, imagination and creativity etc. The 10$^{th}$ and 11$^{th}$ lord Saturn is the strongest planet in this birth chart and obtains own *navamsa*. It is exalted in the 7th house and aspects the ascendant, the ascendant lord Mars, the 5th lord Sun, the 3rd and 6th lord Mercury, the 9th house and the 4th house. Saturn is quite strong and well-placed planet in this birth chart, which has a blessed the native very high position during the major period of Saturn. However, it is believed that Saturn in the 7th house creates delay in the marriage and does not give a beautiful wife, generally. We have established the finding in our various books on marriage that a well disposed Saturn gives a beautiful wife, in addition to high degree of conjugal bliss. Saturn, if exalted in the 7th house, or posited in own sign, does not delay or deny the marriage. The native was married at 23 years of age with an exceptionally beautiful, charming, pretty and very fair complexioned female. However, the analysis of this birth chart indicates the qualification of Chartered Accountant and a very high position in government departments having a control over finance.

*Illustration : 13.3* (**PT**) *Horoscope No.: 179*

Date of birth : 27.04.1960 Time of birth : 00:20:00 hrs
Place of birth : Lucknow Lat 26:50:00 N Long 80:54:00E
Ayanamsa : 23:18:06 Sidereal Time : 14:32:40

| **Pln** | **Degree** | **Rasi** | **Nakshatra** | **Pad** |
|---|---|---|---|---|
| Asc | 1:38:37 | Cap | Uttarasadha | 2 |
| Sun | 13:13:26 | Ari | Asvini | 4 |
| Mon (C) | 23:14:13 | Ari | Bharani | 3 |
| Mar | 25:34:58 | Aqu | P Bhadrapad | 2 |
| Mer | 22:39:59 | Pis | Revati | 2 |
| Jup (R) | 10:14:45 | Sag | Moola | 4 |
| Ven | 28:02:11 | Pis | Revati | 4 |
| Sat (S) | 25:07:37 | Sag | Purvasadha | 4 |

| | | | | |
|---|---|---|---|---|
| Rah (R) | 0:39:11 | Vir | U Phalguni | 2 |
| Ket (R) | 0:39:11 | Pis | P Bhadrapad | 4 |

**Lagna Chart**

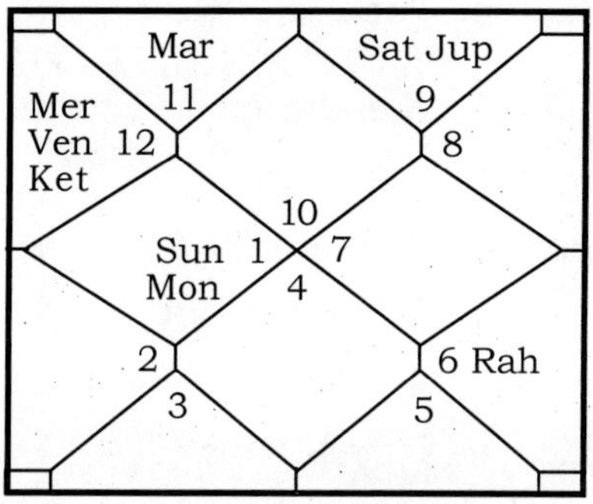


**Navamsa Chart**

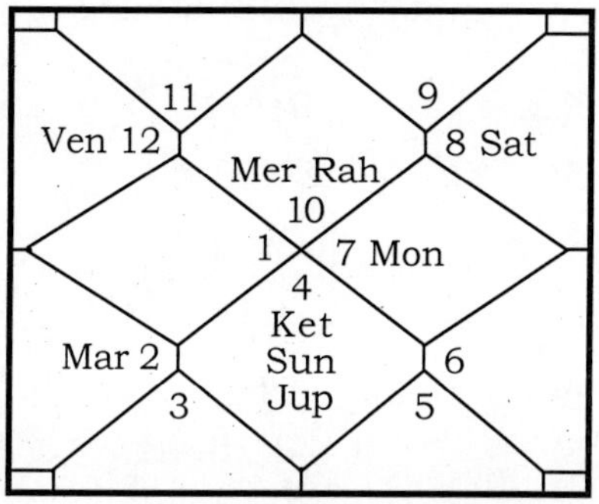


Balance of Vimsottari Dasa of **Ven 5Y 1M 22D**

The native is a very costly lawyer of Income Tax at Delhi. The native was born in Capricorn ascendant. The lord of the 10th house Venus obtains *Vargottam navamsa* and it is associated with 6th and 9th lord Mercury. Venus and Mercury, both, aspect the 9th house, whereas Sun and Moon lend their aspect over the 10th house. Lord of the 4th house, Mars, is placed in the 2nd house, in Jupiter's constellation *Uttra Bhadrapada*. Mars is posited in Saturn's sign Aquarius and is aspected by Saturn as well. 4th house, where Sun and Moon are placed, receives the aspect of Jupiter and 4th lord falls in Jupiter's constellation. Therefore, educational qualification of Chartered Accountant is prominently indicated. Venus is *Atmakaraka* and *Yogakaraka* planet and owns the 10th house. Venus is exalted and obtains *vargottam navamsa*, identical to constellation of Mercury i.e. *Revati*. This also signifies that the occupation of the native will be connected with his educational qualification or Chartered Accountant.

*Illustration : 13.4* (**RM**) *Horoscope No.: 180*

Date of birth : 28.03.1968 Time of birth : 01:48:00 hrs
Place of birth : Lucknow Lat 26:50:00 N Long 80:54:00E
Ayanamsa : 23:24:42 Sidereal Time : 14:02:53

| Pln | Degree | Rasi | Nakshatra | Pad |
|---|---|---|---|---|
| Asc | 23:52:07 | Sag | Purvasadha | 4 |
| Sun | 13:48:45 | Pis | U Bhadrapad | 4 |
| Mon | 1:18:23 | Pis | P Bhadrapad | 4 |
| Mar | 6:28:57 | Ari | Asvini | 2 |
| Mer | 20:15:48 | Aqu | P Bhadrapad | 1 |
| Jup (R) | 3:23:08 | Leo | Magha | 2 |
| Ven | 21:43:32 | Aqu | P Bhadrapad | 1 |
| Sat (C) | 20:54:40 | Pis | Revati | 2 |
| Rah (R/C) | 25:09:43 | Pis | Revati | 3 |
| Ket (R) | 25:09:43 | Vir | Chitra | 1 |

**Lagna Chart**

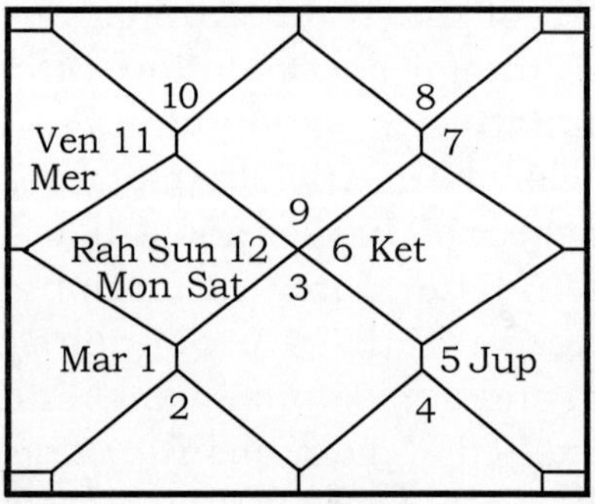


**Navamsa Chart**

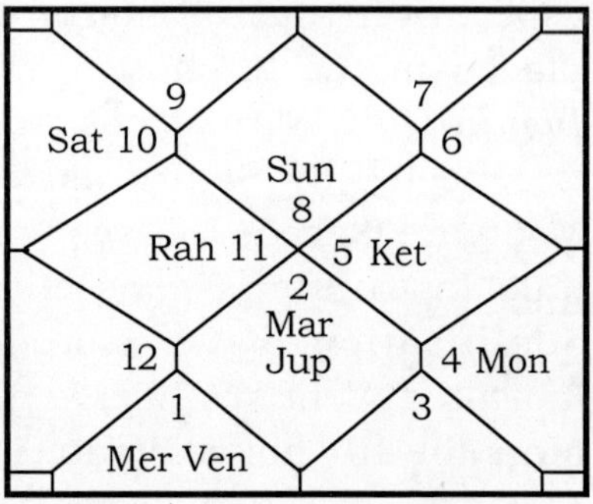


Balance of Vimsottari Dasa of **Jup 2Y 5M 5D**

The name of the native is present in the Guinness Book of World Records for his outstanding professional qualifications. He has as many as 18 professional degrees.

The native was born in Sagittarius ascendant. The 10th house is owned by Mercury, who is associated with 6th and 11th lord Venus. Mercury and Venus jointly aspect *lagna* lord Jupiter, who occupies the 9th house. The ascendant is aspected by its lord Jupiter and Saturn. The 4th house, which indicates educational qualification and certificate education, is occupied by the 9th lord Sun, 2nd and 3rd lord Saturn, 8th lord Moon and Rahu. There is mutual exchange between the 9th lord Sun and 4th lord Jupiter. This is a *Mahayoga,* which indicates that the native will acquire high degree of qualifications. Here, Venus is *Atmakaraka* planet and falls in Jupiter's constellation *Poorva Bhadrapada.* Jupiter, Mercury and Venus aspect each other mutually and this indicates the native will be highly qualified.

Ascendant lord Jupiter and 10th lord Mercury are placed under mutual aspect, identical to 9th and 3rd house, which signifies the qualification of Chartered Accountant as well, in addition to various other qualifications like Ph.D. etc.

*Illustration : 13.5* (**VM**) *Horoscope No.: 181*

Date of birth : 18.10.1958 Time of birth : 08:22:00 hrs
Place of birth : Lucknow Lat 26:50:00 N Long 80:54:00E
Ayanamsa : 23:16:58 Sidereal Time : 9:59:58

| **Pln** | **Degree** | **Rasi** | **Nakshatra** | **Pad** |
|---|---|---|---|---|
| Asc | 29:24:01 | Lib | Visakha | 3 |
| Sun | 0:56:36 | Lib | Chitra | 3 |
| Mon | 12:44:09 | Sag | Moola | 4 |
| Mar (R) | 8:48:21 | Tau | Krittika | 4 |
| Mer (C) | 9:31:42 | Lib | Svati | 1 |
| Jup | 14:55:14 | Lib | Svati | 3 |
| Ven (C) | 24:44:08 | Vir | Chitra | 1 |
| Sat | 28:09:13 | Sco | Jyestha | 4 |

| | | | | |
|---|---|---|---|---|
| Rah (R/D) | 29:05:33 | Vir | Chitra | 2 |
| Ket (R) | 29:05:33 | Pis | Revati | 4 |

**Lagna Chart**

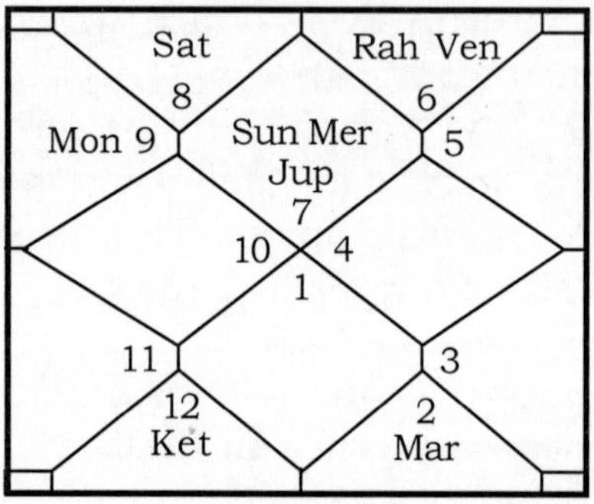


**Navamsa Chart**

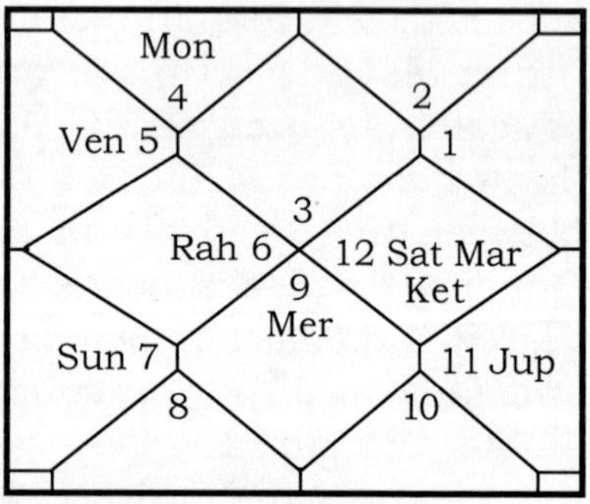


Balance of Vimsottari Dasa of **Ket 0Y 3M 23D**

This lady was highly talented and intelligent, from the very beginning of her educational career. She acquired the qualification of Chartered Accountant at an early age. She joined Punjab National Bank as Chartered Accountant. It was her bad luck that in spite of her brilliant and prosperous career, she suffered from Cancer and met with a pathetic death in her early thirties.

The Sun, Mercury and Jupiter are very well associated in Libra ascendant. $10^{th}$ lord Moon falls in Sagittarius. *Yogakaraka* Saturn is posited in *Jyestha nakshatra,* ruled by Mercury and obtains *navamsa* of Jupiter. $4^{th}$ and $5^{th}$ lord Saturn is *Atmakaraka* planet and obtains *navamsa* of Jupiter. The $9^{th}$ lord Mercury also obtains the *navamsa* of Jupiter. This is a clear indication of her being a Chartered Accountant.

*Illustration : 13.6* **(RP)** *Horoscope No.: 182*

| | | | |
|---|---|---|---|
| Date of birth | : 22.07.1978 | Time of birth : | 11:30:00 hrs |
| Place of birth | : Lucknow | Lat 26:50:00 N | Long 80:54:00E |
| Ayanamsa | : 23:33:27 | Sidereal Time : | 7:22:09 |

| **Pln** | **Degree** | **Rasi** | **Nakshatra** | **Pad** |
|---|---|---|---|---|
| Asc | 24:44:58 | Vir | Chitra | 1 |
| Sun | 5:31:35 | Can | Pushya | 1 |
| Mon | 5:32:32 | Aqu | Dhanishtha | 4 |
| Mar | 28:25:30 | Leo | U Phalguni | 1 |
| Mer | 2:25:48 | Leo | Magha | 1 |
| Jup (C) | 26:54:55 | Gem | Punarvasu | 3 |
| Ven | 17:55:30 | Leo | P Phalguni | 2 |
| Sat | 5:56:49 | Leo | Magha | 2 |
| Rah (R) | 4:46:50 | Vir | U Phalguni | 3 |
| Ket (R) | 4:46:50 | Pis | U Bhadrapad | 1 |

**Lagna Chart**

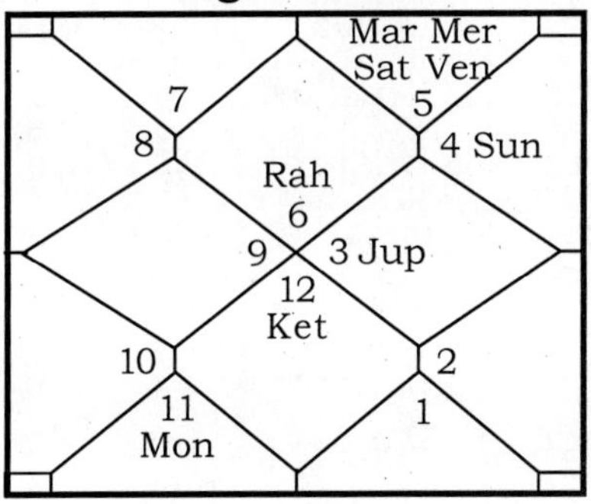


**Navamsa Chart**

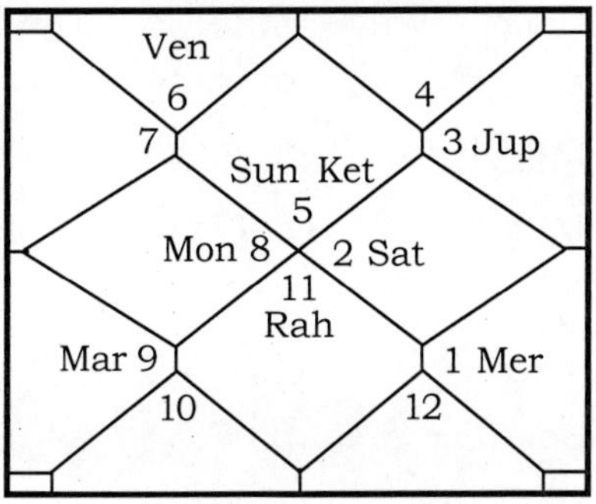


Balance of Vimsottari Dasa of **Mar 0Y 7M 2D**

This horoscope belongs to a lady, who completed her Chartered Accountancy in a very short time.

She was born in Virgo ascendant and the lord of the 4th house, Jupiter, is posited in the 10th house, identical to sign Gemini and aspects the 4th house of its own. The 10th lord Mercury is posited in the 12th house, in association with 2nd and 9th lord Venus, 3rd and 8th lord Mars and 5th and 6th lord Saturn. Mercury obtains the *navamsa* of Mars. Mars obtains *navamsa* of Jupiter and Jupiter obtains *navamsa* of Mercury. Jupiter also obtains *Vargottam navamsa,* in the sign of Mercury, Gemini, and falls in own constellation *Punarvasu.* 2nd and 9th lord Venus obtains the *navamsa* of Mercury. Thus, prominence of Jupiter and Mercury, with regard to 4th and 10th, is clearly visible in this birth chart. This indicates the educational qualification of Chartered Accountant. However, due to strong 12th house, she is not engaged in any occupation so far, in spite of high educational qualification.

*Illustration : 13.7* **(RPT)** *Horoscope No.: 183*

Date of birth : 23.12.1958 Time of birth : 06:30:00 hrs
Place of birth : Lucknow Lat 26:50:00 N Long 80:54:00E
Ayanamsa : 23:17:07 Sidereal Time : 12:27:52

| **Pln** | **Degree** | **Rasi** | **Nakshatra** | **Pad** |
|---|---|---|---|---|
| Asc | 1:32:12 | Sag | Moola | 1 |
| Sun | 7:24:25 | Sag | Moola | 3 |
| Mon | 2:06:55 | Tau | Krittika | 2 |
| Mar | 23:20:31 | Ari | Bharani | 4 |
| Mer | 16:47:55 | Sco | Jyestha | 1 |
| Jup | 28:59:26 | Lib | Visakha | 3 |
| Ven | 17:30:10 | Sag | Purvasadha | 2 |
| Sat (D) | 5:07:51 | Sag | Moola | 2 |
| Rah (R) | 26:23:55 | Vir | Chitra | 1 |
| Ket (R) | 26:23:55 | Pis | Revati | 3 |

**Lagna Chart**

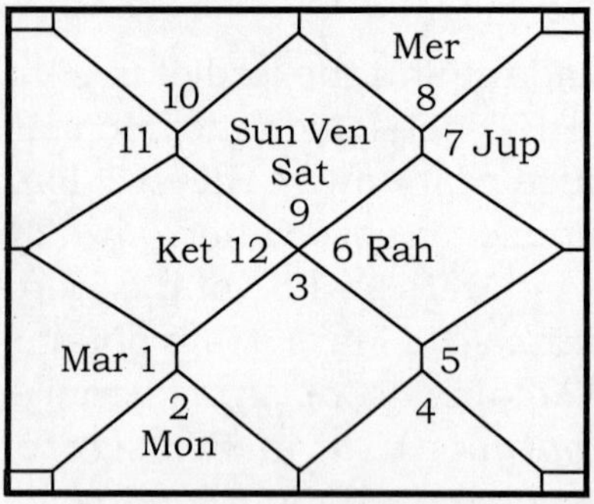


**Navamsa Chart**

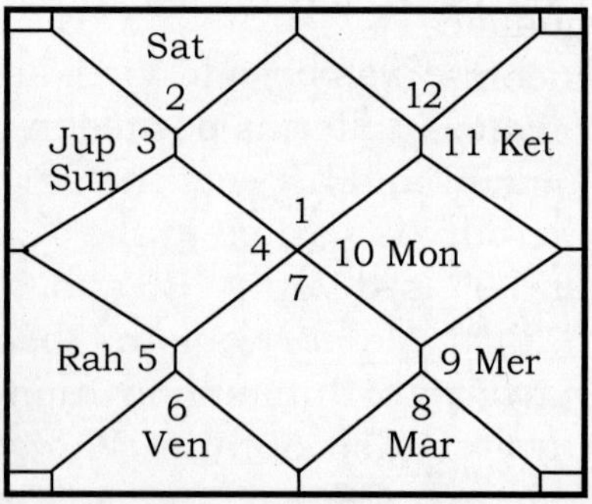


Balance of Vimsottari Dasa of **Sun 3Y 6M 17D**

The native was born in Sagittarius ascendant, whose lord Jupiter occupies the $11^{th}$ house and the $10^{th}$ lord Mercury falls in the $12^{th}$ house, identical to Scorpio sign. The $10^{th}$ lord Mercury is there in own constellation *Jyestha*, in Martian sign Scorpio. Mars joins the $5^{th}$ house, identical to his own sign Aries, and aspects the ascendant lord Jupiter and the $10^{th}$ lord Mercury.

Jupiter is *Atmakaraka* planet in this birth chart, who falls in own constellation *Visakha* and obtains the *navamsa* of Mercury. Thus, the *Atmakaraka* planet Jupiter also indicates that the native should become a Chartered Accountant, as Jupiter is under the influence of Mars, Mercury and Venus. The $10^{th}$ lord Mercury is also under the influence of Mars, Mercury and Moon. This combination of the influence of Mercury, Jupiter and Mars, who are the professional aspect of the native, shows that the native will become a Chartered Accountant.

The $4^{th}$ house is occupied by Ketu and ruled by Jupiter. Ketu is posited in *Revati* constellation, ruled by Mercury and occupies Pisces sign, ruled by Jupiter. The $4^{th}$ house rules over the high education and the educational qualification of the native. Therefore, the native acquired the qualification of C.A. within a short period.

We believe that the $4^{th}$ house should also be examined, along with the other concerning houses, for acquiring the qualification of C.A. The native, who has acquired the qualification of C.A., may become a leading consultant of Income Tax, Sales Tax or he may deal in other kinds of taxation and revenue services, in addition to Bank services joining as Auditor or Accountant etc.

*Illustration : 13.8* **(SS)** *Horoscope No.: 184*

| | | | |
|---|---|---|---|
| Date of birth | : 20.01.1977 | Time of birth : | 01:10:00 hrs |
| Place of birth | : Lucknow | Lat 26:50:00 N | Long 80:54:00E |
| Ayanamsa | : 23:32:21 | Sidereal Time : | 8:59:55 |

| Pln | Degree | Rasi | Nakshatra | Pad |
|---|---|---|---|---|
| Asc | 16:12:00 | Lib | Svati | 3 |
| Sun | 6:05:46 | Cap | Uttarasadha | 3 |
| Mon (D) | 9:04:17 | Cap | Uttarasadha | 4 |
| Mar (C) | 20:37:30 | Sag | Purvasadha | 3 |
| Mer | 13:57:53 | Sag | Purvasadha | 1 |
| Jup | 27:40:03 | Ari | Krittika | 1 |
| Ven | 23:01:55 | Aqu | P Bhadrapad | 1 |
| Sat (R) | 20:59:30 | Can | Aslesha | 2 |
| Rah (R) | 5:21:19 | Lib | Chitra | 4 |
| Ket (R) | 5:21:19 | Ari | Asvini | 2 |

**Lagna Chart**

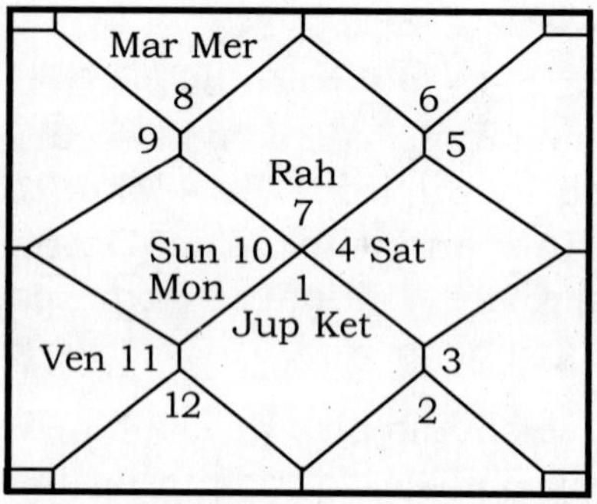


**Navamsa Chart**

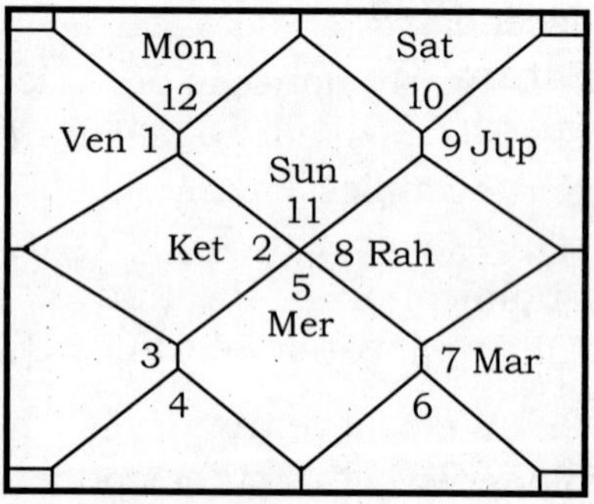


Balance of Vimsottari Dasa of **Sun 0Y 5M 0D**

The native was born in Libra ascendant. *Yogkaraka* Saturn occupies the 10th house in Cancer and falls in *Aslesha* constellation, ruled by Mercury. The 10th lord Moon and 11th lord Sun are well associated in the 4th house and lend their aspect over natal Saturn. In fact, there is a mutual exchange between the 10th lord Moon and 4th lord Saturn. However, 10th lord Moon obtains the *navamsa* of Jupiter, the significator of Chartered Accountancy. Mercury and Mars are also the significators for Chartered Accountant and should be taken into account. The 3rd house has also a concern with educational and writing ability.

In this birth chart, Mars and Mercury both are posited in 3rd house, in Jupiter's sign Sagittarius and both are aspected by Jupiter. In fact, there is mutual exchange between Mars and Jupiter, showing success as Chartered Accountant. Once again, it will not be out of place to mention that Jupiter and Mercury, if influence each other, along with Mars, in one way or the other way, either by conjunction or aspect or by mutual exchange of signs, *navamsas* or *nakshatras*, one is likely to become a successful Chartered Accountant.

Jupiter is *Atmakaraka* planet in this horoscope and falls in the 7th house in Aries. Jupiter aspects the ascendant, the 3rd house, Mars and Mercury, whereas Jupiter is aspected by *Yogkaraka* Saturn. Saturn in the 10th house, for Libra ascendant, is a great asset for the native. In this birth chart, Saturn occupies the 10th house as well as it obtains own *navamsa*. Thus, the 10th house is quite strong and its lord Moon is the strongest planet in this horoscope as it obtains 1.61 *Shadabalas* as well as *navamsa* of Jupiter. Thus, the profession connected with Chartered Accountant is distinctly visible in this birth chart.

Involvement of airy sign i.e. Gemini, Libra and Aquarius, in addition to Mercury and Mars, strengthen the combination of success as Chartered Accountant.

*Illustration : 13.9* **(NA)** *Horoscope No.: 185*

Date of birth : 28.08.1963 Time of birth : 10:15:00 hrs

Place of birth : Dhalpur Lat 26:43:00 N Long 77:53:00E

Ayanamsa : 23:20:41 Sidereal Time : 8:19:18

| **Pln** | **Degree** | **Rasi** | **Nakshatra** | **Pad** |
|---|---|---|---|---|
| Asc | 7:34:44 | Lib | Svati | 1 |
| Sun | 10:49:38 | Leo | Magha | 4 |
| Mon | 20:49:56 | Sco | Jyestha | 2 |

| | | | | |
|---|---|---|---|---|
| Mar | 26:41:10 | Vir | Chitra | 2 |
| Mer | 7:43:26 | Vir | U Phalguni | 4 |
| Jup (R) | 25:34:12 | Pis | Revati | 3 |
| Ven (D) | 10:19:00 | Leo | Magha | 4 |
| Sat (R) | 25:18:49 | Cap | Dhanishtha | 1 |
| Rah | 26:10:17 | Gem | Punarvasu | 2 |
| Ket | 26:10:17 | Sag | Purvasadha | 4 |

**Lagna Chart**

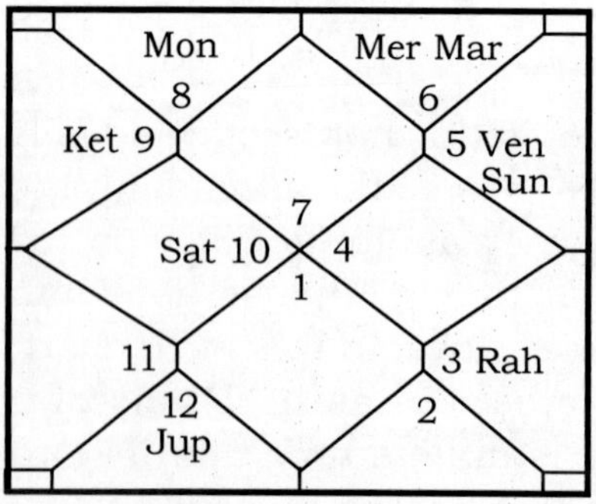


**Navamsa Chart**

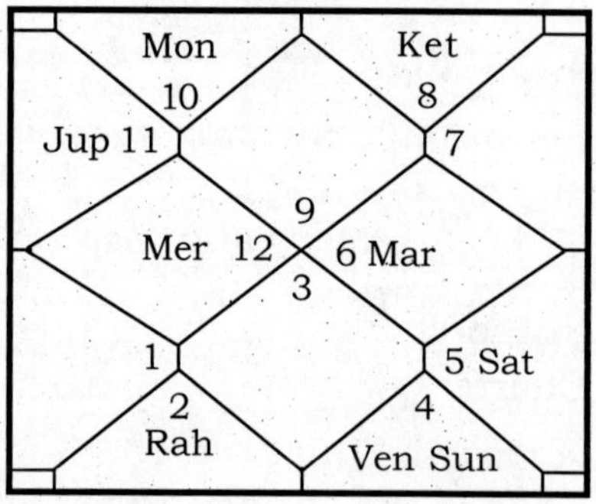


Balance of Vimsottari Dasa of **Mer 11Y 8M 8D**

The native was a famous Income Tax lawyer of Lucknow. He completed Chartered Accountancy within a short period, in spite of his extremely busy engagements as Income Tax lawyer. The native unfortunately could not live long and expired suddenly during the sub-period of Mars in the major period of the Sun. Here, we are dealing with the planetary combinations, for Chartered Accountant, in the birth chart of the native.

The 10th lord Moon occupies the 2nd house, in Scorpio, in Mercury's constellation *Jyestha*. Thus, the 10th house has a collective influence of the Moon, Mars and Mercury. Moon obtains the *navamsa* of *Yogkaraka* Saturn. That is why he was engaged in legal profession.

Mars is *Atmakaraka* planet in this birth chart and it is posited in the 12th house, in sign Virgo and obtains *vargottam navamsa*. This *Atmakaraka* planet is under the influence of Mercury and Jupiter. This strongly indicates that the native will acquire a high degree of accounts.

The lord of the $4^{th}$ and $5^{th}$ house, Saturn, is posited in own sign Capricorn giving rise to *Sasa Mahapurusha Rajyoga*. Saturn falls in *Dhanishtha* constellation, ruled by Mars. Saturn aspects Jupiter, whereas Saturn and Jupiter both lend their aspect over the $10^{th}$ house. Jupiter aspects the $10^{th}$ house, $10^{th}$ lord Moon, the $2^{nd}$ lord Mars and significator Mercury. This is a powerful combination of Chartered Accountancy present in this birth chart. Jupiter falls in own sign Pisces, in Mercury's constellation *Revati* and obtains *navamsa* of Saturn.

Thus, if Jupiter and Mercury influence each other, in one or the other way, and affect the $10^{th}$ house, in addition to the positive effect of Mars, one should plan to work as Chartered Accountant. This is the best use of Astrology.

Chartered Accountancy is a tough qualification and even the bright students can complete the course, only if they work hard on a regular basis. There are so many scholars, who start doing C.A. but fail to complete it. Firm determination, regular hard work and intellectual brain only can make one able to acquire a degree of Chartered Accountancy successfully. The judgement of the same can be made on the basis of the birth chart of the native. The $5^{th}$ and $10^{th}$ houses must be strong along with the $4^{th}$ house.

Jupiter, Mercury and Mars are the significators of Chartered Accountant, in which Mercury should be strong enough without any kind of affliction. If Mercury and Jupiter influence each other, either by mutual aspect or by conjunction or by mutual exchange of their signs, *navamsas* or *nakshatras*, one is likely to do Chartered Accountancy provided Mars has also an influence over the $10^{th}$ house or the significators, Jupiter and Mercury in one or the other way.

*Atmakaraka* planet and lord of the $10^{th}$ house are equally important, along with the lords of the $2^{nd}$, $11^{th}$ and $9^{th}$ houses, which play a prominent role in the judgement of one's profession. The sign, constellation and the *navamsa* of these planets must examined, for each and every profession. The involvement of the $6^{th}$ house with $10^{th}$ lord or lord of the ascendant, indicates livelihood through service, whereas the involvement of $10^{th}$, $11^{th}$ and $2^{nd}$ house, generally, gives rise to independent occupation like consultants and other professionals. However, for business, the $7^{th}$ house and its lord may also influence the professional aspects of the native.

●

CHAPTER-14

# Planets Manage The Management Course

M.B.A. courses are most prevalent and popular globally, nowadays. Mostly students prepare to do M.B.A. as an additional qualification after completion of course of engineering, banking, computer, journalism etc. If following planetary configuration is there, in the birth chart of the native, he is likely to do M.B.A. –

1. Mercury, Venus and Moon are the main significators of M.B.A. course.
2. If Jupiter is also involved, as a supporting significator, one may do M.B.A. in finance successfully.
3. If Mars has a supporting significance, one will do better marketing after doing M.B.A. in marketing.
4. If Saturn's influence is there over the combination of Mercury, Moon and Venus, in respect of profession, one is likely to enter in M.B.A. (H.R.), M.B.A. (I.T.), M.B.A. (Personnel) etc.

Over all prominent role of Mercury, Moon and Venus must be examined. If these planets have an influence over the $10^{th}$, $2^{nd}$ and $11^{th}$ or $3^{rd}$ house, one is likely to do M.B.A. in respective branches.

Apart from the concerning houses of profession, if the combination of these planets has an influence over the $3^{rd}$ and $5^{th}$ house, one will certainly go for M.B.A. Proper examination and careful judgement of a horoscope will reveal that the appropriate profession for the native is business management in a specific or particular branch. This judgement, if made well in time, will be of immense advantage to the native with regard to his professional progression and prosperity.

Many scholars prefer to do M.B.A. after doing B. Tech or M. Tech. etc. In that case, the planetary combination of doing M.B.A. will be stronger and prominent but the planetary combination of an Engineer will also be seen in the birth chart. Involvement of the 8th house will strengthen the possibility of doing M.B.A. and B. Tech or M. Tech. In fact, the 8th house is involved, where number of subordinates or person work under the control of native. It has been observed that the 8th house does play a vital role in the birth charts of Administrative Officers, Engineers and Managers etc.

*Illustration : 14.1* (**SV**) *Horoscope No.: 186*

Date of birth : 16.06.1973 Time of birth : 02:10:00 hrs
Place of birth : Meerut Lat 29:00:00 N Long 77:42:00E
Ayanamsa : 23:29:27 Sidereal Time : 19:26:43

| **Pln** | **Degree** | **Rasi** | **Nakshatra** | **Pad** |
|---|---|---|---|---|
| Asc | 6:48:54 | Ari | Asvini | 3 |
| Sun | 1:05:15 | Gem | Mrigsira | 3 |
| Mon | 1:07:04 | Sag | Moola | 1 |
| Mar | 3:11:39 | Pis | P Bhadrapad | 4 |
| Mer | 24:56:21 | Gem | Punarvasu | 2 |
| Jup (R) | 18:14:13 | Cap | Sravna | 3 |
| Ven | 18:48:25 | Gem | Ardra | 4 |
| Sat (C) | 0:41:17 | Gem | Mrigsira | 3 |
| Rah (R) | 14:06:09 | Sag | Purvasadha | 1 |
| Ket (R/C) | 14:06:09 | Gem | Ardra | 3 |

**Lagna Chart** **Navamsa Chart**

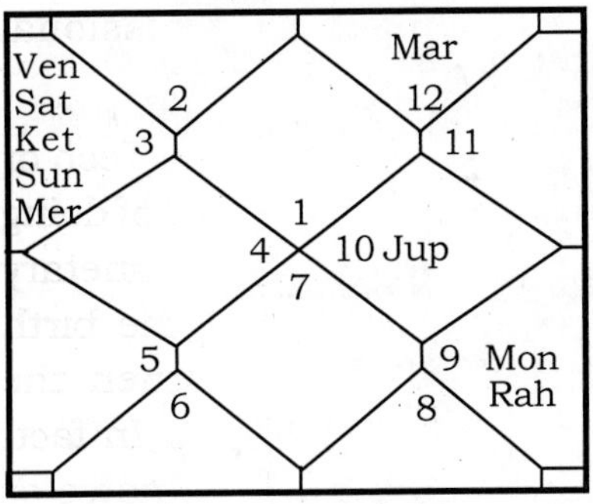


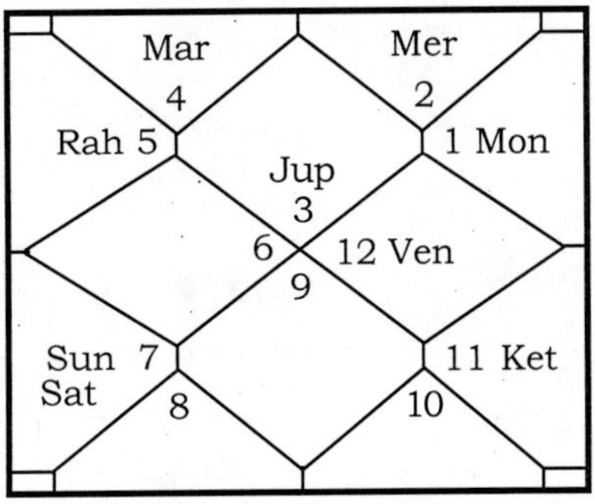


Balance of Vimsottari Dasa of **Ket 6Y 4M 29D**

The native has done M.B.A. in finance from I.I.M., Bangalore. He is drawing several lakhs of rupees per month. He is very much in demand by innumerable multinationals due to his extraordinary performance.

The native was born in Aries ascendant. The lord of the ascendant, Mars, occupies the 12$^{th}$ house and aspects the 3$^{rd}$ house, 10$^{th}$ lord Saturn, 3$^{rd}$ and 6$^{th}$ lord Mercury, 5$^{th}$ lord Sun and 2$^{nd}$ and 7$^{th}$ lord Venus. The lord of the ascendant, Mars, and that of the 10$^{th}$ house, Saturn, have a mutual aspect with each other. For M.B.A., 3$^{rd}$ and 10$^{th}$ houses must be strong, in addition to 1$^{st}$ and 5$^{th}$ house. 9$^{th}$ lord Jupiter is debilitated in the 10$^{th}$ house but debilitated Jupiter is retrograde. Hence, it is giving the effect of exalted Jupiter. However, Mercury is *Atmakaraka* planet in this birth chart and falls in own sign Gemini, in the constellation of Jupiter, *Punarvasu,* and obtains the *navamsa* of Venus, which gives a clear picture of M.B.A. (Finance). Exaltation of 2$^{nd}$ lord Venus, in *navamsa,* justifies and strengthens the combination. The 10$^{th}$ lord Saturn also obtains the *navamsa* of its exaltation. Thus, the lord of the10$^{th}$ house, Saturn, and that of 2$^{nd}$ house, Venus, both obtain the *navamsa* of their exaltation, identical to the sign Libra and Pisces respectively, which are owned by Venus and Jupiter, and clearly show that the native will manage the financial aspect of any concern most successfully.

*Illustration : 14.2* **(VB)** *Horoscope No.: 187*

Date of birth : 20.09.1953 Time of birth : 07:30:00 hrs
Place of birth : Munger Lat 25:24:00 N Long 86:29:00E
Ayanamsa : 23:12:52 Sidereal Time : 7:40:36

| **Pln** | **Degree** | **Rasi** | **Nakshatra** | **Pad** |
|---|---|---|---|---|
| Asc | 29:25:02 | Vir | Chitra | 2 |
| Sun | 3:36:10 | Vir | U Phalguni | 3 |
| Mon | 20:09:07 | Cap | Sravna | 4 |
| Mar | 10:09:17 | Leo | Magha | 4 |
| Mer (C) | 13:56:33 | Vir | Hasta | 2 |
| Jup | 2:14:39 | Gem | Mrigsira | 3 |
| Ven | 1:51:22 | Leo | Magha | 1 |
| Sat | 2:57:26 | Lib | Chitra | 3 |
| Rah (R) | 8:43:34 | Cap | Uttarasadha | 4 |
| Ket (R) | 8:43:34 | Can | Pushya | 2 |

**Lagna Chart**

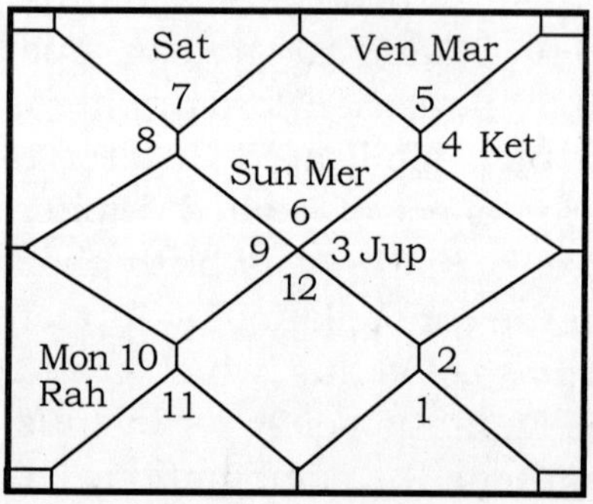


**Navamsa Chart**

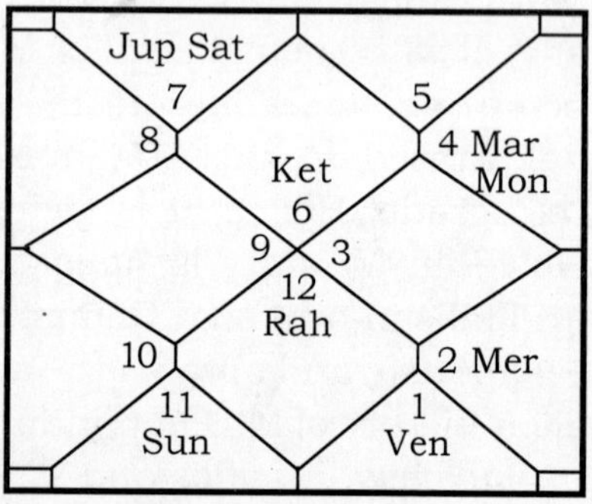


Balance of Vimsottari Dasa of **Mon 2Y 4M 19D**

The beautiful lady of this birth chart is an Executive Director in an multinational organization. She has always been appreciated for her excellent performance and intelligent approach in management. She acquired the educational qualification of M.B.A. and secured a suitable job in reputed and renowned multinational. Following combinations of the management of the business may be noted in this birth chart.

1. The ascendant and the 10th lord Mercury occupies the ascendant, in the sign of its exaltation, and Mercury obtains *navamsa* of Venus.

2. Moon, the *Atmakaraka* planet, owns and aspects the 11th house and obtains *navamsa* of Mars itself. Moon falls in own constellation *Sravna*. Moon is quite strong and very well placed in the 5th house.

3. Placement of Sun and Mercury in the ascendant has given the aptitude for management. Mercury is the lord of the 10th and ascendant both, and its placement in *Hasta* constellation signifies interest towards management. We have found that Mercury and Moon, if have an influence over the houses of profession, one intends to do M.B.A. If Mars is also involved the native will be quite successful manager after doing management. However, Moon, Mercury and Venus are a complete combination of planets, which cultivate the way to go towards the profession connected with management. Thus, Mercury, Moon and Mars, and Mercury, Moon and Venus give success in management. Mars and Mercury are mostly connected with marketing, information technology, human relationship etc. However, Mercury and Venus give success in the management of high degree and make one managing director, chairperson, administrator etc. If Venus is prominent and influence the 10th, 2nd or 11th house, in addition to Mercury and Moon, one will be successful in M.B.A. (finance), M.B.A. (Personnel) etc.

4. In this birth chart, Venus and Mars both are posited in the 12th house and are shifted in the 11th house, and both of these obtain the *navamsa* of Moon and Mars, respectively. This indicates success in the field of management of finance, administration, marketing and

personnel. The lady has done M.B.A. in finance and she is at present an Executive Director in a multinational. Various departments of the organization such as finance, banking, administration, personal, H.R., computer controlling etc. have been headed by her.

*Illustration : 14.3* (**RM**) *Horoscope No.: 188*

Date of birth : 28.03.1968 Time of birth : 01:48:00 hrs
Place of birth : Lucknow Lat 26:50:00 N Long 80:54:00E
Ayanamsa : 23:24:42 Sidereal Time : 14:02:53

| Pln | Degree | Rasi | Nakshatra | Pad |
|---|---|---|---|---|
| Asc | 23:52:07 | Sag | Purvasadha | 4 |
| Sun | 13:48:45 | Pis | U Bhadrapad | 4 |
| Mon | 1:18:23 | Pis | P Bhadrapad | 4 |
| Mar | 6:28:57 | Ari | Asvini | 2 |
| Mer | 20:15:48 | Aqu | P Bhadrapad | 1 |
| Jup (R) | 3:23:08 | Leo | Magha | 2 |
| Ven | 21:43:32 | Aqu | P Bhadrapad | 1 |
| Sat (C) | 20:54:40 | Pis | Revati | 2 |
| Rah (R/C) | 25:09:43 | Pis | Revati | 3 |
| Ket (R) | 25:09:43 | Vir | Chitra | 1 |

**Lagna Chart**

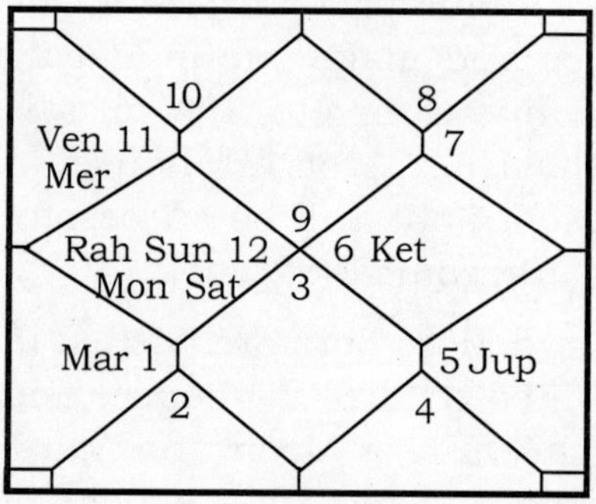


**Navamsa Chart**

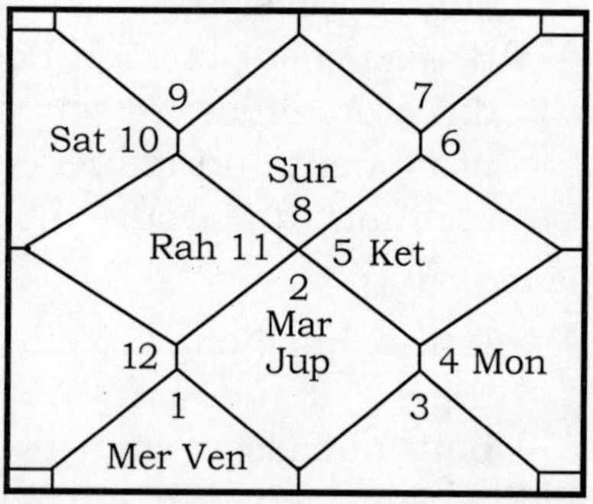


Balance of Vimsottari Dasa of **Jup 2Y 5M 5D**

The native is extraordinary as far as educational qualification and professional degrees are concerned. The name of the native has been placed in Guinness book of records as he has secured successful 18 professional degrees within a short period of 3 years.

The native has done Ph.D. in M.B.A., Finance, as well as M.B.A. Marketing. He was born in Sagittarius ascendant, which obtains Scorpio *navamsa*. The lord of the 10th house, Mercury and that of 11th house, Venus, are placed together in the 3rd house and receive the aspect of ascendant lord Jupiter from the 9th house. This combination is enough to justify his M.B.A. in Finance and Marketing both. However, 10th lord Mercury and 11th lord Venus both obtain the *navamsa* of Mars and Mars obtains the *navamsa* of Venus. Thus, there is mutual exchange of the *navamsa* between the 5th lord Mars and 11th lord Venus. However, four planets i.e. the Sun, Moon, Saturn and Rahu occupy the 4th house and lend their aspect over the 10th house. Here, Moon obtains own *navamsa* and aspects the 10th house along with other planets, Sun and Saturn. The 2nd lord Saturn falls in *Revati* and obtains own *navamsa* Capricorn. The ascendant lord Jupiter obtains the *navamsa* of Venus. This kind of setup of planets, of course, tends one to acquire innumerable number of professional qualifications but it was sure that he would secure M.B.A. degree.

The native has not only done M.B.A. but has also done two Ph.Ds in management courses of finance and marketing. At present, the native is a professor in I.I.M., Lucknow.

*Illustration : 14.4* **(AS)** *Horoscope No.: 189*

Date of birth : 04.12.1964 Time of birth : 16:32:00 hrs

Place of birth : Delhi Lat 28:39:00 N Long 77:13:00E

Ayanamsa : 23:21:43 Sidereal Time : 21:04:02

| **Pln** | **Degree** | **Rasi** | **Nakshatra** | **Pad** |
|---|---|---|---|---|
| Asc | 6:22:19 | Tau | Kriitika | 3 |
| Sun | 18:58:39 | Sco | Jyestha | 1 |

| | | | | |
|---|---|---|---|---|
| Mon (C) | 23:22:58 | Sco | Jyestha | 3 |
| Mar | 20:23:42 | Leo | P Phalguni | 3 |
| Mer | 9:44:32 | Sag | Moola | 3 |
| Jup (R) | 24:58:58 | Ari | Bharani | 4 |
| Ven | 18:13:54 | Lib | Svati | 4 |
| Sat | 5:53:28 | Aqu | Dhanishtha | 4 |
| Rah (R) | 29:37:20 | Tau | Mrigsira | 2 |
| Ket (R/C) | 29:37:20 | Sco | Jyestha | 4 |

**Lagna Chart** **Navamsa Chart**

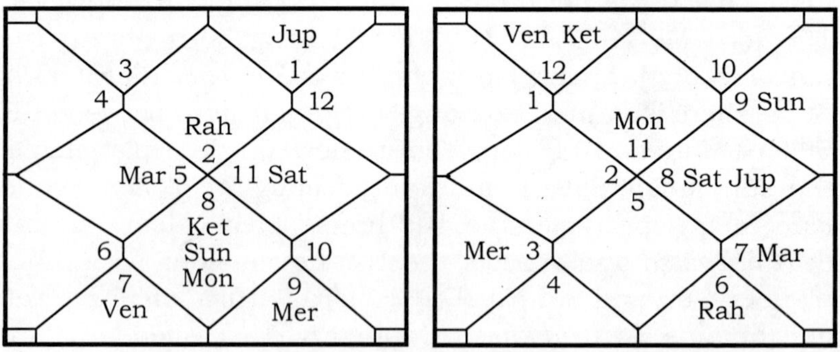


Balance of Vimsottari Dasa of **Mer 8Y 5M 7D**

The native has done M.B.A. from a highly reputed Institute of London. The native is extremely meritorious and he has proved his talent, wherever he has worked so far. He is at present working as General Manager in Asia's largest Plastic and Packaging Industry. His annual salary is in nine figures.

The native was born in Taurus ascendant. *Yogakaraka* Saturn falls in the 10th house of its own giving rise to *Sasa Mahapurusha Rajyoga*. The 10th lord Saturn obtains *navamsa* of Mars and is aspected by Mars as well. Mutual aspect between Mars and Saturn has made the native outstanding, as far as hard and continuous work is concerned. Ascendant lord Venus falls in the 6th house, in own sign Libra, and obtain *navamsa* of its exaltation. Lord of the 3rd house, Moon, falls in Scorpio, in *Jyestha* constellation, ruled by Mars and Mercury, respectively.

The Sun and Moon, both, occupy the 7$^{th}$ house, identical to Scorpio, and both are aspected by the 7$^{th}$ lord Mars and the 10$^{th}$ lord Saturn. Thus, the 3$^{rd}$ lord Moon is under the influence of Mars, Saturn and Mercury, which shows that the native will become a dynamic Manager after doing M.B.A. etc.

The 2$^{nd}$ and 5$^{th}$ lord Mercury obtains own *navamsa* and falls in the 8$^{th}$ house, in Sagittarius. Thus, the 2$^{nd}$ lord Mercury aspects its own 2$^{nd}$ house and is aspected by 8$^{th}$ and 11$^{th}$ lord Jupiter. Mercury in 8$^{th}$ and Jupiter in 12$^{th}$ show that the native will mostly manage international market.

The 11$^{th}$ lord Jupiter is *Atmakaraka* planet, whereas Saturn is *Yogakaraka* planet, as well as 10$^{th}$ lord. Both, Jupiter and Saturn, obtain Scorpio *navamsa* ruled by Mars. Thus, Mercury, Mars, Saturn and Venus, if influence the concerning houses, the native will be a dynamic and meritorious person in the field of Management. Here, Saturn is the strongest planet and obtains *navamsa* of Mars. The native has done M. Tech in Mechanical Engineering in addition to M.B.A. Mercury, Mars and Saturn's collective influence on one's profession makes one a Civil, Mechanical and Metallurgical engineer. Involvement of Venus and Moon will result into additional qualification of M.B.A. marketing.

Involvement of the 8$^{th}$ house further confirms his success in Engineering, Management and Administration etc., especially where the control of number of persons or masses is involved.

*Illustration : 14.5* (**SG**) *Horoscope No.: 190*

| | | | |
|---|---|---|---|
| Date of birth | : 30.06.1971 | Time of birth | : 08:55:00 hrs |
| Place of birth | : Burnpur | Lat 23:40:00 N | Long 86:57:00E |
| Ayanamsa | : 23:27:43 | Sidereal Time | : 3:42:59 |

| Pln | Degree | Rasi | Nakshatra | Pad |
|---|---|---|---|---|
| Asc | 5:25:45 | Leo | Magha | 2 |
| Sun | 14:15:07 | Gem | Ardra | 3 |
| Mon | 7:32:16 | Vir | U Phalguni | 4 |
| Mar | 27:43:26 | Cap | Dhanishtha | 2 |
| Mer (C) | 24:31:56 | Gem | Punarvasu | 2 |
| Jup (R) | 4:02:37 | Sco | Anuradha | 1 |
| Ven | 28:15:59 | Tau | Mrigsira | 2 |
| Sat | 7:52:40 | Tau | Krittika | 4 |
| Rah | 21:38:58 | Cap | Sravna | 4 |
| Ket | 21:38:58 | Can | Aslesha | 2 |

**Lagna Chart**

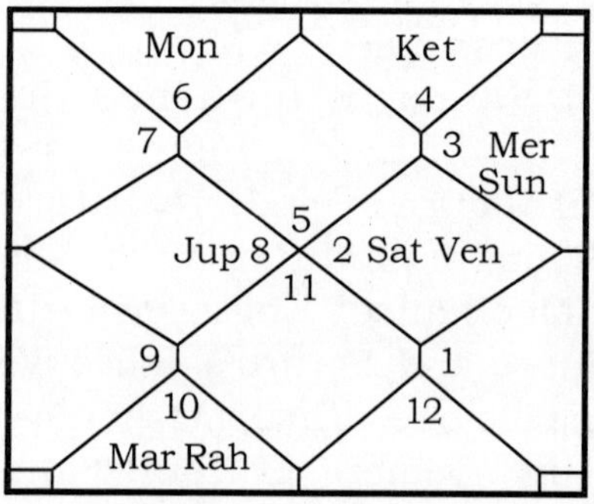


**Navamsa Chart**

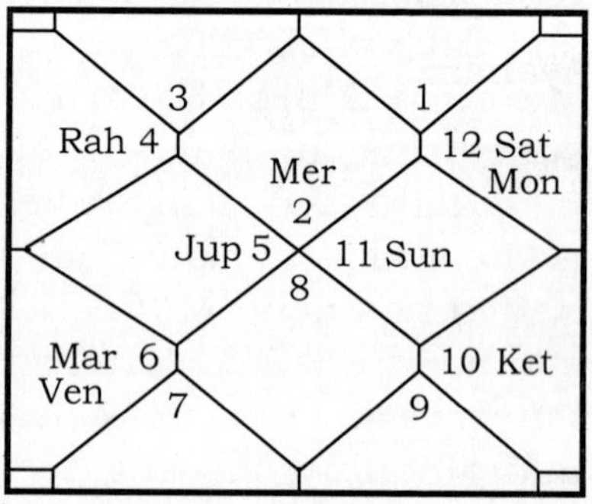


Balance of Vimsottari Dasa of **Sun 1Y 1M 8D**

The native is a Bank Manager in Kotak Mahindra at Dehradun. He has done M.B.A. in Finance from a reputed institute of management. He was born in Leo ascendant, which obtains Taurus *navamsa*. The lord of the 3rd and the 10th house, Venus, occupies the 10th house with 6th and 7th lord Saturn. Venus in Taurus in the 10th has given rise to *Malavya Mahapurusha Rajyoga* and its association with Saturn has added strength to the 10th house with regard to management and controls. Lord of 10th house, Venus, obtains the *navamsa* of Mercury. The 5th lord Jupiter is posited in the 4th house, in Scorpio, in *Mrigsira nakshatra* and obtains the *navamsa* of Sun. Jupiter lends aspect over the 10th house, 10th lord Venus, and the 6th and 7th lord Saturn. Thus, M.B.A. in finance is quite justified. Moon is posited in the 2nd house, in Virgo, in *Uttraphalguni* constellation and Moon obtains the *navamsa* of Jupiter. Venus is *Atmakaraka* planet in this horoscope and falls in *Mrigsira nakshatra* of Mars. Venus obtains *navamsa* of Mercury. Thus, the 10th house is under the influence of Venus, Saturn, Mercury and Jupiter. That has given success to the native in doing M.B.A. in Finance.

*Illustration : 14.6* (**SS**) *Horoscope No.: 191*

Date of birth : 04.09.1971 Time of birth : 14:00:00 hrs
Place of birth : Allahabad Lat 25:27:00 N Long 81:50:00E
Ayanamsa : 23:27:53 Sidereal Time : 12:48:34

| **Pln** | **Degree** | **Rasi** | **Nakshatra** | **Pad** |
|---|---|---|---|---|
| Asc | 6:44:57 | Sag | Moola | 3 |
| Sun | 17:41:47 | Leo | P Phalguni | 2 |
| Mon | 6:18:28 | Aqu | Dhanishtha | 4 |
| Mar (R) | 18:36:23 | Cap | Sravna | 3 |
| Mer (R) | 3:57:19 | Leo | Magha | 2 |
| Jup | 5:38:04 | Sco | Anuradha | 1 |
| Ven (C) | 19:45:49 | Leo | P Phalguni | 2 |
| Sat | 12:51:58 | Tau | Rohini | 1 |
| Rah (R) | 21:03:41 | Cap | Sravna | 4 |
| Ket (R) | 21:03:41 | Can | Aslesha | 2 |

**Lagna Chart**

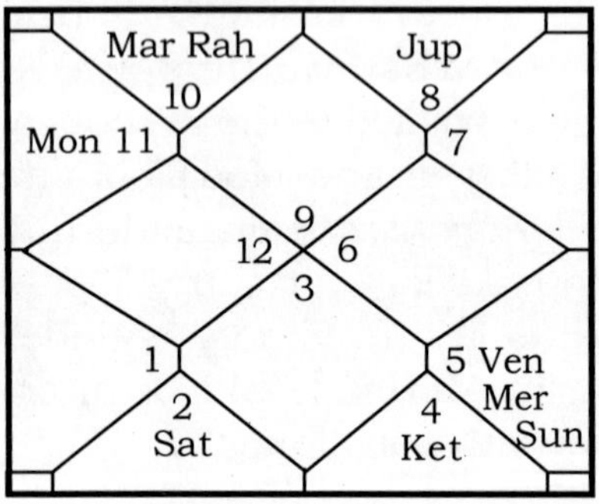


**Navamsa Chart**

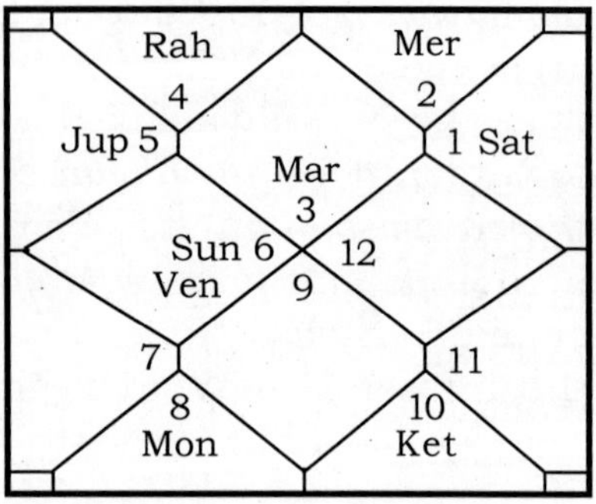


Balance of Vimsottari Dasa of **Mar 0Y 2M 7D**

The native has done M.B.A. from I.I.M., Ahmedabad, in Marketing. At present, he is working in a multinational organization at Bombay. The native was born in Sagittarius ascendant and Gemini *navamsa*. The lord of the 10$^{th}$ house, Mercury, is associated with the 9$^{th}$ lord Sun and 11$^{th}$ lord Venus, in the 9$^{th}$ house. This is splendid combination for all professional and financial aspects of life. The 10$^{th}$ lord Mercury obtains the *navamsa* of Venus, whereas the 11$^{th}$ lord Venus obtains *navamsa* of Mercury i.e. there is mutual exchange of *navamsa* between 10$^{th}$ lord Mercury and 11$^{th}$ lord Venus. Mercury, Venus and the Sun are aspected by the 8$^{th}$ lord Moon and the 5$^{th}$ lord Mars.

Venus is *Atmakaraka* planet who obtains the *navamsa* of the 10$^{th}$ lord Mercury and falls in own constellation *Poorvaphalguni.* Moreover, the 10$^{th}$ lord and Venus are under the influence of Mars and Moon, due to their aspect, which justifies success of the native in M.B.A. The lord of the 9$^{th}$ house, Sun, falls in own sign Leo, occupies *Poorvaphalguni* constellation, ruled by Venus, and Virgo *navamsa,* ruled by Mercury. The Sun is the strongest planet in this birth chart, as it obtains 1.68 *shadbalas.* This shows that the native is fortunate enough to do M.B.A. from a highly reputed institute, and thereafter, to be engaged in a multinational at a very handsome salary.

Involvement of the 8th lord Moon may also be noted, along with the 5th lord Mars, as both of these planets lend their aspect over the lords of the concerning houses and respective planets. The 5th lord Mars falls in Moon's constellations *Sravna* and obtains the *navamsa* of the 10th lord Mercury, whereas the 8th lord Moon falls in Aquarius, in Mars constellation *Dhanishtha*, and obtains *navamsa* of Mars as well. Thus, the involvement of 8th and 5th lords, in addition to 3rd and 10th, is distinctly visible in the birth chart, which explains the qualifications of M.B.A., as well as, the position of Manager in a huge multinational organization, quite prominently.

*Illustration : 14.7* (**GG**) *Horoscope No.: 192*

Date of birth : 16.08.1981 Time of birth : 08:42:00 hrs
Place of birth : Lucknow Lat 26:50:00 N Long 80:54:00E
Ayanamsa : 23:35:47 Sidereal Time : 6:13:20

| **Pln** | **Degree** | **Rasi** | **Nakshatra** | **Pad** |
|---|---|---|---|---|
| Asc | 9:23:01 | Vir | U Phalguni | 4 |
| Sun | 29:34:07 | Can | Aslesha | 4 |
| Mon | 5:03:04 | Aqu | Dhanishtha | 4 |
| Mar | 25:29:34 | Gem | Punarvasu | 2 |
| Mer (C) | 5:37:56 | Leo | Magha | 2 |
| Jup | 15:04:42 | Vir | Hasta | 2 |
| Ven | 3:29:31 | Vir | U Phalguni | 3 |
| Sat | 13:21:44 | Vir | Hasta | 2 |
| Rah (R) | 8:06:40 | Can | Pushya | 2 |
| Ket (R) | 8:06:40 | Cap | Uttarasadha | 4 |

**Lagna Chart**

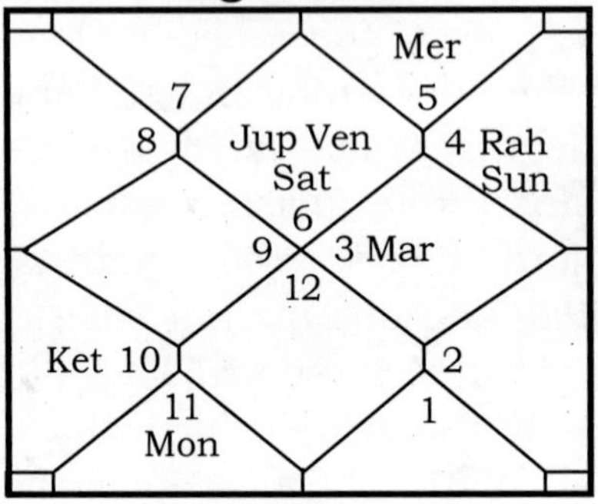


**Navamsa Chart**

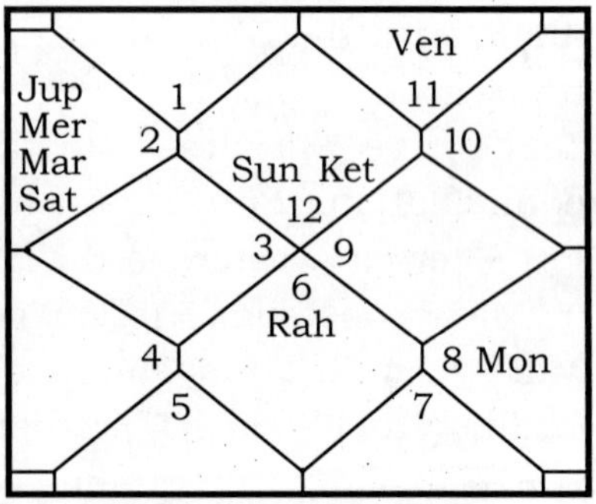


Balance of Vimsottari Dasa of **Mar 0Y 10M 5D**

The native has done M.B.A. from I.I.M., Bangalore. At present, he is working in a multinational as a Divisional Manager.

He was born in Virgo ascendant and Aquarius Moon sign. Lord of the ascendant, Mercury, is posited in the $12^{th}$ house. However, $4^{th}$ and $7^{th}$ lord Jupiter, $5^{th}$ and $6^{th}$ lord Saturn, $2^{nd}$ and $9^{th}$ lord Venus are conjoined in the ascendant i. e. the lords of both the triangles viz. $5^{th}$ and $9^{th}$ lord, Saturn and Venus, are posited in the ascendant. This has added much strength to the ascendant. The $8^{th}$ lord Mars occupies the $10^{th}$ house, and obtains the *navamsa* of Venus. In addition to that, $4^{th}$ and $7^{th}$ lord Jupiter, the lord of $10^{th}$ and ascendant Mercury, and $5^{th}$ and $6^{th}$ lord Saturn obtain *navamsa* of Venus, indicating great success in M.B.A. finance. The Sun is *atmakaraka* planet in this birth chart and it is the strongest planet as well, as it obtains 1.7 *shadabala*. The Sun obtains the *navamsa* of Jupiter and falls in *Aslesha* constellation ruled by Mercury, which confirms M.B.A. in finance branch. Thus, the involvement of $3^{rd}$ and $8^{th}$ lord Mars and $5^{th}$ lord Saturn is there, corresponding to the $10^{th}$ house and the ascendant, due to mutual aspect between both of these planets. The $10^{th}$ and ascendant lord Mercury has a mutual aspect with $5^{th}$ and $6^{th}$ lord Saturn, as there is mutual aspect also between these two planets. These combinations of planets powerfully indicate the success in management course to the native.

*Illustration : 14.8* **(PD)** *Horoscope No.: 193*

Date of birth : 09.11.1974 Time of birth : 11:00:00 hrs
Place of birth : Calcutta Lat 22:30:00 N Long 88:20:00E
Ayanamsa : 23:30:35 Sidereal Time : 14:35:22

| **Pln** | **Degree** | **Rasi** | **Nakshatra** | **Pad** |
|---|---|---|---|---|
| Asc | 4:17:16 | Cap | Uttarasadha | 3 |
| Sun | 22:55:12 | Lib | Visakha | 1 |
| Mon | 20:49:12 | Leo | P Phalguni | 3 |
| Mar (C) | 14:34:08 | Lib | Svati | 3 |
| Mer | 4:03:07 | Lib | Chitra | 4 |
| Jup | 14:31:59 | Aqu | Satabhisha | 3 |
| Ven (C) | 23:35:37 | Lib | Visakha | 2 |
| Sat (R) | 25:19:47 | Gem | Punarvasu | 2 |
| Rah (R) | 17:02:59 | Sco | Jyestha | 1 |
| Ket (R) | 17:02:59 | Tau | Rohini | 3 |

**Lagna Chart**

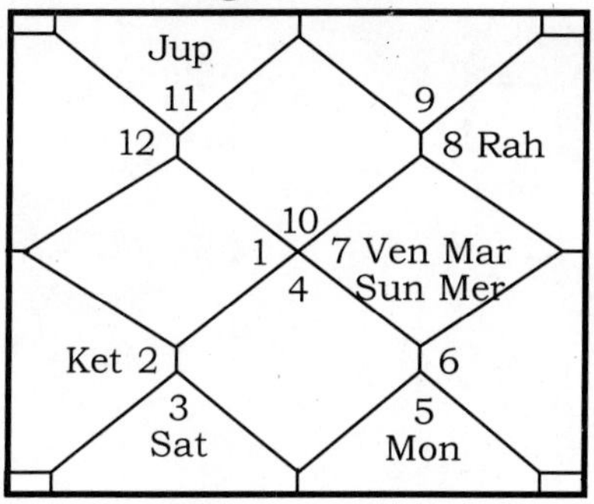


**Navamsa Chart**

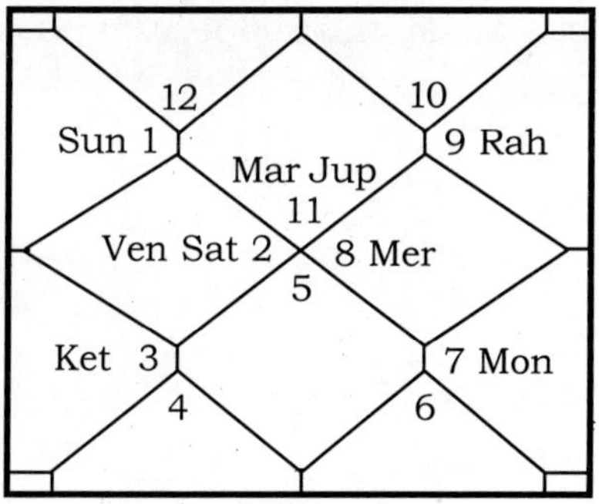


Balance of Vimsottari Dasa of **Ven 8Y 9M 7D**

The native is an Area Manager in Cambridge Book University, Delhi after having done M.B.A., marketing, from Institute of Productivity and Management, Lucknow branch.

He was born in Capricorn ascendant, which falls in Aquarius ascendant. Lord of the 10$^{th}$ house and *Yogakaraka*

Venus joins the 10th house itself giving rise to *Malavya Mahapurusha Rajyoga*. Venus is associated with 9th lord Mercury and 8th lord Sun. Lord of 4th and 11th, Mars, is also associated with Mercury, Venus and the Sun. This is a powerful *Rajyoga* of the conjunction of 9th, 10th and 11th lords in the 10th house itself. The Sun obtains *Neech Bhanga Rajyoga*. 10th lord Venus falls in own sign, Libra and obtains own *navamsa* Taurus, and is associated with Mars and Mercury. This is a clear combination of doing M.B.A. in marketing.

The combination has been further strengthened due to the aspect of 3rd lord Jupiter on the 10th house, the Sun, Mars, Mercury and Venus. Saturn is *atmakaraka* planet in this horoscope. It is retrograde, falls in the 6th house corresponding to Gemini, ruled by Mercury and is aspected by Jupiter. Saturn obtains *navamsa* of Venus and falls in *Punarvasu* constellation. This combination further justifies the study of M.B.A. and service as Area Manager in a reputed organization. Influence of the 3rd house and its lord Jupiter, 8th lord Sun and 5th lord Venus, on the 10th house is present, which strongly indicates high class professional prospects, progression, prosperity and power.

•

## CHAPTER-15

# Astrological Science and Scientists, Discoverers or Inventors

Scientists are the back bone of society. They work for the promotion and advancement of the mankind and humanity. Almighty is the real creator but He creates the things through scientists. This is the tragedy that mostly scientists have been recognized after the death or the proper importance and values have not been given to them during their life time. The Scientists and Philosophers are mostly governed by Mercury and Jupiter. However, in the birth chart of a scientist, Mercury will be more prominent and strong, whereas in the horoscope of a philosopher, Jupiter will have an upper edge over Mercury. But the role of both the planets i.e. Jupiter and Mercury will affect the $10^{th}$ and $5^{th}$ house, in one way or the other. We will study a few cases of scientists hereunder, to know the peculiar astrological findings present in the birth charts of scientists.

1. Mercury and Jupiter must influence the $10^{th}$ house, in one way or the other. If the $10^{th}$ lord finds the place in the sign, constellation or *navamsa* of Jupiter and Mercury, one should think of becoming a Scientist, provided the other conditions are also fulfilled.

2. Mars and Saturn also have a concern with the profession and way of working.

3. The $3^{rd}$, $5^{th}$ and $8^{th}$ houses, or their lords, have also a concern with the occupation of the native.

4. Gemini, Virgo and Aquarius are the signs of intelligence, brightness of mind, sharpness of brain,

creativity with regard to inventions and discoveries etc. Therefore, the involvement of Gemini, Virgo and Aquarius with regard to the ascendant, the 10$^{th}$ house or the 5$^{th}$ house will incline one to become a scientist, discoverer or inventor.

The 8$^{th}$ house from the ascendant and Scorpio sign have significance over the hidden things. Secret things, ideas, researches, discoveries and inventions are the outcome of the 8$^{th}$ house. Therefore, to the best of our intelligence, the 8$^{th}$ house must play a prominent role in the birth charts of Scientists, Inventors, Discoverers and Researchers. If Scorpio sign is involved that will further add strength to the combination.

5. Ketu is a planet of deep intuitions, if the 5$^{th}$ lord and the lord of the ascendant or the ruler of the 10$^{th}$ house fall in the constellation of Ketu e.g. *Asvini*, *Magha* or *Moola*, one will be a great thinker, scientist, inventor, astrologer, researcher, discoverer etc. So, if Ketu has a prominent role to play in one's horoscope, in addition to the influence of Mercury, Jupiter and Mars, on the 10$^{th}$ house or the 2$^{nd}$ and 5$^{th}$ house, one is likely to become a scientist.

6. It has been observed that the native born in Gemini, Scorpio, Aquarius, Taurus and Virgo become great scientists provided Mercury and Jupiter influence the occupation of the native, in addition to Mars and Ketu. It has also been seen that positive role of Saturn on the 10$^{th}$ house provides a deep research oriented brain and profession connected with research, examinations, testing and practical working in laboratories etc.

In fact, well disposed Saturn, if related with 5$^{th}$, 10$^{th}$, 3$^{rd}$ or 8$^{th}$ house, blesses the native with a high degree of vision, on the basis of which one plans his future projects etc.

*Illustration: 15.1* (**Albert Einstein**) *Horoscope No.: 194*

Date of birth : 14.03.1879 Time of birth : 11:30:00 hrs
Place of birth : Ulm Lat 48:23:00 N Long 10:00:00E
Ayanamsa : 22:10:27 Sidereal Time : 22:36:40

| **Pln** | **Degree** | **Rasi** | **Nakshatra** | **Pad** |
|---|---|---|---|---|
| Asc | 15:15:00 | Gem | Ardra | 3 |
| Sun | 1:19:11 | Pis | P Bhadrapad | 4 |
| Mon | 22:09:34 | Sco | Jyestha | 2 |
| Mar | 4:43:47 | Cap | Uttarasadha | 3 |
| Mer (C) | 10:56:35 | Pis | U Bhadrapad | 3 |
| Jup | 5:18:23 | Aqu | Dhanishtha | 4 |
| Ven | 24:47:37 | Pis | Revati | 3 |
| Sat (C) | 12:00:49 | Pis | U Bhadrapad | 3 |
| Rah (R) | 10:28:38 | Cap | Sravna | 1 |
| Ket (R) | 10:28:38 | Can | Pushya | 3 |

**Lagna Chart**

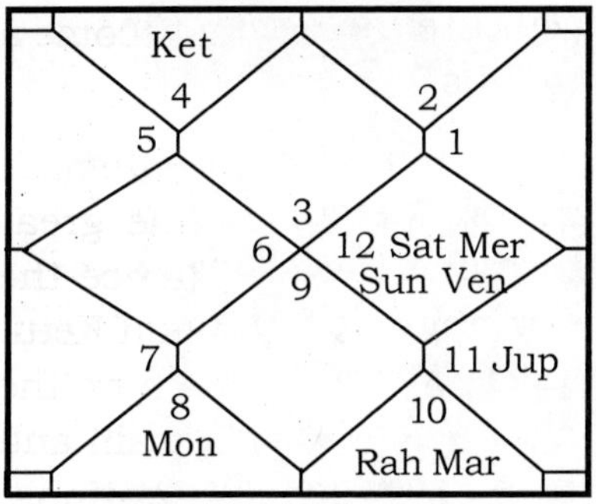


**Navamsa Chart**

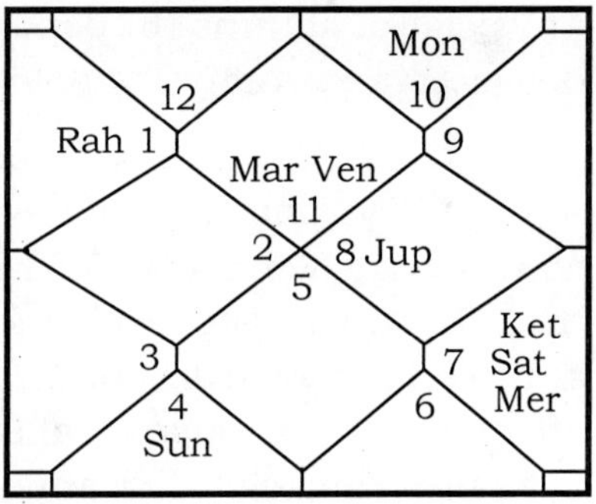


Balance of Vimsottari Dasa of **Mer 9Y 11M 29D**

**Albert Einstein** (March 14, 1879 – April 18, 1955) was a German-born theoretical physicist. He is best known for his theory of relativity and specifically mass-energy equivalence, $E = mc^2$. Einstein received the 1921 Nobel Prize in Physics "for his services to Theoretical Physics, and especially for his discovery of the law of the photoelectric effect."

Einstein's many contributions to physics include his special theory of relativity, which reconciled mechanics with electromagnetism, and his general theory of relativity, which extended the principle of relativity to non-uniform motion, creating a new theory of gravitation. His other contributions include relativistic cosmology, capillary action, critical opalescence, classical problems of statistical mechanics and their application to quantum theory, an explanation of the Brownian movement of molecules, atomic transition probabilities, the quantum theory of a monatomic gas, thermal properties of light with low radiation density (which laid the foundation for the photon theory), a theory of radiation including stimulated emission, the conception of a unified field theory, and the geometrization of physics.

Works by Albert Einstein include more than fifty scientific papers and also non-scientific books. In 1999 Einstein was named *Time* magazine's "Person of the Century", and a poll of prominent physicists named him the greatest physicist of all time. In popular culture the name "Einstein" has become synonymous with genius.

Albert Einstein was born in Gemini ascendant in Aquarius *navamsa*. The ascendant lord Mercury is associated with 5$^{th}$ lord Venus, 9$^{th}$ lord Saturn and the 3$^{rd}$ lord Sun, in the 10$^{th}$ house. This is a unique combination of a renowned and world known scientist. Jupiter, Mercury and Mars, if affect the 10$^{th}$ house, make one a scientist, provided the triangle lords i.e. 1$^{st}$, 5$^{th}$ and 9$^{th}$ also have a concern with the occupation of the native. In this birth chart, lord of all the three triangles are friendly with each other and are conjoined very well in the 10$^{th}$ house. Venus is exalted and obtains Saturn's *navamsa*. *Malavya Mahapurusha Rajyoga* has been formed by Venus. There is mutual exchange between 9$^{th}$ and 10$^{th}$ lords, Jupiter and Saturn. This is called *Mahayoga* or *Maharaja Yoga*.

This is a wonderful horoscope in which unique combinations of a scientist are strongly present. All the concerning houses and planets are very well disposed. Venus is *Atmakaraka* planet, which is exalted in the 10th house and obtains *navamsa* of the 9th lord Saturn. Moreover, Venus falls in *Revati nakshatra,* ruled by Mercury and it is also associated with Mercury.

The Sun is the strongest planet in this birth chart as it obtains 1.75 *Shadabalas*. The Sun obtains *navamsa* of Moon and falls in *Poorva Bhadrapad* constellation, ruled by Jupiter. 10th lord Jupiter falls in Saturn's sign Aquarius and obtains *navamsa* of Mars and falls in *Dhanishtha* constellation, ruled by Mars. Thus, the 10th lord Jupiter is under the prominent influence of Saturn and Mars. Lords of all the three triangles, Mercury, Venus and Jupiter, who are posited in the 10th house, have strengthened strongly the combination of a true and immortal scientist of world wide fame.

Involvement of the concerning signs Gemini, Virgo and Aquarius is also visible in the horoscope of Albert Einstein. He was born in Gemini ascendant. The lord of the 10th house, Jupiter, occupies the Aquarius sign and Virgo sign is aspected by 4th lord Mercury, 5th lord Venus, 3rd lord Sun and 9th lord Saturn. Moreover, 11th lord Mars and 5th lord Venus obtain the Aquarius *navamsa*. The 10th lord Jupiter obtains the *navamsa* of Mars and all other concerning planets i.e. Saturn, Ketu, and Mercury fall in the *navamsa* of the 5th house, Libra. Thus, these 3 planets i.e. Ketu, Mercury and Venus have added a lot, in providing the research oriented brain and deep inclination towards inventions and discoveries. This was the birth chart of great scientist of all times, immortal Mr. Albert Einstein. We have never come across such a potential and strong birth chart, so far, like that of Mr. Albert Einstein.

*Illustration : 15.2* (**Dr. H.J. Bhaba**) *Horoscope No.: 195*

Date of birth : 30.10.1909 Time of birth : 06:00:00 hrs
Place of birth : Patna Lat 25:37:00 N Long 85:12:00E
Ayanamsa : 22:35:34 Sidereal Time : 8:41:34

| **Pln** | **Degree** | **Rasi** | **Nakshatra** | **Pad** |
|---|---|---|---|---|
| Asc | 13:28:52 | Lib | Svati | 3 |
| Sun | 13:21:29 | Lib | Svati | 3 |
| Mon | 28:47:59 | Ari | Krittika | 1 |
| Mar | 3:04:16 | Pis | P Bhadrapad | 4 |
| Mer | 25:05:35 | Vir | Chitra | 1 |
| Jup | 11:06:43 | Vir | Hasta | 1 |
| Ven | 27:47:54 | Sco | Jyestha | 4 |
| Sat (R) | 25:54:25 | Pis | Revati | 3 |
| Rah (R) | 15:06:58 | Tau | Rohini | 2 |
| Ket (R) | 15:06:58 | Sco | Anuradha | 4 |

**Lagna Chart**

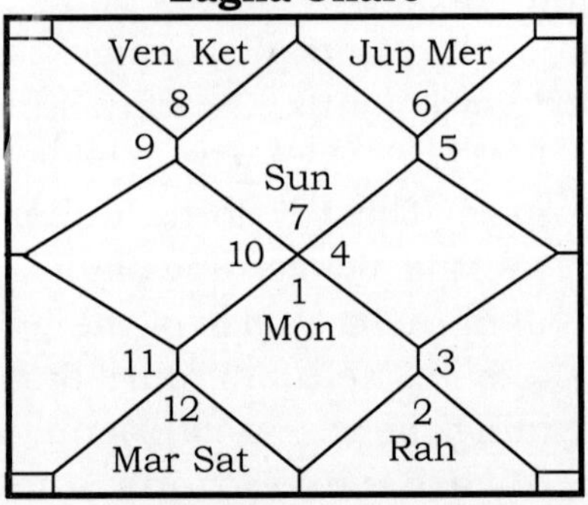


**Navamsa Chart**

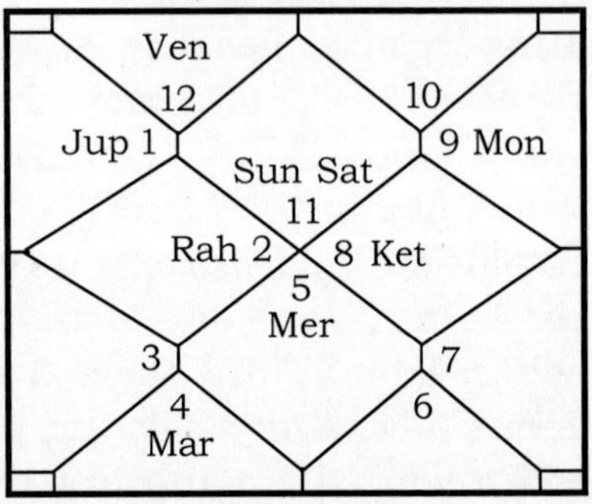


Balance of Vimsottari Dasa of **Sun 5Y 0M 14D**

**Homi Jehangir Bhabha**, FRS (October 30, 1909 – January 24, 1966) was an Indian nuclear physicist of Parsi-Zorastrian heritage, who had a major role in the development of the Indian atomic energy program and is considered to be the father of India's nuclear program. Bhabha was born into a prominent family, through which he was related to Dinshaw

Maneckji Petit, Muhammad Ali Jinnah, Homi K Bhabha and Dorab Tata. After receiving his early education at Bombay schools and at the Royal Institute of Science, he attended Caius College of Cambridge University to pursue studies in mechanical engineering. After taking the mechanical engineering Tripos, he pursued studies under Paul Dirac to complete the Mathematics Tripos. Meanwhile, he worked at the Cavendish Laboratory while working towards his doctorate in theoretical physics under R. H. Fowler. During this time, he embarked on groundbreaking research into the absorption of cosmic rays and electron shower production. Afterwards, he published a string of widely-accepted papers on his theories regarding cosmic ray showers.

World War II broke out in September 1939 while Bhabha was vacationing in India. He chose to remain in India until the war ended. In the meantime, he accepted a position at the Indian Institute of Science in Bangalore, headed by Nobel laureate C.V. Raman. He established the Cosmic Ray Research Unit at the institute, and began to work on the theory of the movement of point particles. In 1945, he established the Tata Institute of Fundamental Research in Bombay, and the Atomic Energy Commission of India three years later. In the 1950s, Bhabha represented India in International Atomic Energy Forums, and served as President of the United Nations Conference on the Peaceful Uses of Atomic Energy in Geneva, Switzerland in 1955. He later served as the member of the Indian Cabinet's Scientific Advisory Committee and set up the Indian National Committee for Space Research with Vikram Sarabhai. In January 1966, Bhabha died in a plane crash near Mont Blanc, while heading to Vienna, Austria to attend a meeting of the International Atomic Energy Agency's Scientific Advisory Committee.

He was born in Libra ascendant with Sun placed therein. Lord of the $10^{th}$ house, Moon, falls in the $7^{th}$ house in Aries opposite to the natal Sun. However, the $10^{th}$ lord Moon obtains *navamsa* of Jupiter. In fact, 9th lord Mercury is associated with the 3rd and 6th lord Jupiter in the sign Virgo. Mars and Saturn are posited in the 6th house and have mutual aspect with Jupiter and Mercury. Thus, the involvement of 4th and 5th lord Saturn and the 2nd and 7th lord Mars is also there.

Ascendant lord Venus, who falls in Scorpio, in *Jyestha* constellation, obtains the *navamsa* of its exaltation. Thus, the ascendant lord Venus is under the influence of Mars, Mercury and Jupiter, which gives a strong aptitude towards research in the field of science, atomic energy etc.

Lord of the 9th house, Mercury, is exalted with Jupiter, in Virgo. 10th lord Moon occupies the 7th house in Aries and obtains *navamsa* of Jupiter. 2nd and 7th lord Mars, falls in Jupiter's sign Pisces and Jupiter's constellation *Poorva Bhadrapada*, whereas *Yogkaraka* Saturn falls in Jupiter's sign Pisces, Mercury's constellation *Revati* and obtains Aquarius *navamsa*. These are the powerful indications of a Scientist like Dr. Homi Jahangir Bhabha.

*Illustration : 15.3* (**Sir J.C. Bose**) *Horoscope No.: 196*

Date of birth : 30.11.1858 Time of birth : 16:25:00 hrs
Place of birth : Mohansingh Lat 22:39:00 N Long 88:23:00E
Ayanamsa : 21:53:19 Sidereal Time : 21:01:02

| **Pln** | **Degree** | **Rasi** | **Nakshatra** | **Pad** |
|---|---|---|---|---|
| Asc | 4:04:49 | Tau | Krittika | 3 |
| Sun | 16:05:35 | Sco | Anuradha | 4 |
| Mon | 19:08:51 | Vir | Hasta | 3 |
| Mar | 20:57:04 | Cap | Sravna | 4 |
| Mer | 2:51:44 | Sag | Moola | 1 |
| Jup (R) | 25:46:21 | Tau | Mrigsira | 1 |
| Ven (R) | 6:46:44 | Sag | Moola | 3 |
| Sat (R) | 20:23:50 | Can | Aslesha | 2 |
| Rah (R) | 11:51:11 | Aqu | Satabhisha | 2 |
| Ket (R) | 11:51:11 | Leo | Magha | 4 |

**Lagna Chart**

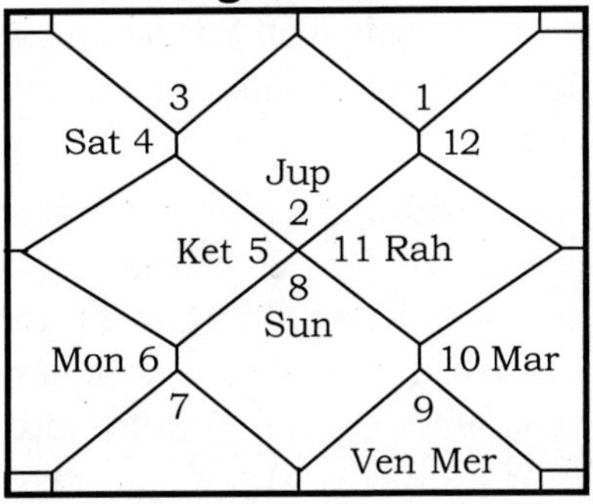


**Navamsa Chart**

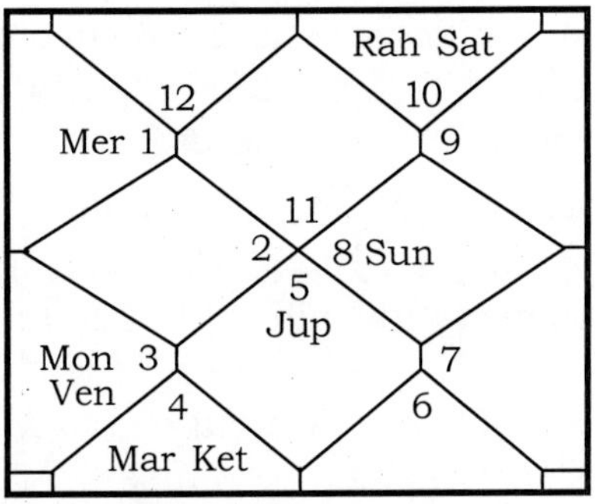


Balance of Vimsottari Dasa of **Mon 3Y 1M 20D**

Sir Jagadish Chandra Bose was a Bengali polymath: a physicist, biologist, botanist, archaeologist, and science fiction writer. He pioneered the investigation of radio and microwave optics, made extremely significant contributions to plant science, and laid the foundations of experimental science in the Indian subcontinent. He is considered the father of radio science, and is also considered the father of Bengali science fiction. He was the first from the Indian subcontinent to get a US patent, in 1904.

Born in Bengal province of British India, Bose completed graduation from St. Xavier's College, Calcutta. Then he went to the University of London to study medicine, but couldn't complete his study due to health problems. He returned to India and joined the Presidency College as a Professor of Physics. There, in spite of racial discrimination, and lack of funding and equipment, Bose carried on his scientific research. He made remarkable progress in his research of remote wireless signaling and was the first to use semiconductor junction to detect radio signals. However, instead of trying to gain commercial benefit from this invention Bose made his inventions public in order to allow others to develop on his research. Subsequently, he made some pioneering discoveries in plant physiology. He used his own invention Cresco graph to measure plant response to various stimuli, and thereby scientifically proved parallelism between animal and plant tissues. Although Bose filed for patent for one of his inventions due to peer pressure, his reluctance to any form of patenting was well known. Now about 70 years after his death, he is being credited for many of his contributions to modern science.

He was born in Taurus ascendant and Aquarius *navamsa*. *Yogakaraka* Saturn occupies the 3$^{rd}$ house and aspects its own 9$^{th}$ house and 3$^{rd}$ lord Moon. Moreover, the lord of the 3$^{rd}$ house, Moon, occupies the 5$^{th}$ house. The 2$^{nd}$ and 5$^{th}$ lord Mercury is associated with the ascendant lord Venus in the 8$^{th}$ house. In fact, 8$^{th}$ house and Scorpio sign indicate hidden things and mysteries, which are discovered by a Scientist. Therefore, the 8$^{th}$ house and the 8$^{th}$ sign should never be ignored in the horoscope of a Scientist. In other words, if the 8$^{th}$ house and Scorpio has a concern with the occupation of the native, along with well disposed Mercury and Jupiter, in addition to the 5$^{th}$ and 3$^{rd}$ housem occupation related with science and research should be predicted.

In this birth chart, Mars and Saturn are posited opposite each other, identical to 9$^{th}$ and 3$^{rd}$ house. We have mentioned above that such kind of influence of Mars and Saturn is generally present in the horoscope of Scientists.

The 8$^{th}$ and 11$^{th}$ lord Jupiter occupies the ascendant, corresponding with *Mrigshira* constellation of Mars. Lord of 10$^{th}$ house, Saturn, obtains own *navamsa* and Mars obtains the *navamsa* of Moon. Thus, Saturn and Mars are opposite each other, even in *navamsa* chart.

Jupiter is *Atmakaraka* planet, which joins the ascendant and falls in the constellation of Mars. The 5$^{th}$ lord Mercury also falls in Jupiter's sign Sagittarius and Ketu's constellation *Moola* and obtains *navamsa* of Mars. These factors, if present in a birth chart, one is likely to become a scientist. Lord of the 3$^{rd}$ house Moon, who falls in own constellation *Hasta* in Mercury's sign Virgo, obtains *navamsa* of Mercury, Gemini. Such planetary combinations strongly justify that the native would be a great scientist, researcher and discoverer. The Moon is the strongest planet in this horoscope, which falls in Virgo, in own constellation and thus obtains *Rashi* and *navamsa* of Mercury, in the 5th & the 3rd house respectively

Thus, all findings as explained by us, which, if present in a birth chart, one is sure to become a scientist, researcher, inventor or discoverer, are very well present in the birth chart of Mr. Jagdish Chandra Bose.

*Illustration : 15.4* **(A.G. Bell)** *Horoscope No.: 197*

Date of birth : 03.03.1847 Time of birth : 07:00:00 hrs
Place of birth : Edinburgh Lat 55:57:00 N Long 03:12:00E
Ayanamsa : 21:43:30 Sidereal Time : 17:28:56

| **Pln** | **Degree** | **Rasi** | **Nakshatra** | **Pad** |
|---|---|---|---|---|
| Asc | 15:22:30 | Aqu | Satabhisha | 3 |
| Sun | 20:23:21 | Aqu | P Bhadrapad | 1 |
| Mon | 2:56:35 | Vir | U Phalguni | 2 |
| Mar | 22:59:06 | Sag | Purvasadha | 3 |
| Mer (C) | 3:08:43 | Pis | P Bhadrapad | 4 |
| Jup | 16:25:01 | Tau | Rohini | 2 |
| Ven | 8:49:52 | Pis | U Bhadrapad | 2 |
| Sat (C) | 12:40:48 | Aqu | Satabhisha | 2 |
| Rah (R) | 27:25:41 | Vir | Chitra | 2 |
| Ket (R) | 27:25:41 | Pis | Revati | 4 |

**Lagna Chart**

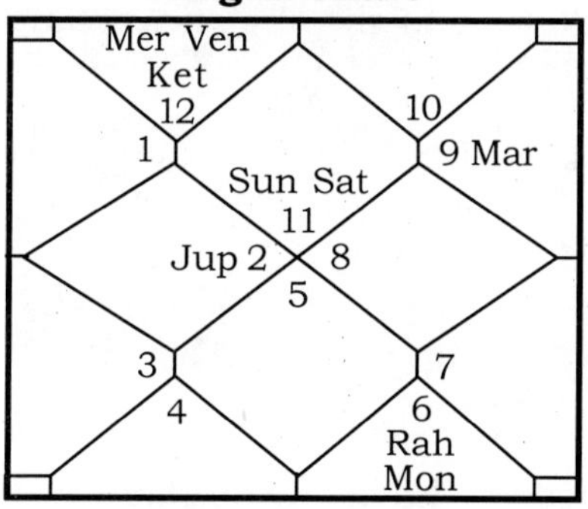


**Navamsa Chart**

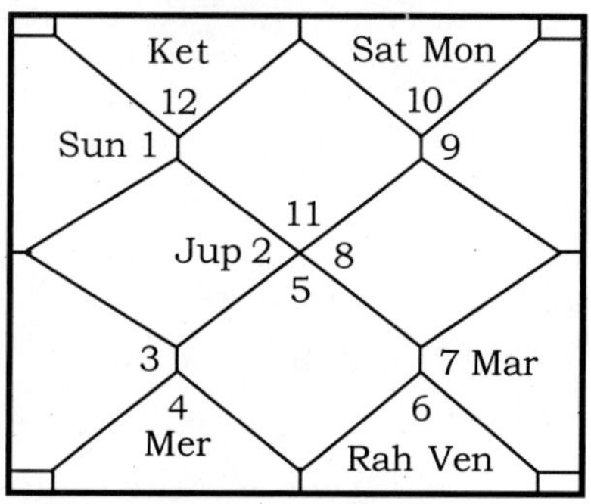


Balance of Vimsottari Dasa of **Sun 3Y 2M 3D**

**Alexander Graham Bell** (3 March 1847 - 2 August 1922) was an eminent scientist, inventor and innovator. Most often associated with the invention of the telephone, Bell was also called "the father of the deaf". His father, grandfather and brother had all been associated with work on elocution and speech, and both his mother and wife were deaf, profoundly influencing Bell's life's work. His research on hearing and speech further led him to experiment with hearing devices that eventually culminated in Bell being awarded the first U.S. patent for the invention of the telephone in 1876.

Many other inventions marked Bell's later life including groundbreaking work in hydrofoils and aeronautics. In 1888, Alexander Graham Bell was one of the founding members of the National Geographic Society. In reflection, Bell considered his most famous invention was an intrusion on his real work as a scientist and refused to have a telephone in his study. Upon Bell's death, all telephones throughout the United States "stilled their ringing for a silent minute in tribute to the man whose yearning to communicate made them possible."

He was born in Aquarius ascendant with the Sun and Saturn placed therein. The lord of the 5$^{th}$ house, Mercury, is associated with *Yogakaraka* Venus and Ketu. Thus, the lords of both the triangles, the 5$^{th}$ and 9$^{th}$, are placed together in the 2$^{nd}$ house and the 10$^{th}$ lord Mars lends it's favourable aspect over the 5$^{th}$ house and 5$^{th}$ lord Mercury, 9$^{th}$ lord Venus and Ketu, in addition to the 2$^{nd}$ and the 6$^{th}$ houses.

Mars is the strongest planet in this birth chart and it is *Atmakaraka* as well. Mars finds place in Jupiter's sign Sagittarius and obtains *navamsa* of *Yogakaraka* Venus. Mars, in fact, is the best placed planet in this birth chart. The 5$^{th}$ lord Mercury occupies the 2$^{nd}$ house, in Jupiter's sign Pisces and Jupiter's constellation *Poorvabhadrpada.*

The 8$^{th}$, 5$^{th}$ and the 3$^{rd}$ houses do have a prominent role to play in the birth charts of Scientists. Here, Mars is the lord of the 3rd and the 10th. The 8th house is occupied by Moon and Rahu, and it is aspected by *Yogakaraka* and benefic Venus, benefic Jupiter, and benefic Mercury. Thus, the 8th house is very well disposed and receives the aspect of its owner Mercury. *Atmakaraka* and strongest planet Mars obtains *navamsa* of Venus, as well as falls in the constellation of Venus and, in addition to this, Mars is the owner of 3rd and the 10th houses. Therefore, the native had interest in voice, music and phone etc., for which Venus is the significator.

This horoscope clearly signifies that the native would become a great scientist and will do innovative research work in the fields for which Venus is the significator.

*Illustration : 15.5* (**HKS**) *Horoscope No.: 198*

Date of birth : 20.09.1943 Time of birth : 05:36:00 hrs
Place of birth : Azamgarh Lat 26:03:00 N Long 83:10:00E
Ayanamsa : 23:04:02 Sidereal Time : 4:30:35

| **Pln** | **Degree** | **Rasi** | **Nakshatra** | **Pad** |
|---|---|---|---|---|
| Asc | 16:53:50 | Leo | P Phalguni | 2 |
| Sun | 3:03:23 | Vir | U Phalguni | 2 |
| Mon | 17:48:25 | Tau | Rohini | 3 |
| Mar | 20:18:06 | Tau | Rohini | 4 |
| Mer (R/C) | 12:36:55 | Vir | Hasta | 1 |
| Jup | 24:20:04 | Can | Aslesha | 3 |
| Ven (R) | 12:23:38 | Leo | Magha | 4 |
| Sat | 3:12:16 | Gem | Mrigsira | 3 |
| Rah (R) | 22:03:03 | Can | Aslesha | 2 |
| Ket (R) | 22:03:03 | Cap | Sravna | 4 |

**Lagna Chart**

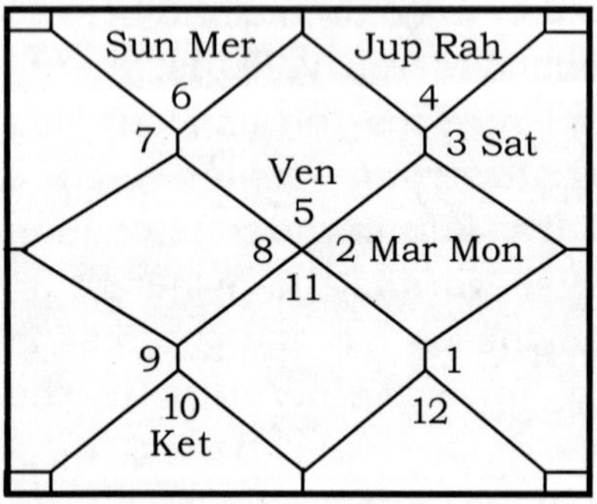


**Navamsa Chart**

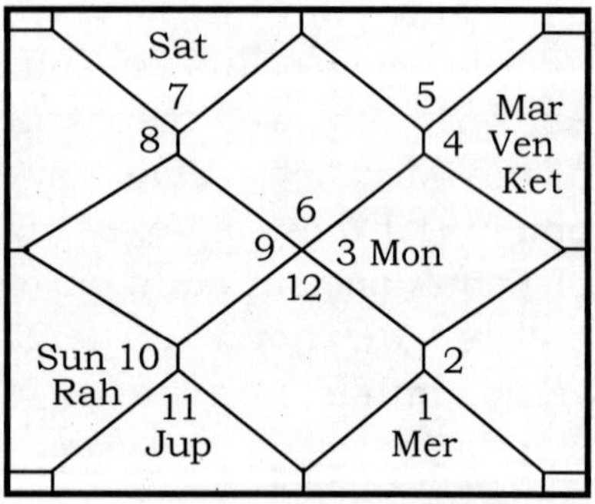


Balance of Vimsottari Dasa of **Mon 4Y 1M 22D**

This is the horoscope of a highly placed scientist in Central Drug Research Institute, Lucknow. He has discovered the Ayurvedic medicines for memory, diabetes etc. after an extensive research of number of years.

He was born in Leo ascendant. The lord of 10th house Venus falls in the ascendant, in Ketu's constellation *Magha* and obtains *navamsa* of Moon, whereas Moon is exalted in the 10th house, which falls in own constellation *Rohini* and Mercury's constellation, Gemini. Venus owns the 3rd house as well and it is quite strong in *shadabalas*. The lord of 5th and 8th house, Jupiter, is exalted in the 12th house, identical to Mercury's constellation *Aslesha*, aspects the 4th, 6th and 8th house. Jupiter is *Atmakaraka* planet in this birth chart and obtains the *navamsa* of the 6th and 7th lord Saturn. Therefore, the native had to do hard work throughout his service in C.D.R.I. and had a tough fight with his superiors. 6th lord Saturn falls in 11th house in Gemini, in the constellation of Mars, whereas Saturn obtains the *navamsa* of his exaltation.

We have seen that Venus also plays the role of a supporting significator in the horoscope of scientists.

*Illustration: 15.6* (**CS**) *Horoscope No.: 199*

Date of birth : 25.07.1970 Time of birth : 21:58:00 hrs
Place of birth : Chandigarh Lat 30:43:00 N Long 76:47:00E
Ayanamsa : 23:26:53 Sidereal Time : 17:46:59

| **Pln** | **Degree** | **Rasi** | **Nakshatra** | **Pad** |
|---|---|---|---|---|
| Asc | 1:46:44 | Pis | P Bhadrapad | 4 |
| Sun | 8:51:11 | Can | Pushya | 2 |
| Mon | 11:41:48 | Ari | Asvini | 4 |
| Mar (D) | 11:18:51 | Can | Pushya | 3 |
| Mer | 27:38:29 | Can | Aslesha | 4 |
| Jup | 4:07:50 | Lib | Chitra | 4 |
| Ven | 21:27:29 | Leo | P Phalguni | 3 |
| Sat | 27:43:54 | Ari | Krittika | 1 |
| Rah | 9:43:56 | Aqu | Satabhisha | 1 |
| Ket | 9:43:56 | Leo | Magha | 3 |

**Lagna Chart**

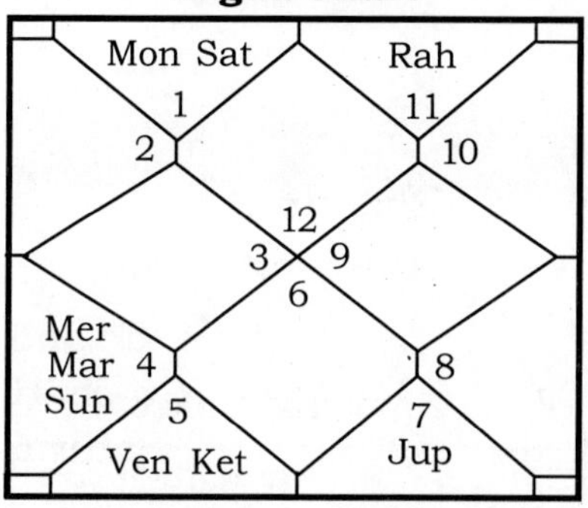


**Navamsa Chart**

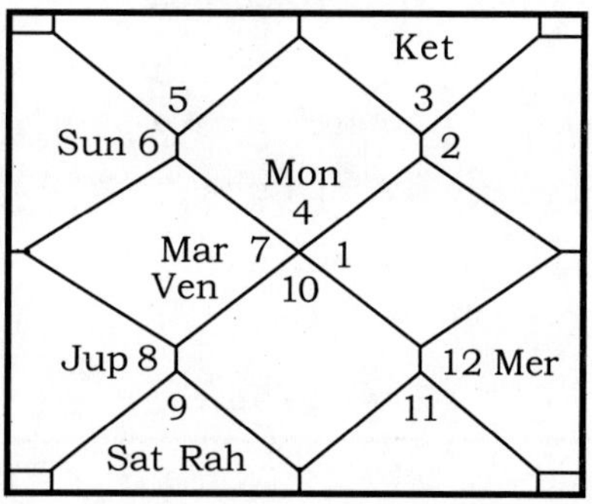


Balance of Vimsottari Dasa of **Ket 0Y 10M 9D**

This female has a tragic story with regard to conjugal bliss but she is outstanding as far as scientific researches are concerned. She is working in Central Drug Research Institute. She has many innovative researches to her credit.

She was born in Pisces ascendant. The lord of 10th house, Jupiter, falls in the 8th house, in Libra and obtains the Scorpio *navamsa,* and falls in *Chitra* constellation, ruled by Mars. The 5th house is occupied by Mars, Mercury and Sun, which shows that she will excel in the field of science. Saturn is *Atmakaraka* planet and joins the 2nd house under debilitation but obtains *navamsa* of Jupiter. Thus, the effect of Jupiter, Mars, Mercury on the 3rd, 5th, 8th and 10th houses justifies her service, interest and inclination in the field of science.

*Illustration : 15.7* (**AA**) *Horoscope No.: 200*

Date of birth : 02.09.1969 Time of birth : 20:45:00 hrs

Place of birth : Indore Lat 22:42:00 N Long 75:54:00E

Ayanamsa : 23:26:02 Sidereal Time : 19:04:58

| **Pln** | **Degree** | **Rasi** | **Nakshatra** | **Pad** |
|---|---|---|---|---|
| Asc | 27:56:50 | Pis | Revati | 4 |
| Sun | 16:31:37 | Leo | P Phalguni | 1 |
| Mon | 4:25:10 | Tau | Krittika | 3 |
| Mar | 25:49:08 | Sco | Jyestha | 3 |
| Mer | 13:34:36 | Vir | Hasta | 2 |
| Jup | 15:05:23 | Vir | Hasta | 2 |
| Ven | 11:55:03 | Can | Pushya | 3 |
| Sat (R) | 15:22:47 | Ari | Bharani | 1 |
| Rah | 27:47:44 | Aqu | P Bhadrapad | 3 |
| Ket (C) | 27:47:44 | Leo | U Phalguni | 1 |

**Lagna Chart**

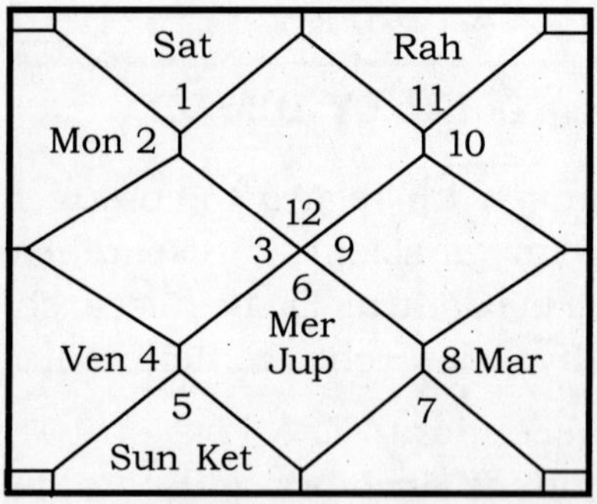


**Navamsa Chart**

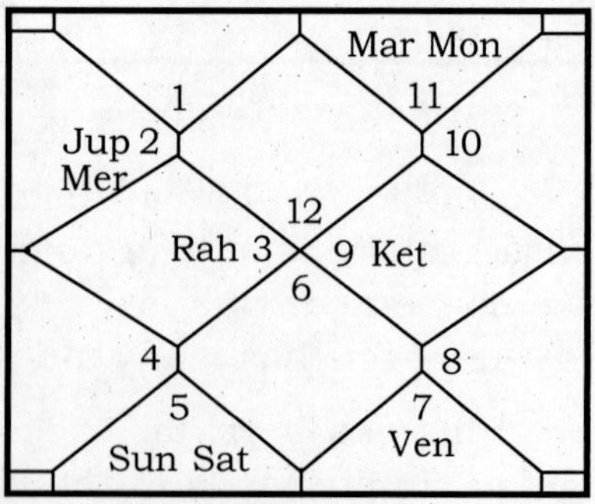


Balance of Vimsottari Dasa of **Sun 2Y 6M 4D**

The native is working as a Scientist in Central Drug Research Institute, Lucknow. He was born in Pisces ascendant. Lord of the $10^{th}$ house, Jupiter, is very well placed in the $7^{th}$ house, in Virgo. Mercury and Jupiter, both, are closely conjoined in *Hasta* constellation and obtain the *navamsa* of Venus. Venus is a supporting significator for scientists and it is placed in the $5^{th}$ house, in Saturn's constellation *Pushya.* Venus also owns the $8^{th}$ house and occupies the $5^{th}$ that gives a research oriented inquisitive brain. Though it is an adverse disposition for children, Venus obtains own *navamsa.*

In this birth chart, Mars is the strongest planet (*Shadabala* 1.74) and *Atmakaraka* as well. Mars is a planet of research, innovative ideas, creativity, supremacy etc., who is posited in own $9^{th}$ house and obtains the *navamsa* of Saturn, whereas it falls in Mercury's constellation *Jyestha.* Thus, Jupiter, Mars, Mercury and supporting significator Venus do influence the $3^{rd}$, $5^{th}$, $8^{th}$ and $10^{th}$ houses, which has made the native the scientist of valuable observations and a researcher.

We have observed that Jupiter, Mars and Mercury make one a scientist, provided these planets have an influence over the $3^{rd}$, $5^{th}$, $8^{th}$ and $10^{th}$ house. Venus should be considered as the supporting significator for scientists. However, the application of these rules should be made quite carefully and properly to reach at the right conclusion.

●

CHAPTER-16

# Astro Calculus for Experts in Calculations i.e. Mathematicians

Here the chief planets are Mercury, Venus and Saturn. Conjunction of the Sun, Venus and Saturn, in airy signs, and in the 1st, 2nd and 5th makes a good mathematician. Conjunction of Mars, Jupiter and Mercury, in airy signs, and in the 2nd or 5th, is another good stellar pattern for a good mathematician. Conjunction of the Moon, Saturn and Mercury in the 2nd or 5th and in airy signs is a good stellar pattern for becoming a good mathematician. The 2nd house stands for oratorical, poetical and intellectual abilities. The 5th house gives inventive genius, and creative talent. If Mars and Mercury influence the 5th house or ascendant, in one or the other way, one is good in mathematical works, calculations, and making and solving complicated programmes of Computer. In fact, Mars and Mercury are the significator of all mathematical works, especially innovative and research oriented inventions and their executions.

*Illustration : 16.1* (**S.R. Iyengar**) *Horoscope No.: 201*

Date of birth : 22.12.1887 Time of birth : 16:25:00 hrs
Place of birth : Tamilnadu Lat 22:39:00 N Long 88:23:00E
Ayanamsa : 22:17:20 Sidereal Time : 22:27:40

| Pln | Degree | Rasi | Nakshatra | Pad |
|---|---|---|---|---|
| Asc | 25:49:41 | Tau | Mrigsira | 1 |
| Sun | 8:01:37 | Sag | Moola | 3 |

| Mon | 9:37:21 | Pis | U Bhadrapad | 2 |
|---|---|---|---|---|
| Mar | 15:51:51 | Vir | Hasta | 2 |
| Mer | 22:53:26 | Sco | Jyestha | 2 |
| Jup | 3:22:08 | Sco | Anuradha | 1 |
| Ven | 22:22:59 | Lib | Visakha | 1 |
| Sat (R) | 13:10:48 | Can | Pushya | 3 |
| Rah (R) | 18:10:06 | Can | Aslesha | 1 |
| Ket (R) | 18:10:06 | Cap | Sravna | 3 |

**Lagna Chart**

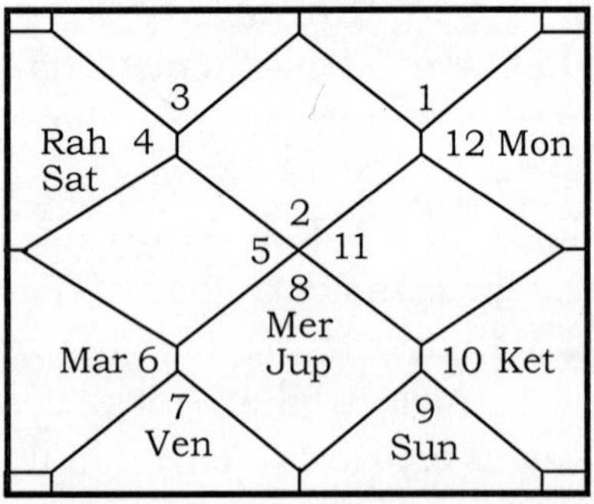


**Navamsa Chart**

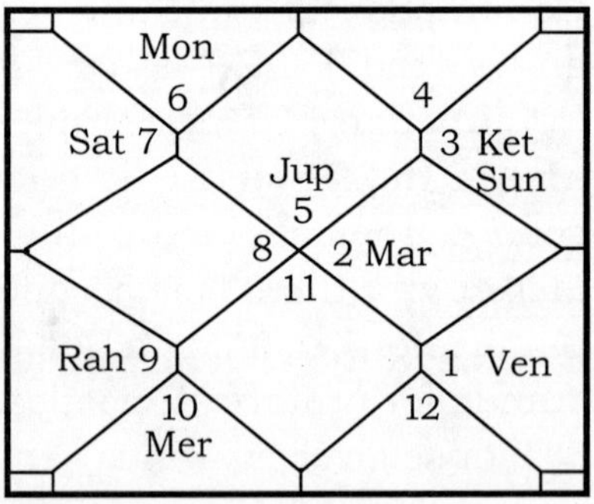


Balance of Vimsottari Dasa of **Sat 10Y 0M 13D**

**Srinivâsa Râmânujan Iyengar** FRS was an Indian mathematician and one of the greatest mathematical geniuses of the 20th century. With almost no formal training in pure mathematics, he made substantial contributions in the areas of mathematical analysis, number theory, infinite series and continued fractions.

Ramanujan, born and raised in Erode, Tamil Nadu, India, first encountered formal mathematics at age ten. He demonstrated a natural ability at mathematics, and was given books on advanced trigonometry by S.L. Loney. He mastered this book by age thirteen, and even discovered theorems of his own. He demonstrated unusual mathematical skills at school, winning accolades and awards. By the age of seventeen, Ramanujan was conducting his own mathematical research on Bernoulli numbers and the Euler–Mascheroni constant. He received a scholarship to study at Government College in Kumbakonam. He failed his non-mathematical coursework, and lost his scholarship. He then joined another college to pursue independent mathematical research. To make a living, he worked as a clerk in the Accountant-General's office at the Madras Port Trust Office. In 1912-1913, Ramanujan sent samples of his theorems to three academics at the University of Cambridge. Only G. H. Hardy recognized his brilliant work, and he asked Ramanujan to study under him at Cambridge.

Ramanujan independently compiled nearly 3900 results (mostly identities and equations) during his short lifetime. Although a small number of these results were actually false and some were already known, most of his claims have now been proven to be correct. He stated results that were both original and highly unconventional, such as the Ramanujan prime and the Ramanujan theta function, and these have inspired a vast amount of further research. However, some of his major discoveries have been rather slow to enter the mathematical mainstream. Recently, Ramanujan's formulae have found applications in the field of crystallography and in string theory. The Ramanujan Journal, an international publication, was launched to publish work in all the areas of mathematics that were influenced by Ramanujan.

Srinivasa Ramanujan was born in Taurus ascendant with Mars in the $5^{th}$ house in Virgo, which is a great combination for being a great mathematician. Mercury is *Atmakaraka* planet in this horoscope, who is posited in own constellation *Jyestha* identical to Martian sign Scorpio, in association with Jupiter. Thus, there is mutual exchange between the $5^{th}$ lord Mercury and the $7^{th}$ lord Mars. The $8^{th}$ and $11^{th}$ lord Jupiter finds its place in Scorpio in *Anuradha* constellation and obtains *navamsa* of the Sun. Lord of the ascendant, Venus, falls in own airy sign Libra in the 6th house. Venus obtains *navamsa* of Mars and Mars obtains *navamsa* of Venus i.e. there is mutual exchange between the *navamsa* of Mars and Venus, in addition to mutual exchange of signs and houses of Mars and Mercury. Thus, Mars is under heavy influence of Mercury, Venus and Moon due to mutual aspects, which made him a mathematician, who created history. No mathematician of his level was ever born. Lord of the 10th house, Saturn, who falls in own constellation *Pushya,* obtains the *navamsa* of its exaltation, falls over the axis of Rahu and Ketu and is aspected by the 8th and 11th lord Jupiter, which also strongly justifes the combination of a unparallel expert in calculation, statistics and mathematic etc.

*Illustration : 16.2* (**N.C. Lahiri**) *Horoscope No.: 202*

Date of birth : 03.04.1906 Time of birth : 24:00:00 hrs
Place of birth : Calcutta Lat 22:30:00 N Long 88:20:00E
Ayanamsa : 22:32:40 Sidereal Time : 12:44:38

| **Pln** | **Degree** | **Rasi** | **Nakshatra** | **Pad** |
|---|---|---|---|---|
| Asc | 8:11:55 | Sag | Moola | 3 |
| Sun | 20:31:39 | Pis | Revati | 2 |
| Mon | 8:50:20 | Can | Pushya | 2 |
| Mar | 19:53:03 | Ari | Bharani | 2 |
| Mer (R/D) | 23:03:00 | Pis | Revati | 2 |
| Jup | 11:32:13 | Tau | Rohini | 1 |
| Ven | 2:30:57 | Ari | Asvini | 1 |
| Sat | 17:19:38 | Aqu | Satabhisha | 4 |
| Rah | 27:01:46 | Can | Aslesha | 4 |
| Ket | 27:01:46 | Cap | Dhanishtha | 2 |

**Lagna Chart**

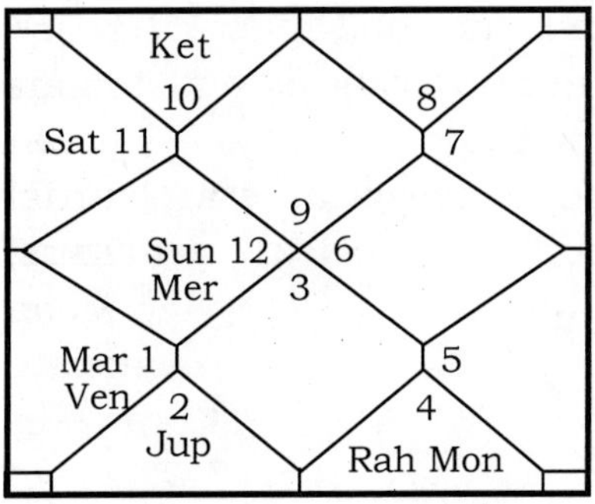


**Navamsa Chart**

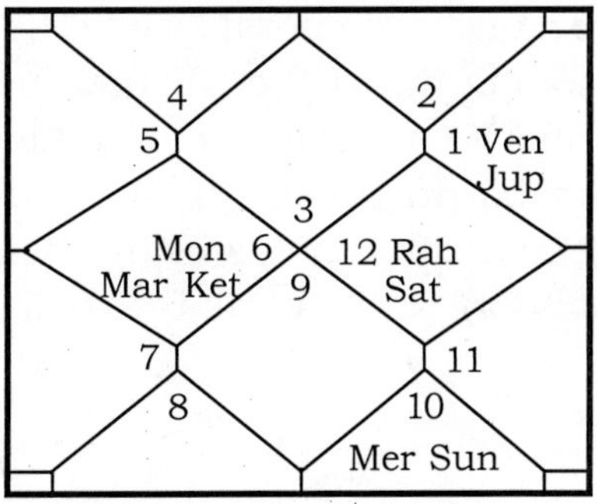


Balance of Vimsottari Dasa of **Sat 11Y 1M 26D**

N.C. Lahiri was a great mathematician. He started world famous Indian Ephemeris, which is most renowned Ephemeris all over the world.

He was born in Sagittarius ascendant, whose lord Jupiter occupies the 6$^{th}$ house. The 10$^{th}$ lord Mercury is posited in the 4$^{th}$ house, in association with the 9$^{th}$ lord Sun and aspects his own 10$^{th}$ house, jointly with Jupiter. Thus, there is a influence of Mercury, Sun and Jupiter on the 10$^{th}$ house. Mars and Venus are posited in the 5$^{th}$ house. 5$^{th}$ lord Mars, who occupies its own house, obtains the *navamsa* of Mercury in association with Moon and Ketu. This indicates that the native will be an excellent mathematician.

Mercury is *Atmakaraka* planet in this birth chart. It is retrograde and falls in *Revati* constellation, ruled by Mercury, and obtains *navamsa* of the 2$^{nd}$ and 3$^{rd}$ lord Saturn. Saturn falls in own sign Aquarius, in the 3$^{rd}$ house, and obtains *navamsa* of Jupiter. Thus, the 3$^{rd}$ lord Saturn, the 5$^{th}$ lord Mars and 8$^{th}$ lord Moon obtain the *navamsa* of Jupiter and Mercury, and are under the influence of each other in *navamsa* chart. Venus obtains *Vargottam navamsa* and is strongest in *shadabalas*. Venus falls in Ketu's constellation *Ashwini*. Conjunction of Venus and Mars in the 5$^{th}$ house, in Aries, inclines one towards the field of calculations and develops interest in Mathematics, Computers, and Statistics etc.

Mr. N.C. Lahiri was a great Mathematician, Astrologer and Astronomer as well. The influence of Jupiter, Mercury, and Sun over the 10th house, Saturn over the 3rd house, Mars and Venus over the 5th house and Moon over the 8th house in Saturn's constellation, in Virgo *navamsa*, is a powerful explanation of his being so good in astrological calculations and all kinds of mathematical work.

## CHAPTER-17

# Entrepreneurship: A Vocation of Life

The societal scenario all around is not that simple and systematic as it was in the yesteryears. With the advance of civilization, modernity has taken new parameters. The socio-cultural and politico-economic organization has become complex indeed and calls for greater and shrewder adoptions of ways in the several walks of life. The social organism-man has to exercise his prudence on right moment in the right direction or he would land in soup. For example, in section of means of ones' livelihood, a thorough comprehension of decisive factors and the specific aptitude of the native have to be reckoned for accurate prophecy. This shall be of immense value as it reflects the forthcoming spectrum of success. The native may engage himself in any business activity or service. This is his option to a certain limit. But the factors, which propel his ship of destiny, may indicate any other possibility. Well, it is at this juncture that clarity of mind plays its vital role and the clarity of mind may be acclaimed with the help of a devoted astrologer.

With a view to understand the likelihood of launching enterprise, one should look into the strength of the *lagna* and the Moon. Further more its significators Sun, Mercury, Saturn and Jupiter should also be strong. In case these planets do not occupy a stronger position, they must be normal in their *balas* but the Sun or Jupiter must be very strong. Again from 7$^{th}$ to 12$^{th}$ house or from 10$^{th}$ to 3$^{rd}$ house, there must be five or more planets. At the time, there must be some relationship between the 11$^{th}$ house and 2$^{nd}$ house, 2$^{nd}$ and 7$^{th}$ house, 10$^{th}$ and 11$^{th}$ house and 10$^{th}$ and 2$^{nd}$ house, in respect to any of the significators. And, if any one planet, as the lord of two business-related houses takes its position in those houses, under the influence of Jupiter or Mercury, then such a situation will auger well in conducting independent business.

All this said, now we shall delineate on specific planetary combinations in the horoscopes of eminent businessmen. These natives run their own proliferating businesses in the Country.

For an independent type of work, the *lagna* and the Moon must be strong, so that they (the natives) may stand, work and think independently. Successful businessmen, doctors, lawyers and consultants etc. always have a strong *lagna* and a powerful Moon.

There are four significators of business. Mercury is most important and other three are the Sun, Saturn and Jupiter.

**MERCURY:**

Mercury has most to do with business as the main significator of trades of all kinds. Mercury governs mental power, way of thinking, intelligence, art of planning, calculation and accounts works etc. In case of an afflicted and weak Mercury, one must never be advised to take-up any business as their means of livelihood, because they will ultimately fail to adjust themselves in their respective trades due to lack of planning and foresightedness. The business requires skill, which will be absent in those who have an afflicted and weak Mercury. Such a person will spoil his business owing to defective planning and bogus accounts or he will regularly suffer with losses. Quality of speech is also under the control of Mercury, so he will not be able to influence others much by his polished way of talking. He will not be clever enough to control an independent work.

**THE SUN:**

'The Sun is most independent' is an universal fact. He represents lot of energy and power to work with much of stamina, vigor and vitality. The persons having weak Sun in their horoscopes cannot work independently and for them it is not wise to take-up a business as their means of livelihood. If the Sun is weak and afflicted, there will be loss of honour, reputation, goodwill, faith, recognition and prestige. One should not work independently, if a powerless Sun is posited in the horoscope and has no good aspect, conjunction or association.

**SATURN:**

Saturn represents labour, patience and the service needed in a trade to offer others. No business can be successful if one does not put sufficient labour and is unable to work hard. In case of weak Saturn, it will definitely be so and such a native will ultimately lose his business if he takes it up as his profession.

**JUPITER:**

Jupiter is the chief controller of wealth. Jupiter governs sincerity, honesty and positive attitude. He makes one to differentiate between right and wrong and also brings the grace of God, without which one can not even dream to become a successful trader. Every business involves money, sale and profit rather this is the main motto of any business or profession. This area involving wealth and profit comes under the rulership of Jupiter. Those, who have a weak Jupiter, begin independent work with lot of input of wealth and in lot many times it is found that even the capital has gone into loss what to say of profit and earnings.

## How to judge the strength of planets:

The strength of planets can easily be judged by an experienced astrologer. The strength depends on placements, ownership, conjunctions, aspect, associations, the sign occupied, the *navamsa* and other *vargas* occupied by the planets. If *graha* and *bhava bala* have been worked out, it is quite simple to define whether the planet has gained the required strength or not. Dr. B. V. Raman has described the way of calculating the exact geometrical strength of the planets and measuring the *bhava bala* numerically in his one of the most valuable work "*Graha and Bhava Balas*". These four significators have been defined to bear the following strength:

| | |
|---|---|
| Sun | 5.00 rupas |
| Mercury | 7.00 rupas |
| Jupiter | 6.50 rupas |
| Saturn | 5.00 rupas |

If any of these four significators is weak in strength, the area covered by that particular planet will suffer in the business undertaken by the native.

**THE TENTH HOUSE:**

For a successful occupation either service or business, the tenth house must be quite strong. If the businessman has weak or afflicted tenth house, he will not gain required success in spite of strong planets. A powerful tenth house means that the native will take up a suitable occupation at appropriate age without loss of any time. He will be successful in his undertakings and endeavours regarding any matter pertaining to his business. There will almost be no obstruction or delay in the achievement of the goal.

This must be borne in mind clearly that the $10^{th}$ house must be judged from the *lagna* or Moon, whichever is stronger. A weak tenth house will result into lot of hindrances, delay, failures and obstructions. One will jump from one business to another resulting into ultimate failure.

So, the four *Karakas,* Mercury, the Sun, Saturn and Jupiter must be strong along with a strong tenth house, the *lagna* and Moon.

Or

If the *lagna* and Moon are normal in strength, and three *karakas* viz. Mercury, Saturn and Jupiter, also obtain just normal strength, one can become a successful trader, provided he has a very strong Sun occupying the *lagna*, $5^{th}$, $9^{th}$, or the $10^{th}$ house.

Or

If the Sun is normal, Jupiter must be very strong in 1st, 4th, 9th or 11th house.

After proper verification of the planetary strength, scrutinize the pattern or placement of the planets. There must be at least 5 planets, as reckoned from the 7th to 12th house or from the 10th to the 3rd house, in the horoscope of an individual, who wishes to take up an independent nature of work.

Or

If the *lagna,* Moon and the significators, the Sun, Mercury, Saturn and Jupiter, all have just normal strength, there must be a relation, by association or aspect, between 1st and 9th or 5th house, or between 10th and 1st or 9th house.

**RULE 1:** The 2nd, 11th, 10th and 7th houses are related with business. In 'How to judge a horoscope', Dr. B. V. Raman has specified that the if lord of the 11th house is placed in 2nd house, with the lord of 2nd house, one will earn through many businesses. This can be interpreted in following ways:

1. (a) The lord of 2nd, in the 11th and 11th in the 2nd, or
   (b) The lord of 2nd in the 11th, with the lord of 11th, or
   (c) The lord of 11th in the 2nd, with the lord 2nd, or
   (d) The lord of 2nd in the 2nd and the lord of 11th in the 11th.
   (e) The lord of 2nd and 11th aspect each other or are associated in a favourable house, i.e. there is a relation between the 11th and 2nd houses.

To illustrate this, following is an ideal example:-

*Illustration : 17.1* (**KKS**) *Horoscope No.: 203*

| Date of birth | : 09.01.1957 | Time of birth | : 04:46:00 hrs |
|---|---|---|---|
| Place of birth | : Kanpur | Lat 26:50:00 N | Long 80:54:00E |
| Ayanamsa | : 23:15:39 | Sidereal Time | : 11:52:31 |

| Pln | Degree | Rasi | Nakshatra | Pad |
|---|---|---|---|---|
| Asc | 23:42:55 | Sco | Jyestha | 3 |
| Sun | 25:10:57 | Sag | Purvasadha | 4 |
| Mon | 21:27:04 | Pis | Revati | 2 |
| Mar | 25:01:20 | Pis | Revati | 3 |
| Mer (R/C) | 29:02:54 | Sag | Uttarasadha | 1 |
| Jup | 8:27:06 | Vir | U Phalguni | 4 |
| Ven | 1:53:31 | Sag | Moola | 1 |
| Sat | 16:52:26 | Sco | Jyestha | 1 |
| Rah | 4:24:02 | Sco | Anuradha | 1 |
| Ket | 4:24:02 | Tau | Krittika | 3 |

**Lagna Chart**

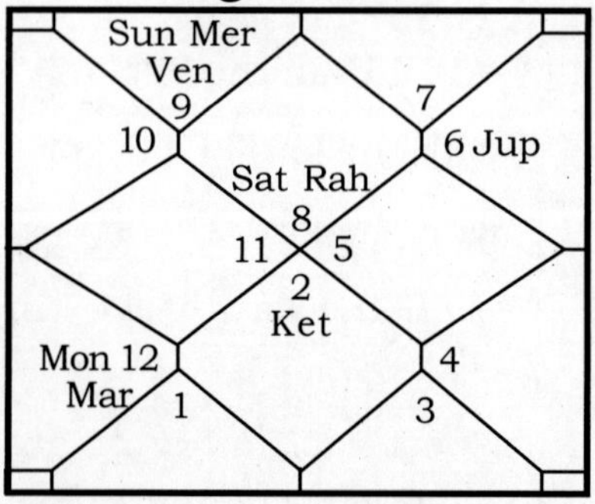


**Navamsa Chart**

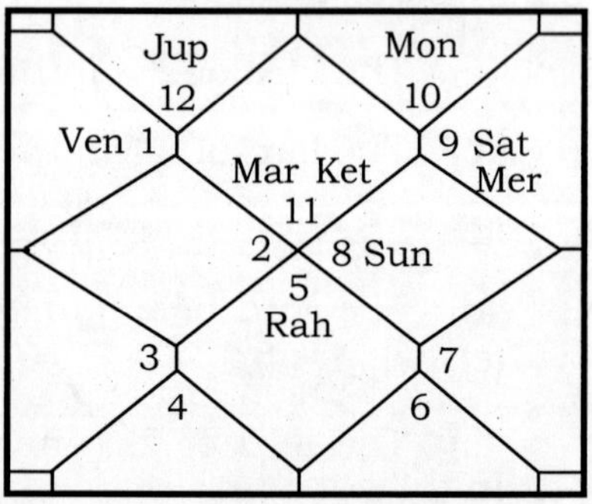


Balance of Vimsottari Dasa of **Mer 10Y 10M 24D**

This is the horoscope of a business magnate of Kanpur who is dealing in steels and is the owner of two very large steel factories and some other businesses. Let us examine the combinations of a successful businessman in this horoscope on the above-mentioned line of judgement.

Both *lagna* and Moon are very strong. Scorpio is the *lagna* and obtains 9.33 *Rupas bhava bala,* while Moon has 6.686 *Rupas graha bala.* However, lord of *lagna,* Mars secures 8.904 *Rupa Bala.* Mercury receives 7.329, Saturn 6.167 and the Sun gets 5.202 *graha Bala.* Saturn is the strongest among all the *Karakas,* as the minimum required strength for Saturn is 5.00 *Rupa* only. So, the native is steel industrialist. The *bhava bala* of the tenth house is 8.33 *Rupa,* which is sufficiently strong to provide an independent occupation to the native. There are six planets posited in the houses as reckoned from the 10$^{th}$ to the 3$^{rd}$ house.

According to rule 1 (a) there is a mutual exchange of the lords of the 2$^{nd}$ & 11$^{th}$ houses. Jupiter occupies the 11$^{th}$ and the main significator, Mercury, is stationed at 2$^{nd}$ house, in association with the Sun, the lord of the 10$^{th}$ house.

**RULE 2 :** If there is a *Sambandh* between the 10$^{th}$ and the 11$^{th}$ lords,

2. (a) If the lord of the 10$^{th}$ occupies 11$^{th}$ and the lord of the 11$^{th}$ occupies 10$^{th}$, or

   (b) If the lord of the 10$^{th}$ is tenanted in the 11$^{th}$ with the lord of the eleventh, or

   (c) If the lord of the 11$^{th}$ occupies 10$^{th}$ in conjunction with the lord of the 10$^{th}$, or

   (d) If the lord of 10$^{th}$ is in the 10$^{th}$ and lord of the 11$^{th}$ in the 11$^{th}$, or

   (e) If the lord of the tenth and eleventh conjoin in a good house or aspect each other favourably.

In the above horoscope lord of the tenth house, the Sun, associates with the lord of the eleventh, Mercury, in the 2$^{nd}$ house as per Rule 2(e).

**RULE 3:** May be defined as the relationship between the lords of the 11$^{th}$ and 7$^{th}$ house.

3. (a) If the lords of the 11$^{th}$ and 7$^{th}$ have mutual exchange, or

(b) If the lord of 7$^{th}$ is in the 11$^{th}$ with the 11$^{th}$ lord, or

(c) If the lord of 11$^{th}$ is in the 7$^{th}$ with 7$^{th}$ lord, or

(d) If the lord of the 7$^{th}$ is in the 7$^{th}$ and the lord of 11$^{th}$ is in the 11$^{th}$ house.

(e) If the lord of 7$^{th}$ and the 11$^{th}$ are under favourable aspect or are associated with each other in a favourable house.

In the above example the lord of the 11$^{th}$, Mercury, conjoins with the lord of 7$^{th}$ house, Venus, in the 2$^{nd}$ house, as per Rule 3 (e).

**RULE 4:**

4. (a) If there is a mutual exchange of the lords of 10$^{th}$ and 7$^{th}$ house, or

(b) If the 7$^{th}$ lord is in the 10$^{th}$ with the 10$^{th}$ lord, or

(c) If the 10$^{th}$ lord is in the 7$^{th}$ with the 7$^{th}$ lord, or

(d) If the 10$^{th}$ lord is in the 10$^{th}$ and 7$^{th}$ lord in the 7$^{th}$, or

(e) If the 10$^{th}$ and the 7$^{th}$ lords are associated with each other in a favourable position or aspect each other beneficially.

In the above example, while considering from the Moon, the lord of the 7$^{th}$ house, Mercury, joins the 10$^{th}$ and the lord of 10$^{th}$, Jupiter, is stationed in the 7$^{th}$ house, as per rule 4(a).

**RULE 5:**

5. (a) If there is a mutual exchange between the lords of the 7$^{th}$ and the 2$^{nd}$ House, or

(b) If the 2$^{nd}$ lord is in the 7$^{th}$ with the 7$^{th}$ lord, or

(c) If the 7$^{th}$ lord is in the 7$^{th}$ and the 2$^{nd}$ lord in the 2$^{nd}$ house, or

(e) If the lords of the 2$^{nd}$ and 7$^{th}$ house have mutual aspect or conjoin in favourable place, i.e. the relationship between the lord of the 2$^{nd}$ house and the lord of the 7$^{th}$ house.

**RULE 6:** If Mercury is tenanted in the $10^{th}$ or $7^{th}$ house, in own or exaltation sign, it tends one towards business, provided other conditions also apply.

**RULE 7:** If the lord of the $4^{th}$ house conjoins with Mars or aspect each other in an angle or $11^{th}$ house and receives the aspect of the $10^{th}$ lord, one becomes successful in business.

**RULE 8:** Mercury is in the $7^{th}$ house and the $7^{th}$ lord in the $2^{nd}$ house or the lord of the $2^{nd}$ house conjoins with Mercury in the $7^{th}$ house.

In the above example lord of the $7^{th}$ house, Venus, is tenanted in the $2^{nd}$ house in conjunction with Mercury assuring the success in business.

**RULE 9:** If Mercury and Venus are associated in the $2^{nd}$ or the $7^{th}$ house success in business can be assured.

**RULE 10:** If the lord of the $2^{nd}$ house is placed favourably, under the full aspect of Mercury, one will be successful in the business matters.

**RULE 11:** If there is a relationship among the lords of $2^{nd}$,$7^{th}$, and $11^{th}$; $2^{nd}$, $7^{th}$, and $10^{th}$; $2^{nd}$, $10^{th}$, and$11^{th}$; $10^{th}$, $11^{th}$, and $7^{th}$, by association, aspect or placement, one will go in for an independent occupation, particularly if Mercury or Jupiter have an influence over these houses.

*Illustration : 17.2* (**RLS**) *Horoscope No.: 204*

Date of birth : 09.07.1949 Time of birth : 16:49:00 hrs
Place of birth : Alwar Lat 27:32:00 N Long 76:35:00E
Ayanamsa : 23:09:01 Sidereal Time : 11:33:36

| Pln | Degree | Rasi | Nakshatra | Pad |
|---|---|---|---|---|
| Asc | 19:22:04 | Sco | Jyestha | 1 |
| Sun | 23:44:48 | Gem | Punarvasu | 2 |
| Mon | 13:11:52 | Sag | Moola | 4 |

| | | | | |
|---|---|---|---|---|
| Mar | 27:28:22 | Tau | Mrigsira | 2 |
| Mer | 5:44:10 | Gem | Mrigsira | 4 |
| Jup (R) | 5:29:41 | Cap | Uttarasadha | 3 |
| Ven | 15:58:17 | Can | Pushya | 4 |
| Sat | 9:58:02 | Leo | Magha | 3 |
| Rah (R) | 28:36:06 | Pis | Revati | 4 |
| Ket (R) | 28:36:06 | Vir | Chitra | 2 |

**Lagna Chart**

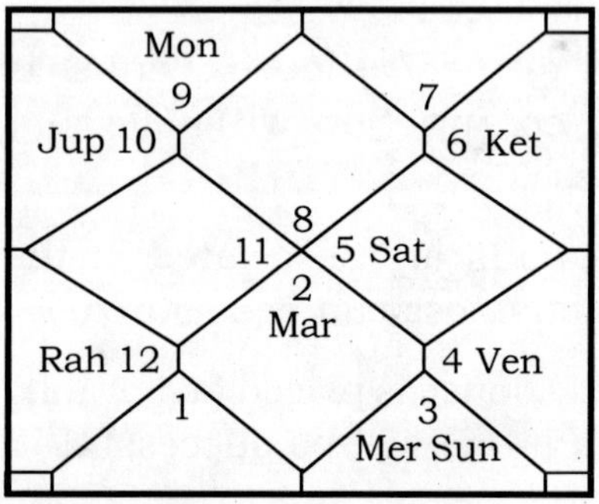


**Navamsa Chart**

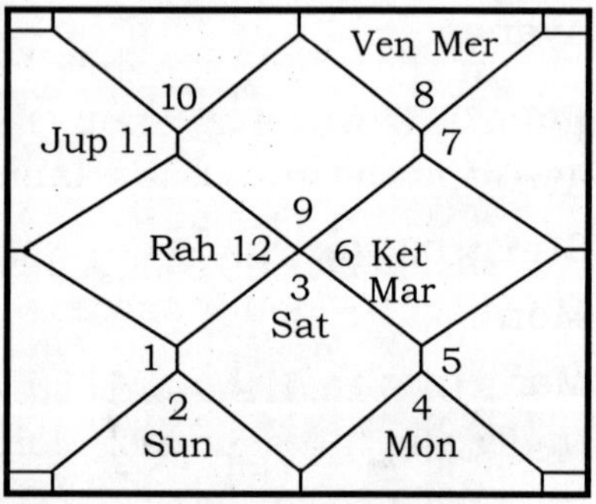


Balance of Vimsottari Dasa of **Ket 0Y 0M 26D**

In this horoscope of a famous businessman of grain and transport, following pattern of disposition of planets is to be noted.

The *lagna* and Moon both are strong but the Moon is slightly stronger than the *lagna*. There are six planets placed in the houses, as reckoned from the 7th to 12th. In *lagna* chart, both, lord of the 2nd house, Jupiter, and the lord of the 7th house, Venus, are under mutual aspect as per rule 5(e). The lords of the 10th and 11th, the Sun and Mercury, are associated and aspect the 2nd house as per 2(e). The lord of 10th house, the Sun, falls in *Punarvasu* constellation ruled by Jupiter. So, the native is mainly dealing in food grains.

The strong Saturn occupies the tenth house receiving the aspect of the *lagnadhipati* Mars. This verifies transport business. Venus represents vehicle, if used for comfort and luxury, whereas Saturn will represent it if used for transport or business purposes. Rule-7 reads that the fourth lord if conjoins with or is aspected by Mars, one adopts business.

Considering the Moon Chart Rule No.6 is applied that Mercury in the 7th should fall in Gemini or Virgo.

*Illustration : 17.3* **(VHD)** *Horoscope No.: 205*

Date of birth : 17.01.1928 Time of birth : 09:45:00 hrs
Place of birth : Jaipur Lat 26:53:00 N Long 75:50:00E
Ayanamsa : 22:50:51 Sidereal Time : 16:59:46

| **Pln** | **Degree** | **Rasi** | **Nakshatra** | **Pad** |
|---|---|---|---|---|
| Asc | 16:21:36 | Aqu | Satabhisha | 3 |
| Sun | 2:57:51 | Cap | Uttarasadha | 2 |
| Mon | 27:46:03 | Lib | Visakha | 3 |
| Mar | 5:45:04 | Sag | Moola | 2 |
| Mer (C) | 8:11:04 | Cap | Uttarasadha | 4 |
| Jup | 6:07:02 | Pis | U Bhadrapad | 1 |
| Ven | 22:50:06 | Sco | Jyestha | 2 |
| Sat | 22:21:21 | Sco | Jyestha | 2 |
| Rah | 25:17:58 | Tau | Mrigsira | 1 |
| Ket | 25:17:58 | Sco | Jyestha | 3 |

**Lagna Chart**

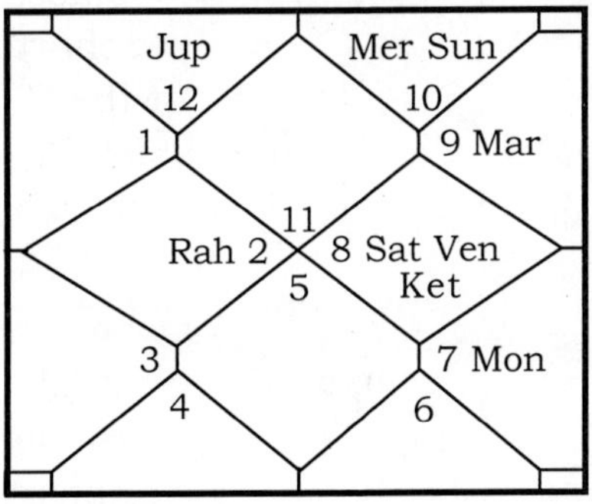


**Navamsa Chart**

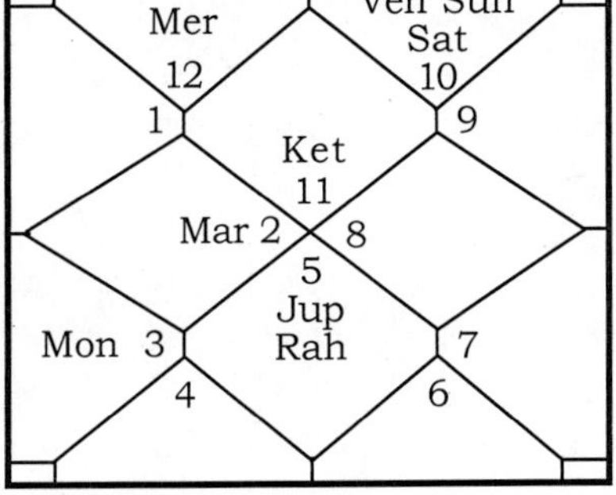


Balance of Vimsottari Dasa of **Jup 6Y 8M 4D**

This is the birth chart of Mr. Vishnu Hari Dalmia, the famous capitalist and industrialist. The following combinations may be noted.

The *lagna* and Moon both are strong. All the four significators, the Sun, Mercury, Saturn and Jupiter are also strong. Eight planets have occupied the houses from $10^{th}$ to $3^{rd}$. Lord of *lagna* and the $2^{nd}$ House, the Saturn, joins the fourth and $9^{th}$ lord Venus is in the $10^{th}$ house. Lord of the $10^{th}$ house, Mars, occupies $11^{th}$, while the $11^{th}$ lord is stationed at $2^{nd}$ house. The main significator of business, Mercury is forming *Vipreet Raj Yoga* and joins $7^{th}$ lord Sun. These planetary patterns made him one of the biggest industrialists of India. Rule No. 11 can also be applied here that the lord of $10^{th}$, Mars, is in $11^{th}$ and $11^{th}$ lord Jupiter is in $2^{nd}$, in own house aspecting the $10^{th}$.

*Illustration : 17.4* (**KKB**) *Horoscope No.: 206*

Date of birth : 11.11.1918 Time of birth : 07:13:00 hrs
Place of birth : Pilani Lat 28:22:00 N Long 75:32:00E
Ayanamsa : 22:43:41 Sidereal Time : 10:02:42

| **Pln** | **Degree** | **Rasi** | **Nakshatra** | **Pad** |
|---|---|---|---|---|
| Asc | 29:58:24 | Lib | Visakha | 3 |
| Sun | 25:08:10 | Lib | Visakha | 2 |
| Mon | 17:19:37 | Cap | Sravna | 3 |
| Mar | 7:00:17 | Sag | Moola | 3 |
| Mer | 10:27:25 | Sco | Anuradha | 3 |
| Jup (R) | 23:00:22 | Gem | Punarvasu | 1 |
| Ven (C) | 21:54:56 | Lib | Visakha | 1 |
| Sat | 4:45:29 | Leo | Magha | 2 |
| Rah (S) | 20:39:26 | Sco | Jyestha | 2 |
| Ket (S) | 20:39:26 | Tau | Rohini | 4 |

**Lagna Chart**

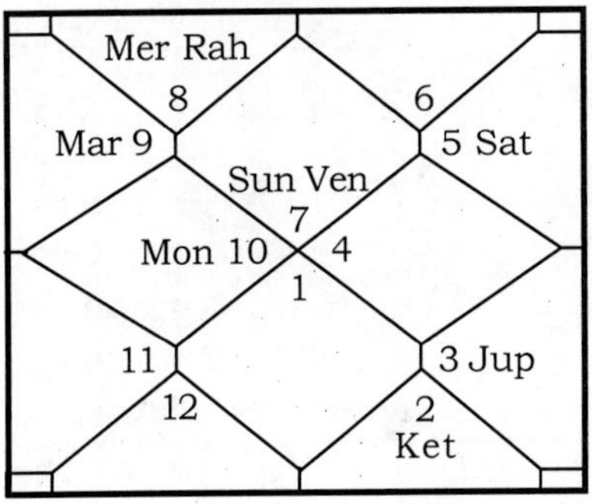


**Navamsa Chart**

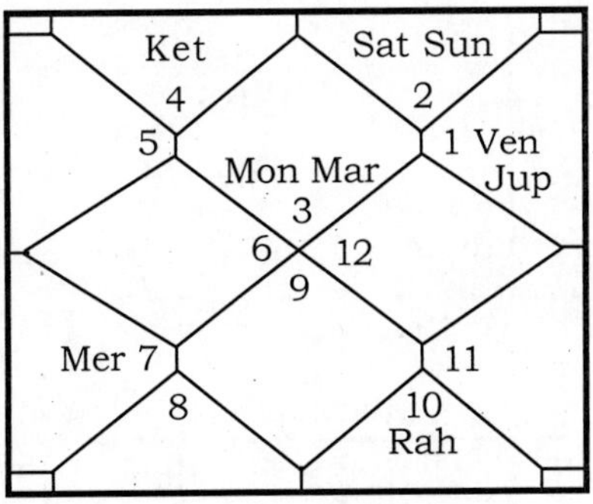


Balance of Vimsottari Dasa of **Mon 4Y 6M 1D**

In this one of the most excellent horoscopes of Mr. K.K. Birla, the *lagna*, Moon and all the four significators are very strong. *Yogakarak* Saturn joins 11th house . And the lord thereof is tenanted in the *lagna*, with the cancellation of debilitation, in conjunction with Venus. Mercury is associated with Rahu in 2nd. Note that the Jupiter aspects the lord of 11th, 1st, 2nd and the 7th i.e. all the houses connected with business are under the influence of well placed Jupiter due to an aspect on their lords, which made Mr. K.K. Birla the biggest industrialist of the Country. Mercury, Rahu in the 2nd house have been found present in the horoscope of many industrialists like Sri. G. D. Birla.

*Illustration : 17.5* (**AR**) *Horoscope No.: 207*

Date of birth : 03.12.1959 Time of birth : 03:44:00 hrs

Place of birth : Lucknow Lat 26:50:00 N Long 80:54:00E

Ayanamsa : 23:17:49 Sidereal Time : 8:21:37

| **Pln** | **Degree** | **Rasi** | **Nakshatra** | **Pad** |
|---|---|---|---|---|
| Asc | 8:06:14 | Lib | Svati | 1 |
| Sun | 16:41:41 | Sco | Jyestha | 1 |
| Mon | 23:02:02 | Sag | Purvasadha | 3 |
| Mar (C) | 6:06:54 | Sco | Anuradha | 1 |

| | | | | |
|---|---|---|---|---|
| Mer (R) | 0:29:01 | Sco | Visakha | 4 |
| Jup (D) | 18:56:28 | Sco | Jyestha | 1 |
| Ven | 1:19:27 | Lib | Chitra | 3 |
| Sat | 12:48:09 | Sag | Moola | 4 |
| Rah (R) | 7:52:25 | Vir | U Phalguni | 4 |
| Ket (R) | 7:52:25 | Pis | U Bhadrapad | 2 |

**Lagna Chart**

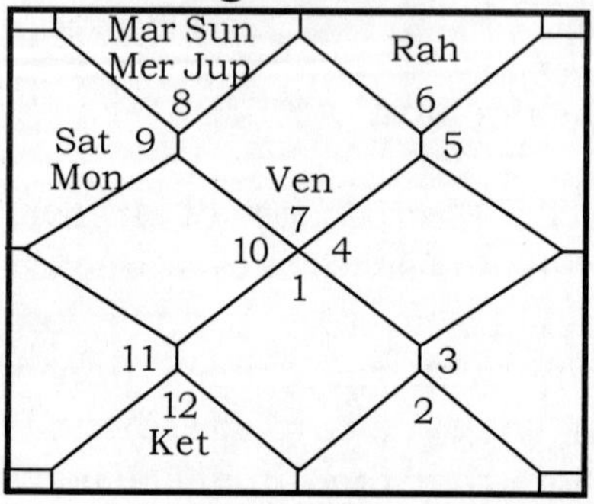


**Navamsa Chart**

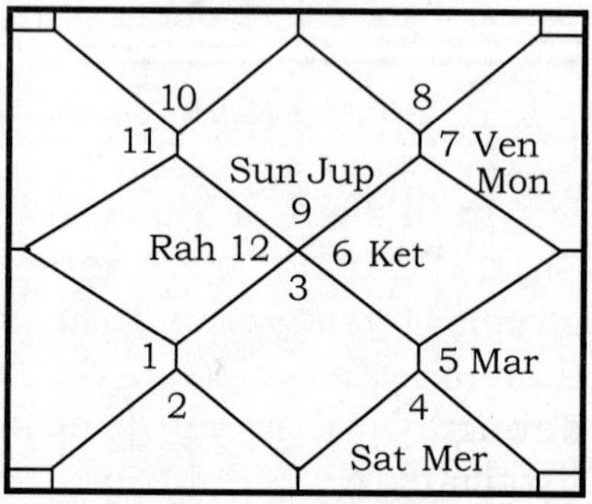


Balance of Vimsottari Dasa of **Ven 5Y 5M 11D**

In this horoscope, all planets signifying trade are strong except Jupiter. The *lagna,* Moon and the 10th house also have moderate strength having 7.22, 8.40 and 7.94 *Rupas bhava bala.* There are 8 planets occupying the houses 10th to the 3rd.

The lord of 11th house, the Sun is placed in the 2nd house with the 2nd and 7th lord Mars, as per Rule 1 and 5 and 7.

1. Association of Retrograde Mercury with these three planets has further strengthened the second house.

The lord of the tenth house, Moon is the strongest planet, as it secures 8.416 *Rupa Graha Bala*, and occupies the *navamsa* of Venus; so the native was advised for the trading in Silver, which brought him on the front rank of silver traders of Lucknow. Dr. B. V. Raman has suggested considering the second house also for the selection of occupation. He writes in 'How to judge a horoscope' 14th Chapter, that an examination of professional prospects would include the study of the 2nd house also as the source of income, which must necessarily be through one's occupation.' The 11th house rules gains and especially in profession that are in the nature of trade gives a clue in which the native would prosper.

In this horoscope the lord of the 2nd house, Mars, is also equally strong, as it obtains 6.739 *Rupa Graha Bala.* Mars indicates bricks, building material, works involving fire, chemist shop, military, mineral etc. The native has also been advised to begin a brick kiln and chemist shop. He followed the advice and has a roaring business of silver, brick Kiln and Chemist shop.

The planetary strength should not be compared in ascending or descending order of *Graha Bala* in *Rupas* but that must be compared in respect to the actual required strength of a planet and excess strength obtained above. For details of this, *Graha and Bhava Balas* of Dr. B. V. Raman may be referred to.

*Illustration : 17.6* **(GDB)** *Horoscope No.: 208*

Date of birth : 14.04.1894 Time of birth : 02:54:00 hrs
Place of birth : Pilani Lat 28:22:00 N Long 75:32:00E
Ayanamsa : 22:22:47 Sidereal Time : 16:22:15

| **Pln** | **Degree** | **Rasi** | **Nakshatra** | **Pad** |
|---|---|---|---|---|
| Asc | 3:55:22 | Aqu | Dhanishtha | 4 |
| Sun | 1:33:28 | Ari | Asvini | 1 |
| Mon | 13:15:51 | Can | Pushya | 3 |
| Mar | 19:15:48 | Cap | Sravna | 3 |
| Mer | 4:09:21 | Pis | U Bhadrapad | 1 |
| Jup | 9:54:07 | Tau | Krittika | 4 |
| Ven | 16:09:36 | Aqu | Satabhisha | 3 |
| Sat (R) | 29:17:14 | Vir | Chitra | 2 |

| | | | | |
|---|---|---|---|---|
| Rah (C) | 17:46:58 | Pis | Revati | 1 |
| Ket | 17:46:58 | Vir | Hasta | 3 |

**Lagna Chart**

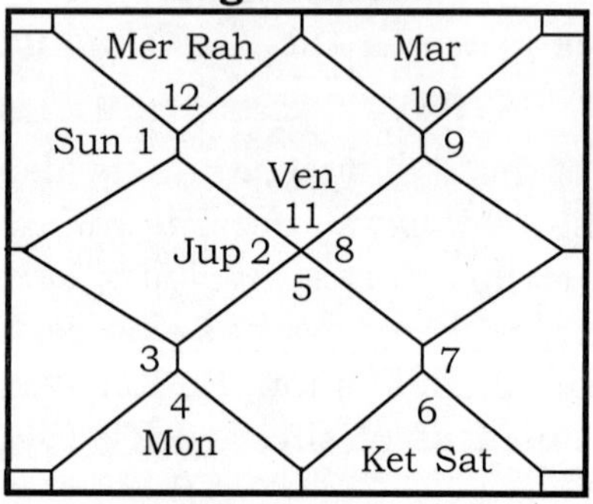


**Navamsa Chart**

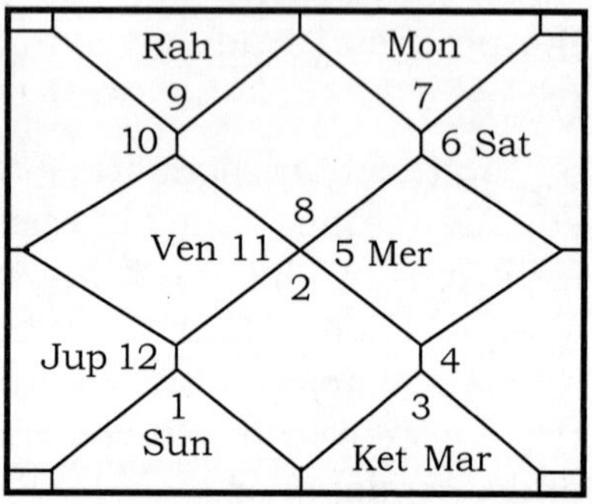


Balance of Vimsottari Dasa of **Sat 4Y 10M 5D**

This is the birth chart of the greatest and exemplary industrialist of the country who started his career from the salary of Rs. 15/- p.m. Shri Ghanshyam Das Birla was pride of our country. In his horoscope, 7th, 3rd and the 10th lords, the Sun and Mars, both are exalted. Moon occupies her own sign Cancer. Mercury occupies 2nd with the cancellation of debilitation in association with *Rahu*. Lord of the 10th Mars is receiving the aspect of lord of 11th house, Jupiter, while the 10th lord Mars is aspecting the 7th lord, the Sun. There are innumerable *Rajyogas* in this horoscope, which is not the subject of this article but we would like to add that the adversities as resultant of the *Kemadrum Yoga* stand cancelled.

*Illustration : 17.7* (**BKA**) *Horoscope No.: 209*

Date of birth : 23.07.1933 Time of birth : 15:26:00 hrs

Place of birth : Alwar Lat 27:32:00 N Long 76:35:00E

Ayanamsa : 22:55:54 Sidereal Time : 11:05:05

| **Pln** | **Degree** | **Rasi** | **Nakshatra** | **Pad** |
|---|---|---|---|---|
| Asc | 13:25:45 | Sco | Anuradha | 4 |
| Sun | 7:08:28 | Can | Pushya | 2 |

| | | | | |
|---|---|---|---|---|
| Mon (C) | 15:31:14 | Can | Pushya | 4 |
| Mar | 16:18:08 | Vir | Hasta | 2 |
| Mer (R/C) | 18:36:47 | Can | Aslesha | 1 |
| Jup | 27:29:15 | Leo | U Phalguni | 1 |
| Ven | 1:51:46 | Leo | Magha | 1 |
| Sat (R) | 21:05:46 | Cap | Sravna | 4 |
| Rah (R) | 5:47:54 | Aqu | Dhanishtha | 4 |
| Ket (R) | 5:47:54 | Leo | Magha | 2 |

**Lagna Chart**

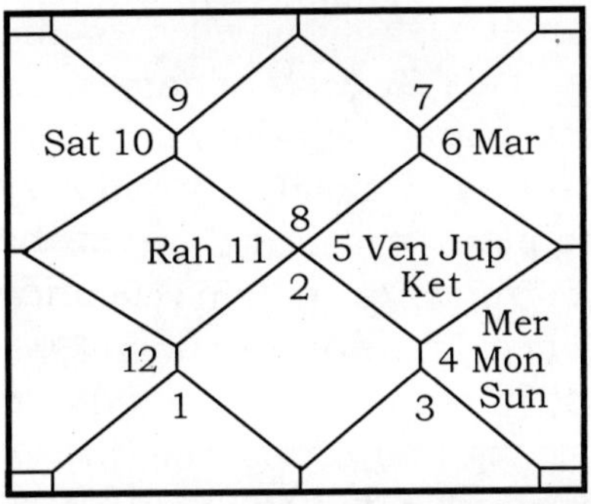


**Navamsa Chart**

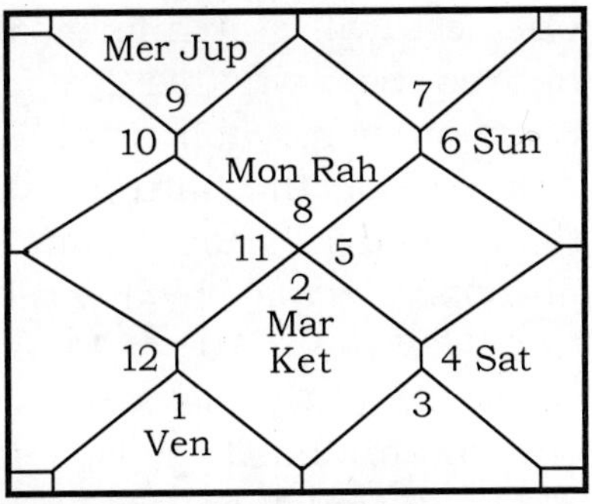


Balance of Vimsottari Dasa of **Sat 1Y 7M 18D**

In this birth chart of a famous rice merchant and owner of several Rice Mills of Rajasthan, planetary strength of the *lagna*, Moon and all the four significators is very encouraging. The tenth house obtains 8.14 *Rupa Graha Bala*. Eight planets have occupied 7th to 12th houses. Conjunction of the 2nd and the 7th lords, Jupiter and Venus, in the 10th house and the conjunction of the 10th and 11th lords, the Sun and Mercury, in the 9th house with the 9th lord, made the native a prominent trader. Lord of the 4th, Saturn, and the lord of the 10th house, the Sun, are under mutual aspect. Lord of the 2nd house, Jupiter, and the lord of the 7th, Venus in the 10th house indicate food grains, *Dal* and rice. The native owns a few *Dal* mills and rice mills and has earned huge amount of wealth through this trade.

The 4th house is 7th from 10th and 10th from 7th, therefore, the fourth house must also be judged in respect to 10th house. In example-1 lord of 4th house, Saturn, is posited in the *lagna* and aspects the 10th. In the example-3 lord of 4th, Venus, is stationed in 10th with the lord of *lagna* Saturn, receiving the aspect of 11th and 12th lord Jupiter. In example-5, the lord of the 4th, the *yogakarak* Venus is posited in the *lagna* and Jupiter, who is placed in the 4th, aspects the 10th and the 10th lord Mars. In the example-6, lord of the 4th, Saturn conjoins with the Sun under the mutual aspect.

Here a few principles of having independent occupation, i.e. business have been enunciated. This is not all. Which business will suit him most must also be advised to the natives. See, whether the *lagna* falls in a stationary sign, common or movable sign. Which planet has the maximum influence on the nature of business? Consider the lord of the 2nd and 10th houses and the planets placed therein and *navamsa* occupied by them. The stronger planet, in reference to the *lagna*, the 10th or 11th will decide the occupation of the native. Mercury plays the most important role in tending one towards business if he is strong and retrograde, in the 2nd or 7th house or 10th or 11th house. Jupiter should also never be overlooked.

If a person is born in certain ascendants, some planets own two concerning houses e.g. (1) Mercury for Leo and Jupiter for the Aquarius ascendant own 2nd and 11th; (2) Mars for Libra and Venus for Aries ascendant own the 2nd and the 7th house; (3) Mercury for Sagittarius and Pisces, and Jupiter for Gemini and Virgo own 7th and the 10th house. If these planets have been posited favourably, in either of these houses, business may be indicated. This will especially be so, if Jupiter or Mercury influence them, by aspect or association, provided the other factors, essential for business as enunciated above, are also found present in the birth chart.

Finally, it may be concluded that the approach in choosing "enterprise" or seeking an employment makes difference in life. It is an undeniable fact that the means of livelihood play crucial role in manifestation of one's unexhausted energies. The analyses of the aforementioned horoscopes are indeed unquestionable testimonies to prove the decisive roles of planetary combinations. A serious and sustained research becomes a prerequisite to serve as guide to choose vocation for success in the world.

## Certain important combinations for Trades or Businessman

1. If Mercury joins the 7th house and the 7th lord occupies 2nd house, the native will be a big trader.
2. If the 2nd lord is placed in the 7th house, in association with Mercury, the native will be a famous businessman.
3. If Mercury and Venus are conjoined in the 7th or 2nd house, the native will be a successful businessman, provided the combination of Mercury and Venus receives the aspect of benefic planets.
4. If the lord of 2nd house is well placed in the sign of benefic planets and the 2nd lord also receives the aspect of Mercury or the 7th lord, one will be a good trader.
5. Mercury is exalted and joins the 7th house and the 2nd house is aspected by the lord of 2nd house, one may work in the organization connected with electricity. One may work in the factory of ammunition.
6. If 10th lord obtains the *navamsa* of Mercury, the native will earn through computers, journalism, writing poetry or novel, editing, translation, painting, publication, law, proofreading etc.
7. If the 10th lord obtains the *navamsa* of Jupiter, one will earn through gold, salt, grains, *Dals*, teaching, law, Judge, *pandit,* prophets, priest, finance business, restaurants, astrology, spiritualism etc.
8. If the 10th lord obtains the *navamsa* of Venus, one gets into business of animals, horses, elephants, cows, precious stones, silver, diamond, milk products, sugar,

gum, perfumes, flowers, incense (*Dhoop*), picture, drama, acting, singing etc.

**9.** If Saturn obtains the *navamas* of *Atmakarka* planet, one will become a prosperous businessman.

**10.** If the $10^{th}$ lord falls in the *navama* of Saturn, one earns through agriculture, travel agents, peon, servants, blacksmith, industry, iron rolling mill, prison, tailor, oil mill, crusher etc.

**11.** If Mercury or Venus join the $10^{th}$ house and the $10^{th}$ falls in the sign of these planets, one will work related to textiles, fabrics, readymade garments etc. He also does so if Jupiter and Venus are placed in quadrant from each other.

## Combination for Various Trades

1. If the $10^{th}$ lord obtains the *navamsa* of the Sun, one will earn through the trade of sugar, pearl, *ghee, gur,* woolen clothes, medicines, gold etc. He may also earn through grains, wood, grass, furniture etc.

2. If Moon is the lord of the *navamsa* occupied by the $10^{th}$ lord, one will do business pertaining to brick, lime, sand, cement, *Shankh*, pearl, earthen toys, wire, oil or cloths etc.

3. If $10^{th}$ lord obtains the *navamsa* of Mars, one will earn through the job of blacksmith, carpentry or machinery related work.

•

# CHAPTER-18

# Miscellany and Remedies

## Concerning Houses and Planets for Ascertaining Direction of Occupation

Ordinarily, the 10th *Bhava* is the one that denotes all particulars relating to one's livelihood including the place or direction where one is likely to earn his livelihood. The sign, falling on the 10th cusp, determines the place or direction of one's occupation. As regards the planets, the lord of the *navamsa* occupied by the 10th lord is of vital significance. The sign in which this lord is placed, the lord of the 10th house and the lord of the Sun sign are of secondary importance. If Moon is strong, then it has to be applied from the Moon sign also. Blending the results of the planets and the signs so arrived, will determine the place or the direction of the profession.

## Leather Merchant

When the 10th house is a *Jeeva Rasi*, it indicates leather. When the 10th is owned and occupied by Jupiter, again leather is indicated. *Jeeva Rasis* are Gemini, Virgo, Sagittarius and Pisces. When these Rasis happen to be the 10th, one will have a vocation related to leather. Mercury and Jupiter are *Jeeva grahas*.

## Iron Merchant

The Sun and Saturn deal with iron. Mars too is the same. Find out *Dhatu Rasi* and its connection with the Moon, Mars, Saturn and Rahu. These indicate iron goods. *Dhatu Rasis* are Aries, Cancer, Libra and Capricorn. Rahu is a *Dhatu Graha*.

## Mining Business

All movable signs indicate *Dhatus* (metals). Moon, Mars, Saturn and Rahu are *Dhatu Grahas. Asvini, Rohini, Punarvasu, Magha, Hasta, Visakha, Moola, Sravna* and *Poorvabhadra* are *Dhatu Nakshatras*. When the house of wealth or house of property is a movable sign, and when *Dhatu Grahas* are posited in the same and when the longitudes of 2 or 4 indicate *Dhatu* constellations, the native is an owner of mines. When the 10$^{th}$ house has *Dhatu* connection as above, the native is employed in mines. The *vargas* of the 2$^{nd}$, 4$^{th}$ and 10$^{th}$ houses may be examined –Prasna Marga.

## Success in Lottery

The 4$^{th}$ & 9$^{th}$ houses represent lotteries. Libra also governs the same. Amongst the planets, Venus and Jupiter may be said to represent the same. The lords of the 4$^{th}$ and 9$^{th}$, and planets posited in the 4$^{th}$ and 9$^{th}$, can also be loooked into.

## Combination for Agriculture

If the lord of the 10$^{th}$ occupies *Katakamsa* (Cancer *navamsa*) and is aspected or joined by Saturn, the native becomes an agricultural demonstrator.

## Pecularities of The Lord of 3$^{rd}$ and 10$^{th}$ House

The lord of the 10$^{th}$ is spoiled by the aspect of the lord of the 3$^{rd}$, while the lord of the 3$^{rd}$ is improved by the aspect of the lord of 10$^{th}$. In the example of Aquarius *lagna*, with Mars being the lord of the 3$^{rd}$ and the 10$^{th}$, if there is no combination or aspect of any other planet, Mars' Dasa will be favourable or unfavourable, according to its strength derived from position and other sources of strength.

## Venus : A Pointer to Profession

Importance should be given to Venus during the examination of the birth chart with regard to professional progression. Venus is a supporting significator of almost all professions. We will not be discussing Venus in detail here, as the book has already become quite exhaustive and voluminous. If, we decide to write a separate book on profession, it will be entitled as **Venus : A Pointer to Profession.**

Taurus is the second sign of the Zodiac and its ruler is Venus. Moon gets exalted here. The second house provides the resources to earn money; it indicates the ways and means to earn money; it shows the tools and implements by which one can earn his livelihood; it reveals one's efforts and strife to earn money. As Venus is the ruler of the second sign of the Zodiac, so its position in a birth chart will indicate the correct vocation, in which one will shine best in his life. If one pursues this vocation vigorously, he will surely attain success and prosperity in it.

## True Nature and Characteristics of Venus

Venus is a planet of harmony and adaptation which finds its expression as 'love'. This love is idealistic and universal. Every work requires unification, co-operation and collaboration. Venus gives beauty, glamour and artistic talent; interest in music, dance, cinema and art. It gives the urge and inspiration to work. So, the most important point is love for work, and Venus gives this passion for work. It is for this reason, Venus's position in a birth chart, and *navamsa* as well, will reveal one's appropriate vocation, wherein he will find love and cheerfulness. This is what is called 'Job Satisfaction'.

Mercury gives the requisite talent, intellect and practical mind to work. The Sun gives the life-force, vital energy and constitutional strength. When these three planets conjoin together in the $1/2/5^{th}$ and in airy signs, it makes one genius.

It also assists the native to make new inventions or new discoveries for the benefit of mankind, if it conjoins with Mercury and the Sun, in the $1/2/5^{th}$ and in airy signs. This is called creation.

## Venus is a strong agent of the Law of *Karma*

A strong Venus, in angle or trine, makes one a very strong man of great personality, which shows that the native had certainly done good and pious deeds in the past birth.

# Remedial Measures and Spiritual Remedies

Many a times, there are innumerable problems and disasters in profession like dismissal, dissatisfaction, distress, demotions, displeasures, disappointments, dejections, termination, reversions, and suspension etc. That happens due to one or the other planetary affliction, malefic *dasa-bhukti* and overall negative influence over the native. To deal with the preventive and remedial measures is out of the scope of this book.

We have written more than fifteen books on the remedies and rectifications of various problems, in Hindi and English as well. A separate book is required for the subject of prevention and rectification of professional problems, disasters and distress etc. However, apart from other specific details of preventive measures, we intend to mention a few most important remedial measures for the reinstatement, to revoke suspension, and for promotion and the like.

**Remedial Measures :**

1. ***Ganapati Atharvshirsh, Purusha Sukta*** and ***Shreesukta*** should be correctly read after *shodshopchaar* worship of Lord Ganapati, Lord Vishnu and Goddess Lakshmi.

2. ***Vaancha Kalplata Stotra*** is one of the most useful remedies for professional progress and prosperity. This will help a lot in promotion and reinstatement as well, if it is done properly under the supervision of learned and experienced *Acharyas*.

3. Following *shlokas* of ***Shree Durga Saptshati*** should be recited for 1100 times everyday by the native, or 18 or 36 *Samput Paath* of *Shree Durga Saptshati* should be done by using the following Samput :

1. ततो वव्रे नृपो राज्यमविभ्रंश्यन्यजन्मनि।
   अत्रैव व निजं राज्यं हतशत्रुबलं बलात्।। (Ch. 13, Sloka 17)

2. यं यं चिन्तयते कामं तं तं प्राप्नोति निश्चितम्।
   परमैश्वर्यमतुलं प्राप्स्यते भूतले पुमान्।।
   (*Devyah Kavacham*, Sloka 44)

3. स्वल्पैरहोभिर्नृपते स्वं राज्यं प्राप्स्यते भवान्।
   हत्वा रिपूनस्खलितं तव तत्र भविष्यति।। (Ch. 13, Sloka 20,21)

4. शरणागतदीनार्तपरित्राणपरायणे ।
   सर्वस्यार्तिहरे देवि नारायणि नमोऽस्तु ते।। (Ch. 11, Sloka 12)

5. एवं देव्या वरं लब्ध्वा सुरथः क्षत्रियर्षभः।। (Ch. 13, Sloka 28)

4. Mantra jaap of Vedic Mantras of the afflicted planets, which are creating problems, tensions, frustration and disappointment in service matters, should also be recited for specified number of times along with *dashansh* (1/10th) *Havan, Tarpan, Marjan* etc.

5. **To revoke suspension or termination :**
   1. All mantras as mentioned above must be done in the same manner and in addition to those, following *Stotras* should also be read for requisite number of times :

श्री गणपति अथर्वशीर्ष स्तोत्र

ॐ नमस्ते गणपतये। त्वमेव प्रत्यक्षं तत्त्वमसि। त्वमेव केवलं कर्तासि। त्वमेव केवलं धर्तासि। त्वमेव केवलं हर्तासि। त्वमेव सर्व खल्विदं ब्रह्मासि। त्वं साक्षादात्मासि नित्यम्। ऋतं वच्मि। सत्यं वच्मि। अव त्वं माम्। अब वक्तारम्। एव श्रोतारम्। अव दातारम्। अव धातारम्। अवानूचानव शिष्यम्। अव पश्चात्तात्। अव पुरस्तात्। अवोत्तरात्तात् अव दक्षिणात्तात्। अव चोर्ध्वात्तात। अवाधरात्तात्। सर्वतो मां पाहि पाहि समन्तात्। त्वं वाङ्गमयस्तवं चिन्मयः। त्वमानन्दमयस्त्वं ब्रह्ममयः। त्वं सच्चिदानन्दोऽ-द्वितीयोऽसि। त्वं प्रत्यक्षब्रह्मासि। त्वं ज्ञानमयो विज्ञानमयोऽसि। सर्व जगदिदं त्वत्तो जायते। सर्व जगदिदं त्वयि

लयमेष्यति। सर्वं जगदिदं त्वयि प्रत्येति। त्वं भूमिरापोऽनलोऽनिलो नभः। त्वं चत्वारि वाक्पदानि। त्वं गुणत्रयातीतः। त्वं देहत्रयातीतः। त्वं कालत्रयातीतः। त्वं मूलाधारस्थितोऽसि नित्यम्। त्वं शक्तित्रयात्मकः। त्वां योगिनो ध्यायन्ति नित्यम्। त्वं ब्रह्मा, त्वं विष्णुस्त्वं रुद्रस्त्वमिन्द्रस्त्वमग्निस्त्वं वायुस्त्वं सूर्यस्त्वं चन्द्रमास्त्वं ब्रह्मभूर्भुवः स्वरोम्। गणादीन्पूर्वमुच्चार्य वर्णादिंस्तदनन्तरम्। अनुस्वारः परतरः। अर्धेन्दुलसितम्। तारेण रुद्धम्। एतत्तवमनुस्वरुपम्। गकारः पूर्वरुपम्। अकारो मध्यमरुपम्। अनुस्वारश्चान्त्यरुपम्। विन्दुरुत्तररुपम्। नादः सन्धानम्। संहिता सन्धिः। सैषा गणेशविद्या। गणक ऋषिः। निचृद्गायत्रीछंदः। गणपतिर्देवता।। ॐ गं गणपतये नमः। एकदन्ताय विद्महे वक्रतुण्डाय धीमहि, तन्नो दन्ती प्रचोदयात्। एकदन्तं चतुर्हस्तं पाशमङ्कुशधारिणम्। अभयं च वरदं हस्तेबिभ्राणं मूषकध्वजम्। रक्तंलम्बोदरं शूर्पकर्णकं रक्तवाससम्। रक्त-गन्धानुलिप्तांगं रक्तपुष्पैः सुपूजितम्।। भक्तानुकम्पिनं देवं जगत्कारणमच्युतम्। आविर्भूतं च सृष्ट्यादौ प्रकृतेः पुरुषात्परम्।। एवं ध्यायति यो नित्यं स योगी योगिनां वरः।। नमो व्रातपतये नमो गणपतये नमः प्रमथपतये नमस्तेऽस्तु लम्बोदरायैकदन्ताय विध्नविनाशिने शिवसुताय श्रीवरदमूर्तये नमो नमः।। एतदथर्वशीर्ष योऽधीते। स ब्रह्मभूयाय कल्पते। स सर्वविघ्नैर्न बाध्यते। स सर्वतः सुखमेधते। स पंचमहापापामुच्यते।। सायमधीयानो दिवसकृतं पापं नाशयति। प्रातरधीयानो रात्रिकृतं पापं नाशयति। सायम्प्रातः प्रयुत्र्जानोऽपापो भवति। सर्वत्राधीयानोऽपविघ्नो भवति। धमार्थकाममोक्षं च विन्दति। इदमथर्वशीर्षमशिष्याय न देयम्। यो यदि मोहाद्दास्यति। स पापीयान्भवति।। सहस्रावर्तनाद्यं यं यं काममधीते तं तमनेन साधयेत्।। अनेन गणपतिमभिषित्र्चति स वाग्मी भवति। चतुर्थ्यामनश्नन्त्र्जपति स विद्यावान्भवति। इत्यथवर्णवाक्यम्। ब्रह्माद्याचरणं विद्यान्न विभेति कदाचनेति। यो दूर्वाकुंरैर्यजति स वैश्रवणोपमो भवति। यो लाजैर्यजति। स यशोवान् भवति। स मेधावान् भवति। यो मोदकसहस्रेण यजति। स वांछितफलमवाप्नोति। यः साज्यसमिद्भिर्यजति स सर्वं लभते स सर्वं लभते। अष्टौ ब्राह्मणान्सम्यग्ग्राहयित्वा सूर्यवर्चस्वी भवति। सूर्यग्रहे महानद्यां प्रतिमासन्निधौ वा जप्त्वा सिद्धमन्त्रो भवति। महाविघ्नात्प्रमुच्यते। महादोषात्प्रमुच्यते। महापापोत्प्रमुच्यति। स सर्वविद्भवति। स सर्वविद्भवति य एवं वेद।। इत्युपनिषत्।।

*।। इति गणपत्यथर्वशीर्षम्।।*

Above *stotra* should be recited 15 times daily, along with one-tenth *Havan, Tarpan* and *Marjan* etc

## NRASINGH KAVACH

**(*For affliction of planets, obstacles in promotions influence of evil spirits and forced Tantrik measures*)**

There are different types of people in the society. Some continuously make advancement as they are desirous of making progress, expansion and development. Their efforts are directed to make themselves better and the best. However, there is one such group of people, who unmindful of their own growth harness their energy towards damaging others. They aim their efforts to injure others, humiliate them, obstruct other's growth and sully their reputation. They are sadists and they do not even hesitate in inflicting fatal harm on their rivals by using Tantrik measures. Nrasingh Kavach and mantras have proved immensely beneficial to persons distressed by evil spirits, afflicted planets, enmity, accidents, recurrent failures, obstructions in promotion and forced Tantrik measures. However, caution is required in its use. If assembling Nrasingh Kavach is not possible then Nrasingh Mantra, given at the end, should be recited for 108 x 11 times (one to 11 Malas) daily to remove any impediment in the path of progress. Enemies are routed and obstacles in promotion are eliminated. Tantrik measures and evil spirits are made ineffective. Nrasingh Mantra should be recited after Shodashopchar worship of God Vishnu, as Nrasingh is incarnation of Lord Vishnu. This experiment is time tested and we have ourselves got amazing benefits when used with caution.

**Method:** Nrasingh Kavach should be engraved on a copper sheet or written on a *Bhojpatra* with *Ashtgandh*, worshipped after being energized and 108 path daily for nine days should be recited. Kavach is also energized by Purashcharan for seven days followed by one-tenth havan and feeding Brahmins, starting form eighth lunar day of dark half to fourteenth lunar day. Such energized Kavach will ward off all impending evils and obstructions in the house where it is placed. It must be, however, kept in mind that worshipping the 'Kavach' daily by offering incense etc will give maximum benefits. Ignoring it will certainly harm the native.

**KAVACH:**

नारद उवाच- इन्द्रिादि देववृन्देश ईड्येश्वर जगत्पते,
महाविष्णोर्नृसिंहस्य कवचं ब्रूहि मे प्रभो।।
यस्य प्रपठनात् विद्वान त्रैलोक्य विजयी भवेत्।

ब्रह्मोवाच- शृणु नारद वक्ष्यामि पुत्रश्रेष्ठ तपोधन,
कवचं नरसिंहस्यस्त्रैलोक्यविजयी भवेत्।

स्रष्टाहं जगतां वत्स पठनात् धारणात् यतः, लक्ष्मीः जगत्त्रयंपाति संहर्ताच महेश्वरः।
पठनात् धारणात् देवाः बहवश्च दिगीश्वराः ब्रह्ममंत्रमयं वक्ष्ये भ्रान्त्यादि विनिवारकम्।।
यस्य प्रसादात् दुर्वासाःस्त्रत्र्यैलोक्य विजयीभवेत् पठनाद्धारणादूयस्य शास्ताच क्रोधभैरवः।
त्रैलोक्य विजयस्यापि कवचस्य प्रजापतिः ऋषिश्छन्दस्तु गायत्री नृसिंहो देवता विभुः।।

क्ष्रौं बीजं मे शिरः पातु चनद्रवर्णो महामनुः,
ओम् उग्रं वीरं महाविष्णुं ज्वलनतं सर्वतोमुखम्।

नृसिंह भीषणं भद्रं मृत्युमृत्युं नमाम्यहम् द्वात्रिंशदक्षरो मंत्रो मंत्रराजः सुरद्रुमः।
कण्ठं पातु ध्रुवं क्ष्रौं हृद् भगवते चक्षुषीमम, नरसिंहाय च ज्वालामालिने पातुकर्णकम्।
दीपदंष्ट्रायच तथा अग्निनेत्राय नासिकाम्, सर्वरक्षोःघ्नायच तथा सर्वभूतहिताय च।।
सर्वज्वर विनाशाय दहदह पदद्वम, रक्ष रक्ष वर्म मंत्रःस्वाहा पातु मुखं मम।।
तारादि रामचन्द्राय नमः पातु हृदं मम क्लीं पायात्पार्श्वयुग्मं च तारो नमः पदं ततः।

नारायणाय नाभिं च आं ह्रीं क्रों क्ष्रौं च हुं फट्,
षडक्षरः कटि पातु ओम् नमो भगवते पदम्।
वासुदेवाय च पृष्ठं क्लीं कृष्णाय क्लीं उरुद्वयम्
क्लीं कृष्णाय सदा पातु जानुनी च मनूत्तमः

क्लीं ग्लौं क्लीं श्यामलांगाय नमः पायात्मदद्वयम् क्ष्रौं नृसिंहाय क्ष्रौं च सर्वांगे मे सादवतु
इति ते कथितं वत्स सर्व मंत्रौध विग्रहम, तवसनेहानमयाख्यातं प्रवक्तव्यं नकसयचित्
गुरुपूजां विधायाय गृह्णीयात् कवचं ततः सर्वपुण्ययुतो भूत्वा सर्वसिद्धियुतोभवेत्।

**Note:** This 'Kavach' is embodiement of Nrasingh mantra. Along with Kavach, recitation of mantra bestows best results. Following is the Mantra:

**'ओम् नरसिंहाय हिरण्यकशिपुवक्षः स्थलविदारणाय त्रिभुवनव्यापकाय भूतप्रेत पिशाचडाकिनीकुलोन्मूलनाय स्तंभोद्‌भवाय समस्त दोषान् हर हर विसर विसर पच पच हन हन कंपय कंपय मथ मथ ह्रीं ह्रीं ह्रीं फट् फट् ठः ठः ठः एहि एहि रुद्रः आज्ञा पयति स्वाहा।'**

6. 18 or 36 *Samput Paath* of **Shree Durga Saptshati** should be done by using the following *Samput*:

    1. **सर्वाबाधाप्रशमनं त्रैलोक्यस्याखिलेश्वरि।**
    **एवमेव त्वया कार्यमस्मद्वैरिविनाशनम्।।** (अ. 11, श्लोक 39)

    2. **ततो वव्रे नृपो राज्यमविभ्रंश्यन्यजन्मनि।**
    **अत्रैव व निजं राज्यं हतशत्रुबलं बलात्।।** (अ. 13, श्लोक 17)

    3. **स्वल्पैरहोभिर्नृपते स्वं राज्यं प्राप्स्यते भवान्।**
    **हत्वा रिपूनस्खलितं तव तत्र भविष्यति।।** (अ. 13, श्लोक 20,21)

    4. **सर्वबाधासु घोरासु वेदनाभ्यर्दितोऽपि वा।**
    **स्मरन्ममैतच्चरितं नरो मुच्येत संकटात्।।**

    5. **करोतु सा नः शुभहेतुरीश्वरी।**
    **शुभानि भद्राण्यभिहन्तु चापदः।।** (अ. 5, श्लोक 81)

    6. **अचिन्त्यरूपचरिते सर्वशत्रुविनाशिनी।**
    **रूपं देहि जयं देहि यशो देहि द्विषो जहि।।** (अर्गलास्तोत्र, श्लोक 8)

    7. **दुर्गे स्मृता हरसि भीतिमशेषजन्तोः**
    **स्वस्थैः स्मृता मतिमतीव शुभाँ ददासि।**
    **दारिद्र्य-दुःख-भयहारिणि का त्वदन्या,**
    **सर्वोपकार-करणाय सदार्द्रचिता।।** (अ. 4, श्लोक 17)

7. If the situation is extremely tough and problematic and grave charges have been framed against the native, ***Shatchandee*** and ***Shatrudree*** paath will also be

extremely useful and will bestow amazing fortune on the native.

8. ***Mahakali Mantra*** and ***Dus Mahavidya Mantra*** will also quite useful, if it is so indicated in the birth chart.

### *1.* MAHAKALI MANTRA

ॐ क्रीं क्रीं क्रीं ॐ हूँ हूँ ह्रीं ह्रीं महाकाली क्रीं क्रीं क्रीं हूँ हूँ ह्रीं ह्रीं स्वाहा।

### *2.* DUS MAHAVIDYA MANTRA

।। श्री गणेशाय नमः ।।

ॐ महाविद्यां प्रवक्ष्यामि महास्तोत्रं प्रकाशये।।

अस्य मनस्साक्षी देवता सविता छन्दः जगदादिः श्री शिवो देवता श्रीशिव प्रीत्यर्थे मनः कामना सिद्ध्यर्थे जपे विनियोगः इति संकल्पः। ॐ महाविद्यां प्रवक्ष्यामि महादेवेन निर्विताम्। चिन्तितां विराटरूपेण मानवोदयनंदिनीम्।। उत्तमां सर्वविद्यानां सर्वभूतवशंकरीम्।।

ॐ कुलकरी वशकरी धेनुकरी दलकरी पुष्टिकरी शवलबलबंधनी सर्वगंकरी सर्वग्रहोच्चाटिनी पुत्रमित्र पौत्रनभोबंधनी मोहनी सर्वकृत्यकारिणी सर्वलोकवशं कारिणी सर्व राजवशं करी सर्वजन प्रमोदिनी, सर्वग्रहमैत्रीकरी, त्वं ऐकाहिकं द्वैयाहिकं, त्रैयाहिकं, पंचाहिकं, षाष्ठाहिकं, साप्ताहिकमाष्ट-माहिकं चातुर्मासिकं षाण्मासिकं सांवत्सरिकं, संध्याहिकं, प्रातर्मध्याहिकं, शीतोष्णमुदकं, वायुकं, कण्ठिकं, कुष्ठरोगमुदररोगं जठररोगं मुखरोगं प्रमेहमुक्ताविक्षिप्तकविस्फोटकादि विनाशाय स्वाहा।।

ॐ विप्र विष्णवे नमः।। ॐ शिं शिवाय नमः।।
ॐ सं सूर्य्याय नमः।। ॐ चं चंद्राय नमः।।
ॐ मं मंगलाय नमः।। ॐ बुं बुधाय नमः।।
ॐ बृं बृहस्पतये नमः।। ॐ शुं शुक्राय नमः।।
ॐ शं शनैश्चराय नमः।। ॐ रां राहवे नमः।।
ॐ कं केतवे नमः।।

ॐ महाशाक्तिक महाशाक्तिक ॐ भूत प्रेत पिशाचराक्षसानां सर्वदृष्टिभयं विनाशाय स्वाहा। ॐ नमो भगवते रुद्राय ॐ सिं सिंहस्य सिंहस्य

दलमृगेन्द्र ॐ ग्राहवृकब्याघ्रादिमृगानहं बध्नामि ॐ श्रोतं बध्नामि ॐ नेत्रं बध्नामि ॐ वाचंबध्नामि ॐ गतिं बध्नामि ॐ आशां बध्नामि, ॐ दिशां बध्नामि, ॐ सर्वबन्धं बध्नामि, ॐ मायां बध्नामि, ॐ सर्वजनान् बध्नामि, ॐ बंधं बध्नामि कुरु कुरु स्वाहा। पंचयोजन विस्तीर्ण मण्डलं मण्डलं कुरु कुरु स्वाहा ॐ नमो भगवते रुद्राय पूर्व दिशायै इन्द्राय ऐरावतारुढाय, बज्रहस्ताय, परिवारसहिताय, दिग्देवताधिपतये इन्द्राय मण्डलं बध्नामि बध्नामि रक्ष रक्ष माचल माचल माक्राम्य माक्राम्य ॐ ह्रां ह्रीं ह्रूं फट् स्वाहा।

ॐ नमो भगवते रुद्राय आग्नेयै अजारुढाय शक्तिहस्ताय परिवार सहिताय, दिग्देवताधिपतये आग्नेयमण्डलं बध्नामि बध्नामि रक्ष रक्ष माचल माचल माक्राम्य माक्राम्य ॐ ह्रां ह्रीं ह्रूं फट् स्वाहा।

ॐ नमो भगवते रुद्राय दक्षिणदिशायै महिषारुढ़ाय शक्तिहस्ताय परिवारसहिताय यमाय दलं बध्नामि बध्नामि रक्ष रक्ष माचल माचल माक्राम्य माक्राम्य ॐ ह्रां ह्रीं ह्रूं फट् स्वाहा।

ॐ नमो भगवते रुद्राय नैर्ऋत्यदिशायै प्रेतमारुढ़ाय खड्गहस्ताय परिवारसहिताय दिग्देवताधिपतये नैर्ऋत्ये मण्डलं बध्नामि बध्नामि रक्ष रक्ष माचल माचल माक्राम्य माक्राम्य ॐ ह्रां ह्रीं ह्रूं फट् स्वाहा।

ॐ नमो भगवते रुद्राय पश्चिमदिशायै मकरारुढ़ाय पाशहस्ताय परिवारसहिताय दिग्देवताधिपतये वरुणाय मण्डलं बध्नामि बध्नामि रक्ष रक्ष माचल माचल माक्राम्य माक्राम्य ॐ ह्रां ह्रीं ह्रूं फट् स्वाहा।

ॐ नमो भगवते रुद्राय वायव्य दिशायै मृगारुढ़ाय पाशहस्ताय परिवारसहिताय दिग्देवताधिपतये वायवे मण्डलं बध्नामि बध्नामि रक्ष रक्ष माचल माचल माक्राम्य माक्राम्य ॐ ह्रां ह्रीं ह्रूं फट् स्वाहा।

ॐ नमो भगवते रुद्राय उत्तर दिशायै पुष्कारुढ़ाय वाणहस्ताय परिवारसहिताय दिग्देवताधिपतये कुबेराय मण्डलं बध्नामि बध्नामि रक्ष रक्ष माचल माचल माक्राम्य माक्राम्य ॐ ह्रां ह्रीं ह्रूं फट् स्वाहा।

ॐ नमो भगवते रुद्राय ईशान्यदिशायै वृषभारुढ़ाय त्रिशूलहस्ताय परिवार सहिताय दिग्देवताधिपतये ईशानाय मण्डलं बध्नामि बध्नामि रक्ष रक्ष माचल माचल माक्राम्य माक्राम्य ॐ ह्रां ह्रीं ह्रूं फट् स्वाहा।

ॐ नमो भगवते रुद्राय रात्रिज्वर दिवाज्वर सायंज्वर प्रातर्ज्वर अग्निज्वर शीतज्वर द्वन्द्वज्वर राक्षसज्वर भूतज्वर पिशाचज्वर दृष्टिजवर स्फितंकाज्वर मतिज्वर माण्डजवर पापिज्वर मतिप्रयोगादिज्वर विनाशाय स्वाहा।

ॐ अक्षिशूल कुक्षिशूल कर्णशूल घ्राणशूल दन्तशूल गण्डशूल शिरश्शूल शिरोर्द्धशूल पादशूल पादार्द्धशूल सर्वांगशूल विनाशाय स्वाहा।

सर्वव्याधिविनाशाय स्वाहा। सव्रशत्रुविनाशाय स्वाहा। अपहृतशोकादि विनाशाय स्वाहा। आत्मरक्षे प्राणरक्षे अग्निरक्षे प्रथमं अग्नि रक्षेते शावकं बध्नामि ॐ ह्रां ह्रीं देहि स्वाहा।

ॐ इन्द्राय देहि स्वाहा।। ॐ स्वर ब्रह्मर्क्षे इति विजाते विष्णु दण्ड ॐ ज्वर ज्वर ईश्वरदण्ड ॐ जं तं नं भंजनिरिति दण्ड ॐ प्रहर प्रहर दण्डं ह्रीं लीं ह्रीं लीं यमदण्ड ॐ नित्ये नित्ये, दण्ड विषये विश्वाश्ववाहिनि हंसिनि शूलिनि गारुडिरक्षे गारुडिरक्षे आयुर्मन्त्रं प्रवक्ष्यामि।

One hundred and twenty five *Paath* (recitations) of the above *stotra*, with one tenth *Havan, Tarpan* and *Marjan,* should be done.

9. **SARVARISHTA NIVARAN STOTRA** along with **Suryopaasna.**

ॐ गं गणपतये नमः। सर्व-विघ्न-विनाशनाय, सर्वारिष्ट-निवारणाय, सर्व-सौख्य-प्रदाय, बालानां बुद्धि-प्रदाय, नाना-प्रकार-धन-वाहन-भूमि-प्रदाय, मनोवांछित-फल-प्रदाय रक्षां कुरु कुरु स्वाहा।।

ॐ गुरवे नमः, ॐ श्रीकृष्णाय नमः, ॐ बलभद्राय नमः, ॐ श्रीरामाय नमः, ॐ हनुमते नमः, ॐ शिवाय नमः, ॐ जगन्नाथाय नमः, ॐ बदरीनारायणाय नमः, ॐ श्री दुर्गा देव्यै नमः।

ॐ सूर्याय नमः, ॐ चन्द्राय नमः, ॐ भौमाय नमः, ॐ बुधाय नमः, ॐ गुरवे नमः, ॐ भृगवे नमः, ॐ शनिश्चराय नमः, ॐ राहवे नमः, ॐ केतवे नमः, ॐ नव-ग्रहाः रक्षां कुरु कुरु नमः।।

ॐ मन्ये वरं हरिहरादय एवं दृष्ट्वा द्रष्टेषु येषु हृदयस्थं त्वयं तोषमेति विविक्षते न भवता भुवि येन नान्य कश्चिमनो हरति नाथ भवान्तरेऽपि। ॐ नमो मणि-भद्रे! जय-विजय-पराजिते! भद्रे! लभ्यं कुरु कुरु स्वाहा।।

ॐ भूर्भुवः स्वः तत्-सवितुर्वरेण्यं भर्गो देवस्य धीमहि धियो योनः प्रचोदयात्।। सर्व विघ्नं शान्तं कुरु कुरु स्वाहा।।

ॐ ऐं ह्रीं क्लीं श्रीबटुक-भैरवाय आपदुद्धारणाय महान्-श्याम-स्वरूपाय दीर्घारिष्ट-विनाशाय नाना-प्रकार-भोग-प्रदाय मम (यजमानस्य वा) सर्वारिष्टं हन हन, पच पच, हर हर, कच कच, राज-द्वारे जयं कुरु कुरु, व्यवहारे लाभं वृद्धिं वृद्धिं, रणे शत्रून् विनाशय विनाशय, पूर्णां आयुः कुरु कुरु, स्त्री-प्राप्तिं कुरु कुरु, हुम् फट् स्वाहा।।

ॐ नमो भगवते वासुदेवाय नमः। ॐ नमो भगवते, विश्व-मूर्तये, नारायणाय, श्रीपुरुषोत्तमाय। रक्ष रक्ष, युग्मदधिकं प्रत्यक्षं परोक्षं वा अजीर्णं पच-पच, विश्व-मूर्तिकान् हन-हन, ऐकाह्निकं द्वाह्निकं त्र्याह्निकं चतुरह्निकं ज्वरं नाशय-नाशय, चतुरग्नि-वातान् अष्टादश-क्षयान् रोगान्, अष्टादश-कुष्ठान हन-हन, सर्व-दोषं भञ्जय- भञ्जय, तत्-सर्वं नाशय-नाशय, शोषय-शोषय, आकर्षय-आकर्षय, मम शत्रुं मारय-मारय, उच्चाटय-उच्चाटय, विद्वेषय-विद्वेषय, स्तम्भय-स्तम्भय, निवारय-निवारय, विघ्नं हन-हन, दह-दह, पच-पच, मथ-मथ, विध्वंसय-विध्वंसय, विद्रावय-विद्रावय-चक्रं गृहीत्वा शीघ्रमागच्छागच्छ, चक्रेण हन-हन, पर-विद्यां छेदय-छेदय, चौरासी-चेटकान् विस्फोटान् नाशय-नाशय, वात-शुष्क-दृष्टि-सर्प-सिंह-व्याघ्र-द्विपद-चतुष्पद अपरे बाह्यं ताराभिः भव्यन्तरिक्षं अन्यान्य-व्यापि-केचिद् देश-काल-स्थान सर्वान् हन-हन, विद्युन्मेघ-नदी-पर्वत, अष्ट व्याधि, सर्व-स्थानानि, रात्रि-दिनं, चौरान् वशय-वशय, सर्वोपद्रव-नाशनाय, पर-सैन्यं विदारय-विदारय, पर-चक्रं निवारय-निवारय, दह-दह, रक्षां कुरु-कुरु, ॐ नमो भगवते, ॐ नमो नारायणाय, हुं फट् स्वाहा।।

ठः ठः ॐ ह्रीं ह्रीं। ॐ ह्रीं क्लीं भुवनेश्वर्याः श्रीं ॐ भैरवाय नमः। हरि ॐ उच्छिष्ट-देव्यै नमः। डाकिनी-सुमुखी-देव्यै, महा-पिशाचिनी ॐ ऐं ठः ठः। ॐ चक्रिण्या अहं रक्षां कुरु-कुरु, सर्व-व्याधि-हरणी-देव्यै नमो नमः। सर्व-प्रकार-बाधा-शमनमरिष्ट-निवारणं कुरु-कुरु फट्। श्रीं ॐ कुब्जिका देव्यै ह्रीं ठः स्वाहा।।

शीघ्रमरिष्ट-निवारणं कुरु-कुरु देवी शाम्बरी क्रीं ठः स्वाहा।।

शारिका-भेदा महा-माया पूर्ण आयुः कुरु। हेमवती मूलं रक्षा कुरु। चामुण्डायै दैव्यै शीघ्र विघ्नं सर्वं वायु-कफ-पित्त-रक्षां कुरु। मन्त्र-तन्त्र-कवच-ग्रह-पीडान् तर, पूर्व-जन्म-दोषान् तर, अन्य-जन्म-दोषान् तर, मातृ-दोषान् तर, पितृ-दोषान तर, मारण-मोहन-उच्चाटन-वशीकरण-स्तम्भन-उन्मूलनं भूत-प्रेत-पिशाच-जात-

जादू-टोना-शमनं कुरु। सन्ति सरस्वत्यै कण्ठिका-देव्यै गल-विस्फोटकायै विक्षिप्त-शमनं महान् ज्वर-क्षयं कुरु स्वाहा।।

सर्व-सामग्री-भोगं सप्त-दिवसं देहि-देहि, रक्षां कुरु, क्षण-क्षण अरिष्ट-निवारणं, दिवस-प्रति-दिवस दुःख-हरणं मङ्गल-करणं कार्य-सिद्धिं कुरु-कुरु। हरि ॐ श्रीरामचन्द्राय नमः। हरि ॐ भूर्भुवः स्वः चन्द्र-तारा-नव-ग्रह-शेषनाग-पृथ्वी-देव्यै आकाशस्य सर्वारिष्ट-निवारणं कुरु-कुरु स्वाहा।।

1. ॐ ऐं ह्रीं श्रीं बटुक-भैरवाय आपदुद्धारणाय सर्व-विघ्न-निवारणायमम रक्षां कुरु-कुरु स्वाहा।।

2. ॐ ऐं ह्री क्लीं श्रीवासुदेवाय नमः, बटुक-भैरवाय आपदुद्धारणाय मम रक्षां कुरु-कुरु स्वाहा।।

3. ॐ ऐं ह्रीं क्लीं श्रीविष्णु-भगवान् मम अपराध-क्षमां कुरु-कुरु, सर्व-विघ्नं विनाशय, मम कामना पूर्णं कुरु-कुरु स्वाहा।।

4. ॐ ऐं ह्रीं क्लीं श्रीबटुक-भैरवाय आपदुद्धारणाय सर्व-विघ्न-निवारणाय मम रक्षां कुरु-कुरु स्वाहा।

5. ॐ ऐं ह्रीं क्लीं श्रीं ॐ श्रीदुर्गा-देवी रुद्राणी-सहिता, रुद्र-देवता काल-भैरव सह, बटुग-भैरवाय, हनुमान सह मकर-ध्वजाय, आपदुद्धारणाय मम सर्व-दोष-क्षमाय कुरु कुरु सकल विघ्न-विनाशाय मम शुभ-माङ्गलिक-कार्य-सिद्धिं कुरु-कुरु स्वाहा।।

एष विद्या-माहात्म्यं च, पुरा मया प्रोक्तं ध्रुवं।
शत-क्रतो तु हन्त्येतान्, सर्वांश्च बलि-दानवाः।।1।।

य पुमान् पठते नित्यं, एतत् स्तोत्रं नित्यात्मना।
तस्य सर्वान् हि सन्ति, यत्र दृष्टि-गतं विषं।।2।।

अन्य दृष्टि-विषंचैव, न देयं संक्रमे ध्रुवम्।
संग्रामे धारयेत्यम्बे, उत्पाता च विसंशय।।3।।

सौभाग्यं जायते तस्य, परमं नात्र संशयः।
द्रुतं सद्यं जयस्तस्य, विघ्नस्तस्य न जायते।।4।।

किमत्र बहुनोक्तेन, सर्व-सौभाग्य-सम्पदा।
लभते नात्र सन्देहो, नान्यथा वचनं भवेत्।।5।।

ग्रहीतो यदि वा यत्नं, बालानां विविधैरपि।
शीतं समुष्णतां याति, उष्णः शीत-मयो भवेत्।।6।।

मान्यथा श्रुतये विद्या, पठति कथितं मया।
भोज-पत्रे लिखेद् यन्त्रं, गोरोचन-मयेन च।।7।।

इमां विद्यां शिरो बध्वा, सर्व-रक्षा करोतु मे।
पुरुषस्याथवा नारी, हस्ते बध्वा विचक्षणः।।8।।

विद्रवन्ति प्रणश्यन्ति, धर्मस्तिष्ठति नित्यशः।
सर्व-शत्रुरधो यान्ति, शीघ्रं ते च पलायनम्।।9।।

Forty recitations of this remarkable stotra have been advised in the '*Sarvarishta Nivaran Khand*' of *Shree Bhrigu Samhita.* As a result childless get the children and unmarried are soon tied into wed lock. Also all evils and diseases like, fever, tuberculosis, leprosy and illnesses due to bile, phlegm and air are cured and obstructions due to evil spirits are removed, by the recitation of this stotra.

If this stotra has to be recited for self, **'मम' या 'मम स-कुटुम्बस्य'** should be spoken or else name and 'gotra' of client should be replaced where **'यजमान'** is written, if has to be done for somebody else.

Sit in front of a Yantra or an idol of any God or Goddess, worship them properly and then recite this stotra. This accomplishes all desires. Wealth comes to poor and unemployed gets a job. Business or trade flourishes. This is tested.

## SURYOPASANA

Sun is the soul of the *KaalPurush.* According to Upnishads, Sun is provider of affluence. It protects us from the effects of ultraviolet and cosmic rays coming from the distant stars.

*Arghya* is dear to Sun God. *Arghya* means offering water in the hands from a vessel, pot or pitcher. Hands of Sun are his rays. Therefore, intending rays of Sun, water so offered is called *Arghya*. Sun God can be worshipped with the same procedure and materials as for other Devtas but it is said that the most important thing which pleases Sun is offering of *Arghya*.

For *Arghya*, take about 2-2½ litre pure water in a copper vessel and put into it *Kumkum*, *Gorochan*, Red Sandal, red flowers of *Kaner*, *Kapoor* etc. Keeping this pot in front, recite the mantra of Sun **"ओम् घृणिः सूर्य आदित्य"** for 108 times and worship Sun God. Then standing on the knees, lift the vessel to the level of head with both hands, pour the water slowly looking at the image of Sun and reciting the mantra.

Mantra: **"ओम् घृणिः सूर्य आदित्य"**

सूर्य गायत्री- **"आदित्याय विद्महे सहस्रकराय धीमहि तन्नो सूर्यः प्रचोदयात्।"**

दक्षाक्षर मंत्र- **"ओम् ह्रीं घृणिः सूर्य आदित्य ह्रीं"**

**Method:** Wake up early in the morning and meditate about Sun God after taking bath etc.

**प्रातः स्मरामि खलु तत्सवितुर्वरेण्यम् रूपं हि मण्डलमृचोथ तनुर्यजूंषि।**
**सामानि यस्य किरणाः प्रभवादिहेतुं, ब्रह्माहरात्मकमलक्ष्यमचिन्त्यरूपम्।।**

**प्रातर्नमामि तरणिं तनुवाङ् मनोभिः ब्रह्मेन्द्रपूर्वक सुरैर्नुत मर्चितं च।**
**वृष्टि प्रमोचन विनिग्रह हेतुभूतं, त्रैलोक्य पालनपरं त्रिगुणात्मकं च।।**

**प्रातर्भजामि सवितार मनन्तशक्ति, पापौघशत्रुभयरोगहरं परं च।**
**तं सर्वलोककलनात्मक कालमूर्ति, गोकण्ठबंधन विमोचनमादिदेवम्।।**

**श्लोकत्रयमिदं भानोः प्रातः प्रातः पठेन्तु यः।**
**स सर्वव्याधि निर्मुक्तः परं सुखभवान्पुयात्।।**

This stuti should be done early in the morning. After bathing, worship Sun God. If red flowers are available, it would be better. Offer *Arghya* to Sun, even if it is plain water and other recommended things could not be mixed.

***Viniyog*** is essential before reciting *Atharvshirsh*, which is as follows:

**अस्य श्रीं सूर्याथर्वशीर्षस्य ब्रह्मा ऋषि आदित्यो देवता गायत्रीछन्दः हंसाद्यग्निनारायणयुक्तं बीजम् हल्लेखा शक्तिः द्विपदादिसर्गसंयुक्तं कीलकम् धर्मार्थकाममोक्षेष जपे विनियोगः।**

**Nyas: ब्रह्मर्षये नमः शिरसि, गायत्री छन्दसे नमः मुखे, आदित्यदेवतायै नमः हृदये, हंसाद्यग्नि नारायणयुक्तबीजाय नमः गुह्ये हृल्लेखा शक्तये नमः पादयोः द्विपदादि सर्गसंयुक्त कीलकाय नमः नाभौ, विनियोगाय नमः सर्वांगे।**

**करन्यास- सां अंगुष्ठाभ्यां नमः, सीं तर्जनीभ्यां नमः सूं मध्यमाभ्यां नमः, सैं अनामिकाभ्यां नमः सौं कनिष्ठाभ्यां नमः सः करतलकरपृष्ठाभ्यां नमः।**

इन्हीं पदों से षडंगन्यास करे- **सां हृदयाय नमः सीं शिरसे स्वाहा, सूं शिखायै वषट्, सैं कवचाय हुम् सौं नेत्रत्रयाय वौषट्, सः अस्त्राय फट्।**

**Dhyaan : रक्ताम्बुज संस्थित. सप्ताश्वरथि, हिरण्यवर्ण चतुर्भुज (दो हाथ में कमल एक वरदान मुद्रा और दूसरा अभय मुद्रा वाला- इस प्रकार चार हाथ वाले) कालचक्र के प्रणेता-भगवान् सूर्य का ध्यान करें।**

Vedic Mantra of Sun is as follows:

**ओम् भूः, ओम् भुवः, ओम् महः ओम् जनः, ओम् तपः ओम् सत्यम् ओम्तत्सवितुर्वरेण्यं भर्गो देवस्य धीमहि धियो यो नः प्रचोदयात्। परोरजमे सावदोम् ओम् आपो ज्योतिरसोमृतम्। ब्रह्मभूर्भुवः स्वरोम्।**

After worshipping the Sun God recite mantra.

10. **Shree Devyatharvashirsh or Devyupnishad**

Shree Durgatharvashirsh is also known by the name of Devyupnishad, which wards off all evils, removes all obstacles and provides Dharma, Arth, Kaama and Moksha. Those, who can not recite Durga Saptashati daily, must recite **Devyatharvashirsh** once every day. Before that, *shodashopchar* worship of Goddess Durga must be performed properly. After that Devyatharvashirsh may be recited with full devotion and dedication. It accomplishes all desires.

## SHREE DEVYATHARVASHIRSH (श्रीदेव्याऽथर्वशीर्षम्)

ॐ सर्वे वै देवा देवीमुपतस्थुः कासि त्वं महादेवी ।1। साब्रवीत् अहं ब्रह्मस्वरूपिणी। मत्तः प्रकृतिपुरुषात्मकं जगत्। शून्यं चाशून्यं च ।2। अहमानन्दानानन्दौ। अहं विज्ञानाविज्ञाने। अहं ब्रह्माब्रह्मणी द्वे ब्राह्मणी वेदितव्ये। इति वाथर्वणी श्रुतिः। अहं पञ्चभूतानि अहं पञ्चतन्मात्राणि। अहमखिलं जगत् ।3। वेदोऽहमवेदोऽहम्। विद्याहमविद्याहम्। अजाहमनजाहम्। अधश्चोर्ध्वं च तीर्यक् चाहम् ।4। अहं रुद्रेभिर्वसुभिश्चरामि। अहमादित्यैरुत देवैः। अहं मित्रावरुणौ विभर्मि। अहमिन्द्राग्नि अहमविश्वना उभा अहं त्वष्टारं पूषणं भगं दधामि। ।5। । अहं विष्णुमुरुक्रमं ब्रह्माणमुत प्रजापतिं दधामि ।6। अहं दधामि द्रविणं हविष्मते सुप्राव्ये यजमानाय सुन्व्रते। अहं राज्ञी सङ्गमनी वसूनां चिकितुषी प्रथमा यज्ञियानाम्। अहं सुवे पितरमस्य मूर्धन्मम योनिरप्स्वन्तः समुद्रे। य एवं वेद। स दैवीं सम्पदमाप्नोति ।7। ते देवा अब्रुवन्-नमो देव्यै महादेव्यै शिवायै सततं नमः। नमः प्रकृत्यै भद्रायै नियताः प्रणताः स्मताम् ।8। तामग्निवर्णां तपसा ज्वलन्तीं वैरोचनीं कर्मफलेषु जुष्टाम्। दुर्गां देवीं शरणं प्रपद्यामहेऽसुरान्नाशयित्र्यै ते नमः ।9। देवीं वाचमजनयन्त देवास्तां विश्वरूपाः पशवो वदन्ति। सा नो मन्द्रेषमूर्जं दुहाना धेनुर्वागस्मानुप सुष्ठुतैतु ।10।

कालरात्रीं ब्रह्मस्तुतां वैष्णवीं स्कन्दमातरम्। सरस्वतीमदितिं दक्षदुहितरं नमामः पावनां शिवाम् ।11। महालक्ष्म्यै च विद्महे सर्वशक्त्यै च धीमहि। तन्नो देवी प्रचोदयात् ।12। अदितिर्ह्यजनिष्ट दक्ष या दुहिता तव। तां देवा अन्वजायन्त भद्रा अमृतबन्धवः ।13। कामे योनिः कमला वज्रपाणिर्गुहा हंसा मातरिश्वाभ्रमिन्द्रः। पुनर्गुहा सकला मायया चा पृथक् विश्वमातादिविद्या ।14। एषाऽऽत्मशक्तिः। एषा विश्वमोहिनी। पाशाङ्कुशधनुर्बाणधरा। एषा श्रीमहाविद्या। य एवं वेद स शोकं तरति ।15।

नमस्ते भगवति मातरस्मान् पाहि सर्वतः ।16। सैषावैष्णवा वसवः। सैवकादश रुद्राः। सैषा द्वादशादित्याः। सैषा विश्वदेवाः सोमपा असोमपाश्च। सैषा यातुधाना असुराः रक्षांसि पिशाच यक्षः सिद्धाः। सैषा सत्त्वरजस्तमांसि। सैषा ब्रह्मविष्णुरुद्ररूपिणी। सैषा प्रजापतीन्द्रमनवः। सैषा ग्रहनक्षत्रज्योतिषि। कलाकाष्ठादिविश्वरूपिणी। तामहं प्रणौमि नित्यम्। पापापहारिणीं देवी भुक्तिमुक्तिप्रदायिनी। अनन्तां विजयां शुद्धां शरण्यां सर्वदा शिवाम् ।17। वियदाकारसंयुक्तं वीतिहोत्रसमन्वितम्। अर्धेन्दुलसितं देव्या बीजं सर्वार्थ-साधकम् ।18। एवमेकाक्षरं मंत्रं यतयः शुद्धचेतसः। ध्यायन्ति परमानन्दमया

ज्ञानाम्बुराशयः ।19। वाङ्माया ब्रह्मसूस्तस्माद् षष्ठ वक्त्रसमन्वितम्। सूर्योऽवामश्रोत्रबिन्दुसंयुक्तष्टात्तृतीयकम्। नारायणेन सयुक्तो वायुश्चाधारयुक् तयः। विच्चे नवार्णकोस्थः महानानन्ददायकः ।20।

हृत्पुण्डरीकमध्यस्थां प्रातः सूर्यसमप्रभाम्। पाशाङ्कुशधरां सौम्यां वरदाभयहस्तकाम्। त्रिनेत्रां रक्तवसनां भक्तकामदुह भजे ।21। भजामि त्वां महादेवि महाभयविनाशिनी। महादारिद्रयशमनी महाकारुण्यरूपिणी ।22। यस्याः स्वरूपं ब्रह्मादयो न जानन्ति तस्मादुच्यते अज्ञेया। यस्याः अन्तो नोप लभ्यते तस्मादुच्यते अनन्ता। यस्याः लक्षं नोपलक्ष्यते तस्मादुच्यते अलक्ष्या। यस्या जननं नोपलभ्यते तस्मादुच्यते अजा। एकैव सर्वत्र वर्तते तस्मादुच्यते एका। एकैव विश्वरूपिणी तस्मादुच्यते अनेका। अत एवोच्यते अज्ञेयानन्ता-लक्ष्याजैकानेका ।23। मन्त्राणां मातृका देवी शब्दानां ज्ञानरूपिणी। ज्ञानानां चिन्मयातीता शून्यानां शून्यसाक्षिणी। यस्याः परतरं नास्ति सैषा दुर्गा प्रकीर्तिता ।24। तां दुर्गां दुर्गमां देवीं दुराचारविघातिनीम्। नमामि भवभीतोऽहं संसारार्णवतारिणीम् ।25।।

इदमूथर्वशीर्षंयोऽधीते स पश्चाथर्वशीर्षफलमवाप्नोति। इदमथर्वशीर्षमज्ञात्वा योऽर्चां स्थापयति शतलक्षं प्रजप्तापि नार्चाशुद्धिं न विन्दति। शतमष्टोत्तरं चास्य पुरश्चर्याविधिः स्मृतः। दशवारं पठेत् यस्तु सद्यः पापैः प्रमुच्यते। महादुर्गाणि तरति महादेव्याः प्रसादतः ।26। सायमधीयानो दिवसकृतं पापं नाशयति। प्रातरधीयानो रात्रिकृतं पापं नाशयति। सायं प्रातः प्रयुञ्जानो अपापो भवति। निशीथे तुरीयसंध्यायां जप्त्वा वाक्सिद्धिर्भवति। नूतनायां प्रतिमायां जप्त्वा देवतासानिध्यं भवति। भौमाश्विन्यां महादेवीसन्निधौ जप्त्वा महामृत्युं तरति। स महामृत्युं तरति। (इत्युपनिषत्) ।।

'*Devyatharvshirsh*' should be read every day after taking bath, sitting on an '*Aasan*' facing east or north. *Dhyaan* and worship of Ma Durga should be done. It is recommended to recite '*Devyatharvshirsh*' once, thrice or five times daily, as far as possible, to propitiate Devi. If it is not possible daily then in *Navratri* worship of nine planets and Ma durga Devi should be done after placing a pitcher (*Kalash*). Thereafter, recite '*Devyatharvashirsh*', which fulfils all desires and accomplishes all ambitions.

**11. For increase and improvement in business :**

1. **ॐ गं गणपतये नमः** should be recited for 1100 times everyday.

2. **ॐ पद्मावती पद्मनेत्रे लक्ष्मीदायिनी सर्वकार्य सिद्धि करि करि ॐ ह्रीं श्रीं पद्मावत्यै नमः।**

This particular measure can be started from a Wednesday. Place energized 'Shree Yantra' on a white cloth, offer water for bathing, and put a tilak of Kesar. Offer incense, lit an earthen lamp and recite above mantras.

After completing the requisite numbers, offer food and clothes to an unwed girl and then put this 'Shree Yantra' in the shop, cash box or place of worship. As long as this 'Shree Yantra' is there and duly worshipped, prosperity and affluence in profession or trade will be there.

For *Purashcharan,* mantra has to be recited 1.25 lakhs times.

**3. Measures to increase sales:**

**"भंवर वीर तू चेला मेरा, खोल दुकान कहा कर मेरा।**
**उठे जो डण्डी बिके जो माल, भंवर वीर सोखे नहीं जाय।।"**

On a Sunday, take some grains of black *Urd* and recite this mantra for twentyone times and spread those grains in the shop. Doing this for four Sundays helps increase the trade. Collect these grains the next day by sweeping and throw them on a roundabout on the road or tie these grains in a cloth and keep it in a pit high in the wall. This has to be done on a Sunday only.

**4. It is written in *BrahmPurana*:**

Stand in the South of your house or village on any Thursday and meditate about Raja Bali. Gain of money would be there.

**5. Gain of money through Mantra:**

ॐ ह्रीं ह्रीं ह्रीं ह्रीं श्रीमेव कुरु-कुरु वांछितमेव ह्रीं ह्रीं नमः।

If there are continous losses in the business which has come at the verge of closure, this mantra may be recited 108 times daily in the morning for 40 days. Losses would be converted into profits.

**6.** Following mantras of Goddess Lakshmi, which fetch Her Blessings and result into much enhancement, prosperity, popularity and improvement in business :

After worshipping Lord Ganapati, *shodashopchar* (16 fold) or *Panchopchar* (5 fold) worship of Goddess lakshmi should be performed. Thereafter, take *Sankalp* (Pledge) and recite following mantras 28, 56, or 108 times daily. Number of mantras should be increased gradually from 28 to 56 and then from 56 to 108 with in a month. Those who are not very conversant and comfortable with Sanskrit, and fear any mistake, may recite *'Shree Sukta'* everyday.

- "ॐ श्रीं ह्रीं ऐं महालक्ष्म्यै कमलधारिण्यै सिंहवाहिन्यै स्वाहा।"
- "ॐ ऐं ह्रीं श्रियै नमो भगवति मम समृद्धौ ज्वल ज्वल मां सर्वसम्पदाम् देहि देहि मम अलक्ष्मीं नाशय नाशय हुं फट् स्वाहा।"
- "श्रीं ह्रीं क्लीं श्रीं सिद्धलक्ष्म्यै नमः।"
- "ॐ श्रीं ह्रीं श्रीं कमले कमलालये प्रसीद प्रसीद श्रीं ह्रीं श्रीं महालक्ष्म्यै नमः।"

For all natives, generally above four mantras are sufficient. But those learned in Sanskrit may also recite following mantras themselves, which bless the natives with wealth, prosperity and property. These mantras are also very beneficial to those who are in business or trade.

ज्ञान-पातक-तमस्तति-तीव्र रश्मि
दौर्भाग्य-भूधर-विदारण-वजमीडे।
रोगर्ति घोर फणि मर्दन पक्षिराजं
लक्ष्मी पदद्वयमनर्थ हरं सुखार्थी।।

अथवा

ओं रं श्रीं ह्रीं धं धनदे रतिप्रिये स्वाहा

## 12. For the amazing victory in Elections :

### VIJAYA SUKTA

In court cases, elections, examination or other spheres of life, when failure is apprehended, recitation of VIJAYA SUKTA, along with Havan, ensures victory and success. At least 11 paath must done daily. Mantra is as follows:

जितमस्माकमुद्भिन्नमस्माकम् मृतमस्माकम् तेजोऽस्माकम् ब्रह्मास्माकं स्वरस्माकं यज्ञोऽस्माक पशवोऽस्माकं प्रजा अस्माकं वीरा अस्माकम्। तस्मादमुं निर्भजामोऽमुमामुष्यायणममुष्याः पुत्रमसौयः सग्राह्याः पाशान्मामोचि। तस्येदं वर्चस्तेजः प्राणामायुर्निवेष्टयामीदमेनमधराञ्चं पादयामि।1।

जितमस्माकमुद्भिन्नमस्माकं मृतमस्मांकं तेजोऽस्माकं ब्रह्मास्माकं स्वरस्माकं यज्ञोऽस्माकं पशवोऽस्माकं प्रजाऽमस्माकं वीरा अस्माकम्। तस्मादमु निर्भजामोऽमुमामुष्यायणममुष्याः पुत्रमसौयः। सोऽभूत्या पाशान्मामोचि। तस्येदं वर्चस्तेजः प्राण तायुर्निवेष्टयामीमेनधराञ्चं पादयामि। 2।

जितमस्माकमुत्भिन्नस्माकम् मृतमस्माकम् तेजोऽस्माकम् ब्रह्मास्माकं स्वरस्माकं यज्ञोऽस्माकं पशवोऽस्माकं प्रजा अस्माकं वीरा अस्माकम्। तस्मादमुं निर्भसामोऽमुमामुष्यायणममुष्याः पुत्रमसाय सोऽभूत्याः पाशान्मामोचि। तस्येदं वर्चस्तेजः प्राणमायुर्निवेष्टयामीवमेनमधराञ्चं पादयामि।3।

जितमस्माकमुद्भिन्नमस्माकम् मृतमस्माकम् तेजोऽस्माकम् ब्रह्मास्माकं स्वरस्माकं यज्ञोऽस्माकं पशवोऽस्माकं प्रजा अस्माकं वीरा अस्माकम्। तस्मादमुं निर्भजामोऽमुमामुष्यायणममुष्याः पुत्रमसौय। सनिर्मूत्या पाशान्मामोचि। तस्येदं वर्चस्तेजः प्राणः मायुर्निवेष्टयामीदमेनधरोञ्चं पादयामि।4।

जितमस्माकमुद्भिन्नमस्माकम् मृतमस्माकम् तेजोऽस्माकम् ब्रह्मास्माकं स्वरस्माकं यज्ञोऽस्माकं पशवोऽस्माकं प्रजा अस्माकं वीरा अस्माकम्। तस्मादमुं निर्भजामोऽमुमामुष्यायणममुष्याः पुत्रमसौय। स पराभूत्यां पाशान्मामोचि। तस्येदं वर्चस्तेजः प्राणः मायुर्निर्वेष्टयामीदमेनधराञ्चं पादयामि ।5।

जितमस्माकमुद्भिन्नमस्माकम् मृतमस्माकम् तेजोऽस्माकम् ब्रह्मास्माकं स्वरस्माकं यज्ञोऽस्माकं पशवोऽस्माकं प्रजा अस्माकं। वीरा अस्माकम् तस्मादमुं निर्भजामोऽमुमामुष्यायणममुष्याः पुत्रमसौय। सदेवजातीनां पाशान्मामोचि। तस्येदं वर्चस्तेजः प्राणः मायुर्निर्वेष्टयामीदमेनधराञ्चं पादयामि ।6।

जितमस्माकमुद्भिन्नमस्माकम् मृतमस्माकम् तेजोऽस्माकम् ब्रह्मास्माकं स्वरस्माकं यज्ञोऽस्माकं पशवोऽस्माकं प्रजा अस्माकं। वीरा अस्माकम् तस्मादमुं निर्भजामोऽमुमामुष्यायणममुष्याः पुत्रमसौय स बृहस्पतिः पाशान्मामोचि। तस्येदं वर्चस्तेजः प्राणः मायुर्निर्वेष्टयामीदमेनधराञ्चं पादयामि ।7।

जितमस्माकमुद्भिन्नमस्माकम् मृतमस्माकम् तेजोऽस्माकम् ब्रह्मास्माकं स्वरस्माकं यज्ञोऽस्माकं पशवोऽस्माकं प्रजा अस्माकं। वीरा अस्माकम् तस्मादमुं निर्भजामोऽमुमामुष्यायणममुष्याः पुत्रमसौय स ऋषीणां पाशान्मामोचि। तस्येदं वर्चस्तेजः प्राणः मायुर्निर्वेष्टयामीदमेनधराञ्चं पादयामि ।8।

जितमस्माकमुद्भिन्नमस्माकम् मृतमस्माकम् तेजोऽस्माकम् ब्रह्मास्माकं स्वरस्माकं यज्ञोऽस्माकं पशवोऽस्माकं प्रजा अस्माकं। वीरा अस्माकम् तस्मादमुं निर्भजामोऽमुमामुष्यायणममुष्याः पुत्रमसौय। स ऋषीणां पाशान्मामोचि। तस्येदं वर्चस्तेजः प्राणः मायुर्निर्वेष्टयामीदमेनधराञ्चं पादयामि ।9।

जितमस्माकमुद्भिन्नमस्माकम् मृतमस्माकम् तेजोऽस्माकम् ब्रह्मास्माकं यज्ञोऽस्माकं पशवोऽस्माकं प्रजा अस्माकं वीरा अस्माकम् तस्मादमुं निर्भजामोऽमुमामुष्यायणममुष्याः पुत्रमसौय। आर्षेयाणां पाशान्मामोचि। तस्येदं वर्चस्तेजः प्राणः। मायुर्निर्वेष्टयामीदमेनधराञ्चं पादयामि ।10।

जितमस्माकमुद्भिन्नमस्माकम् मृतमस्माकम् तेजोऽस्माकम् ब्रह्मास्माकं स्वरस्माकं यज्ञोऽस्माकं पशवोऽस्माकं प्रजा अस्माकं वीरा अस्माकम्। तस्मादमुं निर्भजामोऽमुमामुष्यायणममुष्याः पुत्रमसौय। अङ्गिरसानां पाशान्मामोचि। तस्येदं वर्चस्तेजः प्राणः मायुर्निर्वेष्टयामीदमेनधराञ्चं पादयामि ।11।

जितमस्माकमुद्भिन्नमस्माकम् मृतमस्माकम् तेजोऽस्माकम् ब्रह्मास्माकं स्वरस्माकं

यज्ञोऽस्माकं पशवोऽस्माकं प्रजा अस्माकं वीरा अस्माकम्। तस्मादमुं निर्भजामोऽमुमामुष्यायणममुष्याः पुत्रमसौय। अङ्गिरसानां पाशान्मामोचि। तस्येदं वर्चस्तेजः प्राणः मायुर्निवेष्टयामीदमेनधराञ्चं पादधामि।12।

जितमस्माकमुद्भिन्नमस्माकम् मृतमस्माकम् तेजोऽस्माकम् ब्रह्मास्माकं स्वरस्माकं यज्ञोऽस्माकं पशवोऽस्माकं प्रजा अस्माकं वीरा अस्माकम्। तस्मादमुं निर्भजामोऽमुमामुष्यायणममुष्याः पुत्रमसौय सोऽभूत्याः पाशान्मामोचि। तस्येदं वर्चस्तेजः प्राणः मायुर्निवेष्टयामीदमेनधराञ्चं पादयामि।13।

जितमस्माकमुद्भिन्नमस्माकम् मृतमस्माकम् तेजोऽस्माकम् ब्रह्मास्माकं स्वरस्माकं यज्ञोऽस्माकं पशवोऽस्माकं प्रजा अस्माकं वीरा अस्माकम्। तस्मादमुं निर्भजामोऽमुमामुष्यायणममुष्याः पुत्रमसौय अथर्वणानां पाशान्मामोचि। तस्येदं वर्चस्तेजः प्राणः मायुर्निवेष्टयामीदमेनधराञ्चं पादयामि।14।

जितमस्माकमुद्भिन्नमस्माकम् मृतमस्माकम् तेजोऽस्माकम् ब्रह्मास्माकं स्वरस्माकं यज्ञोऽस्माकं पशवोऽस्माकं प्रजा अस्माकं वीरा अस्माकम्। तस्मादमुं निर्भजामोऽमुमामुष्यायणममुष्याः पुत्रमसौय। स सोऽधमासानां पाशान्मामोचि। तस्येदं वर्चस्तेजः प्राणः मायुर्निवेष्टयामीदमेनधराञ्चं पादयामि।15।

जितमस्माकमुद्भिन्नमस्माकम् मृतमस्माकम् तेजोऽस्माकम् ब्रह्मास्माकं स्वरस्माकं यज्ञोऽस्माकं पशवोऽस्माकं प्रजा अस्माकं वीरा अस्माकम्। तस्मादमुं निर्भजामोऽमुमामुष्यायणममुष्याः पुत्रमसौयः। सोऽहोरात्रयो पाशान्मामोचि। तस्येदं वर्चस्तेजः प्राणः मायुर्निवेष्टयामीदमेनधराञ्चं पादयामि।16।

जितमस्माकमुद्भिन्नमस्माकम् मृतमस्माकम् तेजोऽस्माकम् ब्रह्मास्माकं स्वरस्माकं यज्ञोऽस्माकं पशवोऽस्माकं प्रजा अस्माकं वीरा अस्माकम्। तस्मादमुं निर्भजामोऽमुमामुष्यायणममुष्याः पुत्रमसौयः। स ऋषीणां पाशान्मामोचि। तस्येदं वर्चस्तेजः प्राणः मायुर्निर्विष्टयामीदमेनधराञ्चं पादयामि।17।

जितमस्माकमुद्भिन्नमस्माकम् मृतमस्माकम् तेजोऽस्माकम् ब्रह्मास्माकं स्वरस्माकं यज्ञोऽस्माकं पशवोऽस्माकं प्रजा अस्माकं वीरा अस्माकम्। तस्मादमुं निर्भजामोऽमुमामुष्यायणममुष्याः पुत्रमसौयः स द्यावापृथिवीः पाशान्मामोचि। तस्येदं वर्चस्तेजः प्राणः मायुर्निवेष्टयामीदमेनधराञ्चं पादयामि।18।

जितमस्माकमुद्भिन्नमस्माकम् मृतमस्माकम् तेजोऽस्माकम् ब्रह्मास्माकं स्वरस्माकं यज्ञोऽस्माकं पशवोऽस्माकं प्रजा अस्माकं वीरा अस्माकम्। तस्मादमुं

निर्भजामोऽमुमामुष्यायणममुष्याः पुत्रमसौयः स इन्द्रांग्न्योः पाशान्मामोचि। तस्येदं वर्चस्तेजः प्राणः मायुर्निवेष्टयामीदमेनधराञ्चं पादयामि।19।

जितमस्माकमुद्भिन्नमस्माकम् मृतमस्माकम् तेजोऽस्माकम् ब्रह्मास्माकं स्वरस्माकं यज्ञोऽस्माकं पशवोऽस्माकं प्रजा अस्माकं वीरा अस्माकम्। तस्मादमुं निर्भजामोऽमुमामुष्यायणममुष्याः पुत्रमसौयः स समित्रावरुणयो पाशान्मामोचि। तस्येदं वर्चस्तेजः प्राणः मायुर्निवेष्टयामीदमेनधराञ्चं पादयामि।20।

जितमस्माकमुद्भिन्नमस्माकम् मृतमस्माकम् तेजोऽस्माकम् ब्रह्मास्माकं स्वरस्माकं यज्ञोऽस्माकं पशवोऽस्माकं प्रजा अस्माकं वीरा अस्माकम्। तस्मादमुं निर्भजामोऽमुमामुष्यायणममुष्याः पुत्रमसौयः स राज्ञोवल्स्य पाशान्मामोचि। तस्येदं वर्चस्तेजः प्राणः मायुर्निवेष्टयामीदमेनधराञ्चं पादयामि।21।

जितमस्माकमुद्भिन्नमस्माकम् मृतमस्माकम् तेजोऽस्माकम् ब्रह्मास्माकं स्वरस्माकं यज्ञोऽस्माकं पशवोऽस्माकं प्रजा अस्माकं वीरा अस्माकम्। तस्मादमुं निर्भजामोऽमुमामुष्यायणममुष्याः पुत्रमसौयः स मृत्योः षड्वीशात् पाशान्मामोचि। तस्येदं वर्चस्तेजः प्राणः मायुर्निवेष्टयामीदमेनधराञ्चं पादयामि।22।

जितमस्माकमुद्भिन्नमस्माकमूध्यष्ठॉ विश्वाः पृतना आरतीः तदग्निराहतदुसोम आ हपूषामाधात् सकृतस्य लोके अगन्म स्वः स्वरगन्म स सूर्यस्य ज्योति षागन्म। वस्योभूयाय वसुमानूयज्ञो वसु वशिषीय वसुमान् भूयास वसुमयिधेहि।23।

## For Extraordinary success in Elections :

With the recitation of following mantras, the native gets popularity in public, is inspired to mitigate the agonies of others, rivals are rendered ineffective and he attains high post in government.

इममिन्द्र वर्धय क्षत्रिय म विश मेकवृप कृणु त्वम्।
निरमित्रानक्ष्णुह्यस्य सर्वास्तात् रन्धयास्भा अहमुत्तरेषु।1।

एमं भज ग्रामे अश्वेयु गोषु निष्ट भज यो अमित्रो अस्य।
वर्ष्म क्षत्राणामयमस्तु राजेन्द्र शत्रु रन्धय सर्वमस्मै।।2।।

अयमस्तु धनिपतिर्धनानामयं विशां विश्वपतिरस्तु राजा।
अस्मिन्निन्द्र महि वर्चासि धेह्यवचस कृणुहि शत्रुमस्य।।3।।

अस्मै द्यावापृथिवी भरि बामं दुहाथां धर्म दुधेइव धेनुं।
अय राजा प्रिय इन्द्रस्य भूयात् प्रियो गवामौषधीनां पशूनाम्।।4।।

युनिज्म त उत्तरावन्तमिन्द्र येन जयन्ति न पराजर्तते।
यस्त्वा करदेकवृष जनानामुत राजामुत्तर्म मानवानाम्।।5।।

उद्यरस्त्वमधरे ने सपत्ना ये के च राजन् प्रतिशत्रवस्दे।
एकवृष इन्द्रसखा जिगीवाञ छत्रूयतामा भरा भोजनानि।।6।।

सिंहप्रतीको विशो अद्धि सर्वा व्याघ्रप्रतीकोऽय वाधस्व शत्रुन्।
एकवृष इन्द्र सखा जिगीवाञ छत्रूतामा खिदा भोजनानि।।7।।

After proper execution of above Paath with one tenth Havan, Tarpan and Marjan etc, 9, 18 or 27 Samput Paath of Shree Durga Saptshati with following three mantras should be got done through any learned Acharya.

1. ततो वव्रे नृपो राज्यमविभ्रंश्यन्यजन्मनि।
   अत्रैव व निजं राज्यं हतशत्रुबलं बलात्।।

2. यं यं चिन्तयते कामं तं तं प्राप्नोति निश्चितम्।
   परमैश्वर्यमतुलं प्राप्स्यते भूतले पुमान्।।

3. स्वल्पैरहोभिर्नृपते स्वं राज्यं प्राप्स्यते भवान्।
   हत्वा रिपूनस्खलितं तव तत्र भविष्यति।।

***'Vaanchha Kalplata'*** was composed by Adi Shankaracharya for the beneefit of general masses. With its recital, all ambitions of the native are accomplished. For success in elections, 500 *Paath* of *Vaanchha Kalplata,* done by any experienced and learned Acharya, give beneficial results. All impending obstacles are removed and victoiry is assured. After *Paath* of *Vaanchha Kalplata* one tenth Havan, tarpan, Marjan is not required.

For different and specific ambitions some rare mantra, sukta or stotras have been mentioned here. All these should be executed with care and proper rituals.

Only then these give amazing results. Proper method of their recital and other rituals etc should be learned under the guidance of any learned Acharya or Guru. It is also essential to understand as to which measure is required for which purpose. There are many books in astrology which carry essentials of selection of proper and suitable mantra. Considering the limits of this book these details are not being repeated here, which can be found in any standard work and also in our various books on mantras.

This chapter on remedial measures would be incomplete without the inclusion of *Vaanchha Kalplata* composed by Adi Shankaracharya. This accomplishes all ambitions and has been tested hundreds of times.

This is a large Stotra which is just being introduced here and can be found in a separate book. Having limits of this book in mind, this stotra is not being copied here so that other essential mesures could also find place.

For success in elections and defeat of rivals, this stotra has been found very effective and there remains no doubt about the victory in elections. If, however, *Paath* of Aparajita Stotra is also undertaken through a learned Acharya along with *Vaanchha Kalplata,* victory is attained with greater margin and adversaries are routed incredibly. Aparajita Stotra and mantra is as follows :

## GODDESS APARAJITA

Aparajita is another name of Goddess Durga. Fourth among the eight incarnations of Devi, Vaishnavi is also known as Aparajita. Worshipping of Aparajita as such is quite popular. It is mentioned in 'Hindu Dharm Kosh' on page 38 that :

'........(worship) Aparajita, that is Durga, in War. Her worship is recommended on the tenth lunar day of the bright half of *Ashwin* month.

दशम्यां च नरैः सम्यक् पूजनीयाऽपराजिता,
मोक्षार्थं विजयार्थं च पूर्वोक्त-विधिना नरैः।
नवमी-शेषा-युक्तायां दशम्यामपराजिता,
ददाति विजयं देवी पूजिता जय-वर्द्धिनी।।

that is, for victory and Moksha (emancipation), Aparajita should be worshipped on ninth to tenth lunar day, so that success and triumph is ensured.

It is also mentioned that on this day only, Rama had attacked Lanka, when *Sravana* constellation was rising, in which Devi is worshipped. Seventh lunar day of Bright half of *Bhadrapad* month is also known as 'Aparajita Saptami'

## Mantras of Goddess Aparajita

षड्-विंशत्योत्तर-शताक्षरः तारमाकर्षिणि-पद्मावेशिनि ततो वदेत्, ज्वालामालिनि रमणि रामणि धरणीति च। धारणि तपनोत्युक्तवा तापिनि मनोन्मादिनि, शोषिणीति पदं प्रोच्य ततः सम्मोहिनीति च। तथा नील-पताके च महा-नीले महा-प्रिये, महाग्नेयि महा-चण्डे महा-रौद्रि महेति च। वज्रिणीति तथाऽऽदित्य-रश्मि-जाह्नवि संवदेत्, यम-घण्टे किलि किलि चिन्तामणि-पदं वदेत्। सुरभि-सुरोत्पन्ने च सरस्वतिपदं ततः, सर्व-काम-दुधे प्रोच्य यथा मम मनीषितं। कार्यं तन्मे सिध्यत्वित्ति स्वाहान्तोऽयं मनुर्मतः। षड्द्वादशार्णोमुन्यादि प्रागू-वत् (वैष्णवी-अष्टाक्षर-मनु-वत्) सौख्य-प्रदो मनुः ॐ आकर्षिणि, आवेशिनि, ज्वालामालिनि, रमणि, रामणि, धरणि, धारणि, तपनि, तापिनि, मनोन्मादिनि, शोषिणि, सम्मोहिनि, नीलज्वालामालिनि, रमणि, रामणि, धरणि, धारणि, तपनि, तापिनि, मनोन्मादिनि, शोषिणि, सम्मोहिनि, नील-पताके, महा-नीले, महा-प्रिये, महाग्नेयि, महा-चण्डे, महा-रौद्रि, महा-वज्रिणि, आदित्य-रश्मि-जाह्नवि, यम-घण्टे। किलि किलि, चिन्ता-मणि, सुरभि-सुरोत्पन्ने, सरस्वति, सर्वं-काम दुधे! मम-मनीषितं कार्यं तन्मे सिध्यतु स्वाहा।

## Aparajita Stotra

Proper recital of Aparajita Stotra ensures defeat of all rivals and enemies, cure from illness and end of all problems.

ॐ नमोऽपराजितायै। ॐ अस्या वैष्णव्याः पराया अजिताया महाविद्यायाः।। वामदेव-बृहस्पति-मार्कण्डेया ऋषयः। गायत्र्युष्णिगनुष्टुब्बृहती छन्दांसि लक्ष्मीनृसिंहो

देवता। ॐ क्लीं श्रीं ह्रीं बीजम्। हुं शक्तिः। सकलकामनासिद्ध्यर्थम् अपराजित-विद्यामन्त्रपाठे विनियोगः। ॐ नीलोत्पल-दलश्यामां भुजंगाभरणान्विताम्। शुद्धस्फटिक-संकाशां चन्द्रकोटिनिभाननाम्।। शंखचक्रधरां देवी वैष्णवीमपराजिताम् बालेन्दुशेखरां देवीं वरदाभयदायिनीम।। नमस्कृत्य पपाठैनां मार्कण्डेयो महातपाः। मार्कण्डेय उवाच-शृणुष्वं मुनयः सर्वे सर्वकामार्थसिद्धिदाम्। असिद्धसाधनीं देवीं वैष्णवीमपराजिताम्।। ॐ नमो नारायणाय, नमो भगवते वासुदेवाय, नमोस्त्वनन्ताय, सहस्रशीर्षाय, क्षीरोदार्णवशायिने, शेषभोगपर्य्यङ्काय, गरुड़वाहनाय, अमोघाय, अजाय, अजिताय, पीतवाससे, ॐ वासुदेव, संकर्षण प्रद्युम्न, अनिरुद्ध, हयग्रीव, मत्स्य, कूर्म्म, वाराह, नृसिंह, अच्युत, वामन, त्रिविक्रम, श्रीधर, राम, राम, राम। वरद, वरद, वरदो भव, नमोऽस्तु ते, नमोऽस्तुते, स्वाहा, ॐ असुर-दैत्य-यक्ष-राक्षस-भूत-प्रेत-पिशाच-कूष्माण्ड-सिद्ध-योगिनी-डाकिनी-शाकिनी-स्कन्दग्रहान् उपग्रहान्न- क्षत्रग्रहांश्चान्या् हनहन् पच पच मथ मथ विध्वंसय विध्वंसय विद्रावय विद्रावय चूर्णय चूर्णय शंखेन चक्रेण बज्रेण शूलेनगदया मुसलेन हलेन भस्मीकुरु कुरु स्वाहा। ॐ सहस्रबाहो सहस्रप्रहरणायुध, जय जय, विजय विजय, अजित, अमित, अपराजित, अप्रतिहत, सहस्रनेत्र, ज्वल ज्वल, प्रज्वल प्रज्वल, विश्वरूप बहुरूप, मधुसूदन, महावराह, महापुरुष, वैकुण्ठ, नारायण, पद्मनाभ, गोविन्द, दामोदर, हृषीकेश, केकशव, सर्वासुरोत्सादन, सर्व भूतवशंकर, सर्वदुःस्वप्नप्रभेदन, सर्वयंत्रप्रभञ्जन, सर्वनागाधिमर्दन, सर्वदेवमहेश्वर, सर्वबन्धविमोक्षण, सर्वाहितप्रमर्दन, सर्वज्वरप्रणाशन, सर्वग्रहनिवारण, सर्वपापप्रशमन, जनार्दन, नमोऽस्तुते स्वाहा। विष्णोरियमनुप्रोक्ता सर्वकामफलप्रदा। सर्वसौभाग्यजननी सर्वभीतिविनाशिनी। सर्वैश्च पठितां सिद्धैर्विष्णोः परमवल्लभा। नानया सदृशं किंचिद्दुष्टानां नाशनं परम्। विद्या रहस्या कथिता वैष्णवयेषापराजिता। पठनीया प्रशस्ता वा साक्षात्सत्त्वगुणाश्रया। ॐ शुक्लाम्बरधरं विष्णुं शशिवर्णं चतुर्भुजम्। प्रसन्नवदनं ध्यायेत्सर्वविघ्नोपशान्तये।। अथातः संप्रवक्ष्यामि ह्याभ्यामपराजिताम्। या शक्तिर्मामकी वत्स रजोगुणमयी मता। सर्वसत्त्वमयी साक्षात्सर्वमंत्रमयी च या। या स्मृता पूजिता जप्ता न्यस्ता कर्मणि योजिता। सर्वकामदुधा वत्स ! शृणुष्वैतां ब्रवीमि ते। य इमामपराजितां परमवैष्णवीमप्रतिहतां पठति सिद्धां स्मरति सिद्धां महाविद्यां जपति पठति शृणोति स्मरति धारयति कीर्तयति वा न तस्याग्निवायुवज्रोपलाश-निवर्षभयं, न समुद्रभयं, न ग्रहभयं, न चौरभयं, न शत्रुभयं, न शापभयं वा भवेत्। क्वचिद्रात्र्यन्धकारस्त्रीराजकुलविद्वेषिविषगरगरदवशीकरणविद्वेष्णोचचाटनवधबन्धन भयं वा न भवेत्। एतैर्मन्त्रैरुदाहृतैः सिद्धैः संसिद्धपूजितैः। ॐ नमोऽस्तुते। अभये, अनघे, अजिते, अमिते, अमृते, अपरे, अपराजिते पठति सिद्धे जपति सिद्धे, स्मरति सिद्धे, एकोनाशीतिमे, एकाकिनि, निश्चेतसि, सुद्रुमे, सुगन्धे, एकान्नशे, उमेध्रुवे,

अरुन्धति, गायत्रि, सावित्रि, जातवेदसि, मानस्तोके, सरस्वति, धरणि, धारणि, सौदामनि, अदिति, दिति, विनते, गौरि, गांधारि, मातंगी कृष्णे, यशोदे, सत्यवादिनि, ब्रह्मवादिनि, कालि, कपालिनि, करालनेत्रे, भद्रे, निद्रे, सत्योपयाचनकरि, स्थलगतं जलगतं अन्तरिक्षगतं वा मां रक्ष सर्वोपद्रवेभ्यः स्वाहा। यस्याः प्रणश्यते पुष्पं गर्भो वा पतते यदि। म्रियते बालको यस्याः काकबन्ध्याच या भवेत्। धारयेद्या इमां विद्यामेतैर्दोषैर्न लिप्यते।। गर्भिणी जीववत्सा स्यात्पुत्रिणीस्यान्न संशयः। भूर्जपत्रे त्विमां विद्यां लिखित्वा गन्धचन्दनैः।। एतैर्दोषैर्न लिप्येत सुभगा पुत्रिणी भवेत्। रणे राजकुले द्यूते नित्यं तस्य जयो भवेत्। रणे राजकुले द्यूते नित्यं तस्य जयो भवेत्। शस्त्रं वारयते ह्योषा समरे काण्डदारुणे। गुल्मशूला-क्षिरोगाणां क्षिप्रं नाश्यति च व्यथाम्।। शिरोरोगज्वराणां न नाशिनी सर्वदेहिनाम्। इत्येषा कथिता विद्या अभयाख्याऽपराजिता।। एतस्याः स्मृतिमात्रेण भयं क्वापि न जायते। नोपसर्गा न रोगाश्च न योधा नापि तस्कराः।। न राजानो न सर्पाश्च न द्वेष्टारो न शत्रवः। यक्षराक्षसवेताला न शाकिन्यो न च ग्रहाः।। अग्नेर्भयं न वाताच्च न समुद्रान्न वै विषात्। कार्मणं वा शत्रुकृतं वशीकरणमेव च।। उच्चाटनं स्तम्भनं च विद्वेषणमथापि वा। न किञ्चित्प्रभवेत्तत्र यत्रैषा वर्ततेऽभया। पठेद् वा यदि वा चित्रे पुस्तके वा मुखेऽथवा। हृदि वा द्वारदेशे वा वर्त्तते ह्याभयः पुमान्।। हृदये विन्यसेदेतां ध्यायेद्देवींचतुर्भुजाम्।। रक्तमाल्याम्बरधरां पद्मरागसप्रभाम्। पाशांकुशाभयवरैरलंकृतसुविग्रहाम्।। साधकेभ्यः प्रयच्छनतीं मन्त्रवर्णामृतान्यपि। नातः परतरं किञ्चिद्वशीकरणमनुत्तमम्।। रक्षणं पावनं चापि नात्रकार्या विचारणा। प्रातः कुमारिकाः पूज्याः खाद्यैराभरणैरपि।। तदिदं वाचनीयं स्यात्तत्प्रीत्या प्रीयते तु माम्। ॐ अथातः सम्प्रवक्ष्यामि विद्यामपि महाबलाम्। सर्वदुष्टप्रशमनीं सर्वशत्रुक्षयंकरीम्।। दारिद्र्यदुःखशमनीं दौर्भाग्यव्याधिनाशिनीम्। भूतप्रेतपिशाचानां यक्षगन्धर्व-रक्षसाम्।। डाकिनी शाकिनी-स्कंध-कूष्माण्डानां च नाशिनीम्। महारौद्रीं महाशक्तिं सद्यः प्रत्ययकारिणीम्। गोपनीयं प्रयत्नेन सर्वस्वं पार्वतीपतेः। तामहं ते प्रवक्ष्यामि सावधानमनाः शृणु। एकान्हिकं द्व्यन्हिकं च चातुर्थिकार्द्धमासिकम्। द्वैमासिकं त्रैमासिकं तथा चातुर्मासिकम्। पाञ्चमासिकं षाड्मासिकं वातिक पैतिकज्वरम्। श्लैष्मिकं सान्निपातिकं तथैव सततज्वरम्। मौहूर्तिकं पैत्तिकं शीतज्वरं विषमज्वरम्। द्व्यह्निकं त्र्यह्निकं चैव ज्वरमेकाह्निकं तथा। क्षिप्रं नाशयते नित्यं स्मरणादपराजिता। ॐ ह्रीं हन हन, कालि शर शर, गौरि धम, धम, विद्ये आले ताले माले गंधे बंधे पच पच विद्ये नाशय नाशय पापं हर हर संहारय वा दुःखस्वप्नविनाशिनि कमलस्थिते विनायकमातः रजनि सन्ध्ये, दुन्दुभिनादे, मानसवेगे, शंखिनि, चक्रणि गदिनि वज्रिणि शूलिनि अपस्मृत्युविनाशिनि विश्वेश्वरि द्रविडि द्राविडि द्राविणि केशवदयिते पशुपतिसहिते दुन्दुभिदमनि दुर्म्मदमनि। शबरि किराति मातंगि ॐ द्रं द्रं ज्रं ज्रं क्रं क्रं तुरु तुरु ॐ द्रं कुरु कुरु। ये मां द्विषन्ति

प्रत्यक्षं परोक्षं वा तान् सर्वान् दम दम मर्दय मर्दय तापय तापय गोपय पातय पातय शोषय शोषय उत्साद उत्सादव ब्रह्माणि वैष्णवि माहेश्वरि कौमारि वाराहि नारसिंहि ऐन्द्रि चामुण्डे महालक्ष्मि वैनायिकि औपेन्द्रि आग्नेयि चण्डि नैर्ऋति वायव्ये सौम्ये ऐशानि ऊर्ध्वमधोरक्ष प्रचंडविद्ये इन्द्रोपेन्द्र भगिनि। ॐ नमो देवि जये विजये शांति स्वस्तितुष्टि-पुष्टि-विवर्द्धिनि। कामांकुशे कामदुघे सर्वकामवरप्रदे। सर्वभूतेषु मां प्रियं कुरु कुरु स्वाहा। आकर्षणि आवेशनि। ज्वालामालिनि रमणि, रामणि, धरणि, धारनणि, तपनि तापिनि, मदनि मादिनि, शोषणि संमोहिनि नीलपताके महानीले महागौरि महाश्रिये। महाचांद्रि महासौरि महामायूरि आदित्यरश्मि जाह्नवि। यमघंटे किणि किणि चिन्तामणि। सुगन्धे सुरभे सुरासुरोत्पन्ने सर्वकामदुघे यद्यथा मनीषितं कार्यं तन्मम सिद्ध्यतु स्वाहा। ॐ स्वाहा। ॐ भूः स्वाहा। ॐ भुवः स्वाहा। ॐ स्वः स्वाहा। ॐ महः स्वाहा। ॐ जनः स्वाहा। ॐ तपः स्वाहा। ॐ सत्यं स्वाहा। ॐ भूर्भुवः स्वः स्वाहा। यत एववागतं पापं तत्रैव प्रतिगच्छतु स्वाहेत्योम्। अमोघैषा महाविद्या वैष्णवी चापराजिता। स्वयं विष्णुप्रणीता च सिद्धेयं पाठतः सदा। एषा महाबला नाम कथिता तेऽपराजिता। नानया सदृशी रक्षा त्रिषु लोकेषु विद्यते। तमोगुणमयी साक्षाद्रौद्री शक्तिरियं मता। कृतान्तोऽपि यतो भीतः पादमूले व्यवस्थितः। मूलधारे न्यसेदेतां रात्रावेनां च संस्मरेत्। नीलजीमूतसंकाशां तडित्कपिलकेशिकाम्। उद्यदादित्यसंकाशां नेत्रत्रय-विराजिताम्। शक्तिं त्रिशूलं शंखं च पानपात्रं च विभ्रतीम्। व्याघ्रकर्मपरीधानां किंकिणीजालमण्डिताम्। धावंतीं गगनस्यांतः तादुकाहितपादकाम्। दंष्ट्राकरालवदनां व्यालकुण्डलभूषिताम्। व्यात्तवक्त्रां ललज्जिह्वां भृकुटीकुटिलालकाम्। स्वभक्तद्वेषिणां रक्तं पिबन्तीं पानपात्रतः। सप्तधातून् शोषयन्तीं क्रूरदृष्ट्या विलोकनात्। त्रिशूलेन च तज्जिह्वां कीलयनतीं मुहुर्मुहः। पाशेन बद्धवा तं साधमानयन्तीं तदन्तिके। अर्द्धरात्रस्य समये देवीं ध्यायेन्महाबलाम्। यस्य यस्य बदेन्नाम जपेन्मन्त्रं निशान्तके। तस्य तस्य तथावस्थां कुरुते सापि योगिनी। ॐ बले महाबले असिद्धसाधनी स्वाहेत्या अमोघां पठति सिद्धां श्रीवैष्णवीम्। श्रीमद्पराजितविद्यां ध्यायेत्। दुःस्वप्ने दुरारिष्टे च दुर्निमित्ते तथैव च। व्यवहारे भेवेत्सिद्धिः पठेद्विघ्नोपशान्तये।

यदत्र पाठे जगदम्बिके मया विसर्गबिन्द्वऽक्षरहीनमीडितम्। ततस्तु सम्पूर्णतमं प्रयान्तु मे संकल्पसिद्धिस्तु सदैव जायताम्।।

तव तत्त्वं न जानामि कीदृशेंसि महेश्वरि। यादृशसि महादेवी तादृशायै नमो नमः।।

All above measures bestow victory in elections. Opponents are defeated and victory is ensured. But if *dasha-*

*bhukti* of weak planets is operating and success is doubtful, then 1100 *paath* of ***'Trailokyavijayaprad Kavacham'*** must be got done through any learned Acharya. Though, however, it may be recited at least once by the native himself. This *Trailokyavijayaprad Kavacham,* which is mentioned in 3rd sub chapter of *Brahmand Purana,* composed by Bhargava Rishi, is time tested to ensure success in elections by defeating the rivals. There is no doubt in its efficacy, though however, it should be executed with great care, devotion and dedication with required *Havan, Tarpan, Marjan* etc. according to Vedic rituals.

## Trailokyavijayaprad Kavacham

## ।। त्रैलोक्यविजयप्रदकवचम् ।।

**ब्रह्माण्डपुराणे मध्यमभागे 33 अध्यायः।**

**1-37 श्लोकाः**

सगर उवाच।। श्रुतं सर्वं मुनिश्रेष्ठ कीर्त्यमानं त्वया विभो।। कवचं वद सर्वत्र
त्रैलोक्यविजयप्रदम्।।1।। वसिष्ठ उवाच।। शृणु वत्स प्रवक्ष्यामि कवचं परमाद्भुतम्।।
मंत्रं च सिद्धिदं शश्वत्साधकानां सुखावहम्।।2।। गोपीजनपदस्यांते वल्लभाय
समुच्चरेत्।। स्वाहांतोऽयं महामंत्रो दशार्णो भुक्तिमुक्तिदः।।3।। सदाशिवस्त्वस्य ऋषिः
पंक्तिश्छंद उदाहृतम्।। देवता कृष्ण उदितो विनियोगोऽखिलाप्तये।।4।।
त्रैलोक्यविजयस्याथ कवचस्य प्रजापतिः।। ऋषिश्छंदश्च जगती देवो राजेश्वरः
स्वयम्।।5।। त्रैलोक्यविजयप्राप्तौ विनियोगः प्रकीर्तितः।। प्रणवो मे शिरः पातु
श्रीकृष्णाय नमः सदा।।6।। पायात्कपालं कृष्णाय स्वाहेति सततं मम।। कृष्णोति
पातु नेत्रे मे कृष्णस्वाहेति तारकाम्।।7।। हरये नम इत्येष भ्रूलतां पातु मे सदा।।ॐ।।
गोविन्दाय स्वाहेति नासिकां पातु संततम्।।8।। गोपालाय नमो गण्डं पातु मे सततं
मनुः।। क्लीं कृष्णाय नमः कर्णौ पातु कल्पतरुर्मम।।9।। श्री कृष्णाय नमः पातु
नित्यं मेऽधरयुग्मकम्।। ॐ गोपीशाय स्वाहेति दन्तपंक्तिं ममावतु।।10।। श्री कृष्णेति
रदच्छिद्रं पातु मे त्र्यक्षरो मनुः।। ॐ श्रीकृष्णाय स्वाहेति जिह्विकां पातु मे सदा।।11।।
रामेश्वराय स्वाहेति तालुकं पातु मे सदा।। राधिकेशाय स्वाहेति कंठं मे पातु
सर्वदा।।12।। नमो गोपीगणेशाय ग्रीवां मे पातु सर्वदा।। ॐ गोपेशाय स्वाहेति
स्कंधौ पातु सदा मम।।13।। नमः किशोरवेषाय स्वाहा पृष्ठं ममावतु।। उदरं पातु
मे नित्यं मुकुन्दाय नमो मनुः।।14।। ह्रीं श्रींक्लींकृष्णाय स्वाहा करौ पातु सदा मम।।

ॐ विष्णवे नमः स्वाहा बाहुयुग्मं ममावतु।।15।। ॐ ह्रीं भगवते स्वाहा नखपंक्तिं ममावतु।। नमो नारायणायेति नखरंध्रं ममावतु।।16।। ॐ ह्रीं श्रींपद्मनाभाय नाभिं पातु सदा मम।। ॐ सर्वेशाय स्वाहेति केशान्मम सदाऽवतु।।17।। नमः कृष्णाय स्वाहेति ब्रह्मरंध्रं सदाऽवतु।। ॐ माधवाय स्वाहेति भालं मे सर्वदाऽवतु।।18।। ॐ ह्रीं श्रींरसिकेशाय कटिं मम सदाऽवतु।। नमो गोपीजनेशाय ऊरू पातु सदामम।।19।। ॐ नमो दैत्यनाशाय स्वाहेत्यवतु जानुनी।। यशोदानन्दनायेति नमोंतो जंघकेऽवतु।।20।। रासारंभप्रियायेति स्वाहांतो ह्रीं ममावतु।। वृंवाप्रियाय स्वाहेति सकलांगानि मेऽवतु।।21।। परिपूर्णमनाः कृष्णः प्राच्यां मां सर्वदाऽदावतु।। स्वयं गोलोकनाथो मामाग्नेय्यां दिशि रक्षतु।।22।। पूर्णब्रह्मस्वरूपश्च दक्षिणे मां सदाऽवतु।। नैर्ऋत्यां पातु मां कृष्णः पश्चिमे पातु मां हरिः।।23।। गोविंदः पातु वायव्यामुत्तरे रसिकेश्वरः।। ऐशान्यां मे सदा पातु वृन्दावनविहारकृत्।।24।। वृंदाप्राणेश्वरः शश्वत्पातु मामूर्ध्वदेशतः।। सदैव मामधः पातु बलिध्वंसी महावत्तः।।25।। जले स्थले चांतरिखे नृसिंहः पातु मां सदा।। स्वप्ने जागरणे चैव पातु मां माधवः स्वयम्।।26।। सर्वान्तरात्मा निर्लिप्तः पातु मां सर्वतो विभुः।। इति ते कथितं भूप सर्वाघौघविनाशनम्।।27।। त्रैलोक्यविजयं नाम कवचं परमेशितुः।। मया श्रुतं शिवमुखात्प्रवक्तव्यं न कस्यचित्।।28।। गुरुमभ्यर्च्य विधिवत्कवचं धारयेत्तुयः।। कण्ठे वा दक्षिणे बाहौ सोऽपिविष्णुर्न संशयः।।29।। स साधकोऽवसद्यत्र तत्र वाणीरमे स्थिते।। यदि स्यात्सिद्धकवचो जीवन्मुक्तो न संशयः।।30।। निश्चितं कोटिवर्षाणां पूजायाः फलमाप्नुयात्।। राजसूयसहस्राणि वाजपेयशतानि च।।31।। महादानानि यान्येव भुवश्चापि प्रदक्षिणा।। त्रैलोक्य-विजयस्यास्य कलां नार्हति षोडशीम् ।।32।। व्रतोपवासनियमाः स्वाध्यायाध्यने तथा।। स्नानं च सर्वतीर्थेषु नास्यार्हति कलामपि।।33।। सिद्धत्वममरत्वं च दासत्वं श्रीहरेरपि।। यदि स्यात्सिद्धकवचः सर्वं प्राप्नोति निश्चितम्।।34।। स भवेत्सिद्धकवचो दशलक्षं जपेतु यः।। यो भवेत्सिद्धकवचो विजयी स भवेद् ध्रुवम्।।35।। राज्यं देयं शिरो देयं प्राणा देयाश्च भूपते।। एतन्तु कवचं वत्स न देयं संकटेऽपि च।।36।। मथा प्रकाशितं यत्ते चैतेषां त्राणकारणात्।। ममाज्ञाकरणाच्चैव तद्विद्धि कुलभास्कर।। इदं धृत्वा तु कवचं चक्रवर्त्ती भवान्भव।।37।। इति श्री ब्रह्माण्डे महापुराणे वायुप्रोक्ते मध्यमभागे तृतीय उपोद्धातपादे भार्गवचरिते त्रयस्त्रिंशत्तमोऽध्यायः।।

We have mentioned a few important rectificational measures for the prevention of adversities, disasters, dismissals, suspension, reversions and termination. However, we invite the attention of readers that first of all their horoscopes should be examined by any learned and talented astrologer, so that the exact planetary affliction may be worked out. First of all, *Grahshanti* i.e. the propiation of planets by the recitation of their Vedic Mantras for the specific number of times is most essential.

Other remedial measures should be followed only after proper *Grahshanti*. These remedies and preventive measures have been tested thousands of times at various occasions. And as a result of which, amazing success, happiness and accomplishment of ambitions, promotions, professional progression and prosperity have been there. We pray to almighty to bless the natives with similar astonishing and wonderful auspicious results of the above rectificational measures, if they follow it.

सर्वे भवन्तु सुखिनः सर्वे सन्तु निरामयाः।
सर्वे भद्राणि पश्यन्तु मा कश्चित् दुःख भाग्भवेत्।।
हरि ॐ तत्सत्

•

# Bibliography


Acharya Mukund Daivagya "Jaatak Bhushanam", Ranjan Publications, New Delhi, 1993

Acharya Neeraj, "Vriddh Yavanjatakam", Ranjan Publications, New Delhi, 1994.

Balbhadra Mishra, "Hora Ratnam", Motilal Banarasi Dass Publishers Pvt. Ltd., Delhi, 1979.

Balmukund Pandeyen, "Phalit Prakash", Babu Baijnath Book Seller, Kashi

Bepin Bihari, "Astrological Biographies", Motilal Banarasi Dass Publishers Pvt. Ltd., Delhi.

Bepin Bihari, "The Timing of Events", Motilal Banarasi Dass Publishers Pvt. Ltd., Delhi.

Bhaskaracharya, "Bhav Deepika", Ranjan Publications, New Delhi

Bitthal Dixit, Muhurta Kalpdruma", Ranjan Publications, New Delhi, 2005.

Bhojraj Dwivedi, "Jyotish Yog Sahastri", Motilal Banarasi Dass Publishers Pvt. Ltd., Delhi, 2003.

B.S. Gupta, "Astrological Insights and Experiments", Divya Gyan Kendra, Kurukshetra, 1981.

B.S. Gupta, "Stars and Human Destiny", Sagar Publications, New Delhi

B.V. Raman (Dr.), "A Catechism of Astrology", Raman Publications, Bangalore, 1991.

B.V. Raman (Dr.), "Three Hundred Important Combinations", Motilal Banarasi Dass Publishers Pvt. Ltd., Delhi, 1991.

B.V. Raman (Dr.), "How to Judge A Horoscope (2 Parts)", Motilal Banarasi Dass Publishers Pvt. Ltd., Delhi, 1995.

B.V. Raman (DR.), "Grah Aur Bhavbal (Translation- Om Prakash Palival)", Motilal Banarasi Dass Publishers Pvt. Ltd., Delhi, 1999.

B.V. Raman (Dr.), "Jaatak Nirnaya", Motilal Banarasi Dass Publishers Pvt. Ltd., Delhi, 1995.

B.V. Raman (Dr.), "Notable Horoscopes", Motilal Banarasi Dass Publishers Pvt. Ltd., Delhi, 1995.

B.V. Raman (Dr.), "Hindu Predictive Astrology", IBH Prakashana, Bengaluru. 2009.

Chandra Dutt Pant, "Lagna Chandra Prakash", Motilal Banarasi Dass Publishers Pvt. Ltd., Delhi, 2004.

Col. A.K. Gour, "Professions (Inclination, Fructification and Career Profile)", Alpha Publication, Delhi, 2002.

Daya Shanker, Sharing With Parashar", The Times of Astrolgy, Nishkam Peeth Prakashan, 2005.

Devi Dutt Joshi, "Sugam Jyotish", Motilal Banarasi Dass Publishers Pvt. Ltd., Delhi, 1922.

Devaki Nandan Singh, "Jyotish Ratnakar", Motilal Banarasi Dass Publishers Pvt. Ltd., Delhi, 1983.

Dennis M. Harness David Frawley, "The Nakshatras", Motilal Banarasi Dass Publishers Pvt. Ltd., Delhi.

Dhundhiraj, "Jataka Bharanam", Ranjan Publications, New Delhi

Gauri Shanker Kapoor (Dr.), "Jatak Satyacharya", Ranjan Publications, New Delhi, 2003.

Gayatri Devi Vasudev, "Astrology and the Hoax of Scientific Temper", Motilal Banarasi Dass Publishers Pvt. Ltd., Delhi.

Girija Shankar Shastri (Dr.), "Bharatiya Kundali Vimarsh", Jyotish Karmkand Evam Adhyatm Shodh Sansthan, Allahabad.

Gopesh Kumar Ojha, "Triphala (Jyotisha)", Motilal Banarasi Dass Publishers Pvt. Ltd., Delhi, 1971.

Gopesh Kumar Ojha & Ashutosh Ojha, "The Solar Return or Varshaphal", Motilal Banarasi Dass Publishers Pvt. Ltd., Delhi, 1975.

Gopesh Kumar Ojha, "Sugam Jyotish "Praveshika, Motilal Banarasi Dass Publishers Pvt. Ltd., Delhi, 2002.

Gopesh Kumar Ojha & Ashutosh Ojha, "Aspects in Vedic Astrology", Motilal Banarasi Dass Publishers Pvt. Ltd., Delhi.

Gopesh Kumar Ojha & Ashutosh Ojha, "Astrology and You", Motilal Banarasi Dass Publishers Pvt. Ltd., Delhi, 2002.

Govind Shastri, "Jyotisha Rahasya", Sadhana Pocket Books, Delhi.

G.S. Agarwal, "Practical Vedic Astrology", Sagar Publications, New Delhi.

Harishankar Pathak (Dr.), "Dasaphal Darpan", Chowkhamba Surbharti Prakashan, Varanasi, 2007.

H.N. Katve, "Bhava Vichaar", Nagpur Prakashan, 1970.

H.N. Katave, "Griha Vichaar (Surya, Chandra, Mangal, Buddha, Guru, Shukra, Shani & Rahu-Ketu Griha Vichaar)", Nagpur Prakashan, 1975.

H.N. Katve, "Bhavesh Vichaar", Nagpur Prakashan, 1983.

H.N. Katve, "Dev Rahasya", Nagpur Prakashan, 1983.

Jagjeevan Dass Gupta, "Jyotish Rahasya", Motilal Banarasi Dass Publishers Pvt. Ltd., Delhi, 1985.

Jagjeevan Dass Gupta, "Dasaphal Vichaar", Motilal Banarasi Dass Publishers Pvt. Ltd., Delhi, 2008.

Jagannath Bhasin, "Phalit Sutra", Nav Bharat Printing Press, Delhi, 1974.

Jeevnath, "Bhaav Kutuhalam" (Ed.- Dr. Hari Shankar Pathak), Chowkhamba Surbharti Prakashan, Varanasi, 2004.

Jeevnath Ojha, "Bhava Prakash", Ranjan Publications, New Delhi

Kadalangudi Natesa Shastri, "Jataka Dwadasa Bhava Phala or Hindu Astrological Results", Kadalangudi Publications, Madras.

Kalyan Verma, "Saravali", Ranjan Publications, New Delhi, 1998

Kalidas, "Purva Kalamrita", Ranjan Publications, New Delhi, 1999.

Kalidas, "Uttar Kalamrit", Alpha Publication, Delhi, 2008.

Kalidas, "Jyotirvida Bharanam", Motilal Banarasi Dass Publishers Pvt. Ltd., Delhi, 2011.

Kailash Nath Upadhyay, "Janmang Phal Vichaar", Motilal Banarasi Dass Publishers Pvt. Ltd., Delhi.

Kailash Nath Upadhyay, "Jeevan Phal Darpan", Motilal Banarasi Dass Publishers Pvt. Ltd., Delhi.

Kevalanand Joshi, "Aap Aur Aapki Rashi", Motilal Banarasi Dass Publishers Pvt. Ltd., Delhi, 2000.

Khankhana, "Khetkautukam", Ranjan Publications, New Delhi, 2000.

Krishan Kumar, "Secrets of Varga", Alpha Publications, Delhi, 2002.

Krishna Kumar, "Shadvarg Phalam", Alpha Publications, Delhi, 2003.

Krishna Kumar, "Aajivika Vichaar (Jyotish ke Jharokha Se)", Alpha Publications, Delhi, 2004.

Krishna Kumar, "Bhavphal Vichaar", Alpha Publications, Delhi, 2010.

K.N. Rao, "Advanced Techniques of Astrological Predictions", Bhartiya Prachya Evam Sanatan Vigyan Sansthan, New Delhi.

K.K. Pathak, "Astrology of Professions (Principles and Practices—2 Parts)", Alpha Publications (Publishers), Delhi, 2007.

K. Subramaniam, "K.P. Krishman's Profession", Krishnan & Co., Chennai.

K.C. Saxena, "Venus in Astrology", Sagar Publications, New Delhi.

K.N. Rao, "Ups and Downs in Career", S. Kumar & Associates, Lucknow.

L.R. Choudhary, "Mars and Astrology", Sagar Publications, New Delhi.

L.R. Choudhry, "Transit of Planets", Sagar Publications, New Delhi.

— "Maan Sagari", Sagar Publications, New Delhi, 1954.

Maharishi Parashar, "Brihat Parashar Horoshashtra", Ranjan Publications, New Delhi, 2008.

Maharishi Bhatt Narayan, "Chamatkar Chintamani" (Ed.- Braj Bihari Lal Sharma), Motilal Banarasi Dass Publishers Pvt. Ltd., Delhi, 1981.

Mantreshwar, "Phala Deepika", Motilal Banarasi Dass Publishers Pvt. Ltd., Delhi, 1981.

Mahan Vir Yuli, "Predictive Astrology and Financial Prosperity", Gyan Sagar Publications, Delhi.

Mahendra Nath Kedar, "Bhava Nirnaya, Dasa Evam Gochar Dwara Samay Nirdharan", Bhartiya Prachya & Sanatan Vigyan Sansthan, New Delhi, *Samvat* 2059.

Mahendra Nath Kedar & Shankar Nath Kapoor, "Vivah ka Samay", Bhartiya Prachya Evam Sanatan Vigyan Sansthan, New Delhi, 2012.

M.N. Kedar, "Nine Planets & Twelve Bhavas their Effect on Human Life", Bhartiya Prachya Evam Sanatan Vigyan Sansthan, New Delhi, 2000.

Mukund Ballabh Mishra, "Shadvarga Phal Prakash", Motilal Banarasi Dass Publishers Pvt. Ltd., Delhi.

Mukund Daivagya, "Prasava Chintamani", Ranjan Publications, New Delhi, 1984.

Mukund Daivagya, "Bhava Manjari", Ranjan Publications, New Delhi, 2008.

M.S. Mehta, "Planets and Travel Abroad", Sagar Publications, New Delhi.

M.R. Bhatt, "Fundamentals of Astrology", Motilal Banarasi Dass Publishers Pvt. Ltd., Delhi.

M. Ramkrishna Bhatt (Prof.) (Translator), "Brihat Samhita (English)", Motilal Banarasi Dass Publishers Pvt. Ltd., Delhi

Nemichandra Jyotishacharya (Dr.), "Bhadrabahu Samhita", Bhartiya Gyanpeeth, New Delhi, 2009.

Nemichandra Shastri (Dr.), "Bhartiya Jyotish", Bhartiya Gyanpeeth, New Delhi, 2002.

Nimai Banerjee (Dr.), "Scaling Human Lives", Maa Parameswari Publications, Cuttack, 2001.

N.N. Saha, "Vocational Guidance Through Astrology", Fate & Destiny Publications, Jalandhar.

O.P. Verma, "Secrets of Vimshottari Dasa", Ranjan Publications, New Delhi, 1996.

O.P. Verma, "Profession Through Astrology", Ranjan Publications, New Delhi, 1994.

Pavan Chandoliya, "Jyotish Ke Anubhoot Rahasya", Motilal Banarasi Dass Publishers Pvt. Ltd., Delhi.

Padumnai Chomadri, "Jaatak Deshmarg", Motilal Banarasi Dass Publishers Pvt. Ltd., Delhi, 1992.

Peter West Jologan, "How to Judge a Nativity", Sagar Publications, New Delhi

Pt. Ramyal Ojha, "Phalit Vikas", Ranjan Publications, New Delhi.

Pt. Umashanker Dubey, "Saral Jyotish Gyan", Jagannath Publishing House, Kanpur, 1993.

Pt. Maheedhar Sharma," Shambhu Horaprakash", Khemraj Srikrishna Dass, 1998.

Pt. Mukund Ballabh Mishra, "Phalit Martand", Motilal Banarasi Dass Publishers Pvt. Ltd., Delhi, 1968

Pt. Mahadev Pathak, "Jatak Tatvam", Ranjan Publications, New Delhi, 1988.

Pt. Ramswaroop Sharma, "Jyotisha Sarva Sangrah", Jawahar Book Depot, Meerut, *Samvat* 2052.

Pt. Suryakant Siddhanti, "Brihajjyotissar", Thakur Prasad, Varanasi, 1978.

Pt. Laxmikant Kanyal, "Jyotitatva Prakash", Motilal Banarasi Dass Publishers Pvt. Ltd., Delhi, 2004.

Pt. Sohan Lal Vyas, "Muhurta Parijat", Chowkhambha Vidya Bhawan, 2006.

Prem Kumar Sharma, "The Stars and Your Profession", Rupa & Co., New Delhi.

Prithu Yasho, "Shatpanchashika", Ranjan Publications, New Delhi, 2007.

Prithu Yasho, "Horasaar", Ranjan Publications, New Delhi, 1982.

P.V.R. Rayudu, How to Match Horoscopes for Marriage", Motilal Banarasi Dass Publishers Pvt. Ltd., Delhi.

P.V.R. Rayudu, "How to Read a Horoscope", Motilal Banarasi Dass Publishers Pvt. Ltd., Delhi.

Ramanujacharya, "Bhavarth Ratnakar", U.B.S. Publishers' Distributors Ltd. , 2005.

Ram Dayalu, "Sanket Nidhi", Ranjan Publications, New Delhi, 2003.

R. Santhanam, "Essentials of Astrology", Sagar Publications, New Delhi

R. Santhanam, "Jyotisharnava Navanitam", R. Santhanam Associates, New Delhi.

Rawal Harishankar Surisunu Ganapati, "Muhurta Ganapati", Motilal Banarasi Dass Publishers Pvt. Ltd., Jawahar Nagar, Delhi, 1988.

R.G. Rao, "Profession from the Position of Planets", Sagar Publications, New Delhi, 1995.

Sage Bhrigu, "Bhrigu Sutram" (Ed.-Dr. Gauri Shanker Kapoor), Ranjan Publications, New Delhi, 1981.

Satyacharya, "Satya Jatakam", Ranjan Publications, New Delhi, 2003.

Shankar Adawal (Dr.), "Your Profession (Ups and Downs with Remedial Measures)", Sagar Publications, New Delhi, 2006.

Shailendra Sharma, "Vitta Evam Vratti Prabandh", Mukund Prakashan, Jaipur.

Shailendra Sharma, "Sitaron Ke Sitare", Mukund Prakashan, Jaipur, 1999.

Sri Ganesh Kavi, "Jatakalankar", Ranjan Publications, New Delhi, 1992.

Sriram Daivagya, "Muhurta Chintamani", Chowkhambha Vidya Bhawan, 1972.

Suresh Chandra Mishra, "Jyotisha Sarvasva", Ranjan Publications, New Delhi, 2014.

S.G. Khot, "Jyotish Aur Parivar Niyojan", Motilal Banarasi Dass Publishers Pvt. Ltd., Delhi, 2000.

S.G. Khot, "Laghu Parashari Siddhant", Motilal Banarasi Dass Publishers Pvt. Ltd., Delhi.

S.G. Khot, "Vividh Yoga Chandra Prakash", Motilal Banarasi Dass Publishers Pvt. Ltd., Delhi.

S.P. Walia, "Astrological Guidance to Occupations", D.B. Taraporevala Sons & Co. Pvt. Ltd., Bombay, 1983.

S.S. Chatterjee, "Fortune and Finance", Alpha Publications, Delhi, 2002.

Sukhdev Chaturvedi, "Jyotish Shastra Mein Rog Vichaar", Motilal Banarasi Dass Publishers Pvt. Ltd., Delhi, 1984.

Sumeet Chugh, "Determining Profession and Ups & Downs in Career", Sagar Publications, New Delhi.

Sunita Jha, "Yoga Pushpanjali", Alpha Publications, Delhi, 2003.

— "The Prediction Book of Astrology", Gaurav Publishing House, New Delhi.

Uday Kant Misra (Dr.) & Col. A.K. Gour, "Introduction of Astrology", Alpha Publications, Delhi, 2007.

U.S. Pullippani (Dr.), "Gochar Phal Deepika", Alpha Publications (Publishers), Delhi, 2002.

Vaidyanath, "Jatak Parijat" (Ed.- Dr. Suresh Chandra Mishra), Ranjan Publications, New Delhi, 1979

Varahmihir, "Daivagya Vallabha", Ranjan Publications, New Delhi, 1983.

Varahmihir, "Laghu Jatakam", Chowkhamba Surbharti Prakashan, Varanasi, 1989.

Varahmihir, "Brihajjatakam", Motilal Banarasi Dass Publishers Pvt. Ltd., Delhi, 1994.

Venkatesh Sharma, "Sarvarth Chintamani", Chowkhamba Surbharti Prakashan, Varanasi, 2010

V.K. Chaudhary (Prof.), "Systems Approach for Interpreting Horoscopes", Sagar Publications, New Delhi, 2002.

V.K. Choudhry & K. Rajesh Choudhry, "How to Avert Professional Setbacks", Sagar Publications, New Delhi, 2011.

V.K. Choudhary (Prof.), "Self Learning Course In Astrology", Sagar Publications, New Delhi. 2014.

V. Raghuraman, "Vedic Nadi Astrology & Career", Sterling Publications Pvt. Ltd., Delhi.

## Books written by
# Mrs. Mridula Trivedi & T.P. Trivedi

1. वैवाहिक विलम्ब के विविध आयाम एवं मंत्र (सातवाँ संस्करण)
2. संतान सुख : सर्वांग चिन्तन (छठा संस्करण)
3. वैवाहिक सुख : ज्योतिषीय संदर्भ (पाँचवाँ संस्करण)
4. शत्रु शमन (द्वितीय संस्करण)
5. कालसर्प योग : शोध संज्ञान (तृतीय संस्करण)
6. मेलापक मीमांसा (द्वितीय संस्करण)
7. मंत्र पुष्पांजलि
8. मंत्र संदर्शन
9. विवाह विमर्श (द्वितीय संस्करण)
10. योग शृंखला  प्रथम खण्ड
11. योग शृंखला  द्वितीय खण्ड
12. Foretelling Widowhood
13. पुत्रेष्टि अनुष्ठान
14. पुत्रेष्टि विधान  प्रथम खण्ड
15. पुत्रेष्टि विधान  द्वितीय खण्ड
16. शनि शमन (सिद्धांत पक्ष)
17. शनि शमन (समाधान पक्ष)
18. शारदा सुदीप
19. शारदा प्रदीप
20. भाग्य चिन्तामणि
21. व्याधि विभावरी
22. व्याधि वीथिका
23. शत्रुंजय
24. परिणय निर्णय  मंगली दोषः सन्निहित यथार्थ
25. परिणय निर्णय  मंगली योग : विविध संयोग
26. परिणय निर्णय  वैवाहिक विसंगतियाँः संदर्भ एवं समाधान
27. परिणय निर्णय  विपुल वैवाहिक सुख का आधार : उपयुक्त परिहार
28. परिणय निर्णय  विवाह समय संज्ञान
29. परिणय निर्णय  मुहूर्त मीमांसा
30. शक्ति कुंज (द्वितीय संस्करण)
31. समृद्धि सूत्र : भाग-1 (Astrological Principles of Wealth & Prosperity) (द्वितीय संस्करण)
32. समृद्धि सूत्र : भाग-2 (Astrological Evaluation of Prosperity & Poverty with Observations & Illustrations) (द्वितीय संस्करण)
33. समृद्धि सुधा (Spiritual Measures for Financial Prosperity & Progress) द्वितीय संस्करण
34. समृद्धि सिन्धु (Remedies for Increase in Income & Recognition) द्वितीय संस्करण
35. मंत्र मंजरी (द्वितीय संस्करण)
36. मंत्र मधुवन (द्वितीय संस्करण)
37. A Compendium of Marriage, Vol.-I (IInd Edition)
38. A Compendium of Marriage, Vol.-II (IInd Edition)
39. An Insight into Kuja Dosh
40. Healing Touch of Medical Astrology
41. Proven Principles of Profession
42. व्रत विधान : विवाह एवं संतान
43. वैवाहिक सुख में शनि प्रमुख
44. सुरभित साधना सेतु
45. दीपावली एवं महालक्ष्मी पूजन विधान
46. आयु आकलन
47. वित्त वृद्धि
48. वित्त विचार

49. गीता मंत्र गंगोत्री
50. साधना सरोवर
51. शनि दशा दिग्दर्शन
52. शनि संहिता
53. मृत्युंजय मंत्र संकलन
54. मंत्र मंदाकिनी
55. जातक सारावली–प्रथम भाव
56. जातक सारावली–द्वितीय भाव
57. जातक सारावली–पंचम भाव
58. जातक सारावली–सप्तम भाव
59. जातक सारावली–दशम भाव
60. योग पारिजात–राज योग
61. योग पारिजात–भाग्य योग
62. योग पारिजात–धन योग
63. योग पारिजात–अनुपम योग
64. संतति संहिता
65. शिशु चिन्तन
66. ग्रह योग संक्षेपिका
67. व्यावसायिका
68. व्यवसाय रत्नाकर
69. व्यवसाय विमर्श
70. उद्यम एवं उन्नति
71. Predicting Marriage
72. Shani Shaman (Wooing Saturn)–I
73. Shani Shaman (Wooing Saturn)–II
74. Astrology for Life
75. मंत्र मंथन (दशम संस्करण)
76. मंत्र मंजूषा (दशम संस्करण)
77. विवाह कब होगा?
78. आजीविका के विविध आयाम : मंत्र एवं समाधान
79. Astrology for Overcoming Cancer
80. Natal Planets & Fatal Diseases
81. कतिपय पुत्रप्रदाता व्रत
82. मृत्युंजय कल्पद्रुम
83. दीपावली पूजन प्रविधि : धनार्जन एवं समृद्धि
84. मंत्र संजीवनी
85. महाविद्या प्रतिष्ठान : मंत्र अनुष्ठान
86. मंत्र सृजन
87. नीति निधि
88. शक्ति निकुंज
89. सप्तशती संहिता
90. Pointers to Profession : An Astrological Exposition
91. Astro Equations for Specific Professions
92. Saturn : The King Maker
93. Secrets of Saturn
94. Reunderstanding Saturn
95. Saturn: Maladies & Remedies
96. व्रत व्यावहारिका (In Press)
97. व्रत निहारिका (In Press)
98. Tried & Tested Techniques of Prediction (In Press)
99. Predicting through Navamsa (In Press).
100. Planets and Progeny (In Press)
101. Astro Biography of Celebrities (In Press)
102. राहु-केतु दशा फलदीपिका (In Press)
103. सूर्य दशा फलदीपिका (In Press)
104. चन्द्रमा दशा फलदीपिका (In Press)
105. मंगल दशा फलदीपिका (In Press)
106. बुध दशा फलदीपिका (In Press)
107. बृहस्पति दशा फलदीपिका (In Press)
108. शुक्र दशा फलदीपिका (In Press)
109. शनि दशा फलदीपिका (In Press)